FOLLY BEACH MYSTERY COLLECTION III

FOLLY BEACH MYSTERY COLLECTION III

BILL NOEL

Cover photo and design by Bill Noel

Author photo by Susan Noel

ISBN: 978-1-948374-36-1

Enigma House Press

Goshen, Kentucky

www.enigmahousepress.com

Folly Beach Mysteries

Folly

The Pier

Washout

The Edge

The Marsh

Ghosts

Missing

Final Cut

First Light

Boneyard Beach

Silent Night

Dead Center

Discord

The Folly Beach Mystery Collection

Dark Horse

Joy

The Folly Beach Mystery Collection II

No Joke

Relic

Faith

No Joke

Chapter One

Have you ever seen a stranger and knew, at first glance, that something was wrong? Could it have been the vacant look in his eyes? Or was it the long, wool coat he was wearing over red swim trunks and black patent leather shoes? Maybe it was the seven-foot-long fishing rod he was flinging around over his head like a drum major's baton. And, oh yeah, did I mention he was standing in heavy traffic in the middle of Center Street?

I hadn't noticed any of this until squealing tires and honking horns drew my attention away from gazing in the window of Avocet Properties to the man weaving around the stopped cars while their drivers hurled profanities at him as they came inches from running him down.

He swung the fishing rod at the closest vehicle, encouraging the exasperated driver to maneuver around the gentleman to escape the wrath of the weapon.

I looked around and didn't see anyone moving to save the confused fisherman.

I stepped off the curb, waved for two oncoming vehicles to stop, then sidled up to the stranger. I ducked away from the flailing rod that seemed to have a mind of its own and said, "Could I be of assistance?"

A pickup truck going the other direction zoomed past. The truck's horn blasted; the driver gave us a one-finger wave. At least he hadn't hit us.

The five-foot six-inch tall, thin, mid-seventies rod waver looked at me, blinked twice, and lowered the weapon.

I put my arm around his bony shoulder. Instead of waiting for him to answer, I nudged him to the curb and pointed for him to sit on a rocking chair under the awning of the real estate office.

"Nice fishing rod. Could I see it?" I asked, hoping to get it out of his trembling hand.

He looked at his hand like he was seeing the piece of sporting equipment for the first time. He handed it to me and looked at the street where he'd come so close to being roadkill.

I took the rod and leaned it against the chair on the other side of the stranger.

He shook his head like he was shaking cobwebs out. "Thank you, kind sir, for retrieving me from yon street. May I have your moniker?"

During my sixty-nine years, I'd never been asked that question, yet I assumed he wanted my name.

"Chris Landrum," I said. "And you are?"

He leaned forward then glanced at his fishing rod. "I'm Wallace, umm, Wallace Bentley." He reached to shake my hand.

"Pleased to meet you, Mr. Bentley."

"Call me Wallace." He chuckled. "All my friends, and strangers who save me from getting squashed, call me that."

"Do you live on Folly?"

The temperature was in the mid-seventies, but he pulled his heavy coat around him like he was freezing. He closed his eyes. For a moment, I thought he'd fallen asleep, until his eyes shot open. "Folly … Folly Beach." He rubbed his tongue along his front teeth. "Can't say that I do, Mr. Landrum, Chris. I'm here with friends."

I waited for him to continue. He didn't, so I said, "Friends?"

He looked toward the beach. "Didn't know ocean water was so cold this time of year."

"Sure is. You say you're here with friends. Who are they?"

"Guess that's why surfers wear those skin-tight, black trash bags."

Okay, forget the friends' names. How to reunite him with them was becoming more important. "Wallace, where're your friends?"

"Marvin, he goes by Pete; Salvador, who prefers Sal; Raymond, who prefers Ray. My departed wife, God rest her soul, and I call him Son."

I was beginning to have second thoughts about having rescued the irrational, deranged, or nutty gentleman sharing the rocking chairs with me. I took a deep breath and pretended like we were having a sane conversation.

"Are those your friends?"

"There's one more. I have trouble remembering his name. He's not a friend. He's Sal's brother. That's where we're staying."

I looked around, hoping someone would arrive to collect Wallace.

Several people walked past; none appeared interested.

I didn't blame them, but I couldn't leave him here in his confused state.

He snapped his finger and brought me out of my wish to beam myself anywhere but on this bench. "Got it." He sat back and smiled.

"Got what?"

"Sal's brother's name. Something like Humidor or Thermador." He smiled like that explained everything.

"Like the thing you keep tobacco in, or like the kitchen appliances?"

"Chris, it is Chris, right?"

I nodded.

"You're not making a lick of sense."

Pot calling the kettle black popped into my head. I'd run out of words to share with my new acquaintance.

Wallace said, "Sal's brother, he's a guy who lives down that street that has the river in its back yard."

"Theodore Stull?"

I had retired to Folly Beach, a small, quirky, South Carolina barrier island ten years ago, where I'd received numerous lessons from my equally quirky friends on how one plus one seldom equals two.

"Bingo."

I'd met Theodore Stull a couple of years ago when I joined his walking group. For those who think walking is healthy, I'd respond with five words: It nearly got me killed. Theo, as he preferred to be called, came closer than I had to meeting his Maker because of the group. But that's a story for another time.

"Are your friends at Theo's house?"

Please, please say yes, I thought so I could deliver him to them. Theo lived a short walk from where we were sitting.

"Hear about the dead body?"

Not the answer I was looking for. "What dead body?"

"The one at the beach."

"Tell me about it."

"Sal's seventy-nine, that's years younger than Theo. Do you know Theo?"

I wondered if anyone would notice if I smacked him with a fishing rod.

"Yes, I know Theo. What about a body at the beach?"

"Dead body."

"Did you see a body?"

"That's what I'm trying to tell you, young man."

"Where was it?" Folly Beach had six miles of ocean beachfront, so I hoped he would narrow it down.

"Hard to tell. I don't know much about your island. Just got here a few days ago. Seeing a dead body had a distracting impression on me."

He could say that again.

"When did you see it?"

"Sal thought Theo was losing his mind. He wanted to be here for his brother. That's why we're staying with him."

One more time. "When did you see the body?"

"Must've been today."

"What time did—"

"Could've been yesterday."

I was ready to pull my hair out although, since I was a few hairs shy of bald, I would have to do it figuratively.

"So, you're not certain—"

"I know." He snapped his fingers. "It was January 20, four years ago. Remember it well. That guy, what's-his-name, was sworn in as president. I'll never understand why. Yes, sir, that was the day."

Seconds before I started screaming, a City of Folly Beach patrol car cruised past, and I recognized the driver. Allen Spencer was new on the force the year I'd moved from Middle America. We had numerous conversations over the years. I watched him grow from a young, green beat cop to one of Folly's most experienced law enforcement officials.

He looked my way and nodded.

I waved for him to stop, and he pulled around the corner of the real estate building.

"Hey, Chris, wonderful day, isn't it?" Allen said as he approached the chairs and looked at my new acquaintance.

"Great day, Officer Spencer. Have you met Wallace Bentley?"

Allen moved in front of Wallace and held out his hand. "Don't believe I have. I'm Allen Spencer."

Wallace didn't make eye contact but shook Allen's hand.

The officer focused on the fishing rod. "Going fishing, Wallace?"

Wallace looked over at the pole. "I'm a friend of Sal."

I interrupted their disjointed conversation before it went further off the rails. "Officer Spencer, have a second? I've got a question about the new parking rules on East Arctic."

He looked at me like he had no idea what I was talking about, a look well-founded. I'd made it up. Regardless, he said, "Sure."

I stood. "Wallace, wait here. I'll be back."

I took Allen by the elbow and walked around the corner.

"What stray have you picked up now?"

"Allen, I didn't want to say anything in front of him. Let me tell you what I know."

I proceeded to tell Allen about escorting the oddly-attired man from the center of the street and who he'd said he was visiting. I shared Wallace's story about seeing a dead body at the beach. I'd learned, over the years, that Allen listened to what I had to say, regardless how strange or farfetched it may sound.

I asked if there'd been a report of a death or missing person.

He said there was none he was aware of. Although, it didn't mean much, since there were so many visitors to the island it could be days before someone would've been reported missing.

Allen fiddled with his black leather duty belt then took a deep breath. "Do you put credence in his story?"

"Hard to tell. He had me convinced until he couldn't remember if he'd seen the body today, yesterday, or four years ago. He slipped in and out of reality."

"Sounds like he may need a transport to the psych ward."

"Not yet. He appears harmless. If it's okay, I'll walk him to Theo's to see if his brother's there."

"First, let me see if I can do any better with him."

I smiled. "Have at it."

We returned to Wallace and to a continuation of his story which was as odd as his attire.

I told Wallace I'd shared what he'd said about seeing a body.

Wallace told Allen he had but was confused about when.

I thought it was a major understatement, since his time of the sighting ranged from three hours to the lifespan of a hedgehog.

Wallace seemed to return to the real world when he started describing where he was staying and who he was with. He laughed when Allen said something about Theo being part of a walking group started by another of my friends, Chester Carr. Members of the group called Theo ET which, instead of a comparison to the cute alien from another planet in the old movie by the same name, it meant Energizer Turtle because of Theo's slow pace.

Wallace responded by saying, "That boy's as slow as a turkey trottin' to Thanksgiving dinner."

Allen tried once more to pin down a more accurate time on when Wallace had allegedly seen a body. He was no more successful than I'd been. He looked at me and shrugged.

"Tell you what, Officer Spencer, why don't I walk Wallace to Theo's house? If we can get a better fix on when he saw the body, I'll give you a call?"

Allen turned to Wallace. "That okay with you?"

It was better than him saying, "Is that okay?" or "Would you rather I take you to a padded room in nearby Charleston?"

Wallace agreed with the plan.

Before Allen headed to his patrol car, he said, "You will call me if you learn anything about a body." It wasn't a question.

We started the three-block walk to Theo's. Wallace's gait was quicker than his host, although not much.

Theo owned a large, two-story, elevated home that over-looked the marsh and the Folly River. His two-year old Mercedes was in the drive, so I assumed he was home, or hoped so. My luck continued when Theo opened the mahogany front door. He'd made a fortune after inventing a replacement-window system filled with an exotic energy-saving gas. He'd sold the business to a national window replacement company for several million dollars then moved to Folly. Instead of appearing like a multi-millionaire, most of the time Theo looked homeless. At five-foot-eight, he was a couple of inches shorter than me, had an equal amount of exposed scalp, and looked older than his mid-eighties. He wore a USS Yorktown ball cap, black knee-high support socks and blue jogging shorts. One vestige of his earlier success was his white, button-down dress shirt. The collar and cuffs were frayed, but the shirt had been custom made to fit his trim frame.

Theo looked at Wallace then at me. "Chris, good to see you. I see you met Wallace. What brings you out?"

I started to answer when he added, "Sorry, I'm being rude. Come in."

Theo said it like there was nothing unusual about seeing Wallace standing at the door, sweat running down his cheeks from wearing a wool topcoat in seventy-degree weather, while carrying a fishing rod. We followed Theo to the great room where he had a panoramic view of the Folly River from floor to ceiling windows.

Theo looked up like he was speaking to the heavens, and yelled, "Hey, Sal. Wallace is here."

Theo motioned for us to sit on his oversized latte-colored couch. I heard someone coming down the stairs.

"Well, well, well," boomed the loud voice of the newcomer to the room. "My good friend, Wallace, returns."

Theo said, "Chris, meet my brother, Salvador."

"Call me Sal," said the man whom Theo claimed to be his brother. I say claimed because Sal didn't look or sound anything like Theo. The man who walked over and shook my hand was several years younger and at least five inches taller than Theo. He had long, gray hair, wore black, wide-rimmed glasses that looked like they came off the pages of a style magazine—a magazine from the 1950s. In contrast to Theo's dress shirt, Sal had on an open collar, red and blue striped shirt that would have been at home in a lounge singer's closet, and like the glasses, a closet in the '50s.

"Chris," boomed Sal, "see you met my good buddy, Wallace." He hesitated then chuckled. "You don't have to make a fool out of Wallace. He does it all by himself."

That was a line I didn't want to touch. I didn't have to.

"Chris," Theo said, "Salvador is a stand-up comedian. Done it most of his adult life."

"Adult, huh," Wallace said.

"And so is Wallace," Theo added. "In fact, I have four house guests. All of them make a living in the world of comedy. Wallace's son, Raymond, and another of their friends, Marvin Peters, are somewhere on the island having—"

"Having too many beers," Sal interrupted, "hittin' on some of your charming Southern belle barmaids."

"Now, Sal," Theo said, "you don't know that."

Wallace looked at me. "See why I had to get out of the house?"

That was the sanest thing he'd said since I herded him out of the street.

I looked at Wallace and Sal. "How long will you be visiting?"

"A while," Sal said, clarifying nothing.

Theo elaborated. "They're taking a respite from touring. They've been on the road for a long time."

"How long you ask?" Sal asked and answered, "We started traveling around the country with Daniel Boone. That coon-skinned cap guy couldn't tell a joke if his life depended on it but was a hell of an injun fighter."

If that was as funny as his show, a respite was long overdue.

"We started doing comedy in 1965," Wallace said.

Since he'd said he saw a body either today or four years ago, I wasn't ready to put faith in the year they started.

Theo said, "I believe that is correct, isn't it, Sal?"

Sal must have been running low on jokes. He nodded.

"Nap time," Wallace said, related to nothing.

I took the hint. "Guys, it was nice meeting you. I'd better be running."

Sal said, "Likewise." Wallace yawned.

Theo said he'd walk me out.

I nudged Theo to the front porch, closed the door so Wallace and Sal couldn't hear, then told Theo what'd happened.

He shook his head. "Remember when we first met?"

"Sure."

"Some of my, our, friends thought I was getting Alzheimer's because I seemed to forget things."

I said I remembered.

"Truth be known, it was because I couldn't hear. I was too stubborn to get hearing aids."

When I met Theo, if anyone wanted him to hear what they were saying, they had to speak in a voice the decibel level of Niagara Falls. After two harrowing experiences where he nearly got killed, he decided the electronic aid to his hearing might be a good idea.

"Yes."

"After I almost got killed then got off my high, stubborn, horse and got these, everything changed." He pointed to his hearing aids.

Interesting, but nothing I didn't know.

"There are two reasons I'm telling you this. First, Sal thinks I'm losing my mind. All he remembered before showing up at my door last week was the phone conversations we had before I got the aids. I couldn't hear him. I had to guess what he was talking about. That's not easy to do because he tends to talk comedy, jokes, weird things.

"Anyway, he has a bigger heart than he shows, and came

to make sure I was okay. That's the reason he gave. It may be true, although I'm guessing it's more than that. I don't think they've worked in years, except maybe Wallace's son. He makes regular appearances at clubs and on TV. They came bumming free rooms. They don't think I know. Understand?"

I did, but suspected there was more. "You said two things."

"They're worried about Wallace. As you can tell, his mind wanders from sharp to *huh?* They believe that if he can get settled somewhere for more than a few days, he may not have as many distractions. He can concentrate on seeing things better."

That didn't make much sense. "Do you think it'll work?"

"Probably not."

I shared what Wallace told me about a body, then asked if Theo thought Wallace actually saw one.

"In his mind, he did. In reality, who knows."

I didn't want to call Allen with that analysis, yet knew I'd better. I owed him that much for letting me take Wallace to Theo's. I called when I got home to share what little I'd learned after returning Wallace to his temporary residence.

Allen said it sounded like Wallace might need more psychological help than the others with him could provide. If I thought he didn't appear to be harmful to himself or others, it was okay to let Wallace stay. I thanked him for caring.

"Chris, I told Chief LaMond what your new acquaintance said about a body."

Chief Cindy LaMond and I had been friends since she arrived nine years ago from East Tennessee. She was promoted two years back to chief, or Director of Public Safety, of the Folly Beach Department of Public Safety. For reasons that defied explanation and beat all odds, I'd been involved in several murder investigations since arriving on the island. That would've made sense if my career was in law enforcement.

I'd spent a better—some might say best—part of my life being a tiny cog in the bureaucratic wheel of a large, health-care company in Kentucky. After moving to Folly, I'd owned a modest photo gallery, which didn't defy the odds and, like eighty-percent of small businesses, went belly-up a year ago. I had no business being involved in crimes, much less murder, but when my friends were touched by evil, I felt the need to get involved. Cindy was a part of some of the cases and had proclaimed me as being a murder-magnet; not the legacy I desired to perpetuate.

I sighed. "What did she say?"

Allen chuckled. "I won't tell you what the chief said. It was laced with four letter words."

"Don't suppose love was one of them?"

"She mumbled so many so fast, I could've missed it but I don't think so."

"Figures."

"Tell you what she did do. She said while she didn't think there was a speck of truth to what the delusional fishing-rod waver told us, to be safe, she sent a couple of our guys to walk the dunes. Unless a body is out in the open, I doubt they'll find anything. We're short-handed, so they only had a short time to check."

"Good," I said. "It's an effort. Thanks for following up."

The following morning, I walked next door to Bert's Market for a danish and a cup of complimentary coffee. It wasn't the breakfast of champions, but my chances of becoming the champion of anything were long gone. Bert's was a must-visit location for locals and vacationers in need of food, drink, and the necessities of island life, such as toilet paper, beer, and gossip. The grocery prided itself on never closing. To me, it met the meaning of *if they don't have it, you don't need it.*

I was sipping coffee and talking to a couple of employees who always had a smile plus an occasional bit of information about what was happening to share with customers on the six-mile long, half-mile wide island. Our conversation was interrupted by Charles Fowler.

"Chris, see you're bummin' coffee," Charles said as he winked at the employees.

His use of the word bummin' fell under the definition of irony when spoken by Charles. I met the long-time resident my first week on Folly. For reasons I couldn't articulate, we became best friends. He *retired* to the island at the age of thirty-four, after a less-than-illustrious career on the line at Ford in Detroit, and a few years working for a landscape company where he'd proudly bragged that he'd been a hoer.

He was a couple of years younger than I, more than a few pounds lighter. While I'd been spending thousands of hours a year working, he'd spent an equal number of hours perfecting unemployment. When I opened the photo gallery, Charles appointed himself executive sales manager. Since I'd never paid him, I was glad to let him wear the inflated title.

Bert's employees said they needed to get to work and left Charles and me to do whatever.

He watched them go behind the deli counter. "Rumor is that you've been playing school crossing guard on Center Street."

"Where'd you hear that?"

"Tell you one thing, I didn't hear it from you."

Charles was one of the island's repositories of rumor, fact, and trivia. Two things irritated him more than should bother a rational person. Unless you wanted to hear an earful of nasty, don't call him Chuck, Charlie, or any derivative of Charles, and if you know something that he would deem important, you'd better not dally telling him. I often practiced that second irritant.

"Who told you?"

He huffed. "Amber. She heard it from Marc Salmon, who heard it from—"

Amber was a waitress at the Lost Dog Cafe who knew as much as or more than Charles about the goings-on on the island. Marc was a long-term city councilmember who was in the Dog nearly as often as Amber.

"Got it, that's enough. Did you know Theo Stoll has a brother?"

Charles pulled his shoulders back. "Sure, Salvador. Theo told me a while back that his younger brother was a stand-up comic, had been big back in the heyday of stand up. Why?"

"Did you know Salvador is staying with Theo?"

Charles tilted his head like he was thinking about it. "Is that who was fishing in the street?"

Finally, I knew something that Charles didn't know. "No, it was Wallace Bentley. He—"

"What's that got to do with Theo and Sal?"

Several customers converged on the area where we were standing.

"Grab coffee and let's walk."

Charles got a cup.

I refilled mine and led him up the long block to Center Street then right toward the Folly River.

We'd walked a block before Charles began to pester me about what I knew about Theo and his brother. He would've started the questions sooner but had been distracted by a couple walking two Labs. Four-legged crea-tures were one of the few things that could distract my friend from zeroing in on whatever he wanted to know.

We crossed Center Street and were standing in front of City Hall when Charles pointed at the sidewalk. "Park it, and tell me what herding a fisherman out of the street has to do with Theo and Sal."

The Devil was not in the details to Charles, although he'll bestow the wrath of the Devil on anyone who didn't share all the details. I began with finding Wallace in the street then, after a couple of dozen questions, managed to finish by telling him I escorted Wallace to Theo's house. He wouldn't be satisfied until he knew the color of Wallace's bathing suit, if his shoes were slip on or lace up, and if I knew the brand of fishing rod.

I tried to explain how Wallace seemed to confuse reality with fantasy.

"Don't we all?" Charles asked.

No, I thought and shrugged.

I saved the part about Wallace seeing a body for last. If I'd mentioned it earlier, the conversation would've gone in a different direction. I never would've finished the story.

Charles's eyes bulged. He put his hands on his hips and glared at me. "He said what?"

I repeated what Wallace had said, emphasizing the part about Wallace not knowing if he'd seen it yesterday, the day before, or four years ago.

"How're we going to find it?"

Years ago, Charles decided he was a private detective. He had no formal training, had never been a police officer, yet figured that since he'd been a lifelong reader of detective novels, he knew everything there was to know about the profession. The scary thing was that, over the last decade, he, a cadre of our pals, and I had solved several crimes that had stumped the police.

"You mean the alleged body that had been somewhere along some beach between one day to four years ago?"

"That's the one."

I rolled my eyes.

He looked at his phone. "Whoops. I'm supposed to deliver something for Dude."

Dude Sloan owned the surf shop and had Charles deliver packages to local customers. That, along with helping restaurants clean during busy spells, and providing an extra set of hands for local contractors, provided Charles with enough income to afford his tiny apartment and minimal living expenses.

He turned and started to walk to the surf shop when my phone rang. Charles's nosy factor kicked in. He stopped, then reversed direction.

"Hi, Theo," I said.

Charles leaned closer.

"Sure, what time?"

Charles had no idea what I was talking about but pointed to his chest.

I took the hint. "Can Charles come?"
Charles smiled and nodded.
Theo said, "Could I stop him?"
"No."
I looked at Charles. "Theo's house, noon, tomorrow."
Charles gave a bigger nod as he headed to the surf shop.

Chapter Four

I was in front of Theo's a half hour before the time he asked us over. Charles considered on-time thirty minutes before those of us who pay attention to watches define as on-time. My friend is not constrained by owning a watch, seldom checks the time on his cell phone, yet his altered reality prevails. And, no, it does no good to argue with him. It's easier to adjust to his time.

An older model, silver Lincoln Town Car land yacht was parked behind Theo's Mercedes. Charles jogged up the street, stopped in front of me, panted, and put his hands on his knees.

"You're almost late," I said.

"Nope. Didn't want to keep Theo waiting."

Theo wasn't as familiar with Charles's time-altered universe; he acted surprised to see us on the porch.

"Oh," he said and looked at his watch. "I didn't expect you this early."

Charles said, "We're not ear—"

"Got here quicker than I thought we would," I interrupted before Charles got into a time-wasting discussion about time. "We can come back later."

Theo stepped back, waved us in. "No, no, that's fine. Not sure the others are up."

I didn't see anyone else on the first floor but heard sounds from a television coming from upstairs.

Theo motioned for us sit on the couch in the great room then asked if we wanted coffee. We declined.

He looked at the stairs, joined us on the couch, and whispered, "It's good that I caught you alone. The whole crew will be here this morning. They said they wanted to meet you."

That seemed strange since I'd already met Sal and Wallace.

Charles said, "I'd like to meet your brother and his friends."

That was no surprise since one of Charles's unmet needs was to meet each living soul on earth, plus visitors from other planets who might stumble on earth during their space travels.

Theo bit his upper lip and glanced at the stairs. "Also, wanted to tell you something about Wallace. Chris got a hint when he brought him back yesterday. Charles, Wallace sort of loses touch with reality." Theo shook his head.

Sort of loses touch, I thought. Delusional would better describe him.

Charles said, "Oh."

"Sal told me it's been coming on for years. Said, at first, it was funny. His friends thought it was part of Wallace's act, except it kept getting worse; he did it all the time, not just on stage."

I said, "Has he seen anyone about it?"

"Chris, he's seventy-five. Men his age," Theo tilted his head. "Umm, men his age, and my age, think it's a sign of weakness to get head-doc help. He hasn't and flat out won't.

Sal says Wallace is harmless, the group keeps an eye on him."

Keeps an eye on him like when he was nearly run down in the street. "I hope they're right. He could've been killed yesterday."

"I know. I wanted to ask you to be patient with him. He might not remember what happened. He might not recognize you."

I nodded.

"Think he saw a body?" Charles asked.

Theo looked at the stairs again. "Depends on how close he was to reality at the time. You understand, I barely know him. From what I've seen, I'd give it a fifty-fifty chance. There's something else you need to know. Wallace's son, Raymond is, how shall I say it, he's not personable."

Charles leaned close to Theo. "Meaning?"

Theo lowered his voice so low that I hardly heard him. "He's rude, obnoxious."

"Meaning?" Charles repeated.

"Didn't rude and obnoxious cover it?"

The sound of someone coming down the stairs kept Theo from elaborating.

Sal hit the bottom step, turned toward the couch, and smiled. He wore another colorful, open-collar shirt, black slacks, with untied boat shoes on sockless feet. "Well, if it isn't one of my old brother's only friends. I bet you're Chucky, the bum-looking buddy."

I took a step toward Sal, ostensibly, to shake his hand, but more to be between Charles—Chucky—and Sal so my friend couldn't attack.

"Good to see you again, Carl," Sal said as he grabbed my hand.

I faked a smile. "It's Chris. Good to see you."

Charles moved beside me and reached out for Sal's hand. "And I'm *Charles*."

"Whatever. Glad to see you. Theo says you're a crime-fighting duo. Something about you catch killers before the police figure it out."

"I wouldn't say that. We're—"

Charles interrupted. "Yes, we are."

"You helped save my bro's life a while back," Sal said.

"Theo was the real hero," I said. "He figured out who the killer was and—"

"And was seconds from an untimely trip to meet my Maker," Theo interrupted. "Enough ancient history. I told the guys you'd be stopping by."

"Yeah," Sal said. "He wants you to meet the rest of his houseguests. Don't know why, the rest of them are pretty unlikable."

After Sal's underwhelming greeting, and him thinking that the rest of the crew was unlikable, I wondered how we could get out of the house. The sounds of someone clomping down the steps stopped Sal before he could insult us further.

"Good morning, Wallace," Theo said, as the latest arrival made his way over. He had on a light-blue nurses' scrub top over red and white checkered pajama pants.

Wallace said, "We have visitors?" He wiped his eyes before glancing from Charles to me.

"You remember Chris," Theo said as he patted me on the shoulder. "You met him yesterday. And this is my friend, Charles." He put his other hand on Charles's arm.

Wallace blinked in the direction of Charles, then turned to me. "Can't say I remember. Were you at my show?"

Theo saved me. "Chris met you in town. He brought you to the house."

"Oh," Wallace said, apparently not convinced.

Two more men had made their way down the stairs while Wallace shared his confusion.

Theo said, "Here's the rest of the crew."

"Hi, gentlemen. I'm Marvin Peters, but prefer Pete Marvin."

He, like Sal and Wallace, was in his mid to late seventies, average height, bald, and unlike the others, chubby. From the muscle turned to flab in his forearms, he could've been a weightlifter in earlier times.

Charles and I introduced ourselves as the person we hadn't yet met walked past us on his way to the kitchen.

"That's Ray," Theo said and gave me a sideways look like he was reminding me about the rude, obnoxious one.

Pete started to say something when Ray returned carrying a cup of coffee. He looked to be about fifty, five-foot eleven, and movie-star handsome. It was clear that he got his looks from his mother.

"Who are you again?" he asked, not caring that he interrupted Pete.

We hadn't said who we were in the first place. I let it go and told him our names.

"Why are you disturbing our peaceful morning?"

"They're friends," Theo said. "Remember when we were talking yesterday? You said you would like to meet them since you weren't here when they brought Wallace back? I asked them to stop by this morning."

"Must have been Pete. I wasn't paying attention to what you were yakking about."

Wallace said, "Theo was telling us that they had a friend who owns a country music bar who may let us do our act there."

Wallace had been closer to reality than last night, yet he didn't remember me bringing him back. Strange.

"Sorry, Chris and Charles," Theo said, and waved for us to return to the couch. "That wasn't the reason I wanted you to meet the group. You've been nice to me from the day we met, can't say the same for everyone. I wanted my new acquaintances to meet you. Sure you don't want coffee?"

The phone in the kitchen rang, and Theo left to answer it.

Sal watched him go and leaned closer to Charles and

me. "Glad we have a few seconds without." He nodded toward the kitchen. "The reason I'm here is I've been worried about Theo. We haven't talked often. The last couple of years when I called, he sounded out of it. He couldn't remember much of anything." He waved his hand toward his friends. "We had a break from touring, so I wanted to get over and help. Theo has money. I didn't want anyone taking advantage of him."

"How's he been since you've been here?" I asked.

Ray interrupted, "Old and stuffy."

"A gentleman, a true gentleman," Pete said, as he gave Ray a dirty look.

Sal flipped the back of his hand at Ray like he was flicking away a mosquito. "I don't understand it. He seems fine. Don't know what's going on."

Theo returned. "You talking about me again?"

"Nah. We were saying that since Chris and Charles are here, we'd ask if their friend, Hal, would hire us to do our act in his bar." He turned to me. "Of course, we've performed in large venues all over the country, entertained thousands. We'd like to get back to our roots, you know, intimate venues, closer to our adoring fans. We have all the money we need, so Hal wouldn't have to pay the fees we're accustomed to. Of course, we couldn't work for free. You understand, don't you?"

I glanced at Charles, who leaned back on the couch and folded his arms. Thanks, friend.

"It's Cal, not Hal," I said. "I don't know if he'd be interested. We'll ask."

"I can still picture that SRO crowd in Chicago, Sal," Wallace said. "Tuesday, wasn't it?"

Charles leaned my direction. "SRO means standing room only."

I whispered, "I know."

Sal patted Wallace's back. "Wallace, I believe that was a couple of years back."

Ray blurted, "Damnit, stupid. Join us on planet earth."

Wallace turned to me. "That's my charming son."

I nodded.

Theo said, "I know you two must run, so we won't keep you. I wanted you to meet my guests."

I didn't know we had to run but understood why. Theo was giving us an out. We apologized for having to leave so quickly and said it was nice meeting Theo's friends—Ray excluded. That remained unsaid.

Theo and, for some reason, Wallace walked us to the door.

I took the opportunity to ask, "Have you thought more about the body you saw on the beach?"

Wallace rubbed his chin. "Body?"

I reminded him what he'd said about seeing a dead body. I omitted the multi-year window.

"I said that?"

"Yes."

"Sorry, fine sir. I don't recall that."

Charles looked down as I said goodbye to Wallace and Theo.

As we walked away, Charles said, "Wow, let's do that again. I didn't know comedians could be so funny."

Right, I thought, along with, *Did Wallace see a body?*

Chapter Five

I was to meet Barb Deanelli for supper at Loggerhead's Beach Grill, located across the street from her ocean-front condo. She owned Barb's Books, a used bookstore located on Center Street in the space that had housed my unsuccessful photo gallery. We'd been dating for less than a year.

It was warm for April, so I took a seat on the restaurant's elevated deck and watched for her crossing West Arctic Avenue. I had acquired some of Charles's habits through osmosis. While not a full half-hour early, I arrived at the restaurant before the time we were to meet, enjoyed the warm breeze pushing in from the ocean less than a half block away, and talked to Becca, one of Loggerhead's servers.

Within a minute of the appointed time, Barb gracefully walked across the street. She was my height, much thinner, with short, black hair, and wore linen slacks and one of her several red blouses. She saw me leaning against the railing, waved and, seconds later, arrived at the table and gifted me a smile and a peck on the cheek. She asked if I'd been waiting long.

Not wanting to be accused of being Charles-in-waiting, I stretched the truth, saying that I'd just arrived.

Becca returned, and we each ordered a glass of wine. Barb added a conch fritters appetizer.

Barb watched the server leave, shrugged, and said, "What can I say? I'm starved."

She was four years younger than I, yet her metabolism was that of a twenty-year-old marathon runner. She never gained weight. I hated her for it.

After the traditional winter lull that affected most businesses on the island, vacationers had begun arriving, and Barb's Books reaped the benefits. The downside was that I hadn't seen her as often as I would've liked. I wish I could've said that about business when I owned the gallery.

Our drinks arrived.

Barb took a sip and said, "I hear that a, and I quote, 'stupid ass local' ran in the middle of traffic on the busiest street in town to escort a 'funny looking guy flailing a fishing pole' to the sidewalk." She took another sip.

Barb had moved here from Pennsylvania a little over a year ago, and had already learned how to accumulate gossip and an occasional fact with some of Folly's better practitioners of the art.

I grinned. "Where'd you hear that?"

"Sorry, bookstore owner, book-buyer privilege."

I reminded her that she was no longer practicing law, and that I doubted that there was any such privilege.

"Maybe not. The more important question, was it true?"

Becca delivered the conch fritters.

Barb stuffed one in her mouth, gracefully, of course, and I proceeded to share the entire Theo, Wallace et al. story.

Barb didn't interrupt, something I wasn't accustomed to

from my other friends. When I finished, she asked, "Is Sal anything like his brother?"

It wasn't what I'd expected her to say, although it made sense. Barb was my friend, Dude Sloan's half-sister, and they were less alike than a turnip to a trampoline. Dude was an aging hippie stuck in the 1960s, had never met a sentence that he couldn't mangle, while Barb had been a successful attorney with the ability to use the English language as it was intended. I shared that Sal was different than his brother, although not as different as Barb was from Dude.

"Think he saw a dead body?"

"Good question. He could have, although his credibility tanked when he couldn't decide when he'd seen it. He also said that he performed in Chicago last week, when he was reminded by one of his friends that it'd been two years ago. It seems more fantasy than fact."

"That doesn't mean it couldn't be true."

"I agree. That's why I told Officer Allen Spencer, who shared it with Chief LaMond. Allen said that the chief had a couple of her guys walk part of the beach. I don't know what else to do."

There was little I could add about Theo's friends and the alleged sighting of a body, so I asked if she'd seen Dude lately.

She chuckled and said that he'd stopped in the bookstore to see if she wanted a surfing lesson. I remembered the one and only lesson I'd had with Dude. It was terrible. Wipeout was the one surfing phrase I could identify with. I swore I'd never get on another surfboard, more accurately, never attempt to get on another surfboard.

"What'd you say?"

Barb took a sip, looked in the glass, then at me. "I told the dear, sweet man that there was a better chance of getting me to go shark fishing barehanded." She chuckled. "Dude said, 'Okeydokey, you be sorry.'" Her smile turned serious. "I figured something out. Dude didn't think I'd go surfing. He was using what he knew to reach out to me."

Barb and Dude, other than sharing a father, had little in common. They hadn't lived near each other after high school and had only reconnected a year ago, the result of a horrific event that involved a hired killer who'd been sent to eliminate Barb. One of Dude's loyal employees had given his life to save Dude's half-sister. It wasn't the Hallmark Channel way of bringing estranged siblings together.

"What made you decide that?"

Her smile returned. "Suppose it was because after I said that a surfing lesson was off the table, he plopped down on the floor, crossed his legs yogi style, and said, 'Me be glad you here.' He pointed a finger at me then at his head, before saying, 'Maybe break pumpkin bread together.'"

That be Dude, I thought. "I hope you can spend time together. Dude's one of the good guys. From what I can tell, doesn't have many true friends."

"We're having supper next week. Maybe you can join us. I'll need someone to translate Dudespeak."

I laughed. "That would take someone with a greater Dudespeak vocabulary than I have. Charles often translates it for me. When are you meeting?"

"Don't know. It has something to do with a phase of the moon. I'll get back with him after the weekend to narrow it down."

Dude, in addition to being Folly's leading expert on surfing, and an expert on and still residing in the 1960s, is a worshiper of the sun god, and a student of astronomy. He speaks in solar terms rather than what the rest of us call days, hours, minutes. I find it endearing, and equally confusing. *That be Dude.*

I agreed to join them when Barb figured out when they were breaking pumpkin bread.

She gave a sigh of relief and changed the subject. "Karl and I attended a few comedy clubs in Pennsylvania. I wasn't, and guess I'm still not, big on jokes and many of the stand-up comics we saw felt that, unless their act was filled with profanities and sex jokes, they weren't funny."

Karl was Barb's ex-husband, who had been arrested and disbarred after bribing state legislators and governmental officials. Their breakup was the primary reason that Barb had moved to Folly.

"I went to a comedy club decades ago," I said. "You're right about the subject matter."

Our entrees arrived.

Barb had ordered broiled flounder and in a feeble attempt to eat better I'd selected the fried flounder; it beat a half-pound cheeseburger.

Barb took a bite then turned toward the beach. "The reason I brought it up was, didn't you say Theo's brother and his friends were in their seventies?"

"Three are. Wallace's son is younger, of course. He's probably fifty."

"I thought being a stand-up comic was a young person's game. The ones I saw were in their twenties and thirties."

"I suppose most are, although there've been several famous older comics."

Rodney Dangerfield, George Carlin, and George Burns came to mind.

"I'm sure there are, though it seems rare. My point being, I wonder how long ago it's been since Theo's group performed."

"Sal mentioned that they had a break in their touring. I suppose a break could be a few years. Why?"

"It's the lawyer in me being suspicious. From my experience, things seldom are what they appear. Your friend, Theo, is wealthy and in his eighties. That's an inviting combination for con artists."

"Sal said the reason for being here was to make sure Theo was okay. I know what he'd meant about Theo seeming forgetful, possibly suffering from early onset

Alzheimer's. I also know that Theo's smart and, since he got his hearing aids, he's better. I doubt Sal and his buddies will be here long."

Barb shook her head. "Don't forget, you told me a couple of years ago that Theo came close to giving that con man in his walking group a million dollars."

Point taken. "I'll keep an eye on him."

Barb took another bite, washed it down with water, and patted my hand. "Good. He seems like a nice man who could use a friend like you."

We spent the rest of the meal talking about mundane items, like the unseasonably warm weather and the larger than normal numbers of early vacationers on the island.

She also reminded me that, unlike someone at the table, she had to be at work in the morning. Subtle, it wasn't. I walked her to her condo.

Instead of going home, I headed up Center Street and listened to the live music coming from St. James Gate and Snapper Jack's. I leaned against a wall near where I'd parked Wallace in a rocking chair after helping him out of the street and smiled when I thought of how he'd been dressed. I also remembered that his dress shoes looked like they'd recently been polished.

If he'd seen a body that day, he couldn't have walked far along the beach, or his shoes would've been sand covered. That could mean that the body was in the dunes close to the center of town. I also realized that since he couldn't narrow down when he'd seen the body, if, in fact, he had seen one, his shiny shoes could've meant nothing. If there had been a body and it hasn't been found, it must be back off the beach, probably behind the dunes' line.

Barb was right. While she had to go to work tomorrow, I had little, if anything, to do, so why not spend some of that useless time checking out the dunes closest to where I met Wallace?

Chapter Six

I called Charles at 7:00 the next morning. He'd never resisted waking me when he wanted to share something, or simply to pester me. It was payback time.

He answered with a yawn followed by, "My apartment better be on fire."

I was no fan of caller ID. "I thought you'd be up and hankering for a walk on the beach."

"Only if my apartment's on fire. What's so important to interrupt my beauty sleep?"

"The sun's up, it's a nice day, and I doubt extra sleep will help your beauty. How about meeting me at the Tides in a half hour?"

"Sure," he mumbled before hanging up.

That was the kind of wake-up call I'd received from him more times than I could count. It felt good returning the favor. Besides, I'd spent the last hour thinking about Wallace's claim about seeing a body. I'd feel terrible if there was one out there and I hadn't tried to find it. If Wallace was delusional, or if he'd stumbled on a body in his more distant past, a walk on the beach with a good friend was still a great way to spend the morning.

I was in the lobby of the hotel talking to Jay, a Tides employee and a friend, when Charles stumbled through the front door. He wore cut-off shorts, a Tilley hat that matched mine, and a long-sleeve, white T-shirt with *ASU* in green on the front. Charles has the largest collection of college logoed T-shirts and sweatshirts this side of the Mississippi River— possibly on both sides. I'd given up asking about them; a fact that I knew irritated him, which was more reason not to ask.

Jay hadn't learned. "What's ASU?"

Charles puffed out his chest and grinned. "Adams State University. You know, the one in Alamosa, Colorado."

Jay rubbed his chin. "Oh, that Adams State University."

"Yep, the Grizzlies."

"Interesting," Jay said, before excusing himself. I suspected he'd heard all he wanted to about Adams State.

Charles watched Jay leave, before saying, "Okay, what's up?"

"Couldn't I want to walk on the beach with a friend?"

"That's a remote possibility. Remote if this wasn't the beach where Theo's houseguest said that he'd seen a body. Seems to my sleepy brain that we might be here to gander at more than sun, surf, and sand."

"That'd entered my mind. A couple of Chief LaMond's officers looked to no avail. Besides, Wallace could've been off a few years on when he allegedly saw what he may or may not have seen."

"Those would have been cops who ran down here, ogled college coeds, peeked at a couple of spots along the beach, got tired of getting sand in their shoes, and headed back to their fun job of writing parking tickets." Charles pointed to his chest. "You've realized, after all these years, how outstanding a detective that yours truly is, and you called me to find the dead John or Jane Doe."

"Wow, you got me," I said, not hiding my sarcasm, although he was righter than I'd admit.

"So, what are we waiting for, Beachcomber Chris?"

We walked down the steps from the outside bar to the beach then headed left under the Folly Beach Fishing Pier. If a body had been this close to the pier, it would've already been discovered, so I didn't pay much attention to the dunes until we passed East Second Street where single-family residences dominated the beachfront and fewer people frequented the area.

Charles had brought his Nikon and started snapping photos of yellow flowers snaking through the sand, and shots of one of his favorite subjects, a discarded Doritos package. If I had to describe his photo style, I'd call it eclectic. Others less generous have said he was a trash photographer. Regardless, he loved snapping photos, so I waited while he composed his latest masterpiece. He hated trash on his island as much as he loved photographing it. He picked up the empty package and stuffed it in his pocket.

A couple hundred yards later, I figured, if Wallace had come this far, his shoes would've shown evidence of the walk. "Let's head the other way."

"You're the tour guide, lead on."

We returned to the pier quicker than it had taken us to get to our turn-around spot. It took little time passing the Tides and on the far side of the hotel's parking lot, the long, four-story Charleston Oceanfront Villas condo complex.

Along the next few blocks past the condos, houses were set farther back from the beach than in the direction we had first canvassed, so we spent more time looking at the dunes and the overgrown foliage on the street side of the barrier. Charles seemed less intent on taking photos and spent more time looking for signs of something that shouldn't be there.

I was a couple of strides ahead of my friend and was the first to see an object seriously out of place. Unless someone was looking for it, the body would've gone undetected. Wallace was right.

I stuck my arm out for Charles to stop then grabbed a three-foot long piece of driftwood. I stayed a couple of feet from the partially covered body and used the stick to move underbrush and sea oats away from the head. I was thankful that I hadn't had much breakfast. The face was covered with flies. Charles leaned closer but, from where he was standing, he could only see part of the corpse.

This was a crime scene, so I didn't want to disturb it more than I already had. I took several steps back, motioned Charles to do the same, and punched 911 on my phone.

"Did you recognize him?" Charles asked after I'd told the dispatcher where we were and what we'd found.

"His face was in the shadows. I couldn't see much. Don't think I recognized him."

I heard the siren from a Folly Beach patrol car as it pulled in the parking area adjacent to a path to the beach.

Seconds later, an officer I didn't recognize approached. He had his hand on the butt of his weapon as he glanced around like he expected an armed maniac to jump out at him. "Step back. Keep your hands where I can see them," he barked.

We did as directed while he stepped closer to the body and squinted at it.

He moved to the beach and keyed his mike. "Call the Sheriff's Office. We have a possible 187. Yes, umm, yes."

He keyed off his mike and asked us for identification.

I took out my wallet, and Charles said he didn't have any ID on him. He didn't have credit cards and drove so seldom that he kept his driver's license in his car.

Officer Fisk, according to his name badge, jotted down the information from my license then stared at Charles like he wanted to frisk him to prove that he'd lied about no ID.

"Officer Fisk, my friend and I were walking down the beach when we saw the body." I pointed toward the dunes.

"I'm the one who called 911." I hoped that would alleviate thoughts that we had something to do with the death.

Fisk pointed to the shoreline. "Most people walk out there. It's illegal to walk on the dunes, so what were you doing up here?"

I wasn't ready to get into a discussion about Wallace's comments. I pointed to Charles's camera. "My friend takes photos of the flora and fauna along the beach, especially in the area separating those houses and yards from the beach." I pointed at a pre-Hurricane Hugo cottage close to where we were standing.

Charles looked at me like, "I do?"

I heard a second patrol car approach plus the distinct siren from one of the city's fire trucks. I was relieved to see Allen Spencer scampering down the path to the beach. He was followed by two firefighters who doubled as EMTs.

Officer Fisk pointed toward the body as Allen and the EMTs moved toward the person who had no need for assistance from the medical techs.

The EMTs stayed near the body, and Allen joined the three of us closer to the water. "What do we have?" Allen asked, although I suspected he knew.

Fisk gave a facts-only rundown while glaring at Charles and me like he had caught us, red-handed, killing the guy.

Allen thanked Fisk and told him to get the crime scene tape from his car to mark off the area. Allen was the senior officer on the scene, and he let Fisk know it.

"Who's Officer Friendly?" I asked. "Thought he was going to shoot us for finding a body."

Allen watched Fisk return with the tape. "He's new. He was over in Columbia and worked for the University of South Carolina's Division of Law Enforcement and Safety, or something like that."

Charles said, "Why the piss-poor attitude?"

"He's trying to prove that he's up to the job. He's also pissed because he was one of the guys the chief asked to scout the beach the other day." Allen looked toward the gathered EMTs and Officer Fisk. "The body's well-hidden, so I can see how he missed it. That doesn't mean that he won't catch an earful if the chief finds out that it's the same body the guy with you was talking about."

True, I thought.

Allen, once again, glanced toward the body then turned to me. "I suppose it is the one?"

"Appears to be," I said.

"Crap," Allen said, not an official police code.

No joke, I thought, but remained silent.

Chapter Seven

A series of ominous-looking clouds rolled in while Charles and I were waiting to give a statement to the detective from the Charleston County Sheriff's Office. The Folly Beach Police Department provides the public safety needs of the community, which include both police and fire protection. The department is outstanding, yet relies on the Sheriff's Office when it comes to investigating major crimes. Today's find qualified.

Officer Fisk and an officer who arrived on a black ATV erected a ten-by-ten-foot canopy over the body to protect the scene from the rain that appeared moments from soaking the site.

Detective Callahan from the Sheriff's Office arrived the same time as the rain. He wore a navy sport coat and gray slacks, hardly appropriate beachwear.

Charles and I followed Allen and Callahan to the detective's unmarked vehicle, where the police officials took the front seats. I'd met Callahan three years ago, when he was assigned a murder case involving members of a film crew that had descended like locusts on the island to shoot a movie. A swarm of locusts would've been more welcomed after the filming wreaked havoc on the island and exposed residents to corpses. Callahan had struck me, at the time, as being too young for his position. Nevertheless, he proved to be competent. I was glad to see that he'd caught this case.

The detective wiped the raindrops off his coat sleeves before twisting around in the driver's seat and facing me.

"Mr. Landrum, here we are again. Please don't tell me that you've stumbled on another murder."

Allen answered for me. "I'm afraid he has."

Callahan sighed then took a notebook out of his coat pocket. "Start from the beginning."

I thought about starting from our walk on the beach today, but decided Callahan needed to hear it all. I had to stop several times so he could write down the cast of characters and tidbits from the bio on each of them. The list included Theo, his brother, and the other three stand-up comics.

Allen Spencer chimed in a couple of times to tell the detective that he had met one of Theo's guests and that Chief LaMond had heard most of the story and had dispatched two officers to canvas the area for a body.

"See if I have this right," Callahan said and closed the notebook. "The Folly Beach Police Department heard about the possibility of a body along here three days ago, sent officers to scour the area, they found nothing, yet Mr. Landrum and his friend, Mr. Fowler, have no trouble finding it. Is that correct?"

"Mostly," Allen said.

"Mostly?" Callahan asked.

"Wallace, the gentleman that Chris introduced me to, seemed confused. Remember, he said he could have seen the body that day, or years ago. Even then, all he said was that it was in the dunes. You know how many miles of dunes there are around here?"

Instead of guessing, Callahan glared at Allen. "Yet the

two guys in the back seat walked four blocks from the hotel and found it."

Charles and I were asked by Callahan to tell our story again, plus repeat the names of the people visiting Theo. He gave us his card and asked that we call if we remembered anything else.

We said we would and were dismissed. It was still raining, although not as hard, as we walked back to the hotel and waited for it to end so we could continue home.

Charles slipped his camera under his shirt, pulled his soaked hat down as far as he could on his head, then reminded me that I'd said it was going to be a nice day.

THE RAIN MOVED OUT OVERNIGHT, and Folly Beach was rewarded with a stunning sunrise. The full spectrum of reds reflected off a layer of low clouds closer to the horizon while soothing oranges filtered through the higher clouds closer to the beach. It was the kind of morning that drew me to the island a decade ago. I no longer had the photo gallery, yet I hadn't stopped practicing my lifelong hobby of photography. I grabbed my camera, a light jacket, my Tilley, and headed out to capture images of the early April morning.

My first stop was at the coffee urn near the back of Bert's Market, an activity that I did so often that I could do it blindfolded. With coffee in hand and a camera strap over my shoulder, I walked a block to Center Street, the epicenter of commerce on the island. My first reaction was to turn toward the beach but, after what'd happened yesterday, I headed in the opposite direction.

My quest for the perfect photo, a quest I'd had since I'd taken up photography decades before the word digital had been used to describe a method of making photo images, was put on hold when the sinewy, sixty-six-year-old body of Dude Sloan nearly ran into me.

"Whoops, me be distracted," Dude said as he stopped inches from my feet.

He wore one of his many tie-dyed, psychedelic-colored shirts with a large peace symbol on the front. With his thinning, curly, long gray hair, Dude could be mistaken for Arlo Guthrie, the folk singer.

The surf shop, with all letters lower case for reasons known only to the owner, was a couple of blocks behind me, so I assumed he was headed to work. "Morning, Dude," I said and stepped aside so he could pass. "Heading to work?"

He shook his head. "No, be walking to Portugal."

"Have a safe trip," I said with a straight face.

"Boss," he said with an equally, although more straggly, straight face.

We were in front of the Folly Beach Crab Shack, where one of its employees was sweeping the sidewalk.

Dude moved closer to the road and leaned against a Palmetto tree at the edge of the sidewalk. He appeared to have postponed his walk across the Atlantic.

I said, "I hear you offered Barb surfing lessons."

He rubbed his hand through his week-old beard. "She as stoked about lesson as you were."

I didn't need to be reminded of my ill-fated surfing lesson from years gone by. "She enjoys spending time with you."

"Not as much as she enjoyin' with you." Dude hesitated and slapped his knee. "Aha, me remember news flash." He tilted his head in my direction. "Hear you do it again."

Not having Charles, my Dude translator, with me, I had to ask more questions than I normally would. "What am I doing again?"

"Findin' bod in brambles."

I didn't need a translator for that. "Yes. Where'd you hear it?"

"Folly rumor mill be runnin' three shifts. Like, he told her, her told her, her told he, he told me."

I doubted any of the he's or she's who transported the story to Dude was the person who put the body where I'd found it, so it would be a waste of time to get names. "Did you hear who the man was?"

"*Affirimente.*"

"Who?"

"He be called murder vic."

I sighed. "What about his name?"

"Clueless."

A condition many who didn't know Dude well might agree with. They *be* wrong. While my friend's speech pattern bore a distant resemblance to proper English, his mind was sharp, his sense of humor keen, his concern for others touching.

I nodded like he'd told me something profound.

Dude snapped his fingers. "Speakin' of fractional sis, we be breakin' bread together. You hang with us? Need help understandin' lawyer talk."

I didn't want to tell him that Barb had already invited me. "Love to. When?"

"Soon." He pantomimed talking on a phone. "Let you know."

On any other sidewalk in the universe, our conversation would be considered strange or downright stupid. From my experience, it made perfect sense on Folly Beach, South Carolina. It ended abruptly when two of my most recent acquaintances, Wallace and Marvin, appeared beside us.

Wallace smiled, looked at the woman sweeping the sidewalk, at the light green doors leading to the Crab Shack, and back to Dude and me. "Mushroom walks into a bar. The bartender yells at him to leave, saying 'We don't serve your kind here.' The mushroom says, 'Why not? I'm a fun guy.'"

Marvin laughed, Dude looked at Wallace and blinked,

and I wondered why I hadn't walked in the other direction when I reached Center Street.

After the hilarity died down, Marvin said, "Wallace closes his act with that. Audiences love it." He stopped as if that said it all.

I tried to bring a touch of sanity to the conversation and introduced Dude to the comedians, told him that Marvin Peters preferred to be called Pete, and said that Dude was a good friend who owned the surf shop a couple of blocks from where we stood. I shared that the comedians were visiting Theo.

Dude smiled. "Theo be cool geezer. Be hangin' long?"

Great question. I looked forward to their answer.

"Maybe," Pete said.

I'd waited for that?

"Hear about dead bod Christer found?" Dude asked.

"I found it first," Wallace said.

"Me be confused," Dude said.

I explained to my confused friend that Wallace had told me about seeing a body along the dune line, then I'd shared that information with the police. I didn't think it would be helpful to share when he claimed to have seen it.

"That's right," Wallace said. "I saw the poor soul yesterday afternoon. Tragic, so tragic."

"Why be hangin' with Theo?" Dude asked, oblivious to the fact that Charles and I had discovered the body before Wallace had claimed to have seen it. I wrote the contradiction off to Wallace's escapes from reality.

Pete put his arm around Wallace's shoulder, and said, "Theo's brother, Sal, had several conversations with his brother in recent years and felt Theo may have memory issues. He wanted to be close and asked the rest of us if we wanted to take a break from our grueling touring schedule to spend time here."

"That be kind."

"We've been friends for a long time. It's the least we could do for Sal."

That reminded me of Barb's question about how long it had been since the comics had worked. "Where was your last gig?"

"Up north," Pete said.

"Cool, For Santa at North Pole?" Dude asked.

Pete and Wallace had never been exposed to Dude's sense of humor and didn't respond.

Dude smiled. "Be kiddin'."

"Oh," Pete said. "Good one."

"Santa not alone. Mrs. C plus elves be with him."

Wallace said, "Want to go on the road with us? We could use some new jokes."

Dude nodded. "Me ponder it."

Enough, I thought, and said, "I think Dude has a full-time gig here. When did you perform last?"

Wallace glanced skyward. "Don't recall."

That was no surprise.

Pete added, "It's been a while. Tell us about finding a body. Who was it?"

Wallace jerked his head toward Pete. "Body. What about a body?"

Dude said, "The bod you said you saw other side of last sunset."

Wallace looked at Dude and at me. "I don't understand what he's talking about."

I wondered if it was how Dude said it, or if Wallace had already forgotten what he told us about seeing the body.

"I'll tell you later," Pete said and turned to me. "The last time we talked, you said a good friend of yours owned Cal's Bar. You were going to talk to him about getting us a gig."

That wasn't how I remembered it, but reinforced that I knew Cal, that I'd mention it to him.

"When?" Pete asked.

I avoided the question. "I'll get back with you or Sal after I talk to Cal."

"Good, guess we'd better leave you to your conversation. Sorry to interrupt."

Dude said, "*Adios*."

I said, "Talk to you later."

Wallace said, "What body?"

Chapter Eight

Cal's Country Bar and Burgers, better known as Cal's to everyone, except the IRS, was located a block off Center Street in a building that had seen its better days a decade ago. The interior's condition matched the exterior. The bar hadn't opened for the early drinkers.

Its front door was locked, so I went in the side entrance. Overhead, fluorescent lights, not illuminated when the bar was open, cast a cold, depressing image. The walls were painted dark green with patches of the previous brown paint showing through areas chipped away from contact with tables, chairs, and an occasional inebriated customer taking out his frustration over lost love, lost fortune, or lost keys. The ever-present smell of stale beer and long-ago fried burgers rose from the shredding indoor-outdoor carpet. According to owner, Cal Ballew, those "unique" features made Cal's the perfect country music bar.

Cal was on his knees, fiddling with something behind the ancient Wurlitzer jukebox parked on the edge of the wooden, elevated bandstand sandwiched between the restrooms in back of the room. He heard the door slam behind me and twisted around to see who'd entered.

"Good afternoon, Cal. Need help?"

Cal groaned as he maneuvered his seventy-four-year-old body from kneeling to standing. He reached his six-foot-three-inch, slim frame's full height, and wiped his hands together like he was knocking the dust off. "Not unless you're an electrician. This dang music machine keeps shorting itself out. Know how hard it is to get someone to fix this antique?"

"Not easy?"

"About as rare as plutonium in the parking lot."

I was impressed that the country crooner knew what plutonium was and agreed that there wasn't much of it in the lot.

"I doubt I can help." Far from profound, but true.

"One thing this old bartender can do is get you a drink. What's your pleasure?"

It was still early, so I said Diet Pepsi.

Cal said he thought he could rustle one up, as I followed him to the beat-up, dark, wooden bar along the side of the room. He massaged his lower back as he bent his curved-from-age spine over the cooler. His long, gray hair covered one of his eyes. His signature sweat-stained Stetson, which normally held his hair in place and had traversed most of the South with him for forty plus years, was parked at the other end of the bar.

Cal grabbed a beer then I followed him to one of the dozen tables where he flopped down in a chair. He pointed to the side door. "Since you came in that way instead of the front, I'm guessing you ain't here for alcohol, music, or chillin'."

"Can't slip anything by you, can I?" I didn't remind him another reason for my side door entrance was that the front one was locked.

He smiled. "Truth be told, I reckon you could slip something by me if you were hankerin' to." He pointed his index finger at his head. "Think after four decades on the road sleeping in my car, now seven years trying to keep this place off life support, my brain's as shorted out as that old jukebox."

I had never seen my friend this down, and I'd seen him in a few bad situations, including nearly getting killed. I was also struck by how different the bar and its owner were when illuminated by unforgiving fluorescent lights. When Cal's was lit with a couple of dim lights over the bar, plus neon beer promotional signs, with traditional country music blaring from a healthy jukebox, Cal's came alive and was a popular hangout for locals and vacationers who were fortunate enough to stumble in.

The man who could pass for one of the area's homeless and, who happened to be sitting across from me, would walk on the stage wearing his Stetson, a white rhinestone coat that had travelled as many miles with him as had his hat, and an endearing smile. He'd lean close to an old silver microphone and sing a country classic. I can't guess the number of nights, Cal's voice, image, and sad songs would transport me back to my early years listening to the country greats of the time. A night at Cal's was magical.

I considered it an honor to be his friend, but it was difficult at times to step behind the magical stage and see the realities of his world, and I suppose the real world of most who appear bigger than life when they're on stage.

I told Cal about Theo's houseguests. Cal was a member of the walking group that Theo was a part of, so he knew Theo's experiences on Folly. They weren't close, yet Cal felt a kinship to Theo.

I finished, and Cal asked if I wanted another drink. I declined, and he went for another beer, returned, looked around the empty room, then lowered himself in the chair. He looked at the ceiling, and said, "Stand-up comics and country crooners from my era have a passel of things in common. In the '60s, before comedy clubs began to spring up like rabbits, there weren't many places for comics to perform, so many of them travelled around the country the same way I did. I'd grab a gig wherever I could find one and, occasionally, there were comics sharing the stage. We led nomadic lives." He grinned. "Hell's bells, I've got a couple of ex-wives to prove it. Anyway, we hit tiny towns, tinier towns, towns that weren't even towns."

"That had to be rough."

"If I made enough money to pay for a couple of meals and gas to get to the next town; it was a good gig. I heard that many of the funny guys who were making the rounds were about as successful as I was. Once a few comedy clubs opened, mostly along the left and right coast, some of the guys, or an occasional gal, made it big. Comedy clubs were the thing in the 1970s. One old-timer told me there were more than three hundred of them in the '80s. People laughed more back then."

I was surprised that Cal knew that much about the history of stand-up comedy, and I told him so.

"Chris, if I hadn't taken the road to poverty by being a country singer, I dreamed about being a funny guy."

Cal could be funny but had never struck me as being a comedian. "Did you try?"

He wiggled his hand. "Could have made it big, yes, I sure could have."

"What stopped you?"

"Couple of things. I had a piss-poor memory. Couldn't remember a routine." He shook his head and closed his eyes.

I wondered if he was reliving a time on stage. "The other thing?"

"Couldn't tell jokes."

That'd be an impediment. "I'm glad you couldn't. I can't picture you being anything but a country singer."

"Enough about my past. Why are you telling me about Theo's jokesters?"

"They were wondering if you'd let them do their thing from up there." I pointed to the stage.

"Are they any good?"

"Never heard them."

Cal looked at the stage and at me. "They can't be as bad as some of the singers, and I use that term loosely, that show up open-mic night."

Cal's had open-mic night every Tuesday. The level of talent ranged *from I wonder why they don't have a record deal*, to *I wonder why anyone ever told them that they could sing worth a darn.*

"That's great. I'm sure they'll be thrilled."

"They don't expect to be paid, do they?"

"Afraid so."

"If they think that, they are funny. Pard, I can't afford to pay me. I care a lot more about myself than I do them."

"How about me telling them that they can perform for tips. If they show that they can bring in a big crowd, you'll consider paying them."

Cal rubbed his chin. "That'll work. See if they can do their thing on Sunday night. That's my slowest time. They can't run off too many customers."

On that ringing endorsement, I left Cal, so he could get back to playing electrician.

Chapter Nine

I wondered why I hadn't told Cal about one of the comedians claiming to have seen the body and decided it may've changed his mind about letting the group perform. My mind wandered back to thinking about what Wallace had said and his state of mind when he said it. I didn't wonder long. My phone rang.

"Good afternoon, chief."

"If you think it's a good afternoon, you're in a time zone other than mine. Give me a hint about what's good about it?"

"Well—"

"Never mind," she interrupted. "That's not why I called. Are you roaming around my fair city?"

"If you mean roaming like walking aimlessly, of course not. I am out, was at Cal's, now heading home."

"Crap, if I wanted a definition of roaming, I would've grabbed a dictionary instead of a phone."

"Why did you call stupid, old me?"

"Don't put yourself down. You ain't that stupid. Now old, well."

"Cindy, why'd you call?"

"I learned a couple of things about the body that my crack force couldn't find, yet some senior citizen had no problem stumbling across."

"What?"

"It'll cost you."

I sighed louder than I'd intended.

"No need to get huffy," the chief said. "I'll let you off easy. Meet me at the Surf Bar in five. All I need is an order of fries. Since the head of local law enforcement is supposed to be sober most of the time, you'll get off cheap buying me a Coke."

She hung up before I could say that I'd be delighted to buy her fries and a Coke. She was right, it often cost much more to get information out of her.

The Surf Bar is across the street from the section of City Hall housing the Department of Public Safety. When I arrived, Cindy was at a table near the front door of the rustic bar. The interior was small, and most of the tables were occupied by customers ranging from college students getting an early start on happy hour, a couple of construction workers, whose clothes looked like they had been down-and-dirty in dirt, and a lone middle-aged man, gripping a beer bottle while staring at a surfer video on the monitor in the center of the back bar.

Cindy waved a greeting. She's in her early-fifties, five-foot three, with curly dark hair and a quick smile. Today, it wasn't at full wattage.

"Rough day," I said as I sat opposite her.

She looked at the table, at the dollar bills attached to most every surface, and shook her head. "Do you know how many moving violations my guys handed out yesterday?"

"How many?"

She gave me a tight grin. "Hell if I know. Halfway through the pile of paperwork, I hurled it at the wall. I lied about wanting a Coke. Would you mind going over to the bar to grab me a Blue Moon on tap while I sit here feeling sorry for myself?"

"With fries?"

"If you insist."

I told the bartender what I wanted.

She pulled a Blue Moon for Cindy, handed me a Coke, and said she'd bring the fries to the table when they were ready.

Cindy took two gulps of beer before I settled in the chair. I didn't figure that a pile of moving violations would've put her in the sour mood. We've been friends for years, so I felt comfortable pushing.

"What's bothering you?"

She took another gulp and tapped her fingers on the table. "Nothing."

I stared at her.

She sighed. "Okay, you beat it out of me. The little squirt's beginning to piss me off."

The *little squirt* was how she occasionally described Larry, her husband, although for obvious reasons, never to his face. Larry, who owns Folly's hardware store, had been married to Cindy for seven years. He was a decade older than his wife, at five-foot-one, was a couple of inches shorter, and way more pounds lighter than his spouse would admit to being. I'd known each of them before they met. They were the happiest couple I knew.

"What's he doing?"

"He's beginning to piss and moan about me having to work so much. He forgets that, during the holiday season, he handcuffs himself to the store, and the only time I see him is if I go there to buy a set of Allen wrenches, whatever the hell they are."

Cindy and Larry had gone through a horrific time a couple of years back when he'd been accused of murdering a friend who'd tried to blackmail the hardware-store owner about something from his past. They had weathered the storm and, from what I could tell, were still madly in love.

"Have you talked to him about it?"

"We talking about the same Larry?"

I didn't answer.

"Talking to that squirt about feelings is like talking to a cockroach about its family tree."

The fries arrived, and she asked the server if she could find another beer hanging out somewhere in the bar.

The server said she thought she knew where one was and went in search of it.

Cindy shook her head. "How'd you manage to shanghai the reason for me wanting to talk to you? You want to hear what I know about the body, or not?"

"Yes, although I'm more concerned about you."

She patted my hand. "You're so freakin' sweet. Downright sickening."

"Thanks, I think."

"Don't let it go to your balding head. I spend most of my time dealing with the dregs of society, slobbering drunks, and arrogant vacationers. Compared to what I have to deal with, you're not so bad." She smiled. "Thanks for caring. We'll be okay."

The server had been successful in her search for another beer.

Cindy took a drink, a sip instead of the gulps she'd chugged earlier. A good sign.

"Okay, here's the skinny. The body that my entire police force couldn't find, but you managed to trip over without breaking a sweat, was Michael Hardin. Name ring a bell?"

"No."

"Hmm," she said. "Anyway, he celebrated his forty-seventh, and last, birthday, a couple of months ago. He was well-known by the Charleston Police Department, although not because of his benevolent donations to their orphans' fund. He had a rap sheet the length of a roll of toilet paper.

To sum it up, he'd been a drug dealer. It gets sketchy at that point. According to Detective Callahan, the late Michael Hardin, may've been a confidential informant for their drug unit."

"May have been?"

"He thought it was more than *may have been* but couldn't confirm it. If Hardin had been a CI, that role ended a while back. Hardin made a career change three years ago."

"Became a cop?"

"Funny. He turned to bookmaking, not the kind you read."

"A bookie?"

"Yes, the ancient art of taking bets ain't kosher although, if caught, you don't get thrown in the hoosegow for as long as you do for selling drugs."

"Did he live over here?"

"No, he had an apartment in downtown Charleston although, according to a couple of my guys, he spent quite a bit of time hanging out in some of our restaurants, as well as the Pier."

"Plying his trade?"

"No doubt." Cindy chuckled. "One of my guys said he wasn't too hard to recognize. He wore a straw hat with a feather sticking out the top."

"That rings a bell. I think I saw him a few times. Average size, good tan, well-dressed. I remember the feather. I thought it was strange." I shrugged. "Over here, who knows?"

"That's the one."

"What killed him?"

"Unless he had a massive heart attack while strolling through the dunes, it was blunt force trauma caused by something hard smacking him in the head."

"Has anyone talked to Wallace Bentley since the body's been identified?"

"Callahan did last night. Wallace swore that he'd never

seen anyone dead, or alive, at the beach. The police must've been smoking pot to think that he had."

"Yet Wallace told Allen Spencer and me that he'd seen a body. He'd been confused about how long ago it was."

"Welcome to my world," Cindy said before taking another sip.

"What's next?"

"Let's see. I'm going to wolf down the rest of these fries, finish this beer, head home, see if I can communicate with the cockroach, and—"

"About the murder," I interrupted.

For the second time in an equal number of beers, she said, "Hell if I know."

Chapter Ten

I left Cindy attacking the rest of the fries and stopped at Barb's Books. I could've called, but it was easier to visit. Besides I'd rather see Barb than talk to her on the phone.

A woman was buying four used books, and a man was browsing a shelf of mystery novels when I entered.

Barb saw me at the door and held up one finger, indicating that I should wait.

The customer finished her purchase and nodded to me as she left.

The man continued browsing without paying attention to us.

"Good," Barb said as I approached the counter. "I was getting ready to call. Dude asked if we could move supper to tonight instead of some future moon phase."

I peeked at my watch. "I think I can work it in my busy schedule. Where and when?"

Barb smiled. "Busy schedule?"

"Retirement's a full-time job."

She rolled her eyes. "6:00, the Crab Shack. Think you

can take a break from your full-time job to help me understand what Dude's talking about?"

"For you, anything," I said, as the former browser became a book purchaser. I stepped aside so Barb could take the man's money. On my way out I said I'd see her at 6:00.

I had a couple of hours to kill before I was to begin my translator duties, so I walked to the end of the Folly Beach Fishing Pier. Along the way, I passed a dozen or so men and women watching over fishing rods, hoping to land the catch of the day. Several vacationers strolled along the walkway, hoping to get a glimpse of the dolphins that frolicked nearby, competing with the fishermen for food. At the Atlantic Ocean end of the Pier, I climbed to the second level of the diamond-shaped structure and gazed back at the beach.

The outdoor bar at the Tides was packed, and a rousing volleyball game was in progress at the court between the hotel and the pier. I smiled, thinking about the many hours I'd spent over the years at this spot, reveling in how fortunate I was to live on the Edge of America, as Folly was called, being lucky enough to have a full-time job being retired, and having more friends that I'd accumulated during my life in Kentucky. I thought about how different some of my friends were to the others, to the point that I was asked by both Dude and Barb to serve as a translator. I chuckled when I reminded myself that they were related.

My mood changed as my eyes shifted from the Tides, past the Charleston Oceanfront Villas, to the spot where I discovered the late Michael Hardin. It was ironic how a matter of a few feet can separate the gaiety of the vacationers romping in the surf, soaking up the sun's rays, while the lifeless corpse of someone who would never laugh again had been so close. As much as we would like to think that we are in control of our lives, the reality is that, often, we aren't, and how we erroneously think we know what's happening nearby.

That depressing thought brought me back to what I remembered about Michael Hardin, not finding his lifeless body, but recalling I'd seen him around town. If it wasn't for his straw hat with the feather, I never would've noticed him. The more I thought about it, I realized that I'd seen him on the Pier. He had been talking to two men dressed like they were going to a business meeting rather than taking in the sights.

The three were in animated conversation, their body language hinted that they were arguing. It didn't strike me as unusual at the time, since conventions were often held at the Tides with participants taking breaks at the bar or on the Pier. Now that I knew one was the dead bookie, I wondered if their disagreement was related to betting. Could the two men have had something to do with his death? It was possible, although the incident took place a week or so before Hardin had been killed. I wouldn't be able to identify the men, nor had any idea what they were talking about. I shook the memory out of my head as I watched a young boy squeal when his dad caught a two-foot-long shark and dropped it on the deck in front of his son.

I ARRIVED at the Folly Beach Crab Shack, where Barb and Dude were seated on the outside deck.

Dude waved. "Yo, Chris, hang with us?" Dude was on his best behavior since he called me Chris, not Chrisster, his usual permutation.

I didn't know if they knew that each other had asked me to be part of their breaking pumpkin bread, so I smiled and said that I would.

Neither acted surprised to see me.

Barb scooted over, and I joined her on the bench seat. She kissed my cheek.

Dude said, "Ewe, mushy."

A server arrived, handed Dude a martini, a beer to Barb, then asked if I wanted anything.

I said I would have a white wine.

Dude took a sip and said, "Be bod searchin' again?"

Not how I'd hoped our pleasant evening breaking bread, pumpkin or otherwise, would begin.

"Nope. Been a busy week at the surf shop?" I asked to change the subject.

"Nope."

"I've had more customers than most any week since I opened," Barb said, either understanding my desire to change the subject, or feeling left out of the conversation.

Dude nodded and turned back to me. "Hear who bod was?"

The death was on Dude's mind, and he wasn't to be deterred. "Yes, Michael Hardin."

"Be kiddin'."

"That's what Chief LaMond said."

Barb leaned closer. "Do they know what happened?"

"Nothing, other than someone hit him in the head. No suspects."

Dude closed his eyes and said, "Michael Hardin, Michael Hardin, me know him."

That got my attention. "You do?"

"He be bet taker. Me not above laying down lucre on soccer. Nice chap, pays bets *rapido*."

The server returned with my drink and took our orders.

Barb waited for him to go before saying, "You bet with a bookie?"

Dude shrugged. "Preachers no take bets."

"Do you know if he had enemies?" I asked.

Dude held up his forefinger. "One."

"Who?" I asked.

"Person thought he be baseball," Dude said as he rotated his arms like he was swinging a bat. He grinned and took a sip of martini.

"You don't know who?" I said.

"No. He, me, no best buds."

Barb waved her hand between Dude and me. "Might I suggest we move to a more pleasant topic?"

"You might," Dude said. "What?"

Barb smiled. "Dude, remember when you told me I needed to move here after my divorce?"

He nodded.

"After I was here a week, I thought you were crazy."

Dude said, "Why?"

"Everybody was so nice. I wasn't accustomed to it. They wanted to know all about me, why I was here, what I was doing, suggesting where I should eat. To be honest, it was off-putting."

Dude rubbed his chin. "Like chocolate pudding?"

Barb tilted her head. "No, I mean disconcerting, unpleasant."

Now I knew what Dude had meant about me translating.

Dude smiled. "You be on-putting now?"

"Chris told me that most newcomers either hated or loved Folly. I thought I was one of the former yet, the more I relaxed, the more I realized that the people were sincere and cared about me, a stranger; I began to look at things differently." She laughed. "So, yes, I suppose I've come to realize that most of the people here are on-putting."

"Cool," Dude said. "Talking newcomers, Sal's pals be strange."

Coming from one of the strangest, that was saying something. "What do you mean?"

"Sal and *moi* had confab. He no be surfer. Be fan of canines. Stopped Pluto and me in middle of sidewalk to say

Pluto cute. I say he be. He, Sal, not Pluto, like to confab with Pluto." Dude stopped and waited for a comment.

Pluto was Dude's Australian terrier.

I waited for Barb to say something.

Instead, she looked at me with a glazed look in her eyes.

I took the hint. "Dude, have you met Sal's buddies?"

"Not that know of. Heard."

"What've you heard about them?" Barb asked. She was catching on.

"They be funny men. They be helpin' Theo. They be busted."

The last part got my attention. "Did Sal say that they didn't have any money?"

"No, he say they be stayin' in Theo's *casa*, eatin' Theo's food. Dude knows bummin' when sees it. They be busted."

"Oh," I said.

Dude took that as the end of the discussion about Sal and his friends and started talking about astronomy, one of his favorite subjects.

Barb knew as much about astronomy as I did, which could be summed up in one word: zilch. She moved the conversation back to how well she was doing with her bookstore and how much she liked her condo.

The conversation rambled for the next half hour while food and additional drinks were consumed.

Dude said he needed to get home to let Pluto out.

Barb said she needed to get home to rest up for another busy day in the store.

I said I didn't need to get anywhere and said I would walk Barb home.

To both Barb and my surprise, Dude picked-up the check, and thanked us for "hangin'" with him. He hugged Barb, and said, "Me no be huggin' Chrisster."

Chapter Eleven

I was curious about what Dude shared about Theo's guests being broke, which reminded me that the comedians wanted to meet Cal to talk about performing at his bar. I called Theo's at a reasonable hour the next morning. Apparently, 10:00 fell outside the definition of reasonable for people who'd spent their careers with their work day starting after 9:00 p.m.

Theo was awake and told me that he hadn't heard a mouse stirring upstairs. That wouldn't have surprised me, considering Theo's hearing problem, but he assured me he was wearing his hearing aids and would've heard his guests moving around. I told him why I was calling, and he said he'd have Sal call once he had his first cup of coffee. He added that I wouldn't want to hear from his brother before he had his coffee.

I was pondering whether to have a peanut butter sandwich or a four-day-old muffin for lunch when Sal called. I said good morning.

He mumbled, "What's good about it?"

"It's a lovely day."

"Maybe through your eyes."

He made up for his surliness when he said, "Sorry I'm cranky, mornings aren't my best time of day."

I resisted reminding him it was noon. I asked if his group still wanted to meet Cal.

He said, "Definitely."

I suggested that I could meet them at Cal's tonight and introduce them to the owner.

He said that was great and suggested 9:00.

I swallowed hard, as I knew that was pushing against my bedtime. As a concession to Theo, I agreed.

I wanted to remind—warn—Cal about his visitors, so I stepped into the bar an hour before the comedians were to arrive. There was a decent crowd for a weeknight. From the jukebox, Merle Haggard was telling us he was proud to be from Muskogee, a couple seated by the door were arguing about whether Roger Miller was a better songwriter than Kris Kristofferson, and Cal was tending bar while wearing his Stetson, a fire-engine red T-shirt with the Budweiser logo, and black jogging shorts.

I waved but, before I could say anything, he opened the cooler, grabbed a bottle of Chardonnay, and poured me a glass.

I moved to the bar, thanked him for the drink, and said something about him having a nice crowd.

Cal tipped his hat in the direction of two tables, with five customers at each. "This old cowboy loves conventions at the Tides, especially conventions where the meetings are as dull as a marshmallow in a briar patch."

Cal was from Texas, so I excused some of his sayings. "Great."

The jukebox played Cal Smith's version of "Country Bumpkin," one of the tables of conventioneers sang along, and I reminded Cal about Sal and his crew wanting to talk with him about performing. I told him they were coming tonight.

He pointed to the only empty, large table and said for me to grab it so we could talk when the funny men arrived.

Nine o'clock came and went, as did 9:15. Many customers had departed, leaving the conventioneers and the couple who continued to debate the pluses and minuses of country songwriters.

I was ten minutes from calling it a night when the door opened and Sal entered, followed by Wallace and Pete. Jerry Lee Lewis screaming "Great Balls of Fire" from the jukebox couldn't come close to holding the remaining customers' attention compared to the sight of three seventy-something-year-olds strutting in.

One wore a robin-egg blue three-piece suit, one had on a red sport coat, a white open-collar dress shirt, and a black ascot with white polka dots, and the third gentleman was doing a Johnny Cash imitation, wearing all black. I didn't know how funny their act was, but they looked hilarious.

I peeked at Cal.

His eyes widened; his next move was a combination of head shake plus shoulders slump.

Everyone in the bar was staring at the three men who must've parked their time machine out front.

I was the only person who knew who they were, so I greeted them and led them to the table I'd been saving.

"Sorry we're a tad late," Sal said as he led the group to the table. "Pete couldn't find his ascot."

The Johnny Cash look-alike Wallace chimed in, "I thought I'd burned it. No such luck."

The three took seats around the table.

Sal said, "We wanted Cal to see us at our best. This is our stage wear. I say look professional, be professional."

"What're the chances of us getting beer?" Pete asked.

"Pretty good, pard," Cal said. He was standing behind Sal and looking down at the comedians. Three Buds?"

"That'd be a good start, barkeep. Cool hat."

I moved closer to Cal and introduced the group. I stuck

with first names since I wasn't sure I remembered their last names.

Wallace tipped an imaginary hat to Cal and said, "A dyslexic walks into a bra."

Sal laughed, patted Wallace on the shoulder, and said, "Good one, Wallace." He turned to Cal. "We're comedians. Can't help being funny."

Cal looked at Wallace, without breaking a smile, even after Wallace couldn't help being funny. "I'll grab the drinks."

"Where're Ray and Theo?" I asked the group.

Wallace said, "Theo said it was too late to be running around. Ray, umm, Ray. Oh yeah, my son. He stayed at the house. He was talking to his agent about starring in a TV sitcom."

"Yeah, right," Pete said, "and I'm king of Kansas."

"He may join us later," Sal said, probably to prevent a battle between Wallace and Pete.

Cal returned, set a bottle of Budweiser in front of each comedian, and Pete pulled a pack of Marlboros from his coat pocket.

Cal slipped his hand between Pete and the cigarettes. "Whoa, pard. No smoking in here."

Pete's jaw dropped. "You're joking."

"Nope," Cal said. "You're the comedian. I'm an old country crooner."

Sal leaned toward Cal. "How can you have a country bar without cigarette smoke sucking out oxygen?"

"Well, turtle turd," Pete said poetically. "First, we can't light up at Theo's, now not here. What happened to freedom? I thought one of the Constitution's amendment things gave us the right to smoke in bars."

Wallace nodded, "Sir, we're comedians. Research has found that joke and smoke go together like pigs and pork chops."

Cal pulled his Stetson down lower on his forehead. "Gentlemen, I'm no expert in research and haven't read the Constitution since I was in high school, about the time it was written. In my book, smoke, choke, and croak go together." He pulled a chair from the empty table next to us, turned it around and straddled the back. "Let me tell you something. I spent more nights on the road than there are grains of sand out there on the beach singing in bars, restaurants, on bales of hay on pickup trucks, hell, even highway rest stops. Cigarette smoke was everywhere. I hated it, but it was part of where I performed; probably the same for you guys."

Wallace nodded again.

Sal started to say something, but Cal wasn't done.

"Two of my best buds from yesteryear; danged good singers in their day, died of lung cancer. One smoked like a forest fire. My other friend never stuck a cigarette in his mouth. Hell, he got lung cancer from secondhand smoke, was in hillbilly heaven before the term secondhand smoke was invented."

Sal said, "Sorry."

Cal was on a roll. "I can't stop people from doing stupid things. What I can do is slow them down when they're in here. Like my good buddy, great songwriter, and performer Roger Miller once penned, 'Don't we all have the right to be wrong now and then.'" Cal lowered his head, "Roger died of lung cancer."

That silenced the group.

Pete broke the uneasy silence. "Cal, speaking of dead, did you know the bookie that was dead on the beach?"

"Don't think so. What was his name?"

Wallace stood, smiled at Cal, and said, "What did the fish say when he ran into the wall?"

"Huh?" Cal said.

"Dam," Wallace said, then laughed at his joke.

Pete chuckled, and Sal shook his head.

It was past my bedtime. I began wondering if I was having a bad dream.

The comedians' beers were gone before two more songs finished on the jukebox, and Cal headed to the bar for refills. He returned, and the comedians greeted the bottles like they were their first drinks after being stranded on a desert island.

Cal turned his chair around and scooted up to the table. "Chris, you're always sticking your nose into everything. Do you know who the dead guy was? Ascot man there said he was a bookie." Cal pointed his beer bottle at Pete.

I said, "Name was Michael Hardin. He was—"

"Damn," Cal muttered. "I know him."

Cal's revelation quieted the group. I wanted to hug him for that welcomed event. Instead, I asked how he knew Michael.

"Hard to miss," Cal said, not answering my question. "The boy wore that stupid hat with the bird feather sticking out of it. He was in here all the time."

"I know who you're talking about," I said, "I don't remember seeing him here."

Cal removed his Stetson and ran his hand through his long, gray hair. "He mostly showed up late, probably past your bedtime."

"Was he here with the same people each time?" I asked.

"Nah, most nights he came in by himself. Sat at that table over there." Cal pointed to a table on the far side of the room.

I looked at the table then turned back to Cal. "Did that seem strange?"

"Chris, you know I don't like butting in anyone's business. I never asked him, and couldn't swear to it on a stack of Bibles. If I was a wagering man, I'd put a good helping of greenbacks on Michael taking bets."

Sal chuckled. "If he wasn't dead, you could place your bet with him."

Cal sighed, shook his head, turned away from Sal, and said, "Chris, I've seen a fair amount of betting in my day. Michael would park his rear end at that table, buy a drink or two, and, all casual like, some of my regulars would saunter up to his table, take a seat, lean over, and whisper something. Yes, they would."

Cal stopped and looked around the table like that had explained everything.

"What else happened, Cal?" I asked, hoping for more.

He rubbed his chin. "Let's see. Michael would take one of those flip notepads. You know, like cops carry."

I said I knew.

"He'd open it, write something and, after he finished scribing, the person with him would take cash out of his, occasionally her, pocket and give it to Michael."

Cindy said that Michael had dealt drugs before turning to bookmaking.

"Cal, could he have been dealing drugs instead of taking bets?"

"Suppose so, although I never saw him giving his visitors anything except cash. From what I know about some of his customers, umm, visitors, taking drugs would be a big stretch." Cal looked at the table where he had remembered seeing Michael. "I'll miss him."

Sal leaned closer to the table. "That reminds me. A man goes into a Hallmark Store. He says to the clerk, 'Do you sell sympathy cards?' Clerk said, 'We do.' The man says, 'Could I exchange this Get Well Soon card I bought yesterday?'"

Now I knew I was dreaming.

Sal added, "Get it? It's a dead joke, like that bookie."

Cal and I stared at him.

Pete slapped him on arm. "That joke was funny when Ray told it, remember? That was, before you stole it from him."

Sal said, "Picky, picky. Ray ain't here. It seemed appropriate in light of the gruesome conversation those guys are having." Sal turned to Cal. "While we're talking about jokes, Chris said you were anxious to talk to us about bringing our Comedy Legends World Tour to your fine establishment."

Cal turned to me and mouthed, "Legends. World Tour. Anxious?"

"Sal, I said I'd introduce you to Cal and let him decide if he wanted to add comedy to his nightly offerings."

"Tomato, tomahto," Sal said as he waved his hand in my face. He turned to Cal. "What do you think, Cal, old buddy?"

Cal pushed his Stetson back on his head. "Tell you what, pard. Back when I was making numerous appearances on the Grand Ole Opry, I got to know Sarah Ophelia Colley Cannon and Louis Jones pretty good."

"Who?" interrupted Sal.

Cal grinned. "Sorry, only their good friends called them their real names. You might know them as Minnie Pearl and Grandpa Jones."

"Yes, sir," Sal said. "I didn't know them as well as you did, of course. Everyone in this business knew about those famous country comics. I saw Minnie Pearl in a show once in Birmingham."

Cal looked at Sal and at the other two comics with him. "The point I was going to make is I have a soft spot in my heart for joke tellers. I think, if we can come to terms, I could spare the stage for your show. A Sunday night would work."

Sal took off his glasses and rubbed the bridge of his nose. "Cal, our group has a limited number of open dates on the schedule. I was checking before we came over, and it looks like sometime in the next couple of weeks might work. Let's talk about our fee."

Cal leaned back in the chair and nodded. "Okay, let's. Here's the deal. As an advance, I'll pay you nothing. After you finish, I'll double it."

Sal started to stand.

Cal waved at him to remain seated. "Whoa, pard. I'll tell you what. Before you start, I'll introduce one of you as MC, and I'll tell everyone that tips will be appreciated. During your set, umm, acts, you can plug the tips."

Sal nodded at the other two stand-up comics. "That's several Franklins below our minimum. We're already on Folly, and some of our expenses are being covered by my brother, so we'll do you a favor and give it a go."

"Mighty fine of you, sir," Cal said.

I knew he was being sarcastic, but Sal smiled like he'd negotiated a multi-million-dollar tour.

They agreed to perform Sunday and said they better get back to the house to see how Ray was coming with his TV deal.

I stood, and Cal asked me to hang around. I stayed at the table, and Cal got more drinks for the table of conventioneers who were still enjoying their time away from the hotel.

He returned and scooted his chair closer to mine. "Didn't want to mention it in front of Larry, Curly, and Moe. I figured, since you were nosing into the death of Michael, you need to hear about what happened two nights before he turned up deceased."

I started to deny that I was doing any nosing. Instead, I asked, "What happened?"

"You know Neil Wilson?"

The name sounded familiar, but I wasn't sure. "Tell me about him."

"Big guy, muscle turned to fat. I hear he played football at South Carolina."

"I know who you mean. Looks like a tall fire hydrant on steroids."

"That's him," Cal said. "He works security at a couple of places in Charleston. A few months ago, he asked if I needed a bouncer. He said he lived in an apartment on Ashley Avenue and was trying to find extra work close to home. I told him that I couldn't afford my part-time cook and me."

"I've seen him in Bert's. What about him?"

"He sashayed in, lumbered in, and made a beeline toward Michael Hardin. It was the last night I saw Michael at his office table. It was crowded, so I didn't hear what they were talking about. A few minutes later, I heard Neil bellow something like, 'Over my dead body.' He smacked the door so hard on the way out I thought the hinges were going to pop off."

"Any idea what it was about?"

"You're the detective. Knowing what I know about Michael, it must've had to do with money. If I had to guess, I'd say Neil owed Michael a piss-pot full of it."

"Enough to kill him over?"

Cal nodded. "You bet."

Chapter Twelve

I got up later and hungrier than usual. Last night at Cal's had pushed me past my normal bedtime, so I walked to Bert's for coffee and a two-pack of donuts, where I saw Chester Carr talking to Denise, one of the clerks. I had known Chester for several years, first when he worked at Bert's, much better two years ago, when he formed a senior-citizen walking group that I had joined to learn more about an alleged blackmailer among the walkers. That experience nearly got Theo and Chester killed, not to mention me almost losing my life.

"Morning, Chris," Denise said, interrupting her conversation with Chester.

I returned her greeting, acknowledged Chester. With the late Michael Hardin fresh on my mind, I asked Chester if he could spare a few minutes when he was finished talking to Denise.

He nodded.

I continued to the coffee urn.

Before I took my first sip, Chester was beside me. "Been missing you and Charles walking with us."

Chester was approaching ninety, stood five-foot six and, in the words of Charles's late Aunt Melinda, was "a spittin' image of Mr. Magoo."

"Sorry, Chester. I need to start back."

"I've heard that before. What's up?"

"Do you know Michael Hardin?"

Chester took his Coke-bottle-thick glasses off to rub his left eye. He returned the glasses to their rightful place. "Would that be the Michael Hardin you and Charles found out past the Oceanfront Villas?"

I smiled. "The same."

"Yeah, I knew him. Nice guy. I hated to hear what happened, although, I'm not surprised."

"Why?"

"I heard he was pushing drugs a few years back. Seldom anything good comes from that. After he got in deep doo-doo with the cops, he switched directions to become a book-ie." Chester looked around and whispered, "I heard that he'd spent time in prison. That's a rumor; he didn't tell me. I'd guess that participants in both of those careers have shorter life spans than the average clerk in here."

That was hard to argue with. I asked if he knew anything more specific.

"Mind you, I never placed a bet with Michael," he said. "Don't suppose I ever will now. I know a few who did."

The store was crowded, and we were in the line of traffic to the coffee. If I'd learned anything from years of frequenting Bert's, it's not to stand between morning customers and their caffeine.

"Let's step outside."

It was in the low seventies and pleasant, so Chester followed me to the tree-shaded, parking area between the store and my house.

Chester took a sip of coffee and said, "You trying to catch whoever killed Michael?"

"Not really. I'd seen him a few times, was trying to learn more about him."

"That sounds like yes to me."

I shrugged. "Know if he had enemies?"

Chester watched a rusting, classic Fiat carrying a surfboard drive past then turned to me. "I didn't know him well. He was always pleasant. It seems he had a booming bookmaking business from the number of people I saw him huddled with. Betters lose more often than they win, so I reckon some of them could've been mad, but heck, it wasn't Michael's fault they lost."

"You weren't aware of anyone angry with him?"

"Not off the top of my head."

"Do you know Neil Wilson?"

"Doesn't ring a bell. Who's he?"

"Someone I hear had a beef with Michael."

"Describe him."

"Big guy," I said. "Played college football, works security in Charleston. I don't know him. I've seen him in Bert's a couple of times, but never talked to him."

"Still doesn't ring a bell. What was his problem with Michael?"

"Not sure. I heard they had an argument in Cal's."

Chester shuffled his feet in the sandy parking lot. "Now that you mention an argument, I do recall something. Don't know why I didn't think of it earlier. It was, oh, a couple of weeks back, when I saw Michael on the sidewalk in front of Snapper Jack's. He was puffin' on a cigarette and waving his arm around like he was being attacked by a swarm of bees." Chester hesitated and smiled. "I can picture it now. Sort of funny." He hesitated again and watched another vehicle drive by.

"And?" I said, channeling Charles's lack of patience.

"Sorry, my train of thought ran off the tracks."

"Michael fighting off a swarm of bees."

"Oh, yeah. Weren't bees. I was coming up from behind him, didn't see the other person until I got beside Michael."

"Other person?"

"Yeah, Michael was blocking my view. He was in a heated discussion with Janice."

"Janice?"

"Yeah, you may know her, Janice Raque. Nice little lady. She's in her late fifties, about five-foot three, short brown hair with bunches of gray sneaking in. She spends a lot of time walking the beach, hunting shark teeth."

That described several people. I didn't know if I knew her or not. "What about her?"

"She's usually chirpy, big smile, easy laugh. Not that day. She looked like she was ready to knee Michael in the, umm, well, somewhere that'd get his attention."

Chester stopped talking. I was beginning to wonder if I'd have to knee him to get him to finish whatever he was trying to tell me. "What was she upset about?"

"Couldn't tell you. I didn't want to stop and get in the middle of it. I did hear her say something about him not doing what he was supposed to do, how it cost her big bucks."

"Any idea what?"

"Nope, but I can tell you that dear, sweet Janice was royally freakin' out."

He didn't think about that when I asked if he knew someone who might have been angry at Michael?

"Do me a favor. Let me know if you hear anything else about Janice and Michael, or if you hear anything about anyone else mad at him."

Chester laughed. "So, you want to know because you're *not* trying to figure out who killed him?"

"Correct," I said, wondering if it sounded as insincere to Chester as it had to me.

"If you say so."

That answered the question.

Chapter Thirteen

According to Chester and Cal, Neil Wilson and Janice Raque had issues with Michael Hardin. Could their anger have escalated to murder? I had a nodding relationship with Neil, but didn't know Janice. If anyone knew more about them, it would be Charles. It was a gorgeous day, so I walked eight blocks to his Sandbar Lane apartment.

He gave me a less-than-welcoming reception, as he motioned me in. He looked like he hadn't shaved for a week. His long-sleeved Virginia Commonwealth University T-shirt had a mustard stain between the m's in Commonwealth. His hair was a mess, matching the rest of him.

Charles was one of the most positive people I knew. He could find good in the most obnoxious people, liked most everyone, and was a walking, talking ambassador for Folly Beach.

A year ago, his long-term significant other, Heather Lee, an aspiring country music singer, had decided at the urging of a Tennessee music agent to move to Nashville to seek fame. To no one's surprise, Charles moved with her. To no one's surprise, Heather was a failure in Music City. She had been a regular performer at Cal's open-mic nights, entertaining the audience with her enthusiasm and positive stage presence. Her singing sucked. That wasn't enough to stop her from following her dream; a dream that became a nightmare when her agent was murdered. She skyrocketed to the top of the suspect chart with a bullet.

I helped prove her innocent through luck and with assistance from friends. The experience convinced her to lower her expectations and remain a big fish in the small pond in the country music world on Folly.

Charles and Heather returned to the beachside community, yet Heather never returned to her former, cheerful self. She slipped out of town, leaving Charles a note, asking that he not try to find her.

He was devastated. While he's shown glimmers of his former self, there've been bouts of despair. It seems I caught him in the middle of one of those downs.

"Up for a walk?" I asked as he looked around the room for somewhere for me to sit.

Charles had one of the largest collections of books outside the Library of Congress. Floor to ceiling bookshelves covered three walls in the living room, nearly as many in the other rooms, including the bathroom. Plus, each horizontal surface, including the two chairs in the living room, held stacks of reading material.

He muttered, "I guess."

That was the right answer, since it would've taken a forklift to clear a spot for me to sit. Some of my fondest memories had been when we walked agenda-free around the island. We were photographers, and the island was a photo-rich environment, so we'd spent hours taking photos, although that was a good excuse to talk about whatever came to mind.

We left the large, gravel and shell parking lot when Charles said, "What direction?"

I was more interested in helping my friend than where we walked. "Your call."

"I'm not in the mood to find more bodies, so let's not go to the beach."

I turned right on West Indian Avenue then walked a couple of blocks before he spoke again.

Charles kicked a rock out of the road and mumbled, "The only two women I've loved. One dead, one gone."

Four years ago, Charles's Aunt Melinda, whom he hadn't seen for many years, moved to Folly from Detroit, Charles's hometown. She had brought her boundless enthusiasm, friendliness, and endearing charm with her. She also brought a diagnosis of terminal cancer and died less than a year after arriving. Charles was still not over her passing. Now with Heather gone, he was struggling to return to the man I'd known for years.

"Charles, there's nothing I can say to lessen the pain, but there're many people here who think the world of you. They'd do anything to help."

He kicked another rock. "That's what's keeping me sane."

I started to joke about his sanity, something I could've done before all of this happened. He would've responded to my insult with a smart aleck remark, and we would have continued our walk. After Heather moved, his friends were on thinner ice, weighing their words carefully. His sense of humor had been a casualty of the loss of his two loves.

We walked another block before he said, "Learn anything new about Michael Hardin?"

I took that as a sign of hope that he was looking past his problems. I told him what Cal said about Michael Hardin's argument with Neil Wilson.

Charles stopped. "Big guy, six-foot two or three, lives out East Ashley?"

"That's the one. How well do you know him?"

"I don't. He was in Bert's talking to Norman. When he

left, I asked Norman who he was, and he said his first name was Neil, but forgot the last name. He told me where the guy lived and said he was asking if the store wanted to hire him to provide overnight security when foot traffic was low and alcohol levels high. Neil told the clerk that they could pay him anything. He was desperate for work. It seems that Neil had two part-time jobs in Charleston."

"What did Norman tell him?"

"They didn't need help."

"It sounds like he could've owed Michael Hardin money."

"Hmm," Charles said. He bobbed his head up and down. "A good way to wipe out a loan is to wipe out the loaner. Think he killed him?"

"Don't know. I was going to tell Cindy."

Charles stopped in the middle of the street and pointed to the pocket holding my phone. "What're you waiting for?"

I started to say that I thought there was a better place than in the middle of the street to make the call. My argument against calling the chief would have fallen on deaf ears, so I moved to the sandy berm. I tapped her number, thinking there's something unsettling about having the chief on speed dial.

She answered with a growl. "What trouble are you going to cause me now?"

I smiled. "Afternoon, Cindy. Pleasant day, isn't it. I'm with Charles. "We—"

"Crap, double trouble. Want to know what's been so strange about today? Until now, that is."

"What?" I said, as Charles waved his hand at the phone, which was his signal for me to put it on speaker. I did.

"Glad you asked. Today has been peaceful. My competent police and fire departments haven't brought me any impossible situations, and not a single house has burned down. So I wait on the edge of my chair to hear how you plan to ruin it."

I assured her I didn't plan to and then told her about my conversations with Cal and Chester. I made the mistake of asking if she'd learned anything about people who'd been betting with Michael Hardin and might have reason to do him in.

"Gee, Chris, why hadn't I thought of that? I sleep better at night knowing that some of my citizens, you know, those without any law enforcement training, are always thinking of things that we, the dumb cops, would never think of on our own."

I stifled a smart remark for the same reason that I'd withheld one from Charles earlier. Cindy had been in a bad mood the last two times we'd talked. Today's disposition wasn't an improvement.

"I know you and your folks are doing what you can. I was curious if anyone had looked closer at Neil Wilson and Janice Raque."

"Hang on a sec," she said. I heard papers rustling in the background. She returned to the phone. "I was looking through the reports of interviews my guys conducted. I know who Janice is. Let's see, yes, Officer Fisk interviewed her yesterday. She claims to have been visiting friends in Charleston around the time that Michael lost his last bet. Neil Wilson hasn't been interviewed by my folks."

Charles leaned closer to the phone. "Cindy, he'd be a good one to talk to."

"Chris, you sound like Charles, your worthless friend."

"Cute," Charles said. "What about it? Neil had a reason to make the bookie disappear."

"We haven't talked to him, Chris," Cindy said with an emphasis on Chris. "That doesn't mean the Sheriff's Office hasn't. I've told you before, their folks often treat us local yokels like we're a few thousand cells short of having half a brain. To keep you from pestering me more than you already have, I'll share what you learned with Detective Callahan."

"Thank you," I said. "Who else is on the list?"

I didn't think Cindy had heard my question. She hesitated, then said, "NOYFB."

She had me on that one. "What?"

"It's police code for none of your, umm, freakin' business," she said and hung up.

Charles stared at the silent phone. "Chris, I think she made that up."

We started walking toward the center of town, with a rejuvenated bounce in Charles's step. He had something to think about that didn't involve Melinda or Heather.

I was a step behind him when he stopped. "Know what we need to do?"

I was afraid to ask, but did anyway, "What?"

"You knew Michael Hardin."

"Barely," I said.

"And you found his body."

"Yes."

"It's fate, you knowing who he was and finding his body. That says it all."

"What does it say?"

"You've got to figure out who killed him. The best news is I'll help." He smiled and nodded. "You're welcome."

Tell me again why I decided to visit Charles's apartment.

Charles looked at his bare wrist. "Whoops. I have to deliver two packages for the surf shop. While I'm doing that, you start working on a strategy to figure out who killed bookie man."

Charles picked up extra cash making local deliveries for Dude. Up until when Charles had purchased a car to make the move to Nashville, all his deliveries were within a few blocks of the surf shop. He could now travel farther, yet Dude said he preferred to use "them big ole brown clunky trucks" for those deliveries. That's UPS for those who don't know Dudespeak.

Before Charles left me standing in the street, I asked

what he would be contributing to the task of finding the killer. He'd said that, since I was the college graduate, I would need to strategize, outline our alternatives, and design a plan of action. I repeated my question about his contribution, to which he said, "I'll come up with all the stupid ideas so you can shoot them down. That'll help you figure it out."

I bit my tongue and didn't remind him that he claimed to be the private detective, nor had I agreed to his half-baked idea that it was fate that I should figure it out. I shared what I knew with Cindy. Her job, and the job of the Sheriff's Office in Charleston, was to catch bad guys. I had no reason to get involved.

I was sticking to that story.

Chapter Fourteen

T he phone rang as I settled into my kitchen chair, preparing a labor-lite lunch of peanut butter on rye and Doritos.

"Chris, this is Theo. Could I ask a favor?"

I told him he could ask, although I couldn't promise that I'd be able to do whatever it was.

"Fair enough. Could you come to the house? There's something I'd like to talk to you about while the guys are out. I'd come to you, but I'm waiting for a plumber."

I was intrigued enough to tell him yes. I finished my sandwich on the ride over and was greeted by Theo before I'd reached the top step to his porch. He was dressed in blue jogging shorts, a T-shirt with Maryland Terrapins in red block letters, and his usual knee-high support socks. I hoped he wasn't taking sartorial lessons from Charles. He looked around like he was afraid someone was watching then waved me in. He led me to the great room filled with sturdy, light-colored, wood furniture, and original oil paintings on the walls. I sat on the couch and waited for him to tell me why I'd been invited.

Theo apologized twice for asking me to come on short notice. He fiddled with the elastic waistband on his shorts, went to the large windows overlooking the marsh and the Folly River, stared out, then returned to the couch. He was nervous, and I was starting to catch his affliction. Theo was getting to the reason for the meeting, as slow as he walked. He had the reputation in the walking group as being slower than coal turning to a diamond. With the average speed of the walkers zipping along at zero miles per hour, that was telling.

Before I started pacing with him, I asked, "What's bothering you?"

He looked at me like he'd forgotten that I was there. "I don't know how to start. I'm not sure, don't know what to do."

"Have a seat, and start at the beginning."

He slowly lowered himself onto the couch and again adjusted his shorts. "I've been robbed. I think it's one of the guys."

That wasn't on my list of things I figured Theo had called about. "Tell me about it."

He took a deep breath then pointed at the table against the wall. "See those silver figurines?"

My eyesight wasn't what it'd been years ago, but I couldn't miss three, six inch to a foot-high sculptures. One was a cat, another the head of an eagle, the tallest, a llama. I'd seen them during previous visits but paid little attention since to me they were merely dust catchers. I nodded.

"The designer we hired to furnish the house said they would add a touch of life to the room. They'd be exceptional conversation pieces. I thought they were hunks of silver that cost more than my first car. My wife, God rest her soul, said I had to buy whatever the designer recommended, so I bit my tongue, wrote the checks."

His story was interesting, although I didn't see what it had to do with him being robbed. "Okay."

Theo sighed again. "Three days ago, there were four."

"Oh."

"A silver frog was perched beside the llama."

"You think one of the guys took it?"

"Chris, I'm embarrassed to say that silly little frog cost $700. I was an inventor, an engineer by trade, so I had to do a lot of math. Granted, I'm not a math savant, but I sure as shootin' can tell the difference between three and four critters over there."

"Could something else have happened to it? Misplaced, or could someone else have taken it?"

"I have a cleaning lady who's been with us, just me now, since I moved here. I'd trust her with my life. A couple of workers have been in the house in the last couple of days. They could have swiped it, but I don't think so."

"Why not?"

"There's more."

Theo's phone rang before he could elaborate. He answered it and moved to the kitchen.

I went over to the table and lifted the cat figurine. I was struck by how heavy it was and by its intricately-detailed features.

"Danged plumber," Theo said as he came back in the room. "He can't get here until tomorrow. Sorry for having you come over. I could've met you somewhere."

"That's okay. You said there was more."

"I keep a safe in my closet. It's one that's fireproof, but not heavy. You could easily carry it off if you wanted to."

"It's gone?"

"No, but I keep $3,000 or so in it. If I ever need cash, I want it handy. Stupid, but I've always done it. This morning, I was in there to get money for the plumber, the danged one who isn't coming until tomorrow. He gives a cash discount. I'd forgotten to get it from the bank, so I went to the safe. Now, I don't know exactly how much I had, but it was more than what was there this morning. I'd guess it's $900 short.

None of the workers who've been here were on the second floor, so they couldn't have taken it."

"Was it locked?"

"No. I'm usually alone here. I wanted to keep the money safe from fire, not theft."

"Have you filed a police report?"

"And tell them what? A little statue's missing, and there's some cash gone. Or, hey, my brother, or one of his pals, is a thief."

"It probably wouldn't help, but you never know."

"I might call the cops." He shrugged. "I'm not leaning that way."

"You really think it was Sal, or one of his friends?"

"Honest to God, Chris, I don't want it to be." He sighed. "Regardless what I want, it's probably one or more of them."

"Do they think you wouldn't notice things missing?"

Theo fiddled with his shorts again and stared out the window. "When they showed up, I was excited to see them, at least to see Sal. I didn't know the others. I became less excited when Sal said he was afraid that I was having memory troubles, thought it would be good for them to hang out here to help me. I told him that my memory was fine, or as fine as an old man's memory can be. Since I got these, everything was okay." He pointed to his hearing aids. "He beat around several bushes before the real reason for them coming started to come out. I could be off, although, I'd bet I'm not. They're broke, pennies away from being flat broke."

"Did he tell you that?"

"Not in so many words." He shook his head. "Do you know what they've paid for since showing up?"

"Not much?"

"How about not anything? They've made up stories about how checks from their investment portfolios have been delayed, or residuals from television appearances from the 1980s are being held up by agents and lawyers, or, oh, never mind."

"You don't believe it?"

"You know I've been fortunate. I sold my company for a tidy sum. I'm not as stupid to the ways of business as some may think. From living as long as I have, I can detect some things a mile away."

"Such as?"

"Such as pure, unadulterated bullshit."

"Any idea who did it?"

"Not really. I hope it isn't my brother. That's hope only. It could be any of them. If, umm, never mind."

"What?"

"If I had to guess, I'd say Wallace."

"Why?"

"His memory has me buffaloed. One minute, he's making sense, knows what's going on." Theo pointed to the top of his head. "Other times, he starts talking about something from the past, or forgets what he said seconds earlier, or looks off in space like he's seeing life in another dimension. It wouldn't take much imagination to see him stealing without knowing he did it, or, this is terrible to say, I've thought, a couple of times, that he's faking his problems."

"What makes you say that?"

"He forgets things or changes the subject when it's to his advantage. It's like when he doesn't want to answer something, he goes into his mental disappearing act. I can't put my finger on it. It's a feeling, that's all."

"You could be right," I said. "That doesn't make him a thief."

"I know. They're all broke, so any of them could've taken the money or snatched the frog to hock."

Or more than one of them working together, I thought. "What do you want me to do?"

Theo smiled for the first time since I'd arrived. "Listening to this old man spew accusations helps. I don't know that there's anything you can do. I was certain that if there was anyone on Folly who might be able to help, it'd be you."

I was glad Theo felt that way. I told him that I agreed with him when he said he didn't know anything I could do.

"Think about it," Theo said. "Next time you run into them, maybe you could pay more attention, or ask questions that could get one of them to say something suspicious. Crap, I have no idea."

I told him that I would.

He thanked me for listening and said our discussion made him want to take a nap.

In a matter of five hours, not only was I challenged to find a killer, but I added finding a thief to my to-do list.

I n addition to today's near-impossible challenges, I added getting a good meal to my expanding list. The peanut butter sandwich worked for a few hours but, unless I wanted to fix another one for supper, I'd have to leave the house to find food. I made the block-long walk to St. James Gate, on the corner of Center Street and Ashley Avenue. The Irish restaurant was one of the easiest locations to give directions to since it faced the town's only traffic light and was painted black, not a typical beach color.

I'd been told that the deep browns and blacks that dominated the interior would be at home among the many pubs in Dublin. I was greeted by a smiling hostess and seven men sitting at the bar, most likely drinking one of the many craft beers the restaurant was known for. I wasn't a beer drinker, so the subtleties of the various brews were lost on me. I did know the restaurant served outstanding fish and chips.

The tables were full, so I sat at the bar where the bartender was in front of me as soon as I was situated. He said he was Richard and asked what I wanted to drink. He didn't let it show, but I suspected Richard was disappointed when I said I wanted water instead of Guinness. He smiled when he figured his tip would increase when I ordered food.

Richard was quick with the water, while I was much slower trying to figure out what I could do to help Theo or the police. I had suspected that Sal and his friends weren't as successful as they wanted everyone to believe, so I wasn't surprised by Theo's comments about them being broke. I could see one, or more of them, stealing cash, while wondering if he, or they, would have enough contacts in the area to fence the figurine. I realized that I was staring at a rerun of a golf tournament on the flat screen television on the wall behind the bar rather than thinking about my challenges. The fish and chips were delivered with a flourish. Richard set the plate in front of me and said, "In cod we trust."

I responded with a chuckle and bit my tongue, not to ask if he was ready to go on the road with the Legends comedy tour.

I was alternating between taking bites of cod and glancing at the television when a familiar face slid onto the seat next to me. I'd seen the man a couple of times. Unlike Charles, whose goal in life was to meet every human on earth, I normally wouldn't have spoken to the newcomer. Recent events made me more curious.

"Aren't you Neil Wilson?"

"Yes," he replied. He then turned to Richard and said, "Guinness."

Richard went to get Neil the drink that I was supposed to order.

Neil seemed larger up close than he had when I'd seen him in Bert's. He said, "I've seen you in Bert's. You're?"

"Chris Landrum."

Neil's eyes narrowed. "Yeah, I've heard about you."

"Good, I hope."

"Mostly. Someone there told me you live near the store and help the police when they're stumped."

That wasn't how I wanted the suspect in Michael Hardin's murder to think about me.

"Luck. People exaggerate."

He smiled. "Ain't that the truth?" He shifted on the chair trying to get his tall, wide frame comfortable.

"Work around here?"

I knew he didn't yet know what else to say. He hadn't had his first Guinness, so it was too early to ask if he killed Michael Hardin.

"Private security in Charleston and bouncer in a bar," he said as Richard delivered the beer.

"Oh."

"Know any jobs over here? I need to pick up something to keep me busy."

He sipped his beer and yawned. My eyes had adjusted to the dark interior, and I noticed that his were bloodshot. I wondered if it was from lack of sleep or alcohol.

"Afraid not," I said. "Give me a number. I'll call if I hear of anything."

He nodded but didn't offer a number. He returned to his drink, and I continued to eat. All we shared for the next fifteen minutes was the golf replay. He ordered a second beer while I wondered how to get him talking about Michael Hardin.

I didn't have to. The bartender did it for me. "Hey, Neil. That was terrible about your friend."

Neil said, "Friend?"

"Michael Hardin."

Neil turned from the TV to Richard. "Terrible." He said and stared in his mug like he was watching a fly doing the backstroke in the brew.

"Weren't you close?" Richard said.

Go, Richard, go!

"Not really," Neil said, as he continued watching whatever was happening in his mug. "More a business relationship."

Richard took the bar towel from his shoulder and started drying a mug. "All I know is I saw the two of you in here a few times. Hear what happened?"

"Nothing other than he was killed." He shook his head. "He was a nice guy. Don't know what the world's coming to."

Neil turned back to his mug, and I was afraid the conversation would go the same direction as had Michael.

I said, "What business were you and Michael in together?"

He looked at me. I was afraid he wasn't going to answer until he said, "I was one of his customers."

Richard had returned from getting more beer for two men at the other end of the bar, and said, "Michael was a bookie."

I refrained from shouting, *Thank you nosy Richard.* "I heard that. Someone told me he had several customers on the island. I never met him. From what I hear, he did a good business and was honest."

Richard was summoned by a thirsty customer, and Neil glanced back at the golf match. I figured our conversation was over, so was surprised when he faced me. His arm, the size of a giant sequoia, brushed against me as he turned. I reminded myself to never arm wrestle him.

"Michael was a good guy. I know some fellas who're constant losers. Michael gave them extra time to pay. You don't find that happening anywhere else. I'd done quite well with him. I hate that he's gone."

That was far from the version that Cal had shared. I couldn't figure out how to bring up the argument that Cal had told me about and his speculation that Neil owed Michael a *piss-pot full* of money; couldn't bring it up without Neil inflicting harm on me. I thought about asking where he was when Michael was killed, which would have been a wasted question since I hadn't heard when it happened. Besides, what would've been an innocent way to ask?

"You knew him pretty well," I said. "Have any idea who may've killed him?"

"Not really. He and I were good, but there are always disgruntled customers." He shook his head for the second time. "I suppose one of them could've fallen in the trap of killing the messenger. I see that a lot at my bar job, drunken show-offs, trying to pick fights with poor bartenders minding their own business doing their job. They're pissed about something and take it out on whoever happens to be around. Michael didn't lose horse races, games, tennis matches, or whatever. All he did was take bets. He didn't hold a gun to anyone's head to bet with him." He gave one more shake of his head. "Damn world's going all to hell."

I couldn't argue with that. I was searching for something to say when he grabbed a bar napkin and wrote a number on it. "Here. I'd appreciate it if you'd give me a call if you hear of any work."

I said that I would.

He gulped down the rest of his beer and mumbled that he needed to get home to get some sleep. He punctuated it with another yawn as he slid off the chair.

All I concluded from my conversation with Neil was that he was a world-class liar. I didn't know if he was responsible for Michael Hardin's death. I equally knew Cal had told me the truth about Neil's tirade directed at Michael. Neil probably hadn't stolen the figurine or the money from Theo, but he was now at the top of my suspect list for killing the bookie.

Chapter Sixteen

Boring another hole in my belt hinted that I needed to cut back on my traditional French toast breakfast at the Lost Dog Cafe. Over the last month, I'd been successful, so decided to celebrate my lower caloric intake by having French toast. Did that make sense? Of course not. Did that stop me? Nope. I rationalized it by walking instead of driving several blocks to the Dog where I was greeted by Amber, my favorite server. She was approaching fifty, five-foot five, with long auburn hair pulled in a ponytail. We had dated for a couple of years when I first arrived on Folly and have remained friends ever since; a relationship I cherished. It was already a good day. It was made better when she led me to my favorite table.

With a radiant smile, she said, "Coffee and fresh fruit parfait?"

"Out of mud-covered gravel?" I asked the lady, whose sense of humor equaled her beauty.

She knew I was more likely to order gravel than fresh fruit parfait.

"How about French toast?"

"You took the words right out of my mouth."

"But not the calories," she said as she punched my arm then left to put in the order.

She returned with coffee. "Wrangle any more guys fishing for mackerel in the middle of Center Street?"

In addition to being great at her job, Amber was exceptional at collecting rumors.

"No."

"How about bodies in the bush?"

I sighed. "No."

"You're slipping. Figure out who killed the bookie?"

"Who said I was trying?"

"Let's see." She rubbed her chin. "Chester Carr said you were sticking your nose in again. Charles told me that you almost have it figured out. Dude—"

I looked toward the window leading to the kitchen. "Think my food's ready?"

She laughed and headed to the kitchen.

Marc Salmon was standing beside my table before Amber returned with my celebratory breakfast. "Morning, Chris." He stared at the seat across from me.

I took the hint. "Join me."

"I can spare a few. Houston isn't here yet."

Marc and his fellow councilmember, Houston Bass, met most mornings in the Dog. Marc claimed they discuss the "intricacies of the difficult issues" facing the council. Granted, they could be overheard discussing the business of governing the island, although most of the time, they were chewing on breakfast and the rumor *de jour*. It was said they had a decent handle on the "pulse of the community," and a firm grip on "all the gossip worth repeating."

Amber returned, set a mug of coffee in front of Marc, and told me my food would be up as soon as the cook stuffs the calories in.

I faked a smile and watched her move to a nearby table

to see if there was anything else she could do for the couple seated there.

Marc took a sip, and said, "What's the latest on the dead guy?"

"I suspect you know more than I do."

He chuckled. "Won't know until you tell me what you know."

The gossip-collecting councilmember came by his reputation honestly. I shared what little I knew, skipping over my conversation with Neil Wilson.

"Nothing new there," he said, more to himself than to me.

"Got a question," I said.

"Shoot."

"Do you know Janice Raque?"

"Why?"

"I asked first."

A childish comment, I admit. Unless I got Marc talking, I'd never get anything out of him.

"Yes, she is one of our fine citizens, attends some of the council meetings, and shares her opinions whether asked or not. She lives at Mariner's Cay."

Mariner's Cay is a condo complex and marina on Folly Road the other side of the Folly River, but a short walk to the retail stores and restaurants on the island, as well as the beach. I wasn't about to ask Marc if he thought she was capable of killing the bookie and found it hard to believe he didn't know anything else about her.

"Is that it?"

He looked up from his mug and narrowed his eyes, irritated that I was disappointed because he didn't know more about Janice.

"She's married. I suppose he lives with her. I've only seen him once, and she clams up when anyone asks about him." Marc smiled. "She smiles a lot. She's also a bit feisty if you ask her something she doesn't want to talk about."

Marc said it like he had first-hand experience.

Amber returned with three plates, set the one with French toast in front of me, and took the other two to a couple behind us.

Marc pointed to the door and started to stand. "There's Houston, better get to discussing city business."

He grabbed his mug and was gone before I could ask, "What city business?"

Amber returned, looked around the room, and took the seat that Marc had vacated. "Heard you talking about Janice Raque."

"I was asking Marc what he knew about her. You know her?"

"She's been in a few times. Don't know much about her, except that she's got a temper and a gambling problem."

"How do you know?"

Amber leaned closer to the table. "A couple of weeks ago, she was sitting right over there." Amber pointed to a table in the center of the room. "Shantel, a server on her second day, was waiting on her. Somehow, Shantel grabbed the wrong plate and plopped it down in front of Janice. Well, you would've thought that Shantel took a plate of wiggly-worms to the bitty. I was afraid Janice was going to stab poor Shantel with her butter knife."

"What happened?"

"Zack was the manager on duty. He was nearby and stepped between Shantel and Janice. He managed to settle down the knife-wielding woman. Janice didn't apologize to Shantel. She did leave a decent tip; probably because we comped breakfast."

"You mentioned a gambling problem."

Amber saw a customer on the other side of the room raise her hand. She said she'd be back. My breakfast was getting cold, but it didn't stop me from sopping it in syrup and enjoying each bite.

Amber returned and said, "That's what I hear."

I assumed she was talking about Janice's gambling problem, "What did you hear about it?"

"Now, mind you, this came from someone who's accurate more often than not. I can't swear to how true it is. From what I hear, Janice placed a large bet on a horserace with a bookie. The horse she bet won, and she would've won, get this, $3,500."

"Would have won?"

"Good catch. Janice called in her bet with the bookie. The next day, the bookie told her she didn't get it in before the race went off. The person who told me said Janice wasn't spittin' nails, she was spittin' railroad spikes. She didn't have to pay the bet, but lost a ton of money because it wasn't placed. She swore she had it in plenty early. Who knows?"

"That's bad, though it doesn't mean she has a gambling problem."

"Oh," Amber said, "Didn't I tell you that she already owed the bookie $3,000 before that bet? She planned that the bet she won, and didn't win, would get her out of the hole."

I nodded. "The bookie was Michael Hardin?"

Amber smiled.

Chapter Seventeen

The Comedy Legends World Tour was mere hours from its Folly Beach debut. Theo had called three times since sunrise. During the first call, he said that Sal told him, before going to bed, to call me first thing in the morning to see what time their *opening act*, a.k.a. Country Cal Ballew, would finish his first set.

I promised myself not to tell Cal about his *opening act* status. If I had, the Legends tour would have been cancelled, as Cal would say, "in a hummingbird's heartbeat." I told Theo I'd have to ask Cal and suggested that he could call him instead of me relaying the information. He said he didn't want to bother the bar's owner. I took it as a compliment that he felt comfortable pestering me, or so I told myself.

I gave Cal a couple of hours to wake up before I called. He said that the *funny guys* should be ready to go on at 9:00, that he'd be starting his second set at 10:00 sharp. He repeated *10:00 sharp*.

Theo called a second time before I could call with the starting time. "Sal wants to know if there will be reporters from the Charleston television stations at the performance. If so, did they want to interview the Legends before or after the performance?

I started to ask if he was serious. Instead, I said, "They'll be there if Cal's is on fire."

"Oh. I'll tell them you weren't sure."

Wise. With the public relations questions out of the way, I told Theo what Cal said about their starting time.

His third call came two hours before Cal was to begin his set.

"Chris, Sal wanted to let you know that I will be chauffeuring the Legends in my Mercedes. Sal said all the top promoters they've worked with provided a limo to their *sold-out performances*." He lowered his voice. "He wanted me to wear a chauffeur's outfit, including one of those silly hats. I said, 'No way.'" He chuckled. "Actually, I said, 'Hell no!'"

Visions of trick-or-treat popped in my head. "Why a limo?'"

I heard him sigh. "Sal said if television cameras are there, it's a good visual for the Legends' arrival."

I told him I'd keep that in mind and that I'd see him tonight. I also wondered if anyone would notice if I jumped off the Folly Pier rather than attend the Comedy Legends' Folly debut.

Charles said he'd meet me at the bar an hour before Cal started his set. We could get a good table for the historic event. That meant my friend would be there by 6:30, so I walked four blocks to Cal's and was there around the time I figured Charles would show. I was surprised to see Charles and Pete, or Marvin Peters, at the front of the room, sliding together three tables near the raised stage. They had already moved eight chairs to the tables. I waved at Cal, who was standing behind the bar, drying a wine glass. He cocked his head in the direction of Charles and Pete.

Johnny Cash was singing "Ring of Fire," from the Wurlitzer as I headed over to see what Charles was doing.

"Good timing," Charles said. "We're done."

I smiled and shook Pete's hand. He was dressed in raggedy jeans and a black T-shirt with *THE COMEDY STORE* in red and white letters on the front. It looked as old as Pete.

He saw me looking at his shirt. "In addition to being one of the Legends, I'm filling in as advance man. Our regular guy couldn't make flight arrangements. Got to make sure the venue's ready. I'll walk back to Theo's and get in my stage garb before our grand entrance."

It was more than I wanted to know. "Oh."

He looked at his watch. "Better get going. Got to get dressed then decide which jokes to open with." He nodded goodbye to Charles and me then went to the bar to shake Cal's hand and thank him for his hospitality, things I figured a good advance man would do.

The bar was beginning to fill. I knew some of the regulars, plus several newcomers. I asked Charles about them, and he said that Sal had taped posters around town announcing the Legends' Tour and left a stack of flyers at the Tides.

Charles looked around for Cal and whispered, "You may not want to mention the posters to Cal. Seems his name was left off." He rolled his eyes. "An oversight, I'm sure."

"Right."

The sounds of Tanya Tucker's "Delta Dawn" and the smell of frying burgers filled the air. All but two tables were occupied, so Cal had a grin on his face as he made his way over to Charles and me.

"Best Sunday crowd I've had since, well, since I don't know when. Word must've gotten around that I'm doing a couple of sets. Don't usually sing on Sundays, you know."

Charles looked at me and gave an abbreviated shake of his head, roughly translated as, "Don't you dare mention the posters."

I didn't need the reminder. "Great group, Cal. Word got around."

Cal looked at the empty seats at the double table. "What time is my undercard getting here?"

In addition to not telling Cal that the comedians are considering him their opening act, I won't mention to the comedians that Cal has called them his undercard. It's beginning to look like a night to keep my mouth shut.

Charles helped me with that plan when he said, "Don't know. I'm sure they'll want to hear you sing."

"No doubt," Cal said. "Chris, you did tell them when they'll go on, and off?"

I told him I'd shared that information with Theo.

He nodded and said that he'd better help Joy, his server, distribute beer to his "adoring fans."

Charles watched the country crooner head to the bar. "It'd be best if we could keep the 'undercard' and the 'opening act' as far away from each other as possible. I'm not big on bar brawls."

I agreed and noticed a couple at a table between us and the bar. The room was dark, and I couldn't make out their features, but thought the woman looked familiar and fit the description I'd been given of Janice Raque. I asked Charles if he knew who they were.

He squinted in the direction of the couple. "Not certain, but I think the woman's Janice Raque. I've seen her a few times but remembered because of her unusual last name. Why?"

I gave him a rundown on what I'd heard about Janice and her relationship with Michael Hardin.

"When were you going to tell me?"

Charles was peeved that I knew something and hadn't shared it a millisecond after I'd learned it.

I told him that we hadn't had a chance to talk recently.

He reminded me that he had a phone.

I conceded that I could've called and gave a half-hearted apology.

He huffed but seemed mollified. Jumping off the Pier was becoming more appealing.

Randy Travis had finished "On the Other Hand" when a blaring automobile horn grabbed the attention of all but the noisiest customers. It continued to fill the air with its irritating bellowing.

Charles headed out to see what was going on.

I followed, but not as enthusiastically.

Theo's Mercedes was in front of the bar; its horn continued to blow. The back door opened, and out stepped three-fourths of the Legends. Sal was out first, dressed in the same robin-egg blue three-piece suit he'd worn when he first met Cal. Wallace, in all black, was next to scoot out of the seat, followed by Marvin Peters, excuse me, Pete Marvin. Yes, he had on his red sport coat and black ascot. They reminded me of going to the circus when I was a kid and watching approximately seventy-five colorfully dressed clowns exit a Volkswagen. Ray Bentley stepped out of the front passenger's seat. He wore jeans, faded green T-shirt, and looked like he would rather be anywhere but here.

The three clowns, excuse me, comedians from the back seat looked around, probably for television cameras. Theo was still in the Mercedes limo and wiggled his finger for me to stick my head in the window.

"They made me sit on the horn, something about alerting the media that they're here."

In the dim light of the car's interior, I saw Theo blush. I felt his pain.

We watched the comedians straightening their clothes, pulling their shoulders back, and entering Cal's like they were entering Madison Square Garden to perform for thousands.

It wasn't an exaggeration to think this would be one of the longest nights of my life.

Chapter Eighteen

"Guys and gals," came Cal's powerful voice through an oversized speaker on each side of the stage. He wore his trademark rhinestone-adorned white coat, black jeans, cowboy boots, and Stetson, with his gray hair inching out around the sides. "Thanks for coming out. Ya'll are in for a treat. Not only will I be performing country classics and my top-ten hit, we have a group of comedians from out of town who've agreed to share their funny business with us." He looked over, nodded to the tables where Sal and his group were seated with Theo, Charles, and me. He clapped his hands in the direction of the entertainers like he was applauding their attendance. The only other sounds coming from the room were beer bottles clanking, plus a man at the bar asking about his burger.

"Without further ado, I'll kick off the festivities with 'Hey, Good Lookin',' a ditty made famous by my good friend Hank Williams Sr."

I knew ole Hank and Cal were good friends because Cal had confided that he met the fabled country singer twice; the second time, Hank had called him "buddy."

Wallace whispered to Sal, "That tall drink of water needs to work on his introduction of the Legends."

Cal finished his first song and swung into "Your Cheatin' Heart," another Hank Sr. classic. He'd performed the same songs for more than forty years, yet sold them to the audience like it was the first time. The noise level in the full room rose in time with the volume of Cal's singing.

I turned from the stage just in time to see the man who had been with a woman who fit the description of Janice Raque push his chair back, throw cash on the table, and storm out.

Cal's server, Joy, a new addition to the staff, had been behind the man as he exited before she came to our table to see if we needed more drinks.

I tilted my head toward Janice's table. "What's going on over there?"

Joy looked the direction I'd nodded. "Nothing unusual, I hear. That's Horace and Janice. I'm told they come in every so often, get in a fight most every time. One of them usually charges out. Good tippers though. Why?"

"Curious. What do they fight about?"

"You name it. One of the other servers told me if Horace says the sky is up, she'll say it's down. If he says water's wet, she'll argue it's as dry as the desert. Gotta keep moving. Cal's croonin' turns beer sippers to guzzlers. Ya'll need anything else?"

Sal said, "Another round for all of us. Stick it on Theo's tab."

Joy said it'd be right up, Cal switched to songs from another of his "good friends," George Jones, and Wallace kept glancing at his watch, no doubt wondering how much longer he'd have to listen to the undercard.

From the stage, Cal said, "I'm going to finish my first set with 'Don't We All Have the Right,' a song made famous by my good friend, the late Roger Miller."

Three minutes later, he finished the song with, "Don't we all have the right to be wrong now and then?"

A nice round of applause filled the room, none louder than from the comedians. I suspected because he was finished rather than appreciation for his singing.

Cal's curved spine leaned toward the silver mic. "Now, guys and gals, Cal's is privileged to have some funny guys entertaining until I start my next set in an hour. I'm plum piss-poor at remembering names, so I'll let Theo Stoll's brother Sal serve as MC for their part of the show." He snapped his fingers. "Almost forgot, Cal's doesn't have a budget large enough to pay the group their normal rate, so feel free to slip some paper money out of your pocket, after you pay your bar tab, that is. Before you leave, slip the cash in a bucket that I'll be parking on the corner of the stage."

I glanced over at Sal and could almost read his mind thinking, *He ain't paying us anything, much less something from his budget,* and, *That was a "plum piss-poor" way to turn the stage over to the Legends.* He gritted his teeth and faked a smile as he made his way to the mic.

"Thank you, Cal, for the nic—umm, introduction. I'm Sal Stoll. I'm honored to be one of the stand-up comics who'll entertain you tonight. I'll also be master of cere-monies and will introduce my fellow famous comedians so they can bring hilarity to your evening." He paused, looked around the room. "I was over at my brother Theo's this morning. There was a tap on the door." Sal gave a stage nod. "Yep, his plumber has a strange sense of humor."

The other comedians laughed like it was the funniest thing they'd ever heard.

A handful of others in the room chuckled.

Once again, I considered jumping off the Pier.

Sal smiled. "Now that we're off to a good start, let me bring to the stage one of the best comics who ever stood behind a microphone. He's travelled all over the country, bringing laughs to thousands, no, millions, at comedy clubs,

Las Vegas stages, and television variety shows. Let's have a big hand for Pete Marvin."

Pete moved to the microphone, lifted it off the stand, and unwrapped the cord from the stand. In the stage lights, I noticed how much more frayed his and Sal's outfits were. "Thanks Sal." Pete stepped toward the front of the stage and tapped on an imaginary door. "Knock, knock." He moved to the other side of the door. "Who's there?" He scooted back to the spot where he'd said, "knock, knock." Held his arms out wide. "It's me, ladies and germs. Your entertainment!"

That got a laugh from the comedians.

No one else in the room cracked a smile. Several groaned.

Sal leaned over toward me. "That gets them every time. They were expecting a knock, knock joke. What makes comedy funny is the unexpected."

I suspected the most stupid, childish knock-knock joke would've been funnier. But, hey, what'd I know about comedy? After all, Pete was the Legend.

Pete didn't let the lack of laughter deter him. "This morning, Theo over there," he hesitated and pointed at Theo, "told me to follow my dreams. Now Theo's a wise man, so I followed his advice. I went back to bed."

That did garner laughs from some customers, probably from those who had consumed the most beer. There was hope.

I began to lose faith after Pete shared several more jokes. From what I could tell, customers at three of the tables thought he was funny. That would have been good if there weren't four times that many tables in Cal's. One of the three tables was occupied by the rest of the Legends.

Pete looked around, gave a wide stage smile, then thanked the audience for being so enthusiastic. I wondered if he'd been in the same room as I had for the last ten minutes.

"Now I'm going to welcome Sal back to the stage to share his unique brand of humor."

I wondered if unique could mean the same thing as not funny.

Sal returned and took the mic from Pete.

"Let's give Pete another big hand," Sal said and clapped his hands together with the sound echoing through the speakers.

How had I missed the first big hand the audience had given Pete? He returned to the table and received pats on the back from Wallace, Ray, and Theo.

Sal waited for the applause from two drunks by the back door to die down, leaned toward the microphone, and looked at Cal who was standing by the bar. "Hey, Cal, I didn't know you were Chinese."

Cal looked at Sal and held out his hands like, "What're you talking about?"

Sal pointed to Cal's guitar on top of its case in the back corner of the stage. "That last song you sang, remember: 'Don't we all have the right to be Wong now and then?'"

Pete slapped his hands on his knees and leaned over to me. "Sal loves to bring local flavor to his set. See how he weaved in the country music?"

I saw how he'd insulted the owner of the bar who was giving Sal a chance to perform. I said, "Hmm."

"Speaking of Cal's," Sal continued from the stage, "a termite walked in here last night. It said, 'Is the bar tender here?'"

I heard three people laughing behind me but didn't turn to see who they were. I was confident Cal wasn't one of them.

Sal did three jokes about marriage, and a couple about priests, before saying, "Time for me to get off the stage to turn it over to Wallace. Before I go, here's one for the road. A snake slithers into Cal's, and my country buddy refused to serve him. The snake was miffed, if snakes can be miffed. It asked Cal why. Old Cal tipped his fancy hat to the snake. 'You can't hold your alcohol.'"

That did bring laughter from a couple of tables that had been acting like they were at a funeral visitation rather than a comedy show.

Sal thanked the audience for being so attentive then introduced Wallace.

Wallace bounded on the stage with a burst of energy that I hadn't seen from him during our fateful meeting in the street, or the other times I'd seen him. He grabbed the mic, thanked Sal for the kind introduction, gazed out at the audience, and said, "Yes, I know what you're thinking. You expected a comedian. Instead you got Johnny Cash." He moved his hand up and down his all-black garb. "Before I upstage Cal and burst into 'I Walk the Line,' let me give you some advice. You may want to write some of this down, so I'll give you time to get out a pen and paper."

He looked at his watch then at the audience. If he was waiting for pens and paper to appear, it would be a long night.

"Okay, here goes. First, no matter what they tell you at the store, don't waste money on expensive binoculars." He paused, looked around before leaning closer to the tables, and whispered in the microphone, "All you have to do is stand closer to what you want to see."

There were chuckles from two ladies at the bar and from a couple of tables near the rear.

"Thank you," Wallace said. "Here's something that's even more important. Never get in line in the bank behind someone wearing a ski mask."

I heard a few more chuckles, a smattering of laughter, and, of course, more than a smattering from the comedians at our table. Apparently, they thought their reactions would be contagious. They were wrong.

Wallace smiled at the audience. "Thank you, thank you. Ready yet for 'I Walk the Line'?"

"No," yelled a man leaning against the bar.

I'd venture to guess that he was speaking for most everyone in the room, although, I wondered if Wallace's singing was worse than his opening jokes.

Wallace smiled. "Your loss. Okay, did you hear about the proctologist who …" Wallace hesitated, looked at the floor, then stared at the silver microphone. "I remember once, while I was headlining in Vegas at the Sands. Been a while back. Well, umm, who's that singer who's called green eyes?"

Ray, Wallace's son, was sitting beside me. He mumbled something, looked at his dad, and yelled, "Frank Sinatra, old blue eyes."

Wallace smiled, "That's it, Frank Sinatra. What was I saying about him?" He looked at the audience.

I was expecting, no, hoping for a joke.

Most of the others in the room were wondering where Wallace was going with the story.

Wallace shook his head and giggled. "Did you hear about the agnostic dyslexic insomniac? He stayed up all night wondering if there was a dog."

That received the most laughs of anything Wallace had said. I wondered if it was because the audience felt it was that funny or were relieved that he managed to share a whole joke.

Wallace took a deep breath and laughed. "That's more like it. Hey, when we got here, Cal told me that beer won't make you smarter. Wrong. I said it made Bud wiser."

Cal pulled a chair up beside me on my right. He leaned over and said, "Know where I can get a shepherd's hook to yank him off the stage?"

Charles said, "Don't know many shepherds on Folly."

"Not many?" I said.

"Okay, none."

From the stage, Wallace said, "Did I tell you about that

time I found little Ray out back smoking … what was it again, Ray?"

Ray slammed his hand on the table and whispered something to Sal, who started to respond, before Ray said, "No! I'm out of here." He pushed his chair back, shoved his way past a couple at the table behind us, and stomped out of the building.

Most of the patrons didn't notice; they were staring at Wallace, probably wondering what he would say, or not say, next.

Pete said something to Sal, who stood and moved to the side of the stage.

Wallace saw him, looked at his watch, and shook his head. "Sorry folks, out of time. Won't be able to sing my big hit." He turned to Sal and said, "Want me to introduce Ray, or are you?"

Sal rushed to the microphone, took it out of Wallace's hand, and put his arm around the much shorter comedian.

"Ladies and gents, we're running a bit long. I know you want to hear more tunes from the legendary Cal Ballew, so Ray has agreed to skip his set. Let's put our hands together for Pete, Wallace, and, of course, me." He took an extended bow, while the audience gave a more than generous round of applause.

Cal's next set wasn't scheduled to begin for twenty minutes. Like the professional he was, he strapped his Martin acoustic guitar over his shoulder then took the microphone from Sal.

"Great job, boys. Great job. Now Sal is too humble to ask, but remember, the tip bucket is right there." He pointed to the tin bucket on the corner of the stage. "Be sure to plop some big bucks in there for these here Legends of Comedy."

I wouldn't have associated the word humble with Sal. Cal had been nice to remind the audience about tips.

Cal strummed a chord on his Martin. "Now, let's go

back a few years. Here's one made famous by my good buddy Roy Acuff called 'Wabash Cannonball.'"

Charles tapped me on the arm. "Chris, have we been here a week yet?"

It was the funniest thing I'd heard all night.

Chapter Nineteen

Cal had been kind enough to give the stand-up comics the stage, so I wanted to support him and stay until the bitter end, emphasis on bitter. There was little more I wanted to say to the comics, and Charles had remained quiet—quiet for Charles. I hoped that Theo's guests would leave.

Instead, they stayed at the table and ordered two more rounds of beer during Cal's second set. Most of the customers had drifted out. Those who remained spent more time staring at their drinks than paying attention to what was happening on the stage.

Janice was still at a table, so I thought it would be a good time to meet her. Cal began John Anderson's hit, "Would You Catch a Falling Star," as I walked to Janice's table.

"Oh," I said, like I'd just noticed her. "Aren't you Janice Raque?"

Her eyes narrowed. Instead of saying anything, she nodded.

"Thought so. I was on my way to the bar and saw you. I'm Chris Landrum. You were talking to Michael Hardin one afternoon in Bert's. Someone told me who you were. Just wanted to say hi."

I didn't remember seeing her before and hoped, at some point, that she'd had a conversation with Michael in Bert's.

She maintained her skeptical look. "You know Michael?"

"Not well," I said.

"He handle your bets?"

"No, but I know several of his customers. You?"

"Huh, yeah. Some of the biggest mistakes I've ever made. Can't say I'm sorry. He got what he deserved."

I moved to the seat across from her. She didn't ask me to leave.

"Mistakes?"

Cal was singing "Chiseled in Stone," so I leaned closer to Janice to hear her.

"He cheated me out of a lot of money. You're fortunate you didn't give him any."

"Sorry to hear it. Any idea who killed him?"

She looked to see where I had come before staring at me. "You a cop?"

I chuckled and shook my head. "Hardly. I'm here with some friends. We were over there talking about Michael's murder. You knew him, so I thought I'd ask."

"You can tell your friends that I didn't. The cops have already talked to me." She grabbed her purse off the floor. "I gotta go. Nice meeting you."

She headed to the exit without looking back. None of her words, body language, or attitude said that she thought it was nice meeting me.

I returned to our table where Charles whispered, "You need to work on your pick-up lines. She left like you'd stuck her butt with a straight pin."

Cal finished his song. I started to respond when I heard Wallace tell Sal, "I know I killed him."

I turned to Wallace and started to ask the comedian what he meant.

Charles also heard him. He pivoted away from me and said, "Kill who, Wallace?"

Sal slipped his arm around Wallace then turned to Charles. "Wallace said that we killed the audience. Isn't that right, Wallace?" Before Wallace responded, Sal added, "That means we were a hit."

Wallace had a glazed look in his eyes. Each of the comics had consumed several beers, so I didn't know if the look was alcohol-induced, or if he was drifting from reality.

Theo was behind Wallace, and he shook his head.

From the stage, Cal said he was taking a "pause for the cause," as opposed to having to "take a piss," as he often announced. He was on his best behavior in front of the Legends.

Sal took advantage of the quieter room to say, "Well, Theo, Charles, Chris, what'd you think of our show? Like Wallace said, I think we killed them."

I was relieved at not having to say a slow death by razor blades, when Pete said, "We were a little rusty. I screwed up a couple of jokes. It's been a few nights since we preformed."

"Few nights," Wallace said. "How about months?"

Sal jumped in, "He's always joking. Good one, Wallace."

Charles, the peacemaker, said, "I've been a regular at Cal's since our friend took over seven years ago. That's the best comedy show I've seen in here."

"I've got to agree with Charles," Cal said as he walked over to the table.

I wondered if the comedians realized that it was the only comedy show in Cal's history. I also wondered how I could bring the conversation back to what I heard Wallace say and not what Sal wanted us to believe Wallace had said.

Wallace tapped his beer bottle on the table and pointed it at Pete. "Pete, remember the other night when we were waiting in the green room to appear with Johnny Carson on the Tonight Show? You said I should tell my joke about the Rabbi and the priest. Remember what I said?"

Pete said, "Now Wallace, that was a few years—"

Wallace laughed. "I said not that joke, because … Umm, guess it was funnier then."

Sal said, "Think we'd better call it a night. We're not as young as we used to be."

Theo said, "Good idea, I'll get the car, the limo."

Cal headed to the stage to finish his set, the comics wobbled out of the bar, and I wondered what Wallace meant about killing someone.

Charles and I were the only customers left when Cal finished singing.

Joy was picking up bottles from the tables.

"I'm too old for these late nights," Cal said as he flopped down in a chair at our table.

Joy yelled from across the room and asked if he wanted anything.

"Peace, quiet, two new feet, a new ticker."

She grinned. "How about a beer?"

Joy was back to the table with his drink before he said that it was his next choice.

Cal took a gulp and said, "Now that they're gone, what'd you think about their show?"

I said, "They had some good jokes but, like Pete told us, they were rusty. I could tell they were better back in the day."

Charles smiled. "Looked more like the over-the-hill gang than the Legends. And what's with Wallace? Forgetting lines, screwing up times, *The Tonight Show* the other night. Get real."

"Think the geezer's gone bonkers," Cal said.

That showed the singer's high-level grasp of psychiatry. Or did it? Granted, I'd seen Wallace dazed, confused, and struggling to maintain a grasp of reality. I'd also seen him remember some of his routine and appear normal during a couple of conversations. And there was his statement about killing someone.

"Charles, what's your take on his comment about killing him?"

"Don't know. I'm certain it didn't have anything to do with their performances."

Cal leaned forward. "What're you talking about?"

I explained what Wallace had said while Cal was singing.

Cal took another draw on his beer, slipped a chair in front of him, and put his feet up on the seat. "Think he was talking about Michael Hardin?"

Charles glanced at me then back at Cal before pointing his cane at the stage. "The boy's performance up there was schizoid: memory accurate, memory sucked, loss-of-reality powerful. From what you said, his other performance, the one in the middle of the street, would qualify for a strait-jacket. Think I'm leaning toward Cal's bonkers diagnosis although, by the time they left, they were a few beers passed soused. They were all jabbering nonsense." He looked at the table where Janice Raque had been seated. "Why'd you leave our outstanding company to hit on that Raque chick?"

Cal pointed at me. "In the middle of my set."

I smiled at the aging singer. "Guilty. I wanted to see how she'd react to me mentioning Michael Hardin."

"Well?" Charles said with his usual amount of patience.

"Don't think she'll be sending flowers to his funeral."

Cal took his feet off the chair and leaned toward me. "Think she killed him?"

I shrugged.

"What'd she say?" asked Charles, not satisfied with my shrug.

I filled in the details, at least, the few I knew from our brief conversation.

Charles said, "That the best you can do?"

I said it was. Charles stretched and clasped his hands behind his head. "This's been quite a night. Got to see some Legends, or maybe that's Legends in their minds, right up on Cal's stage. Got to know about two people who might've killed the bookie. And got to watch Chris stay up two hours past his bedtime. Will wonders never cease?"

I didn't know about all that, but knew I was leaving Cal's with more questions than when I'd entered. Did the "Legends" believe that they were Legends of comedy? I didn't, but wondered if they did. Did Janice have something to do with Michael's death? Then there's Wallace. Did he kill someone, or see someone get killed? If he did, why did he say what he did?

Chapter Twenty

The phone rang not long after I'd fallen asleep. I wasn't aware of research to back me up although, from personal experience, the odds were mighty slim, like being-struck-by-a-meteor slim, that a call at three o'clock in the morning would bring good news. It only took me saying, "Hello," to confirm my suspicion.

"Could you come to the house? Oh, yeah, this is Theo."

"What's wrong?"

"It's dreadful. My God, horrible. Dead, he's dead. Please come."

"Who's dead?"

"Please."

I was sitting on the edge of the bed and realized that Theo was so shaken, it'd be useless to ask anything else.

"On my way."

I shook the cobwebs out of my head, got dressed, and drove through the deserted streets to Theo's. It became apparent as soon as I turned on his street that I wasn't the first person summoned. Flashing red and blue lights from two Folly Beach patrol cars, one fire engine, an ambulance from Charleston, and two unmarked police vehicles reflected off street signs, each other, and windows from nearby houses.

I pulled off the street a half-block behind the emergency vehicles and headed toward a familiar face, Officer Trula Bishop, who was standing in the middle of the street ready to direct traffic for any curious citizens who might be driving by. Traffic at this hour could be counted on one finger, so she had little to do.

"Good morning, Mr. Chris."

I'd met Officer Bishop shortly after she'd started on the force three years ago. We'd talked on numerous occasions, and she'd helped me out a couple of times when I'd managed to find myself in awkward situations.

I nodded toward Theo's house. "Trula, what's going on?"

Instead of answering, she looked at her watch, then said, "What brings you out at this ungodly hour?"

"Theo Stoll, the owner of the house, called to ask me to come over."

She smiled. "Then you know what happened."

"No. Theo sounded in shock. That's all I know."

She nodded like that'd made sense. "Seems that someone fell down the steps, broke his neck. Killed him."

I exhaled. "Who?"

"Don't know. I haven't been in. Two officers and the chief were already on the scene. She asked me to stay out here to keep riffraff, like you, away."

She was teasing about me being riffraff, or so I hoped. I asked if it was okay for me to see what had happened. I reminded her that the owner requested my presence.

"If I had to shoot you to keep you away," she smiled, "I'd get in trouble for shooting wildlife out of season." She flicked her wrist toward the house. "There should be one of our guys at the door. Check with him before you go in."

I thanked her and wished her well on riffraff patrol.

I reached the door and lucked out, the second time since arriving.

Officer Allen Spencer met me. "Chris, is there some reason that I see you at as many death scenes as I see the coroner?"

He said it with a smile, although it was only a slight exaggeration.

I shrugged and told him that Theo called. Then I asked what'd happened.

Allen moved aside.

I moved to the entry and saw several cops, medics, plus someone from the coroner's office standing around a body at the bottom of stairs. The object of their attention was already in a body bag. The coroner, with the help of one of the cops, was hefting it on a stretcher. I asked Allen who was killed.

He moved me out of the doorway, so the body could be wheeled out, and said, "One of the visitors staying at the house with Mr. Stoll, in fact, the son of one of the visitors."

"Raymond Bentley?"

"Think that's it."

Theo and two of his houseguests were seated in the great room. I wanted to learn what I could before joining them.

"How'd it happen?"

"According to Mr. Stoll, Theo, not his brother, the group performed at Cal's last night. They consumed more adult beverages than their bodies could handle. Mr. Stoll said he was driving for the group and had a couple of beers, but the others were inebriated when they dragged in here around midnight. He said they barely staggered their way upstairs."

"Did anyone see what happened?"

"You're beginning to sound like the chief."

"She's my role model," I said, smiled, and reworded my question. "Witnesses?"

Allen looked toward the group in the great room. "I was

second on the scene. Officer Fish beat me by a few minutes. When I got here, the body was where it was when you came in, Theo and the others were where they are now, and Fisk was calling the Sheriff's Office. If any of the guys in there, except for Theo, had been driving and I pulled them over, they'd be spending the night in the drunk tank. Their eyes are redder than Santa's suit. They weren't making sense. When the ambulance got here on a wasted trip, they'd settled down. From what I could gather, they'd been in their rooms when it happened."

"Who else is here?"

"The chief and Detective Callahan got here fast. They had each of the guys move to separate rooms, so they could question them individually. Callahan is still with one of them."

"No one saw him fall."

"Only Raymond Bentley." Allen shook his head. "He won't be telling us much."

Chief LaMond started down the steps and saw me talking to Allen. Instead of greeting me with an insult, she said, "Hi, Chris."

"Chief," I said then waited for her to say something snarky.

"Glad you're here."

If I had false teeth, they would've fallen out when my jaw dropped. "You are?"

"Theo asked if he could call you," She looked around the stairs to the group gathered in the great room. "He was so shaken that I was afraid he was going to drop dead in the middle of my crime scene. I was beginning to worry about him so, in a moment of weakness, I said he could call."

I asked her the same question I'd asked Allen. She said that from the statements each of the guys made, no one saw him fall. They claim that when they got home from Cal's, they were pooped and went to their rooms.

"Did they tell you Ray left Cal's before the others?"

"One of them did." She flipped open her notebook. "Marvin Peters, who said he would rather go by Pete Marvin." She shook her head. "Hell, I'd rather go by Jennifer Lawrence, but I'm stuck with Cindy LaMond."

"Pete's the only one who mentioned Ray leaving Cal's? That seems strange."

"Detective Callahan is upstairs talking to Theo's brother, so I don't know what he's said. The confused one, Wallace, is so out of it, I doubt he knows if he was at Cal's tonight, umm, last night, or climbing the Eiffel Tower. That boy's got a spittoon full of screws loose."

"Anything else?"

"Crap, Chris, want me to email you the police report when we get it finished? Even better, if the coroner's wagon hadn't skedaddled, I'd let you go with them to help with the autopsy."

I bit my lower lip to keep me from smiling. "So, nothing else?"

Cindy pointed toward the great room. "Get in there. Work your calming charm on poor Theo."

I saluted, said, "Yes, chief," and joined the comics and *poor Theo.*

Sal's questioning must have ended because he was back in the room, wearing blue and white horizontal striped pajama bottoms with a navy-blue top. He stared at the floor and held his head between his hands. Pete was staring out the window at total darkness. His bright red PJs would've made a stop light feel anemic. Wallace had on the same clothes he wore in Cal's. The only things missing were shoes and socks.

Theo looked up. Not only did he look up, but he pushed himself off the couch and hugged me. His white robe tickled my chin. His arms were more powerful than I would've imagined. I had to pull them away to break his grasp.

"Thank you for coming. I didn't know what to do. Didn't know who to call."

I was pleased that he felt comfortable calling, although I would've preferred a more decent hour. I told him I was glad to come.

He turned to the other three sitting on the couch. "Guys, Chris is here."

They weren't as happy to see me as Theo had been.

Only Sal's nod acknowledged my presence. He didn't speak.

I was confident that I knew, but still asked Theo what happened. He told me the same story I'd heard from the police. He added that he was asleep when he heard commotion in the hall outside his bedroom. One in the group screamed for someone to call an ambulance. Theo didn't know who yelled. He ran to the top of the stairs, looked down, saw Ray, and called 911.

"How's Wallace?" I whispered, although Ray's father looked like he was in a trance and couldn't hear anything.

Theo glanced over at him and whispered, "How do you think? He found his son dead at the bottom of the steps. I can't imagine what's going through his head."

Wallace must've sensed that we were talking about him. He shook his head, looked at Theo and me, and said, "My wife wanted to see the world, so I bought her an Atlas."

I smiled, and Theo faked a laugh.

Pete returned to the couch and put his arm around his friend. "It's okay, Wallace. Everything will be fine."

And I thought Wallace was the one losing touch with reality.

Cindy and Detective Callahan conferred by the front door while the comics, Theo, and I sat in the great room.

The detective left.

Cindy came in, said the police were done in the house, and told the assembled group to call if anyone thought of anything he hadn't shared. If the guys heard her, they didn't acknowledge it.

Theo and I walked Cindy to the door.

We watched her go, then Theo looked back at the group, still unmoving in the other room. "Chris, could you spare a few more minutes?"

I would've been hard-pressed to come up with a reason to be somewhere other than in bed at 4:00 in the morning. I nodded.

Theo ushered me to an office off the kitchen. "Chris, do you think Ray's death was anything other than an accident?"

"Why ask?"

Theo closed the door. "Just letting my mind run amok."

"Go on."

"Sal's the only one of the group I knew before they showed up at my door. Ray has been fighting with each of them since the day they arrived. He may be funny on stage but, from what I saw, he was a royal asshole. He made fun of the others behind their backs. He kept bragging about how many high-paying, prestigious gigs he had recently, and never hesitated to tell the others they were has-beens."

"Did he get along with his dad?"

"Not that I could tell. When Wallace was making sense, not that often, I might add, he tried to defend his overbearing, obnoxious son. He talked about how horrible a childhood Ray had with Wallace traveling all the time. Wallace may've taken up for Ray although, if you ask me, Ray treated his dad like crap. The others tried to get Ray to calm down." Theo smiled for the first time tonight. "I remember a couple of days ago, Pete had to step between Ray and Wallace to keep Ray from punching his dad. Pete pointed his seventy-five-year-old bony finger in fifty-year-old Ray's face, and said something like, 'You're fortunate that I don't flatten your nose.'"

"Was he serious?"

"I don't know. After he said it, Ray laughed, and Pete joined in. Besides, each of the other guys felt that way about Ray and told him so since they were here."

"Because Ray was obnoxious doesn't mean someone killed him."

"True," Theo said. "I don't know about Ray because he left Cal's before the rest of us. I know the other guys had so much to drink that they were probably seeing double when we got here." He smiled for a second time. "Doubt they'd know which of the two Rays they were seeing to push him down the steps."

"Theo, do you know what got Ray so upset that he stomped out of Cal's? Wallace made that joke saying that he remembered when Ray was young and was smoking something. Why did that bother him so much?"

"That may've been the last straw. I'll tell you it was only part of a larger hay bale. Ray was pissed when they piled in the car for me to take them to Cal's. Before you ask, I don't know why."

"Was Ray here when you got home?"

"I think so, but I didn't see him. His door was closed, so I figured he was in his room."

"What was he wearing when you found him?"

"Same thing he had on at Cal's. Why?"

"Curious. A minute ago, you mentioned something about when Wallace was making sense. He seemed to be having a tough time with reality when he was performing. Has he been getting worse?"

Theo looked at the closed door. "You know I don't like to talk unkindly about anyone."

Other than calling Ray a royal asshole, I thought. I motioned for him to continue.

"I never know what year he's living in. One minute he's as coherent as can be; the next, he's talking about something that happened three decades ago."

"What do the others think?"

"They go back a long way. Other than Ray, they get along well, occasionally finishing each other's jokes. They listen when one of them tells a story that I know the others must've heard countless times. I think they would do anything for each other. That's all to say that, if they know Wallace is drifting out of reality, no one mentioned it. Think it's something they've come to expect."

I didn't know how to casually broach the topic, so I didn't try. "Remember the other day when Wallace said he'd seen a body. He was confused about when?"

"Sure, turned out to be that bookie."

"Remember last night when Wallace said something about *killing him*?"

"When Sal jumped in and tried to make us believe that Wallace was referring to killing the audience?"

Theo was old by many standards. In the walking group, he had been teased about being as fast as a snail on Ambien, but anyone who thought he wasn't as sharp as a chef's knife didn't know him. It wasn't by accident that he'd been a successful business owner and inventor.

"Exactly," I said. "Any idea what he was talking about?"

"No. I wanted to get him aside later and ask. Then this happened." Theo waved toward the stairs.

"To answer your question about what I thought, I wasn't here, so I have no idea what happened. Unless someone changes his story, none of your guests saw what happened."

"That's what I figured. Anyway, thanks for coming out in the middle of the night. I suppose I need to get back in there to escort the guys to their rooms. I doubt anyone will go back to sleep."

Theo walked with me to the door. The others hadn't moved since Theo and I'd been talking.

"Chris," Theo said as I was stepping off the porch.

I stopped and looked at him.

"You'll figure it out, won't you?"

"I'll try."

"Good."

The thing was, I didn't know what I'd agreed to figure out.

Chapter Twenty-One

I grabbed a quick supper at Planet Follywood and headed home for what I hoped to be an evening without thinking of what had happened at Theo's this morning or playing over in my mind the trauma of finding the bookie's body. Television was no help. I watched two sitcoms touted as the best of the year. Compared to the TV shows, I began thinking that Sal and the rest of the Legends might be funnier than I'd first thought.

I turned the TV off and grabbed a copy of a photography magazine and flipped through pages until I realized that I wasn't paying attention to what I was seeing. Regardless how hard I tried, I kept coming back to the dead bookie, Wallace's confusion over having seen the body, plus his confusion about nearly everything, and Ray's abrupt exit from the giant comedy club called Earth. And, why in heaven's name did I tell Theo that I would try to figure it out, whatever *it* was?

The death will be ruled accidental, unless the medical examiner comes up with something to indicate otherwise. Ray was inebriated, staying in a strange house, and it was early in the morning; all factors that could contribute to him falling.

So why did I keep coming back to it? Was it because it happened close to when I discovered Michael Hardin, the death where there was no question about cause? How about because Wallace said something about seeing Michael Hardin's body? He was also within a few feet of Ray when he fell? Were the deaths related? Or did I think it was suspicious because Ray was not liked by the others? He made fun of them. He arrived at Cal's angry, then when something was said stormed out. Add to that, he was rude, egotistical, disrespectful. Or was my imagination working overtime?

I wanted to call Theo to see how he was doing but figured he'd be exhausted, with luck, asleep. I called Charles after I left Theo and got his answering machine. I'd left a message but hadn't heard from him. That wasn't unusual since he had the irritating habit of leaving his phone in his apartment then forgetting to check messages.

I tried his number again with better luck. I asked if he ever checked his messages.

He gave feeble excuses about the phone being in another pair of slacks, about the battery being dead, he never got important calls anyway. After a litany of these he got around to asking why I'd called.

I shared what happened at Theo's. In return, I was the recipient of a thirty-second rant that could be summed up with him wanting to know why I didn't spend every waking hour since I left Theo's trying to find him so I could tell him about it. He was irritated with himself, taking it out on me. That's what friends are for, or so I continued telling myself.

He calmed and said, "Do you think Ray's death was accidental?"

"There's nothing to indicate that it wasn't, although, it strikes me as strange coming so close on the heels of his father claiming to see the body of the bookie, and how others in the house didn't like Ray. That's only a gut feeling."

"You told Theo you would figure out what happened."

"No, I told him I'd try."

"How are we going to do that?"

"We?"

"You need my help."

"I do?"

"You said Wallace drifted in and out of reality. The whole group is delusional about their success. From what I heard at Cal's, they seem confused about how funny they are."

I waited, but no more was forthcoming.

"So?"

"Who do you know who's an expert on drifting in and out of reality? Who have you accused of thinking he's funnier than he is? When you think of delusional, who comes to mind?"

"You?"

"Duh. These are my kind of people. You need me."

I started to respond when he interrupted. "For the candle on top of the icing, on top of the chocolate cake, don't forget, I was with you when you found Michael Hardin. I'm smack dab in the middle of being connected to the case."

Somewhere between the icing and the cake, I took a deep breath and realized that I didn't know about Theo, but I knew that I was exhausted. I told Charles I'd think about it and we could talk tomorrow. I hadn't planned to think about it; I wanted to get off the phone.

THE NEXT MORNING, I brewed a pot of coffee instead of going next door to Bert's for a dose of caffeine. Charles and I had agreed to meet at noon at the Dog, which meant

11:30, so I had a few hours to kill. I sat at the kitchen table and flipped through the photography magazine I'd skimmed yesterday. I had little interest in reading the reviews of the latest, greatest cameras with numerous features more than the twelve-year-old digital Nikon that'd served me well, nor did I care about the newest drone technology that gave photographers the ability to view the earth from three hundred feet. Perhaps my age was showing. I had enough trouble capturing interesting images from my five-foot-ten vantage point. What the magazine did achieve was keeping my mind off the murder, the theft, and the motives of Theo's guests.

The more I looked at the magazine, the more I thought about my numerous walks around the island with Charles and how happy I was having someone with whom to share my interests. Photography was the excuse we often used to make the lengthy treks. We did take photos, yet the best part of the trips were our conversations. Other than an interest in photography and being retired, we had little in common.

It'd taken me a few years to realize that, while Charles was seldom without something to say, talking about his past was not among the things he dwelt on. I knew the basics: where he was born, about being raised by his grandmother, what he'd done before coming to Folly, how he'd spent his time while on the island. But, after the hundreds of hours we'd spent together, he'd never revealed why he wore long-sleeve shirts, regardless of the weather; why he carried a hand-carved, wooden cane, even though he was as mobile as anyone I knew, or, why he'd accumulated more college and university sweatshirts and T-shirts than the marsh had oysters. It wasn't for the lack of asking, although I'd given up after the first couple of years, once I realized that the answers were as elusive as catching a rainbow.

I was with him when he met Heather. I observed their growing romantic relationship until she left a few months ago. I learned how much he loved his Aunt Melinda during her brief time with him until she succumbed to cancer.

He was getting over these heartbreaking losses, yet still had a way to go. Each time I thought he was making progress, he said something about Melinda, Heather, or acted depressed. I didn't think it was clinical depression, but bouts of sadness and anger over them being gone. His self-proclaimed position of executive sales manager at Landrum Gallery had given him purpose and a feeling that he was accomplishing something—something that he'd felt lacking before I'd come along. It was unavoidable, yet I knew how much I'd hurt him when I closed the gallery.

I poured another cup of coffee, threw the magazine in the trash, and realized, as strange as it may seem, the happiest, most energized and self-confident I had seen my friend over the last three years was when we were up to our eyeballs in police business, things that we shouldn't be involved with. Good or bad luck, depending upon who was telling the story, had propelled us into situations that almost cost us our lives. Falling on the side of good luck, we helped the police catch people who had killed some of our acquaintances, were out to kill someone close to us, and nearly had succeeded in ending our lives.

That realization gave me a different perspective on what I was going to say at lunch. My initial thought was to remind him that whatever had happened wasn't our concern, that it was in the competent hands of the police. Neither of us knew the bookie. We had seen him a few times but, on an island as small as Folly, that wasn't unusual. The death of Ray Bentley appeared to be a case of an inebriated man missing the top step and tumbling to the hereafter. Tragic, yes, and sad that it was Wallace's son, who happened to be a friend of Sal, who happened to be Theo's brother, who was one of our friends. It was still an accident. Yes, I'd told Theo that I would try, but we'd be better off leaving it to the authorities.

The best way to help my friend was to agree with him, do everything I could do to find out what had happened and who was responsible for Michael's death. We may not succeed, but I'd be doing something to bring back the positive, helpful, cheery friend whom I'd come to love.

I arrived at the Dog at 11:30 to find Charles at a booth along the back wall.

He looked at his imaginary watch and nodded his head to indicate that I was on time.

I slid in opposite him and noticed his eyes were red, his eyelids at half-staff. "Rough night?" I asked.

"Trouble sleeping. So, how're we going to catch the killer?"

Amber was quick to the table, set a mug of coffee in front of me, and asked if I knew what I wanted for lunch.

I thanked her for the coffee, although I'd had too much of the stuff, and said, "Mahi Salad."

Amber put her hand over her heart. "Whoa. That's almost healthy."

I smiled. "I'll get over it."

"No doubt," she said then asked if Charles needed anything else.

He told her no, and she headed to the kitchen with my almost-healthy order.

This is where I would normally argue that the police

were paid to catch the killer. It was none of our business. Instead, I said, "I think we need to start by learning everything we can about Michael Hardin. Who else placed bets with him? Did anyone have stories about how he'd cheated them? Did anyone owe him a large amount of money?"

Charles's eyes opened wider. "Really? I thought you'd tell me to butt out."

"You said *we* needed to figure out what was going on. It's a good idea."

He sighed. "Thanks a lot. Now you've done gone and screwed up everything I planned on spending all day arguing with you about."

"Like what?"

"Like you were going to say we that we didn't know Michael Hardin, so we had no reason to stick in our noses. I was going to say that it was true, but our friend, Theo's brother, is a friend of Wallace Bentley, Wallace said he saw the body, or said he saw a body. That made it our business. Sal's friend got killed at the house where he was staying, the house of our friend, Theo. See?"

"You're right."

Charles pointed his fork at me. "You messin' with me?"

"I'm agreeing."

He leaned back in the booth and stared at me like I was a three-headed sloth.

Amber returned with my salad and a hot dog for Charles that he'd ordered before I arrived. She said, "What's wrong, Charles? You look like you've seen the Ghost of Christmas Past."

Charles continued to stare at me. "An alien's done swooped down and planted itself in Chris's brain."

Amber smiled. "That explains the Mahi Salad." She patted my balding head and left to see if the couple seated in the middle of the room needed anything. She didn't appear as worried as Charles.

Charles blinked twice, took a bite of hot dog, looked

around the room, then back at me. "Think I'm over the shock. How do we find out who else had reason to kill the bookie?"

I pointed to the table on the other side of the room, where Chief Cindy LaMond was lunching with two of her officers. I saw them when I came in and started thinking about Charles's question before he asked it. "First, we need to find out who the police have eliminated as suspects."

"And you think Cindy's just going to waltz over here to tell us?"

I laughed. "No, she'll say it's not our concern. If we keep meddling in her job, she'll shoot us before the killer does."

"That'll help us how?"

"I didn't say she wouldn't tell us. I said she'd first give us a bucket of grief."

"How are we going to get her over here without her lunch mates?"

"I'll figure something out."

Before I had a chance to do much figuring, Chester Carr magically appeared beside our booth.

He nodded at Charles and said to me, "Thought I'd find you here."

I didn't ask why. First, because it didn't matter. Second, because Charles was asking him to join us.

Chester slid in beside Charles. "We're halfway through a .5 group walk. Made it all the way to the River Park, where I left the rest of the folks gasping for air."

Chester started the .5 walking group two years ago. The name came from the half-mile distance Chester wanted the group to walk, from the end of East Ashley Avenue to Lighthouse Inlet, where we could view the iconic Morris Island Lighthouse, then trek back to East Ashley. One of the requirements to be in the group was that the member had to be sixty or older. That, along with the physical condition, or lack of condition, of most of the members made a .5 mile walk as easily attainable as hiking to the top of Pikes Peak. Regardless, the name stuck.

Charles faked surprise. "You deserted your group?"

Chester said, "Since you think you're too good to walk with us, I couldn't tell you what I found out if I stayed with the others."

That perked Charles up.

I said, "What?"

"You asked me to let you know I if learned anything new about the bookie?"

"Yes."

"After the .5 group left the Pier to head up Center Street without two of its members who're sitting here feeding their faces—"

"Subtle," I interrupted. "You were walking up the street, and?"

"David Darnell was talking about how busy his insurance business is recently. Most of us couldn't care less about insurance, so we weren't paying attention, until he said something about Horace Raque. That's Janice's husband, remember, the lady I told you about who was arguing with Michael Hardin?"

"I remember."

"David was telling funny stories about things his clients say. David's a big talker. It's a wonder anyone has time to buy insurance with him doing all the talking." Chester shrugged. "'Course David's semi-retired, so I guess it doesn't matter if he sells anything."

Charles took the words out of my mouth when he said, "What'd he say about Horace?"

"Horace, right. I missed the first of it. I didn't want him to know that I wasn't listening, so I didn't have him start over. Horace was talking to David about car insurance then got off track and said he didn't need more life insurance." Chester closed his eyes, opened them, and tapped his finger on the table. "Oh, yeah, David laughed. He said that

Horace told him that as mad as Janice gets, he's afraid she'd kill him. He didn't want to give her added incentive with a bigger policy."

"Was Horace serious?" I asked.

Chester looked across the room at Chief LaMond's table and turned back to me. "David thought Horace was joking. I don't know. Remember how mad Janice was at the bookie? She has a temper. I can see her being that mad at Horace. I sure can."

"Did Darnell say anything else?"

"Yeah, he went off on a story about one of his customers driving into a ditch. The guy swore that a fly landed on his nose and made him veer off the road."

"Anything more about Horace?" Charles said.

"No, but I reckoned since you and Chris are detectives, you'd figure what David said was a clue."

Every other time we'd been accused of what Charles's imagination had created, I denied it. Not today.

"Yes, it was," Charles said.

Chester started to slip out of the booth before saying, "I'll try to catch up with the crew. Shouldn't be hard at their speed."

I thanked him for coming to find us. As Chester walked away, Charles cleared his throat and nearly fell out of the booth leaning toward the table where Cindy and her officers had been. The two cops waved goodbye to the chief and headed to the door. Cindy looked our way. I motioned her over, and Charles pointed at the seat Chester had vacated.

Cindy looked at the seat, at Charles, then at me. "Am I going to regret this?"

Charles said, "Of course not."

I didn't lie to her; I smiled as she joined us. I'd wager it wasn't her first choice.

Charles asked, "How's your day?"

Cindy pointed to the table where she had been seated. "One of my guys told me he was quitting and moving to his wife's hometown somewhere in the middle of God's country in Arkansas. The other one said his doctor recommended he take a leave of absence because of job stress. Can you believe that?"

I could, but I limited my response to, "I'm sorry."

"Now two troublemakers summon me over. So, Charles, how do you think my day's been?"

Charles smiled. "Looks like it sucked until you joined us."

"I assume the two of you didn't ask me over to see what kind of day I was having. What's up?"

"Chris wanted to know who you and the Sheriff's Office are figurin' as suspects in Michael Hardin's murder." Charles pointed his fork at me. "He thought it was one of the bookie's disgruntled customers."

Cindy glared at me. "He did?"

"That's not exactly right, Cindy," I said, although it wasn't far off. "I was curious how the investigation was going."

Cindy shook her head. "If I could stick you behind bars for lying to a police chief, that salad would be the last good meal you'd be getting in the next few weeks, months, maybe years."

"Chief," Charles said, "before you haul Chris's pasty white rear end off to the hoosegow, do you have any good suspects?"

"There's room for both of you," Cindy said, looked to see if anyone was nearby, and sighed. "I was on the phone with Detective Callahan before my department was reduced by two. He'd taken the bookie's notebook as evidence and has a detective following up on the names in it. The word most of Michael's clients shared was that he was a stand-up guy, honored his losses. If there was such a place, they'd nominate him for the Bookie Hall of Fame."

"Not everyone believed that," I said.

Cindy looked around, got Amber's attention, and

ordered a Diet Coke. I took it as a sign that she wasn't going to rush out.

"Chris, there's nothing to indicate that his death was related to his bookmaking. It could be anything. Someone could have hated that damned hat with a feather in it. Who knows?"

I nodded. "Anything to say he was reverting to his drug-pushing career?"

"None that's come out."

"What about Janice Raque?"

"What about her?"

"How solid is her alibi?"

"She claimed to be visiting friends, but there're holes in the timeframe. Two women she'd visited live on opposite sides of Charleston and there was a significant gap between when they saw her. Have you heard anything more about her?"

"Chester Carr was in here a little while. Said that while he was with his walking group this morning—"

Cindy interrupted, "Crawling group."

She'd told me a couple of months ago that when Chester's group gets to some of Folly's intersections, one of her cops often stopped traffic to let them cross like a raft of ducks.

"Okay, crawling group. Anyway, David Darnell was telling him something that Horace, Janice's husband, told David."

"Do I need a subpoena to get it out of you?"

I told her what Horace had said about Janice getting so mad that he was afraid she'd kill him, and she didn't need an additional incentive by having more life insurance.

Cindy looked down at the table. "Chris, you're single, so I'll forgive your ignorance. We married chicks are always telling our husbands that we're going to kill them. Crap, some of the time we mean it. But you know how many of us do it?"

"Can't say that I do."

"How many?" asked trivia collector Charles.

"Don't know," Cindy said. "It ain't many, otherwise there wouldn't be any married women left. They'd all be in jail, which thinking about it, doesn't sound bad. Three square meals a day; we don't have to cook. No nagging husbands." She looked off into space.

"Janice Raque still a suspect?" I said to bring Cindy back from dreaming about an idyllic life in prison.

"Detective Callahan is trying to pin down her alibi. She may be."

"What about Neil Wilson? The last time we talked, you didn't know if anyone had questioned him."

"He was on Callahan's list. Neil was at work in Charleston around the time the bookie was killed. Like Janice, there's a gap in his alibi since the ME can't pin down the time of death as accurately as I'd like." She sipped her Diet Coke and looked at her watch. "Guys, I'd love to stay and let you tell me who killed Michael, but I've got a budget committee meeting at City Hall. I can't tell you how excited I am about it."

"One more question," I said. "Is there anything suspicious about Raymond Bentley's death?"

"Chris, is there a possibility, even a teeny-weeny, remote possibility that somewhere in your circuit-shorted brain that could entertain the thought that a person could die of something other than being murdered?"

"Yes."

Charles waved his hand in front of Cindy. "What about Ray?"

Cindy shook her head. "I'm beginning to look forward to my meeting in City Hall. No, no, and no, there's nothing to indicate that anything other than a damned drunk man fell down the steps and prematurely ended his career in comedy. Is that clear enough?"

She didn't wait for an answer.

Charles watched her go and said, "So, which of Theo's guests shoved Ray down the steps?"

We discussed the possibilities for twenty minutes before deciding two things. First, when it came to people who may've killed Michael, we had no idea, although, we could identify two possible suspects, but acknowledged that considering Michael's profession, that number could swell dramatically. Second, we decided that our lunch was outstanding, even if the Mahi Salad was healthy.

Chapter Twenty-Three

I called Theo late that afternoon to see how he and his houseguests were doing.

His voice cracked as he spoke, yet insisted he was okay. He shared that, earlier in the afternoon, Pete had taken Wallace to the funeral home in Charleston to make arrangements once Ray's body was released from the coroner's office.

I asked if he'd heard anything from the police. He said that Detective Callahan had returned to ask more questions, saying that they were "routine" and to "follow up" from his middle of the night visit. I doubted there was anything routine about them. Theo was still traumatized, so I didn't share my thoughts. Callahan hadn't said anything new about what the coroner found, although he told Theo that he was still investigating the death.

"Has Wallace said anything about funeral plans?"

Theo hesitated before saying, "He's the only family they have left, and Ray didn't have close friends. His son wanted to be cremated with no funeral. Wallace tried to make a joke out of it by saying that they would be able to carry Ray's ashes to gigs. To be honest, I'm not sure it'd been discussed and would venture to guess the decision was because Wallace didn't have money for a funeral."

"You still think they're broke?"

"Wallace asked if I could lend him the money for the funeral home. He fabricated some far-flung story about CDs not maturing until November. I gave him my credit card."

"You don't believe him?"

"I know broke when I see it. Besides, Wallace first said his CDs were maturing in June, changed it to early next year, now November. I can't tell if he thinks I don't remember what he told me, or if he doesn't remember."

"How's he taking the death?"

"Don't know. He'd been in his room until he left with Pete."

"Is he still getting confused?"

"I suppose."

"What's that mean?"

"I hate to say anything, because I don't know him like his pals do. Like I mentioned before, it seems his confusion comes at the most opportune times."

"You still think he's faking it?"

"Honest to God, I don't know. Something doesn't feel right about it. Again, I don't know him enough to tell."

Have you asked Sal?"

"I tried. He kept changing the subject."

"Are they sticking to the story that no one saw what happened?"

"Funny thing is, none of them are saying anything. They're acting like nothing happened."

"They could be in shock."

"I know I am. I don't know what to say or do around them. I'm sick about what happened, yet, well, I'm sick."

Theo was leaving words on the table, so in the spirit of Charles, I said, "What aren't you saying?"

"I hate saying this. I don't know how much longer I'll be

able to stand company. Sal's my brother, but we're not close. I've gotten comfortable being in the house by myself."

"I understand and feel the same way. Have they said anything about leaving?"

"Nothing. My gut says they don't intend to go anywhere. They haven't mentioned scheduled appearances outside the area. With the tragic death of Ray, this wasn't time to broach the subject."

I told him to call if he needed anything. He asked if I knew of any good comedian exterminators. If it hadn't been so close to the tragic death in his house, it would've been funny. I wished him a peaceful evening.

<hr>

THE CHAMBER OF COMMERCE perfectly described the next day. The temperature was in the low seventies, a breeze was blowing out of the west, with not a cloud to be seen. I decided to walk two blocks to the ocean and stroll along the beach. After yesterday's healthy Mahi salad, and now a walk in the sand, I could picture pounds falling off my slightly overweight frame, my cholesterol sinking to acceptable levels, and contemplating running in a mini-marathon. I wondered how different I was than reality-challenged Wallace. I started to laugh at the comparison, when I saw Pete Marvin sitting in the sand with his bare feet touching the water as each wave inched ashore. No one was nearby, and he was staring at the horizon like he was watching for his ship to come in.

Pete was so focused that I hesitated to approach then figured, if I wanted to learn as much as possible about Ray's death, this would be my chance. I said, "Hi."

He looked up and for a second didn't appear to recognize me.

A smile appeared on his face. "Oh, hi, Chris, you startled me. Have a seat. Wiggle your toes in my kiddie pool."

I lowered my body to the sand, keeping my feet back from the water lapping over his feet.

"A terrible thing about Ray," I said as I scooted my deck shoes in the sand. "Are you okay?"

He shook his head. "It could've been any of us. We had too much to drink. Theo's steps are steep." He shook his head again. "You never know. It could as easily have been me."

"Were you and Ray close?"

"Not really. I've been friends with Wallace since Columbus sailed the ocean blue. I've known Ray since before he was born. Don't get me wrong, I liked him as Wallace's son." He hesitated and chuckled. "He was easier to like when he was a kid. The older he got, the harder it was to be around him. He'd diss his dad, as well as the rest of us. The other day he told Sal that Sal's IQ came back negative. He called us old farts, said we were as funny as a toadstool. The only time he showed a sense of humor, or for that matter, humility, was when he was on stage. He could be funny standing behind a microphone. When the spotlight was turned off, so was his sense of humor."

I'd heard that many comedians weren't that funny when not preforming. Pete had more experience with them than I had, so I said, "Is that unusual for comedians?"

"There are more like that than you might think. Still, most of them, most of us, aren't always hostile. Some of us even like other people, something Ray lacked."

"Have you always been a stand-up comic?"

"Wanted to be a boxer when I was young. After entering a few amateur bouts and getting the snot knocked out of me, I decided on something less dangerous."

I pointed to his tree-trunk-sized arms. "Looks like you would've been good at boxing."

He laughed. "After I kept getting whipped, I started weightlifting." He patted his left forearm. "These things used to be all muscle back in the day. I bulked up then got tired of exercising, watched them turn to flab. That's when I turned to comedy. I hung out in some bars. When the bartenders got bored, they asked me to tell a few jokes. Wasn't long after that when I met Sal."

"Guess it was safer than boxing."

"Safer, no less brutal. I was decent at it. I figured I wouldn't be good enough to do it for a living, not a successful living. For a few years, I switched to the management side of comedy. I got to know a lot of the guys on the tour. A couple of them asked if I wanted to be their manager, booking gigs, helping them with their money, stuff like that. That's when I learned that most were nice guys. Oh, sure, some had problems, drink, drugs, anger, paranoia, but most were okay."

"Do you manage any now?"

His laugh came easily, and he shared another one with me. "Can't seem to manage myself. Nah. Gave up managing a decade ago and re-hitched up with Sal, and with his buddy Wallace. We've been together ever since."

"When did Ray start traveling with you?"

"A year ago. He kept telling everybody that he's between big TV deals. If you ask me, it's bullshit. He's worked more than the rest of us, although, I think TV deals were in his imagination. It doesn't matter now." He looked out to sea, then back at me. "Ray was a prick. His dad's a good guy. For that reason, I hated to see anything bad happen to Ray. It could've been any of us."

"Where're the rest of the guys?"

"They're torn up about the accident. Sal was heading upstairs to see if he could get some sleep. None of us got much after it happened. Poor Wallace said he needed to get away and took the Lincoln to Charleston. He made up some story about buying new stage duds. I think he wanted to get out of the house. I hope he makes it okay."

"Is there a reason he might not?"

"He lost his son. His memory is on the fritz. And, he's

driving around in a strange town in a car the size of the Queen Mary. What do you think?"

"He does seem confused at times," I said, stating the obvious.

"I suppose. I'd better get back." Pete hopped up, brushed sand off his feet, and slipped his shoes on. "Good talking to you."

I watched him go and repeated what he had said about Wallace's confusion: "I suppose." Something about the way he'd said it didn't feel right.

Chapter Twenty-Four

On the way home, I stopped at Bert's to grab a sandwich. Ty, one of the clerks, was kneeling and in a deep conversation with a mid-sized dog that appeared to be a pure-bred mongrel. The clerk was conversing with the dog; the dog was waiting for Ty to give it a treat.

The pooch, person conversation ended, the dog gobbled down the treat, Ty looked up at me, and said, "Want a treat?"

I declined, so Ty stood and wiped off his knees, before asking, "Hear about that funny guy falling down the stairs at Theo Stoll's house?"

I told him that I had.

"Don't know why I bother telling you anything. I'm beginning to think you know about terrible things before they happen. And I thought Charles's ex-gal Heather was the psychic."

I thought about how much truth there was in his comment. "Theo's a friend. He called me after it happened. Tragic."

"Speaking of tragic," Ty said, "you figured out who killed the bookie?"

I rolled my eyes. "It's in good hands with the police."

"You're one of the best I've run in to for not answering a question while the person asking thinks you did."

"Thanks, I think."

Ty held his head back and laughed.

"What's so funny?" someone said from behind me.

I turned to see Neil Wilson. He wouldn't have been easy to miss as his six-foot-three, former college football player frame towered over me. He wore black slacks and a light-weight, black jacket with a generic red, white, and blue shield-shaped patch on the arm. *SECURITY* was printed in the middle of the patch. He was holding a six-pack of Budweiser and looking over my head at Ty.

"I was asking Chris if he'd figured out who killed Michael Hardin. He was avoiding answering me."

I stepped out of the way of their conversation.

Neil looked at the clerk but nodded toward me. "Why would he figure it out?"

Ty smiled. "Chris gets in the middle of every murder. He claims to be a simple, retired bureaucrat, but there're rumors he's like one of those superheroes you see in the movies. He's got a tight-fitting, stretchy body suit under that red golf shirt."

Neil turned to me like he was waiting for me to pull my shirt off and bend steel barehanded.

"Ty's teasing. He knows I've lucked into helping the police a couple of times."

Neil seemed unconvinced and I was in a hurry to change the subject. "Had any luck finding a job?"

Neil set the six-pack on the table beside us and started to answer.

Ty interrupted and said he needed to get back to work.

Neil crossed his arms. "Not yet. Hear of anything?"

I told him that I hadn't but still had his number in case anything came up.

"So, you're trying to help the cops catch the guy who killed Hardin?"

"No," I said. This was the last conversation I wanted to have with the giant of a man who I considered a suspect.

"Anyway, I hope the cops hurry up and catch whoever did it. Would you believe one of them came to my work, pulled me in the office, and started asking questions?"

I did believe it since Cindy had already told me. "What kind of questions?"

"Where I was when he was killed. Word was that I owed Michael a few dollars. I guess the cops thought I was a suspect."

"You had an alibi, didn't you?"

His eyes narrowed as he smiled. "You playing superhero?"

I'd hoped Neil had forgotten Ty's comment. I smiled. "Do I look like a superhero? The police chief, Cindy LaMond, is a friend. The other day we were talking. She said they'd interviewed several people who may've had a motive. She told me that they all had alibis, so I figured you might've been one of them."

"They asked about a four-hour block. I figured that's when he was killed. I told them I was working about that time. I think they verified it with my boss. That was the end of it."

"Good."

Neil picked up the six-pack. "Better get this home before it gets warm. Don't forget, you said you'd let me know if you hear of work. Don't have to be security. I've also done some cooking in my day."

As he left, I couldn't help remembering that Cindy had said that his alibi was for only some of the hours, then how he'd lied to me about feeling bad about Michael's death.

I got home and chewed on my sandwich and on what

Neil had said. I didn't know what the police were thinking. To me, the security guard was a prime suspect. I called Cindy and was rewarded with her voicemail. It was late, so I told her I didn't need anything important. I asked her to call in the morning.

Fifteen minutes later, the phone rang. Cindy must've missed talking to me so much that she couldn't wait until the morning. I was wrong, something that was happening far more often than I liked.

In a barely-audible voice, I heard, "Chris, this is Theo."

"Hi, Theo. Is everything okay?"

"Umm, yes."

"Why're you whispering?" I asked, hoping he didn't want me to come to his house.

"I'm in the kitchen. Can't talk. Sal and Wallace are in the other room."

I heard glasses clanking. Theo yelled, "I'm on my way, guys." He went back to whispering. Can you meet me at the Dog in the morning?"

"What time?"

"Seven, if you can make it. Not a creature will be stirring around here that early. No one will miss me."

"I'll be there. What's going—"

The phone went dead.

Chapter Twenty-Five

Theo was easy to recognize when he entered the Dog. He wore his USS Yorktown ball cap, an oversized, white T-shirt, Carolina-blue jogging shorts, and knee-length black support socks. He's always looked older than mid-eighties. Today, he looked like he could be starring in a zombie movie. His eyes were blood-red from what I could see of them. They were half closed. I worried that he wouldn't make it to the booth.

Amber arrived at the same time and asked if Theo wanted coffee. He perked up, lowered himself onto the bench seat with great effort and a groan, and told her, "Yes, lots."

"Rough night?" I asked.

He bowed his head like he was praying and mumbled something that I couldn't understand. I asked him to repeat it.

"I'm scared. Don't know what to do. Chris, I'm at wits' end."

I leaned closer to my distraught friend. "What's going on?"

Amber set coffee in front of Theo.

He didn't look up, so I thanked her.

She shrugged, and I told her I'd wave if we needed anything.

Theo put his hands around the mug but didn't lift it. "Wallace and Pete spent a lot of time yesterday talking about their trip to the funeral home. I was in and out of the room. I swear to God, Wallace told Pete a thousand times what the funeral director said. Pete listened, listened, and listened. If Wallace had repeated himself that many times, I would've walked away. Anyway, that's not why I'm upset."

"You think Wallace kept forgetting he'd told Pete, or was nervous and kept repeating it?"

"Hard to tell. It's what he told me later that made me call you."

Theo blew across the coffee and took a sip. I wanted to ask if Wallace and Pete had learned anything else about Ray's death yet didn't want to interrupt whatever Theo wanted to share.

He set the coffee down. I motioned for him to continue.

"Pete must've gotten tired of listening to Wallace, said he had to do something in his room. I was coming out of the kitchen when Wallace asked me to walk out back with him. I followed him to the deck. He stretched out in a chair, I sat next to him, and he told me." Theo sighed and looked in his mug like his next words would appear on the surface of the liquid. "You know what he told me?"

Of course, I didn't, so I remained silent.

"Said he killed the bookie. Wallace said it to me right there on my deck." He shook his head. "What should I do?"

"Was he serious?"

"Sounded like it."

"Remember, he told me that he'd seen the body, yet was confused about when it was. You told me that he seemed to drift in and out of reality."

"You weren't there, Chris. The man looked me in the

eye, said he smacked the bookie in the head and left him in the weeds."

"I find it hard to believe he knew Michael Hardin. Did he say why?"

"I was so taken back that I couldn't speak, much less ask questions. What should I do?"

"You need to tell the police."

He took a deep breath then looked down. "I know … I know. I don't want to get anyone in trouble. They're my houseguests."

"Theo, I understand, but the police need to know."

"What if poor Wallace was hallucinating, or confused? He could've made it all up?"

"That's possible. The police will figure it out."

"I hate to impose, but would you go with me?"

That wouldn't have been in the top one-hundred items on my to-do list, but Theo was a friend.

"Of course. Let me call Chief LaMond to see if she can meet us at her office."

She answered on the second ring. "Crap, Chris. I just got your message from last night. Is there a reason why you couldn't wait until I got coffee in my bloodstream before pestering me again? I was going to call, scout's honor."

"That's not why I'm calling. Theo Stoll and I are at the Dog. He has something to tell you. Could we stop by your office in a few minutes?"

"I'll do one better. Where do you think I was going to get my caffeine fix? Don't answer, I'm pulling in front of the Dog. I'll be there before you can say, 'Cindy LaMond, you're the best police chief in the world.'"

She wasn't far off. She was standing at our booth, motioning for Theo to move over before I finished telling him she was on her way.

Cindy smiled. "Who said cops are never there when you need them?"

She was too cheerful for Theo. He didn't return her

smile, and I would rather have had our conversation in the privacy of the chief's office. That wasn't in the cards.

Amber was quick to the booth with Cindy's coffee and asked if Theo and I needed anything.

I deferred to Theo, who said he was fine. I said the same.

Cindy took a sip, exhaled, and said, "So, what'd you call about last night?"

"It can wait. Theo has something to tell you." I motioned to him.

Three false starts later, he told her about his conversation with Wallace.

She asked the same question I posed. "Was he serious?"

Theo gave the same response.

Cindy turned to me. "What do you think?"

"I wasn't there. From my conversations with Wallace, it could've been something out of his fantasy world."

Theo interrupted. "You're right, you weren't there. I'm no expert on warped minds, but I think he was serious."

Cindy said, "Where is he now?"

"My houseguests operate on three time zones west of here. They were asleep when I left the house. They're sawing logs in their, in my beds."

Cindy looked at her watch. "Tell you what, Theo. Mosey on home, I'll come-a-callin' in a couple of hours."

Theo nodded. "Are you going to tell him where you heard it?"

"Did he tell anyone else?"

"I don't know."

"He'll know, unless he told other folks. I won't mention you unless I have to."

Theo nodded. "Will you arrest him?"

"Theo, I'll start by talking to him and play it by ear. That's all I can promise." She glanced at her watch. "Head on home. I'll be there in a couple of hours."

Theo had looked beaten down when he came in; he

looked like he'd been run over by the comedians' Lincoln when he shuffled out.

Cindy shook her head as she watched Theo leave. "What's your take, Chris?"

"Wallace is a mystery. There's no doubt he confuses reality on a regular basis, yet I keep getting the feeling that it may be more fake than real. Theo said the same thing."

"What makes you and Theo believe that?"

"Gut feelings. It appears that Wallace's at his worst when it suits his need, if that makes sense."

"Not much. I'll take your word. What doesn't make sense is that, after you dragged him out of the middle of Center Street, he felt the need to tell you he'd seen a body. I never would've made a connection between Theo's visitor and the death of a bookie."

I caught Amber's eye. I motioned her over, ordered French toast, then asked if Cindy wanted anything to eat. She said that she didn't want to be rude and sit there and watch me eat, so she told Amber to double the order.

"If Wallace was having trouble with reality, he could've stumbled on the body, was confused about when he'd seen it. If the comedian was faking mental problems, and killed the bookie, he might have seen someone notice him near the body. Acting confused and claiming to see it, would explain why he was there."

Cindy looked at the ceiling and said, "Why would he confess to Theo?"

"Great question. That'll be up to Folly's *best police chief in the world* and the detectives from the Sheriff's Office to figure out."

"Thanks."

I smiled. "Glad I could help."

"So, what'd you call about last night?"

I told her about my conversation with Neil Wilson and asked if she had learned anything more about his alibi or if

Detective Callahan had made progress. I told her about Neil asking if I was playing a superhero.

She laughed until coffee spouted out the side of her mouth.

I told her I didn't think it was that funny.

She said she agreed. It wasn't funny, it was hilarious.

Our food arrived and I said, "Callahan learn anything?"

"Don't guess it matters. It seems we've got a confessor bunking at Theo's."

Chapter Twenty-Six

Cindy called as I was sitting down for a supper feast of Velveeta on rye. "Didn't disturb anything important, did I?"

"No, the Food Channel just left after filming me fixing supper."

She laughed. "And you think Wallace has problems with reality."

"Speaking of Wallace, did you catch up with him?"

"I did. At eleven-hundred today, I knocked on the door of one Theodore Stoll and was greeted by the homeowner, who looked more like he wanted to slam the door in my face than welcome me to his far-from-humble abode."

I interrupted, "Chief, are you auditioning for a movie role as a stuffy cop? You sound like you're reading a poorly written script."

"The mayor's been on my ass, umm, excuse me, on my case—again—to start acting and sounding like a professional law enforcement official. I'm practicing."

The mayor, Brian Newman, had been the city's police

chief for many years before being elected mayor three years ago.

"He's failing."

"Affirmative. Now, if I may continue. Against his wishes and better judgment, Theo let me in. He headed upstairs to get Wallace. Half past an eternity later, Theo inched his way down the stairs with Wallace following. The old comic was dressed in black and looked like Theo's shadow as they made it to the great room where I'd been twiddling my thumbs."

I took a bite of sandwich instead of twiddling my thumbs while waiting for the Cindy to get to the reason for the call.

"Theo made an inane excuse why he had to go back upstairs, and left Wallace with me. I told the funny guy that I'd heard that he had confided in *some people* that he'd killed Michael Hardin. When I told Theo later, he was pleased that Wallace didn't ask who."

"What did Wallace say?"

"He looked at me like someone would look at the devil walking down the street while wiggling his bony finger for the person to follow him. Wallace's body shook like he was exorcising bad memories. He said, 'I did? When did I say that?'"

"Cindy, that's what I meant about him drifting out of reality at opportune times."

"Hang on, Food Channel star, it gets weirder."

"I'm not surprised."

"Let me get my notes." Papers rustled in the background. "I'm back. Wallace looked at me and said, 'I found a shell on the beach. Luckily, it didn't explode.'"

"He told a joke?"

"I'll say yes if you add *stupid* in front of *joke*."

"What'd he say next?"

"Let me get the exact quote. Here it is, he said, 'Ha, ha, ha.'"

I sighed. "After that?"

"He said, 'Speaking of the beach, did you say I killed someone out there?' He pointed toward the ocean. I repeated what I told him when I first came in, to which he said, 'Oh yeah, I remember.' I thought we were getting somewhere. I was wrong, way wrong. I asked him what he remembered. The poor boy looked around the room. He put his finger to his lips like he was trying to hush me. He slipped four steps under reality and said that he, and this is a quote, 'Conked a man with a candlestick in the library.'"

"Was that another joke?"

Cindy hesitated and then continued, "Chris, my professional opinion is that Mr. Wallace Bentley is, in official police lingo, wacko. After he described the murder, he grinned and held out his hands like he wanted me to slap on handcuffs."

"What'd you do?"

"Pinched myself to make sure I wasn't dreaming. I wasn't. I asked if he knew where he was, what day it was, if he knew who he was staying with, even his name. I wanted to see how far from reality he'd drifted."

"What'd he say?"

"Funny thing, he knew the answers, even told me that he was at the funeral home yesterday making arrangements for his son's cremation. He knew the name of the funeral director, how much the cremation cost, where he and Pete had gone to eat after leaving the mortuary." Cindy hesitated and said, "He put his head down and started crying and saying how much he was going to miss Ray and how horrible a father he'd been to his only child. It was an awkward ten minutes before he wiped his eyes and asked if I had more questions."

"Did you?"

"I asked him to tell me again about the body on the beach. He cocked his head and frowned before saying,

'Sorry, I don't know what you're talking about.' That's all he said."

"What are you doing with him?"

"I told him I didn't have anything else to ask and for him to go upstairs and send Theo down. Wallace left, Theo returned. I wanted to see if he could remember exactly what Wallace told him about killing someone. Maybe he knew something specific that would help determine if Wallace killed Michael. He didn't. Wallace hadn't told him when he killed him, or where. All he said was he smacked him in the head. Theo didn't know about the candlestick in the library."

"Now what?"

"My hands are tied. Wallace didn't say anything that led me to believe the crime he'd committed had been anywhere other than in his warped head. Michael's murder was committed by a one-inch thick oak branch, not a candlestick, nowhere near a library. What was I to do? He didn't appear to be an immediate threat to himself, or others so, when he came back downstairs, I smiled, thanked him for his time and for sharing his flight into fantasy."

On that note, she said she needed to help her husband clean out a closet and invited me to help.

I declined the generous offer.

She wasn't surprised.

Cindy was right about Wallace not giving her anything to implicate him in Michael's death, and I couldn't think of anything that would tie him to the bookie. Wallace and his friends were new to Folly so, most likely, he wouldn't have known that Michael existed. So why did I have such an uneasy feeling about Wallace's sojourns in and out of reality?

Neil Wilson struck me as a better suspect. He owed the bookie a bundle and had lied about liking Michael. He had size and strength to send Michael to the great bookmaking joint in the sky with a blow to the head; his alibi had a hole in it. I would also add Janice Raque to the suspect pool. Her alibi had as many holes in it, as did Neil's; she had a quick temper and had been seen arguing with Michael.

I finished my sandwich, used my culinary talents to unwrap a Hershey bar for dessert, and wondered what I could do to unwrap the truth about Michael Hardin's death.

Chapter Twenty-Seven

The next two days were taken up with the type of hassles that come from owning an older home in a humidity-rich beach community. I got an expensive respite from thinking about Michael Hardin, his two customers, and the comedians, when the air conditioner decided to take time off.

After I'd called the AC repair shop, stared at my watch for four hours waiting for someone to fix it, a tech arrived, rolled up his sleeves, and stuck his head in the unit's innards. He fiddled with the mechanism and said, "Hmm" and "That's what I was afraid of," which I translated as expensive, before he said that a blown electronic something-or-other in the unit needed to be replaced.

He didn't have what it needed, so he had to go to the parts house to get one. While I waited for his return, the power in the kitchen kicked off, apparently, a sympathy strike for the silent air conditioner. A call to an electrician was next, followed by laughter from the lady who answered the phone when I asked if someone could come to the house today.

The first half of the next day was spent waiting for an electrician, but at least a working air conditioner made the wait tolerable. I knew as much about the AC unit and the house electrical system serving the kitchen as I knew about the Huli Wigmen tribe in Papua, New Guinea. My contribution to both technicians was to point to the electrical box and the air conditioner.

Cindy called while I was listening to the electrician ramble on at an extraordinary high hourly rate about why I needed five hundred dollars' worth of repairs.

I asked if I could call her back.

She said I could and, if I was lucky, she'd answer.

My checkbook was one more check and several hundred dollars lighter when I returned her call.

She answered with, "What are you pestering me about now?"

I reminded her that I was returning her call.

"Whatever. The coroner's office called this morning with the autopsy results on Ray Bentley."

I waited for her to continue, but she didn't say anything.

"Well?"

"Hold your palomino, I'm trying to find it. Okay, got it. Let's see, he says in all sorts of words I don't understand, but I think they mean Ray is still dead. Wait, there's more. In laymen's terms, Ray died of a broken neck."

"No surprise."

"Since you think every death is murder, I should add that the coroner said there were no signs of a struggle. Ray's BAC, that's blood alcohol content for you common citizens, was .16, twice the threshold for drunken driving. He wasn't in a vehicle when he tumbled down the steps, so he won't be posthumously cited for a traffic violation."

"It was accidental?"

"It looks like he was so drunk that he didn't see the stairs and staggered straight when the floor fell out from under him. The medical examiner agreed. It's ruled accidental, a result of alcohol, stupidity, and gravity. I added the last two."

I asked if Cindy found it strange that one of Theo's houseguests claims to have seen a body, presumably Michael Hardin, or has killed the bookie, depending upon his mood and, days later, another of his houseguests falls to his death.

"Of course I find it strange," Cindy said. "If you've been a cop as long as I have, you'll have seen way more things strange than normal. Still, I can't see a connection between the two. Can you?"

I hated to, but I agreed.

Cindy said, "Welcome to my world of strange."

MY SPIRITS WERE LIFTED when I met Barb for supper at Rita's Seaside Grille. It was a couple of hours before sunset, and still warm, so I arrived at the restaurant before Barb and was fortunate enough to commandeer the last available patio table.

Rita's was on a prime piece of property across the street from the Pier, catty-corner from the Tides Hotel. Customers were standing two deep at the outdoor bar. The rest of the tables were filled with a mix of locals, vacationers, and four men at one table who probably had played hooky from a meeting at the hotel. They wore coats and ties and appeared as uncomfortable as balloons at a porcupine party. The din of festive diners was a welcomed relief after spending hours in silence in my house the last two days.

My spirits were boosted further when I saw Barb walk across the street. She wore a short-sleeve red blouse, tan linen slacks, and a gleaming, white smile as she weaved her way around two tables and greeted me with a kiss.

The server had been waiting for her to arrive, was quick to the table, and asked if she needed a drink.

"Do I ever?" she asked before ordering a bottle of Sam Adams Rebel IPA, way more words in the beer's name than the beer choices of my other friends.

"Rough day?" I asked.

"Not really, but super busy with customers arriving in bunches. I can sit there for an hour without anyone coming in, then a couple of people are buying books, three are waiting to sell books, and someone wants to talk about the muse, or some amorphic symbolism in a book she 'loved, simply loved.'"

I'd spent several years in the space when it was the unsuccessful Landrum Gallery, so she lost me on *people buying*. I nodded like I understood as her drink arrived.

She took a sip and asked about my day. I shared my fascinating AC and electric stories while she pretended to be interested. After her heart rate slowed after being so excited about my air conditioner's new electronic part, she told me someone had come in the store who claimed to know me. I asked who. She said she'd tell me later. Her priority was getting food. I waved for the server, and Barb ordered fish and shrimp tacos, while I went with the fried shrimp basket.

The server left, and I said, "Back to your story?"

"An older guy, I'd guess in his mid-seventies, all-black clothes. His hair was so black it looked like he put shoe polish on it. He looked like he was going to a Halloween party. It was one of the times the store was empty. The gentleman walked over to me and said, 'Hi, I'm Wallace Bentley, you may have heard of me. I'm a comedian. Who might such a lovely lady as you be?'"

"What'd you say?"

"I smiled, told him my name and said I had heard of him. I didn't tell him it was because you screwed-up his fishing trip in the middle of Center Street."

"Wise," I said. "How'd he seem?"

"Flirty, smarmy. Why?"

I told her about Wallace's son's accident, how he'd told Chief LaMond about killing someone, and how delusional he had appeared to be when confessing.

"He seemed fine, well, not fine, but didn't say anything that was out of the ordinary—ordinary for a smarmy flirt."

"Why'd he come in?"

"After we talked, he strolled around the store like he was killing time rather than looking for anything, then he bought a book on Jewish humor. He paid from a wad of cash and asked if I had other joke books. I told him I didn't think so." Barb chuckled. "He said that was okay. Said that, unlike one of his friends, he was funny enough without stealing jokes. I thought that was humorous since he'd just bought a book of jokes."

"He say anything else?"

"He said if I wanted to have a smokin' good time with a man's man, I was looking at him. I told him I'd keep that in mind. I wanted to tell him that he was a funny guy, but I smiled instead."

It didn't sound like Wallace was too broken up by his son's death. Either that, or he was doing something he appears to do well, avoiding reality.

Our food arrived, and Barb asked if I'd heard anything new about the death of the bookie I gave her my thoughts about Neil Wilson and Janice Raque.

Being a good attorney, she homed in on the differences between what I knew and what I suspected. I knew what she was getting at, but we weren't in court. She asked if I'd shared my thoughts with the police.

I told her that I did.

She reached across the table and put her hand on mine. "You've done all you can. Now it's up to them."

I nodded, recognizing it was time to drop the subject.

We spent the next hour enjoying a perfect evening watching diners around us soaking in the island's atmosphere while enjoying a delightful meal.

I was again reminded why I had chosen to retire on Folly Beach. The best part of the evening, other than spending it with a lovely lady, was that I didn't give another thought to the murder, or murders.

Chapter Twenty-Eight

Theo called the next afternoon to tell me Ray's body had been cremated. He'd taken Wallace to the funeral home to pick up the cremains.

I asked how Wallace was, and Theo said he was quite well for someone who'd just lost a son. He went on to mention that, during the trip, the comic never strayed from reality. I thought that was a good sign, although curious.

Theo then admitted that there was another reason for his call. Sal cornered him as soon as he got back from the funeral home and wanted him to call me to see if I'd meet him at Cal's tonight. Theo said Sal thought that, since I was such a good friend of the bar owner, it'd be good if I was with Sal when he asked about another appearance. I could tell Cal how good the idea was.

I'd rather have another visit by an electrician than pimp for Sal and his band of comedians, so I asked Theo what he wanted me to do.

He stated that Sal was his brother and that family members must stick together. Not a rousing yes.

I told him that if he was there, I'd be.

I entered the nearly-full bar as the distinct voice of Hank Williams Sr. singing "I'm So Lonesome I Could Cry" filled the air, along with the comforting smell of frying hamburgers. Two couples at a nearby table were clinking their beer bottles together toasting something. At another table, four middle-aged women were laughing. Cal was behind the bar, pointing a finger at Chester Carr, who stood in front of the bar nodding at Cal.

There were two empty tables beside the stage and nobody else entering, so I didn't have to rush to grab one. I headed to the bar to say hi to Chester and warn Cal about Sal's visit.

"Chris," Cal said as he tipped his Stetson my direction. "Glad you're here. Tell this old man I'm right."

I smiled and turned to Chester. "Old man, Cal's right."

Cal pulled his shoulders back. "I told you so."

Chester shook his head. "Chris, you don't know what he's talking about."

I patted Chester's shoulder. "Don't need to. It's his bar, so he's right."

Cal slid a beer to Chester. "Chester, you could learn a lot by paying attention to this here youngster." He pointed at me.

Cal's mood was often influenced by the size of the crowd. He was excited about the mid-week numbers. My mood was influenced by someone calling me a youngster. Maybe tonight wouldn't be as bad as I'd anticipated.

From the jukebox, Johnny Cash was bemoaning how bad his Sunday morning was, two men stepped up to the bar and asked for more Buds, and Chester put a damper on my mood when he asked if I'd caught the bookie's killer. I would rather he'd told me what he and Cal had been arguing about. I said no.

He took a sip, looked around the room, and leaned closer to me. "If you ask me, it's Janice Raque."

"What makes you think that, other than the argument you told me about?"

Chester looked around again, then turned to me, "Last night—"

Cal set a glass of wine in front of me, nodded in Chester's direction, and interrupted, "You convinced my pard here that I'm always right?"

"Yes," Chester said before I could. "You're always right, Cal. You remember when I was in here last night sitting by the table near the door?"

"I'm old, not senile. Of course, I remember. You were with Horace and Janice Raque. Am I right, or am I right?"

"Did you notice that Horace left before Janice?"

"That slipped by me. What's your point?"

Chester motioned for Cal to lean closer. "I was telling Chris that I think Janice killed Michael Hardin."

Cal took off his hat and rubbed his hand through his hair. "Because her husband left before she did?"

Chester shook his head. "You know why he left?"

"I'm a broken-down, country-singing barkeep, not a psychic."

"Why'd he leave? I asked, hoping to move the deteriorating conversation along.

"Janice started to tell me how much she lost when the bookie claimed he didn't place her bet in time. Horace snarled at her and said that he's sick of hearing her tell that story and how happy she is that the blankety-blank bookie's dead."

Somehow, I'd missed how that made her a murderer. I said, "Is that why you think she killed him?"

Chester hesitated and whispered, "When Horace was storming out, Janice mumbled, "That's why I freakin' killed him."

"Whoa," Cal said. "That came from nowhere. You sure that's what she said?"

"I barely heard her. It surprised me. I asked her what

she said. She looked embarrassed, like she didn't know that she said it out loud."

Cal reached over the bar and punched Chester on the arm. "Don't keep us in suspense. What'd she say?"

"She stammered, 'I, umm, said, I'm glad Michael is dead.'"

"You sure that's what she said?" Cal asked.

Chester tapped his beer bottle on the bar. "That's what she told me. That ain't what I heard. Not what I think I heard."

Two men at the other end of the bar called for more drinks.

"Damn, just when it's getting good," Cal said and moved to the thirsty customers.

"Chester, you want to tell the chief what you heard?"

"Chris, that's all I've thought about since last night. I've tried to think how I could've misunderstood her. If I didn't, if she was serious, umm, it was loud in here. My hearing's not what it used to be. The more I ponder it, the more I'm not sure. I don't feel comfortable blabbing to the police."

"Sure?"

"Yes."

Roy Acuff's version of "Blue Eyes Crying in the Rain" filled the room as Sal sauntered in wearing his three-piece, robin-egg blue suit. He was followed by Pete and Theo.

Sal saw me and shrugged.

I motioned them to the empty table by the stage and turned back to Chester. I offered to go with him to see the chief if that'd help. He promised to keep my offer in mind, threw a ten-dollar bill on the bar, said he was tired, and wanted to get home.

Sal and Pete had taken seats at the table; Theo was talking to a nearby couple. I moved to the newcomers, even though I would rather have spent more time trying to convince Chester to share his story with the police.

Theo finished talking with the women, and he and I took the two vacant chairs.

Sal thanked me for meeting them and waved for the harried server to take our order.

She was quick to the table and said it would be a few minutes before she could get back with the drinks.

I asked, "Where's Wallace?"

Theo looked at Sal and answered, "He stayed home. Said he was torn up by Ray's death, didn't feel like seeing anyone."

"News to me," Sal said. "Wallace couldn't stand being around Ray when he was alive. Now he wants to stay in his room to stare at a box of ashes."

Pete spoke for the first time. "Ray's a lot nicer in a box than when he was alive."

"Come on, Pete," Sal said, "that's a horrible thing to say."

Pete smiled. "It's true."

Cal brought our drinks and welcomed my table mates.

Sal moved around the table to shake Cal's hand. "Great to see you again, good buddy. How's business?"

Cal shook Sal's hand and gave me a sideways look. He'd told me that, after several decades of being on the road entertaining and encountering countless managers, promoters, and bar owners trying to take advantage of him, he could spot BS a mile away. He was even better spotting it at three feet.

"Good," was all Cal said before Sal interrupted and asked the singer to join us. He reached over to pull another chair to the table before Cal could escape.

Cal looked around and didn't see anyone needing his attention. He gave me a dirty look as he sat.

Sal smiled. "Pete, Wallace, and I were checking and uncovered a couple of open slots in our schedule. We thought since you were so happy with our performance, we'd be willing to do an encore. We know we can't compete with your incredible singing talents, but we could give you a break you know, fill in between your sets. What do ya think?"

I don't know what Cal thought, but I thought it was the biggest crock I'd heard in Cal's.

"Tell you what, guys," Cal said and set his Stetson on the table, "Chris knows this, but you may not. Each Tuesday, I have open mic night for crooners. We draw a good crowd and a handful of wannabes. I was thinking we could try a few open mic nights for comedians. I've had customers mention it, even say they might could lay some jokes on an audience. We could do it Sunday nights. If you could work it in your busy schedule, we could feature the Legends Tour the first few weeks to get us off to a rousing start. I bet the newcomers could learn a bunch from you professionals. How about it?"

Not only could Cal spot BS, but he could also sling it. It was interesting that he chose his slowest night of the week and, with other joke tellers, there was a chance of hearing something funny from the stage.

Sal looked at Pete then turned to Cal. "Of course, we'll have to talk to our agent and our booking company. There's a decent chance we'll be able to break free to help you get your event off to a good start. Our business manager will want to know the pay."

Without hesitation, Cal said, "Same as last time."

Sal stared at the ceiling then at Cal. "That'll work."

Pete said, "Now, about something else, smoking. It's a proven fact that people don't hear things as funny unless there's smoke in their eyes. Seems I've seen folks smoking in a couple of places over here. So, it can be okay during our performances, right?"

Cal said, "I'm a country singer. I don't tell jokes or funny stories. I'll tell you what I do. I make payments on this bar. I own those speakers up there." He pointed to the stage. "I own that big ole silver microphone that's hooked into my amp that's hooked to the speakers. And, I make the rules. When ya'll asked about smoking the last time, it was no joke when I said no, N-O. If you don't like it, there's the door." Cal glared at Pete. "That clear enough?"

Sal put his hand in front of Pete. "Don't get all worked up, Cal. Pete was just asking,"

Cal nodded. "I think that Dylan guy said it good when he warbled 'The Times They Are a-Changin'.' Change your hang-up about people puffin'."

Cal had said he couldn't tell a joke, yet he's talking about changing, talk coming from a man who's so stuck in the 1960s that he thinks music written after that should be banned.

"Good point, Cal," Sal said. "It's easy to see why you have such a successful bar. We'll let you get back to your job. Someone will call you tomorrow to let you know what our support staff says about the Legends headlining Sunday."

Headlining. Support staff. Sal was funny.

Cal was quick to leave. No one was waiting for drinks, so it was to escape from the Legends rather than to get back to bartending.

I finished my drink and left Theo and his houseguests enjoying drinks, country classics, conversation, and a night out of the house where Ray had fallen to his death and his dad was conversing with his son's ashes.

Chapter Twenty-Nine

Charles was waiting for me the next morning at the Dog. I'd called him on my way home from Cal's to see if he had breakfast plans. He said that he did but, because I was such a good friend, and had offered to pick up the tab, he'd shift his schedule around to free up breakfast—all that to say he had nothing to do.

Amber and I arrived at the table at the same time, and she placed a steaming hot mug of coffee in front of me.

A group of five ladies on the other side of the room waved for Amber's attention.

She acknowledged their signal but, before she left, she said, "When it slows down, I've got something to tell you."

We ordered, and Amber moved to the other table.

Charles watched her go. "What does she want to tell you?"

I shook my head and took a sip.

He continued to stare at Amber. "Suppose we'll have to wait until she gets back." He ran his hand through his hair. "I've been thinking."

I nodded in response since that was his second comment that didn't warrant a response.

"Aren't you going to ask what I've been thinking?"

I smiled. "No, you're going to tell me whether I ask or not."

"You're no fun. Anyway, I did a heap of pondering last night. I think Neil Wilson killed the bookie."

"Go on."

Charles tapped the table with his forefinger. "First, he owed money." He tapped again. "Second, he could no more pay it than I could become Governor of South Carolina." Another tap. "Third, he's a brute. It would've been easy for him to clobber the life out of the bookie." One more tap. "In addition to being big, he's a cop, so he's got hand-to-hand combat training. Bookie-man wouldn't have had a chance." He hesitated and looked at the ceiling. "And, whatever the next number is, Cindy said Neil didn't have an alibi. That enough reasons?"

I didn't think a security guard would be considered a cop. I also questioned whether Neil had combat training, hand-to-hand or otherwise. I didn't think Charles's reasons were anywhere close to proving Neil's guilt. I couldn't fault him for trying and didn't want to challenge him since he's been so fragile. My guess was that he's thinking about the bookie's death more to get his mind off losing Heather than to solve the murder.

"Good points. The police know all of that, so I doubt they've cleared Neil."

Charles peeked at his wrist, then looked around the room. "When's Amber coming back?"

"Patience, she'll be here. You could be right about Neil. Let me throw something else in the mix."

I shared what Chester told me about Janice, what he thought she said about killing Michael, and what she told him she'd said after he questioned her about it. Charles asked if Chester was sure he heard her say that she killed him. It was the same question I'd asked, so I gave Charles the same answer I'd received.

"When were you going to tell me? Why'd you let me go on about Neil when you already knew who the killer was? Why did—"

I held my coffee mug up in his face. "Could I have stopped you?"

Charles bit his lower lip and said, "No, but—"

Amber was standing by the table, set our breakfast down, and interrupted Charles. "I've only got a minute. I figured you'd want to know that Janice was in yesterday, got here right before closing. Remember her temper tantrum when Shantel got Janice's order wrong?"

I nodded.

"She did it again. This time, she was mad when she walked in the door, and didn't try to hide it. Shantel was stuck with her. I was behind the counter by the coffee urn. Since I knew what happened the last time, I kept an eye on them. Shantel bent over backwards to be nice. Janice ordered. Shantel went to put the order in and bring Janice water. I thought Janice was going to knock the water on the floor. She pounded the table and said, 'Could you be any slower?' Poor Shantel didn't know what to do. She'd done everything right, had the water there as quick as any of us could have." Amber rolled her eyes. "I would've been tempted to smack Janice. Shantel apologized, backpedaled from the table, then went to the kitchen to get away from the irate customer. Next thing I know, Janice slammed her chair against the chair behind her and was out the door. She didn't pay for anything." Amber shook her head. "Shantel was in tears."

"That's terrible."

Amber looked around, didn't see anyone seeking her attention, and said, "That doesn't prove anything, other than Janice is a hothead and won't be on Shantel's

Christmas card list. I figured you'd want to know since you're trying to catch the bookie's killer."

I thanked her, and she headed back to work.

Charles said, "Okay, you've got me. Neil just slipped to number two on my list."

"Like Amber said, all it proves is that Janice has an explosive temper."

"True, but when you add that to what Chester told you, it paints a nasty picture about good ole Janice. You need to tell Cindy." He took a bite of breakfast then pointed to my phone.

"I don't want to talk to her from here. I'll call later."

"You bet you will. I'll be there to make sure you don't leave anything out."

I changed the subject and told him about the comedy Legends meeting with Cal and the decision to hold open-mic comedy night on Sundays, that is, if the Legends' staff approves.

"Staff, you mean their imaginary manager?"

"That's the one."

"Cal figures if he can get some amateurs to embarrass themselves on his stage, his customer won't have to be exposed all night to the Legends."

I said, "Do you blame him?"

"Cal didn't get old by being stupid."

We continued eating and agreeing on Cal's wisdom.

Charles said he knew a couple of folks who might have the guts or were stupid enough to stand on stage and try to be funny. He would try to recruit them. I wanted to ask if he was okay, but decided he'd tell me he was whether he was or not. I kept the conversation light and was pleased to see him smile more than he had the last few times we'd been together.

He stuffed the last bite in his mouth then pointed at my phone.

I took the hint, asked Amber for the check, paid, and

Charles followed me to the small park adjacent to the Dog. Instead of calling Cindy, I punched in Chester's number. He must've had the phone in his hand because he answered before I heard it ring. "Hi, Chester."

Charles flailed around like he was being attacked by a gaggle of gnats and mouthed, "That's not the chief."

I held my hand over the mic and said, "Chill."

"No, I wasn't talking to you, Chester. I wanted to see if you were certain about what you told me that Janice said about killing the bookie."

"Chris, I was up half the night thinking about it. I'm not sure. I think that's what she said. I'd hate to get her in trouble if I'm wrong."

"That's all I wanted to know."

"I wish I could be more helpful."

I told him I knew and wished him a pleasant day.

Charles put his hand over his eyes and shook his head. "Don't suppose you're going to call Cindy?"

"Not until I have something to tell her."

Charles sat back on the bench. "George W. Bush said, 'When I take action, I'm not going to fire a two-million-dollar missile at a ten-dollar empty tent and hit a camel in the butt. I'm going to be decisive.'"

I agreed, and the phone rang.

Charles said, "See, Chester changed his mind."

I didn't know about Chester, since Theo was on the other end of the call.

"Chris, could you come to the house?"

"When?"

"Now. The guys are still in bed. I have something to tell, no, to show you."

"Can Charles come?"

"Will that take longer? I want to show you before the guys wake up."

I told him that Charles was with me. We could be there in a couple of minutes.

Chapter Thirty

Charles and I were at Theo's door and greeted by the homeowner whispering for us to keep our voices low so we wouldn't wake his guests. We moved to the great room and sat close together on his oversized couch.

Theo whispered, "Notice anything different?"

It was the kind of question I hate. It was up there with someone asking if I'd heard the latest.

"Different?" I repeated back to Theo.

Charles looked at Theo. "You look older than I remembered."

"Not me," Theo said. "Anything different in the room?" He stared at the table along the side of the room, the table holding his silver figurines.

A silver frog was next to the eagle, cat, and llama that he had shown me during a previous visit.

I walked over and lifted the frog. "Is this the one that was missing?"

"One and the same."

Charles said, "So it didn't croak after all."

I carried the figurine to the couch and sat so I could keep my voice low. "How'd you get it back?"

"Don't know," Theo said. "I came in yesterday afternoon, saw something behind the table. It was on the floor in the corner."

I turned it over in my hands. "Could it have been there all along?"

Theo shook his head. "It's possible, although I would have thought the cleaning lady, or I, would've noticed."

Charles moved to the table and put his hand in the gap between the table and the wall. "The space is wide enough for it to fall."

Theo shrugged.

Charles said, "Frog's hop. I'm certain that silver ones don't hoppity hop on their own. If someone knocked it off, he, or she, would've heard it smack the floor."

"I agree," Theo said.

I pointed to the ceiling. "Do you think one of them took it and put it behind the table so it looked like it'd fallen?"

"That was my thought."

Charles said, "Why would someone steal it then bring it back?"

I stared at the frog. "He could've felt guilty about taking it, figured this was a way to return it without raising suspicion. Or he tried to hock it and couldn't find anyone who'd give him much for it. What about the missing money?"

"Still gone."

I returned the frog to the table, and Charles said, "Any idea which one of your guests absconded with the frog and the moolah?"

Theo shook his head.

Charles replied, "Come on, Theo, you have an idea."

"Could've been any of them."

"How about Wallace?" Charles asked. "He could've been in one of his weirdo moods. He took it then came to his senses and brought it back."

"Could be. If he did, his good sense wasn't strong enough for him to bring the money back."

"Sal?" I asked.

"I hate to think so." He shrugged. "We've had so little contact during the last couple of decades that I can't rule him out."

"What's all the racket down here? Did I hear my name mentioned?" Sal said as he came down the stairs.

Without skipping a beat, Theo said, "We were talking about your appearance tomorrow at Cal's. They were saying how excited they were to see the Legends perform again."

Charles turned to me and whispered, "We were?"

I smiled, said hi, and agreed with Theo about how happy we were.

"Fantastic," Sal said. "I think our performances will blow you away. Heard if there're amateurs who'll try their hand at comedy before Cal turns the show over to the pros?"

Charles said, "I know a couple of folks who might tell some jokes."

Sal headed to the coffee pot in the kitchen and poured a cup. I looked at Theo and wondered how he wanted to handle us being here. I didn't have to wonder long.

He said, "Chris, sorry you and Charles have to run. It would've been nice if you could have spent more time with my houseguests."

Charles returned Theo's lie. "Me too. We must get going. Besides, we'll get to spend time with them tomorrow at Cal's."

Theo mouthed, "Thank you."

I took one more look at the silver frog before we let ourselves out.

"WHAT ARE the chances that that ugly, expensive frog hopped itself off the table?" Charles asked as we stood in front of Pewter Hardware a block from Theo's house.

"Zero. Theo didn't tell his guests it was gone. It makes more sense that whoever took it couldn't unload it then brought it back, hoping that Theo wouldn't notice it'd been missing. Let's see if Larry's here."

In addition to being Chief LaMond's husband and owner of the city's only hardware store, Larry had a checkered past and had spent eight years at taxpayer's expense after getting caught burglarizing homes. He'd used those years to reevaluate his career choice, moved to Folly, and became one of its most upstanding citizens.

"What're you going to do, ask if someone tried to pay for a Weed Eater with a silver frog?"

I rolled my eyes and told him to follow me as I opened the door to the compact store. The building was empty, except for Larry standing behind the counter, fiddling with a toaster-sized electric motor, and Brandon, Larry's only full-time employee, who was at the far side of the store restocking a rack of electrical tape.

Brandon looked up as the bell over the door announced our arrival. He saw who it was and went back to restocking.

Larry smiled, set the motor down, wiped his hands on a grease-stained towel, and said, "Welcome. What can I do for you today?"

Charles made an overblown stage wave in my direction. "This ought to be interesting."

Larry turned to me.

"Got a question." I said. "How easy would it be to find someone to buy a less-than-legally acquired, expensive, silver figurine?"

Larry tilted his head and frowned. "I would know that how?"

I held up my hand and said in a voice low enough so

Brandon couldn't hear. "Because I value your wisdom and vast experience."

Larry smiled. "That's a subtle way to say I used to be a thief who had relied on fences to unload my, umm, regifted items."

"Larry," Charles said, "I like the way you said it better."

Larry ignored him. "How valuable?"

"Seven hundred dollars."

"Most pawn shops would avoid it. They'd want to be sure of the person pawning it. How did he get it? Why was he hocking it? Those kinds of things. Even then, the owner would give you little for it. Now if the person hocking the item found a, how shall I say it, less than upstanding dealer, he might buy it no questions asked, but not for much. Nowadays, those guys are harder and harder to find, or so I've been told. Most likely they wouldn't have a shop, would do business through word of mouth."

"How easy would it be for someone from out of town to find one of those dealers?"

Larry stepped out from behind the counter and glanced over at Brandon. "Near impossible. No one would trust a stranger for fear that he was an undercover cop. Why?"

I shared what had happened at Theo's and why I'd suspected one of his guests.

Larry shook his head. "Chris, it's possible that the thief could luck out and stumble across someone who would give him a decent price. Possible, although I wouldn't bet on it."

Chapter Thirty-One

I arrived at Cal's an hour before the first-ever open-mic comedy night and second appearance by the world-famous, in their minds, Legends tour group. The island was blanketed by an April shower. While it was too early to know if it would bring May flowers, it was apparent that it didn't bring a large crowd. Two tables were occupied, one man sat at the bar and was in deep conversation with Cal. Two servers huddled in a corner, probably bemoaning why they were both there with so few customers.

Theo had asked me to save room for his group, so I slid the same two tables together that we occupied during the Legends previous appearance, set my Tilley on them to mark my turf, and went to see Cal.

The bar owner finished his conversation with the lone bar customer and tilted his Stetson at me. "Did you see a bus full of thirsty customers parked out front?"

"It's early. The rain's supposed to stop. Folks will turn out."

"Sure as holy hyenas, I hope so, or those gals will string me up." He hesitated and tilted his head in the direction of the frowning servers. "I told them that tips would be flowing as free as the tide tonight."

It was shy of a busload, but four people stepped in the door, looked around, and moved to the table closest to the stage.

"See," I said, "the crowd is arriving."

Cal watched the group take seats and Joy approach them to take their order. "That's part of the entertainment. The one who looks like a fat piñata is Vernon. He's a comedian, well he's a bean counter, but tonight he's playing comedian."

The man Cal referred to was in his thirties, with pasty white skin, and dressed in a colorful Hawaiian shirt and cut-off jeans. He looked more like a blimp caught in a paint store explosion than a piñata.

"How do you know?"

"He came in last night. Said he was here to, 'analyze the assets and liabilities of the venue' before tonight's appearance."

"That's how you knew he was an accountant?"

"Hell's bells, no. I said to him, "You want to dumb that down for this ole cowboy?' Then he told me he was an accountant and apologized for his highfalutin' talk."

Charles arrived next and shook the rain off his Tilley. He noticed my hat on the table, threw his beside mine, then joined Cal and me. He was wearing a navy-blue long-sleeve T-shirt with the head of a lion and the word *EMERSON* in gold on the front. "Where're the thousands of Legends' fans?"

I suspected he knew the answer but, since Cal looked so down about the numbers, I told him that I was sure they were on their way.

"They may need a boat to get here," Charles said.

Their ship must have come in because, during the next few minutes, three more groups of soaked customers arrived and griped about the rain as they commandeered tables.

Cassis and Kristin had added smiles to their faces and a bounce to their steps as the rushed to serve the newcomers.

Cal began to get more enthusiastic about the crowd when two more people arrived. He got Charles a Bud Light, a glass of wine for me, and pointed at Charles's shirt. "Emerson?"

Charles smiled. "Wondered if anyone'd notice."

Cal asked, "What's the deal?"

I knew better than to comment on Charles's shirts.

"It's in Boston. The only college in the US of A that has what?"

"One fewer T-shirt?" I said.

"Wrong."

"I'll bite," Cal said. "What?"

"A bachelor's degree in comedic arts."

Cal said, "You're kiddin'."

"I didn't go there so I can't be kiddin'," Charles said like it made sense. "I got it for tonight."

I was impressed but didn't dare tell my friend.

"Wow," Cal said, "I'd love to hear more, but I'd better start acting like a bartender."

Charles and I left him grabbing drinks for Kristin then moved to the tables.

Charles looked at the table, where the colorful accountant was talking to the others with him. "I see Vernon made it."

"You know him?"

"I'm why he's here. I met him in Mr. John's Beach Store. He was gabbing with that skinny chick sitting with him. She was laughing at something he said. I didn't hear what it was, but figured it was funny, so I introduced myself and asked if he was a comedian."

Charles could get away with something like that. "What'd he say?"

"He looked at me like I was a tarantula he wanted to stomp on, then he grinned. He told me that he was an accountant, although some of the folks in his office told him he should be a stand-up comic. That was coming from accountants, so I didn't think he had to be funny to impress them. The lady with him, her name's Tanya, said he should go for it. I told him about open-mic comedy night. There he is."

"Don't know how funny he is, but his shirt will get laughs."

"Ah, ha," Charles said as he looked at the door. "There's my other recruit. Maybe I should supplement my private detective income as an agent to the stars."

He was looking at two women, both appeared to be in their late-twenties, with short, dark hair, wearing white blouses and skinny jeans.

"Both comedians?" I asked.

"Not sure about both. The one on the left is. That's Franny Foster. She works at Harris-Teeter. Every time I'm in there, she's talking about her three kids and her worthless husband. She's downright funny, so I invited her."

Franny waved at Charles as she followed the lady with her to a table.

There was one vacant table left, and Joy and Kristin were busy. Cal was in a better mood as he looked at his watch before moving to the stage.

He tapped the large, silver microphone. "Guys and gals, listen up. This is a big night for Cal's. You're in for quite a treat. We're going to unplug the jukebox and bring to this here stage some of the finest joke tellers that ever stepped foot on Folly Beach. That's right, we'll be opening with some locals who think, no, who know, that they're as funny as those funny guys you see on TV. Then, as quick as you can shake a hickory stick, you'll be laughing your as—umm, your rear end off when the true Legends of comedy get here." He held up both hands like he was holding back the excitement of the crowd.

It worked. No one applauded, laughed, or showed signs of excitement.

"So, let's get the fun beginning. Raise your hand if you want to share some jokes with us."

Two hands went up: Vernon and Franny.

"Fantastic," Cal said. "Let's begin with the young man who looks like he just got here from Hawaii. Vernon, umm, what's your last name again?"

The roly-poly man said, "Moore."

"Bring it on, Vernon Moore."

The three-other people at Vernon's table applauded as he moved to the microphone.

He squeezed it like it was a snake trying to wiggle free. "Hi, I'm Vernon Moore, and this is my first appearance here." He chuckled. "Umm, it's my first appearance anywhere. I've been told that I'm funny, and my sweet wife, Tanya, said I could prove it to you. So here goes." He hesitated, took a deep breath, then said, "During the day, I'm an accountant in downtown Charleston. Yep, I'm one of them. There are three kinds of accountants in the world, those who can count, and those who can't." He nodded his head toward the room.

Two of the three people at his table laughed. They must've been accountants.

"Okay," Vernon continued, "You know the definition of an economist?" Vernon waved his hand at the audience. No one knew. "It's someone who doesn't have enough personality to be an accountant."

Charles leaned over to me. "Is it midnight yet?"

"Do you know when a person decides to be an accountant?" Apparently, no one knew that answer, either. "When he realizes he doesn't have enough charisma to be an undertaker."

That elicited chuckles from several people who weren't sitting at his table.

Vernon was on a roll. He shared a few more accountant

jokes, and I was beginning to wonder where the Legends were.

Vernon said, "I'd better finish up so, remember, if you ever want to drive an accountant insane, tie him to a chair, stand in front of him, and fold a roadmap the wrong way. Thank you, thank you." He bowed and received a standing ovation—from three people at his table.

Polite applause was sprinkled throughout the rest of the room.

Cal put his arm around Vernon and said, "Great job, great job. Let's hear it again for Vernon Moore."

Vernon returned to his adoring fans, and Cal motioned to the woman who'd said she wanted to perform.

She walked to the stage like she was stepping on eggshells.

Cal met her, leaned close, while she whispered something to the country crooner.

Cal grabbed the mic and said, "Folks, put your hands together on this historic night. Give a big round of applause for Miss Franny Foster."

Most of the patrons applauded, and Franny said, "Evening guys, like Vernon, this is my first time behind a microphone. As handsome Cal said, I'm Franny and I'm frazzled. I came out tonight with my friend, Laurie, to get out of the house. You see, I have three tikes at home, actually, it's four, because my husband's thirty years old, or ten in kiddie years." She sighed. "Let me tell you how smart he is. He put a knocker on our front door. Seems he thought it'd help him win the no-bell prize." It may have been my imagination, but it appeared that most of the women in the room laughed.

"I know, I know," Franny continued, "I've learned never to argue with an idiot. He'll drag you down to his level then beat you with experience."

This time, it wasn't my imagination.

Franny shook her head and frowned. "I don't know

who's lazier, my hubby, or our dog Darwin. Whenever someone knocks on the door, Darwin looks at me like I should bark."

More laughter. Franny smiled, and said, "My husband claims I'm always negative. Yesterday, we were halfway to Columbia when he said, 'All you do is complain. Gee, I remembered the car seat, I remembered the diapers, I remembered the stroller. And all you do is gripe about me forgetting the baby.'"

Even Cal laughed.

Franny started another joke when she was interrupted by the constant blaring of a car horn.

I closed my eyes and shook my head. The Legends had arrived.

Charles asked if I wanted to go out and meet them.

I told him I'd rather slither under the table.

He said it wasn't a bad idea.

We turned out attention back to Franny who was trying to pretend that the horn wasn't disrupting her set.

"And kids," she said. "Don't get me started about kids. The other night, I came home and saw Timmy, my oldest, who's nine, sitting on a big stuffed horse and writing something. Now, being a keen observer, I asked him what in the world was he doing. He looked at me with his big brown eyes and said, 'Our teacher told us to write an essay on our favorite animal. That's why I'm sitting here and why sis is sitting on the goldfish bowl.'"

Cal's front door flung open and, for all practical purposes, Franny's performance was over.

Chapter Thirty-Two

In walked Sal, shoulders pulled back, looking as confident as LeBron James playing in a middle-school basketball game. His robin-egg blue, three-piece suit was replaced by a shiny, off-white suit and black dress shoes.

Pete was next through the door. Instead of his red sports coat, he wore a bright orange coat with a brown ascot.

I wouldn't have been surprised to see him followed in by Wallace in a red, white, and blue jumpsuit, with an elephant wearing a top hat. I was disappointed when Wallace walked in the door wearing a black shirt, slacks, and shoes. His wardrobe was black and new; the shirt showing packaging creases. He carried a plastic Walmart bag. It wasn't black.

Sal looked at Franny, gave her a thumbs-up, and moved, along with his companions, to the table. Their attire was loud enough to make up for his silence.

Franny seemed to lose her place, stammered, and said, "My time's up. Remember, folks, it's true that women don't work as hard as men." Two women in the audience groaned. Franny held up her hand and smiled. "It's because we get it right the first time. Thanks."

Maybe it was because they had a beer or two, or because they thought Franny was funny, the crowd applauded, not just the lady at Franny's table. Sal yelled, "Bravo!"

He'd heard a grand total of one joke. The comic must've figured that if he praised her performance, she'd do the same when he finished.

The reason didn't matter to Franny, she beamed from ear to ear and nodded in Sal's direction. After all, how often does a legend of comedy praise a mother with three toddlers, four counting her hubby, after her first gig?

Cal had his arm around Franny. He echoed Sal's remark when he told the audience that he was taking a fifteen-minute break for everyone to order more drinks before he brought on the world-famous Legends of Comedy.

Theo had parked the Legends' limo and joined us while Krista and Joy were taking Charles and my reorder plus orders from the others.

"Nice outfits," Charles said to the Legends.

Sal said, "We wanted to look our best tonight. Wallace thought we could be good role models for the aspiring comics who came out to tell a few jokes. It's called leading by example."

"Good idea," I said, yet thought they looked like examples for aspiring clowns rather than comics.

Joy and Kristin returned with drinks when I noticed Janice Raque seated at the bar. She was by herself, so I went to say hi. She recognized me and said it was good to see me. I was surprised by her good mood. I asked if she was alone.

She said yes, so I asked if she wanted to join our group. She looked over to see who *our group* was, and said, "Why not?"

Charles saw us coming. He pulled an extra chair from a nearby table and patted its seat for Janice.

I introduced her to the group. If they cared, they hid it well. I wrote it off to nerves, or it could have been they truly didn't care. Theo, who didn't have to worry about his comedy performance, said he knew Janice and was glad that she joined us.

"Where's Horace?" Theo asked like he just realized that Janice was by herself.

"Don't know, don't care, don't ask," she said, then turned to Wallace. "I was sorry to hear about your son."

I was surprised that she knew about Ray. Charles beat me to asking, "How'd you hear?"

She hesitated and said, "Can't keep anything under rocks around here."

Cryptic, I thought, and so did Charles. "Who told you?"

Before she answered, Cal blew into the microphone, tapped it with his knuckles, and said, "Here's what we've all been waiting for. Let me bring up to the stage Mr. Sal, umm," he glanced at a piece of paper in his hand. "Salvador Stoll. He's going to serve as master of ceremonies for the Legends. It's all yours, Sal."

Sal looked like a skinny, short version of Colonel Sanders as he grabbed the mic like he owned it. "Thank you, Cal. Let's have a hand for the best bar owner in this half of the country."

Mild applause followed, some of it was because the people knew Cal and showed their appreciation, some was muted by people who were probably trying to figure out who the best bar owner was in the other half of the country.

"How about the great performances by the comics who opened for us tonight?"

Applause rang out from the tables where the previous performers were seated. Sal nodded. "Great job, folks." He paused and smiled. "I was sitting over there a few minutes ago when my good friend, Chris, asked me if there were any famous men born on my birthday. I said, nope, only babies." Sal laughed at his joke and said, "Speaking of birthdays, I asked my wife what she wanted for her birthday. She said something with diamonds. Being the generous, accommodating husband that I am, I gave her a pack of playing cards." He laughed again. "And if you think that's funny, wait until you hear what my good friend, Pete Marvin, will be laying on you. I'll be back in a little while. Until then, let me present nationally-known comedian, entertainer extraordinaire, Pete Marvin."

I leaned over to Theo while Pete was making his way to the mic. "Those new outfits must've cost a pretty penny."

"Don't know. They didn't use my credit card."

I thought it strange since he'd said he'd been footing all their bills. "Where'd the money come from?"

"Pete said he got a payment he was owed by one of the clubs where they'd played last year."

"Do you believe him?"

"No reason not to. It was fine with me since I wasn't forking out the cash."

No reason other than someone stealing money from his house. I didn't share that thought.

Pete was introducing himself to the crowd as if Sal hadn't already.

"I don't know about you," Pete said, "I want to die peacefully in my sleep like my grandfather." He paused. "Not screaming and yelling like the passengers in his car."

Scattered laughter came from some of the tables, along with a spattering of groans. I wondered how sensitive a death joke was this close to Wallace's son's demise.

"The other day, I read where four out of five people suffer from diarrhea. Yep, four out of five. Does that mean one person likes it?"

The dead joke wasn't so bad after all.

"Speaking of my grandfather," Pete continued without waiting for the silence to die down, "I remember when he gave my grandmother a cemetery plot for her birthday." He shook his head. "Was she ever pissed. The next year, he didn't give her anything. That irritated her even more. She asked him why he didn't get her a gift. Gramps said, 'You didn't use what I gave you last year.'"

Three men at a table behind us thought it was funny, probably the reason they were in Cal's without their wives.

Pete told a few more jokes that received increased amounts of laughter. I could see how he'd been a success on the comedy club circuit. He finished, took a couple of bows, and introduced his "good friend," Wallace Bentley, the "star of comedy shows, television, and movies."

The room was full, Cal smiled like he'd discovered a way to increase Sunday business. Joy and Kristin were scurrying around the bar, distributing drinks while earning the kind of tips that they'd anticipated.

Wallace pushed up from the table, grabbed the Walmart sack, and moved toward the stage like he was walking in a pool of Jell-O. He set the bag on the corner of the stage and moved to the microphone. His shiny, black hair glistened in the lone stage light.

"Wasn't Pete great?" Wallace asked and applauded in the direction of Pete. His face smiled, but his eyes and clenched fist screamed pain.

Pete gave what I suspected was intended to be a humble nod but looked more like he was drifting asleep with his chin bouncing off his chest.

Wallace turned to the crowd and said, "Before I begin, I'd like to dedicate my performance to my son, Ray. He was a wonderful kid, a fabulous entertainer. He joins me tonight on the stage. He's gone now but will always be with me during my performances." Wallace moved away from the mic and stooped down in front of the Walmart bag. He pulled a rectangular, bronze box the size of a shoebox out and set it next to the mic stand."

A couple of people in the back of the room laughed, two tables of customers moaned, most everyone else didn't know how to react. Was it a joke? Was he serious? What do we do now? Everyone at our table understood.

The comedians bowed their heads. I peeked at Charles and couldn't tell if he was rolling his eyes or shaking his head.

Janice mumbled, "Shit."

"Thank you," Wallace said.

For what, I didn't know.

He pointed at Pete. "Pete's a good friend. I love him like a mosquito, but tell you the truth, he comes from a stupid family." He then pointed to a table on the other side of the room. "How stupid, you ask. In the Civil War, his ancestors fought for the West."

Nervous laughter from not knowing what to do after Wallace's introduction of Ray, turned sincere.

"His sister's so dumb, blondes made jokes about her."

More laughter.

"Then there's my good friend, Sal. Wave Sal."

Sal frowned then waved.

Wallace nodded then gave a stage whisper into the mic. "Don't tell anyone, but Sal told me that his brother, Theo, the old codger sitting beside him, is so dumb that he once sold his car for gas money."

Most everyone in the room, except for Theo, Charles, and I, thought it was one of the funniest things they'd ever heard—proof that cigarette smoke wasn't a requirement for people thinking things were funny. A couple of hours guzzling beer made the difference.

Wallace continued with a couple more jokes about marriage and two about humorous road signs he'd seen.

Most of his jokes were funny, but that's not what surprised me the most. He'd been on stage for fifteen minutes and transitioned from one joke to the next. Not once had he lost his place. He didn't drift into the past, and he seemed to have a grasp on reality. This was not the Wallace I'd become accustomed to observing. Instead of listening to his joke about a drunken hippo, my mind wandered back to what Theo had said about Wallace's lapses in reality coming at times that were convenient. Was it all an act?

I returned to reality when I heard him say, "Let me leave you with two bits of advice. First, when everything seems to be coming your way, you're in the wrong lane. And folks, a day without a smile is a day wasted. Thank you."

Sincere laughter and applause followed as Wallace bowed twice before reaching down and lifting the container holding his son. He kissed the box and walked back to the table.

It could have been the poor lighting, but I thought I saw a tear roll down his cheek. Was Wallace a killer, a man grappling with reality, or a grieving father?

Or, all three?

Chapter Thirty-Three

It was after midnight before the party at Cal's broke up. The comics were on a high after their performances. While Sal kept referring to the large venues where they had entertained on *numerous occasions*, the three seemed exhilarated by the reception they'd received at lowly Cal's.

Janice had drifted away after Wallace finished his set.

Several customers stopped by the table to congratulate the entertainers, which, boosted by several beers, gave them, as Sal had interpreted their comments to mean, "A night to remember."

The main thing I remembered as I fell out of bed the next morning was how late I'd stayed at the bar. I also remembered that, in a moment of weakness, I'd agreed to meet Charles for breakfast. Fortunately, showing a glimmer of wisdom, I'd suggested we meet at 9:00, an hour or so later than we usually frequented the Dog.

My friend was already in the booth when I arrived. He made a weak effort to goad me into feeling guilty about being late, which, of course, I wasn't.

Amber was quick with coffee, quick to let me know she

knew where we'd spent last night. She asked if I had as much fun as Charles. I told her I didn't know since I didn't know how much fun Charles had. She told me comedy wasn't my forte. I told her I was serious. She said, "Whatever," before leaving to wait on another table.

Charles took a sip, rubbed his temples, and said, "Thomas Jefferson said, 'Beer, if drunk in moderation, softens the temper, cheers the spirit, and promotes health.' If last night's an indication, somewhere along the line, moderation must have been thrown out the window. I'm irritated, nowhere near cheered, and feel like I've been run over by a bull elephant."

He looked like it as well. He had on the Emerson College T-shirt he'd worn at Cal's, and his hair looked like it'd spent time in a food blender.

"What's wrong? Didn't you have a good time?"

He continued to rub his temples. "The guys were funnier than I thought they'd be. The wannabes weren't bad. I thought Franny was as good as Sal. But … oh, never mind."

"Charles?"

He lifted his mug then set it back down. "When the funny men were on stage, I kept thinking of Heather and how much she lived for standing behind that microphone, strumming and singing. I kept thinking about how much I liked … no, how much I loved her, how much I prayed that she could've had the life she wanted." He hesitated and looked toward the door. "Kept thinking about how I failed her, how I couldn't give her the one thing she wanted with all her heart and soul." He looked at me with his bloodshot eyes. "Now, she's gone."

I was at a loss for words when Charles looked at the door a second time and smiled.

I turned to see Cal in the entry.

Charles waved him over.

I thought Charles looked bad, although he actually

looked like a GQ model compared to Cal. I must've missed the memo about wearing the same clothes from yesterday. Cal's rhinestone-covered coat appeared to have been run over by the same bull elephant that had stomped on Charles. His shirt was so wrinkled it made a mummy's face look Botoxed.

Cal put his arm around Amber's waist and whispered something to her before making his way to the table.

"What're you doing up this early?" I asked.

Cal removed his Stetson, put it on the seat beside him, and to no avail, ran his hand through his unruly hair. "Can't be up unless you've been down," he said, sounding like a line from a country song.

Charles asked, "You haven't been to bed?"

"Does it show?"

Instead of screaming yes, I said, "How come?"

"Was 2:00 when I ran out the last bunch of drunks. I had to do a heap of cyphering to try to get my cash drawer to balance."

Charles said, "Did it?"

"Nope."

Charles was on the hunt. "Off by how much?"

"Two big ones."

"Two hundred dollars," Charles said.

"That's what I said?"

Charles nodded, although it wasn't what Cal had said. "What happened to it?"

"If I knew that, I wouldn't be here looking like cow crap. I ain't got a clue."

I said, "Think it was stolen?"

"Did you miss *ain't got a clue*?"

I was tempted to smile, but Cal was serious.

Charles said, "What are you going to do?"

Amber set a mug of coffee in front of Cal.

"Thank ya darlin'," Cal said, as only he can without sounding sexist.

He took a sip then said, "Nothing I can do. No use crying over spilt C notes. Hell, it was a great night. Ain't ever seen that many customers on a Sunday, and I hate to admit, the Legends weren't half bad."

It was interesting how money disappeared whenever the Legends were around. "Are you going to have them back next Sunday?"

Cal chuckled. "Before he left, Sal inched up to me, said that he'd have to confab with his business manager. If a mutually prosperous arrangement could be lassoed, the Legends could break free for another gig. To this old cowpoke's ears, that meant I'd be hard pressed to stop them from doing their thing. They've got a business manager like I've got a mansion in Beverly Hills."

I said, "The tips were enough to keep them coming back?"

"Not bad, but I'll tell you one thing, they didn't come close to covering the tab for the Legends. The buds at Budweiser live for groups like the beer-guzzling Legends. My horse would've choked on the roll of cash Wallace pulled out of his pocket to pay for their night of partying."

That got Charles's attention, although not for the reason that struck me. He said, "You have a horse?"

Cal shook his head. "Charles, you read all those books, so I thought you'd grasp symbolism if I laid some on you. I ain't got a camel, a chimpanzee, or a horse. Wallace had a roll of cash."

Charles said, "Thought the funny guys were broke. Where'd he get a wad of cash?"

"Do I look like a money tracing, FBI bean counter?"

"A forensic accountant," Charles corrected.

Cal smiled. "See, you do get something out of those books. I don't have an idea the size of an atom where he got it. It was cash. That green stuff spends pretty good in Cal's."

Charles would be, in Cal vernacular, a great bronc rider. Once he grabs on, there's no letting go. "He didn't say—"

"Charles," Cal interrupted, "I don't know."

Charles paused and let Cal's definitive statement soak in before trying another approach. "What else did he say?"

"Charles, I ain't Leonard Bernstein, that Watergate reporter. I ain't got a recorder or one of those photogenic memories."

"Carl Bernstein," Charles corrected, referring to one of the reporters who uncovered the Watergate scandal, further proof that he'd read most of his books.

"Whoever. The point is, Wallace didn't share where the money came from. He was too curious to give me the history of his paper money."

"Curious about what?" I asked.

"Remember when Janice came over?"

I reminded him that I was the one who invited her to the table.

"After she left, Wallace asked me who she was. I figured, since everyone kept calling her Janice, that wasn't what he was searching for. I told him about her and her hubby and that she'd come in the bar a few times. I'm practicing being as nosy as you, Charles, so I asked him why he wanted to know."

Charles smiled and said, "You're a wise man, Cal. What'd he say?"

"Wallace said she looked familiar. I told him he could've seen her in the bar. He said that wasn't it. He thought he remembered seeing her somewhere in town."

Charles said, "He didn't say where?"

"Charles, my memory bank's overdrawn. He didn't say where. I didn't ask. That's that."

My memory bank wasn't in as poor a shape as Cal's. Something began to click. Wallace had told me that he'd seen the body of someone, presumably Michael Hardin, near the beach. Janice was irate with Michael because of a bet he claimed she didn't place, and she owed him money. According to both Cal and Amber, Janice has a quick temper. It didn't take an Olympic-length leap to think that Wallace, during a period where he and reality had split ways, could have seen Janice near Michael's body.

Chapter Thirty-Four

Charles said he needed to go back to his apartment to clean. He once told me that he cleans every eight months, whether it needs it or not. I took it as another sign of depression. Cal said he had to get home, needed to "sleep a spell" before opening the bar.

I wished him well and realized that I didn't have to be anywhere, or do anything, but wasn't ready to go home. It turned out to be a gorgeous day. The rain that disrupted Cal's open-mic comedy night had moved out to sea. It was in the mid-seventies with a few puffy, white clouds filtering the sun. A walk to the end of the Folly Pier would meet my need to avoid going home. On the way to the end of the pier, I stopped twice to take in the view of the beach and the Atlantic, to savor the moment and how fortunate I was to live where thousands of people save money all year to vacation.

I reached the end of the structure and saw a familiar face seated on one of the wooden benches, looking out at the waves. I almost didn't recognize Marvin Peters, a.k.a.

Pete Marvin, since he wasn't in stage garb. He looked like thousands of other locals and vacationers in his tan shorts, a short-sleeve Reebok T-shirt, and tennis shoes.

He stared at me, did a double take before smiling recognition.

"Great show," I said as I leaned against the railing near his bench.

His smile widened. "You think so?"

I crossed my fingers. "Sure. Thought all of you were great."

"I appreciate that, but my timing was off. You'd be surprised how rusty I get after a layoff. Suppose it's like a pro athlete after off-season."

This could be a chance to get a non-PR version of what they've been doing.

"You've been off a while?"

"Wallace and Sal would kill me if they heard me say this." He looked around like they might be hiding behind the steps to the second level of the pier. "Hell, I don't care. Until that first night in Cal's, we hadn't had a gig in five months." He chuckled. "I'd say we're down to our last penny, but that'd make us sound rich."

"I'm surprised. You're so good, I would have figured you'd be booked all the time."

A little sucking up couldn't hurt, and it may keep him talking.

"I appreciate the smoke you're puffing up my butt. Stand-up comedy is a young person's game. Sure, there are a few old farts still making it. For most of us, big shows, big crowds, big paychecks are in the rearview mirror."

"Sorry."

"Don't get me wrong, entertaining is what keeps us going, and, umm, if you tell Cal I said this, I'll hunt you down and feed you to the sharks out there." He hesitated and pointed out to sea. "We'd play his bar without as much as tips, if he'd let us." He looked down and back at the ocean. "Sal and I would. Don't know about Wallace, poor guy." He looked down again.

"Why poor guy?"

His brow wrinkled. "We've been together a long time. When Sal first thought his brother was having Alzheimer's problems, he talked us into coming with him. He's a good guy, wanted to do what he could to help his brother. Hell, it's not like we had anything else to do, so we said why not. Wallace, sometimes, has trouble with what's real. He came, but he didn't like us butting in Theo's world, and hates us bumming off him. When we discovered that Theo's mind was okay, his problem was his hearing, Wallace flipped. He said we needed to move on and make some money."

Now that Pete had opened the door, I figured that I'd better slip through before it slams shut.

"Curious. I was thinking about Wallace's confusing things. Did he say anything about seeing the dead body on the beach?"

"I've been hanging with Wallace for years. A long time ago, he had trouble with prescription drugs. He had a bad leg break from a car wreck, got hooked on pain pills. He worked his way out of it. God knows, it wasn't easy. I don't know if it had anything to do with that or not, but his memory started slipping. He slips back in time, now more than ever."

I wondered if he'd forgotten my question about Wallace seeing a body. I didn't want to stop him from sharing. Charles would kick me out of the nosy club, but I was determined to wait.

"What do you mean?"

"Don't get me wrong, Wallace is a good friend; he'd do anything for the rest of us. Some days, I'm not certain that he knows what decade he's in. Other times, he's as lucid as an astronaut." He smiled. "About now, I reckon that you're wondering where I'm going with this story, if I'm going to get to your question about the dead guy."

I returned his smile. "It crossed my mind."

"I'm saying this because Wallace told me about the body. He could've been remembering something from thirty years ago as easily as what had happened the day he said it."

"What'd he say?"

"Said he was walking on the beach. Instead of walking near the water, he decided to move closer to the dune's fences that are up by the line of whatever those tall things are."

"Sea oats," I said.

"If you say so. Anyway, he was up there, saw a clump of dead guy, that's how he said it, clump. Said he was sure the guy was dead because of how his head was twisted."

"He say anything else?"

"He mumbled something about a person nearby."

"Did he say anything else about the person?"

"Don't recall."

Wallace had to be talking about Michael Hardin, not something he dredged from ancient history.

"Pete, I found the body. Wallace's description was spot on. Did he say anything that led you to believe that what he was talking about took place in the past, not the day before he told you?"

"No."

This is where it was going to get tricky. I knew what his answer was going to be.

"You know that Wallace had told a couple of people that he killed the man."

Pete looked out to sea and gave a tentative nod.

"Could he have?"

I was prepared for an outburst and a robust denial.

Pete continued to look out to sea. "It's possible."

That stopped me. I waited for him to continue, but he didn't.

I tiptoed on. "Why?"

"Remember what I said about us being broke?"

I nodded.

He turned back to me. "Did you notice our new stage outfits?"

"Yes."

"Theo's been paying for everything since we got here. He's been super generous. Wallace bought the outfits. Don't know where he got the money. He also bought our drinks after the show."

"You think he killed the bookie to rob him?"

"Wallace would never have hurt the guy, never would hurt anybody, unless the man put up a fight. Even then, he only would've tried to stop him. Wallace is a good man, a good friend."

"Did Wallace say anything about what he found? Tell me again what he said about a person being nearby."

"Just what I told you. A woman was nearby."

"You didn't say it was a woman."

He shrugged. "That's what he said."

That reminded me how Cal said that Wallace had asked him about Janice when he met her at open-mic night.

"Did Wallace say anything about a woman named Janice? She was at our table at Cal's."

"I remember someone introducing a gal. I don't remember her name. Wallace didn't mention anyone by name after that. He was excited that so many people enjoyed the show. Why do you ask?"

"Just curious. Wallace asked Cal about her, and I thought she might've been mentioned."

Pete smiled. "In his younger days, Wallace prided himself on being able to woo the young ladies from the audience into, umm, more intimate venues. He forgets that he's not the stud he used to be. It doesn't surprise me that he was asking about a chick. He must've forgotten by the time we got back to Theo's."

"Would you be willing to tell the police what you told me about Wallace and the body?"

He shook his head. "The police have already talked to Wallace. He told us he confessed to killing the man. I suppose they checked it out and didn't believe him since he's still on the free side of prison bars."

I don't know what Wallace had told Pete about his confession, but I knew he told the police that he killed the bookie with a candlestick in the library. Pete's version made more sense. I wasn't in a position to push him.

"Remember anything else he said?"

"Chris, I wasn't avoiding your question about talking to the police. Okay, I guess I was. You must understand, Wallace gets confused. When he was telling me about the body, he could have been talking about something from his memory that he thought he saw forty years ago. I don't want to get my friend in trouble over something that may not have happened in this century. Something that may not have ever happened. Memory is a strange thing, often wrong. You understand, don't you?"

"Sure," I lied.

Pete stood, straightened his shorts, and leaned on the railing and looked toward the Tides. "Enough about poor Wallace, how long have you been here?"

I gave him an abbreviated history of discovering Folly, retiring here, owning a gallery.

He listened without interrupting, something I wasn't accustomed to.

"Theo tells me you're some sort of detective that helps the police catch bad guys. That's got to be fascinating."

I told him that I had been lucky a couple of times, although I wasn't anything more than a retired bureaucrat living his last years on Folly Beach.

"Theo said you saved his life."

I told him that Theo was the hero and how he'd given me information that helped catch the killer.

Pete said Theo didn't take any of the credit. That's why he admired him so much.

I agreed with Pete then asked him, one more time, if he would be willing to go to the police. One more time, he said no.

I didn't tell him that I would.

Chapter Thirty-Five

Barb told me that if I picked up a pizza at Woody's she'd provide drinks so we could enjoy supper from her fourth-floor balcony overlooking the Atlantic and the Folly Beach Fishing Pier. She didn't have to say it twice. I arrived sharing a smile, a kiss, and a large pizza.

The weather was perfect, as was the company. Over the first slice of the Woody specialty pizza, I shared my strange conversation with Pete. Barb asked if I believed what he said Wallace had told him.

"Good question. You know about most of my conversations with Wallace. If you'd asked me after the first couple of times I talked with him, I'd say he was so far outside the realm of reality, that I wouldn't believe anything he said."

Barb poured a second glass of wine and said, "You've changed your mind?"

"Theo said he thought Wallace might be faking some of his problems; said he seems to use confusion when it's convenient. At open-mic night Wallace gave a flawless performance. He didn't miss a punchline, he remembered all the jokes. He was in total control."

Barb took a sip and said, "Mel Tillis."

She'd been around my friends too long.

"Mel Tillis what?"

She smiled. "And you claim to be a country music fan."

"I am, so?"

"Mel Tillis was a chronic stutterer—"

"Except when he was singing," I interrupted.

"His speech disfluency disappeared when he performed."

"You think that's what happened when Wallace was behind the microphone?"

"Possibly."

"I would agree except, the first time I saw the Legends perform, Wallace was all over the map. Coherent one moment, out of it the next."

"Let's say Theo is right. Wallace uses his problem when it's in his best interest. The first time he performed was close to the time he claimed to have seen a body. Maybe he wanted to confuse everyone about his mental state. That would support his absurd statement to the police that the bookie was killed with, what did you say?"

"A candlestick in the library."

"Yes."

I shook my head. "It's all confusing."

"Perhaps Wallace wants it to be."

"Why did he say anything in the first place? Granted, his behavior was anything but normal when I pulled him out of the street, but why bring up a body?"

"You said before that he could've feared that someone saw him near the body. He wanted to give himself a reasonable explanation for seeing it while not being the killer."

"Yes."

"Makes sense."

She plopped a second slice of pizza on my plate, added another one to hers, and I said, "But why did he tell me that he saw a body, tell Pete that he saw a body, and told Theo he killed the person, then told the police the fantasy about a candlestick?"

"Chris, I'm a bookstore owner and former lawyer for the wealthy. I'm not a psychiatrist. It sounds like you'd need one to understand Wallace."

"No argument there. Let me add something else. Both Amber at the Dog and Cal told me one of their customers, Janice Raque, was angry at the bookie for not placing a bet she thought he should have. She owed him several thousand dollars. The bet would've paid him off with money to spare. They also told me Janice has a temper and blew up at a waitress in the Dog and at her husband in Cal's."

"Another suspect."

"Yes, and it gets stranger. At open-mic night, I saw Janice at a table by herself and invited her to join the group. Wallace asked about her after she left, and Pete told me that, when Wallace was talking to him about finding the body, he said that there was a woman nearby."

"You think it was Janice?"

I shrugged.

"That supposition wouldn't get you far in court." She held her hand up, palm facing me. "Don't say it, I know we're not in court. That is an interesting coincidence."

"I asked Pete if he would tell the police what he shared about Wallace."

"He said no."

"Correct."

"Why would he? Why would he want to get his friend in trouble? Wallace didn't tell him that he killed the bookie. Wallace had already been interviewed by the police. What could he have said to them?"

"The police think that Wallace is a kook, but they don't know about the money."

"What money?"

I told her about what Pete had said about Wallace paying for the stage outfits and the bar tab.

"Didn't Theo tell you that someone stole a statue and money from his house? It was probably one of his house-guests, right?"

"Yes."

"Wouldn't that explain where Wallace got money?"

"Yes, but what if the murder and the theft from the house were unrelated?"

"Wallace could've stolen the stuff from Theo's, and Janice killed the bookie."

I nodded.

Barb smiled. "Wallace could've seen Janice near the body and still be right about seeing the bookie without being the killer."

"Even if Pete didn't want to share what he told me with the police, I need to tell them, at least tell Cindy. She can share it with the Sheriff's Office."

"I agree," Barb said, "If you allow me to slip on my old attorney hat for a minute, I don't see a shred of admissible evidence in what you've said."

"I didn't think there was. It might give them a kickstart to the investigation that doesn't appear to be going anywhere."

She waved her hand toward the ocean. "Is this a fantastic evening, or what?"

It was Barb's way of saying that our depressing conversation about murder was over.

I told her that it was fantastic.

And so was the rest of the evening.

Chapter Thirty-Six

The next morning, I thought about walking to Bert's for coffee, thought about driving to the Dog for breakfast, and thought about what Barb had said about looking at the theft at Theo's and the murder of Michael Hardin being unrelated.

After more thought than I could handle, I fixed coffee at home, ate stale coffee cake for breakfast, and spent the rest of the time trying to figure out what I knew and didn't know about the offenses. The obvious thing I didn't know was who committed them, and that was only the beginning of the list. What was Wallace's true state of mind? Could Janice or Neil have killed Michael? And could Ray's tumble down the stairs have been something other than an accident? What I did know was that, regardless if he wanted me to or not, I had to tell Cindy about what Pete shared. The sooner the better.

She answered with, "What now?"

"I learned something yesterday from one of Theo's houseguests I think you need to know."

"Where are you?"

"Home."

"I'll be there in five minutes."

She was gone. No insults, no interrogation, no smart-aleck remark. What had happened to the Cindy LaMond I'd come to love?

She pulled her pickup truck in the drive, and I met her on the front porch. She walked past me into the living room and said, "Coffee?"

I led her into the kitchen and poured her some in my cleanest dirty mug.

She took a sip then plopped down on a kitchen chair.

"You okay?" I asked.

She held up the cup of coffee. "Working on it."

It didn't appear that she was succeeding. "What's wrong?"

"Tired."

It was more than that, so I played Charles. "Why?"

She looked at me, took another sip, and sighed. "I didn't get home last night, correction, this morning until two something. College students, a busload of them, were on the beach, acting like infants playing in a sandbox. Their Pablum had a high alcoholic content. They were raising such a ruckus that it woke up two families from Tennessee renting a beach house.

"Three of my guys and I had to pretend that we were adults and put a stop to the horsing around. We didn't haul any of the students away, although it took longer than it should have to round them up and herd them on their bus. The driver was sober, so he could get them off the island and out of our hair." She took another sip and shrugged.

It didn't sound like something that would put her in a foul mood. "And?"

"Larry decided that three this morning was the perfect time to express extreme displeasure about me being out. He was pissed, pissed on hormones. He dredged up every time in the last year he thought I should've been home rather than serving and protecting the citizens of this fine island. I wasn't in the best mood and blew a gasket. No blows were thrown but every profanity known in the Western World bounced off the walls."

Cindy and Larry were two of my favorite people and I hated to hear about their early morning fight. They were stubborn, opinionated, and madly in love with each other.

"What happened?"

"Not much. Neither of us wanted to act like things were normal, so neither of us slept in the bed. Larry spread out on the couch; I slept in the truck." She stopped and stared at me. "If I hear that you tell anybody about this, you'll be sleeping in a coffin."

"It doesn't leave this room."

"So, what in the hell did you drag me over here for?"

Instead of answering, I gave it one last try. "Are you going to be okay?"

"Of course, we are, I hope. I'm heading to the hardware store as soon as I leave here to give the little squirt a big hug, tell him I'll try to get home earlier, and see what happens. If that doesn't work, I'm moving in with you. Did you forget why you wanted to talk to me?"

I squeezed her shoulder.

Again, she asked why she was here.

I told her everything that Wallace had said to Pete about seeing a body and a woman. I also told her how Wallace reacted to Janice at the open-mic night, plus what Pete said about Wallace paying for drinks and their new stage clothes.

She asked if Pete thought Wallace had been making sense or was in one of his back-to-the-past moods.

I said I thought he was making sense.

She asked if he mentioned a candlestick beating in the library.

I shook my head.

"Why was Pete telling you?"

"He's worried about Wallace. I wouldn't be surprised if

he isn't afraid that Wallace might break and kill someone else."

"The best I can do is talk to Wallace again. I didn't know about him paying for drinks and their costumes, so that's a reason to reintroduce myself. Thanks for letting me know."

I wished her luck.

"I'll need it. Also, thanks for letting me dump on you about Larry. We'll be fine."

CINDY LEFT, and I had second thoughts about what I'd shared. Regardless, the police now know as much as I do. With luck and their resources, they should be able to get to the bottom of it. If Wallace hadn't killed Michael Hardin, there was still a good chance he'd stolen Theo's money and figurine.

As the old saying goes, *Man cannot live on stale coffee cake alone.* Okay, I made that up. Anyway, I was still hungry and decided to walk to Snapper Jack's for lunch. The colorful, multi-level restaurant faced the island's only traffic light and was popular with residents and vacationers. The eatery was crowded for early in the week.

Instead of taking up a table, I sat at the bar and faced a bank of flat-screen televisions and a college-aged bartender wearing a black Snapper Jack's T-shirt. She asked what I needed. I said a glass of wine and a menu. She smiled and said she thought she could handle it.

I was staring at one of ESPN's 300 channels on the set in front of me when I was startled by a tap on the shoulder. I turned to see Neil Wilson smiling at me.

"Is this seat taken?" he asked as he pointed to the empty chair beside me.

I told him, "No."

He sat, looked at the television, and said, "You a sports fan?"

"Not particularly. I was daydreaming more than watching."

The bartender set my wine and a menu in front of me.

I asked Neil if I could buy him a drink.

He said yes before I got the question out and told the bartender he wanted Corona.

"How's your job search?"

"Remember the other day when I told you the cops came to my job and questioned me about that dead guy?"

"Yes."

"Know what my boss did yesterday?"

I said I didn't.

"Fired me."

The bartender slipped a Corona in front of Neil.

"Why?"

"Get this, he said it was bad for the image of his company to have cops interrogating his security guard about a murder. Can you believe that? It's a damned plastic fabrication plant. They make toys, for God's sake. You would've thought they built freakin' computer chips for the Pentagon."

I didn't tell him, but agreed that it seemed drastic.

"That's too bad."

"Yeah, and he threw up an old arrest from years ago that found its way on my background search when I was hired. He told me when he hired me that since the arrest was more than ten years old, he was willing to take a chance on me. The chance lasted until I was doing my civic duty and answering the cop's questions." He took a long draw on his beer and repeated, "Can you believe that?"

I didn't know what to believe, but wondered if there was something about the firing that he hadn't told me. He was here and seemed open to talking, so this would be a good chance to see what he would say about his relationship with Michael Hardin.

"Want some lunch?" I slid a menu in front of him.

"You buying?"

"Yes."

He waved for the bartender. He ordered fish tacos. I went with a chicken finger basket, and he added another Corona.

"I know the police learned you were working when Michael Hardin was killed. You'd bet with him, so I wondered if you could think of anyone who would've wanted him dead." I didn't mention there was a big hole in his alibi and that I was aware that he owed the bookie a significant amount of money.

"He was a nice guy. I can't imagine anyone would kill him."

Other than to wiggle out of paying off a huge debt, I thought. I also wondered how Wallace, who had been on the island for a few short days, could've known the bookie.

"I'd seen Michael around town a few times, but never talked to him. Did he take bets from anyone?"

Neil smiled for the first time. "Bookmaking is illegal, you know. Over the years, I've known a few bookies. You could say gambling is one of my hobbies." He pointed to one of the TVs playing highlights from last night's NBA games. "Won some, lost some. Most bookies are careful about who they deal with. Not just anybody could go to them. Most new clients are referrals from someone the bookie trusts. Understandable, don't you think?"

I agreed.

"Not Neil. What got him so much business was that he'd take bets from anyone. Well, not anyone. If he thought someone was an undercover cop, he'd act like he didn't know what the person was talking about."

No one would confuse seventy-five-year-old Wallace Bentley for an undercover cop.

Our food arrived, and Neil inhaled a large chunk of fish taco.

"Let me ask you something else," I said.

His mouth was full. He mumbled, "You're playing cop, trying to catch the person who killed Michael."

I didn't deny it. "I'm curious. Someone I know may've had something to do with the death. I was wondering if anyone else had information that would help the police."

"What's the question?"

"Did Michael carry a lot of money?"

"One reason Michael was so popular was that he paid winnings right away. Some guys make you wait a day before shelling out. Most betters I know need the money, need it now."

"So, he would've carried a substantial amount of cash?"

"Depends on what events were being bet on that day but, yes, I wouldn't be surprised if he'd be pocketing hundreds, even thousands some days."

Yet no money was on him when I found his body.

Time for a little white lie. "I hear he would carry some customers."

Neil swallowed another bite and smiled. "Yeah, he trusted a few of us. I owed him a little. He wasn't pressuring me to pay, knew I was good for it."

Other than asking if he killed Michael Hardin, I didn't see how I could get more from him.

"He sounds like a nice guy."

"Yes. It's my turn to ask something."

"What?"

"Are you sure you don't know anyone hiring? I was stretched thin before the idiot fired me. I've got one low-paying, part-time gig and no money."

"I don't, Neil. But I'll ask around. You'll be the first if I hear anything."

We finished lunch with minimal conversation. He wanted to talk about the pro basketball games guys on television were jabbering about. I had little, if any, interest and limited my comments to, "Hmm" and "Yeah." Dude would have been proud of my vocabulary.

"Sure you've got this?" Neil asked as he waved at his empty plate.

"Yes."

"Thanks, you're a pal." He headed to the exit.

Yeah, a pal who's trying to pin a murder on you.

Chapter Thirty-Seven

On the walk home, I reviewed my talk with Neil, leaving out anything about pro basketball. I hadn't learned much. He confirmed what I already knew about Michael Hardin. I'd learned that Neil had been fired and was desperate for a job, although the termination occurred after Michael was murdered so that, alone, couldn't have precipitated the killing. To listen to him, you'd think he and Michael were good buddies. Neil liked the bookie, and owing him a little money was no big deal. I figured none of that was true. Had I expected him to admit being so desperate that he'd killed Michael? If Barb was right that the thefts at Theo's were separate from the murder, Neil was my prime suspect.

I started thinking about what I knew about Janice Raque, the other suspect, when the phone rang.

Theo's name was on the screen. "Hi, Theo, what's up?"

"This is Sal, his brother. Is this Chris?"

"Yes," I said. "Is Theo okay?"

"Can you come to his house? Like now."

I heard noises in the background and repeated, "Is he okay?"

"Umm, sort of. Are you coming?"

Sal either didn't want to or was unable to tell me what was going on. "Yes."

I pulled in front of Theo's a couple of minutes later. I was relieved to see there were no ambulances, fire trucks, or police cars surrounding it. On the other hand, Chief LaMond's vehicle was in the drive.

Sal greeted me with, "Thank God, you're here."

I saw Pete on the couch with a drink in his hand and staring out the window at the Folly River. "What's going on?"

He pointed at the steps to the second floor. He didn't say anything, so I hoped he meant that I should go upstairs. A wide, center hall divided the second-floor rooms. This was the first time I'd been upstairs, and it was apparent that it had been decorated by the same professional who did the first floor. The wall covering had a muted floral pattern that was complimented by a patterned fabric on the two upholstered chairs on one side of the hall. Three original oils depicting serene Lowcountry scenes were on the opposite wall. They were the only serene things I found. One of the chairs was occupied by Theo, the other held Cindy LaMond.

I faced the chief, who was tapping her foot on the floor. She looked up and shrugged. Theo was twisting the sleeve of his T-shirt like he was wringing water out of it.

Cindy said, "What're you doing here?"

"Sal called and asked me to come."

She exhaled. "Okay, stay out of the way."

"Out of the way of what?"

Cindy pointed to a closed bedroom door, in a low voice said, "We have a bit of a problem."

Theo let go of his sleeve and said, "Thanks for coming.

Sal said you were the one friend he knew I had. He thought I needed someone with me. Sorry for the inconvenience."

I nodded at Theo then turned to Cindy. "Problem?"

She stared at the closed door. "I stopped by to ask Wallace some questions." She hesitated and patted Theo on the knee. "He told me that Wallace, Sal, and Pete were in the kitchen and asked me to follow him. We got to the kitchen, where things went sideways."

Theo made an audible groan and put his head down between his hands.

"What happened?"

"The funny guys were standing around the island drinking beer. Sal saw me with Theo, smiled and said, 'Umm, correct me if I get it wrong, Theo. 'Three seniors were out for a stroll. One of them said, 'It's windy.' Another one said, 'No way. It's Thursday.' The last one says, 'Me too. Let's have a beer.' I thought I was there to ask Wallace questions, not to be the audience at a comedy show. Sal slapped his knee, and Pete laughed at the joke. Wallace shot out of the room like a chicken with its tail feathers on fire."

Theo groaned again.

"Then?" I said.

"Wallace took off up the steps, went in his room, and slammed the door. Theo and I followed and asked him to come out. I told him I had a couple of routine questions. I emphasized routine. As you can see, he hasn't taken kindly to my request."

I turned toward Theo. "Does he have any weapons?"

"Been down that road," Cindy responded before Theo could. "He doesn't, well, not that Theo knows about. Sal followed us up and said that Wallace could stab us with his rapier wit. I didn't need more jokes and sent him downstairs."

"How long's he been holed up in there?"

Cindy looked at the door. "Half hour, tops."

I said, "Plan?"

"I don't want to go all SWAT on him. The door's got one of those little holes in the knob. I could get in with this." She held up a three-inch-long, thin wire that unlocks many interior residential doors. "Wouldn't have to kick it in. I called Officer Spencer and asked him to come in silently to join us. He should be here any minute. Before you came up, I told Wallace that I'd give him a few minutes to think. I'd be waiting out here."

"What'd he say?"

"Something about hell freezing over." She glared at the door. "I'm not waiting that long."

I said, "Think he's a danger to himself?"

"We can hear movement in the room and he mumbles something every once in a while, so he's going strong."

I heard the front door open and Sal talking to someone. Seconds later, I heard the heavy footsteps of Allen Spencer as he bounded up the stairs. He looked around, and Cindy gave him a thirty-second recap of the situation. I had always been impressed how calm Cindy became when faced with tricky situations. This would qualify.

Cindy leaned close to Theo and said, "Theo, this is your house. Do I have permission to search Wallace's bedroom once we finagle him out?"

"Oh," Theo said, like he'd returned from being zoned out. "Umm, sure, whatever you need, Chief."

Cindy stood and moved to the side of Wallace's door. "Wallace, this is Chief LaMond. I've got a couple of easy questions I'd like to ask you. How about you open the door and come on out? I'll ask my questions and be on my way."

The only sounds I heard were Sal and Pete talking downstairs.

Cindy tapped on the door. "Wallace, tell you what. Theo will go downstairs and get you something to drink while I'll come in and ask my questions. How's that sound?" She pointed at the stairs and Theo headed down.

Cindy closed her eyes and shook her head.

Allen moved to the other side of the door and rested his hand on his handgun.

Cindy started to insert the wire in the door knob, when the door swung open. Cindy jumped, and Allen started to pull his gun when Wallace stuck his head out the door. "Here for my next show?"

"Wallace," she said, "how about you and I move over to those chairs so I can get my questions out of the way?"

He was dressed in black. For the first time, I noticed that he was the same height as Cindy, although she outweighed him by thirty pounds. She appeared comfortable with that advantage in case he didn't cooperate.

Wallace smiled, said, "Why not?" then sat in one of the chairs.

"Officer Spencer," Cindy said as she took the other seat, "why don't you look around Wallace's bedroom while he and I talk?"

Wallace jumped up and pointed to his room. "You can't do that. You need a search warrant."

Cindy held her hand in front of him. "That's okay, Wallace. It's Theo's house. He said we could look. Have a seat, and let me ask you something."

Officer Spencer went in the room, Wallace returned to his seat, and I moved to the corner of the hall.

Cindy smiled and leaned toward Wallace. "I was wondering why you ran when you saw me stopping by to visit my friend Theo."

She said it like two friends having a conversation rather than an interrogation.

"I've been a little jittery. I've also had a couple of bad experiences with police over the years."

Cindy nodded and smiled. "That explains it. You don't have to be afraid of me." Her smile widened. "Someone said you'd been generous, bought your friends their new stage clothes. I must say, from what I've heard from people who were at your performance at Cal's, you all looked professional."

Wallace smiled. "Thank you."

Cindy chuckled. "I even heard you bought the drinks that night. That was nice of you."

Wallace leaned back in the chair, his shoulders relaxed, and he nodded.

Cindy leaned closer to him. "Somebody told me that it'd been some time since you'd received a lot of the money that you'd been owed by promoters or royalty checks. That's irritating, isn't it?"

He tilted his head and eyes narrowed. "Sure is."

"So, I was wondering about something. You can help me figure it out. Where'd you get the money for the clothes and drinks?"

It wasn't the best timing, but Theo returned and handed Wallace a canned Coke.

Wallace took a sip without taking his eyes off the chief.

"Chief LaMond, why am I getting the idea you didn't show up to visit your good friend Theo? Are you accusing me of something?"

"No, I'm trying—"

Wallace interrupted. "I already confessed that I killed that guy on the beach. You'd looked at me like I was an organ grinder's monkey. You didn't bother to arrest me." He leaned down, slammed the Coke can on the floor, and stood.

Cindy put out her hand. "Calm down, Wallace. I'd rather clear up these questions here. If you'd rather, we could go over to City Hall."

He looked toward the stairs and returned to the chair. His fists were clenched. If Cindy wasn't larger, I was afraid he was going to pounce on her.

"The money," he said and repeated, "the money. Oh, yeah, I got a cash advance when I used Theo's credit card at the grocery." He turned to Theo. "Sorry, I should've told you."

Officer Spencer cleared his throat. He was standing in the doorway to Wallace's room and holding an orange and red credit card. "Chief, could I borrow you a moment?"

She looked at her officer then said to Wallace, "Give me a minute. Chris, why don't you talk with Wallace until I get back?"

I translated is as, "Don't let Wallace bolt." I asked if he wanted anything to eat.

He said no and looked toward his room. "Chris, those cops need twice as much sense to be half-wits."

I was glad he hadn't shared that statement, joke, or whatever it was with Cindy, or he may've found himself getting an ant's eye view of the polished wood floor.

Cindy, followed by Allen Spencer, returned to the hall. She sat, scooted closer to Wallace, and waved the MasterCard in front of the comedian. "Wallace, please explain this."

Wallace looked at the card and shook his head. "Never seen it before."

"You sure?"

"That's what I said. Where'd you get it?"

"Officer Spencer found it under your mattress."

"Must've been there forever. Is it Theo's?"

"It appears to belong to Michael S. Hardin. That name familiar?"

Wallace stared at the card, looked at the floor, then back at Cindy. "How could I forget? That's the guy I told you I killed." He closed his eyes and whispered, "I did it, I knew I did." He shook his head. "Where did I get the candlestick?"

"Wallace," I said, "how do you know you killed him?"

"Oh, umm. I was told I did. I think it was in a dream, or one of the guys told me. I remember standing over him. He was dead."

I asked. "What guy told you?"

"Pete," he hesitated, "or could've been Sal." He snapped his fingers. "No, it was Ray."

Cindy held her hand in Wallace's face. "Before you say anything else, I'm going to have Officer Spencer read you your rights."

Allen Spencer Mirandized Wallace.

The comic slumped in the chair and came close to slipping out of it.

Cindy then told Spencer to take Wallace to the jail in Charleston.

Allen asked what he should charge him with, and Cindy said the murder of Michael Hardin. Allen took hold of Wallace's elbow as he escorted him to the steps.

Wallace stopped and turned to Theo. "I never saw that card. Honest to God."

Theo moved to the chair that Wallace had vacated and looked at Cindy. "I think there's something wrong with him —something wrong with his head."

Cindy reached out to touch Theo's leg. "Theo, that's for someone else to determine. My job is to haul the fish in; someone else has to weigh them."

I said, "Did Allen Spencer find anything else that would implicate Wallace?"

"Isn't the dead guys MasterCard enough?"

I shrugged.

"Chris, don't tell me you don't think he did it. He was broke, yet came into money to buy clothes and pay a hefty bar tab. He parked the dead guy's credit card under his bed and, oh, yeah, there's one other little pesky detail, he confessed."

"Cindy, he confessed to killing someone in the library with a candlestick. He seemed surprised when you sprung the credit card on him."

Cindy looked at her hand and at me. "Surprised because we found it, not that he didn't know it was there. Where did he get the money?"

I turned to Theo. "Why don't you tell her about the missing cash?"

Cindy turned to Theo so quickly that she could've sprained her neck. "Missing cash?"

Theo's face turned a dull shade of red. He told her about the missing money and the disappearing and reappearing silver frog.

Cindy started to take notes, but her pen didn't touch the notebook. Instead, she pointed the writing instrument at Theo. "You didn't think the heist was important enough to tell the cops?"

"Chief, I'm sorry. It had to be one of my houseguests, one of my brother's friends. I didn't want any of them to get in trouble."

I also thought it could have been his brother but didn't think it needed to be said.

Cindy mumbled, more to herself than to us, "The clothes and bar tab could have come from that money and not Michael Hardin." She sat straight in the chair and looked at Theo. "Any other crimes you didn't think I needed to know about?"

Theo said, "No, Chief. Again, I'm sorry."

"If you'll excuse me. I've got to get to the jail and try to make some sense out of this mess. Maybe Wallace will confess to killing JFK so we can clear up that conspiracy."

Theo's guests weren't the only comedians in the house.

Cindy left.

Sal and Pete were waiting for Theo and me at the bottom of the stairs. They were talking over top each other. Their basic question was, *What's going on?*

We moved to the great room, where Theo and I tag teamed them with an explanation.

Sal said, "He needs to be in the psych ward instead of jail. He's been losing it, more and more each day."

"Sal," I said, "weren't you suspicious when he bought

you the new clothes? Did he tell you where he got the money?"

"No. I figured—don't know what I figured."

Pete added, "Theo, Wallace told me that you gave him the money. He could've been lying. The bookie probably had a bundle on him and, if Wallace killed him, he would've taken the cash and the credit card. Poor Wallace's been so confused, poor man. What can we do for him?"

Theo said, "He needs a lawyer. I'll call the one I use for estate planning. He'll be able to recommend a good defense attorney."

"He can't afford it," Pete said.

Theo replied, "I'll take care of it."

Pete shook his head. "That isn't fair to you. Won't a good lawyer cost a bundle?"

"Yes," Theo said. "If there's a chance that he's innocent, he'll need all the help he can get."

"What can we do?" Sal asked.

Theo said, "Damned if I know."

I couldn't have said it better.

Chapter Thirty-Eight

"Charles, I've got a story for you," I said on the phone before I pulled out of Theo's drive. "Where are you?"

My friend had trained me well. I knew the sooner I shared what happened with him the better. And, if by some strange circumstance he heard it from someone else, I'd never hear the end of it. He was in front of the Baptist Church and walking on his way to nowhere; said he was tired of being cooped up in his apartment, feeling sorry about his miserable life. That was more information than I wanted and suggested that I meet him in the Folly River Park, across the street from the church, and a couple of blocks from Theo's house.

The park was small, but popular, as it was within easy walking distance of the main business district. It was the home to art shows hosted by the Folly Beach Arts and Crafts Guild in warmer months, and Christmas decorations during the holiday season. Its pavilion was the site of musical performances throughout the year. It occasionally provided a shady spot for Charles and me to hang out.

I parked and saw my friend sitting at one of the picnic tables. He was leaned back on the table and looked like he may have slept under it. His Tilley was tilted sideways on his head, his hair was sneaking out from under the hat, his tennis shoes were untied, and his orange Tennessee Volunteers long-sleeve T-shirt had a rip on the sleeve.

"Been wrestling a bear?" I asked as I sat beside him on the bench.

"Funny," he said without a glimmer of cheer. "What's so important to interrupt my mindless, boring, depressing walk to nowhere?"

My first thought was if I should have waited another day to tell him about my trip to Theo's. I also figured that what I had to share could bring him out of his funk, at least momentarily. I started with the call from Sal and shared the highlights of my visit ending with Wallace being hauled off to jail and the conversation I had with Theo, Sal, and Pete.

Charles was clearly depressed since he didn't interrupt countless times.

I finished, and he said, "Let's walk out to the river."

A narrow walking pier went from the park over some of the marsh and ended a few feet over the Folly River. Charles didn't speak as we made our way to the river end of the pier. We leaned against the railing, watched traffic cross the bridge, and a fishing boat meander under it.

Charles continued to stare at the boat. "What's your take?"

I told him about seeing Neil Wilson and how, until this morning, I was leaning toward him as being the killer. I also shared my gut feeling that Janice could have done it.

"You eliminated them because the card was in Wallace's room?"

"Sure."

"You said Wallace seemed surprised that the credit card was there."

"True."

"And Wallace claims to have killed the bookie with a candlestick?"

"That's what he said."

"That says the boy's off his rocker, not that he's a killer. Let's say he needs to be in a padded cell rather than in a jail cell, then who put the card under the mattress to frame him?"

Charles was becoming more animated the more we talked. Bad topic; good sign. I saw the Charles of earlier days inching his way back.

"Sal, Pete, even Theo."

"Yes," Charles said, and rubbed his three-day old beard. "Don't forget Ray. He could've put it there before he took his tumble."

"Or Ray," I conceded. "If the bookie was killed for money and credit cards, it wouldn't have been Theo. He has all the money he'll ever need."

"That leaves the living houseguests, plus Ray. All had access to the room."

I was almost convinced it was one of the houseguests when I remembered what Neil had said about when he was hired in the job from which he'd been terminated. His boss had hired him, despite him having a record that dated back several years. It was a stretch, but I wondered what his crime had been. Cindy talked to him about the murder and could have run him through her databases. I made the mistake of mentioning this to Charles.

"Call her."

My choices were to get yelled at by Charles if I didn't call, or get yelled at by Cindy if I did. Charles was showing signs of improving, so I chose to incur the wrath of the chief.

Cindy greeted me with, "This better be good."

"Got a question." She could decide if it was good or not. "You said you'd questioned Neil Wilson about where he was when Michael Hardin was killed."

"Yes, and—"

I interrupted, "Did you run a criminal check on him?"

"Do you sit for hours at home in your big, plush easy chair thinking up things to make my life miserable, or do they just come to you?"

I chuckled and said, "Some of us have the gift."

"No."

"No to me having the gift, or no to checking his background?"

She sighed. "You have the gift. No, I didn't check. Dare I ask why?"

I shared what he told me about his recent termination and how he mentioned being arrested several years ago.

Cindy said she'd check when she got to a computer and let me know.

Charles was pestering me about when she would let me know before I had time to return the phone to my pocket. The old Charles was in sight.

We left the park and walked down Center Street toward the ocean. The sidewalks were more crowded than I'd seen since last summer. We stopped in front of Mr. John's Beach Store.

Charles looked at a large, inflated float shaped like a frog that was hanging on a pole at the side of the building and said, "Ray may've killed the bookie and hid the credit card in Wallace's room, but he didn't steal the cash from Theo and take the stupid silver frog."

"He was dead when the frog reappeared."

"Yep," Charles said. "Unless his ghost brought it back, or the frog hopped back, you can mark him off the money and frog heist suspect list. That leaves Sal, Wallace, Pete, and Theo, who would have to be nuttier than Wallace to take his own stuff."

"Other than Wallace's confession that won't hold up, what do we know about the other three comics?"

Before answering, Charles stooped to pet a dog that was

leading its master down the street. "You've been with them more than I have. I know they ain't knee-slappin' funny for being Legends. They probably played their last gig for George Washington and are broker than an amoeba. Speaking of Washington, he said, 'Truth will ultimately prevail where there are pains to bring it to light.'"

Getting to the truth has been a pain, and I was clueless about what to do next. Other than Charles stating the obvious, I didn't know how we, or the police, were closer to knowing what happened. Other than stumbling on the body and seeing Theo hurt from his experiences with his houseguests, I couldn't come up with a good reason to be involved. It would be easy to accept that the police had the killer in jail. It likely was the same person who stole money from Theo. Case closed.

Why did I have the feeling that I knew something or heard something that would lead to a different ending?

I WAS SITTING IN, as Cindy called it, my big, plush easy chair and instead of thinking of things to make her life miserable, thinking about each interaction I'd had with the comics. I thought of several things, but none of them brought me closer to what had been nagging at me. I got a reprieve when the phone rang. Cindy's name was on the screen.

"Good evening, Chief."

"If you say so. It's been such a fun-filled afternoon, I thought I'd fallen asleep and dreamed I was being followed around by a camera filming an episode of *America's Biggest Idiots*."

"What happened?"

"When I was a teeny-tiny sprout in East Tennessee, our next-door neighbor had an old billy goat. Ornery thing, about as smart as a piece of chalk, but not as useful. He'd sit in the corner of the yard and watch cars go by. Half the time, he'd run along the fence, thinking he was a dog chasing the car. Other times, he'd stand in the middle of his pen, think he was a Mexican jumping bean, and jump straight up in the air. Occasionally, he thought he was a gymnast. He'd stick his head on the ground and somehow push off with his back legs and throw his rear end up in the air and balance himself in his front legs and head. Get the picture?"

I said yes, but I wondered why I was hearing about her tiny-sprout days.

"Chris, Wallace Bentley makes that old goat look like Albert Einstein."

I repeated, "What happened?"

"Officer Spencer almost ran into a garbage truck when Wallace stripped naked and mooned an eighty-seven-year-old granny following the cop car in her 1977 Ford Granada. After he got to the interrogation room, he told Detective Callahan, in such a sincere voice, that he could be mistaken for the Pope, yes, he'd killed Michael Hardin, and had killed Adolph Hitler, and while he was at it, admitted killing David Letterman, who, unless you know something I don't know, is still walking among the living."

"Oh."

"You won't find this hard to believe. Instead of sticking him in one of the fine, well-appointed prison cells provided by the County of Charleston, Wallace is over at the hospital, handcuffed to a bed being evaluated by a head doc."

"That's too bad."

"There was a high-powered lawyer at the jail to talk with him but, after a few seconds, she decided that psychiatric care was needed more than legal care. The lawyer said Theo Stoll hired her. That was generous of your friend. So far, it's not going to help Wallace."

"Do you think he was faking?"

"Not after what I saw and heard today."

"Thanks for letting me know."

"Other than playing ringmaster in a three-ring circus, I did one useful thing for you. You're welcome."

"What?"

"Your boy, Neil Wilson, was arrested twelve years ago after he and three of his buddies got hopped up on something and broke into a drug store. It was in a town in Arkansas where everybody knew everybody. The guys got off light. Seems some of their parents were good friends with the pharmacist, and some were friends with the local judge. Neil had a shortage of influential friends and got the short end of the stick and spent two years behind bars."

"Why'd he get the short straw?"

"Seems he was the one who picked the drugstore lock. The other three guys just happened to follow him in. That was their story. They stuck to it, saw the light, and were back roaming the streets three months later."

I heard Larry in the background asking Cindy something. She said, "Yes, dear," and whispered to me, "Gotta go. I'm back in good graces with the shrimp. Need to keep it that way."

She didn't wait for me to say goodbye.

Chapter Thirty-Nine

The simplest explanation for everything was that Wallace met Michael Hardin, learned he was a bookie, and tried to rob him. Michael put up a fight, and Wallace hit him hard enough to kill him, or Wallace intended to kill the bookie and rob him. Often the simplest explanation turns out to not be so simple. If that's what happened, why did Wallace tell me he had seen a body? That admission was the first thing tying him to the crime. Next, why did he go off the deep end with the story that he killed Michael with a candlestick in the library? Two things could have accounted for that. He could've decided once suspicion had been raised about him, to make up the far-fetched story to craft an insanity defense, or he had actually hopped off the sane train.

I didn't have answers for those questions, although I knew that Wallace had come into an unexplained amount of money. It could have come from the bookie, or was the money taken from Theo? If Wallace stole it from Theo, it was possible that he didn't kill the bookie. That led me back to why he had said that he'd seen a body in the first place.

The simplest answer is that he saw the body, but hadn't been the killer.

Then what about Neil Wilson? He owed the bookie and had asked me if I knew of part-time jobs. He was desperate for work, which meant that he didn't have the money to pay the debt. Now I learn that he possessed lock-picking skills, which meant that he could've broken into Theo's house and planted Michael Hardin's credit card in Wallace's room. If he killed Michael and planted the card, how did he know anything about Wallace? Silly question, I realized.

Rumors fly around Folly as fast as a speeding bullet, and it was no secret that Wallace claimed to have seen a body. Neil had been questioned by the police and could've figured they knew about the holes in his alibi, so he had to deflect guilt. What better way than to frame an outsider, someone who would have little community support, someone who was having troubles with reality, someone who had already said he'd seen a body, presumably that of Michael Hardin.

Returning to Barb's thought, there could have been two separate crimes and two criminals. The most likely candidates for stealing Theo's money and taking and returning the frog, would've been one or more of the houseguests.

The most likely person to have killed Michael Hardin would be Sal, Wallace, Pete, or even Ray, who could have killed him and slipped the credit card under Wallace's mattress days before his death. Add Neil Wilson as a long shot and, if I was objective, an even longer shot would be Theo. What about Janice Raque? She thought Michael Hardin cheated her out of enough money to pay off her debts. She has a temper and told more than one person that she resented the bookie. Each of them could be the killer but considering how difficult it would have been for Neil, or Janice, to have put the credit card in Wallace's room, they would be down the list. If I marked Neil and Janice off, and removed Theo, because he didn't need the money and I had known him long enough to trust him, that left Sal, Wallace, Pete, and Ray.

Sal, Wallace, Pete, Ray. I said the names several times and remembered something that was said the first time the comedians had been in Cal's. It didn't strike me as unusual at the time but, the more I think about it, the stranger it seems. Who said it? For the life of me, I couldn't remember. Cal had been there, so maybe he'd remember. A late afternoon walk to Cal's would get me out of the house and, with luck, an answer.

A dozen or so folks were enjoying drinks, conversation, and country classics from the jukebox. The bar's owner was wiping off the counter and singing along with Jimmy Rogers. Cal had his Stetson tilted back and wore a green Polo shirt instead of his rhinestone coat.

He waved me over. "What brings you out so early?"

I told him I had a question about the first time he'd met the comedians.

"It'd better be easy. I'd have to strain my brain to remember what happened this morning."

He looked around then pointed to a vacant table nearest the bar. "Lasso that table and I'll have Joy take care of the customers."

I headed to the table as Cal headed to the storage room to find the server.

A minute later, Cal set his Stetson on the table and said, "Okay, what's on your mind?"

"What do you remember about the first night the group came in and talked to you about appearing here?"

He ran his fingers through his long, gray hair. "They were late. Pissed me off, since I was already tired. You'd said they were coming at 9:00. They didn't strut in until, well, a lot later. Speaking of strutting in, they looked like they were on their way to a Halloween party."

I chuckled, and Cal continued, "What else? Let's see, okay, they told a couple of corny jokes, and one of them, maybe it was Pete, started raising a ruckus about smoking. It's coming back to me now. Pete brought it up, remember, because of the one with the silly ascot. Wallace, the nutty one, started tag teaming me about smoking. Something about being funnier if the customers were puffin' on a cigarette, cigar, pipe, or funny weed. If they weren't staying with Theo, I'd have thrown the whole lot of them out the door. How am I doing?"

"Not bad." It wasn't what I was fishing for. "Do you recall one of them saying something about the death of the bookie?"

Cal rubbed his chin and tapped his fingers on the table. "Can't say that I do. Why?"

"At the time, little was known about Michael Hardin's death. Most folks didn't know who the victim was, fewer knew he was a bookie. One of the comics asked about the death and used the term bookie."

"Yeah, that was the first time I heard who he was. I think you're the one who told me. What's so important about that? Some people must've known."

"Yes, but Theo's houseguests weren't from here. They'd been on the island only a few days. Doesn't it seem unlikely that they would've known who or what Michael was?"

"I thought everyone knew that. Hasn't the nutty one confessed? I hear he was hauled off to jail. He would've been the one who knew the bookie was a bookie and said it that night. Mystery solved."

Cal made sense, but I didn't think it was Wallace. I said, "Could've been."

"There you go, that solves it."

I wasn't convinced. "Remember anything else they said?"

"Sure do. I didn't think they were that funny up there on the stage." He pointed at the microphone. "But when Sal referred to them wanting to perform in here as part of the Comedy Legends World Tour, that was danged hilarious. They should've saved that joke for their performance."

"They were serious."

Cal smiled. "That's what I thought when they said it. That's why I didn't laugh, even though it hurt my innards not to."

"Remember anything else?"

"Afraid not. Do the police think it's someone other than the one who needs to be in the looney bin?"

"They arrested Wallace because they found Michael's credit card in his room. That was the reason more than his confession."

"It seems to my withering brain that you don't buy into that."

"I'm not sure."

"You're playing detective?"

"Trying to wrap my hands around what's going on. Theo is a friend. I'd hate to see him caught up in something that isn't resolved. He's already hired an attorney for Wallace, he's putting up the group in his house, covering their expenses while they're there. It looks like they have no plans to leave."

"Except the nutty one."

"True."

"You'll figure it out."

"I wish I had your confidence."

Cal looked at Joy who appeared to have things under control and turned back to me. "Let me change gears. I learned something yesterday that I think you'd be interested in."

"About the comedians?"

"Nope, about Janice Raque. Remember, you, Chester, and I were confabbing about her? You said folks mentioned her ferocious temper?"

"Yes."

"Rumor is that Horace packed up his belongings and

skipped out on her. Somebody told me that somebody told them that he found a young chickadee over in Mt. Pleasant that he'd rather spend time, dusk 'til dawn time with, than with his beloved spouse. Looks like he decided to extend that time to twenty-four-seven. To this old observer of heartbreaks, I'd say that's why she's been on such a tear. I feel sorry for her. She's not as bad as she's been made out to be."

That could explain her tantrums in the Dog, explain arguing with the bookie.

"That's too bad. What's she going to do?"

"Don't know. She doesn't work so, unless the creep Horace keeps paying on her condo in Mariner's Cay, she'll have to find somewhere else to live. Tell you what, I won't miss her bickering with hubby every time she's here."

Joy came to the table and said she was sorry to interrupt, but she needed Cal at the bar, something about the credit card machine had a mind of its own and wasn't charging enough.

Cal said he couldn't have that.

Janice wasn't high on my list of suspects since she would've been the least likely candidate to have put the credit card in Wallace's room. She had now all but fallen off the list after hearing what Cal had shared about Horace. Where did that leave me?

I listened to Freddy Fender sing "Before the Next Teardrop Falls" then headed home. I had learned a couple of things. My number one question still hadn't been answered.

Chapter Forty

Theo had been in Cal's during the comedians' visit to the bar, when they had asked its owner if they could perform, plus when the conversation turned to the identity of the body found at the beach. A morning walk to his house would give me some much-needed exercise, a chance to breathe the fresh morning air, and with luck, get the answer to the question that had been nagging me for the last twenty-four hours.

It was almost 9:00 in the morning and, according to Theo, the middle of the night for his houseguests, so I was surprised that the Lincoln wasn't in the drive. Theo's Mercedes was there, so I rang the doorbell. It took a long time for anyone to answer, and I was beginning to think that Theo had left with the comedians. I turned to leave when he opened the door.

He rubbed his eyes and was moving slower than his normal slow pace.

"Is this a bad time?" I asked.

"No, come on in. Had a late night. The guys are shook about Wallace."

I followed him to the kitchen and was quick to accept his offer of coffee.

We each got a cup, and he pointed at the table.

I sat, sipped coffee, and said, "Are they gone? Their car wasn't here."

"Sal was up early, early for the guys, and said he was so traumatized by Wallace's situation that he needed to go for a drive. He asked if I wanted to go. I declined. I couldn't see an upside to being stuck in a car with my upset brother."

"Where was he going?"

"I don't know. When I asked him, he said the same thing.

"Did Pete go with him?"

"He's upstairs sawing logs."

"Have you heard anything about Wallace?"

"Sal called the hospital, but they wouldn't tell him anything. They referred him to the Sheriff's Office. He didn't figure he could get anything out of them and decided to wait for the police, or Wallace's attorney to call."

"Think Sal went to the hospital to see Wallace?"

"No, the hospital told him yesterday that no one would be allowed in. It's nice that you stopped by, although something tells me it's not for coffee."

"I have a question. Remember the first night you brought your houseguests to Cal's?"

"When Wallace and Pete tried to snooker Cal into letting people smoke in his bar? The only smoke I saw was coming out of Cal's ears as he lambasted them for trying to change his rules."

I smiled. "That's the night."

"What's the question?"

I asked the same thing I asked Cal and got the same answer. Theo didn't remember who among his group said anything about the bookie. He did remember how shocked Cal had been when I told him the identity of the body, but that was all.

I got a refill on my drink, then said, "You don't sound happy about your guests."

"Chris, I've been hospitable. I've given them room and board, paid for all sorts of stuff they claim to need, and listened to their jokes, banter, moaning and groaning." He held his thumb and forefinger three inches apart. "I'm about this close to telling them that they've overstayed their welcome. I hate to be rude, but I'm surprised that my brother thought he could bring his friends here and expect me to be their den mother and bank." He stood, walked to the window, and looked out before returning to the chair. "Am I being unfair?"

"You've been more than generous."

"The worse thing is their sniping. You'd think they can't stand each other." He hesitated. "Maybe they can't."

"What do you mean?"

"Remember when Ray stormed out of Cal's the first time they performed there?"

"When Wallace was joking about something Ray did when he was young?"

"Yeah, I thought that was what it was about, but the guys had been bitching at each other all night. Then Pete said something about the stupid joke, Ray nearly hit him and said something like, 'At least all he kills is the audience.' That's one example. Here's another, last night, after poor Wallace was hauled out, Sal said he got what he deserved. Gee, Chris, those guys are supposed to be friends."

"It sounds like they're getting on each other's nerves as much as they're bothering you."

"What can I do about it? I can't throw my brother out; the others don't have anywhere to go."

I heard someone clomping down the stairs. "What's all the racket down here?" Pete said as he came in the kitchen.

Theo glared at him. "If it's okay with you, my friend and I are having a peaceful conversation."

I had never heard Theo that sharp with anyone. He was right about his houseguests getting to him.

"Well excuse me, Mr. Touchy. Hi, Chris, sorry to interrupt."

Pete nodded my direction. "Did you hear that, after Theo's honeymoon, he said he felt like a new man? So did his wife."

Theo's wife had died six months after moving to Folly, so I wanted to tell Theo that I'd help him pack their stuff. Instead, I frowned as Pete laughed at his inappropriate, untimely joke.

Pete poured a cup of coffee and said, "If you guys can get along without me, I'll take this upstairs."

Neither of us responded.

"I rest my case." Theo said after Pete was gone.

INSTEAD OF HEADING home after leaving Theo's, I went to the Dog for a late breakfast. The restaurant was packed, with a handful of customers waiting around the front door for a table. I didn't want to hog too much real estate, so I told the hostess I'd be okay sitting at the bar, where there was a short wait before a seat became available. Zack, one of the managers, asked if I wanted coffee. I declined. Amber wasn't around to scold me, so I said French toast was all I needed. I was watching the cooks do their thing on the other side of the food pass-through, when I felt a tap on the shoulder.

I turned to see Chief LaMond grin before she said, "Thought that was the back of your bald head."

I returned her smile. "Why don't you go ahead and say fat, old, and ugly while you're at it?"

"Now Chris, don't be hard on yourself. You're not that ugly."

I realized that insults from my friends were ways they

showed that they cared. I then wondered if it was true of Theo's houseguests.

Cindy inched closer and nudged the man sitting to my right. He scooted his plate over and offered her his seat. She thanked him for his act of chivalry, which I suspected was more because she was chief. Either way, it worked.

"Any update on Wallace?"

Zack asked if she wanted anything. She said she's already had seventy-three cups of coffee this morning and better not add any more.

She leaned closer to me. "Detective Callahan called to say that Wallace was worse last night than he'd been since we hauled him in. As you know, that was already bad."

"What's he doing?"

"Callahan said that, every time someone looks the poor guy's way, he cracks a joke." She hesitated, and continued, "Well, he cracks part of a joke. Either the punchline is unrelated to the first part, or doesn't make a whit of sense. Callahan said the hospital staff isn't in stitches."

Convenient, I thought. "Do they think he's faking?"

"Callahan said that the head docs will need time to come to a definitive diagnosis." She retrieved a notebook from her rear pocket and flipped through a few pages. "They were throwing out terms like dissociative identity disorder, schizophrenia, dissociative amnesia, and other psychobabble that to this lowly cop meant nutzoid. None of the docs have bandied about the word faker."

I was more confused than before. Even if one of those diagnoses was accurate, whether he knew what he was doing or not, he could have killed Michael.

"Chris, I'd love to stay and carry on an intellectual conversation about various psychiatric nomenclatures and taxonomies. Instead, I've got a meeting with one of my nutty officers who'd rather hand out tickets to vacationers whose cars have their tires an inch on the pavement than stopping people driving thirty miles an hour over the speed limit on Arctic."

I smiled. "Nomenclatures and taxonomies?"

Cindy elbowed me and said, "And you thought I was just another pretty face."

She hopped up and was gone before I could tell her that I was impressed, impressed with her vocabulary as well as her pretty face.

Chapter Forty-One

I was at Bert's the next day, grabbing an early-morning cup of coffee and a cinnamon roll, when Charles called to ask if I was up for a walk. We often took strolls around the island, but my friend seldom called this early to suggest one. I agreed to meet him in front of City Hall.

Charles would've been hard to miss. He was standing in front of the salmon-colored seat of local government and wearing a gold long-sleeve T-shirt with *Grambling State University* in black letters on the chest, and orange shorts that went as well with the T-shirt as would a flute in a rap band. His head was covered with a more traditional canvas, Tilley, with his feet covered with green-trimmed tennis shoes.

I chose not to mention his fashion statement, or maybe his getting dressed in the dark. Instead, I asked, "What direction?"

He waved in the direction of the Folly Pier. "The Pier or bust."

The two-block walk didn't rate *or bust*. I was pleased with what appeared to be a good mood from the man who hadn't exhibited many lately. "Lead on."

We crossed Cooper and waited for the traffic light to turn red before crossing Ashley. After another block, we were standing at the steps leading up to the structure and Pier 101 restaurant. Charles hadn't said more than a dozen words during the walk. The only words out of his mouth were when he carried on a brief conversation with a Dalmatian that was escorting its owner past us on the sidewalk. If Charles ever failed to talk to a passing canine, I'd know he was close to being committed.

The walk was a wise, albeit silent, choice. The sky was cloudless, the temperature a perfect, seventy-two degrees. We were far from the only people taking advantage of the weather. The Pier was more crowded than I'd seen in months. Groups of vacationers, apparent from chalky-white skin and resort clothing, competed for space with fishermen who lined sections of the railings. A couple with a man in a wheelchair and the woman walking along beside him, maneuvered around groups. They appeared to be enjoying the view, as well as the Pier's level surface.

Charles suggested that we go to the two story, diamond-shaped structure at the end.

We found a vacant picnic table shaded by the second-story roof, where he gazed at the beach and the Tides. He didn't speak for a long time. There was something on his mind, and I didn't want to give him an excuse not to tell me. I remained silent.

Charles leaned toward me but continued to gaze at the shore. "Remember when we first met?"

"Of course."

He smiled but didn't turn from looking at the hotel. "I had to spend a lot of time teaching you everything Folly. You were like a lost puppy in the middle of I-26."

"I don't think—"

"This isn't the spot where you argue," he interrupted. "Hear me out."

I nodded.

"I don't know what I saw in you. You were a stiff, prim and proper bureaucrat, whose sense of adventure was ordering onion rings instead of French fries. Anyway, I suppose my superhuman wisdom saw potential to turn that old you into a true Folly person."

"I think you—"

He waved his Tilley in my face. "What part of 'hear me out' befuddled you?"

I didn't know whether to laugh or apologize, so I stared at him.

"The point is that you gave me purpose, a challenge, something to do that was bigger than thinking about myself. You stumbled on a murder and, without my help, I'd be sitting here today talking to your ghost."

That wasn't how I remembered it.

"You opened the photo gallery and hired me—never paid me but hired me—to help run it. That was another challenge that I, if I say so myself, met with flying colors. I don't need to mention the close scrapes we've found ourselves in. Some gave me purpose, some gave me ulcers. Along came Heather, who gave me a chance at love, something that I never thought would happen."

He hesitated and looked down at the wooden deck, shook his head, and looked at me for the first time. "Franklin Roosevelt said, 'Be sincere, be brief, be seated.'"

Too late, I thought.

"Bottom line is that I'm rudderless, and don't know what to do about it."

He seldom admitted shortcomings. I had to think before responding.

"Charles, you're a wonderful person. You're liked by everyone you meet. Those who know you best love you. You've helped countless people. You've saved lives. How many people can say that?"

"History," he interrupted. "That's all history, some ancient, some recent. Still history."

I didn't want to get in a philosophic discussion about everything that all of us have accomplished is history. "Charles, that's true of all of us. You've led, you're leading, a good life, you've meant much to so many, and the world, especially the small corner of it on Folly Beach, is a much better place because of it. What makes you think you will change and not continue to bring joy to others?"

"Nothing, but—"

"But nothing. You don't know what's going to happen tomorrow. That's true. Neither do I, nor does anyone. What happened with you and Heather was sad. I think you loved each other. For whatever reason, it didn't work. Was it your fault? Some. Was it her fault? Some. Does that mean you won't find happiness with someone else? Absolutely not. The one thing I've learned about you is that you are at your best and feel the best about yourself when you're helping others. Is there a reason to think that you won't continue to do that?"

"I suppose not. You're right about it making me feel good."

"So, you're not rudderless, you simply don't know what direction your helping will turn you toward."

Charles smiled for the second time since we'd arrived on the pier. "So your best pep talk is I'm lost, don't know what direction I'm going, and not to worry. I won't run aground?"

I returned his smile. "Something like that."

"That's honest to God stupid, but I think I understand. I still don't hurt any less about losing Heather."

"You won't for a long time."

He picked at the cuticle on his left hand, stood, and looked over the railing to the deck below before returning to the bench. "Okay, have you got this mess with Theo, the funny guys, the dead bookie, and the missing, unmissing frog figured out?"

That was the Charles I'd come to admire and make fun of at every opportunity. Getting involved in someone else's problems was the quickest way to bring him out of his funk. I was determined to help him along the way. I told him what I'd learned about Wallace and his current state, about Horace leaving Janice, plus the latest on Neil, including that he'd been in prison a decade ago. He listened without interrupting which told me he wasn't over feeling rudderless.

I finished summarizing, and he said, "What again did Theo tell you that Ray said to, umm, Pete I guess, before Ray charged out of Cal's during the comedians first appearance?"

"Something about Wallace killing the audience. I'm not sure of the exact words. Why?"

"Could that mean Ray was implying that Wallace killed something other than the audience?"

"I don't know. Theo wasn't clear about what he heard. He said all of them were down each other's throats the entire night, even before they got to Cal's."

"Don't suppose we can go right to the horse's mouth to find out since Ray bounced down the steps to the hereafter."

"I'll ask Pete."

"You do that." Charles hesitated before saying, "See, I'm already helping."

I put my arm around his shoulder. "Yes, you are."

"My rudder's on the mend. Why don't we mosey over to Theo's house and see if the sleeping beauties are awake yet, so we can ask Pete?"

It was still before 10:00. I told Charles that from what I had seen on previous visits, Theo may be awake, but the odds that Pete and Sal were vertical were near zero.

"If our p.m. is their a.m., I'll meet you outside Theo's at two. Don't be late."

I told him that was a plan, not one I would have preferred, although it was one that would keep Charles involved in something other than himself. Instead of talking to Pete, I'd rather talk to Theo first. I was unclear what he had said about what Ray told Pete about killing the audience. It may have been nothing, but the word killing still stuck with me.

———

I WAS STANDING at the bottom of Theo's steps at 1:30, looking around for my friend. Instead of seeing Charles, my phone rang. His name was on the screen.

"Guess what?" Charles said.

I smiled. "You got a pet aardvark."

"Guess again."

"Why don't you tell me?"

"You're still no fun. Okay, Dude has me delivering a wetsuit for some guy from London, the one in England, who's staying at a big ole mansion out West Ashley Avenue. Something about the guy doesn't have a car with him. He just absolutely has to surf this afternoon, *old chap*, and needs the *bloody* wetsuit."

I was surprised. "Dude, the master of the annihilated vocabulary, said it like that?"

"Course not. That's my interpretation of whatever he said."

"Are you saying you're not coming to Theo's?"

"No. I'll be a couple of minutes late. Must go, the Brit's awaitin' to catch a wave."

I told him that I'd wait for him in the vacant lot across the street.

He said, "Cheers."

I turned to cross the street, when the front door opened.

Pete stuck his head out and yelled, "You selling encyclopedias or wanting me to join the Mormons?"

I smiled. "Yeah, you buying or converting?"

He motioned me up the steps and said, "Got a question that's been bothering me since 1979. If everybody says you're not supposed to eat at night, why's there a lightbulb in the refrigerator?"

I humored him with a smile, thought, *Once a comedian, always a comedian,* and followed him into the house.

Before I could tell him that Charles was on his way, Pete patted me on the back and said, "Heard anything about Wallace or the dead bookie?"

Then it hit me. I was looking at the person who first asked about the dead bookie. I was looking at the man who wouldn't have had any reason to know the occupation of the man found murdered at the beach. Unless ....

How do I ease out of here or stall for Charles to arrive? *Stay calm,* I told myself. *Act natural.* I told him that I hadn't heard anything about the bookie or Wallace, and said, "Is Theo here?"

Pete pushed the front door closed. "Yep, Old ET's roaming around upstairs. Go on up."

I looked at the steps leading to the second floor. "I don't want to bother him. I'll come back later."

I turned and saw Pete several feet behind me. He looked like anything but a comedian. I saw nothing funny about the pistol in his right hand, the pistol pointed at my heart.

The same moment I noticed the gun, the front door flung open. Charles stepped in and saw me standing by the stairs. Pete had moved behind the door and out of Charles's line of sight.

Charles was breathing heavily, took a deep breath, and said, "Hope it's okay for me to barge in. I saw the door close, so I figured you'd be close."

Pete stepped out from behind the door and slammed Charles's head with the weapon. My friend's eyes rolled up in his head and he hit the floor like a sack of rocks. He didn't utter a sound on the way down.

I started to kneel to see how he was when Pete slammed the door, mumbled a string of profanities, and again, pointed the pistol at me.

Chapter Forty-Two

"Let me help my friend," I said, staring at the gun.

Pete motioned for me to go up the stairs. "He'll be fine. That's the least of your worries."

Charles still didn't make a sound. I was afraid he was dead but didn't get a chance to check.

Pete barked, "Upstairs. Now!"

He was four feet behind me, too far away for me to reach the firearm. I shook my head and started up the steps.

Pete said, "Know what Theo said about you?"

I walked up two more steps when he said, "Stop. Change of plans."

I stopped and waited for directions.

He appeared indecisive, looked up the stairs, and said, "We're going to the kitchen." He waved the handgun in that direction.

I descended the steps, glanced down at Charles's unmoving body, and headed toward the kitchen.

"What'd Theo say about me?"

"After you left the first time I met you, the old coot kept going on, and on, and on, about how you singlehandedly caught more killers than all the cops in South Carolina combined. Sal and Wallace laughed like they thought he was joking. I figured he was exaggerating. Either way, I stuck that bit of trivia in here." He hesitated then, with his free hand, pointed to his head.

"You killed Michael Hardin," I said, to keep him talking.

"I've got the mic. You'll get your turn."

The only sound I heard was coming from Pete, so I assumed either Theo wasn't in the house or, if he was, he was unable to say anything, like my friend splayed out on the entry floor. I waited for him to continue.

"I wasn't worried. Poor Wallace was doing a bang-up job convincing everyone that he killed the guy. He was nearby when the bookie took his last breath but didn't get there soon enough to see what happened. He was so out of it, he couldn't tell if he saw what he saw, or if he imagined it." He hesitated and chuckled. "Saw, see, seesaw, there's a joke in there somewhere. I bet you don't think it's funny." His smile turned to a frown. "The poor guy's been losing it for years. The rest of us have been propping him up, pretending he's sane." He chucked again. "I would've loved to have seen his face when the cop showed him the credit card that magically appeared under his mattress. That would've been worth the price of admission."

"I didn't—"

He waved the gun in my face.

I closed my mouth.

We entered the kitchen, Pete looked around, then back at me. "I kept seeing you nosing around. You weren't buying Wallace's confession. You were looking at each of us like we were criminals, not hilarious Legends. It damned near hurt my feelings. I knew, as sure as I'm standing here, that you were going to be a thorn in my side. I don't know how, but you were going to figure it out. You understand why I couldn't have that, don't you? Know what my plan was?"

"What?"

Pete appeared distracted like he was trying to find something in the kitchen. I faced him and with my right hand, slipped the phone out of my back pocket. If I could tap 911, the dispatcher might hear our conversation and trace the call. I slid my finger over the screen to unlock it and glanced back to see the phone icon.

Two things happened. Pete looked at my hand holding the phone, and the phone rang. Pete lunged toward me as I saw Chief LaMond's name on the screen.

Before I hit the answer button, Pete smacked the phone out of my hand. He muttered a profanity as the device hit the floor. The screen cracked on impact. The rest of the phone met instant death when Pete stomped on it. His arm holding the gun bounced around like it had a mind of its own, but not for long.

Pete took a deep breath, moved the gun in its previous position pointing at my head, then grinned like nothing had happened. "I was going to get you and Wallace somewhere together and put a bullet in your meddling body. You'd be able to visit the bookie guy. Poor Wallace is so brain-rattled that I could convince him that he shot you, then sit back and watch him confess to a second murder. Poor, pitiful Wallace would spend the rest of his days in a nuthouse. I'd mourn the loss of one of Theo's friends, and be so sad about poor Wallace." He shook his head and made a clicking sound with his mouth.

Pete slammed the butt of the gun against the wall. I jumped. He laughed. "Wallace screwed my plan up when he went loony. He got the cops interested enough to find the credit card and haul him off before my perfect crime could commence. When Wallace was at his best, oh so many years ago, he had trouble with timing. Even you, one of the least funny people I know, could understand how that could mess up a joke." He looked down at the gun, then back at me. "A recent study found that women who carry a little extra weight live longer than men who mention it."

I sighed. How could I get the gun away without getting killed?

"See, knew you didn't have a sense of humor. That was funny."

"Why'd you kill the bookie?" I asked, to stall.

He laughed, again. "Who said I killed him. Think I'm stupid? If I said I did it, I'd be admitting to a crime. Now shut up and let me think about plan B, that being how to get rid of you and get away with it. I've almost got it, so chill." He chuckled. "That was funny, wasn't it?" He looked around the room.

I inched my way toward the patio door.

He twirled back to me. "My humorless friend, where do you think you're going?"

I stopped.

He smiled, not the kind he would use on stage, but one teemed with anger. He motioned with the gun for me to sit. "I'm getting long in the tooth, not as fast as I used to be, but bullets are swift."

I sat. He hadn't admitting to killing the bookie, so I tried another theory that had been rattling around in my head. "Why'd you push Ray down the stairs?"

His eyes narrowed, and he nodded. "Theo was right about you. Didn't you pay attention to the idiot cops? Poor drunken Ray got up in the middle of the night in a strange house. It was dark up there." He pointed the gun to the ceiling before returning it to my head. "Everyone knows he stumbled out in the hall in a drunken stupor and fell down the steps. A tragic accident."

I needed to keep him talking. "Did he know you killed Michael Hardin?"

Pete sighed. "There you go again. Did I say I killed the bookie, or anyone else for that matter?"

I didn't respond.

"Okay, let's pretend I'm not only a comedy legend but, in my spare time, I'm a genie. If you're stupid enough to make your last wish a question about a damned bookie, I'll answer. Yes, I killed him."

"Why?"

"Sal fed his brother some fantasy about us being successful, playing all over the country to sold-out crowds, rolling in dough. Fed him the story that the reason we showed up here was out of concern for Theo." He shrugged. "Suppose some of that's true. Sal was worried about Theo. When we got here, it took us seven minutes to figure out that Theo was in better shape than we were. There was nothing wrong with his mind. Years ago, we were hot stuff on the comedy tour. The key words being *years ago*." He looked over my head and shook his head. "I told you before, we're broke. That's a condition I'm not comfortable with."

"So, you killed him for money?"

"Duh."

I didn't know what I'd hoped would happen. What I knew was, the longer I kept him talking, the better chance something would happen—or so I prayed.

"How'd you meet Michael or learn he had money on him?"

"You know what, it's like hanging around in this house with two old farts who think everything they say is a joke, one son of a … umm, son of one of the old farts who thinks the only jokes in the house are the rest of us, and took every opportunity to make fun of us or put us down?"

"No, I don't—"

He waved the gun in my face. "Then, there's the slowest moving human in history who tries to be nice to each of us, but grates on my nerves like a piece of sandpaper. That's a long way to say that I got out of here every chance I could. I walked around, would've liked to plant my ass on a barstool at one of your bars, but didn't have enough money to buy a used beer."

He hadn't answered my question but was helping me stall. "So?"

"I was out on that long pier, saw some well-dressed guy wearing a god-awful looking hat with, would you believe, a feather sticking out the top. He was scrunched up against another guy. He looked around like he was hawking meth. I figured he was a dope dealer. One thing those guys have in common, other than selling death in a plastic bag, is a roll of cash. I thought there goes my bank, walking down the beach. I jogged down the handicap ramp then followed him out past where people were sunning themselves in front of the hotel."

Still no sounds from Charles.

"A robbery gone bad."

"You make it sound so cold. I wanted a permanent loan, not to hurt him. He was a drug dealer. It would've been stupid for him to go to the cops about being robbed. I caught up with him and didn't think there was anyone nearby. I pulled this out of my pocket and said for him to give me his money. The damn dealer looked at the gun, up at my face, said something like he didn't want any trouble, then asked if he owed me money. That confused the hell out of me. Why would a drug dealer owe me money? I asked him why. He acted like I should know." Pete rolled his eyes. "The guy said he was a bookie."

"Because taking bets wasn't as big a crime as selling drugs, you thought that he might go to the police to report a robbery, and—"

"I couldn't have that, could I?"

"Shooting him would draw too much attention."

"Sure would. Your god of the sea, Neptune, left a piece of wood by the bookie's feet. Unfortunate for him, he lunged for it. It all happened before I could think. He was a lot younger than me, but not as quick." He shook his head. "I grabbed the wood, swung it at him before he got to me. He was deader than a doornail, as they say. I found a bundle of cash in his pocket, grabbed it, and casually strolled away." He hesitated and shook his head again. "Did you know there are more than 300 million people living in this country?"

I didn't think this was a time to show off. I stared at him and waited for his point.

"Out of all 300 million, what are the odds that the one person who happened to come by after I took the guys money was Wallace? Whatever the odds, it was lucky for me. Lucky because he didn't see me—lucky that he was so out of it he confessed just because he happened to see the body. Considering where he is now, it was unlucky for Wallace. If the bookie was still alive, he could have taken bets on what would happen next."

"Why'd you kill Ray?"

"Do you ever stop asking questions?"

"You told me about the bookie. We both know you don't plan to let me live to tell anyone, so you might as well tell me."

"Perceptive fellow, aren't you? You're right. Why'd I kill Ray? Good question. It could've been because he was one of the most obnoxious humans I've ever known. Believe me, I've known my share. I didn't think he knew anything until the day we went to Cal's to ask—beg—for a gig. Ray came up to me and in his self-righteous, cocky, demeaning way, said something like, 'I know what you did.' I played dumb, acted like I didn't know what he was talking about. He said killing the guy was the only way I could have come up with the money I started spending. Said he'd make me pay. At Cal's, he made that smartass comment about all Wallace killed was the audience. When we got back here, Ray was in his room. After everybody either went to sleep or were in an alcohol-induced coma, I went to his room to have it out."

"What'd he say?"

"He was so drunk, I had trouble figuring out what he was saying. He laughed and said I'd get mine. Then he made a mistake, turned out to be a deadly one. He stumbled to the hall and announced he was going for a beer. Let's just leave it at me helping him down the stairs." Pete gave me another sinister smile and tapped his non-gun toting hand on the granite island. "Got it?"

"Got what?"

"Plan B. Your grand finale."

Chapter Forty-Three

I had hoped to find a way to distract the gun-toting comedian before he came up with an alternative plan to kill me and, if he wasn't already dead, kill Charles. That was not to be.

He kept the gun trained on me, stepped back to the sink, and grabbed the purple dish-washing gloves from the top drawer. "Take baby steps to the great room. Don't try anything funny. Pretend like your and your friend's lives depend on it." He chuckled. "I suppose they do. For a few minutes."

He was still too far away for me to reach, so I followed his instructions. I was in the center of the room as he moved to look out the double doors leading to the deck.

"You're so nosy about everything, I think you'll be interested in hearing Plan B."

"Yes," I said, in hopes it may give me a way to thwart it.

"It's more painful than Plan A." He laughed. "More painful for me, no different for you." He waved the gun in front of his face. "You won't be around for most of the plan, so I'll give you a preview. First, we will drag your friend's body to the kitchen where he's going to be on the floor near the door. You're going to be lying on the floor about right where you are now. You'll be dead. If your friend isn't already, he will be shortly."

"You don't want to—"

"Shut up. I'm telling the story. Here's where my pain comes in. I'm going to shoot myself in the arm. A flesh wound, you know, the kind that'll bleed all over Theo's ritzy room." He chuckled. "Hell, I'll drip some on his expensive couch just to piss him off." He held the purple elbow-length gloves out for me to see. "Oh, yeah, in case you were wondering why I have these with me, I'm going to wear one on my gun hand. Want to hear more?"

I said yes, hoping for a miracle.

He moved the pistol to his other hand, pointed the forefinger on the hand that previously held the deadly weapon, and pointed it at his upper arm. "Bang, two shots, or three shots in case Charles ain't already visiting the bookie. See, no gunshot residue on my hand or arm. Look at me, Mr. Policeman, I couldn't have done it." He grinned. "Anyway, with my arm feeling like it'd been bit by an alligator, I'm going to walk out there, fill the gloves with sand and tie the ends together. It's such a lovely day, I'll stroll to the end of Theo's private pier, throw the gun and gloves in the river, never to be seen again.

"I'll come back in, call 911, and tell the cops about a masked intruder who slipped in the back door. You know, the door I'll leave unlocked after depositing the gun and gloves. The guy was in a rage and going to rob Theo. Everyone knows he has money. Instead of money, the intruder found you, Charles, and me. Wow, was the gunman surprised? That's why he hit Charles over the head and shot us. He must've panicked. He ran out instead of stealing anything. Such a terrible thing to have happen." He shook his head, and grinned. "There it is, Plan B."

"The police are good. What makes you think you'll get away with it?"

"You give them too much credit. What reason would I have for shooting you? What kind of fool would they think I was to shoot myself? Don't forget, poor old Wallace has already admitting to killing the bookie. Everyone knows that Wallace's evil sperm, Ray, got himself drunk and fell down the stairs. You see, everything is solved, except catching the bad guy who came in here, killed you, killed your buddy, and thought he'd done the same to me. Yep, the perfect crime. Sadly, I won't even get to hear an appreciative audience give me a standing ovation. *C'est la vie.*"

He was so proud of his plan that I thought he was going to take a bow, regardless if there was an audience or not.

He didn't get a chance. The front door swung open. Theo yelled, "I'm back!"

Things happened so quickly that I wasn't sure of the sequence of events. I think Pete jumped back and twisted his body, so it faced the open front door.

Theo stared at Charles on the floor then at Pete, and said, "What's going—"

His question was interrupted by a gunshot. Theo collapsed.

I took two steps to the table along the wall and grabbed the silver frog.

Pete jerked back around to me, and yelled, "Stop!"

I swung my arm, and the frog caught him on the side of the head.

He staggered and fell to one knee.

Before I could get away, he grabbed my other arm as he raised his gun hand.

I didn't have as much leverage. I yanked my arm as far as I could, managed to bring the frog back around, and caught his wrist with the silver amphibian.

The gun bounced on the floor.

Pete screamed, bared his teeth, and reached for the firearm with his good hand.

He may have been a weightlifter in years gone by, but most of Pete's muscles had turned to flab. I still couldn't afford to let him get a solid grip on me. I kicked the gun under the couch, then hit him one more time with the frog.

He went down for the count. I thanked Wallace, or whomever had taken the frog, for returning it.

Pete wasn't moving, so I rushed to Theo lying half in the doorway. I didn't see a bullet hole or blood on my friend. I gave a sigh of relief. I grabbed Theo's phone and punched in 911. The second-best thing I heard was the dispatcher saying that emergency vehicles were on their way. The best thing I heard was a moan coming from Charles as he slowly moved his arm to the back of his head. I breathed another sigh of relief when Theo started to sit up.

Charles slowly sat, closed his eyes, and said, "Sorry I was late to the party. What'd I miss?"

I alternated between catching my breath and laughing although, if pressed, I wouldn't be able to tell what was so funny. Being alive trumped funny.

Sirens came from all directions before Charles regained his composure. "What happened?"

Theo had moved to a seated position and leaned back against the doorframe. "I'll second that question."

I told them they'd have to wait to be part of my audience when I told the police.

Chapter Forty-Four

"How come 'you're a peach' is a complement but 'you're bananas' is an insult?" Sal asked the standing room only crowd at Cal's. "Why are we allowing fruit discrimination to tear society apart?"

The room was not torn apart with uproarious laughter, although a sizable number of patrons laughed, a handful applauded. I attributed most of it to the clusters of empty beer bottles sitting on many of the tables. I attributed the laughter coming from those sitting at the two tables I'd pulled together two hours ago to several things, none of which were the jokes Sal was sharing from the stage.

It'd been two weeks—two traumatic weeks—since my near-death experience at Theo's. Tonight, I would've laughed if Sal was reading the phone book. I was alive, something I wouldn't have put money on that fateful day.

Charles, who'd spent the first week after being assaulted in his apartment, complaining about headaches, finally ventured out to tonight's performance. He leaned my direction. "Think he really got someone to pay him real money for telling those jokes?"

Cindy and Larry LaMond were sitting beside Charles. "Hush," Larry said, "I'm trying to listen. That guy's funny."

Cindy put her arm around her husband. "Larry thinks a can of Drano's funny. He doesn't get out much." She kissed him on the cheek.

"Eww," Charles said as he rolled his eyes.

Despite a concussion and incessant complaining about headaches, he'd shown more life and enthusiasm the last two weeks than I had seen in months. As tragic as it may have been, he seemed to thrive when first, there was something bad happening, and second, when he could help be part of the solution, albeit a painful part. I was thrilled to see him back to being Charles.

Sal continued unfazed. "Don't know why those prospectors out west during the gold rush had so much trouble. All they had to do was dig where the gold was. Who knows, maybe they needed the exercise."

"Larry thinks that's funny?" Charles asked.

"So did one guy over there," I said tilting my head toward the table where I thought I heard laughter, or maybe someone belching.

Sal said, "Any married man should forget his mistakes. There's no use in two people remembering the same thing."

A spattering of laughter followed, along with a couple of groans.

Sal reached for a bottle of water on the floor.

Theo took advantage of the break in the hilarity. "Guys, thanks for coming out. This has been a rough time for Sal. He feels horrible about subjecting me and all of you to Wallace, Ray, and don't even get him started on Pete."

"Any news on Wallace?" Barb asked.

Over the last fourteen days, she heard more about the group of comedians than anyone should have been subjected to. I'd spent several hours in her bookstore, talking about the near-tragic events, then when we went to the Dog for breakfast, 5,000 of Folly's 2,000 locals had stopped by our table to ask about the comedians and to share their experiences with the funny men.

Theo looked at the stage where Sal was still sipping water. "Afraid he's going to be in the psychiatric ward for a long time. At least Pete's confession got him off the hook for killing the bookie."

"What about stealing your money?" she asked.

Theo glanced at Sal and turned to face Barb. "I'm not pressing charges. I told Cindy I might have misplaced the cash."

Barb grinned. "Did she believe you?"

"Can't imagine she did, but she let it slide. Poor Wallace will be going through enough misery without adding that to his plate. Besides, he brought the frog back. That little hunk of silver ended up making it possible for Chris and me to be here tonight."

Sal tapped on the mic to regain everyone's attention and smiled. "Two construction workers were building a wooden storage shed. One worker was surprised to see the other going through the box of nails and throwing out half of them and said, 'Why are you doing that?' The other worker said, 'Those nails have the heads on the wrong end.' The first worker said, 'You idiot. They're for the other side of the shed.'"

The joke received the best response of the evening, and even Sal laughed. I suspected it was more from relief than thinking what he'd said was that funny.

Cal joined us after helping Joy and Kristin deliver beers to his thirsty crowd. He looked toward the entry, waved at someone, and said, "Neil, tomorrow, 5:00. See you then."

I turned and saw Neil leaving. "Cal, what's that about?"

He looked toward the door. "I figured, with all the new funny business I'll be bringing in, I'll need more help in the kitchen. Did you know Neil's a cook?"

I told him that I did.

"He's going to be using that talent working here."

"That's great."

Cal pulled his chair close to Charles, Barb, and me.

"Cal," Barb said, "I hear you're going to let Sal do comedy between your sets on the weekends."

Cal pushed his Stetson back. "He's spent a lot of time in here since the frog conking at Theo's. He's not a bad guy. According to Theo, the old broken-down comedian's going to become a permanent resident of our island." Cal leaned closer to Barb. "Tell him this, and I'll swear on a stack of Lenny Bruce albums that I never said it. I think we could become friends."

Charles, who apparently had been suffering withdrawal symptoms from not being the center of attention, tapped Cal on the arm. "Woodrow Wilson said, 'Friendship is the only cement that will ever hold the world together.'"

Sal must have been channeling Woodrow Wilson when he said, "Folks, it's been great being here with you tonight. I hope you come back Friday, when I'll be sharing the stage with my good friend, the legendary Country Cal. And, speaking of friends, let me finish with an observation. Friends wave red flags when you have a bad idea. Real friends pick up a camera."

Relic

A FOLLY BEACH MYSTERY

Chapter One

A disestablished Coast Guard station, now known as Lighthouse Inlet Heritage Preserve, anchors the east end of Folly Beach, a tiny, barrier island located fewer than a dozen miles from downtown Charleston, South Carolina. This morning, I knew it as the place where Charles Fowler and I planned to shoot sunrise photos of the iconic Morris Island Lighthouse, precariously perched on the deteriorating Morris Island, visible from the Preserve. Tumultuous, early-July thunderstorms had rolled through overnight, jarring me awake three times, the final time a little after 5:00 a.m. I hoped that Charles would have seen the wisdom of postponing our photo shoot for another day.

Wisdom and Charles seldom appear in the same breath, so I wasn't surprised when his fist pounded on my door, with his annoyed voice saying, "Chris, we're late."

I shook my head, opened the door, and stood face-to-face with my best friend. Charles was a year younger than I. Although, this morning, my body felt like it was a decade older than my sixty-eight years. True, I've never been a decade older, so am guessing what it would feel like. Regard-less, I wasn't ready to slosh through soaked sand and prickly sandspurs to listen to Charles pontificate on things in which I had no interest. After spending hundreds of hours with him since I'd moved to Folly, I knew it'd be a waste of words to point out the obvious reasons to not venture out.

Twenty minutes later, I finished dressing, grabbed my camera, and mumbled words that meant stupid, moronic idea, all while listening to Charles share how excited he was to be going on another photo adventure. We drove three miles to the end of East Ashley Avenue, the entrance to the Preserve.

Most days, street parking was at a premium since this was the entry to one of the most popular spots on the island. Today, there was one other vehicle parked on the sandy berm along the dead-end road, no surprise since it was still fifteen minutes until sunrise. To get to the best view of the lighthouse, we'd have to walk a quarter of a mile, much of it on what was once the road through the Coast Guard prop-erty, then the rest of the way over deep sand descending to the inlet.

I parked about a hundred feet from the stanchion, blocking all but emergency vehicles from entering the prop-erty, and was grabbing my camera from the back seat when Charles pointed to the other vehicle parked off the road between us and the stanchion. "Fitzsimmons."

"Strange name for a car," I said, to irritate the man who dragged me out of the house before sunrise.

"No, dummy. It's Anthony and Laurie Fitzsimmons' car."

"How do you know?"

"You know other Volcanic Orange MINI Cooper convertibles?"

I didn't even know that one. One of Charles's goals was to get to know every human on Folly, probably each human in South Carolina, plus their pets.

"Who're the Fitzsimmons?"

He pointed his hand-carved wooden cane at the MINI. "Met them in town last week. I was walking down Center Street, minding my own business, when they stopped me, asked if I went to Jacksonville University."

He almost lost me on *minding his own business*, an activity I'd never witnessed. Instead, I recovered. "Why'd they ask that?"

"Suppose because I was wearing a Jacksonville University T-shirt with Nellie on it."

"Who, or what, is Nellie?"

He sighed, unbelieving that someone wouldn't know Nellie. "The mascot, a dolphin."

In addition to Charles carrying a cane for no apparent reason, his torso was usually covered by a college, or university, T-shirt in summer, sweatshirt in winter, always long-sleeved. I don't ask why. It would be another waste of words.

"Again, why'd they ask about Jacksonville University?"

"They're from there, the city, not the university. Anthony was a high school math teacher; Laurie taught drama."

"Vacationers?"

"Retired last month to move here."

Lightning lit the sky off to the east; thunder rumbled in the distance. The weatherman said that the rain was out of the area, but I began to wonder. It didn't stop Charles from tapping his cane on the pavement while heading to the entrance.

I followed. "They buy a house?"

"Chris, give me a break. I didn't have time to get their life history, bank statements, Social Security numbers, blood types." He shrugged. "Anthony said they were late for something. They had to go."

Which meant my uber-nosy friend may not have their blood types, yet it wouldn't have stopped him from interrogating them at a level that would make the CIA drool.

"Wonder why their car's here?" Charles said, more to himself than to me.

"Maybe that's their house." I pointed to a cottage near the car. There were five houses within a stone's throw from where we were standing. No lights were on in any of them, so they were either vacant vacation rentals, or the residents were still asleep, making them wiser than the two of us.

"Could be," Charles said with little conviction. He veered off the path to the Preserve to approach the MINI. He leaned close to the driver's side window then jumped back like he'd seen a ghost. He stumbled then regained his balance.

"What is it?"

He put his finger to his lips and whispered, "Laurie's in there."

"Asleep?"

"Hope so."

The MINI's door swung open, startling both of us.

Charles said, "Not asleep now."

"Crap! You scared me to death," said the car's occupant. She stepped out of the vehicle, twisted her shoulders around, like she was loosening a strained muscle. She stared at us, before saying, "Who the hell are you?"

"Laurie, it's me, Charles. We met in town the other day. Didn't mean to scare you."

Laurie stood five-foot-three, petite, with short, dark hair, and a bewildered look on her face. "We met in town?"

That was a blow to Charles's *everyone knows me* ego. He reminded her where they'd met.

Her look softened. "Oh, I remember. You're the guy with the long-sleeved Jacksonville University shirt standing in the blazing sun."

The sky began to lighten. Laurie's hair was matted; her tan slacks wet from the knees down. I stepped closer and told her I was Chris Landrum, Charles's friend, that we were on our way to the end of the island to photograph the lighthouse. I added that we were sorry to startle her.

Today's temperature was to reach the mid-80s, although the gusty breeze off the ocean, and the lack of sunshine, had the temperature currently hovering in the low 70s. Laurie wrapped her arms around her chest. She was shivering.

"Are you okay?" I asked.

"Umm, yes."

Charles stepped closer to her. "Where's Anthony?" He looked around, like he expected to see Laurie's husband pop up from behind the car.

Laurie looked down at the sandy berm, glanced back at her car, then turned to Charles. "He's… well, supposed to be with me. Umm, he's."

I waited for her to continue. She looked at Charles, at me, back at the ground, then said nothing.

"Laurie, you're shivering," I said. "Why don't we get in your car, where we can turn on the heat?"

"Good idea," Charles said before Laurie could respond. He was already on the way to the passenger side of the vehicle.

"Okay," Laurie said, barely above a whisper.

I held the door open while she climbed in and turned on the ignition. Charles opened the passenger door, moved a flashlight off the seat, pushed the front passenger seat up, and squeezed his five-foot eight, one hundred fifty-pound frame in the back seat. I walked around to the front passenger's seat. In the glow of the interior light, I saw gray roots from Laurie's brown hair. Even with her hair in disarray and wrinkled clothing she was attractive. She stared out the windshield and continued her silence. I was determined to wait for her to tell us what was going on.

Charles, a stranger to patience, leaned forward while pushing aside a four-foot long metal detector behind him on the seat. "Where's Anthony?" He said it like he hadn't already asked.

Laurie rested her arms on the steering wheel and leaned against her forearm. "He's … I don't know where he is."

"Help us understand," I said as calmly as possible.

She turned to Charles then back to me. "We were in whatever that's called out there." She pointed to the Preserve.

Charles, a stickler for details, said, "Lighthouse Inlet Heritage Preserve."

Laurie said, "Whatever."

I agreed with her. "Go on."

"We got here around seven… umm, last night now. We got caught up in, umm, our activities, didn't notice how dark it was getting."

"Activities?" Charles interrupted.

Laurie jerked her head toward Charles then glanced at the metal detector beside him. "Are you cops?"

It was a strange question. Before I answered, Charles said, "I'm a private detective, my friend here and I help the police occasionally."

Charles, who hasn't had a steady job since moving to Folly some thirty-two years ago, popped out of bed one morning, deciding that he wanted to be a private detective. He'd never studied the profession, nor apprenticed under a licensed private investigator, a requirement in South Carolina. He hadn't let those troublesome barriers stand in the way of self-proclaiming what he was, if only in his mind. When pressed, he'd said he read enough novels about private investigators to be "more than qualified," whatever that meant.

"Laurie," I said, "we're not police. Why?"

Charles said. "Humph."

She started to say something, hesitated, before continuing, "We were looking for Civil War relics in the woods when it started pouring. It was the first time that we'd, umm, explored that area. We got turned around."

The question about us being the police was beginning to make sense. It was illegal to use metal detectors, or to remove artifacts from the Preserve, owned by Charleston County.

Charles said, "What happened?"

"Before we knew it, we couldn't see five feet in front of us. The rain got harder. Lightning everywhere, thunder deafening. We were lost. Thank God we had flashlights." She took a deep breath. "We knew there was a trail somewhere. Umm, yes, we were on a sandy trail, maybe off it a little." She closed her eyes, her head vibrated like a tuning fork.

Charles said, "Then what?"

Laurie opened her eyes and blinked a couple of times. "Where was I?"

"On a trail," I said.

"We were? Oh, I guess so. Did I say we were lost?"

I nodded.

"It was really, really dark. Anthony told me to stay where I was. He'd find the way to the car." She hesitated, her hands trembled. "I told him we should stick together. He said no, for me to wait. I kept waiting for him to come back. I was huddled down under the densest tree cover I could find, anywhere to stay dry. It didn't work. God, the rain kept getting harder, thunder boomed, lightning turned the sky to daylight. I was so scared."

"What time was that?" Charles pushed, "What happened next?"

"Time, I don't know. Like I said, it was after dark. Maybe ten, or eleven. I waited and waited. It seemed like hours. The rain eased, so I couldn't just sit there. I started walking in the direction of the ocean. At least, I thought that was the direction I was going. It was cloudy, but I could see a glimmer of moonlight when I broke through the woods. I saw the ocean, saw the beach. I figured that, if I turned right and started walking, I'd get to the houses near where we parked. Those over there."

She pointed to the structures adjacent the Preserve. "I saw the houses, so I had an idea where I was. Guys, I was so happy. Anthony would be in the car, waiting until the rain died down, to come get me. I knew he would." She turned, looked out the side window, then whispered, "He wasn't here. Why did I let him go? Why?"

Charles and I remained silent.

Laurie smacked her hand on the steering wheel. "If we'd gone together, I'd know where he was." She leaned forward. "Now I don't."

Then, she fainted.

Chapter Two

Other than Laurie being wet, exhausted, confused, and passed out, I had no idea what else might be wrong. I called 9-1-1 and told the dispatcher that help was needed at the east end of Ashley.

You'd have thought there was a three-alarm fire at the Preserve. In addition to the longest street on the island, next to Runway 15/33 at the Charleston International airport, Ashley Avenue is one of the straightest paved areas nearby. If it weren't for traffic, a twenty-five mile-per-hour speed limit, and regular police patrols, it'd be a perfect dragstrip. I saw strobing emergency lights, heard sirens from two patrol cars and two fire trucks long before they arrived.

The first responders earned their reputation. They were hitting their brakes five minutes after I called. Officer Trula Bishop was the first to arrive. Charles moved to the front seat of the MINI while I met Bishop behind the orange car.

"Mr. Chris, was that you who called?"

I nodded then gave her an abbreviated version of what'd happened. She told me not to run off then moved to the passenger side of the MINI to motion for Charles to get out so she could check on the distressed driver. Most Folly Beach Public Service Officers were cross-trained as EMTs and fire-fighters. This allows the small force to respond to not only police situations, but also to fight fires and stabilize those in medical distress until an ambulance arrives from Charleston.

The first fire engine squealed to a halt. Two firefighter/paramedics were next to the MINI. Officer Bishop let them do their thing and returned to me. Charles was close behind her as she suggested we might be more comfortable in her vehicle. I'd known Bishop since she joined the force three years ago. She was an outstanding officer, also one of the few females on the force. I also knew her suggestion to join her in her car was closer akin to a command. I got to the patrol car first and climbed in the back seat.

"Okay, Mr. Chris, what have you and your buddy got yourself into now?"

Charles answered before I could. "We were going for an early-morning saunter to take pictures of the lighthouse."

Bishop put her hand up, palm facing my friend's face. "Charles, is Chris a ventriloquist, or are you answering for him?"

I told you that she was outstanding. I smiled then took over for Charles giving her the unabridged version of what'd happened.

"She was asleep in her car with wet clothes," Bishop said, like she was trying to wrap her head around what we'd found. "How long was she asleep? When did she get back to the car? How could she fall asleep with her husband missing?"

I shook my head. "Don't know. She fainted before we learned more than what I told you."

"Were there other vehicles here when you found her?"

"Only her volcanic orange MINI Cooper," Charles said, providing Bishop more than she needed to know about the car.

Bishop pointed to the nearby houses. "Any lights?"

"No," I said. "No sign of life."

One of the EMTs tapped on the driver's side window. Bishop lowered the window, and the medic whispered something. She responded with, "Okay, keep me posted."

The EMT returned to the MINI when Charles said, "What?"

"Two things," Bishop said. "The ambulance is five minutes out."

"And?" Charles interrupted.

Officer Bishop glared at Charles then turned to me. "His patient is mumbling something about her husband should have come relic hunting with her tonight instead of…"

"Instead of what?" Charles asked.

"She didn't say. Her eyes rolled up in her head, and she was out again."

Charles twisted in the seat to look at the MINI. "Does that mean Anthony wasn't with her? That doesn't make sense."

"All I know, Charles, is what my guy said. You talked to her. Did she say anything that would make you think she was alone?"

"No, the opposite," Charles said.

A Charleston County EMS ambulance pulled up behind the MINI, followed by a silver Ford F-150 pickup truck occupied by Cindy LaMond, the island's director of public safety, aka police chief. Two EMTs from the ambulance rushed to the MINI, while Chief LaMond walked to where we were seated. She was in her early fifties, five-foot-three, well built with curly dark hair. She was also a close friend whom I'd known since she moved to Folly nine years ago.

Cindy glanced at the MINI then bent down and looked in the window of Bishop's patrol car.

"Crocodile crap," Cindy said, unchieflike. "When was the last time I rolled up on a crime scene without having to look at the two of you with your scraggly, wrinkled, Cheshire-cat-grinning faces, ready to ruin my day?”

“Good morning, Chief LaMond,” I said. “Nice to see you this morning.”

Cindy rubbed her lower back. “Get out of the car. My aching back doesn’t take kindly to being bent like this.”

The three of us exited and stood beside Cindy facing the MINI. “Okay, let’s hear it?”

Bishop gave a police-speak version of what she knew. The chief turned to me to ask if that summed it up.

I said that it did as I watched the EMTs load Laurie Fitzsimmons in the ambulance.

Cindy walked over and looked in the MINI.

The rest of us followed.

“Okay,” she said, “here’s my question. How could whatever her name is, and her husband, get that lost back there?” She nodded toward the entry to the old Coast Guard property. “Hell, it’s not that big.”

“Eighty acres,” added my trivia-collecting friend Charles.

Cindy glared at him then continued, “As I was saying, if you walk one direction, you hit the marsh, another, and you’re staring at the lighthouse, head another way, and you’re tippy- toeing in the Atlantic Ocean. Go the fourth direction and, *voila*, you’re here at that god-awful orange car.”

Charles pointed his cane at the MINI. “Volcanic orange.”

Cindy lowered her head. “Charles, sayeth I in all sincerity, who gives a crap about the color’s name? Can anyone answer my geography question?”

I glanced at Charles, waiting for him to give a more detailed answer than anyone would have wanted. He didn’t say anything, nor did Officer Bishop. I offered, “It’s unlikely any of us would get lost, but she told us they were new here, it was storming, dark, plus it was their first visit out there. It's possible."

"So, was Mr. umm," Cindy looked at Bishop.

Bishop said, "Anthony Fitzsimmons."

Cindy nodded. "Was he with her, or not?"

"She told us he was," I replied.

Bishop added, "And told the EMT he wasn't."

It was nearly 8:00, the lingering clouds from last night's storm were offshore. Bishop said, since it was lighter, she'd walk around the MINI to see if she could find evidence that anyone else had been there.

Cindy called dispatch, requesting that more members of the Folly Beach Department of Public Safety join her at the end of the island. She leaned against Bishop's patrol car and rubbed the bridge of her nose.

I said, "Cindy, you okay?"

"Sure, umm… no. Chris, I'm three officers short. I have no business being out here fighting mosquitos, listening to you two blabbering, when I have a pile of paperwork taller than Mt. Rainier in the office." She pointed at the stanchion leading to the Preserve. "Now, we have Mr. Fitzsimmons missing, or not, depending on which mood his wife is in."

A City of Folly Beach SUV parked behind the second fire truck. Three men and one woman exited then gathered around their boss. She told them to grab the guys who were already here, spread out, and start a grid search for the missing spouse.

"Do we have a description?" said one of the officers I hadn't seen before.

Cindy closed her eyes then slammed her hand on the hood of Bishop's car. "Tell you what, officer. Round up every man you find out there, bring him in, and we'll figure out if he's Mr. Fitzsimmons." Under her breath, she uttered, "Idiot."

No, she was not okay.

The search party spread out and started their slow

canvass of the eighty-acre Preserve. Cindy said that, if she didn't get back up to full staffing soon, she'd reduce the force by one more with her resignation. Charles said he and I were going to continue toward the lighthouse to do what we came to do, although we were too late to capture images of the sunrise casting its glow on the lighthouse.

Cindy said, "If you think I'm dumb enough to believe that crock, then I don't need to be chief of anything."

She knew Charles well. The last thing on his and, to be honest, my mind was to take photos. I had no idea what happened overnight. Laurie's confusion about Anthony being with her, or not, muddied the story even more. What was clear was there was a chance that Anthony was somewhere on the property, so Charles and I wanted to be nearby when he was found. Charles's nosy gene had invaded my system.

The distance from where we found Laurie to the beach overlooking the Morris Island Lighthouse was paved, all but the last hundred yards. The road, built to serve the Coast Guard, bisects the wooded area between the ocean to our right, and the marsh to the left.

"More than fifty kinds of birds have been seen back here," Charles said as we walked along the road.

"You tell me that each time we're here."

In addition to collecting long-sleeve T-shirts, Charles collected books; enough to stock his apartment with nearly as many books as are housed in the Folly Beach Branch of the Charleston County Library. He also collected trivia and quotes from United States presidents, and was generous with spewing trivia and quotes at anyone who'll listen. In my case, I had given up listening five years ago. It hadn't stopped him from sharing.

"I know. I also know your memory ain't what it was when you were a young whippersnapper. I've got to keep telling you."

"If you say so."

I normally didn't mind his banter. Walking along this path reminded me of my first time here some ten years ago, when I had looked forward to a peaceful morning photographing the lighthouse. Instead, I happened upon a murder. That fateful discovery catapulted me into a nightmare that nearly got me killed, not quite a chamber of commerce preferred introduction to Folly Beach. That walk also allowed me to meet Charles, plus a handful of Folly folks who've become my friends.

We reached the spot where the paved road ended. Then, a sandy path led the way to the beach. I was startled from reliving the past when one of the police officers to my right yelled, "Over here!"

Charles stopped, pointed his cane the direction of the sound. "He's calling us."

He wasn't directing his comment at us, yet it didn't stop Charles from nudging me in the direction of the voice. The wind-swept trees and shrubs along the right side of the path made it impossible to see who'd called, plus there wasn't a path in that direction. Two officers emerged from the less-densely foliaged area on the other side of the path, shoved their way between the prickly shrubs, then maneuvered toward the sound of the officer who'd repeated his call. A City of Folly Beach ATV parked beside us. Its driver joined the two officers into the shrub-filled space.

Charles and I followed. Between the mushy sand, standing water from the overnight storm, and prickly underbrush, it was slow going. The officers in front of us had created a semblance of a path for us to reach the spot where the police were gathered. It didn't take a devotee of TV crime shows, or a coroner, to determine three things: The person they were staring at was male. The man splayed out in the sand had taken his last breath. And, if I could find anyone dumb enough to bet with, I'd wager my life savings on the unfortunate soul being Anthony, the late husband of Laurie Fitzsimmons.

Chief LaMond was next to arrive. She waved her officers away from the body, took in the surroundings, told two of her guys to tape off the scene, then glared at Charles and me.

She shook her head, pointed her finger at the two of us before pointing the direction of the road.

"Get the hell out of my crime scene!"

Told you she wasn't okay.

Chapter Three

Charles was surprisingly quiet on the drive to town after we'd been evicted from the crime scene. His only comment was that he was scheduled to make a delivery for our friend, Dude Sloan, owner of the surf shop. Charles picked up a few dollars making on-island deliveries for Dude, helping restaurants clean after busy weekends and, until recently, when he'd started complaining about debilitating arthritis in his hands, provided help for contractors who needed extra hands on projects. None of these *jobs* had burdened Charles with reported income, withholding taxes, or those burdensome IRS regulations. His expenses were minimal, so little more than petty cash was needed to meet his standard of living. I dropped him in front of the surf shop then continued to the Lost Dog Cafe for an early lunch.

The Dog, located a half-block off Center Street, Folly's center of commerce, was my favorite breakfast, and lunch spot. The kitchen in my cottage is used about as often as a Wiccan priest attends services at the Baptist church, so I was in the restaurant more often than many of its servers. As usual, the popular restaurant was packed, the closest parking spot two blocks away. The hostess told me that there would be a fifteen-minute wait. I was on my way outside to wait for a table when I heard a familiar voice call my name. I turned to find Theodore Stoll, pointing to an empty chair beside his brother, Salvadore. I must've been distracted by the morning's discovery to miss seeing them when I came in. Theo had on an orange T-shirt; Sal wore a red, orange, and florescent green striped shirt that looked like it belonged in a 1960s lounge singer's closet.

I joined the men, and Theo said, "What's this I hear about you finding a body at the old Coast Guard station?"

Sal didn't give me a chance to answer. He removed his black, wide-rimmed glasses that looked like he'd had them since the 1950s and said, "Is it a full, or a part-time job, you have bebopping around Folly finding bodies?"

Theo followed with, "Who was it? Who killed him?"

I held up my hand. "Whoa. Good morning, guys."

Theo pointed his fork at me. "Okay, let's try again. Good morning, Chris."

"Better."

I'd met Theo a couple years ago when Charles and I joined a senior walking group at the behest of Larry LaMond, a friend of mine who's Chief LaMond's husband, to find anything we could about another member of the group who'd been suspected of trying to blackmail Larry. It hadn't entered my mind that a benign senior walking group could nearly cost the lives of so many people. Anyway, that's a story for another time.

Theo was the butt of jokes by others in the group, who'd nicknamed him ET for Energizer Turtle, rather than for the lovable alien from the movie *ET*. For the group to call Theo slow was hypocritical since the average walking speed of the others in the group was the speed of an earthworm. Sal, at age seventy-nine, was nine years younger than his brother. He'd moved in with Theo earlier this year. He was a stand-up comedian who'd spent many years on the road before giving up the nomadic life to live comfortably in Theo's McMansion.

Sal said, "With the polite stuff finished, answer Theo's question."

I wanted to ask which of Theo's three questions he wanted me to answer. Instead, I told him that, yes, I was at the Preserve when a body was found. I asked how he'd heard about it.

"Amber," he said, like it was all I needed to know.

It was. I'd known Amber Lewis since I moved to Folly. She was the longest-tenured server at the Dog, was also the go-to person if you're in need of a friendly, warm, smiling face, or the latest gossip.

As if on cue, she arrived at the table, patted me on the shoulder, and said, "Good morning, trouble magnet. Did finding another body stir up your appetite?"

"How'd you hear about it?" I thought it was a legitimate question since the lifeless Anthony Fitzsimmons was discovered less than two hours ago.

Amber nodded toward the counter, where three diners were in deep conversation. One wore a police uniform, so I knew the answer before Amber said anything.

"Officer Timmons told me. He said the guy had been shot. He didn't know who did it. Sad, so sad. I told Theo, since you're friends."

"Enough gibberish," interrupted Sal. "I need more tea."

Amber frowned at him. "You'll get more as soon as I get done talking to Chris and seeing if he wants anything to eat." She turned back to me. "Are you okay?"

Amber and I had dated my first couple of years on Folly. We had remained friends since then. I could count on her being concerned.

"I suppose so. Did you know Anthony and Laurie Fitzsimmons?"

"A smidgen. They'd been in a couple of times. They're

retired teachers, bought an old house, are fixing it up." She chuckled. "Laurie was fascinated by the dog photos on the walls. She kept asking if all of them had been here. I told her that a few had. Although, since there are a couple of hundred photos, many were given to us by people long after they left. Some had never set a paw on our dog-friendly patios."

Sal waved his hand in Amber's face. "You think talking about these damn dogs is more important than my tea?"

Amber gave him her best faux smile. "Of course not, Theo's rude brother. I'll stop being nice to customers and scamper over there to get you your tea because you are certainly the most important person in the building."

Sal smiled. "Miss Amber, I spent a half century around comedians. You're going to have to do better than that to insult me."

She rubbed her hand in his long, gray hair. "I love a challenge." She headed behind the counter to get Sal's tea.

I said to Theo, "Did you know Anthony and Laurie?"

"Nope."

"Me, either," said Sal. "What's a dog kennel?"

I started to ask why he wanted to know.

He held up his hand. "A barking lot."

I grinned.

Theo said, "I'm trying to housebreak my brother's habit of telling jokes.

"You're failing," I said.

Theo sighed as he shook his head.

Sal said, "You two old farts have no sense of humor. Enough about the dead guy I didn't know. Theo, tell Chris about the call."

Theo twisted his napkin as he looked at his half-eaten chicken salad croissant. "He doesn't care about—"

"Doesn't care about what?" Amber interrupted then set a fresh glass of tea in front of Sal.

"Nothing," Theo said. "Chris, were you going to order?"

Amber turned my way until I ordered a Mahi salad."

She put her hand over her heart. "Lordy, Lordy, Chris ordering something healthy. Not sure my heart can take it."

Theo leaned closer to Sal and whispered, "Amber's been trying to get Chris to eat healthier since forever."

Amber was good at many things, succeeding with that task wasn't one of them. She was right, although knowing and doing were two different things. I was a few pounds overweight, which I rationalized as a byproduct of aging. Rationalizing was one of my strengths.

"I owe it all to you, Amber."

She winked. "Yeah, right," then headed over to the kitchen.

I turned to Theo. "What call?"

Another of my strengths was listening. I never thought it was a strength until I observed many others who only want to hear what they have to say and appear oblivious to the thoughts, feelings, and words of those around them. Besides, Charles's nosiness was rubbing off on me.

"Okay. You know my son died a year or so ago. He—"

My turn to interrupt. "Son? Theo, I didn't know you had children."

"Oh. I thought I must've told you."

I shook my head.

Theo turned to Sal. "Why'd you have to bring it up?"

Sal held his hands out to his side in a *who me* motion.

"Yes, Chris," Theo said, "Theodore Jr, he went by Teddy. Probably my biggest failure. It's hard to talk about. We were never close. I spent all my time working. Eunice had to raise him nearly by herself. Teddy went out west to college, where he stayed. The only time we saw him was when he came home for the holidays." He shook his head. "He didn't do that often. Eunice and I tried to stay in touch, but he wouldn't return our calls. He was a chef, worked all the time. He said that he couldn't come to see us and discouraged us from visiting. He opened his own restaurant. Poor Eunice and I never saw it." He sighed. "I was a terrible dad."

"Not so great a brother, either," Sal added.

I supposed that was a joke. If it was, Sal was joking with the wrong audience.

I said, "Go on, Theo."

He stared at his plate, like he was studying his chicken salad. I didn't think he was going to respond, until he said, "He got married. Know how I found out? Got an invitation in the mail, an invitation postmarked a week after the wedding."

"I'm sorry, Theo."

He looked down at his plate, sipped his water, closed his eyes. Sal, for once, didn't crack a joke. I waited for Theo to continue.

He didn't get a chance. Charles stormed in the door, looked around, and made a beeline for our table.

"Guess who I just talked to. Guess what he said."

Sal looked at my out-of-breath friend, and said, "Big Bird. He squawked that you're a lunatic."

Charles opened his mouth, stared at Sal, then shut his mouth.

"It was a joke, Charles," I said. "Theo was saying something important. Can it wait?"

"Oh, sorry."

I asked Charles to have a seat. He judiciously did and remained quiet, a near miracle.

I turned to Theo. "You were saying?"

"Not now, Chris. I can't." He stood as he waved to Amber for their check. He leaned close to me. "Later." He dropped money on the table then told Sal that they were leaving. It was as quick as I'd ever seen Theo move. His green jogging shorts swished as he headed to the exit. Sal followed two-steps behind him.

Charles watched them go. "What'd I interrupt?"

"Nothing," I said, not wanting to get in an extended conversation about Theo's son and whatever he wanted to tell me, reluctantly tell me. "Who'd you run into?"

"You know old man Gant?"

"Abraham Gant?"

"That's the one."

I didn't know much about him, other than he'd lived on Folly most of his life and retired from the South Carolina Highway Patrol.

"What about him?"

"I was peddling back to town from, delivering a wet suit for Dude. Took it to a chubby guy living out near the end of East Huron. Don't know how he's going to wiggle into the suit. He said—"

"Charles, Abraham Gant?"

"No wonder you never know what's going on. Anyway, I parked my bike beside the Crab Shack, was headed in to enjoy a brew. Gant was standing on the corner by the bicycle rack. Did you know he preferred to be called Captain Gant?"

"No. How do you know?"

"Suppose because the first time I met him he said call me Captain Gant." Charles smiled. "Thought it sounded silly. First thing I thought of was Captain America, Captain Hook, Captain D's, Captain Midnight, Captain Crunch, Captain—"

"Your point, Charles?"

"Okay, okay. Captain was his last rank when he was a cop. Anyway, I said, 'Howdy.' That's all it took."

"For what?"

"For him to start ranting about relic hunters, scavengers. Now, here's the important part, Anthony Fitzsimmons."

"Explain?"

"Captain stuck his shriveled-up forefinger in my chest,

said something like, 'Did you hear that old, blankety-blank scoundrel was killed?' He didn't say blankety-blank."

"Was he talking about Anthony?"

"Duh, of course. That's my point. How did Captain know about the murder? We'd just stumbled on it."

"What else did he say?"

"I'd heard he was eccentric, but didn't know about what. Now, I do. The old boy gets all riled up on the topic of the past, about what kinds of things happened then."

"Like what?"

"Ghosts, things, people from the past. Says what happened back there needed to stay back there. What's buried should stay buried. He spouted off something about the past is the past because it's not now. He said people who go digging up bones, or old stuff, are the scourge of the earth."

I was certain that what Charles said didn't make sense. "So?"

"Hang on, I'm getting to the good part. Captain Gant said those people who dig up the past should, now get this, be shot. Yep, that's what he said. S.H.O.T."

Chapter Four

I left the Dog after agreeing that Gant's comment warranted a call to Chief LaMond. I didn't believe his mini-rant amounted to a confession yet, unless I agreed to tell Cindy, I'd never hear the last of it. Of course, Charles could've called her. He said that she'd believe me before taking his word. History told me he was right.

A stop at the post office rewarded me with a brochure offering a "deal of a lifetime" on a "miracle" hearing aid that was about the size of a gnat but would allow me to hear the tiniest sounds, or not miss important words spoken by family and friends. I didn't know about hearing the tiniest sounds, something that seemed to be a distraction rather than an improvement, but knew my friends made sure they never let any of their "important words" get past me. I dropped the deal of a lifetime in the trash before calling Chief LaMond.

She answered with, "What took you so long to pester me about this morning?"

"Good afternoon, Cindy."

"Tell me one good thing about it. Come on, tell me one."

Cindy's moods occasionally ranged from mad at the world to life's grand. I was a good enough friend, so she didn't hesitate sharing both ends of the spectrum. Her frustrations with her no-win job occasionally seeped into her relationship with those who knew her deeper than by title. There weren't many of us in that category, so I gave her benefit of the doubt, if she appeared to be taking her frustrations out on me.

"It's a beautiful July afternoon."

"Oh, wait, let me get out of this rickety chair, stand on my tippy-toes so I can look over this damned pile of folders chock full of crap I need to review and, oh yeah, hang on while I throw the office phone in the trash so I don't have to see the red light blinking, the screen showing I have twenty-seven voicemail messages." She groaned. "Hell, yes, it does look like a beautiful day out there. Hope you're enjoying the heck out of it. Back to my question, what took you so long to pester me about this morning?"

I moved the phone away from my face, so she wouldn't hear my chuckle.

"Sorry to bother you. I was talking to Charles, who shared a conversation he had with Abraham Gant."

Cindy interrupted, "That's Captain Gant to you."

"Yes, Captain Gant told Charles something about the past needing to stay in the past, that people who dig it up should be shot."

Cindy sighed. "Let me guess. Your *faux* detective friend used his *faux* detective skills to figure that Captain Gant killed Anthony Fitzsimmons."

"That was his thought."

"Chris, do you know how many people Captain Gant has shared his warped views with about relic hunters, grave robbers, heck, anyone who happens to stump their toe on a Civil War frying pan uncovered by a storm?"

"No."

"Me, either. It's a bunch. I've heard it from several of our fine citizens. He's freely shared those views for years with anyone who'd listen. Tell Charles to go back to doing what he does best. That would be nothing, in case you're not sure."

"I'll do that, Cindy. Have you learned anything new about the murder?"

"I'm disappointed it took you this long to butt in. If it would be any of your business, which it is not, the answer is, "No.' "

"Have you heard how Laurie Fitzsimmons is doing?"

"That I can answer. The hospital kept her a couple of hours. She was Ubered home after being told to drink plenty of liquids, get plenty of rest. One of the Sheriff's Office detectives is going to talk to her this evening."

The Folly Beach Department of Public Safety was responsible for law enforcement, fire protection, even animal control on the island but, because of the size of the department, major crimes were investigated by the Charleston County Sheriff's Office.

"Which detective?" I asked, realizing how sad it was that this retired insurance company bureaucrat would even ask. Since moving to Folly, I'd, unfortunately, encountered several detectives and on a more positive note, had dated one.

"Callahan."

I'd met Michael Callahan a few years ago, when he was lead detective in the murder investigation of a stockbroker. A friend of mine was the prime suspect before Charles and I stumbled on information that helped prove our friend innocent.

"Good. So no suspects?"

Before hanging up she said, "One, Abraham Gant."

I TOOK part of the doctor's advice to Laurie and took a nap before I was to meet Barbara Deanelli for supper at Rita's. Barb owned Barb's Books, a used bookstore which occupied the space that formerly housed Landrum Gallery, a photo gallery owned by, and creatively named for, yours truly. Owning a gallery featuring my photos had been a lifelong dream. Once it became reality, it turned to a nightmare, where costs exceeded income by amounts approaching the national debt. I shuttered the door two years ago. The space morphed into Barb's Books.

Barbara moved to Folly from Pennsylvania after her attorney husband, now ex-husband, was arrested for bribing state officials. Barb, also an attorney, had no knowledge of her hubby's nefarious activities, yet was judged *guilty by wedding ring.* She moved to Folly to restart her life, and be near her half-brother, Dude Sloan. Dude and Barb were as alike as Viagra was to Venus, yet, over the last year, he had managed to find common ground to inch closer.

To secure a table on the patio, I was at the restaurant a half hour before I was to meet Barb. Rita's was on the corner of Center Street and East Arctic Avenue, a prime location on the island. It's across the street from the Folly Beach Fishing Pier, cattycorner from the Tides Hotel, and across Center Street from the iconic Sand Dollar Social Club.

I was sipping on the house Pinot Grigio when Barb appeared in the doorway. She was my height at five-foot-nine, at sixty-five, three years younger than I, way thinner, with short black hair. She was wearing one of her trademark red blouses. Tonight, she had on tan shorts. Her perfectly coordinated, and probably expensive, attire contrasted with my faded blue polo shirt and wrinkled gray shorts. She didn't seem to mind my scruffy clothes, as she kissed my forehead, pointed at my wineglass, and said, "Where's mine?"

Kim, the server, was quick to the table and said she

would get Barb's drink, "before you could say please." It arrived before Barb could tell me how busy the bookstore had been this afternoon. I would have been hard-pressed to tell anyone that the gallery had been that busy, ever.

Barb and I had been, as some of my friends called it, an item for a year or so. She had been slow to acclimate to the unhurried pace, and bohemian attitude, of many of the island's residents. She wouldn't admit it, yet I could see the mellowing in her hard-driving tendencies, and skepticism about the motives of others. Folly was becoming a part of her attitudes, and her behavior. It was a delight to see.

"Got a rumor to bounce off you," she said before looking around for Kim. "First, I have to get something to fill this empty stomach." She waved to Kim. "Blue crab and artichoke dip, please. I'm starved."

Kim nodded and headed to the kitchen. Barb could out eat a sumo wrestler, yet she was model-thin. I fluctuated between envying, and hating, her metabolism.

Barb told me about a customer who'd vacationed on Folly for the last nineteen years, staying at a different house, or condo, each year. I didn't see what was so unusual, but Barb couldn't imagine someone moving around that much. I wondered what that story had to do with the rumor she'd mentioned before she ordered the crab and artichoke dip.

"Did she tell you the rumor you mentioned?"

"No, I got off track. Now, for the rumor. This afternoon, one of my regulars told me a tale about a body the police found this morning at the old Coast Guard property. The customer didn't know who he was, or the circumstances about his demise."

Kim set the appetizer in front of Barb.

The story took a back seat to Barb's need to fill her stomach. Two bites later, she continued. "The customer didn't know anything about the body. Know what she did know?"

I was afraid that I did. "What?"

"An old geezer named Chris Landrum was the guy who called the police. Seems he was there with another geezer, Charles Fowler, plus a lady the customer didn't know." Barb pointed a fried tortilla chip at me. "It's funny that I'd hear something like that from a stranger rather than from the person sitting across from me."

Her hazel eyes showed a glimmer of what I hoped was humor.

"I didn't want to interrupt your day at the store. I figured I'd tell you tonight." I stuffed a chip in my mouth.

"So you thought a pleasant supper would be the perfect time to talk about a dead body and being out with another woman?"

"Well, umm, I—"

Barb laughed. "Kidding." Her smile faded. "Are you okay?"

I said that I was and proceeded to tell her about my fateful morning. Barb was a good listener, rare among my friends. She used her law school training, plus years of listening to clients, to grasp everything I said.

She chewed another chip, wiped her mouth with her napkin, before saying, "I've only been out there once. It didn't seem that large an area. Is it possible to be lost as long as Ms. Fitzsimmons said they were?"

"It's hard to understand, although she was a stranger to the area. That, combined with it being dark and stormy, could make it possible."

"You said they're in their late fifties."

I nodded.

"Did she seem in good health?"

"What do you mean?"

"Did she appear healthy? Any noticeable handicaps?"

"As far as I could tell she was okay. Why?"

"It's strange that a person in good health who, after being separated from her husband in a strange place, not knowing what was going on, would, after finding her way back to the car, fall asleep. I'd be worried sick, wouldn't be able to sleep."

"Putting it that way, yes, it's strange. What're you saying?"

Kim returned to ask if we were ready to order. Barb quickly said that she was and ordered the flounder. I was a sucker for Rita's hamburgers, so I ordered one.

"What am I saying?" Barb said as Kim moved toward the kitchen. "Suppose I'm a bookstore owner playing lawyer. Usually, when things don't make sense, there's more to it than meets the eye. If I was a defense attorney representing someone who'd been accused of murdering Mr. Fitzsimmons, someone other than his wife, that is, I'd be looking for suspects to throw at the jury. Ms. Fitzsimmons would be number one. She may be as innocent as a newborn, yet her unlikely story would go a long way toward creating reasonable doubt for my client."

I told her that the police would see the same things.

Barb said that she hoped so.

"Speaking of suspects," I said. "Do you know Abraham Gant?"

She nodded. "Cranky guy, insists on being called Captain?"

"So you know him?"

"Little, other than he stops in the store about once a week. Cranky, feisty fellow. Why?"

I told her about Gant's encounter with Charles.

"He's a history buff, spends most of his time browsing the history, or biography, sections. He bought a few books about the Civil War, one on slavery. He may not want anyone to literally dig up things from the past, yet he reads a lot about the past. That seems to be a form of dredging up history."

I seldom read anything other than the newspaper, and that's not often, so I didn't know how many books Barb had on the Civil War. She gave one of her endearing laughs when I asked.

"I've gotten several in, sold them as quickly to your friend William Hansel. He, like Gant, is a history buff."

"The Civil War?"

"He stops every Friday on his way home from the College of Charleston. He said he's a professor of Hospitality and Tourism, is deeply involved with Preserve the Past, the group with the goal of raising money to preserve the Morris Island Lighthouse. He always asks if I have anything new on the Civil War. William is one of my favorite customers. Others could learn a thing or two from him about politeness."

Our entrees arrived and the conversation, once again, took a back seat to eating. The sun was lowering itself behind the second story of St. James Gate up the street. While it was still in the upper eighties, we were in the shade, and comfortable. Neither Barb, nor I, returned to the topic of murder. We spent the next hour watching the steady stream of people walking along the nearby sidewalk, enjoying each other's company.

After leaving Rita's, we walked four blocks up Center Street, listened to the live music coming from Snapper Jack's upstairs outside bar, and the Crab Shack, before heading back down the street to her oceanfront condo. The day ended much more pleasantly than it had begun.

Chapter Five

Barb's questions about Laurie's actions stayed with me well into the next day. True, it was unusual that Laurie would find her way back to the car only to fall asleep while her husband's whereabouts was in question or if he was with her at all, yet did it rise to the level of making her a murder suspect? It wasn't my problem to solve, that was tasked to the capable hands of Detective Callahan from the Sheriff's Office and Chief LaMond of the Folly Beach Department of Public Safety.

Barb mentioning William Hansel reminded me that it had been several weeks since I'd talked to my friend. He was probably home from work so why not take the short, four-block walk to his house. I needed to lose a few pounds so, despite my aversion to exercise, the walk would do me good. Remember, I said to myself, it was simply me wanting to talk to an old friend, burning calories in the process, not anything to do with Anthony Fitzsimmons' death. Honest.

William's wife had died seventeen years ago, so he lived alone in a quaint, pre-Hurricane Hugo cottage on West Cooper Avenue, two blocks from Center Street. He greeted me at the door, like there was nothing unusual about me dropping by unexpectedly.

"Ah, my friend," he said in his deep bass voice as he waved me in. He was thin, roughly my height, and four years younger than I. "To what do I owe the pleasure of your company?"

"Did I catch you at a bad time?"

"On the contrary. I just arrived home and changed from professorial attire to my gardening wardrobe."

If you took my friend sentence-challenged Dude's average words spoken, add it to William's, then divide the sum by two, you would come close to a normal sentence. William was a wonderful person with the best intentions but, occasionally, it was hard to stay awake once he started talking.

His gardening *wardrobe* consisted of jeans with a hole in the left knee, a long-sleeved denim shirt, and tennis shoes.

"Don't let me keep you from whatever you were going to do."

"Nonsense. The precocious, invasive weeds in my garden will wait until later for me to eradicate them. Is it possible that you have an agenda for today's visit?"

See my point?

"No. It's been a while since we've talked, so I thought I'd stop by."

"I'm pleased that you did. Could I interest you in iced tea?"

"If it's no trouble."

William headed to the kitchen, and I sat on the flower-patterned, wingback sofa facing a similarly-patterned wing-back chair. I gazed around the room to, once again, be struck by the feminine touches. Cream-colored doilies topped each table with glass angel figurines strategically placed on the coffee table. I had never asked, nor had William offered, but I suspected the house looked exactly as it had before his wife's death.

William returned to hand me tea in a vintage, cut crystal drinking glass. He offered sugar from a white sugar bowl. I declined, and William took a seat in the wingback chair.

He took a sip then said, "Chris, I value our friendship immensely, and I thoroughly enjoy our conversations. I also feel I'm well enough acquainted with you to share what my intuition tells me."

"That would be?"

"You did not appear at my door simply to *shoot the bull*, as my students would say. If I am mistaken, I apologize. If not, perhaps you would like to share your reason."

"Did you hear about the body found at the Lighthouse Inlet Heritage Preserve?"

"I was paying for gas this morning at Circle K, where I heard the person in front of me say something to the clerk about a deceased gentleman. I, of course, am not prone to infuse myself in conversations, unless invited, so I didn't learn anything further. Perhaps that is the body to which you refer."

I gave him a brief rundown about the body, and the circumstances under which it was found.

"Oh, my heavens, that's tragic. I am not familiar with them. Do they live on our island?"

I told him what little I knew.

"What were they doing in the Preserve overnight? My understanding is that it closes at sunset, albeit it's a rule difficult to enforce since there are no barriers around the property."

"Hunting Civil War relics. They got caught in the rain, then darkness set in. There was a metal detector in the car."

William frowned. "Collecting artifacts from the Civil War, or any other previous visitors or inhabitants of Folly, is strictly prohibited in the Preserve."

"That might be the reason they were there late in the day. There would've been few, if any, others nearby."

William looked in his tea glass, at one of the glass angel

figurines on the table, then back at me. "It would appear someone else was there, unless Mrs. Fitzsimmons killed her spouse. Are you taking it upon yourself to investigate who might have terminated the gentleman's life?"

"Nothing like that. I found it interesting that she told me they were looking for relics. I'd heard you were a Civil War buff. I knew you had a strong interest in saving the lighthouse, but I wasn't aware of your interest in the Civil War."

"Quite frankly, I had little interest in the infamous conflict, until I learned about the gravesite of the nineteen soldiers from the 55th Massachusetts Volunteer Regiment found on the western end of Folly. The regiment was composed of free-born African Americans trained near Boston before heading south to fight the Confederacy.

"I perhaps had learned some about this during my secondary schooling, although if I had, it was long forgotten. I share a common race with those brave soldiers, so I took an interest in their plight before expanding that interest to the entire milieu and personality of those who fought in that war that divided our country."

"Barb told me you were a regular, always in search of books on the Civil War."

"That, and to gaze at the lovely bookstore proprietress." He winked at me and chuckled.

"That I can identify with."

"Are there specific questions that I might answer about the horrific time in our country's history?"

"Any ideas what the Fitzsimmons may've been looking for?"

"The gravesite I referred to is on the opposite end of the island from the Preserve although, from what I read, the eastern portion of Folly Island was important to the Federal army as a strategic base for the battle to take Fort Sumter. They constructed roads, primitive forts, living quarters, even an artillery battery out there." He shook his head. "I can't imagine how miserable it must have been surviving in the jungle-like foliage, the extreme summer heat, humidity, exposure to the ocean, lack of adequate shelter, and sanitation."

"What would've been left at those sites to pique the interest of the Fitzsimmons?"

"I would imagine little of monetary worth. Anything left would consist of trinkets of steel, or other metals, cookware, uniform buttons, tools. Remember a while back when Hurricane Matthew visited out humble island?"

I nodded.

"A man found a dozen or so rusted cannonballs on the beach near the Preserve. They were rendered harmless, yet would have been valuable to someone who collected, legally or illegally, ordnance from the Civil or other wars." William looked out the window, started to speak, then hesitated.

"What?"

"Chris, as I have shared with you on more than one occasion, I look askance at rumors and gossip. More than askance, I abhor them."

"But?"

"There've been rumors going around for decades that a British ship, or possibly more than one, sailed from Canada, carrying a cargo of guns and gold to the soldiers. One of those ships, the Constance Decimer, sank. It was later discovered near Charleston with no gold found. Old-timers swear that there were several other ships carrying gold.

"None of this has been proven, that's why I put it in the broad category of rumor. If the Fitzsimmons heard some of these stories, it's conceivable they thought the east end of the island could be the final resting place of the precious metal." William smiled. "Of course, there are an equal number of rumors that a hundred years before the Civil War, pirates sailed up and down the coast robbing merchant ships of gold, silver, other valuable commodities. Some of those pirate vessels were reputed to hide their bounty on the coastal islands, Folly included. Yet again, these are only rumors."

"I've heard stories about pirates."

"Does any of this help?"

"A little," I said. "One more question. Do you know Abraham Gant?"

"Captain Gant?"

"Yes."

"What about him?"

"Someone mentioned that he has strong opinions about relic hunters."

William smiled. "If by strong you mean that he thinks they all should be wiped off the face of the planet then, yes, he is opinionated. He'd attended a couple of Preserve the Past meetings. He seemed to be sitting on a cushion of nails, quick to comment on most anything. Once, when dear sweet Francene Gregory suggested that some excavating around the lighthouse might give the group a better idea of what it was like during the structure's earlier days, the Captain uttered something about sacrilege then stormed out of the room. He's not been back, nor has his presence been missed."

"Is that all you know about him?"

"Yes. It's more than I want to know."

We moved to a topic that was dearer to his heart, his garden, and ended on a lighter note. He told me not to be a stranger; I told him that he was welcome at my house.

I left the air-conditioned comfort and stepped into the heat that felt twenty degrees hotter than when I arrived. Add sweltering humidity, and I questioned the wisdom of walking instead of driving to William's. Instead of trekking all the way home, I stopped at the Surf Bar, located halfway between William's house and mine. An advantage of being retired was that most of the time I didn't have to be anywhere. I had a twinge of guilt about that freedom, as compared to most everyone else who had to work for a living. The twinge this time lasted until I grabbed a stool at the rustic bar and ordered a glass of wine. There were five other customers.

My appearance raised the average age of those present by roughly ten years. The popular bar catered to a younger crowd and, on most weekends, featured live music by groups I'd never heard of. From what I'd seen on how packed the bar was on weekend nights, I was in the minority when it came to knowing about the rock, funk, or whatever name captured today's popular music.

A couple of rock songs I did recognize filled the room, and the sound system was turned to a level more fitting to my elderly ears. That was fortunate since I heard my phone ring. Charles's name was on the screen.

He said, "Want to go with me tomorrow?"

"Hello, Charles."

I had been trying to get my friends to start conversations with radical words like, "hello," or even the shorter version, "hi." I'd been as successful as the pet collie I had as a child had been at climbing a telephone pole to catch a squirrel. Actually, the collie was more successful. It managed to leap three feet up the pole.

"Hi, Chris. So want to go?"

This wasn't the time to attempt a lesson in phone etiquette. "Where?"

"Gee, get with the program. To see Laurie."

"Silly me. Why didn't I know that?"

He ignored my comment. "Are you going, or not?"

"Charles, why are you, we, going to see Laurie?"

"To see if she's okay."

To paraphrase the Good Book, or possibly The Byrds, for everything there is a season. This is not the time, the season, to try to find out Charles's motivations. 'Tis the time to say, "Sure. What time?"

We agreed on a time, and I ordered a second glass of wine. I had a hunch that I'd need it.

<h1 style="text-align:center">Chapter Six</h1>

Charles told me that he'd used his "well-honed investigative skills" to learn that the Fitzsimmons's house was eight blocks off Center Street on East Erie Avenue. His well-honed investigation consisted of asking Officer Bishop where Laurie lived. With temperatures in the upper eighties, neither of us wanted to walk. He'd told me to pick him up at 10:00, so I was in his parking lot at 9:30 the next morning. On time, to him, meant thirty minutes before the rest of the world's interpretation.

He stepped out the door of his compact Sandbar Lane apartment, spotted my car, and looked at his wrist, where normal people wore a watch. Charles, never accused of being normal, didn't own a timepiece. He wore a long-sleeved, green and white, Bismarck State College T-shirt, tan shorts with a black ink stain on the pocket, and Adidas tennis shoes. His graying, ill-kept hair was sticking out the side of his canvas Tilley hat.

"Glad you made it on time," he said.

I smiled as he slid in the passenger seat and tossed his cane in the back seat. Two minutes later, we were driving east on Erie Avenue, while Charles looked for the address he'd been given. The houses on the left side of the road backed up to the marsh and the Folly River, giving them magnificent views of the sunset. The residences on the right didn't have nearly as good a view. Most were older with a sizable number built before Hurricane Hugo devastated the island in 1989.

Charles spotted the Fitzsimmons house a half block before East Erie made a sharp right turn to become Eighth Street East. The house was set back from the road on a lot surrounded by large live oaks, three palmetto trees, and straggly underbrush. My realtor friend, Bob Howard, would've described the house as "in need of some TLC." In non-realtor-speak, the word "dump" would have been appropriate. The one-story house had wood plank siding with several boards missing. The roof was covered with pine needles with mildew around the edges. Two sawhorses were near the front door with a four-by-eight-foot sheet of plywood spanning them. A red toolbox was shaded by the plywood, with an orange extension cord snaking from the side of the house to the sawhorses. A narrow gravel drive weaved around the trees. The MINI Cooper was in front of the house.

I was reluctant to go to the door, a reluctance not shared by my passenger. He grabbed his cane, bounded out of the car, then scampered to the door, as if he was late for a meeting with Laurie.

Well-worn front steps squeaked as we climbed them. The front door had been painted red, but had faded to pink; the brass-plated door knob had long lost its luster. Not seeing a doorbell, Charles knocked. There was no response, or sounds, coming from the house, so Charles glanced at me standing behind him, shrugged, and knocked again. Still nothing. He asked if we should leave when the door opened a couple of inches.

Laurie peeked out; her eyes darted from Charles to me.

"Can I help you?"

"Hey, Laurie," Charles said like we were lifelong friends. "It's Charles and Chris. Remember, we were at your car the other morning?"

The door opened a couple more inches. The sunlight shone on her. Her eyes were bloodshot, her hair uncombed. Our visit was not a good idea.

"You were there when they took me to the hospital," she said, more of a question than statement.

"We were," Charles said. "Chris and I were nearby, and wanted to stop to see if you were okay, or needed anything. Have a few minutes?"

"Oh, umm, I guess." She slowly opened the door the rest of the way while motioning us in.

She wore a bulky, quilted robe, and was barefoot. She pointed to the living room to the right. "Have a seat while I throw something on." She headed toward the back of the house.

We sat on a burgundy-colored, leather sofa that appeared new. A black leather La-Z-Boy recliner was at a right angle to the sofa facing a large, flat-screen television. Nothing else was in the room. The new furnishings contrasted with the cheap wood-panel walls.

The double-hung window was missing all but the casing and jamb. Heavy, transparent plastic covered the entire window and was duct taped to the casing. An exposed electrical junction box was in the center of the ceiling which, at one time, must've held a ceiling fan, or a light. In front of the sofa, there was an eight-by-ten-foot dark green indoor/outdoor carpet that I suspected was hiding flaws in the floor.

Laurie returned. She had run a brush through her hair, put on a starched, white blouse, a black and white striped skirt, plus a forced smile.

I smiled, hoping it seemed sincerer than hers. "We didn't mean to intrude. I know this is a terrible time. We wanted to offer our deepest sympathy for your loss."

"Thank you," she whispered then turned to Charles. "I'm sorry, tell me your names again."

We reintroduced ourselves as she moved to the La-Z-Boy. Her petite frame was swallowed by the chair.

"I apologize for my memory," she said. "It's coming back now. You were at the car when I woke up. Charles, I also remember meeting you on the street when we asked if you were from Jacksonville."

Charles smiled. "That's right." He looked around the room. "You have a nice house. I'm so sorry you have to start your retirement on such a tragic note."

I wondered what house Charles was talking about. I kept my mouth shut.

"Thank you. Were you still there when they… when they found Anthony?"

Charles lowered his gaze to the floor. "Sadly, we were. We are so sorry."

Laurie stared at the spot on the floor where Charles had been looking. "I didn't know, umm, they didn't tell me about his passing until a detective came to the hospital. He waited for the doctor to release me." Tears filled her eyes. "Oh, God, if only I'd gone with him when he tried to find his way out of the woods. Why did I tell him to go ahead, that I'd be okay where I was? He might still be with us if I'd gone."

She was no longer confused about if he'd been with her that night like she'd told the EMTs.

Charles leaned forward. "You don't know that, Laurie. If you'd gone, maybe you'd have been… well, not with us now."

"I don't know."

Charles continued to lean toward Laurie. "Any idea who could've done it?"

I was beginning to get a hint of another reason Charles wanted to visit the grieving widow.

"No. We hardly know anyone here. We're retired teachers. Who'd want to kill us?"

"Did Anthony have enemies?" Charles continued.

"None."

Her tears had stopped flowing, and she seemed more comfortable talking.

I said, "You told us you all were in the old Coast Guard property searching for Civil War relics. Find any?"

She eyes opened wide. "I said that?"

I nodded and wondered if I should mention that she'd told the EMTs that Anthony wasn't there.

"No, nothing."

"Did anyone here know you'd be there?"

She shook her head. "The person who shot poor Anthony must be a nutjob, an escapee from a mental hospital who was there for… for, I don't know why. Poor Anthony was only trying to find his way to the car. Why did it happen?"

I said, "They'll catch whoever did it."

She slammed her fist on the armrest. "Will that bring my husband back?"

"No," Charles whispered.

Laurie shook her head. "I'm being a horrible hostess. Can I get you something to drink?"

Charles smiled. "Water would be nice. Could I help?"

Laurie declined his offer then went to the kitchen. Charles leaned toward me. "It'll calm her. She needs someone to talk to."

She was quick to return with a plastic cup of water for each of us, even though I hadn't indicated that I wanted any. She went to the kitchen to get her cup then returned to the La-Z- Boy.

"How come you decided to retire to Folly?" Charles

asked, as if the previous discussion of finding the body had never happened.

Laurie took a sip then stared in the cup. "My grandfather grew up here in the '30s. My parents and I used to come up from Florida each summer for a week or two. I remember Granddaddy spinning tall tales about various characters who lived here. He'd go on about how he thought the police were no better than the crooks yet, if anything bad ever happened to someone, all the people, good or bad, would band together to help whoever was having problems."

"The police aren't corrupt now," Charles interjected. "People still hang together if anything bad happens. You could say that's why we're here. What was your grandfather's name again?"

She hadn't said the first time.

"Harnell Levi." She smiled. "He was a character. Know what else Granddaddy talked about all the time?"

Of course, we didn't. I said, "What?"

"Buried relics. Civil War valuables. He said that he knew there was a lot of it. He just hadn't had time to look. I took it all with a grain of salt. Figured, if it was here, then someone would've found it by now. When I told Anthony about Granddaddy's stories, he took them to heart, started doing research." She stopped, took a sip of water, stared at the plastic covering the window. "If I hadn't told him those stories, he'd be with me today, tomorrow, and…"

"Again, Laurie, we're so sorry," I said. "We won't take more of your time. Is there someone we can call to be with you? Relatives?"

"Thank you, no. Anthony's only living relatives are distant cousins. They live in Miami. He never had contact with them. I doubt they'll come to his funeral. Mine are in Seattle. We're not close. Two friends are coming up from Jacksonville tomorrow. They're going to stay a few days to help with funeral arrangements."

"Good," Charles said. "Let me give you my number. Please call if there's anything you need or if Chris and I can help."

She took the number then walked us to the door. "Thanks again for stopping by. Sorry I wasn't good company."

The inside of the car felt like we were in an oven with the heat turned to 350 degrees. I switched the air conditioner to high and turned to Charles.

"What do you think?" I asked.

"What do I think about what? The poor lady lost her husband. Now, she's stranded on an island where she doesn't know anyone. She's a mess. That's what I think."

"I agree, although did you catch what she said about why they were separated the night Anthony was killed?"

"Sure. She said she told him to try to find his way back to the car, that she'd be okay where she was."

"Yes, that's what she said today. Remember what she told us when we found her at her car?"

Charles rubbed his three-day old whiskers. "Sure. Umm, maybe."

"She said Anthony told her to stay where she was. He'd find the trail to the car. She then told him they had to stick together."

"Now that you mention it, yeah. Two different stories?"

I nodded. "She could've been confused that night. The rain, being lost, sleeping in the car, being confronted by two men she didn't know."

"We need to tell Cindy?"

"I don't know."

"I do," Charles grabbed my phone off the console and handed it to me.

The chief's voicemail kicked in after five rings. Charles rolled his eyes, like Cindy had the nerve not to take such an important call. I left her a message to call when she had a chance.

Charles looked over at the house. "I'll grant you that Laurie could've been confused about her stories, or she's having trouble keeping her story straight. Remember, when she was talking to the EMTs she was confused about if Anthony was even there. Confusion would be simple, if it's all a lie."

<h1 style="text-align:center">Chapter Seven</h1>

I began the next day with a cinnamon Danish from my next-door neighbor, Bert's Market. My culinary skills exceeded a butterfly's ability to bake a cherry pie, but not by much. If it wasn't for Bert's, the island's only grocery, and the Lost Dog Cafe, I would've shriveled up and blown away. The humidity was low, the temperature cooler than it had been for a couple of weeks, so I took the Danish, a cup of complimentary coffee, then walked two blocks to the Folly Beach Fishing Pier.

After walking to the far end of the thousand-foot long structure, I stopped to observe five surfers sitting on their boards, waiting for a wave, and two men on paddleboards creating their own excitement by paddling through the calm surf. Chief LaMond hadn't returned my call, so I was tempted to call her until I realized that the inconsistencies in Laurie's stories were minor, easily explained. I didn't want to be an alarmist, or worse, a Charles. I also replayed the rest of the conversation with Laurie, but nothing else struck me as important.

Laurie saying that she and her family weren't close

reminded me of what Theo had confided about his son. I also remembered Charles interrupting his story. Did Theo want to tell me more, or what was important about a phone call that Sal mentioned? One way to find out. I didn't know him as well as I knew William, so I wasn't comfortable showing up at his door unannounced.

Instead of calling Cindy, I punched Theo's number in the phone. I told him I felt bad that our conversation at the Dog had been interrupted and wondered if he wanted to share more. He said he would, then hesitated before saying it really wasn't anything to burden me with. That was all it took. I asked if he wanted to meet for lunch. He said he would but had promised to take Sal to the mall for shoes. I told him I was nearby and could come to his house. He hesitated before saying okay.

When Theo opened the door I had to bite my tongue not to laugh. He was wearing red, white, and blue striped jogging shorts, well, they'd be called jogging shorts on anyone other than Theo. On him, shuffling shorts came to mind. He also wore a tank-top T-shirt, or as trivia-collecting Charles had informed me was called an A-shirt, the *A* standing for athletic. It had a paint stain on the side. Rounding out his attire were his knee-length, black, support socks.

Theo waved me in, then ushered me to the great room where floor to ceiling windows provided a panoramic view of the marsh and the Folly River. I'd been in the room several times, was always impressed with the high-end, aka expensive, furnishings, with original oil paintings on three walls. Theo had founded a window-replacement company where he discovered a gas he sandwiched between two panes of glass, helping keep cold air in when it's hot outside, warm air in during the winter. He'd tried to explain the chemistry to me, although all I understood was that he'd sold the company for several million dollars.

"Where's Sal?" I asked after I took a seat on the over-sized, latte-colored leather sofa.

Theo pointed toward the ceiling. "Still asleep. He seldom stirs before noon. After years performing late nights in comedy clubs, his circadian rhythm pattern is asunder. When we saw you at the Dog, I had to wake him up to go with me."

In non-technical talk, I supposed that meant that Sal slept late. "You were used to living alone. How are things working out with him?"

"It's been an adjustment. He stays out of my way, spends most of his time in his room. After sleeping in hotel rooms for decades, he says he's comfortable in the small space. That's fine with me. How about coffee?"

I said it sounded good then followed him to the kitchen that looked like it was taken from the pages of *Charleston Living Magazine*.

"At the Dog, you were talking about your son. Sal mentioned a call, but you didn't get to tell me about it."

I stopped hoping he'd pick up on the conversation. He handed me the drink, then we returned to the great room.

"I told you I wasn't a good dad. His mom was great, encouraged him in school. He had straight A's in high school. I wanted him to follow in my footsteps and go into engineering, maybe law school. In hindsight, it was a mistake. We had a major blowout over it. He rebelled, left home the week he finished high school. Chris, I shouldn't have pushed."

Theo looked at the floor and shook his head.

"What happened?"

"He moved to Southern California, taking a series of low-paying restaurant jobs. The only reason I know is because he kept in contact with his mother. Eunice told me that he worked his way up to be a cook at better restaurants. We didn't hear anything for five years, then we got a note saying he and another guy were opening a fish restaurant, said he was happier than he'd ever been." He shook his head like he was shaking out memories. "Did I tell you he got married?"

"You'd mentioned it before Charles interrupted."

"Sure you want to hear this?"

I said that I did.

"The next time I heard from him was when we got the wedding invitation, got it after the wedding. When Eunice died, I found the name of his restaurant in one of the letters he'd sent her. I called. It was strange talking to Teddy after all those years. You know what he told me?"

I shook my head.

"It was busy season. He couldn't get away to come to the funeral. He sent a big arrangement of flowers to the funeral home. Chris, I hate to admit it, but I wanted to hurl them in the trash." Theo twisted the corner of a throw pillow in his lap.

"Theo, you don't have to tell me unless you want to. You said he died a year or so ago. What happened?"

Theo stared out the window. A walking pier extended from the back of the house, across a narrow strip of marsh, to the edge of the river.

"I was out at the end of the pier, this time of day, in fact. The phone rang. A female voice with an accent, possibly Caribbean, asked if I was Theodore Stoll, father of Theodore Jr. I told her I was and asked who she was. Her name was Grace, said she was my son's wife. He was dead." He stared at the pillow in his hands. "I was stunned."

"What happened?"

"Grace, umm, Teddy's wife, said he was on his motorcycle on the way to work when a car swerved to avoid hitting a dog. It struck Teddy's front wheel. The motorcycle flipped, Teddy was thrown over the handlebars, his head hit the raised curb. He wasn't wearing a helmet. Killed instantly."

"I'm sorry."

He shook his head. "It took me a few minutes to grasp what she'd said. Finally, I asked about funeral arrangements while mentally trying to figure out how I could get there. I needn't have. The woman said he'd been cremated. She and Teddy's friends spread his ashes in the Pacific." Theo threw the pillow across the room. "My son didn't want me around when he was alive. Didn't want me there in death."

I repeated how sorry I was.

After a long pause, Theo said, "You asked about the call. Grace said she was on the way to Charleston. She wants to meet me. Chris, I don't know one iota about the woman." He held his arms out, palms up. "Why would she want to meet me? Why would I want to meet her?"

"Don't suppose you'll know until you meet her. When's she getting here?"

"Two days." He stared out the window before turning back to me. "Will you go with me?"

***

CHIEF LAMOND RETURNED my call that evening and apologized for taking so long, something about a two-day training session in Charleston for local police chiefs. I asked how the sessions were. She unceremoniously said that she had learned more painting her toenails while daydreaming about Brad Pitt. She added the meals were better than Larry could fix on his outdoor grill. That meant the meals were nothing to write a culinary magazine about since Larry was almost as good a "chef" as I was. I told her that I was sorry, she added a couple of her native East Tennessee profanities, then added that her officers benefitted by her being at the meetings instead of pestering them. She ran out of steam griping about the training session then finally asked why I'd called.

"Couple of reasons. I was curious if you've learned anything else about Anthony Fitzsimmons's death, or—"

"I knew it," she interrupted. "Larry owes me a steak dinner at Halls Chophouse. Halleluiah!"

Halls was one of the top restaurants in Charleston.

"Let me guess. He bet I wouldn't call to ask about the death?"

"Yep, the boy will never learn. That's after I told him you already left the message."

"Congratulations. So have you learned anything?"

"Hang on a second. Let me get the taste of that scrumptious filet mignon out of my mouth before I scream at you for sticking your cute little nose in police business, business that's none of your business."

"Cindy, I'm not butting in. Charles and I found Laurie. I was curious."

"Butting in, nosy, curious, inquisitive, all the same. You, and I suppose your sidekick, are for what, the seventieth time, playing detective, assuming the highly-trained police professionals couldn't find their noses during allergy season."

I choked back a chuckle. "So anything new?"

Cindy uttered a loud sigh, followed by, "Autopsy results indicate time of death was Sunday between midnight and 4:00 a.m. Cause of death didn't need an autopsy to determine. A bullet hole in the head ruled out prostate cancer. Even us dumb cops got that right." She hesitated and said, "This is the point where you're supposed to say, 'Now, chief, that's not true. I have faith that you and the other cops will figure it out. I will stay out of your way to let you do your job.' "

"Did you learn anything else?"

Another sigh. "Not really. The rain washed away any prints. The shot was from close range. A couple of the nearby houses were occupied, everyone claimed that they were asleep after midnight, didn't hear, or see, anything. None of them even said they saw the glow-in-the-dark, orange car parked near their house. A lot of lightning was nearby so, if anyone heard the gunshot, it could've been mistaken for thunder. That's about it. Don't worry. I'm sitting here at my expensive police-chief desk waiting for the damn killer to walk in to confess. To think, you don't believe us cops know what we're doing."

"Cindy, I know you know what—"

"Chris, no need to say it. I'm frustrated, letting off steam. We have nothing. It feels like crap. You called for two reasons."

I could almost hear her shout *butting in* before I told her the second reason. "Charles and I went to see Laurie Fitzsimmons yesterday. She said—"

"That's not butting in?" the chief shouted as I moved the phone away from my ear.

"Charles thought—"

"That's two damn words that should never be neighbors."

"We thought since Laurie told him that she and her husband were new to Folly that they might not know many people here. We wanted to see if she needed anything."

"Chris, that's about the biggest pile of moose manure I've heard this year and, believe me, I've heard piles of it."

It was my turn to sigh. "Chief, do you want to hear what we learned or want to continue your harangue?"

"What did you and your social worker friend learn when you went to help the damsel in distress?"

"When we found her that morning, she said Anthony told her to stay where she was. He'd find the trail to the car. She told him that they had to stick together."

"So?"

"When we met yesterday, she said that she told Anthony to try to find his way back to the car, that she'd be okay where she was. Don't you think those are significant differences?"

"Chris, they're different but, under the circumstances, doesn't it make sense that she could've been confused, especially when you first met her? Her husband was missing. She'd been asleep. It'd been storming. She was in a strange place. And, you and Charles appeared out of nowhere. If I ran into someone looking like Charles under those circumstances, he'd scare the, well, you know what, out of me."

"You're right, of course."

"But you don't believe it?"

"Cindy, my gut tells me it's more than confusion."

"Is your theory she killed him?"

"Okay, I'm butting in a little. If I was a detective, I wouldn't rule it out."

"You do realize you're not a detective."

"Of course not, chief."

"Right. What do you and your fake private eye friend think her motive was?"

"No idea."

"If she was asleep, had been out there all night, what did she do with the gun?"

"No idea."

"That helps. I don't know how I'd keep Folly safe without such incredible citizen support."

Cindy was good at passing out grief and sarcasm. She was also an exceptional law enforcement official. From numerous discussions over the years, I knew that she'd taken me seriously. Even if she didn't acknowledge it, she'd follow up on whatever I shared. She was a good cop, an even better friend.

"Cindy, what's going to happen next?"

"No idea."

Chapter Eight

I ran into Dude Sloan the next morning in front of Planet Follywood. After a brief discussion, the only kind possible with Dude; I agreed to have lunch with him at Loggerhead's. We'd often talked but seldom broke bread together, so I was looking forward to the meal, sitting outside on a beautiful summer afternoon, while sharing partial sentences with the surf shop owner.

I was seated on the deck at a table near the railing overlooking the Oceanfront Villas, an expansive four-story, oceanfront, condo complex, when Dude appeared at the top of the steps. The aging surfer was five years younger than I, three inches shorter, a ton of pounds lighter. His face looked like a cross between Arlo Guthrie and Willie Nelson. He wore one of his many florescent tie-dyed T-shirts with a peace symbol dominating the front, along with one of his many confused looks on his face. He spotted me then weaved his way around several tables. The patio was nearly full, with two servers working at Mach speed to keep up.

Dude looked at me then at his watch. "Christer be early."

It was a malady I'd caught from Charles.

I pointed to a chair on the opposite side of the table. "I wanted to make sure we got a table."

Dude looked around at the crowded seating area. "It worked."

Tiffany, a server who'd waited on me several times, always with a friendly smile, and a kind comment, was quick to the table and asked Dude if he wanted something to drink.

He looked at the glass of white wine in front of me. He said, "Martini, *tres* green fruitees. stuck with wood." He grinned at Tiffany. "Please."

Tiffany looked at me, still with the smile on her face, and shrugged.

"Gin martini with three olives," I said.

Dudespeak often required a translator, and like gin martinis, was an acquired taste. Tiffany seemed satisfied as she headed to the outdoor bar.

"Be snugglin' with fractional sis?"

Since I'd started dating Barb, Dude's half-sister, a little over a year ago, he'd gone out of his way to have more contact with me. We talked a couple of times a week at the Dog, and he and Pluto, his Australian Terrier, had stopped by the house a few times. He and Barb had never been close; their professional lives had little in common until she moved to Folly. Their current common interest was they both owned retail stores, although the surf shop had been wildly successful for years while Barb's Books was new, struggling to gain a profitable customer base. They'd become closer a year ago when a tragic event touched each of them. They're now protective of each other.

"We had supper the other night."

"*Donde?*"

As If Dudespeak wasn't hard enough to understand, he's been throwing in Spanish. I'd asked if he was learning Spanish. He'd responded with, "*Un poco,*" which I'd remembered from high school Spanish as meaning "a little." I suspected that *donde* meant "where," so I told him Rita's.

Tiffany returned with Dude's martini. He took a sip, gave a thumb's up, and said, "Cool."

Brief, but English. We told Tiffany to give us a few minutes and we'd order. There were a couple of groups waiting for tables, several people seated appeared to be ready to leave, so I didn't feel rushed. We were in the shade of a large umbrella and I was in no hurry to leave the deck. I asked about business. He threw together a handful of words that meant business was good. He asked if I'd heard about the murder, if so, was I helping the police catch the killer. I told him yes and no. He didn't seem to believe me, so I changed the subject to the weather.

I hadn't paid attention, but the table beside us had opened. The hostess was seating three people, one being Laurie Fitzsimmons. She wore a mid-thigh length black skirt, and a dark gray blouse. She looked much better than when Charles and I visited her house. She sat on the opposite side of the man and woman, a couple about Laurie's age. The man was overweight, mostly bald, average height. His companion was slightly taller than the man, not heavy, not thin with no memorable features.

Laurie glanced at us and looked surprised. "Oh, hi, umm ..."

"Chris," I said.

"Chris, of course." She smiled. "It's good to see you."

Her forced smile, added to the way she held her arms across her chest, didn't seem to share her words.

Dude, not to be left out, said, "I be Dude, bud of Christer. Who be you?"

This was Laurie's first exposure to Dude, so she probably wouldn't know how to respond. I stepped in, figuratively, and introduced Laurie to my surfer friend. Laurie told us her friends were Dean and Gail Clark.

I remembered that she'd said that a couple from Jacksonville was coming to be with her for a few days.

"Dean, Gail," I said, nodding their direction. "Nice to meet you. Are you from Jacksonville?"

Dean started to answer, when Gail interrupted, "Yes, we're here to help Laurie get through the next few days."

I said, "Sorry you're here under such terrible circumstances." Our tables were three feet apart. With the crowd noises, it was difficult hearing, plus I felt like I was intruding on their private time. "I'll let you get to your meal."

Laurie gave a sincerer smile. "Good seeing you again."

Dude, seeming oblivious to my desire to let them have their privacy, said, "Slip slide tables together. You be joining us."

Laurie looked at our table. "Thank you, Dude, but—"

Gail interrupted, "Great idea. It'd be nice for us to get to know Laurie's friends."

Friends wouldn't be how I'd describe our relationship since I'd only seen Laurie twice. She'd known Dude for as long as it takes to smack a mosquito that just bit my arm. Before I could say, "Thanks, but no thanks," Gail was *slip sliding* their table our way. Tiffany returned to our combined tables to see if Dude and I were ready to order, and if Laurie, Gail, and Dean wanted drinks. I said Dude and I would wait a little longer. Gail, without input from Laurie, or Dean, ordered a bottle of white wine.

Gail turned to me. "Laurie wanted to sit in her house and order pizza. I told her she needed to get out, get fresh air, get her mind off Anthony's death."

Laurie looked at the menu, ignoring what was being said.

Dude waved his hand toward Dean. "Be from gator state?"

Had he missed Gail's earlier answer to the same question?

"Jacksonville," Gail said, answering for Dean. "We've

been friends with Laurie and Anthony for years. Neither of us have kids. We have lots in common. Played cards a couple of times a month. Dean and Anthony are, sorry, were history buffs. The second Laurie called to tell us what happened, I said we'd be up to stay through the funeral. I don't work so I had the time." She hesitated, nodded toward Dean. "My husband taught for five years with Laurie and Anthony, before taking over his dad's tire business."

I wondered if Dean was permitted to speak when he was at work. I'd wager it was rare at home.

Dude bobbed his head. "Cool."

Tiffany returned with the bottle of wine and set glasses in front of the newcomers. "Ready to order?"

Gail said not yet, again, without consulting her tablemates.

Dean took advantage of the break in discussion. He turned to me. "Have you known Anthony and Laurie since they moved here?"

"Not really," I said. "I met Laurie the day Anthony died."

"Oh," said Gail. "I thought you, oh well, never mind. Did she tell you Dean and I were supposed to be here that day? We were going relic hunting with them, but Dean had to go to a tire retailers' meeting in Tallahassee." She put her hand on Laurie's hand. "If we'd been here, Anthony may still be with us. Laurie, I'm so sorry."

Dude leaned toward Dean. "Me found injun head penny once. Be relic?"

Dean leaned closer to Dude. "Well, it could—"

"By the strict definition of relic, yes," Gail interrupted. "Our interest is more in line with artifacts from the Civil War. Anthony had been telling us about the history of Folly Beach during that war. Laurie's grandfather told her stories years ago. We were excited about joining our friends. Again Laurie, sorry we couldn't be here."

"You're not as sorry as I am," Laurie said. "Let's order. I'm certain Chris and Dude aren't interested."

Gail waved Tiffany to the table, and each of them ordered. I was pleased Gail didn't order for everyone. Tiffany looked at me, I nodded for Dude to say if he was ready. He and I ordered, while Laurie started talking to Gail and Dean about funeral arrangements. I heard Gail tell Laurie that Dean had to get back to the store in the morning, but she would be staying until after the funeral. Dean would return for the funeral then take Gail home the following day.

We ate mostly in silence. Our tables were touching, although our conversations, however brief, remained apart. Dude was determined to tell me about four vacationers from Maine who were in the surf shop where they got in an argument about who was the best surfer. It seems none of them had ever been on a surfboard. They were arguing based on how athletic they were on the golf course. Dude thought it was hilarious; I thought it was mildly amusing.

Dude and I finished before Laurie, Dean, and Gail, so we waved bye. I told them it was nice meeting them and again expressed condolences to Laurie.

On our way down the steps, Dude said, "Gail chick be big bundle of bull."

Not necessarily articulate, yet one-hundred percent accurate.

Chapter Nine

The next morning, low-hanging clouds and light rain blanketed the area, so I was surprised to hear a knock on the door a little after eight. I was even more surprised to see Charles standing on the screened-in front porch. He wore a purple, long-sleeve, T-shirt with Alcorn State University in gold, block letters on the front, a canvas Tilley hat with water dripping off the brim and carrying a bag from Bert's Market. His classic 1961 Schwinn bicycle leaned against the front of the house. I wondered why he'd peddled over rather than driving. I didn't ask.

He pushed his way past me on his way to the kitchen. "You're a wimp, so I figured you wouldn't come out to meet me for breakfast. You're a pitiful excuse for a cook, so I figured you wouldn't have anything here to eat. I picked up donuts next door, figured we could eat in your never-used kitchen."

What I figured was that it was too late to say, "Good morning, Charles. How are you today? What brings you out on such a lousy morning?"

I may be a pitiful excuse as a cook, if that good, but I

was a wiz at fixing coffee in a Mr. Coffee machine. Charles found one of my three clean mugs, poured a cup, plopped down on a kitchen chair, and tore open the box of prepackaged donuts. He seldom appeared at my door without an agenda. If I asked what it was, he'd respond by saying something like, "Couldn't I want to see a friend?" I wasn't ready to play that game, so I sipped my drink waiting for the agenda to unfold. It didn't take long.

"I was thinking," he said then took a bite of donut.

"Would you like to share what?"

He pointed the mug at me. "Harnell Levi."

It took me a couple of seconds to remember who that was. "Laurie Fitzsimmons's grandfather."

Charles shrugged. "You know any other Harnell Levis?"

"I didn't know the one who was Laurie's grandfather. What about him?"

"The geezer died six or seven years ago. I knew him from when I did some cleaning at the Sandbar Restaurant."

The Sandbar Restaurant had been behind Charles's apartment building, and was one of Folly's most popular eating spots for ages but has been closed a few years. It'd overlooked the Folly River, and had a memorable view of sunset.

"Why didn't you tell Laurie you knew him?"

Charles started on his second donut, took a sip of his drink, then said, "Teddy Roosevelt said, 'If you could kick a person in the pants responsible for most of your trouble, you wouldn't sit for a month.' That was old man Levi. Figured if I couldn't say anything good about her gramps, I'd better keep my mouth shut."

"Tell me about him."

"The old coot was short, doubt more than five one, portly, if he could smile, I never saw it. The old man was plum cranky. He was also paranoid, always looking around like a KGB agent was hiding around every corner. I never saw him when he wasn't mumbling something, or whispering."

"What about?"

"Best I could decipher, he'd found some Civil War arti-facts. Told me once he'd been a prospector in the old west. It didn't make a lick of sense since the old west was long gone before he could've been there. Some of his mumble-talk was about relics and other stuff, said he knew where it was."

"Other stuff, like what?"

"He never said. Probably wasn't frankincense, or myrrh. I'd lean toward silver, or gold."

"You never heard him say silver or gold."

"Nope. He was one weird dude."

"Laurie seemed to have been close to him. If he talked to you about *relics and other stuff,* he probably shared more with his granddaughter. You think that's why they were hunting relics?"

"Yep."

"And he claimed to know where some were."

"Yep."

"It's possible that they either found something of value, or had a good idea where to look, then someone else found out about it. That could've been motive for killing Anthony."

"Yep."

I hoped that Charles would stop imitating Dude and add something more to the discussion. "If that's true, who would've known? Laurie and Anthony hadn't been here long. If they truly had an idea where to find buried relics, or treasure, why would they tell anyone?"

"Therein lies the mystery."

After three more donuts, two more cups of coffee, Charles noticed the rain had stopped. He decided that he needed to get to his apartment before the weather turned worse. On his way out, he said I should meet with Chief

LaMond to tell her what he'd learned from Harnell Levi. I asked why he didn't want to meet with her. He said that she would believe me before believing him. I said I'd think about it.

The phone rang before I could give it more thought. Theo called to remind me that I'd agreed to go with him when he met with his daughter-in-law. I told him that I remembered.

"Good," he said. "She just called, said she's in Charleston, and asked if I could visit today. Are you available?"

Even if I didn't want to go, I didn't have enough time to think up a reason why I couldn't. Besides, I was curious about his daughter-in-law.

"Sure."

"Great. I'll pick you up at noon."

THEO WASN'T as time obsessed as Charles, so it was five after twelve when his late-model, black Mercedes pulled in the drive. Knowing that Theo walked at turtle speed, I'd been watching, so I could meet him at the car before he got out. He thanked me for going three times before we'd made the short trip off island, twice more on the half-hour ride to the hotel.

Theo's daughter-in-law was staying at a Comfort Inn near downtown Charleston. Theo was to call her cell once he was at the hotel. He was slower than usual as we walked from the car to the lobby of the attractive, seven-story building. It took him a couple of minutes to catch his breath after he flopped down on a sofa in the lobby. He was breathing heavily as he stared at his phone.

"Are you okay?" I asked.

"Scared. Chris, I don't know if I can do this."

"It'll be fine. Besides, you're in better shape than she is.

Imagine how she must feel meeting her late husband's father."

Theo smiled. "Good point." He tapped her number in his phone.

She was quick to answer. Theo said he was in the lobby but, before he could say anything else, she must've said she'd be down.

"She sounded excited," Theo said as he stood and walked to the large windows overlooking the parking lot. When the elevator door opened, Theo jerked around to look in its direction. Two men dressed in seersucker suits, and engrossed in a conversation, emerged. Theo sighed as he returned to the sofa.

The elevator door opened again, a dark-skinned woman stepped into the lobby. She was short, roughly five-foot-two, trim, in her early-fifties, with a short-cropped Afro haircut. She had on a black blouse, dark-gray Capri pants, and flip-flops. We stood and looked her way.

Theo whispered, "Think that's her?"

The woman saw us standing fifteen feet away, smiled, then headed over. Theo's question was answered.

She stopped in front of us, nodded, and said, "Gentlemen, would one of you happen to be Theo Stoll?"

Theo said that he was.

The woman's smile increased; she held out her arms and wrapped them around his waist. He got a startled look on his face, which, fortunately, the hugger couldn't see.

"Then, fine, sir, I am honored to say that I am Grace, your daughter-in-law."

Her Caribbean accent, combined with an endearing smile, made her both pleasant to look at and listen to. She unhooked her arms from Theo's waist and took a step back. Theo struggled with what to say, so I stepped forward, told her who I was, adding that I was Theo's friend. The center of the lobby wasn't the best place to continue our conversation, so I asked if she was thirsty.

"A drink would be pleasant," she said as she continued to smile. Her teeth were glowing white, and flawless.

Theo didn't respond.

I ushered them to the breakfast area then to a booth along the wall as far as possible from three guests huddled around a laptop. Large photos of scenic spots in downtown Charleston adorned the walls. I went to get drinks from a refrigerator in the corner of the room. Theo had found his voice by the time I returned.

"How was your trip?" he asked.

She smiled. "Long, exhausting. I'm pleased to finally have reached my destination after four days on the road. Thank you for meeting me. I know this must be awkward."

Theo smiled for the first time. "True for you as well."

Grace took a sip of orange juice. "Yes. I don't know how to say this other than to say, I'm so sorry for the death of your son."

Theo shook his head but didn't respond.

I said, "Grace, I'm sorry for your loss."

"Thank you. It was devastating."

Theo's head jerked up, he leaned closer to his daughter-in-law. "You must know I had little contact with him. I didn't know he was getting married until I got the wedding invitation. I only knew your name because it was on the invitation I received days after the event." He took a deep breath. "Grace, I don't want to sound insensitive." He took another breath. "Why did you come all the way across the country? What do you want?"

I was startled by Theo's stinging words to someone whom he'd just met moments earlier. Grace jerked back like Theo had slapped her.

The conversation went downhill from there.

"Mr. Stoll, I'm terribly troubled that I've offended you. I was aware of your lack of closeness with Teddy, but—"

"Lack of closeness," Theo shot back. "I hear nothing from him in years. He couldn't find time to attend his mother's funeral. Then, he gets married to someone I'd never heard of. Now, you appear out of nowhere, smiling like everything's hunky-dory." He sighed. "Like we're one big happy family."

Grace's shoulders appeared to fold inward; she sank down in her seat; a tear appeared in the corner of her eye. I was shocked. I'd never seen Theo this agitated. He glared at her while shaking his head.

"Grace," I said, "I hope you understand that hearing from you and now your arrival has thrown Theo's world upside down. Perhaps you would like to share with him, with us, what inspired you to come from L.A. Did you say you were on the road for four days? That had to be a grueling trip."

Theo continued to glare while remaining silent.

His daughter-in-law looked at him, then turned to me. "Yes, Mr. Landrum. Last night was the first night I stayed in a hotel since leaving California."

"Where'd you stay on the road?"

"I have a sleeping bag in the food truck. It wasn't horrible; rough on the back." She tried to smile. It fell short.

I wondered if that meant she didn't have any money. It was best not to ask. "Do you have family on the East Coast?"

"Just…" she nodded toward Theo.

Theo's glare softened, although not much. He tapped his finger on the table. "Where's your family?"

"I grew up in Topeka, Kansas. Mom was from there. Dad was from a tiny, tiny town you've never heard of near Kingston, Jamaica. My parents are no longer with us. It is my understanding that you are Teddy's only living family."

Theo shook his head. "Teddy has an uncle. My brother, Salvadore, lives with me."

"Oh, I am sorry. Teddy didn't mention him."

Theo tapped his fingers harder on the table. "Of course, he didn't. Probably didn't remember him. He would've had to stay in contact with his family to know about such things."

Grace lowered her head. She didn't need more grief from Theo, so I moved the conversation to more positive topics. "Charleston is a beautiful city. How long will you will be visiting?"

She looked at Theo. In a low, singsong voice said, "I'm moving here."

"For good," Theo said.

"Mr. Stoll, I couldn't stay in California. Our restaurant, the business that Teddy and I built from scratch, the business we had another partner in before he stole most of our profits before absconding, went under. Teddy died there. I have nothing but bad memories from California. I tried, but couldn't remain there. I know no one in Kansas who is still living. I never got to know any of Dad's relatives in Jamaica. Truth be told, I've never been to Jamaica." She hesitated then continued. "I thought I could know at least one person here and open my food truck. Perhaps it was a mistake to think that."

Theo waved his arm around the room. "Will you stay here?"

"I wish. This is a lovely place. The bed felt so good last evening. My resources are limited, so I will be staying in my truck until I've saved enough to find an apartment. Thank you for asking."

In the Pollyanna world in which Charles resides, the one I occasionally visit, this would be where Theo offers Grace a room at his house which is ten times larger than he needs. Even though Sal is there, he has extra bedrooms collecting dust. I know him to be a kind, compassionate, trusting soul, regardless of today's behavior.

Theo nodded to Grace. "You've spent several nights in it, so I suppose it's comfortable. With your experience, you should be able to find business for your food truck."

She smiled, something I wouldn't have been able to

muster under similar circumstances. "That's what I'm counting on. Do you know if they grant food trucks permission to set-up on the island where you live?"

There are a couple of food trucks that have seasonal locations on Folly, although I didn't know anything about the requirements for operating one. I also realized I had no idea what Grace sold out of her truck.

"Grace, there've been a couple. What type of food do you sell?"

"We, umm, I've tried several things. It's been hit or miss. Hamburgers didn't do as well as anticipated. Sub sandwiches fell flat. Our niche seems to be hot dogs. Not just run of the mill mustard, or ketchup on hot dogs. I sell fifteen combinations, ranging from the traditional Chicago-style dog, to one I call the 'everything but the kitchen sink dog.' "

She looked at her watch. "You must be terribly busy, so I don't want to keep you. Besides, the hotel privileged me with a late check-out time, so I need to start moving out. Mr. Stoll, umm, Mr. Landrum, it was a true honor to meet you. I'm sorry it had to be under such unpleasant circumstances."

She stood and reached to shake Theo's hand.

He offered it to her, although it was as enthusiastic as if he would reach to shake a polar bear's paw.

She gave it a brief shake then reached for my hand. I felt terrible for her, yet I didn't know what to do. We shook, then I gave her a quick hug, before she headed to the bank of elevators.

We were in the car ten minutes before Theo said anything other than agreeing with me about the heavy traffic. I wanted to ask why he was so cold, no, make that rude, yet I knew he'd talk when he was ready.

We were five miles from Folly when he said, "I was shocked she's black. I was stunned with the realization I not only had no idea who she was, I didn't have a clue who my son was, or who he'd become. She drove all the way across the country to… to what? What does she want from me? What on God's green earth should I have said to a total stranger?"

"Theo, you know as much about her as I do, so I don't have answers. There may be an ulterior motive for her being here. I get that. You were burned earlier this year when Sal brought three comedians with him who, for all practical purposes, moved into your house."

"Damned near got me killed."

"Yes, despite that, look how you and Sal have bonded after years of being strangers."

"So?"

"So, you don't know what Grace wants. She didn't ask for anything. It's possible she meant it when she said you were her only family left. She loved Teddy; she may hope to find some of him in you."

Theo didn't say anything as he stared at the road in front of us.

"Theo, do you have a problem with her being black?"

I knew Theo and William were friends from their time together in the walking group, I didn't remember him ever saying anything derogatory about anyone because of race.

"Chris, I'm eighty-seven years old. I grew up in a time when race relations weren't what they are now. I wouldn't say my parents were racist, wouldn't say I was yet, when I was young, black people had their place. It wasn't the same as ours. It was the way it was. Segregation, although I didn't know what the word meant, was the law of the land. I'm an old dog, but think I can learn a few new tricks."

"When I had my company, two of my top engineers were black, African American. They were great engineers, great people. That's a lot of words to say I probably have vestiges of racism in me. I think I've overcome most of it. Yes, I was shocked when I saw Grace. Was it because of her color? I honestly don't know." He smiled for the first time since being in the car. "Hell, Chris, I would have been just as shocked if she was six-foot-five, or if her hair was glow-in-the-dark purple."

"You're saying your reaction was because she was different than you'd expected?"

"I'd like to think so."

Theo returned to silence until we got to his house, when he said, "You know what that doesn't answer?"

"What?"

"Why she's here."

Chapter Ten

I didn't have time to think about Theo's antagonistic reaction to Grace. The phone rang as I walked in the house.

The conversation opened with Charles's machine-gunning me with, "What's she like? What did Theo say? Does she have a dog? When will I meet her?"

I gave him a brief rundown of our meeting. I made it through the first minute of the summary before Charles did what he does best, interrupt with more questions. I proceeded to tell him, in no particular order, what Grace looked like, what she had on, how Theo reacted to her, how long it had taken her to drive from California, and if she had a dog. I was unable to tell him what her food truck looked like since we hadn't seen it. Most importantly, I couldn't tell him why she was here.

After more elaboration than necessary, he asked, "What does she want?"

"I don't know."

"Why didn't you ask her?"

"Charles, it wasn't my place. She was here to see Theo."

"Seems to me that's a little strange. I think Theo has a legitimate point thinking she wants something. He's rich, has a big house, is old as dirt, and just as fast. Sure, Sal's Theo's blood relative, but after him who's in line to get Theo's wealth when he kicks the bucket?"

"Charles, when did you get so jaded? Theo's not going to let her pull anything over on him. He's bright, but considering the way he reacted, I'd be surprised if he'll reach out to her, much less rush to put her in his will."

"Have you already shed enough brain cells to forget how Theo was hours from being taken in two years ago by a con artist? Nearly gave him a million bucks."

"I haven't forgotten. You didn't see how Theo reacted to Grace. He was borderline nuclear. If she'd asked for money for a soft drink from the vending machine, I think he would've turned her down."

"Whatever," Charles said, then took a deep breath. "Now let me tell you why I really called. Laurie Fitzsimmons called."

"Oh."

"Yeah, oh. Know what she wanted?"

"You want me to guess?"

"No. She wants to have supper."

"Did she say why?"

"I suppose because she's hungry."

"You know what I mean."

"She didn't say. Remember Gail, Laurie's friend from Jacksonville?"

"Sure."

"She's still here, hubby headed home. Laurie and Gail are going to St. James Gate tomorrow night. She asked me to join them. Does that sound strange, or what?"

"What'd you say?"

"After I got over the shock, I said, 'Why not? Chris and I'd love to join you.'"

"Charles, did she invite me?"

"No. I did. Why?"

"Never mind. What'd she say?"

"She mumbled something, held her hand over the phone, then said something to I assume Gail. She returned with, this is a direct quote, 'Six-thirty, meet you there,' and hung up."

Hanging up was something I should've done as soon as Charles said, "I suppose because she was hungry." Theo asking me to go with him to meet his daughter-in-law, now Charles asking, correction, telling me I was having supper with Laurie, a person I'd met twice, and Gail, someone whom I'd met once. Do I look like a human psychiatric service animal?

IN CHARLES'S WORLD, six-thirty meant six o'clock, so I was standing in front of St. James Gate when he walked up wearing a long-sleeved, gray T-shirt with what looked like an eagle over University of North Florida in blue on the front. Unlike his unlimited supply of T-shirts, he had on the same frayed, tan shorts that had been with him since we'd first met.

He pointed to the logo on his shirt. "Bet you think it's an eagle."

He would've been hurt if he knew I hadn't given it any thought. I shrugged.

"It's an osprey."

Instead of saying, *Who gives a flying flip?* I said, "Oh."

"Wore it in honor of Gail. It's in Jacksonville, you know." He peeked in the restaurant's open front window. "Speaking of Gail, are the ladies here?"

I reminded him that Laurie probably assumed that six-thirty meant six-thirty. He responded with an articulate, "Whatever."

Erik Swartz, a friend of mine, walked up behind

Charles, said "Hi," then pointed at Charles's T-shirt. "Eagle?"

"Osprey," I said before Charles could go into an extended explanation of who knows what.

Erik said, "Oh."

My thought exactly.

Erik turned to me. "Glad I ran into you. Figured out who killed Anthony?"

"We're working on it," Charles said, before I could deny trying and telling Erik it was in good hands with the police. "Did you know him?"

Erik nodded toward the restaurant's door. "Not really. I met him in there once. I stopped by to talk to John, the owner, about a musician I was booking. I had to wait, so I grabbed a beer and started talking to Anthony, who was drinking a Guinness a couple of chairs over."

Erik was a talented musician who booked musical acts in a few local businesses.

Charles said, "What'd you talk about?"

"Nothing really. I asked how long he lived here. He said he retired from teaching a few weeks earlier. He and his wife bought a house."

"Anything else?" Charles the Nosy asked.

"Nothing important. I was trying to make conversation until John was free. I asked what he was planning to do now that he was retired."

Erik chuckled.

"Funny, now that I think about it, he said something about not doing much, except fixing up the house. He said it needed a lot of work. I said it sounded like a money pit; he smiled, said I hit the roofing nail on the head. He said for me not to worry. He laughed, said he'd dig up the money to pay for it."

I said, "Do you think he literally meant dig up the money?"

"Didn't at the time. After what happened, I'm not

sure. I hear he was out at the old Coast Guard station with a metal detector. He must've been looking for something."

Erik laughed.

"He could've been looking for all that gold that rumors have been flying around about for decades."

Charles had been neglected long enough. "Think there's gold buried on Folly?"

"Talk's cheap. I've been around here going on a dozen years and have heard stories about buried treasure. If you ask me, which you did, I think I have as good a chance stumping my toe on a gold brick here on the sidewalk as Anthony would with a metal detector." He looked at his watch. "Gotta run, guys. Nice talking to you."

Charles watched Erik walk away then looked at his empty wrist. "Laurie and her friend are late."

Of course, they weren't. I started to tell him so, when I saw them crossing the street.

Laurie wore an oversized, black blouse over black slacks, and an oversized frown. She was still in mourning. Gail, a half-foot taller than Laurie, wasn't as grieved. She had on a celery-colored blouse with a tan skirt.

Gail smiled when she saw Charles, then pointed at the logo on his shirt. "Ozzie the Osprey."

Charles smiled, like he'd stumbled on a gold brick on the sidewalk.

Gail ignored her friend and shook Charles's hand. "Thank you for joining us."

"My pleasure," said Charles. "I hope you don't mind if I brought Chris with me. If we play it right, we'll get him to pay."

Laurie said, "It's okay."

Not quite a resounding yes.

I told the ladies that it was nice to see them again then suggested we go in before the restaurant filled.

It was fortunate that we arrived when we had because it

was nearly full. We were seated at a table in the front corner of the restaurant that had just been vacated.

A server finishing cleaning the table asked what we wanted to drink.

The ladies each ordered a Guinness, Charles stuck with a Bud Light. I ordered white wine.

Laurie seemed ill at ease, something her friend didn't share. Gail said, "Do you know why we chose here?"

I shook my head; Charles said, "Why?"

"This was Anthony and Laurie's favorite restaurant. They ate here two or three times a week. Isn't that right, Laurie?"

"Yes, we——"

Gail interrupted, "That's why I thought it'd be a good place tonight. Isn't that right, dear?"

Laurie nodded, probably because she knew she wouldn't be able to get a complete sentence out without Gail interrupting.

The server returned with our drinks, and Laurie was quick to take a sip. I didn't blame her. I told the server to give us a few minutes to decide on what to order.

Gail said, "Anthony's funeral will be Friday. I begged Laurie to take the body back to Jacksonville so their former teaching buddies could attend. But, no; she said, 'Don't be silly.' Folly was now home; Anthony would be buried near where she lives." She reached over and patted Laurie's leg. "I told her not to worry. Dean would come back, and I'd already be here for the service. Isn't that right, Laurie?"

Laurie took a larger gulp of beer, turned to Gail, and said, "I don't think our friends want to hear about a funeral. Let's talk about something more pleasant."

Gail said, "Oh. I was mentioning it because I'm sure they'll want to attend. Isn't that right, guys?"

"Tell us where and when, we'll be there," Charles said without glancing my way.

"See," said Gail. "There'll be a graveside service at two

o'clock at the Holy Cross Cemetery, on, what's the name of the street, Laurie?"

Laurie looked at her drink and mumbled, "Ft. Johnson Road."

Charles said, "You can count on us."

"Now," Gail said, "that's out of the way. Charles, Laurie tells me that you're a private detective. That must be exciting, must be dangerous."

"I don't know about exciting. Dangerous, definitely. I, along with some of my friends, including Chris here, have helped the police a few times."

Gail turned to Laurie. "Why don't you ask Charles to help find the person who, murd… umm, took poor Anthony's life?"

This didn't appear to be the way to turn the conversation to more pleasant topics, so I said, "Gail, I know the detective from the sheriff's office assigned to the case. I also know the Folly Beach Police Chief. They're both good at their job. I have confidence they're doing what they can to solve it."

Laurie appeared to perk up. "That detective, think his name's Callahan, came to see me yesterday. He had me go over what happened again. There's no doubt he's thorough."

The server returned, we ordered, and the conversation drifted to lighter topics.

Gail asked how long Charles and I had been on Folly and what I had done before retiring. She talked about a factory where she'd worked before it moved its operation offshore. She shared way more information than we needed about how Dean had quit teaching, how he'd taken over his dad's tire store.

I started to tune out the conversation when Gail began telling us how the two couples had met, how neither had any children, how they shared a common interest in history and cooking, plus how they played bridge twice a month. Most I'd already heard.

Telephone calls were seldom pleasant interruptions, but I was pleased when my phone rang around the time Gail was telling us a "fascinating" story about the time she and Laurie had prepared the "most delicious" bison meal for their husbands.

Chief LaMond said, "What's that noise in the background? Am I interrupting something?"

I wanted to scream, *"Yes, thank you!"* Instead, I told her who I was with and that she wasn't interrupting.

"Interesting. Can you stop by the office in the morning? I've got a couple of things to share about the murder."

We agreed on a time. I returned the phone to my pocket while wondering why Cindy had said, "Interesting," then realized that the interruption hadn't slowed Gail from regaling Charles with more "fascinating" tales.

I had little interest in most of what she was saying, although it was nice that the topics veered away from Anthony's untimely demise. Laurie interjected how much better it was living on Folly, with its laid-back residents, and slower pace. Gail continued to finish most of Laurie's sentences. Laurie didn't seem to mind. I would've been tempted to smack her annoying friend.

The food arrived, and we ate in silence before Charles leaned toward Laurie. "That reminds me, I was wondering if there were other cars out there when you arrived with Anthony. When Chris and I got there, we only saw your MINI."

I wondered what Laurie, more accurately, Gail had said that reminded Charles of that. I didn't ask since I was interested in her answer.

Laurie blinked a couple of times. "It seems like there were three or four. There weren't as many when I got back to the car after stumbling around finding my way out. I think there were two. Why?"

She must've understood that one of the vehicles could've belonged to the killer, that is if she hadn't killed her husband. I asked, "Do you remember what they were?"

"Not really. I'm not good about cars. Most look alike."

"What color were they?" Charles asked.

"It was dark. I couldn't tell. They weren't white, or silver. They were dark. Could've been black, gray, blue. I don't know."

I said, "You never saw anyone after you entered the Preserve?"

"No," Laurie said. "Oh, I get it. One of cars could've belonged to the person who shot Anthony."

"Possible," I said. "Although they could've belonged to the people staying at the nearby houses."

"It doesn't matter. I couldn't identify any of them. Besides, Anthony is still dead." She lowered her head and put her hand over her face.

So much for a lighter topic.

Chapter Eleven

After Laurie and Gail headed to Laurie's house, I told Charles about the meeting with Cindy. As expected, he asked if he could join us. I told him that it was fine with me. If the chief didn't want him there, then she'd kick him out, preventing me from having to bear the grief of telling him, "No."

The Folly Beach Department of Public Safety was in the salmon-colored City Hall. The main entrance to the seat of local government was on Center Street, but the entry to the stairs to Cindy's office was around the corner on Cooper Avenue, directly across from the Surf Bar. The door was open, and Cindy was behind her oversized desk, staring at a foot-high pile of manila folders when I knocked on the doorframe. She looked up, glanced at her watch, and said, "Well, if it isn't Tweedledumb and Tweedledumber."

She wasn't smiling, so I took the higher road. "Morning, chief. Do you have time to meet with us?"

"Us, as in the person I asked to come by, plus his shadow?"

"Yes."

She pushed the pile of folders aside, waved for me to close the door, then motioned us to the chairs in front of her desk.

"This job's going to be the death of me," she said as she turned to the large window behind her. "You know how many loud-noise complaints this serve-and-protect office received last night?"

I said, "No."

Charles said, "Seventeen."

Cindy stared at him, like he was a tarantula crawling up her arm. "Nine. What in blue blazes am I supposed to do about it? Do I have my guys run all over town to see if their eardrums burst when they should be patrolling for bad guys? The death of me yet."

I said, "Sorry, Cindy," before Charles asked about each complaint.

"Never mind. That's not why I asked *Chris* to stop by." She paused, stared at Charles long enough for him to get the message, before turning to me. "I've known you long enough to know you're getting as nosy as your buddy sitting there."

"Inquisitive," Charles corrected.

Cindy rolled her eyes. "So, Chris, since you, and yes, you, too, Charles, awakened the sleeping Mrs. Fitzsimmons the morning we found her late husband, you'll have your antenna up, soaking in all the local gossip about what we've learned. Most of what you hear will be pure BS. I know that you'll keep whatever I tell you in confidence. You will, too, Charles. Right?"

Charles nodded. I couldn't see if he had his fingers crossed.

Cindy returned his nod. "Chris, I have a couple more questions about the morning you two found Mrs. Fitzsim-mons. Something still doesn't feel right. I can't put my finger on it."

"Fire away."

Cindy tapped her desk. "Was she really asleep when you found her?"

"I have no way of knowing. She acted startled when she jumped out of the car. Her eyes were bloodshot, her hair a mess. I'd say yes."

Cindy smiled. "I know I'd be startled if someone looking like Charles stuck his face against my window. What do you think, Charles?"

"I agree with Chris."

I was pleased that he ignored the chief's insult. I said, "Why?"

The chief tilted her head. "If Larry and I were out there in a storm that was pitch black, and if we got separated and I found my way to the car, the last thing I'd do would be to fall asleep. I'd be worried, I'd call for help, I'd stare out the window. Fall asleep, never. Would you?"

That'd bothered me from the beginning. "I hope not."

Charles said, "I wouldn't have been able to sleep."

"Exactly," Cindy said. "Let me ask something else. Do you believe her story?"

Charles glanced at me before saying, "I don't know what Chris thinks. It makes sense to me, all except falling asleep."

I nodded. "We're all different. It seems strange, although I couldn't say how Laurie would react in the same situation. What do you and Detective Callahan think?"

"Callahan isn't sharing much. You know the sheriff's office and lowly city cops aren't always on the same page. Hell, most of the time, they don't put us in the same book. All to say, I don't know what he thinks."

"What about you?" I said.

Cindy said, "Tell me about your supper with Mrs. Fitzsimmons and her friend, umm, what's her name?"

"Gail," Charles said before I made the transition from asking what Cindy thought about Laurie being asleep to our dinner. "We met Laurie and Gail at St. James Gate. Gail's from Jacksonville, has been friends with Laurie for years. They played bridge—"

Cindy put her hand in front of Charles's face. "Whoa. Hold the history lesson. All I want to know is why were you having supper with them?"

I thought, *Please don't say because they were hungry.*

"Laurie sort of bonded with us after we woke her up. She wanted to tell us about Anthony's funeral. Come to think of it, she didn't say why."

I said, "Cindy, why do you ask?"

"I'm trying to get a better picture of Laurie. Tell me about what you talked about." She pointed a finger at Charles. "Not what you had to eat, not who else you talked to, not all those itsy-bitsy facts you accumulate, you know, the ones having nothing to do with anything. Let me narrow it down more. Was anything said that could have anything to do with Anthony's death?"

That said volumes about what she thought about Laurie's story. "You think she's lying?"

Cindy sighed. "Did you miss my question about dinner?"

I said, "Laurie wanted to talk about their past, until Gail said she heard that Charles had helped the police catch bad guys. She asked him if he could find Anthony's killer."

Charles waved his hand in the air. "She asked both of us."

"Oh, great, just what we need. Where did she hear that?"

Charles said, "Laurie told her."

Cindy turned to me. "What did you tell her?"

"The police were good, that they'd figure it out, that there wasn't any need for us to be involved."

"Thanks, I suppose. Anything else?"

Charles said, "I asked her how many cars were nearby when they got to the Preserve, then how many were there when she came back to the car."

Cindy rolled her eyes. "How does that say that you didn't need to get involved?" She exhaled. "Never mind. What was her answer?"

I shared what Laurie had said. After Cindy mumbled something about us being nosy, butting in police business, how she should be shot for talking to us about the case, she said Laurie's story about the other vehicles was consistent with what she'd told the police at the scene.

"Cindy," I said, "do you think she killed her husband?"

She shook her head. "Don't know. What I do know is her story's fishy, could be true yet, still fishy. She had opportunity. We haven't found the gun, so there's no way to know about means. And the big question, until late yesterday, was motive."

"It would have been easy for whoever killed him to fling the gun in the ocean," Charles said as he made a throwing motion. "Splash, it's gone."

"Never to be found," Cindy added.

I wasn't paying attention to their recreating flinging a gun. "Cindy, what do you mean about motive and late yesterday?"

"Before I tell you, let me ask, did Laurie say anything to indicate she and her hubby had problems with each other?"

"No," I said.

"Like problems enough to kill him over?" Charles said.

Cindy said, "That'd be the kind."

Charles shook his head. "Not that I heard."

"Chris, back to your question," Cindy said and pointed at me. "It's nice that one of you listens to what I'm saying. Len, one of my officers, was talking to his insurance agent yesterday about a life insurance policy. He got married a few months ago and, now, his wife's pregnant. We have a good policy through the office, but he wanted to add to it in case, well, in case something happens. Anyway, you know the agent, David Darnell."

I nodded.

"David asked Len if we'd caught the killer. Len said, "No," then David said the Fitzsimmons were his clients. Len, being a good cop, told me what David said, so I called the agent to ask about the Fitzsimmons' insurance. He started to give me the runaround about needing a warrant to get that information. I said I would and started to hang up. Good ole David stopped me, said since Anthony was no longer among the living he guessed it was okay to share that Anthony and Laurie had taken out a half-million-dollar life insurance policy on each other."

"Motive," I said.

Cindy shrugged. "Know when the policy was written?"

"When?" Charles blurted.

"Two months ago."

Chapter Twelve

I stopped at Bert's for bread after meeting with Chief LaMond. My last loaf had turned several shades of blue and green, attractive colors in a painting, not so much for lunch. Mary Ewing, one of the store's personable clerks greeted me at the door. A thin, attractive, twenty-something, she gave a high-wattage smile. "Hi, Mr. Landrum."

I'd met Mary a couple of years ago, when she and her two young daughters were homeless. With the assistance of surfer friends, they were squatting in vacant vacation rentals. True, the assistance came in the form of breaking into houses, although the intentions were admirable. Since then, a local minister helped her find legal living arrangements.

"Mary, I've told you, please call me Chris. How are the girls?"

Her smile increased. "Joanie turned four last week." She laughed. "Big sister, Jewel, threw her a party."

"Jewel's eight?"

"Going on twenty."

"I bet it was fun."

"Joanie said it was the best birthday she'd ever had. The two women we share the house with were there, one had her five-year old son, the other lady brought the three kids she babysits. It was a hoot."

"I can imagine."

Mary started to respond, looked over my shoulder, then waved. "Hi, Captain."

I turned to see Abraham Gant return Mary's wave. He was in his mid-eighties, probably had been six-foot tall during his heyday but was now around five-foot-nine.

"How's my favorite clerk?" Gant said as he hugged Mary.

Mary told him that she was fine.

"Who's your friend, Mary?"

"Captain, this is, Mr. Landrum, I mean Chris. We've known each other nearly as long as I've been here."

Gant gripped my hand and smiled. Calling his grip bone-crushing would've been an exaggeration, although not by much.

"Chris, I'm Captain Gant. If you're a friend of Mary, you're a friend of mine."

Mary patted me on the back. "Captain, you two have something in common."

He laughed. "Something other than being old farts and having you as a friend?"

I was glad that Mary considered me a friend, although I didn't see any humor in the octogenarian Captain thinking I was an old fart, or otherwise.

I turned to Mary. "What do we have in common?"

"Both were law enforcement. Chris, the Captain is retired from the South Carolina Highway Patrol. He was a captain so that's where his name came from."

Gant turned to me. "Were you a cop?"

"No, I—"

Mary interrupted. "Chris helps the police. If you can believe it, he's caught some killers. He's—"

My turn to interrupt. "Some friends and I've been fortunate a time or two when we learned things that the police weren't aware of. It helped them solve a couple of murders. Nothing like what you spent your career doing."

Gant's smile lessened. "Oh, you stuck your nose where it didn't belong?"

Time to change the subject. "We were fortunate to help the police. How long have you lived on Folly?"

I didn't think he was going to answer. Finally, he said, "My parents moved here in the late 1930s. Dad was in the Coast Guard. I wasn't much older than Joanie." He smiled at Mary.

I said, "I've been here ten years. I wish I'd been here longer. It's great hearing stories from the old-timers. Do you know Charles Fowler? He's a good friend who's lived here way more years than I have."

"The T-shirt guy, sure, although I don't know him well. We run into each other occasionally."

"Hate to interrupt, guys," Mary said. "Work calls."

I said it was nice talking to her then the Captain gave her a fatherly, grandfatherly hug.

"She's so sweet," Gant said as Mary moved behind the counter to check out a woman carrying a white poodle.

"Charles said you'd told him about Anthony Fitzsimmons' death."

"I told him about it, but should've known he already knew. Your friend has a reputation for knowing everything that goes on."

I remembered Charles's comment about being surprised that Gant knew about the death such a brief time after the body was found.

I smiled. "He does have a way of accumulating rumors, sometimes the truth. How'd you hear about the body?"

Gant stared at me like I was a suspect in a crime. "Don't recall. Must've heard it from someone at breakfast. Why?"

"No reason."

"Did you know the SOB?"

"I never met Anthony. Charles talked to him and his wife once. I take it you didn't like him."

"He had me fooled. Met him in Planet Follywood, where he started up a conversation. He and the Mrs. bought a house here, retired schoolteachers, he said. After I told him I'd been here since the invention of fire, he asked me all sorts of questions about what island life was like way back when. I don't get to share my stories much anymore. Most of my cronies are gone; most of the youngsters don't care. He wondered if I knew his wife's grandfather, Harnell Levi. I told him, 'Yes,' although I didn't know him well." Gant grinned. "I didn't tell him Harnell was a serious nut case who was ignored by most folks."

"Nut case?"

"The old guy was always blabbing about treasure, pirates' gold, striking it rich. He reminded me of those old, scruffy prospectors in black and white movies who were always chewing tobacco, telling anyone who'd listen about gold in *them thar hills*."

"No one took Harnell seriously?"

Gant shook his head. "What would you think if you saw an old man walking down the beach carrying a rusty shovel while singing 'Some Enchanted Evening' at the top of his lungs?"

"Good point."

Gant's smile faded. "Anyway, Anthony and I were getting along pretty good, until he said his hobby was relic hunting. He went on and on about digging up the past."

"What happened?"

"I'll say it once, only once." Gant pointed to the concrete floor. "What's buried should stay buried. Period. Those who've come before us lived their lives the best they could. Some were good. Some were bad. All are gone. They need to stay gone. We have no right digging them up, no right digging up their things, their bones, their past. I'm not saying there're ghosts, not saying there ain't. There've been stories over the years of people on Folly seeing ghosts of soldiers, of nurses, of average folks. I haven't seen any, myself. I'll tell you what, I know of honest people who've seen them. Relic hunters, and people digging for buried treasure, are disturbing the souls of the wonderful people who've come before us. Bad things should happen to them. It's illegal to go digging up anything out where the SOB was murdered." He glared at me. "Got him killed."

"Have you heard rumors about who might've killed him?"

"Chris, I don't traffic in rumors."

"If he was killed because of what he was doing, I wonder who knew he'd be there."

Gant rubbed his hand through his short, gray hair and stared at me. "Twenty-five years ago, it would've been my job to figure that out. I'm glad it isn't. Know why?"

I shook my head.

"He deserved what he got."

Gant pivoted and walked away, nearly running over Stanley Kremitz as he stormed out the door. I couldn't help but wonder if Gant knew that Anthony Fitzsimmons was going to be at the Lighthouse Inlet Heritage Preserve that fateful evening.

Stanley was my height, thin, in his late sixties, although he looked older. He moved to my side then looked at the door. "What'd you do to put a bee in his bonnet?"

Stanley was a friend of Chester Carr, a man I'd met five years ago. I'd become better acquainted with Chester two years ago when Charles and I joined a walking group he'd formed.

"We were talking about the man killed at the old Coast Guard property. Apparently, Gant didn't take too kindly to him."

"People in glass houses shouldn't throw stones."

If Stanley wasn't Chester's friend, I'd avoid him or, as he

would say, "I'd avoid him like the plague." He was a nice man, friendly, but had never met a cliché he didn't like, or worse, repeat.

"What do you know about him?"

"You know I always look on the bright side. That's hard to do when it comes to Gant, who insists on being called Captain. He's got a quick temper. It doesn't take much to set him off."

"Think he'd get mad enough to shoot someone?"

"He was a state cop. He'd know how to pull the trigger. You can take that to the bank."

The store was getting crowded, and I ushered the retired pipefitter out of the aisle, and said, "Did you know Anthony and Laurie Fitzsimmons?"

"A little. Met them in here, right back there by the bin of fruits." He laughed. "Laurie was picking up an apple. I stepped up and said an apple a day keeps the doctor away. She must've thought I was weird. Stared at me like I was a three-headed hippo." He rolled his eyes. "Go figure."

I didn't see anything wrong with Laurie's reaction. "Was that it?"

"No. Anthony found humor in what I'd said. He told me who they were. I said it was nice meeting them. Laurie finally seemed to catch on that I was teasing. They're both retired teachers, live here full-time now."

"Did you know about them relic hunting?"

"Anthony had a pack of batteries in his hand, so I made a joke about using them to run the apple she had in her hand. You know, like the Apple i-stuff, the iPhone. They didn't laugh. Can you believe that?"

Absolutely, I thought. "Looking for relics?"

"Yeah," Stanley said. "Anthony finally said they needed batteries for flashlights. It was as bright as Charmin outside. I joked about them not needing flashlights. Anthony, or maybe it was Laurie, said they like to fish around in wooded areas. They sometimes need the extra light to see. That begged the question, fishing around for what, so I asked. Anthony glanced at his wife then said something about them having an interest in the Civil War. They've heard that old military stuff, buttons, other metal things can be found around here. I asked if they'd found anything."

"Had they?"

"Anthony looked around, like he was about to tell me where the fountain of youth was and didn't want anyone else to hear. Then, he looked at Laurie. I didn't see her reaction. Anthony sure did. He changed direction in mid-stream and said, 'Nope,' they hadn't found anything."

"Was that it?"

"I suppose."

He didn't sound convincing, so I said, "You sure?"

"Yeah. Terrible about what happened to him that morning. I hear Laurie was the only other person out there, and she didn't see what happened. Someone said she didn't know anything happened to Anthony until the morning. Chester tells me you're good friends with the chief of police. Is that how she tells it?"

I thought it was a strange question, one that I wasn't comfortable answering, well, answering truthfully. "Don't know. We haven't talked about it."

Chapter Thirteen

I met Charles the next morning for a late breakfast at the
Dog. After sparring with Amber about my choice of
French toast, over her ongoing crusade to get me to eat
healthier, Charles asked for the latest on Anthony's death. I
told him I didn't know anything new, then shared my
conversations with Gant and Stanley Kremitz.

Charles rubbed his three-day-old beard. "Gant goes
apoplectic when anyone mentions ghosts, or diggin' up
bones. The old boy's got a bag of screws loose when it
comes to the past. I still think it's possible he shot Anthony."

"He became agitated talking about Anthony and relic
hunting. I asked if he'd known Laurie's grandfather. He
said, "Yes' then shared that Harnell was considered a nut. I
couldn't tell if that was Gant's opinion because Harnell was
digging for buried treasure, of if others felt that way."

"Chris, it bothers me that Gant knew about Anthony's
death so soon after the body was discovered. Plus, being a
retired state police officer would've given him the skill to
kill."

"I don't know how he heard about it, but you don't need to be a retired cop to be able to shoot someone. Don't forget, people who weren't in law enforcement have shot at us."

Charles held out his arms, wiggled his left leg. "Shot at by amateurs. We're alive. Anthony ain't."

Amber returned with breakfast, and to add sanity to our conversation. She asked if we'd heard about the heavy rains that were supposed to hit this afternoon, or the sale at two T-shirt stores.

I answered, "Yes" to the rain. I didn't care about the sale.

Charles added that he would've been interested in the sale if they sold college T-shirts. They didn't, so he wasn't.

Amber left to wait on a family of five who'd taken a table in the center of the room, when Chief LaMond entered and headed our way.

She motioned for Charles to slide over, sat beside him, then said, "Have you heard?"

"Heard what?" I asked.

Cindy opened her mouth wide, raised her hand, and made a motion with her forefinger, like she was making a mark on a whiteboard. She said, "Is this a historic day, or what?"

I said, "What're you talking about?"

"I never thought I'd live to see the day when something bad happens on *my* island, when you didn't know about it before I did. Damned historic day."

Charles jerked his head toward Cindy, almost knocking over his bell jar of water with his hand. "What happened?"

"Be patient," she said. "I'm savoring the moment." She took a notebook out of her pocket. "At nine-hundred this morning, Mrs. Anthony Fitzsimmons called 9-1-1 to report that an unknown person attempted to make her the late Mrs. Fitzsimmons. She—"

"Whoa!" Charles interrupted. "Details?"

"Thought that'd get your attention. Laurie called to report someone fired a shot through her window. We responded posthaste, for you amateurs, that's police talk for super swift. Our mayor looks askance at citizens being shot at. Go figure. Officer Bishop was first on scene. She reported that Laurie wasn't hit, whoever pulled the trigger was long gone. I was nearby, got there next."

Charles did what he does best. He interrupted, again. "Did she see who it was?"

"Shut up and listen. You'll find out," Cindy said, doing what she does best. "She didn't see anyone. That would've been too easy. She said she was in the bedroom when the first thing she knew was the window beside her shattered. She jumped back, tripped on the side of the bed. By the time she got to her window, the perp was gone, plus there was a bullet hole in the wall on the opposite side of the room."

"Where was Gail Clark?" I asked.

Cindy flipped a page in her notebook. "Gail Clark, oh, yeah, her Florida friend. Laurie sent Gail to Harris Teeter to get food for lunch." Cindy smiled. "She, Laurie, that is, said she needed alone time. Something about being tired of Gail finishing her sentences. Said she was finishing sentences that Laurie was only thinking about. Seems nerves are frayed between the friends."

"Any witnesses?" I asked.

"No. The bedroom faces a vacant lot with lots of trees, shrubbery, weeds as tall as me. Whoever was in there could've been doing a naked rain dance, and no one would've noticed."

I took a sip of coffee and said, "Don't suppose Laurie had any thoughts on who it was?"

Cindy shook her head. "She's pretty torn up. Hell, I would be, too, if someone took a shot at me when all I was doing was standing in my bedroom. Think of how much worse it is for her, considering it came a few days after her husband was murdered, came the day before his funeral."

Charles said, "Don't suppose the shooter left the gun and his driver's license?"

Cindy cocked her head. "Gee, Charles. We forgot to check. No wonder you think you're a detective."

I said, "What happens now?"

"Detective Callahan's been to the house. He's having crime techs search for anything that might've been left in the vacant lot. I doubt they'll have any luck." She pointed to Charles. "Unless he, or she, left a driver's license."

I looked around to see if anyone was near enough to hear, then asked, "Cindy, could she have faked it, took the shot herself?"

Charles stared at me. Cindy nodded. "That entered my mind. You think she did it to deflect suspicion that she killed her husband?"

I shrugged. "It still strikes me as strange that, after getting lost from her husband in the middle of the night, she'd find her way back to the car then fall asleep. Add to that, the half-million-dollar insurance policy would be a strong motive."

Cindy continued to nod. "It's an interesting coincidence that she sent her friend to the grocery before the incident."

Charles took a sip of his drink then said, "Did you search her house for a gun?"

"On what grounds? The woman calls us in hysterics to report being shot at. We show up and say 'That's terrible. While we're here, can we search your underwear drawer?'"

Charles said, "That mean, 'No'?"

"Can't fool you, Charles."

"Trying to help."

"Thank you," Cindy said, slobbering sarcasm.

"While we're talking about possible suspects, I was talking to Abraham Gant yesterday. He—"

Cindy waved her hand in my face. "Captain Gant, to you."

"Captain Gant went on a rant about relic hunters, specifically about Anthony Fitzsimmons."

"That's nothing new. Rant and Gant not only rhyme, they're redundant."

"True, although I thought it was a bit strong when he said Fitzsimmons got what was coming to him."

"Let me see if I have this straight," Cindy said, "You think Laurie and the captain were standing outside Laurie's window this morning shooting up her bedroom?"

I sighed. "No, I'm saying each had a motive for killing Anthony."

Charles said, "Add Gail Clark to the list."

"Why?" Cindy asked.

"She leaves Laurie to go to the grocery, then someone shoots through the window."

I shook my head. "Motive?"

"Don't know." Charles motioned toward Cindy. "That's for you to figure out."

"Halleluiah," Cindy said. "*Faux* detective Charles finally leaving something for us civil servants to do." She looked at her watch. "I've had about all the fun I can have with you two. Got to get back to the office to pretend like I know what I'm doing." She stood and took a step toward the door, before turning back to us. "I can't believe I knew something before you did."

I asked Charles why he thought Gail was a suspect, other than being out of the house when the shot was fired. His phone rang before he answered. Up until a year ago, he didn't have a cell phone, or an answering machine. The reason he got the phone was because he and his then girl-friend, Heather Lee, had moved to Nashville for her to pursue a music career. He wanted to be able to give me updates on their move. Her career never got off the ground, so they returned to Folly. Not long after, Heather left Charles. He kept the phone.

The phone conversation was brief. The half of it I heard consisted of, "Yes," and "Okay, we're on our way."

"Where?" I asked as he slipped the phone in his pocket.

"Laurie's."

Chapter Fourteen

The house looked as much a work in progress as it had during our first visit. The only difference being, instead of Laurie greeting us, Gail met us at the door. She motioned us in saying Laurie was in the kitchen.

Laurie wrapped her arms around Charles, like he was a long-lost relative. She had tears in her eyes as she loosened her grip and stepped back. She gave me a hug that lasted half as long as the one she'd given Charles.

"You won't believe what happened," she said in Charles's direction.

Charles didn't admit he knew. "What?"

Gail, from the doorway, said, "Laurie, perhaps your friends would like coffee."

"Oh, sure. Sorry for being rude. Coffee, brownies? The next-door neighbor brought over more than we could ever eat."

I said coffee, not because I wanted it, but hoping it'd calm Laurie if she was doing something. Charles glared at me, like I was keeping her from telling what'd happened. Charles and I took chairs at the kitchen table. Gail grabbed one of the two remaining chairs, like she expected to be waited on by the woman who'd been the alleged target of a bullet hours earlier.

Laurie delivered a plate of brownies then went for our drinks.

"Nice kitchen," Charles said as he looked around.

This time, he wasn't simply being kind. Much of the house needed work, but the kitchen was immaculate. New stainless-steel appliances fit the spaces between the granite countertops. White cabinets and a white subway-tile backsplash were the perfect contrast from the mint green walls.

Laurie rubbed her hand over the granite counters. "Thank you. Anthony thought I was spending too much. After seeing the finished kitchen, he said it was wonderful." She looked at the tile floor and whispered. "He'll never get to enjoy it."

Gail interrupted Laurie's melancholy moment. "Laurie, don't you need to tell your friends why you called?"

Laurie brought our coffee before taking the remaining seat. She glanced toward the bedroom. "Somebody tried to kill me." She looked in her cup as she slowly shook her head.

Gail reached to squeeze her friend's arm. "Now, dear, tell your friends everything."

Laurie twisted her arm out from under Gail's hold and turned to Charles. "We'd been trying to see what food we needed for the next few days. People brought plenty to eat, but we were out of the basics. I was feeling queasy, so Gail offered to go to Harris Teeter. She left. I want in the bedroom to tidy up. To be honest, I thought about lying back down. Instead, I came in here to get a glass of water when I heard it." Her gaze returned to the cup.

"Tell them," Gail said.

She was as impatient as Charles.

Laurie continued, "All I remember is shattering glass. My first thought was, *That's just what I need, a rock breaking the window. Anthony's funeral tomorrow, now this*. I went in the bedroom ready to look out and scream at some kid when I realized there was a hole in the wall opposite the window, glass all over the floor." She glanced at me and turned to Charles. "Guys, if it'd been seconds earlier, I'd be dead."

Chief LaMond already answered the question, but I asked, anyway. "Laurie, did you see anyone?"

"I was scared, so confused. When I realized it was someone shooting, I ducked, afraid to look outside. By the time I got the nerve to peek, I didn't see much. There was someone walking out of the lot next door, or I thought there was. I was so scared."

She'd told Cindy she hadn't seen anyone.

"Can you describe the person?"

"Not really. I think it was a guy. He could've had on a ball cap, no, he did have one on."

"Height, age, weight, anything else about him?" I asked.

"No. By the time I saw him, he was past the tree line, so I didn't get a good look. Even if I got a clear view, it might not have been the person who shot at me. I was so shaken that it may've been a minute or two before I looked out the window. I don't know, honest."

"Did you tell the police what you saw?"

"I don't remember. I was shaking when they got here, my stomach was doing somersaults." She wiped a tear from her cheek then smiled for the first time. "I wasn't my best."

"Of course, you weren't, dear," Gail said as she returned her hand to Laurie's arm.

Charles looked toward the bedroom. "Laurie, do you feel like showing us where it happened?"

Gail responded for Laurie. "I don't think she—"

Laurie stood. "Yes."

We followed her to the bedroom. The room was painted a soothing green, a shade darker than the kitchen. A queen-size sleigh bed was against the far wall with its bedspread, covering the sheets, although not neatly. A large double-hung window was on the left side with a piece of cardboard covering the lower half. The wood paneling on the opposite wall had a two-inch diameter hole a couple of feet below the ceiling. It looked like it had been made by a woodpecker, although more likely the work of the crime techs digging out the bullet.

Laurie saw us looking at the window. "Chief LaMond's husband owns a hardware store. She called while she was here. He rushed over. He didn't have a piece of glass that fit, so he taped the cardboard up there until he could fix it. The black officer, Bishop, I believe, swept up the glass. Such nice people."

I told her that I'd known Cindy, her husband, and Officer Bishop for years and that they exemplified most of the people on Folly who would do anything to help their neighbors. I added, "Laurie, you said you were in here then went to the kitchen before the shot was fired?"

"Yes, went to get a drink."

Charles stood on his tiptoes to see out the top half of the window, and said all he could see from that angle was the top of the trees in the adjacent lot.

Laurie's hands began to shake, so I suggested that we return to the kitchen.

This time, Gail refilled our cups while Laurie put her elbows on the table, her head between her hands.

In a couple of minutes, her breathing returned to normal, and her hands stopped shaking.

Charles said, "Is there anything we can do?"

Instead of answering, she said, "I don't know what I'll do. I don't know how I'll live, how I'll afford it."

Gail returned to the table. "Now, dear, the insurance will keep you from having to worry."

"Insurance?" Charles said, never fearing to tread where no man should go.

Laurie moved her hands from her face, glared at Gail, and turned to Charles. "When we retired, Anthony insisted we take out a large insurance policy. I argued it was morbid, that we shouldn't do it. He said it was his way to show his love for me. He never wanted to leave me wanting." Tears rolled down her cheeks.

Once again, Gail put her hand on Laurie's arm. She shook it off and rushed to the bathroom.

Gail watched her go. "Anthony was a wise man. Laurie will need that money. All she has is her teachers' pension, and a house that needs more work than they expected. Dean and I tried to talk them out of buying this place." She glanced at the closed bathroom door. "I think she was sure they'd find a buried treasure, not have to worry about money."

"What made them so sure?" I asked.

"Her grandfather gave them—"

Laurie opened the bathroom door, Gail stopped mid-sentence.

"Chris, Charles," Laurie said, "I hate to run you off. I need to lie down."

We stood, and Laurie gave me a hug and thanked me for coming. She moved to Charles, squeezed him, whispered something, then escorted us to the door.

Charles didn't say anything until we were in the car with the air-conditioning blowing full blast. "Chris, how many times did Laurie say she'd been in her bedroom then went to the kitchen when she heard the window shatter?"

"Twice that I recall. No need to say it. Laurie told Cindy she was in the bedroom when the bullet hit."

"Good old Abe Lincoln said, 'Be sure to put your feet in the right place, then stand firm.' Seems that Laurie had to do some fancy footwork to be in two places at the same time."

"A red flag, yes. It's also possible she was traumatized, confused when she talked to Cindy."

"Do you believe that?"

"Don't know. Either way, we need to tell the chief. She can follow up."

Charles looked back at the house. "You bet we do. And how about the insurance policy that Laurie argued against buying? Sounds fishy."

"Maybe," I said.

"Without a psychic, it's going to be hard to ask Anthony." He adjusted the air flow. "Why did she latch on us?"

"Latched onto you. I was along because you invited me."

"Strange," Charles said. "I didn't think she was going to let go once she got her arms around me."

"What'd she whisper when we were leaving?"

"Don't be a stranger."

"Oh."

" 'Oh,' is right."

I DEPOSITED Charles at his apartment and went home to called Chief LaMond to tell her what we'd learned.

"Why were you and your nosy friend there?"

I told her I was there because my nosy friend invited me. He was there because Laurie called him.

"Why did she call Charles?"

I thought about how happy she'd been to see him. I'd wondered the same thing. Instead of going into the hugging and whispering, I said, "Don't know. He's one of the few people she knows here."

After a moment of silence, Cindy said, "With those non-answers out of the way, why are you calling?"

I shared the discrepancy between what Laurie had told the police about where she was when the shot was fired opposed to what she'd told us.

Cindy said that it was interesting, although, in the grand scheme of things, considering the amount of stress that

Laurie had been under when she'd told her version to the police, it wasn't that unusual. She went on a mini tirade about how many of the witnesses she interviewed over the years told stories that proved to be nowhere near what happened. She pointed out that they weren't intentionally lying, their stories were "royally screwed up" by shock, selective memory, other "psychological gibberish" that the "ignorant police chief from the hills of Tennessee" wasn't bright enough to understand.

I wasn't going to argue, although she's one of the smartest people I know. She proved it when she ended by saying she'd talk to Laurie again.

In a rare concession, she thanked me for calling. Of course, she ended the call on a more familiar note. "Oh, yeah, if I find out you two are sticking your snotty noses where they don't belong, I'll throw both of you in jail, charge you with driving a police chief coocoo."

She hung up before I could say, "I love you, too."

The phone rang, so I thought she was going to give me another chance.

No such luck.

"Chris, this is Theo. Could I buy you a drink?"

I'd never heard those words from Theo. "Yes."

"Good, could you meet me at The Washout. It's a nice night, I'd like to walk. I'll leave now, be there in a half hour."

The Washout was a ten-minute walk from Theo's house, so thirty minutes sounded about right for the man who moves slower than the Lincoln Memorial.

I live three times as far from the restaurant, as does Theo, so I made the trek and was sitting at the outside bar fifteen minutes after hanging up. A conversation with the bartender about the hot weather, and the rash of vacationers on the island, and twenty minutes later, an out-of-breath Theo limped up to the bar.

He wiped sweat off his forehead, took the seat beside

me, and said, "Whew. You would think all the walking I do would have me in better shape for these long excursions."

His white T-shirt was gray from sweat. I was afraid, instead of ordering him a drink, I'd have to order an ambulance. Theo took a gulp of water from the glass the observant bartender set in front of him, then said, "I hope I didn't take you away from anything important."

I didn't tell him that my other options had been to ponder a solution for world peace, wonder if climate change was real, or fixing a peanut butter sandwich for supper. I stuck with, "I wasn't busy."

"I suppose you're wondering why I asked you to meet me."

"It crossed my mind." I left out, *about fifty times.*

He took another gulp. "I would've invited you to the house, except Sal was there. Don't get me wrong, my brother's wonderful. It's great getting to know him, again, after all the years he was on the road. It's nice having family nearby. It's been lonely since I lost Eunice." He hesitated and looked at his glass. "Did you know that we'd been married fifty-two years?"

He'd told me several times. "That's a long time, Theo. You must miss her terribly."

"Yes," he whispered. "Anyway, it's good that Sal is living with me."

He sighed, as I waited for "but." I didn't have long to wait.

"But my brother is driving me crazy. Chris, not a day goes by, correct that, not an hour goes by without him telling a joke. The old boy's got a million of them. They must've been funny forty years ago, when he shared them with a room full of drunks at a smoky comedy club in Oshkosh, Wisconsin. Occasionally, one of them strikes my funny bone. By occasionally, I mean one in a hundred. The old boy's going to joke me to death."

"Have you said anything to him?"

"I've tried. He nods like he's listening."

"And?"

"He cracks a joke. Anyway, that's not your problem, not the reason I wanted us to share a drink."

The bartender returned to give us the chance to order drinks, something other than water. We each asked for a glass of white wine, the bartender said, "No problem," a phrase which, in my opinion, had no place in the vocabulary of any server or bartender. He left to get our drinks.

"Chris, was I too hard on Grace?"

I wasn't ready for the transition from Sal to Grace. When in doubt, I turn the question around, something that'll never work with Charles. "Do you think you were?"

Our drinks arrived, Theo took a sip before saying, "She took me by surprise. I didn't know what to think, what to expect. When she stepped off the elevator, I didn't know what to do." He shook his head. "I blew it."

"Theo, I can't imagine what must've been going through your mind. It'd been years since you had contact with your son. Then, you learned he was gone. Now there was a stranger saying that she's your daughter-in-law. I don't know how I would've reacted."

"Chris, it's not her fault Teddy is dead. Why did I take it out on her?"

"You were shocked. You didn't know her. You didn't know what to expect. You didn't know why she came across the country. All reasons to be skeptical."

"Not a reason to be rude. For heaven's sake, she's my daughter-in-law."

"You could've handled it better. That's easy to say now. If I were in your shoes, I'm not sure I would've done anything differently. What're you thinking?"

"She said she was going to live out of her food truck. That tells me she doesn't have much money. She asked about moving her truck to Folly. That means she wants to be here. She didn't ask for anything. Is it possible she's sincere about wanting to be near her father-in-law, to be near me?"

"It's possible." I repeated, "What're you thinking?"

He leaned over to pull up his black, knee-high support stockings. In such a faint voice, I nearly missed what he was saying. "Asking her if she wants to move in my house until she gets on her feet enough to get a place of her own."

"Oh."

"Think it's a good idea?"

I smiled at the thought of the incongruity of Theo's house inhabited by an over-the-hills comedian, a half-Jamaican widow, and a retired engineer. All I said was, "I don't know. You still aren't sure what, if anything, she wants."

Theo watched a mini-van turn on West Hudson Avenue from Center Street. He then turned back to me. "I think it's a good idea. I'll call her tonight."

"What does Sal think?"

"Don't know, haven't told him."

"That should be interesting."

"He'll probably have a joke about a Jamaican, a comedian, and a geezer walking into a bar."

"Theo, you're a tough audience."

He chuckled, the result I'd been hoping for. He turned serious. "Chris, I'm dominating the conversation. Have you heard anything else about the murder of the retired schoolteacher?"

"Not much. Laurie called Charles, so we went to see her today."

"I didn't know they were friends."

With everything going on with Theo, I didn't need to discuss the attempt on her life. "She'd met him once before we found her in her car the day of her husband's murder. Seems she's bonded with him."

"That's great. Charles is a good person to have on your side. When's the husband's funeral?"

"In the morning."

"Should I go?"

"Did you know them?"

"Never met. I thought going to the funeral would be the Folly thing to do."

"I'm sure the widow would appreciate it." I gave him the details. He said he'd better get home to call Grace.

"Are you going to talk to Sal before you call her?"

"No. If she says, "No," he didn't need to know I offered. If she says, 'Yes,' I can show him I may not know jokes, but I can spring a surprise."

Go, Theo, go!

Chapter Fifteen

Anthony's graveside service was to be held eight miles from Folly in the Holy Cross Cemetery on Ft. Johnson Road. The temperature was in the mid-eighties, with humidity pushing the heat index to near triple digits. A low cloud cover kept direct sun off the mourners. I was pleased by the number who attended considering how few people the Fitzsimmonses knew on Folly. Two rows of white folding chairs were in front of the coffin with Laurie, Gail and Dean Clark occupying the front row.

Both ladies wore long, black dresses. Dean looked out of place in a navy, three-piece suit. Everyone else was casually dressed, including Charles in one of his few non-logoed, long-sleeved T-shirts. Good to his word, Theo was there and, as a concession to his age, was offered a seat in the second row. He was joined by William Hansel and three ladies I didn't recognize. Stanley Kremitz and a woman I assumed to be his wife were standing with a group of six others behind the row of chairs. Charles and I joined that group.

The service was brief, a good thing considering the

stifling heat. The women beside Theo spent most of the service waving their faces with fans featuring an image of a church on them. The fans gave them away as regulars at Lowcountry outdoor funerals. I worried about Theo since he didn't have a fan, and his face turned redder as the service progressed. Dean sat ramrod straight, and Gail kept her arm around Laurie's shoulder while she had her head bowed the entire time.

As the service ended, I moved behind Theo to see if he was okay. He said he would be as soon as he was in his air-conditioned car. Charles went to offer condolences to Laurie, William joined Theo and me for the short walk to our vehicles. I wanted to make sure Theo made it safely to his car before speaking to the widow. By the time Theo was resting in air-conditioned comfort, Laurie was walking toward the three elderly ladies who'd been seated behind her. She had on black, high heel shoes and gingerly traversed the bed of pine needles near her car. The ladies took turns hugging the widow before they became engrossed in conversation.

Stanley led the woman he was with over to me. "Chris, allow me to introduce my better half, Veronica."

I said that it was nice to meet her and appreciated them attending.

"I didn't know the deceased," Veronica said as she squeezed Stanley's arm. "Stan had met them, so I thought it would be nice for the widow to see that her island neighbors were sympathetic to her loss."

Stanley nodded a couple of times. "Every cloud has a silver lining."

I was trying to come up with a cliché that meant, *How do I get away from Stanley* when Veronica said they were in a hurry to meet a friend in Charleston? I pretended I hated to see them go.

Charles moved beside me. I told him that I wanted to speak to Laurie. He said that there was no need because we were meeting her, and the Clarks, for lunch at the Crab Shack.

We got in the car, and I said, "Charles, I don't want to infringe on Laurie's time of grief."

"It was her idea. She insisted that we join them."

"We?"

"Sure," Charles said while adjusting the air-conditioning vent. "She asked me to have lunch with them. I told her you were driving. She nodded meaning she wanted both of us."

Not my interpretation. Arguing with Charles would have been as fruitful as arguing with the live oaks standing sentry around the perimeter of the cemetery.

Charles wiped sweat from his neck as we pulled back on Ft. Johnson Road. He pointed his thumb toward the back window. "Ever been to Ft. Johnson? It's a mile behind us."

"No."

"It goes back a long way. Named after Sir Nathaniel Johnson back in seventeen-something. He was the Proprietary Governor of the Carolinas, whatever that is."

Charles was somewhat of a history buff. My interest in history ended when I was in the ninth grade and the teacher, Old-Bitty Jenkins, asked me what Abe Lincoln and Jefferson Davis had in common. I said they were both dead. She threw a piece of chalk at me. Apparently, I was right, but also wrong.

"Oh," I said, showing little interest.

He mumbled something about the fort's role during the American Revolution, then during the Civil War, and how most of the land now belonged to the South Carolina Wildlife, and Marine Resources Department. I zoned out until I heard him finish the lesson with something about the College of Charleston having its Grice Marine Laboratory on part of the land.

I knew Charles enough to know something was bothering him. He was using the history lesson to take his mind off whatever it was.

The roar of the air conditioner lessened the temperature in the car until it reached a comfortable level. "What's bothering you?"

He readjusted the air vent again. "I'm worried about Laurie. Gail's leaving tomorrow. She'll be alone. She knows a few people at the most. She said that she's still not over being shot at. What's going to happen to her?"

Was someone trying to kill her, or did she fire the gun to deflect suspicion that she killed her husband? I shared that question with Charles.

"Don't be ridiculous. Of course, she didn't fake it. Did you see how torn up she was back there?"

I didn't remind him that she'd taught drama.

"Charles, remember eight years ago when that guy who lived at the Edge shot himself in the arm with the crossbow?"

The Edge was a large seaside boardinghouse owned by a lady who rented rooms to those who couldn't afford the costlier condos along the beach. It was destroyed by a hurricane, a hurricane with the added assistance of a killer who came within moments of ending Charles's and my lives.

"Duh, nearly got us killed."

"Yes, he shot himself so the police would think he was a victim like the two people he'd killed."

"Did you miss the part about not forgetting what happened?"

Then why was he being so dense about what I was suggesting?

"Charles, don't you see how this could be the same thing?"

He shook his head. "This is different."

"How?"

He slammed his hand on the center console. "It just is." He then whispered, "Chris, it just is."

Not another word was spoken, until we found a parking spot across Center Street from the restaurant.

THE FOLLY BEACH Crab Shack was one of the island's longest-tenured restaurants. Laurie and the Clarks hadn't arrived, so we had the choice of a table on the covered patio or inside. I would've preferred the patio but, after standing in the heat at the funeral, and considering the clothing worn by our luncheon companions, we opted for inside.

A server appeared with water for each of us when the other three arrived and were escorted to the table. Laurie and Gail had replaced their high heels with flats. Dean had abandoned his tie, vest, and suit coat. He looked like he'd walked through a sprinkler. We stood as Laurie hugged each of us then took the chair beside Charles. The Clarks sat on the other side of the table.

"Thank you for choosing inside," Gail said. "The cool air feels good. We were afraid you'd be on the patio."

The newcomers were quick to say water when the server, who announced she was Selene and would be taking care of us, returned to ask what they wanted to drink. The color in their faces had turned from standing-in-a-sauna red to pale Caucasian.

Laurie glanced at me then turned to Charles. "Thank you for coming to the funeral. It was nice seeing so many people there who I don't know that well."

Gail added, "Laurie's worried about being here with so few friends. Dean and I've encouraged her to move back home."

Laurie jerked her head toward Gail. "Gail, I appreciate your offer. I told you in the car that this is my home. I'm not going anywhere. Let's talk about something else. I'm certain these gentlemen aren't interested."

She didn't know Charles.

"Laurie," he said, "you're one of us now. Look how many people attended the funeral. They were there for you.

We stick together. You don't have to worry about making friends."

Gail interrupted, "I'm just saying—"

Laurie interrupted Gail's interruption, "I'm saying the topic is closed. Let's order."

I motioned for Selene before the women exchanged blows. Charles put his arm around Laurie's shoulder, showing which side he was on. Dean asked Gail if she wanted to head home this afternoon instead of in the morning.

She looked at the menu then said, "No. I promised Laurie we'd stay to help straighten up the house."

"It's not that big a mess," Laurie said, subtly sharing her vote on the Clarks leaving early. "I can take care of it."

Dean had leaned back in the chair and watched the antagonistic ping-pong match between the women before saying, "Either way is fine with me."

Gail said, "What time is your meeting tomorrow?"

"After lunch," Dean said. "There'll be time if we leave in the morning."

"Then, it's final," Gail said, "We'll wait until tomorrow."

Laurie's glare looked more hostile than one of grief. Selene had stood at the table with pen in hand waiting for the debate to end before offering to take our order. We ordered, and the conversation took a more civil turn. Laurie talked about the restaurant's colorful walls and the murals. Gail talked about the considerable number of restaurants on Center Street, while Dean stuffed his mouth with peanuts he scooped from a barrel beside the patio door. We ate in silence for a few minutes after the food arrived.

The silence was broken when Laurie said, more to herself than to the rest of us, "All Anthony dreamed about was moving here, finding buried treasure. He said we wouldn't have to worry about money again."

Gail, in a gesture of peace, put her hand on Laurie's arm. "Yes, dear, I know. We'll miss him terribly."

I'd heard, over the years, that Civil War relics had been found on Folly Beach. Uniform buttons, belt buckles, knives, cooking utensils, and cannonballs were the items I'd heard most often mentioned. If that was what the Fitzsimmons were looking for, I couldn't see how they could benefit financially to where they wouldn't have to worry about money.

Charles must've had similar thoughts. "Laurie, what kind of buried treasure were you looking for?" His face broke into one of his loveable smiles that made it difficult to be mad at him regardless how personal the question. "Is there a pot of gold out there I don't know about?"

She dropped her fork on the plate. "No, of course not. It was… nothing. Gail, I think I need to get home. This has been a draining morning."

Gail looked at Laurie's plate. "You sure you don't want to finish eating?"

Dean said, "Gail, didn't you hear her. She's ready to go."

Charles said not to worry about the check, he'd get it. Laurie stood before Gail could give her more grief about finishing lunch, or moving back to Florida, or whatever else she wanted to gripe about. Charles was quick to his feet. He gave Laurie a hug before the trio made their way to the exit.

Charles watched them go. "Wow. If those are best friends, I'd hate to hear Laurie's enemies."

I agreed, yet didn't say anything. I was reeling from Charles's offer to pick up the check.

Chapter Sixteen

William Hansel and Theo entered the restaurant while we were eating. They didn't appear as bothered by the heat since they were on the patio. Charles and I finished. He paid, then suggested we visit William and Theo.

As we approached their table, William looked up from his fish sandwich and smiled. "I see where you gentlemen were engaged in social intercourse with the widow and her acquaintances from Florida."

Uninvited, Charles pulled up a chair. "If that means we were talking with them, yep."

The professor smiled, took a sip of iced tea, and Theo said, "William convinced me we were hungry after leaving the cemetery."

I didn't think it was necessary for him to explain why they were at a restaurant at lunch time.

I said, "William, I was pleased to see you at the funeral."

He nodded. "As you know, I wasn't familiar with the family, yet when Theo indicated an interest in attending I felt compelled to accompany him. I postulated that attendance would be minimal, so I didn't want Mrs. Fitzsimmons to feel that no one was saddened over her spouse's passing."

Theo nodded. "I'm glad he did. I didn't want to go by myself. As cruel it is to say, I didn't want to invite Sal. I was afraid he'd see those gathered as an audience and start cracking jokes."

Charles said, "Wise."

Selene brought fresh glasses of water to Charles and me then told us to wave if we needed anything.

William took another bite then said, "Chris, I've been thinking about what you said about buried treasure being on Folly. I did some research in the college library, found several references to buried artifacts in proximity to our location. In addition to the gold from the Civil War I told you about, I found information on historic occurrences a hundred years prior to the Civil War."

"Rumors about pirate ships you mentioned?"

"Precisely."

Charles leaned closer to William. "What'd you learn?"

William glanced at the ceiling, like he was recalling something from the far reaches of his memory. "According to two sources, pirates frequented the waters off Folly in addition to other barrier islands. They hid their vessels in and around the isolated islands and pounced upon unsuspecting supply ships sailing to coastal locations." He stopped and took another bite.

Charles, who doesn't take kindly to interruptions in something he wants to hear, said, "What happened?"

I said, "Charles, let the man eat."

William smiled. "Are you familiar with an English gentleman named Edward Teach?"

I shook my head.

Charles said, "Who's he?"

"Perhaps you are familiar with his more common moniker, Blackbeard."

Theo raised his hand. William pointed at him.

Theo said, "One of the most famous pirates to sail the ocean blue. He had a house on Folly."

"Correct."

Charles, who didn't want to be left out, added, "I knew that. A hurricane blew his house away."

You know my opinion of history, so I remained silent.

"Mr. Teach, Blackbeard, is the subject of numerous myths, rumors, perhaps an occasional fact. What does appear to be substantiated is that in his day he had one of the mightiest ships ever to sail. He used it to his full advantage. His ship carried more than forty cannons, making it more formidable than any other he encountered."

William paused and glanced around the patio before continuing. "Blackbeard was also three hundred years ahead of those who make a living in our media-saturated, image-obsessed world by aiding politicians or successful businesspersons with how they are perceived by the public. Before going in battle, the famous pirate would garb himself in black, affix pistols to his torso, then at that point don a large, black captain's hat."

"Scary," said Charles.

William looked at him with a gaze I suspected he used on students who had the audacity to interrupt the professor's lecture. "There's more, Charles."

Charles waved his palm in William's face as an apology.

"One reference book said he would put slow-burning fuses in his greasy black hair and beard then ignite them. The fuses sputtered giving off smoke, which gave Blackbeard the appearance of the devil rising from the depths of hell. When opposing ship captains saw the spectacle, gentlemen, they surrendered without firing a shot."

Charles switched from saying scary to uttering, "Cool."

William ignored him. "One of Mr. Teach's travelling companions for a time was Stede Bonnet, another famous pirate."

Charles said, "Hanged at the Battery in Charleston."

"How do you know that?" I asked.

Charles smiled. "Historic marker at the Battery. It says Stede, and twenty-nine of his crew, were hanged in seventeen something. Sorry, don't remember the year. Another pirate dude and nineteen members of his crew were also hanged there. Their bodies were thrown in the nearby marsh that was eventually filled in. That area now houses some of the mansions in the Battery."

"1718," William added, showing his penchant for accuracy.

Enough of the history lesson about what happened in Charleston. I wanted to get back to Folly and buried treasure. "William, did any of the references specifically say Blackbeard, or other pirates, buried their bounty on Folly?"

"Mind you, I didn't spend a great deal of time in the library. I found no documented references to pirates burying or hiding their ill-gained treasures on our island."

Charles said, "That doesn't mean they didn't."

"Of course not," William said. "I did find references to handed-down stories about buried treasures, but none of them mentioned Folly, or Coffin Island, as it was then called."

Charles rubbed his chin. "So Laurie and her late husband were on a quest with nothing to indicate it would pay off?"

"I can't speak to their intentions," William said. "There were no documented instances that I could find. I did discover one interesting tidbit, albeit not footnoted with credible citations. You see, I'm constantly reminding my students that if they are going to reference something in their papers, they must cite the source. That's so future—"

Charles interrupted, "The tidbit, William?"

"Yes, of course. There were stories that one large cache of gold and silver was buried along the North or South Carolina coast. The interesting part of the stories was that instant death would come to anyone who sought the cache."

Charles said, "A curse?"

"That was the inference. I do not believe in curses. Research shows there is always a rational explanation when some event is attributed to the amorphous concept of a curse."

Charles said, "So you're saying that there's no research that proves that curses are real. And by curses, you mean those things that can't be proven because, well, because they're curses?"

William chuckled. "Charles, that's why I teach travel and tourism. Mysticism, mythology, and theology are outside my area of expertise."

"So, the curse could be real?" Charles said.

At times such as this, it was difficult to tell if Charles was serious, obstinate, or trying to provoke a reaction.

Before William answered, Theo leaned forward, wiped his mouth with a napkin, and said, "I bet Anthony Fitzsimmons believes in curses."

I didn't know whether to laugh or agree. Instead of either, I stated the obvious, "We'll never know."

Chapter Seventeen

Theo hadn't mentioned his daughter-in-law while at the Crab Shack, so I was curious if he'd asked her to stay at his house. I conceded that after knowing Charles for nearly a decade, I was becoming more like him. I rationalized that it wasn't a bad thing, although it had gotten me in trouble more than once. With that said, I didn't see any harm in calling Theo.

Sal answered so I asked if Theo was home.

"Hey, Chris, if Theo tells you that I kicked him in the butt, it's true."

I was used to my friends' penchant for answering the phone in, shall I say, a nonconventional manner. Sal's response was a new one.

"Why?"

"I didn't mean to, Theo turned around." Sal broke into laughter.

I wanted to ask if he'd started a dial-a-joke business but was afraid it'd encourage him. I repeated, "Is he there?"

Instead of answering, I heard rustling in the background, before Theo said, "Hang on while I move to the kitchen."

The sound of Sal's laughter lessened.

Theo said, "Sorry about that. I'm making progress, breaking my brother of his exasperating habit of seeing every person as a victim of his humor. He'd never admit it, although it's clear to me that he uses humor, what he thinks as humor, as a shield against others seeing his insecurities."

"Good luck."

"I'll need it. The good thing around the house is that I can turn off my hearing aids. Oh, well, he's my brother, I love him." He paused, before saying, "I don't suppose you called to hear a joke, or me gripe about Sal."

"True. I was wondering if you talked to Grace."

"Last night. I told her there was plenty of room, that she was welcome to move in until she got on her feet." Theo sighed. "She thanked me then turned me down."

"Why?"

"She repeated what she'd told us at the hotel about coming to South Carolina to be near Teddy's dad so we could see each other. She said she didn't come to be a burden on anyone. I told her she wouldn't be a burden, that there was plenty of room, that she wouldn't be in the way. Know what she told me?"

"What?"

"She said she drove by the house yesterday, saw how big it was. I asked why she didn't stop. She said she didn't see a car in the drive, so figured I wasn't here. She said the real reason was to get a layout of the island to see a good place to set up her food truck."

"Is she still living in the truck?"

"Yes."

"What're you going to do?"

"What can I do? She made it clear she didn't want to stay here. She was polite, didn't sound angry, yet was clear about her intentions."

"Did she find somewhere she could set up?"

"She didn't say."

"Think she knows what she needs to do to operate a food truck on Folly? I assume there're health department permits, inspections, specific local regulations about opening a business. When I opened my gallery I had my friend, Sean Aker, help me through the bureaucratic maze."

"Chris, I have no idea. She had the truck in California, so I assume she knows the hoops to jump through. She seems self-sufficient so I'm sure she'll be able to take care of it. I plan to call in a couple of days to see what she's learned. I'll offer help, financial or otherwise, if she needs a lawyer to get her business set up. If she does, I'll recommend Sean."

I wished him luck a second time.

He thanked me, then added, "I was thinking after lunch about what you told us Laurie and her husband said about finding treasure. It had me confused."

"Why?"

"If Anthony thought there was even a ghost of a chance, pun intended, in finding something of value, he must've known more than vague rumors about treasure being buried, or relics from the Civil War."

Theo had an excellent point. Laurie sounded confident they were going to discover something countless people had failed to find since the Civil War ended more than a century and a half ago. Laurie and Anthony were new to the area, so they hadn't been here long enough to explore each nook and cranny. So, what did they know? How did they learn it? Even more important, if it existed, where was the treasure? I told Theo I agreed and asked if he had any idea how they might've known.

"No. What I can tell you is Sal would have a joke about it."

No doubt, I thought.

I moved to the chair in the living room and reflected on

the day that began with a funeral, continued with an awkward, tense lunch with Laurie, Dean, Gail, and Charles, then ended with a sophomoric joke and Theo making a generous offer to Grace only to have it rejected.

I was starting to drift to sleep in the chair when Charles called.

"Guess where we're going tomorrow morning?"

I didn't have the energy to ask how I could possibly know. "Where?"

"Laurie's house."

If I wasn't fully awake when he started the conversation, I was now. "Why?"

"She called and invited us to coffee."

"Us?"

"Not exactly."

"What exactly?"

"Something like, 'Charles, could you stop by the house in the morning around nine?' "

"She invited you."

"There's no reason to get so picky about it. Would you go with me? She sounded like there was something strange going on. I'd feel more comfortable with you there."

"Strange, how?"

"Can't put my finger on it. Strange."

"That helps. What's she going to say if you show up at her door with me in tow?"

"I'll let you know in the morning."

I rolled my eyes at the phone. "What do you think she wants?"

"I'll let you know in the morning."

I surrendered. He said he had to deliver a surfboard for the surf shop and would meet me at Laurie's house. She wanted him to be there at nine, so I knew he'd be there at 8:30, Charles Standard Time.

I'm certain he said, "Thank you." Of course, I couldn't hear it since he'd hung up.

Chapter Eighteen

I pulled in Laurie's gravel drive and parked behind Charles's Toyota Venza and Laurie's MINI. Charles stepped out of his vehicle. He had on navy shorts, and a long-sleeved, gray T-shirt with IPFW in blue letters on the front. I had stopped asking about the shirts years ago, although it'd never stopped him from sharing, in my opinion, worthless information about his logo ware. I was clueless about what the letters stood for and comfortable remaining that way.

Fortunately, he didn't feel the need to enlighten me. He said, "On time, good."

We walked up Laurie's steps thirty minutes early, and one person more than she'd invited. I stood behind Charles, wishing myself invisible as the homeowner opened the door. She'd abandoned her black, mourning clothes. She had on a baby-blue blouse and tan slacks, a drastic contrast from our first visit when she was in a quilted robe. Her face looked refreshed, with no remnants of tears.

"Oh," she said. "You're early," proving that she didn't

know Charles enough to know about his time quirk. She glanced around Charles. "Hi, Chris."

Charles said, "Is it okay if my friend came with me?"

I didn't expect her to say, "No."

"I suppose, come on in."

Not quite an open-arms welcome, although, under the circumstances it wasn't bad.

We followed her to the kitchen, where she asked how we liked our coffee. We said black.

"Good. I have all this food the good people of Folly have given me, but I don't have cream." She got two mugs out of the cabinet and poured our drinks. She handed a mug to Charles and said, "What's IPFW, a union?"

"Thanks for asking," he said as he glanced at me. "It's Indiana University, Purdue University Fort Wayne."

"Oh," she said.

My sentiments exactly.

"Did you go to school there?"

Further proof that she didn't know Charles that well.

"No. I thought the shirt was interesting."

"Oh," she said, for the third time. She walked us to the living room where we sat on the sofa. Laurie took the Lazy Boy.

"Did your company get off okay?" I asked.

"Yes, thank goodness. Dean has a meeting with his banker this afternoon, so I think Gail would've stayed forever if her ride hadn't been leaving. I love her to death; she'd do anything for me. As you could tell from lunch, she'd smother me with kindness, and advice. As wonderful as she is, smothering is still smothering." She turned to Charles. "That's why I asked Charles over. I wanted to apologize for getting him in the middle of our carping."

The use of *him* wasn't lost on me, so I waited for the only person she'd invited to respond.

"Laurie," Charles said. "I hadn't given it a thought. We

were glad you invited us, weren't bothered a bit. Were we, Chris?"

Yes, it bothered me, yes, I felt uncomfortable horning in on her grief. Of course, I said, "No. It was fine."

"Thank you. I feel better with that out of the way."

Charles said, "Has Gail always been that pushy?"

Laurie looked at the floor. "I don't know what's gotten into her. She wasn't always that bad. Honest, she wasn't."

I didn't think she expected a response, especially since we didn't know Gail at all. It didn't stop Charles.

"You've been friends a long time. I'm sure Anthony's death struck her hard. Maybe that's why."

Laurie looked up from the floor. "You're a wise man, Charles. That's probably it."

It was the first time I'd heard Charles called wise without being followed by another word for donkey.

The wise man said, "Are you going to be okay?"

"I think so. I hope so. I don't know what I'll do without Anthony. He did everything for me. Perhaps Gail was right about me moving back to Jacksonville. I don't know many people here. And what about that bullet that nearly killed me? Somebody killed Anthony, somebody was trying to kill me, Charles. I don't know what to think. What's to say they won't try again?"

Charles looked over at me, expecting me to respond. She was talking to Charles, so I stayed out of it. He took the hint.

"Any idea who it might've been?"

She jerked her head toward Charles. "No. Why kill Anthony? I know he could be difficult. Lordy, we had our differences, but no one knew him here. So why kill him? What have we done to make someone that angry?" She jumped out of the chair and grabbed our mugs. "Let me get you more." She headed to the kitchen without waiting for us to respond.

I looked at Charles, who shrugged.

Laurie returned with refills. Her hands were shaking as she handed us the mugs. Not knowing what to say, I took a sip as she returned to the La-Z-Boy.

"Laurie," Charles said, "could Anthony's death, umm, murder, have something to do with what you were looking for out there?"

"Why? All we were doing was looking for Civil War relics."

I took a gamble. "Laurie, when we were at lunch, you mentioned that Anthony said something about you not having to worry after you found the buried treasure. What was—"

She leaned up in her chair so fast that I thought she might fall out. "You must've misunderstood. I wouldn't have said buried treasure. Heavens, that sounds like gold, silver, or something more valuable than what we were looking for. They may have worth, but nothing like buried treasure. A simple misunderstanding." She leaned back.

I hadn't heard her incorrectly at lunch. "I misunderstood. Sorry."

"Are you a treasure hunter?" She had leaned back yet her words were as sharp as they were seconds earlier.

I smiled. "Far from it. I'd never thought about it. Why?"

"Nothing. I was curious."

Curious, and ill at ease with the topic.

"I know it's none of my business," Charles said. "Are you going to be okay financially?"

"It's okay to ask, Charles," she said as her smile returned. "I'm glad you're concerned. I think so. Anthony had insisted on that nice insurance policy. I have my teachers' retirement."

"If you ever need anything, don't feel bad about calling."

"Charles, thank you for the offer. I may take you up on it. I appreciate you, umm, both of you, stopping by. I know you must be busy, so I won't keep you."

A dismissal, albeit a polite one. We stood, thanked her for the coffee, and reiterated that she could call Charles if she needed anything.

On the drive home, I asked myself two questions. First, why did Laurie really ask Charles over? She could've told him on the phone she was sorry about how he was caught in an awkward situation at lunch. That would've been as effective and easier than Charles going to her house. The second question was why did she lie about what she'd said at lunch concerning a buried treasure? The drive home was too short for me to come up with adequate answers. What I did come up with was a need to learn the truth.

DESPITE THE FOOD Laurie's neighbors had brought, all she had offered Charles and me was coffee. I parked in the drive but, instead of going in the house, I walked next door to Bert's Market to grab something to quench my hunger. I found a Reuben sandwich that I could microwave at home, and found Abraham, excuse me, Captain Gant pulling a six-pack of Budweiser out of the wall cooler. He lowered the beer to his side and gave me a vague smile of recognition.

"Hi, Captain," I said, and in case he didn't remember, added, "I'm Chris."

"Of course. I may be old, but I'm not senile."

Old, not senile, and cranky, I thought, before I said something about it being a muggy day and that it looked like it would rain tomorrow.

"We need the rain," he said.

I turned to walk away when he said, "Glad I ran into you." He set the beer on the floor. "Have you heard if the police have suspects in the damned relic hunter's murder?"

I thought it was a strange question. He was the retired cop, not me.

"No, why do you think I'd know?"

"I hear rumors. Someone said you're good friends with the chief. I thought she might've shared something."

"We're friends although she—"

"You know what she accused me of?"

Irritating interrupting came to mind. I said that I didn't.

"She questioned me a half hour yesterday, accusing me of taking a shot at the damned relic hunter's wife. How stupid is that?"

I didn't think it was stupid since I'd suggested it to Cindy. "Why'd she think that?"

"She was playing it close to the vest. Admirable, I suppose. That's how I would've handled it back in the day when I interrogated suspects. The chief didn't say why I was a suspect. I figure it was because of how I'd badmouthed the couple for meddling in the past, things they had no damned business doing."

"What'd you tell her?"

He glared at me. "Young man, it's none of your damned business what I told her." His glare turned to a wicked smile. He put his hand near my face, palm out. "I have nothing to hide. I was at a doctor's appointment in Charleston. Told the chief there was a herd of sick people in the waiting room the entire two hours. That's right, two hours waiting. Ought to be a law about that. I had to sit there listening to people cough, wheeze, spew germs. If I wasn't sick when I got there, I damned well could've been when I left. There were witnesses galore. The damned doc couldn't vouch for most of that time because he didn't see me for two hours. Did I already say that?"

I nodded. "Good alibi."

Abraham was at the top of my suspect list. Even if he didn't take a shot at Laurie, he could've killed Anthony.

"Not saying I wouldn't have had a desire to kill the damned woman for her and her husband digging for buried treasure. It's pathetic how people meddle where they shouldn't. I'm not sorry someone's trying to end her meddling life. I'm only saying it wasn't me."

That was today's second reference to buried treasure.

"Captain, my understanding is that they were searching for Civil War relics. What do you mean about buried treasure?"

He looked around the store and leaned closer to me, like he was about to whisper the nuclear missile launch code. "Remember when I told you about the grandfather of the woman I was accused of trying to shoot?"

"Harnell Levi. You said he was a nut."

"Good recall."

"You said he was always talking about pirates, about treasure."

"Meddling in the past. Horrible."

I didn't want him to get on another rant about those who dig up the past. "Do you think he told his granddaughter about buried treasure and that's what they were hunting?"

"Sure do."

"People have searched here, plus on the other barrier islands for decades. They haven't found anything other than Civil War items, or skeletons. What makes you think the Fitzsimmonses would have a chance at finding something of value?"

He rubbed the side of his face and looked around again. "I didn't take it too serious at the time. Hell, I didn't take anything the old coot said serious. Didn't give it a thought, until the damned relic hunter was killed."

"Take what seriously?"

Gant nodded. "The map."

"Map?"

"In addition to running around singing show tunes, talking about Nazi subs he claimed to see, and looking like a character actor out of a B cowboy movie, when the old codger got a few of those in his system," Gant pointed to the six-pack on the floor, "he'd spout off about a treasure map that was going to lead him to riches."

"Was he serious?"

"Serious as a delusional, screwed-up, old codger can be."

"Where'd he get this supposed treasure map?"

"As far as I know he never said."

"Anyone ever see it?"

"I never heard about him showing it to anyone."

"Except Laurie?"

"Speculation, my friend. Pure speculation."

A little sucking up may be fruitful. "You're a former law enforcement officer, a good one I've heard. You have good instincts, decades of experience. Any thoughts on who had reason to shoot Anthony Fitzsimmons?"

He smiled. "Flattery, not a bad technique." His smile disappeared as quickly as it had appeared. "Back in the day, if I was looking for a killer, I'd start with the spouse. The relic hunter's wife. Does she have motive? Money's always a big one? Did hubby have a lot of it? Was he worth more dead than alive? Then there's love. Was he having an affair, or did she love someone else, and her husband was an albatross around her neck, a problem she needed to eliminate?"

"I don't know—"

He ignored me. "Then you get reasons that are flat out stupid. Did she get mad at him because he wanted to watch a NASCAR race when she wanted to watch a Hallmark movie, or she didn't like the way he criticized her for the way she cooked pork chops? Stupid reasons, yet I've seen spouses killed because of them."

"Who else would you consider besides the wife?"

Abraham looked at his hand and held up three fingers. "My third choice would be someone who knew about the treasure, someone who wanted to get it before the dead guy found it."

"If Anthony had the map you mentioned, why wouldn't

the killer wait until he dug up whatever was out there then steal it?"

"That's what I said or meant to say. How do you know he didn't?"

"It doesn't make sense that they found something. If they found the treasure, why wouldn't she have said something to the police, or to me when Charles and I found her in the car? As far as I know, the police didn't find a shovel or where digging had taken place."

Gant grinned and shrugged. "They didn't find a murder weapon either, did they? It would've been easy to throw the gun and whatever he had been digging with in the ocean. It'd been raining hard. With the land low out there, it could've flooded, washed sand and crap into wherever he'd been digging. Tons of unanswered questions, ain't there? That's why they call it a mystery."

"True."

"I'll tell you one thing, mister. It's a mystery for the police to figure out. It's nothing for a retired state police officer or a whatever you are to waste time with."

I wasn't about to argue. I'm also far from a mathematician and have trouble balancing my own check book, yet I realized something Gant had said didn't compute.

"You said your third choice was someone who knew about the treasure hunt. Who's your second choice?"

His smile returned. "You're looking at him."

He picked up the six pack of Bud, turned, and walked to the cash register leaving me staring at the cooler and thinking how much simpler life would be if Charles and I had decided to drive to Charleston to take photos of the mansions overlooked the bay rather than traipsing off to the old Coast Guard property that fateful morning. I also thought that Abraham had a good point that whatever had happened to Anthony Fitzsimmons was none of my business. It would better be left to the police.

Finally, I wondered why that wouldn't be the case.

Chapter Nineteen

The next morning, the heavy rain that Abraham and I wasted time talking about had done its damage, and eased. A puddle the size of Lake Erie was in the front yard as water cascaded off the roof of the screened-in porch. An hour later, the rain ended, and I decided to make a visit to Barb's Books. She was standing by the large plate glass window, gazing at the traffic passing on Center Street, a practice that consumed hours of my time when the space had been my gallery.

She smiled. "Thank goodness, someone enters."

She had on another red blouse. As a concession to the summer temperatures, and the custom of many island retail employees, she wore shorts and tennis shoes.

"Slow day?"

"Including you, I can count today's customers on one finger."

"Suppose I should buy something."

She rolled her eyes. "How many books have you bought since I've been open?"

"Counting on one hand, zero fingers."

"Don't ruin your perfect record. Can I interest you in a Diet Pepsi?"

"You twisted my arm," I followed her to the office. I looked around, again marveling how different the office looked than when it was Landrum Gallery's office, snack bar, and hang out for my friends.

She said as she handed me a drink, "Let's head up front so I don't miss any of the customers who don't come in."

I was pleased she was acclimating to the quirky character of many of the island's residents. I joined her as she returned to the staring spot at the front window then shared my conversation with Captain Gant.

Barb listened with the intensity of an attorney, took a sip of Diet Root Beer, before saying, "It's interesting how he included himself in his list of suspects. That was an effective way to deflect guilt."

"What do you mean?"

"You said he smiled when he added his name to the list. It was as if he threw it in as an absurdity, like who could possibly think he was the killer. Also, he has a solid alibi for when someone shot at Laurie."

"True. Depending upon what version Laurie gives, she was either in the bedroom or in the kitchen when the shot was fired."

"You think she faked it?"

I shrugged

"The police know Laurie's conflicting stories?"

"Yes."

"They're following up?"

I was heading into a trap. I nodded.

She mirrored my nod. "So, you're stepping aside, leaving it to the police?"

The sun had started to break through the clouds, as I muttered, "Yes," and changed the subject. "Looks like it's going to be an enjoyable day."

She gave me a skeptical expression, then agreed about the weather. Before I said I should head home we agreed to meet for supper in a couple of days.

I turned onto East Ashley Avenue, where I saw a white, Chevy step van parked at the entrance to a large gravel lot that's the prime parking area for beachgoers and customers to the central business district's restaurants and stores. The van had been converted into a food truck and had a large red and brown oval logo on the side with a rendering of a hot dog slathered with mustard. Above the hot dog were the words *Hot Diggity Dog!* Underneath the cartoon-looking hot dog, it read, *Gourmet Hot Dogs.* I didn't have to be a detective to know it belonged to Theo's daughter-in-law.

I pulled in a parking space in front of Cool Breeze Bike Rental across the street from the truck. I waved at Matty, the bike rental's owner, told him I'd be just a minute, and crossed the street to the food truck. The six-foot long service window was closed. No one answered after I knocked twice. I walked around the vehicle to see if Grace was nearby. She wasn't, so I took a closer look at the vehicle.

There was a dent on the back corner on the passenger's side. I thought there would be more than that if I had to back the truck into parking spaces. The tires weren't bald, although I suspected they'd have trouble passing a safety inspection. It appeared a miracle that Grace had safely made the twenty-three-hundred-mile trip from California.

I knocked one more time in case she'd been sleeping. No response, so I headed back to my car.

Matty was leaning against my hood. He smiled. "If you'd told me where you were going, I could've saved you a trip."

The truck was Grace's only means of motorized transportation, so I knew she couldn't have gone far. "You know where she went?"

He waved in the direction of Center Street less than a block away. "When she started walking that way, I should have asked for a written itinerary and how long she'd be gone. I didn't know you'd be asking, so I didn't."

I smiled at my friend. "You don't know where she went?"

"No. Now that you're standing in my parking area, keeping hundreds of vacationers from getting to my business which will probably put me out of work, let me ask something. Who is she? Why is that oversized hot dog stand parked there? Oh, yeah, where's the lady from who parked it?"

I wasn't certain if Matty knew Theo. Even if he did, I doubted Theo would want him to know Grace's story about why she was here.

"Someone I recently met, name's Grace. She wants to open a food truck on Folly. Why'd you ask where she's from?"

"She came over an hour ago to tell me her name. She gave me the cutest smile I'd seen in years. She has a delightful accent."

"If she told you her name, why ask who she is?"

"There's a difference between a name and who someone is."

True. I still didn't want to get in an extended conversation about Theo's daughter-in-law. "She's Jamaican, came from California."

"Yep. Knew she wasn't from around here. Mighty cute sounding. Is she thinking of opening her business there?"

"I don't know."

"Hope so. She's pleasant to listen to, and look at."

"If you see her, tell her I stopped by."

"You got it. Besides, that'll give me an excuse to share some facetime with her cute Jamaican accent, and lovely smile."

I smiled. "Since when have you ever needed an excuse to talk to someone?"

He smiled. "Now get your car out of here so real customers can get in."

Chapter Twenty

The sun had concluded its work for the day while I was on my screened-in porch watching cars pass in front of the house, many carrying surfboards. I smiled, thinking about my ill-fated attempt at surfing with Dude, when the phone rang.

"Chris, this is Matty. Did I catch you at an inconvenient time?"

Matty was an interesting man, as Folly as anyone can be. This was the first time he'd called. I was tempted to ask him to teach telephone etiquette to my friends. As great as that temptation was, I decided it was more important to hear what he wanted.

"It's fine. What's going on?"

"You were asking about the lady with the food truck, so I figured you'd want to know something's going on over there. Two patrol cars are parked beside the truck. Now, Chief LaMond just rolled up."

"Any idea what happened?"

"Nah. The good news is there aren't firetrucks, or ambulances."

That was good, although it didn't answer my question. I started the block-long walk to the truck with the phone still to my ear. "You don't have any idea what happened?"

"I don't think they're there to buy hot dogs. If you'd mosey over, you could con your buddy, the chief, into telling you."

"I'm on my way."

"Good. I'll leave it in your capable hands."

I was a half block from the food truck and saw flashing lights from the patrol cars. One of the cars was exiting the lot when I crossed the street in front of Grace's vehicle. Its door was standing open, its owner sitting on the slide-out step. She wore a pink sundress, and her arms were waving around, like she was describing something to the chief who was standing in front of her, taking notes. Grace was backlit from the light inside the truck, so I couldn't see her expression.

Chief LaMond looked up when she saw me approach, pointed her pen at me, and said, "What took you so long. You're usually attracted to commotion, like a mosquito to my lovely, ivory-hued arms."

Theo's daughter-in-law stood then turned so I could see her face. "Hello, Mr. Landrum."

Cindy glanced at me then looked at Grace. "You know this fossil?"

"Yes, mon. Mr. Landrum is a friend of, umm, someone I know."

It didn't appear that Grace wanted to get into her relationship with Theo. "What happened, chief?"

Cindy glanced at her notebook. "Someone broke in Ms. Stoll's truck. I was taking down basic information, was about to ask her if she was related to Theodore Stoll when you stuck you nose in official police business, again."

Grace's head jerked toward Cindy. "Are you familiar with Mr. Stoll?"

She was about to get her first lesson in everyone-knows-everyone on Folly.

"Most definitely," Cindy said. "Known him ever since he moved her. Your relationship?"

"I was married to Teddy, his son."

"Oh."

That threw Cindy. Now, for my contribution to the conversation. "Theo's son and Grace lived in California. Theodore Jr., Teddy, was killed in a motorcycle accident a while back. Grace has moved here to open her business." I looked at Grace to see if she wanted me to say more.

She took it from there. "I needed to leave California, thought being closer to my father-in-law could be a good thing." She waved her hand toward the truck. "Now, this."

"Was anything taken?" I asked Grace, sensing she was uncomfortable saying more about her family.

"I don't think so. I was eating supper at that place called Planet Follywood. All the money I have was with me." She tilted her head toward the truck. "Everything in there is a mess. I can't tell what could be missing."

I asked, "How'd they get in?"

She started to respond when Cindy said, "Chris, why don't you let me play cop and ask the questions?"

"Sorry."

"Grace, how did they get in?"

I turned my head so Grace wouldn't see me smile.

"The old girl has some age on her." Grace pointed at the truck. "She'd be old enough to drink in most states. Has more than a few dings. Her air conditioning works only when it wants to. Her door ain't quite as secure as Fort Know, mon."

The space between the door and the jam had a quarter-inch gap which was wider near the handle.

Cindy nodded, wrote something in the notebook, pointed in the door, and said, "Anything broken, or just thrown around?"

Grace stepped in the truck, and Cindy followed. I was behind Cindy and while the truck was old enough to drink, the interior had been converted to a food truck much later. Even with equipment strewn around, I could tell it was nearly new. Grace picked a large pot off the floor and set it on the counter.

"It had been a bakery delivery vehicle in Los Angeles before we bought it. Teddy found a company in LA that converts step trucks into food trucks. We worked with them to have the interior custom outfitted. We did some of the work ourselves. I'll pat myself on the back and say that I'm handy with tools; in fact, helped remodel a couple of restaurants in my younger days.

"Even with doing much ourselves, it was still many thousand dollars later before this became our pride and joy. The good thing about it is it's built to travel, to go over bumpy roads, to have a hard life. In other words, it would take a lot to break anything in here. At first glance, I don't see anything beyond repair."

Cindy nodded as she looked around. "Ms. Stoll, can you think of anyone who would do this?"

Grace looked at the floor as she leaned against the aluminum prep table. "Chief, I pulled onto your quaint island two days ago. I have only spoken to dear Theo, Mr. Landrum here, that nice man across the street with the bicycles, and Melody, the server at Planet Follywood. I do not know anyone else." She shook her head. "What reason could I have accumulated for someone to want to do this to *Hot Diggity Dog!*?"

Cindy picked up tongs from the floor, looked around, then set them on the counter. "Grace, it could be as simple as someone seeing the truck; not seeing anyone around; thinking there could be money inside; breaking in to steal it; getting frustrated when he or she couldn't find anything worth stealing; then made this mess."

Grace dropped the tongs that Cindy had put on the

counter in the compact sink and sighed. "I hope that it's as simple as that."

Me, too, I thought.

Cindy patted Grace on the arm. "Grace, would you like me to help put things back together?"

"Oh, dear, Chief, you are way too kind. Thank you, but no. I will have it together in a jiff."

Cindy nodded. "That's all I can do here. I'll have some of my guys ask around to see if anyone remembers seeing someone lurking around. I doubt it'll help. Anyway, we'll try." Cindy hesitated, then glanced at the sleeping bag rolled up between the driver's seat and the passenger's seat. "Grace, where are you staying?"

She followed Cindy's stare. "In the truck."

The Chief said, "Where are you parking overnight?"

Grace lowered her eyes. "Last night over on the other corner of the lot. I was hoping to stay here tonight."

Cindy slowly shook her head. "I'm afraid that's not possible. Motor homes aren't permitted to house occupants on Folly. Technically, your truck falls under that classification. Sorry."

"Where can I—"

Cindy held her hand up. "There's Walmart five miles up Folly Road on the left. Check with their manager. They let people park their motorhomes overnight in their lot."

"Thank you, Chief."

"I know you've been here only a couple of days, probably haven't had time, but have you applied for a retail food establishment permit from the South Carolina Department of Health and Environmental Control?"

"I was going to work on the application tonight."

"Great," Cindy said. "What about a permit to operate on Folly?"

"I'll check on that tomorrow."

Cindy said, "I've pestered you enough. It's nice meeting you. Sorry it's under these circumstances." She started toward the door, hesitated, pulled a card out of her pocket, and handed it to Grace. "Give me a call if you think of anything that might help. In case you don't already know, Chris, while he's often a pain in my posterior, is a good guy. He can be trusted."

She was out the door before I could say, "Awe, shucks."

Grace stared at the open door. "She seems like a nice person."

"She's the best. Let me help you get straightened up."

"No way, fine sir. I'll do it later. It's not like it's going anywhere. Do you mind if I sit down? This has been one long day."

I followed her to the front of the truck as she moved the sleeping bag from between the seats. She took the driver's seat while I moved to the passenger's seat.

"Are you okay?"

Grace was staring out the window at the lights from Pier 101, the restaurant at the Folly Pier across the parking lot. She didn't say anything for a minute, then in her lilting voice said, "If someone told me six months ago that I'd be a widow, sitting in a ransacked food truck, staring at the Atlantic Ocean, I'd say they'd been smoking too much wacky weed." Tears began flowing down her cheeks.

Other than an occasional sniffle, we sat in silence, staring straight ahead.

Ten minutes later, in a low voice, she said, "Dawg nyam yu suppa,"

"What?"

"Oh, sorry, it's a Jamaican phrase that literally means, "Dog will eat your supper." She looked at me as she attempted to smile. "It means I will be punished, something bad will happen to me, for some reason. Like what could be worse than your supper being given to a dog." She sighed. "What did I do to deserve this?"

"Bad things happen to the best of us, often for no reason."

"Mr. Landrum, I'm so terribly sorry. You don't know me. Here I am, a middle-aged woman, acting like a sniveling baby taking up your time."

I touched her arm. "It's okay, Grace. It's okay."

"Thank you." She turned to look toward the food prep area.

"Would you like me to call your father-in-law? He has room in his house. He'd love for you to stay there. You can park the truck in his drive until you find somewhere of you own."

"No way." She sighed. "He treated me like pig dung when we met." She returned to staring out the front window. "I don't blame him. Here I was, a stranger, trying to be family. The whole time I was driving from California; I knew he and Teddy had a horrible relationship. Besides, Mr. Stoll has a right to think I must want something. Why wouldn't he think that? No way will I stay there, or ask him for anything." She slammed her hand on the steering wheel. "No way."

"Grace, I've known Theo for a couple of years. I've been with him in rough situations. I've seen how loyal he was to his friends, even when it would have been better otherwise. Don't judge him without getting to know him."

"Perhaps another time, mon. Now, I'd better get *Hot Diggity Dog!* to Walmart before she gets towed. Thank you for coming to check on me, Mr. Landrum."

She was pulling out of the parking lot before I had time to cross the road on my way home.

Chapter Twenty-One

Charles and I agreed to meet for breakfast at the Dog, so I wasn't surprised to see him at a table on the front patio when I arrived. I was glad he was there because the restaurant was packed. Plus, there was a couple accompanied by their collie waiting for an outdoor seat.

"Guess who called last night," Charles said as soon as I sat.

"Mick Jagger," I said then took a sip of water that he'd had the server leave for me.

"You suck at guessing."

Amber was at the table before I could offer a second guess. She pointed her pen at me. "Found more bodies?"

"No. Good morning, Amber," I said, practicing the lost art of politeness. "How are you this beautiful morning?"

She smiled. "You're the first person who asked me that today. I'm fine." She pointed her pen at the wall between the patio and the inside dining area. "Guess what he's saying in there about Anthony's death?"

"Who's he?"

"Who's your favorite councilmember who's here nearly each day with another councilmember, the one who'd rather spread gossip than butter?"

Finally, a question I could answer. "Marc Salmon."

"Bingo. Are you ready to hear what he's saying?"

Two in a row I could answer. The day was looking up. "Yes."

"Said Anthony was shot because he stumbled on a drug deal. According to Marc, drug dealers were bringing dope on shore out there because it's isolated, nobody'd be there after dark. Something about Anthony being at the wrong place at the wrong time."

That made sense, but I wondered how Marc heard about it. "Who told Marc?"

Amber shrugged. "Didn't ask. Needy customers keep interrupting his story. Want to me to find out?"

Charles said, "You bet."

I added, "If you can without letting him know who's asking."

Amber saluted then asked if I was ready to order yogurt.

I said, "French toast," to which she said, "Surprise, surprise."

Charles watched her leave. "You ready for me to tell you?"

I'd forgotten what he was talking about. "Sure."

He said, "Laurie."

It was coming back to me. A call. "What'd she want?"

"Thought you'd never ask. She wants me to come see her."

"Why?"

"Didn't say."

"Why do you think?"

"Get real, Chris. Who wouldn't want this charming, handsome, wise, witty fellow to visit?"

I wanted to add *delusional*. Instead, I repeated, "Why do you think?"

"No idea."

That was more like it.

"When?"

He looked at his wrist. "As soon as you're done eating."

I knew the answer to the next question before I asked. "Did she say she wanted me to come?"

"Not in those words."

"How did she say it?"

"The last time we were there, she hadn't mentioned you coming, yet she invited both of us in. See. she wants both of us."

I was ready to point out the lack of logic in his thinking when Amber returned, refilled my cup, and whispered, "Captain Gant."

"Gant told Marc about the drug deal gone bad."

"Yep." Amber grinned like she'd solved the Rubik's Cube.

Charles said, "He say anything else?"

"Yep. He said, 'Ready for the check.' " Her grin turned to a smile as she tapped the top of Charles's head before walking away.

I asked Charles, "What do you make of that?"

"He was ready to leave, wanted to pay."

"You know what I mean."

"His story makes sense. It was late, so nobody would be there. One of the cars Laurie saw could've been the person waiting to pick up the drugs. After Anthony got separated from Laurie, he could've stumbled on the deal. Then, bang!"

I looked at the increasing crowd waiting for tables. "Or, it could be Captain Gant, dreaming up the story to lead police on a wild goose chase."

"That, too."

"CHARLES, thanks for coming. I see you brought your friend," Laurie said as she opened the door. She looked like she was ready to go to a party in a lavender blouse, white linen slacks, and low-heel, black dress shoes.

Her comment about Charles bringing a friend was spoken with little enthusiasm, or else I was projecting awkwardness about being there. Regardless, she didn't turn me away, then asked if we wanted something to drink. We said, "Water" and followed her to the kitchen, where she grabbed three plastic water bottles out of the refrigerator. We headed to the living room.

Laurie looked at her lap, picked a speck of lint off her linen slacks, looked up at Charles, and smiled. "I suppose you're wondering why I asked you over."

Charles returned her smile. "I was curious."

I leaned back on the sofa and remained quiet.

"The last two years Anthony and I were teaching, all we talked about was moving here when we retired. We batted scenarios around like a volleyball." She picked another piece of lint off her slacks and shook her head. "We'd be retired, still in our fifties, too young to not do something. We talked about getting part-time jobs." She giggled. "Anthony wanted to work at that shop on the pier so he could look out the window and see the ocean.

"I'm a morning person and thought it'd be interesting working at a breakfast restaurant, like the Lost Dog Café, or the Black Magic Cafe. We talked about getting a boat; nothing big, nothing oceangoing, simply something we could use to explore the marsh or nearby rivers. We talked about taking an Alaskan cruise. The boat and the cruise were only dreams because we didn't have the money. She hesitated and looked down at her slacks. Apparently, she couldn't find more lint, so she looked back at us. "Charles, do you know what we never dreamed about, never gave a second of thought to?"

"What?"

"One of us being gone. Charles, Anthony's gone. Gone forever."

Charles whispered. "I'm sorry."

Laurie put her hand on her forehead and closed her eyes. "I'm scared."

Charles said, "Is there anything we can do to help?"

Laurie moved her hand from her face. "Guys, you're the only friends I have here. Sure, I've talked to people at the stores, I even know a few of their names. I was shocked by how many came to the funeral. I don't really know them."

"It takes time," I said. "When I moved here, I didn't know anyone. Then, so many people showed me kindness and true warmth that I felt welcomed."

Laurie looked at me as if she just realized I was there. "I know I must keep my head up and move forward. Maybe—"

Charles interrupted, "Teddy Roosevelt said, 'By acting as if I was not afraid, I gradually cease to be afraid.' "

Laurie cocked her head at Charles.

He said, "I get inspiration from presidents."

"Oh," she said. "I hope you, umm, President Roosevelt was right. It doesn't help now. I'm alone and, my God, Charles, someone tried to kill me." She jumped up, started toward the kitchen, turned, and looked at us. "What can I do?"

If, as I suspected, she'd killed her husband, she was a great actress. It still wasn't clear why she asked Charles to stop by.

"Laurie," I said. "Unless you remember something that you haven't shared with the police, I doubt there's anything you can do about what happened to Anthony, or the person who shot at the house. The police are good. They'll do what they can."

She glanced at Charles and looked at me. "That night at the Lighthouse Preserve is all a blur. I think I told them everything."

I remembered the rumor that Marc Salmon was spreading. "Laurie, I know the rain was heavy, the thunder loud. Do you remember other sounds?"

"Like the gunshot? I could've but didn't tell any difference between it and thunder."

"I was thinking more like a boat motor."

"A boat?"

Charles was feeling left out of the conversation. "We heard a rumor that someone may've been delivering drugs by boat to someone near where Anthony was killed."

"You're saying Anthony saw something he shouldn't have, paid for it with his life. Is that why he was killed?"

"We don't know," I added. "That's why I was wondering if you heard a boat."

"Not really."

"You don't remember anything else about the cars that were out there when you got back to the car?"

She shook her head and looked toward the bedroom door. "If that's what happened, why did somebody shoot at me?"

It was possible that if the death was drug related, the killer could've seen Laurie then figured she saw him. Possible, although unlikely since there was a gap between when she and Anthony got separated and when he was shot.

"Laurie, I'm sure the police have heard the rumor. They'll investigate."

She returned to hunting lint on her slacks, and whispered, "I hope so."

Charles said, "They'll figure it out."

"Good," she said and shook her head. "Sorry I dumped all that on you. That's not why I asked you over. Gail and Dean are coming back tomorrow for the weekend. They want to take me to supper. I told them not to. A four-hour drive to get here for supper. Stupid. Of course, Gail wouldn't listen." She sighed. "Charles, could you come with us? I'm not ready to hear Gail spend all night telling me why

I should move to Jacksonville, or griping about the condition of the house, or that I need to sell it. Whatever else her gripe of the day is."

"I don't want to take time away from you, and your friends."

"Please."

Charles smiled. "Sure."

"Thank you."

The mood was broken when Charles said, "Can Chris come? He could be my date."

"Oh. I don't want to impose. I'm sure he has better things to do than spend time with strangers."

"No, he doesn't."

Laurie faked a smile. "He's welcome to join us."

She wasn't as good an actress as I thought she was.

Chapter Twenty-Two

Charles and his "date" were to meet the others at Taco Boy on Center Street. I told Charles that I'd meet him in front of the popular restaurant and was there thirty minutes early. My friend was next door to Taco Boy, leaning against the green, brick wall of the Palms gift shop. He wore a long-sleeved, royal blue T-shirt with Gators on the front, and orange shorts that matched the color of Gators.

Instead of saying "Hi," or anything normal people might utter, he pointed his cane at the outdoor patio at Taco Boy and said, "How about eating outside? It's in the shade."

I reminded him that, when we ate with the same group after the funeral, they preferred air-conditioned comfort.

He reminded me that it was twenty degrees cooler than it was after the funeral. Besides, he liked the outdoor tables which were a couple of feet from the sidewalk, so he could check out the people walking by and talk to their pets.

I hadn't been invited, so I deferred to Charles.

One of the six-foot-long picnic-style tables on the patio was available. After Charles assured the hostess that there would be three others, she seated us. A server was quick to the table, told us he was Timothy, and asked if others would be joining us. I told him there'd be more, so we'd wait for them before ordering.

"Wrong," Charles said. "An order of nachos and a Cadillac Margarita for me. I suppose the boring guy beside me wants white wine, the cheapest you have."

Timothy looked at me as I shrugged. He said, "No problem," and headed to the bar.

Charles leaned past me to set his Tilley on the wide railing separating the patio from the sidewalk. "What can I say? I'm starved. I have a feeling I'll need the margarita, and more, before the night's over."

Bud Light was usually the most exotic drink my friend ordered.

Charles said, "Do you still think Laurie shot Anthony?"

"Not as much as I did before yesterday."

"Good. I told you she didn't."

"Charles, she still could have. She has the strongest motive. I have trouble wrapping my arms around the odds on Anthony being at such a desolate place stumbling on a drug deal."

He looked past me at the retro Christmas lights that were strung along the railing, waved at a couple passing by, then said, "I don't think she killed him. I do have a feeling she's lying about searching for Civil War relics."

"I agree."

Before we got over the shock of agreeing on something, our nachos and drinks arrived. Laurie may've been lying about something, but Charles hadn't been when he'd said he was starved. He'd stuffed three nachos in his mouth before the waiter asked if we wanted anything else. I looked at the cheese oozing out the corner of Charles's mouth and said, "Extra napkins."

"No problem."

I inwardly snarled at the server.

With Charles stuffing his mouth, I figured it'd be an appropriate time to tell him about Grace and what happened at her food truck. Eating kept questions to a minimum. For Charles, minimum meant no more than one each thirty seconds. He managed to garble out one of his most often asked questions less than a minute into my description.

"Why didn't you call me?"

There was never an acceptable answer, so I didn't try, and continued the story. By the time Charles got around to asking what kind of hot dogs *Hot Diggity Dog!* sold, I was saved when he spotted Laurie, Dean, and Gail walking toward the entry. He yelled for them as he pointed to the table, like they wouldn't know it was where they'd be joining us.

A few seconds later, they arrived. Charles slid closer to me so that Laurie could sit on our side of the bench seat. Dean and Gail moved to the other side but, before sitting, Gail said, "Don't you think it's too hot out here?" She pointed to the door to the inside dining room. "I saw a nice table in there. Let's move."

Laurie glared at her. "This is fine. Our friends are already here."

A great way to start a pleasant meal, I thought.

Dean smiled as he slid across the bench seat. Gail mumbled something under her breath then followed her husband.

She noticed Charles's T-shirt, wrinkled up her nose, and said, "I hate the Gators. Do you have to throw it in my face?"

For one of the few times, Charles was speechless. Laurie saved him when she smiled. "I'm sure that, since you're from Florida, Charles was trying to make you feel at home. Now, Charles, what's good to eat here?"

As if on cue, Timothy appeared to ask if anyone needed drinks.

Charles was quick to say another margarita, I said I was fine.

Each of the others ordered beer.

Charles proceeded to tell the visitors that, since the restaurant was named Taco Boy, they couldn't go wrong with tacos.

Whether Gail bought it, or she didn't want to talk to anyone who threw the University of Florida *in her face*, she didn't ask him about the multiple taco options.

Laurie asked Dean if business was good at the tire store. I suspected it was to steer the conversation away from the growing rift between Gail and Charles.

"Not bad."

"Not bad, crap," Gail said. "How about sucking wind. With Costco, Walmart, and every big box store under the sun selling tires by discounting the hell out of them, mom and pop shops can't compete."

"It's not that bad, dear."

"Tell that to our damned banker."

Timothy returned with drinks, and I was about to tell him I needed more wine, a lot more. Instead, I asked if everyone was ready to order.

Gail said, "Yeah, tacos. They better be good."

Seventeen different taco iterations were on the menu, so she wasn't going to get off that easy. Timothy did a respectable job of describing the most popular choices, did an even better job of not throwing Gail's beer in her face. The rest of us ordered, and Timothy left the table, probably contemplating a career change.

Dean smiled at Laurie and turned to Charles, "Laurie tells us you've been good friends and have stopped by the house to see if she was okay. She said you've also kept her up on what the police are doing to catch the horrible person who shot Anthony. She's here by herself and needs—"

"Needs to move back to Jacksonville," interrupted Gail.

I hoped we weren't going to rehash that discussion.

Laurie had made it clear that this was her home. Couldn't Gail let it go?

Laurie reached across the table and put her hand on Gail's hand. "Now, dear, I know you're concerned about me. I appreciate that, I really do. I'll be fine."

Laurie was trying a new tact. I hoped it'd be more effective than getting angry, like she did the last time Gail shared her feelings about Laurie returning to Florida.

Gail pulled her hand away then balled her fist. "Don't come crying to me the next time someone shoots at you."

Charles leaned toward the Clarks. "How long will you be staying?"

He was trying to diffuse the tense situation. I hoped their answer would be that they were leaving after supper, if not sooner.

Charles succeeded, although I didn't get the answer I wanted, when Gail took a deep breath, faked a smile, then said, "We'll head back Sunday evening. Dean has to go to some dingy hotel in Miami all next week for the annual meeting on something about tires."

Dean added, "Independent Tire Dealers of the South."

Charles smiled. "Sounds interesting."

Really, Charles?

"Not terribly interesting," Dean said. "These meetings are critical if we're going to compete with the big guys, if we're going to stay in business."

Our food arrived, saving me from having to listen to more about tires dealers, independent, or otherwise. The taco put Gail in a better mood. She asked several non-hostile questions about how Charles and I had come to Folly, what were some of the best places to visit in Charleston, and what Laurie's plans were to remodel her house. She used neutral terms, like it needed *tender loving care*, or *a few upgrades*, rather than calling it dump like she had the last time she went on a rant about its condition.

We ordered more drinks, Timothy managed to deliver

them to us with no problem. Customers at the tables around us came and went. Despite the way it had begun, the evening, the conversation, and the warmth expressed by the Clarks and Laurie continued on the uptick.

I was finally relaxing while enjoying the company when Gail said, "Laurie tells us that you think poor Anthony came across drug dealers out there in the middle of nowhere. That's what got him killed."

I said, "That's a rumor going around. There's never a shortage of rumors when something bad happens. I don't know if it's true."

Gail said, "Is that what the police think?"

"I don't know."

"I thought you were friends with the chief," Gail added, not letting it go.

"We're friends. That doesn't mean she talks about investigations. The lead on the case is a detective from the Charleston County Sheriff's Office."

Gail pointed her beer bottle at me. "I don't know what I'd do if anything happened to Laurie." She set the bottle on the table and stared at it. "I can't help but think that, if Dean and I'd been here that night instead of in Florida, Anthony may still be with us."

Dean added, "Or we'd all be dead."

"Enough!" Laurie said. "Don't ruin a wonderful evening with friends. What's past is past. I'll be fine."

Her comment reminded me of Abraham Gant's views on the past. I need to call Cindy in the morning to see if she had any information about the captain. It made more sense that he could've been the killer than the unlikely event Anthony stumbled on a drug deal.

The evening ended on a more pleasant note than it had begun. Gail thanked Charles and me for keeping an eye on Laurie. Laurie thanked us for putting up with her and her friends squabbling. I lied when I told her it was okay, also when I told Gail and Dean I enjoyed spending time with them. Charles grinned as he covered *Gators* with his hand on our way to the exit.

We got to the sidewalk where Laurie, Gail, and Dean headed one way, Charles started the other direction, stopped, and smiled. "That was fun. Let's do it again."

I smacked his arm.

Chapter Twenty-Three

A low cloud cover hung over the city, keeping the temperature mild for July so, instead of driving, I walked three blocks to City Hall. Chief LaMond's door was open a couple of inches, so I could see her sipping coffee as she flipped through manila folders. She looked up when I tapped on the door.

"Unless you've come to confess to a murder, or give me a new car, turn around and let me see your chunky butt waddle away."

I took that as she'd love to talk to me. I pushed the door open, stepped in the cluttered office, and smiled. "Morning, Chief. Having a good day?"

She pointed to a pile of papers on the side of the desk. "You know how many calls for service your itty-bitty, under-staffed, underpaid police department got the last twelve months?"

"A lot?"

"Nearly eighteen thousand."

"Wow."

"Number of citations and warnings, you know, the bad kind, not for good citizenship?"

"A lot?"

"Thirty-eight hundred."

"That is a lot."

"Ya think! That doesn't count more than seven thousand parking tickets."

"Your point?" I asked, although she would tell me whether I asked, or not.

She waved a computer printout in my face. "The point of all these numbers I have to talk to the city council about next week is that I don't have frickin' time to waste talking to you about whatever you made the trip here for."

"Sorry, Cindy. I didn't mean to—"

She threw the printout in the air. "Hell, you talked me into it. Let's walk down the street to get some good coffee, not the crap your tax dollars pay for."

Cindy jogged down the steps to the sidewalk, like someone would catch her and tie her to her desk if she dallied.

I didn't need to ask where we were going as she led me two blocks to the Black Magic Cafe, a coffee shop and breakfast/lunch restaurant. It was close to Cindy's office so she could often be found sipping a drink in the popular business whenever she wanted to escape the bureaucratic burdens of her job. She grabbed one of the outdoor tables while I went for our drinks.

Five minutes later, I returned with two colorful Black Magic mugs.

"Chris, I don't suppose you were wandering around City Hall when you happened to stumble in my office. Why did I let you buy me coffee?"

I blew across the hot liquid. "True." I smiled. "Wandering around City Hall isn't something I often do. You should be honored you're the reason I was there."

"How lucky can a girl be? Did you forget my question?"

"I was wondering if you learned anything more about the break-in at the food truck."

"Nary a thing. I also have no idea who broke in the baby-crap-green Volkswagen minivan the night before last and stole, if you can believe this, an 8-track tape player, or who swiped two baseball bats out of the yard of a vacation rental on East Hudson last Tuesday, or—"

"Got it. You have more problems than cops to solve them. The answer is, no clues, no cameras, no witnesses, no idea who broke in."

"Couldn't have said it better myself." She took a sip of her drink. "Nothing appeared to be taken, so vandalism slips a far piece down the priority list. Sorry."

"I knew it'd be a longshot."

"A longshot means there's a shot. I wouldn't give it that good a chance."

"Any news on Anthony Fitzsimmons's murder?"

"Keep with the questions, and you'll be buying me lunch, and a diamond bracelet."

"News?"

"You'll be pleased that I listen to you, sometimes. I casual-like talked with Captain Gant."

"Casual-like?"

"I didn't want him to think he was a suspect, didn't want to get his Captain Crunch knickers in a twist. I asked if he knew about the shooting. He acted insulted I asked, said that of course, he knew about it. If he said he didn't, I would've arrested him for not being a true Folly resident. Anyway, he did what he's known for. He went on a tirade about the blankety-blank screwballs who're digging up the past."

"Don't suppose he confessed during the outburst?"

Cindy chuckled. "Not even after he finished the rant when I teased him with, 'You sound mighty angry at Mr. Fitzsimmons. You didn't kill him, did you?'"

"What'd he say?"

"The old boy didn't see much amusement. He snarled

then growled out words that sounded like, 'If you think I did, prove it.' I displayed my enchanting smile and told him I didn't think he did but, to satisfy the detective from the Sheriff's Office, I needed to ask where he was when Fitzsimmons was killed." She took another sip.

"What'd he say?"

"He said, 'Asleep, asleep by myself.' He repeated that, if I thought he shot the blankety-blank grave robber, prove it. His quote was, 'That's for me to know, you to find out.' "

"That's all he said?"

"No, he ended our fun-filled conversation telling me to get my rear in gear, go pester someone else."

"Anything else?"

"Not about Captain. Detective Callahan and I talked to Laurie again. I didn't think it'd do any good. There are only so many ways she can say she didn't see anything, or anyone, that night. She didn't vary from her previous story, yet… never mind."

"Yet what?"

"Something keeps tugging at my instincts. She's not telling everything."

"Like what?"

"Chris, instinct-tugging ain't specific. I don't know." She hesitated and looked around the patio. "Lord, strike me down with lightning. I can't believe I'm about to ask this." She sighed. "Why don't you and, yes, I'm saying it, Charles, make another run at her? For some logic-defying reason, she seems to trust you two."

I told her about last night's dinner with Laurie and her friends from Jacksonville.

"See, she's taken a likin' to Charles. She'll tell him things. He has a way of nosin' into secrets. Don't tell him I said that."

I said that we'd try.

She told me she had to get back to the mountain of paperwork.

I promised not to tell Charles what Cindy had said about him *nosin' into secrets.*

BLACK MAGIC WAS three blocks from Theo's house. I was making efforts to get more exercise, so I took a chance he'd be home and welcoming guests. The clock hadn't reached noon, so I also hoped that, if Theo was there, Sal was asleep. No such luck. Instead of Theo answering the door, I was greeted by black, wide-rimmed glasses magnifying the sleepy eyes of Theo's brother. I was amazed that anyone could be sleepy wearing a red, orange, and luminous green shirt, the same shirt he had on the last time I'd seen him.

Sal blinked twice, ran a hand through his long, gray hair that hadn't touched a comb this morning, and smiled. "What do you call a sleeping bull?"

I'd transitioned from someone at the door to an audience. "What?"

"A bulldozer." He slapped his knee and laughed.

I asked if Theo was home.

"Ah, Theo. Did you know he had to retake his driver's test?"

Why, again, did I decide to visit Theo?

"No."

"Yep, he got eight out of ten. The other two guys jumped out of the way."

I faked another smile then repeated my question about Theo being home.

Sal sighed and pushed his glasses up on his nose. "You're a tough audience. You remind me of a group of Masons I entertained back in Toledo, or was it Oshkosh? I was getting to my best material when—"

"Is Theo here?"

He stepped aside and waved me in. "Kitchen."

I waited for another joke. Instead, Sal huffed and

headed toward the great room, while I went to the kitchen. Theo was standing at the granite-covered island, slathering butter on a bagel. He wore a lightweight navy-blue robe. Red and white striped pajama pants stuck out the bottom.

He turned, saw me, and jumped back. "Didn't hear you come in."

"Didn't mean to startle you."

"What? Hang on, let me get my hearing aids." He left the room, and I heard him clomping up the stairs, leaving me staring at his breakfast and listening to Sal in the great room singing "Danke Schoen." It was horrible, but at least it wasn't a joke.

An eternity later, Theo returned. He'd changed into red jogging shorts, a T-shirt with the Nike swish on the chest, plus his signature knee-high support socks. Theo and Sal's attire reminded me of men leaving a homeless shelter on their way to panhandle.

"Sorry I took so long," Theo pointed to his ear. "Couldn't find these. I try not to put them in when we're here alone."

Wiser words couldn't have been spoken. I told him I was nearby and thought I'd stop to see if there was news about Grace. He thanked me then asked if I wanted a bagel. I declined but told him to go ahead and eat.

"Let me heat it then we can go out on the deck. It's a beautiful day." He lowered his voice as he looked toward the great room. "I don't want Sal to hear."

He poured us coffee while his breakfast was heating and grabbed the bagel, coffee, and headed at Theo-speed through the great room to the door to the deck. Sal was crooning his version of "Ain't That a Shame" that'd have Fats Domino rolling over in his grave. He ignored us as we slipped through the door onto the sun-drenched deck over-looking Theo's private pier leading to the Folly River.

After closing the door, Theo pointed toward the great room. "See why I don't wear these around him?"

"Yes, yes, yes."

"I didn't want him to hear us discussing Grace. He doesn't know I'm trying to get her to move in."

We sat in two chairs shaded by a large umbrella on the corner of the deck.

"Have you talked to her since she turned you down?"

"No, the more I thought about it, the more I think her staying here is a good idea. I called yesterday afternoon, got her voicemail. I left a message asking her to call. I'd hoped she'd call last night. No such luck."

I told him about the break-in at her food truck. He seemed shocked. He asked who'd do such a thing. I told him what little I knew. He said that he was glad the police had gotten involved but, then, I shared what Cindy had said about it being a low priority. What I didn't share was how Grace had said that she wouldn't stay with her father-in-law or her comment about how poorly he'd treated her.

"Chris, what should I do if she doesn't return my call? I feel horrible about how I treated her. I want to apologize."

"Chief LaMond told her she couldn't stay on Folly in the truck, so you might check the Walmart lot. She may also move her truck to the space across the street from Cool Breeze Bike Rental where I found her."

"I could try."

I smiled. "Or you could stay here and listen to Sal's combination concert and stand-up comedy act."

Chapter Twenty-Four

I arrived on Folly ten years ago from my hometown in Kentucky, and my life changed. Some say that it changed for the worse, most swear for the better. My existence had been uneventful before I crossed the bridge to the island the first time. I had the good fortune to be born into what in the late-40s had been considered a normal family, with two well-adjusted parents, and no siblings to fight, or compete, with.

I graduated with average grades from an average high school; attended college where I continued to earn average grades; graduated and bounced around in a few unrewarding jobs until landing with a large insurance company, where I had an average job in its human resources department. Like many in my generation, I married my high-school sweetheart; unfortunately, like many of my peers, divorced after twenty average years. I stumbled upon Folly while attending a seminar in Charleston. One visit to the island, discovering one body near the beach, and being stalked by one murderer, the concept of average was yanked out from under me.

I accumulated more friends than I had during my half century in Kentucky. By friends, I'm not talking about people whom I know casually and proclaim to be friends. I'm talking about people who would literally give their lives for me. I knew that, because on a few occasions, some almost had. As surprising as it was, I would've done the same for them.

Charles Fowler was at the top of the list. We met my first week on the island. Once I realized that he wasn't your average wacko, nor was he a killer, we'd become friends. We were also as opposite as possible. I was average; Charles was anything but. I'd worked my entire adult life; Charles had spent the last thirty-two years treating work as if it was a terminal disease. I was an introvert; Charles has never met a man, woman, child, dog, or cat he didn't want to make friends with. There are other differences, but suffice to say, we had little in common.

One thing I'd learned over the last decade was that friendships, true friendships, know no boundaries. Opposites didn't necessarily attract, yet they didn't stop us from becoming close. I also learned that my friendships, true friendships, were cemented when I shared traumatic experiences with others. That's what changed my life. Well, that and becoming embroiled in murder investigations, getting shot at more than once, getting close to becoming incinerated in a house fire, moments from drowning at the hands of a murderer, and not to mention nearly getting killed in a sabotaged automobile, and on another occasion, run over by another vehicle.

I was dragged, often by Charles, more than once kicking and screaming more, into situations, deadly situations, that should have been left up to law enforcement professionals. I'd been told that, unless I acted, those committing horrific deeds would go unpunished. As the arguments went, since I knew the victims, however slightly, I "had" to get involved. After a while, I started believing it. I suppose that's why I couldn't shake the feeling that I shouldn't, couldn't, stand idly by while whoever killed Anthony Fitzsimmons remained on the loose. The question was, What could I do about it?

There were two suspects that I'd met, Laurie and Captain Gant, plus the mysterious drug dealer, or dealers, who, to my knowledge, no one I know had met. Laurie would've had the most obvious motive: insurance. Gant didn't like Anthony, or for that matter, anyone who had the nerve to dig for anything from the past. He had motive, means, and hadn't hesitated to express disdain for Anthony. Was that reason enough to kill? Possibly, although it didn't seem strong enough. Which brings me to the drug dealer who might've been seen by Anthony, thus inflicting upon him a death sentence. Was it possible? Sure. What could I do about it? No clue.

With all that cluttering my brain, I pulled denial, one of my most often used tools, out of my tool box, and headed to Barb's Books for what I hoped to be a pleasant conversation with the lady whom I found far more fascinating than Theo, or Laurie. She was unquestionably more attractive. I was forced to observe her appearance from across the room. There were six customers in the store with three vying for Barb's attention. Two more potential customers entered while I was waiting, so I decided to return later. I left the store and came inches from bumping into Stanley Kremitz.

He stopped when he saw me, nodded toward the bookstore, and said, "Looks like books are selling like hotcakes."

I couldn't come up with an appropriate cliché. "Sure are."

"Glad I saw you," he said as he nudged me closer to the building out of the line of foot traffic. "I've been thinking of something I wanted to share. I learned the other day that Laurie, you know, the wife of the guy who was killed out at the end of the island."

I nodded.

"I learned Harnell Levi was her grandpa. Did you know that?"

I nodded again.

"I knew old man, Levi, back in the day. He was a mean old bastard, yes he was. Getting along with him wasn't a bed of roses, although somehow I managed to stay on his good side." Stanley looked around, leaned closer, and whispered. "When he was, shall I say, under the weather, he didn't have a good side."

"Under the weather?"

Stanley mouthed, "Drunker than a skunk."

"Was he often *under the weather?*"

"Yes. I didn't know him when he was a young whipper-snapper. In his twilight years, he was often drunk. I avoided him when I could, but I too had a fondness for the hops. I spent more than a few hours in local bars bending elbows with him."

Interesting story, I suppose. Now, get to the point, Stanley. "You said you wanted to share something."

"Tell you what, Chris. Why don't you let me buy you a drink at Rita's? The sidewalk isn't the place for me to share what I know."

I could count on one hand the number of times someone offered to buy me a drink, so it didn't take much effort to convince me. Besides, I wanted to know what he had to say. We walked in silence two short blocks to the restaurant's outside bar. We each ordered wine and took the first sip before Stanley spoke.

"Now to what I wanted to share. One night, I remember it clearly, Harnell and I were sipping beer, swapping tales. Other than the bartender, we were the only two in the joint. Harnell told me he knew where gold was buried on Folly. I figured it as an overdose of alcohol pickling his brain. I didn't take him seriously. Not at first, you see. I asked him to tell me more. He started rambling about pirates hijacking a ship coming from England carrying tons of gold to the good ole' US of A, which wasn't the US of A at the time. I figure a rose by any other name is still a rose. Harnell said he got the information from an old sea captain he crossed paths with, said it was a fact."

"Stanley, there've been stories for ages about pirates' bounty, gold, and everything else of value, buried along the coast. What made Harnell think it was true?"

"Chris, that's the same thing I asked him. Know what he told me?"

"What?"

"He had a map to the treasure. He said the old-timer who told him about the gold knew he didn't have long on this earth, wasn't able to search any longer, so he traded the map to Harnell for a few drinks. If Harnell was to be believed, the old-timer died three days later."

It sounded like another tall tale. "Stanley, did you see the map?"

"I asked him about it. Boy, did he get defensive. Said I wanted to get my grimy hands on it so I could steal the treasure right out from under him. He was coming close to screaming. I wrote it off as him being pickled, not really accusing me of wanting to steal it."

"If the old-timer had a map, why didn't he find the treasure?"

"Chris, that's another question I posed. I'm beginning to think you and I are as alike as two peas in a pod."

Not on your life, I thought. "What'd he say?"

"He reminded me that the map was drawn a couple of hundred years earlier, that it'd been bent, folded, wrinkled bunches of times. The next person who got it must've redrawn it. That could've happened more than once. The point being the *X marks the spot* could've gotten off during each redrawing. Also, hurricanes and storms that've hit in all that time, redefined where the beach is, changing the shape of the island. Erosion, vegetation, growing, then dying, walking paths made and covered over, all those things made the original map hard to follow. All Harnell was sure of was that the treasure was buried on what became the Coast Guard property."

"I can see that. If it'd been buried by pirates, what's to say the treasure wasn't dug up by people who had the map?"

"Two peas in a pod, yes we are. That was my question to Harnell. He figured since the map was still around it was an indication no one had found the treasure. If they had, why need the map?"

"Stanley, if pirates buried treasure it would've been a hundred years before the Civil War. That property was used by the military during that period. Later, the Coast Guard built several buildings and roads on the same grounds. Even if the person who had the map didn't find the treasure, there would've been a good chance it was uncovered by someone."

"That could be true. Hmm, it'd be unlikely that it's still out there. Yet let's say it's still buried. Remember, Harnell was the Fitzsimmons's woman's grandpa. If he didn't find the treasure, he could've given her the map."

"She and her husband could've been searching for the treasure rather than Civil War relics like she said."

Stanley slapped me on my back. "Two peas, Chris. Two peas."

My phone rang before Stanley could share more clichés.

"Mr. Landrum, umm, Chris, this is Grace. Is this a good time to talk?"

It wasn't, but I was curious. "Yes."

"I've been thinking about Theo's offer. I don't know him as well as you do, and you've been nice to me. Would it be too much to ask if you could go with me to see him?"

I told her I'd be glad to, so we decided on a time in the morning.

Stanley had paid for our drinks while I was talking to

Grace. He stood, patted me on the back, and said. "Yep, we're two peas. Birds of a feather flock together."

He turned and left. I turned and ordered another glass of wine. I'd earned it.

Chapter Twenty-Five

I called Theo the next morning for three reasons: To warn him that Grace and I would be knocking on his door at ten o'clock so he'd have a chance to get dressed before we got there; and, most importantly, to decide if he wanted to tell Sal about her prior to our arrival. Grace didn't need an impromptu stand-up comedy routine interfering with whatever she wanted to share with her father-in-law. Theo was surprised that Grace wanted to see him. He thanked me for the warning, said he'd put on his finest, and assured me Sal would be dead to the world that early in the day.

I parked behind Theo's Mercedes. Before I unbuckled my seat belt, *Hot Diggity Dog!* pulled in behind me. Grace bounded out the door, wearing a blue and white sundress, sandals, and a shell necklace. She stretched her arms over her head as she smiled in my direction.

"Good morning, Mr. Landrum."

I was only seventeen years older than Theo's daughter-in-law, yet felt ancient compared to her trim, athletic figure and cheerful demeanor. "Please call me Chris."

"Okay, mon." Her smile faded as she nodded toward the house. "Do you think it's acceptable to visit?"

"Yes. I called to make sure he'd be home. He was pleased you were coming."

Her smile returned as she followed me up the steps. Theo opened the door before we reached the top step. He'd heeded my advice. I'd never seen him so well put together. He had on a Hawaiian shirt which I'd never seen, and from the packaging creases, I suspected it was its debut. To complement his attire, he wore white shorts and tan, canvas Crocs. Black, knee-high, support stockings that I'd never seen him without, were nowhere to be seen. His legs were as white as his shorts.

"You look lovely today," he said as he grabbed Grace's hand. "Please, come in."

He wasn't as appreciative of my faded-blue golf shirt. I followed them to the great room where the host invited us to sit then asked if we wanted something to drink. Grace said tea if he had any, if not, coffee would be fine. There was no tea, so she and I settled for coffee as Theo headed to the kitchen.

Grace looked around the room with her mouth open. "Oh, my God, this is magnificent."

"It's one of the nicest homes on the island."

She looked out the large windows. "The view, incredible."

Theo returned with a bamboo tray holding three cups of coffee. "I didn't know if you needed cream or sugar, so I brought both."

We said black was fine.

"Where might your brother be?" Grace asked and looked around, as if she expected Sal to step out from behind a piece of furniture.

Theo pointed to the ceiling. "This is his middle of the night. He spent decades performing at clubs, often didn't go on stage until ten or eleven. His performances ended months ago, yet his day still doesn't begin until the rest of us are thinking about lunch."

Grace nodded. "Teddy and I had similar hours when we had the restaurant. I never adjusted well to it." She jerked her head toward Theo. "I apologize; I didn't mean to speak of your son. It must be painful to you."

Theo smiled. "That's okay, dear."

This was a much kinder, gentler Theo than Grace had been exposed to during their first meeting.

She said, "Thank you."

"Chris tells me someone broke into your food truck."

"A mess they made. I haven't detected anything stolen."

Theo nodded. "Do you know why?"

"No. It can't be because someone has something against me. I haven't been here long enough. The police believe the person was looking for valuables. When finding nothing but cooking supplies, he, or she, became angry. Out of frustration created a mess. My father would say, 'Puss inna bag,' a Jamaican phrase that means 'a cat in a bag.'"

I was pleased when Theo said, "What?" It kept me from asking, and sounding, stupid.

Grace chuckled. "Not knowing what you're getting before seeing it. You can't tell what a cat is like if it's in a bag. The person who broke in didn't know what he was going to find. It was with great fortune that all my money, as meager as it is, was in my purse instead of in the truck."

"That's frightening. Dear, do you think it's safe staying in your truck?"

"I believe so. The manager at Walmart indicated I could continue to park overnight in their lot a few more evenings. It's well-lighted."

"What'll you do, then?" Theo asked. "Have you got all the permits needed to start selling hot dogs?"

"I have the paperwork, but haven't submitted it yet. I'm

afraid it may take longer than I'd anticipated." She sipped her drink and looked at the floor. "Mr. Stoll, that's what I wanted to talk to you about. You graciously offered to allow me to stay in your wonderful house until I could get my feet on the ground. I'm afraid I reacted discourteously toward the offer, I must confess, toward you. I do not want to be a burden on anyone. You don't know me. Considering the strained relationship you had with Teddy, you would have no reason to be so kind in my direction." She turned to me. "Mr. Landrum has convinced me I should reconsider being so stubborn. Perhaps he's right." Her gaze returned to Theo. "Might I enquire if your generous offer is still available?"

"Grace, your negative reaction to me was justified. I admit, when we met at the hotel, I was shocked, riddled with emotions regarding my son. I had pent-up anger from years gone by. That had nothing to do with you. I'm also old-fashioned and, while I'm embarrassed to admit it, I was shocked to see that you were, umm, Jamaican."

"Black," interrupted Grace.

Theo lowered his head.

Grace smiled. "Mr. Stoll, I grew up in Topeka, Kansas, where more than nine out of ten residents are white. My father was a black man from Jamaica. My mom's skin was as white as your legs. There is nothing you can say I haven't heard since the day I first learned the difference between red and green, blue and yellow, black and white. Dad would say, 'Yu tink she mi born big?' which literally means 'You think I was born big, or old?'" In other words, don't take me for a fool. I wasn't born yesterday."

I smiled. Theo nodded.

"Besides," she said, "I know you white folk can't dance, can't sing worth a lick, cooking, get real, and when it comes to sports, forget it. But, hey, mon, we'll tolerate you."

Theo made the greatest response possible. He laughed, stood, leaned down, to give Grace a hug.

He stepped back. "Mrs. Stoll, I'd be honored if you would move in here. You can stay as long as you like. My home is your home."

Chapter Twenty-Six

Theo and Grace said that they had a lot to talk about. She moved the truck so I could get my car out of the drive to let them spend time alone. Theo wanted me to stay and see Sal's reaction to having a new housemate. I needed a plethora of Sal's jokes like I needed malaria. I declined and left that "fun" experience to Grace and Theo.

It was still before noon, also known as wake-up time in Sal's time zone, so I gave Charles a call to see if he wanted to make a grocery run to Harris Teeter. He laughed, saying that me making a grocery run was like our obese, icono-clastic friend Bob Howard making a run to, well, a run anywhere. He added that I could pick him up and take him somewhere he needed to go. I asked where. The answer would have to wait, he'd already hung up.

Charles was waiting for me in the parking area in front of his apartment. He slid in the passenger's seat and said, "You're late."

I said, "Where to?"

"Laurie's house."

I slammed on the brakes. "Why?"

"She called, said she wanted to talk to me about something important."

"What?"

He shrugged.

"She asked for you, not for you and me?"

"So?"

Another shrug.

Instead of getting in a discussion about the difference between asking for Charles, as opposed to asking for Charles and Chris, I said, "Don't you find it strange that she keeps calling?"

He glanced at me as he tapped his cane on the floorboard. "Sure. You've known me long enough to know strange is my thing. The real question is strange why, not that it's strange."

I understood, proving I knew him better than he thought. What I didn't understand was how Laurie would react to seeing me tagging along with the person she asked to come visit. I didn't have to wait long. She opened the door wearing a tan, button-down blouse, and navy slacks, and greeted Charles with a hug and a stare at me that would bring fear to a lion tamer.

"Oh, I see Mr. Landrum is with you."

Oh, I thought, and wished myself invisible.

Charles pretended not to see her glare. "Yes, he'd stopped by my place after you called and offered to drive. It's okay, isn't it?"

Historical revisionism was one of Charles's many talents.

"Yes. Come in gentlemen."

A plate of brownies was on the table beside the sofa with orchestra music playing in the background. She asked if we wanted coffee, and Charles said we'd love some before I had a chance to say no. She headed to the kitchen as Charles noted that the room had been straightened up since our last visit. Laurie returned, handed each of us a mug, pointed out the fresh-baked brownies, and sat in the chair opposite the sofa.

Charles grabbed a paper napkin, a brownie, and asked if I wanted one.

I declined.

Laurie said, "Baked them this morning. Thought you'd like them."

"You didn't have to do that," Charles said while wiping a crumb off his lower lip.

Laurie chuckled. "Idle hands are the devil's workshop, or something like that."

"Proverbs," Charles said.

Laurie looked impressed, so did I. I thought, unless a president said it, Charles didn't know it.

"I believe you're right," she said. "Anyway, I wanted to share something with you to get your take on it."

"Share away." Charles said then took another bite.

Laurie took a deep breath and looked at her hands folded in her lap. "That lady chief stopped by last evening. She was polite. The chief told me again how sorry she was about Anthony's death."

Chief LaMond didn't make house calls without a reason. Expressing sympathy would've been a good enough reason. "Did she want anything else?"

Laurie frowned like she hadn't been talking to me. That was reinforced when she said, "Charles, she wondered if Anthony had a gun. I told her he bought one years ago. I thought it was a stupid idea, stupid and dangerous. She asked if she could see it."

Charles said, "What'd you tell her?"

She shook her head. "I told her no because he sold it. He eventually agreed with me, finally saying he didn't need it. The chief asked who he sold it to. I told her Anthony never told me."

I said, "Why'd she ask about the gun?"

"At first she didn't say. She kept asking if I was certain I didn't know who bought it from Anthony. After a while, she said the bullet that killed Anthony and the one shot at me were from the same gun."

Charles was reaching for another brownie then hesitated. "Did she think it was from Anthony's gun?"

"She didn't know since she'd need the gun to run the ballistics test. She was thinking Anthony may have carried it with him on our relic hunt, the killer took it from him, shot Anthony with his own gun. I told her that couldn't be right since he no longer owned it."

Most likely, before she made the house call Cindy would've checked records in Florida and learned about Anthony buying a handgun. My guess was that Cindy was becoming as suspicious about Laurie's involvement in her husband's death as I was. I also found it convenient for Laurie to say that Anthony sold the weapon.

Laurie started to say something. Instead, she stood, said she would get us more coffee, and headed to the kitchen. I was left in the room wondering why she'd really asked Charles over.

The sound of shattering glass and an eardrum-shattering scream coming from the kitchen broke the silence. Charles leapt to his feet. His drink sloshed on his University of Arkansas T-shirt. He cursed and clanked the mug down on the table.

I didn't have to deal with spilled coffee and beat Charles to the kitchen. Laurie was huddled down in front of the sink. Shards from the shattered window over the sink were on the counter, in the sink, on the floor, and in Laurie's hair. Window glass mixed with broken pieces of curved glass from the carafe from the coffee maker. Hot liquid spread over the counter and dripped down the front of the cabinet.

I bent so I was lower than the windowsill and inched over to Laurie. "Are you hit?"

She was shaking all over but managed to mutter, "Don't think so."

"Can you move?"

She nodded.

I said, "Stay low, move to the living room."

Charles saw that Laurie wasn't injured. He dashed to the back door, slowly opened it, then peeked around the corner in the direction the shot had come from.

Laurie crawled to the living room, remained on the floor, and leaned against the sofa.

"Think they're gone," Charles said as he returned then squatted down beside Laurie who was still shaking. He put his arm around her shoulder.

I punched 9-1-1 on my phone, gave a quick report to the emergency operator, then went into the kitchen to see what I could see out the window. Whoever took the shot was gone, the large lot was deceivingly peaceful, as it was bathed in a beautiful, sunny day at the beach.

Laurie, with coffee splattered on the front of her blouse, moved to the sofa and was comforted by Charles.

I went to the front door to greet the emergency responders. A patrol car, siren blaring, slid to the sandy curb in front of the house.

Allen Spencer, a cop I'd known since he was a rookie on the force years ago, scampered out.

I met him at the door to assure him that no one was injured. He radioed we wouldn't need the EMTs that had been dispatched. I led him to the living room. I heard the siren from another patrol car in the distance. Allen looked at Laurie and Charles on the sofa. Laurie had her head down and didn't look at the newest arrival. Charles nodded and told the officer Laurie was shaken but okay. Spencer moved to the kitchen, cautiously walked around the glass on the floor, then looked out the damaged window.

A second patrol car skidded to a stop behind Spencer's

and Trula Bishop was quick to the door. "Here we are again, Mr. Chris. What now?"

I led her to the kitchen, where Spencer was surveying the scene. Bishop, like Spencer, was careful not to step in the glass, or the coffee. Fortunately, there was no blood to avoid. I shared what'd happened, while Spencer headed outside to see if he could see where the shooter had been.

Bishop went to the living room and motioned for Charles to move to the other side of the room. Bishop replaced Charles on the sofa. In a calming voice, told Laurie who she was, then asked her what she'd seen.

Laurie tensed, as if she didn't realize that Charles was no longer beside her.

Bishop touched Laurie's arm. "It's okay, you're safe. If you could tell me what you saw, it might help us catch whoever did this."

Laurie looked down and touched her damp blouse. "Charles and Chris were here on the sofa. I went to get more coffee." She, again, rubbed her hand on the blouse. "Picked up the pot, turned to bring it in here when the window shattered. Scared the hell out of me. I screamed, dropped the carafe. Glass flew everywhere, so did coffee. I ducked, umm, Chris came in. Then… then, nothing. I was in here and you came."

"Miss Laurie," Bishop said, "did you look out the window either before it was shattered or after?"

She rubbed her forehead, shook her head. "If I did, it was a glance. I didn't notice anything other than it was a gorgeous day. Sorry."

"That's okay. Do you know why someone would want to shoot you?"

Laurie moved her hand away from her face then turned facing Officer Bishop. "Officer, I haven't the faintest idea why someone killed my husband. I don't have a clue why someone shot at me the other day. Now—" She twisted around to face the kitchen. "No…"

Spencer stood in the doorway. "Officer Bishop, there wasn't anything out there. It's a big field. With so many trees, someone could hide and not be seen from the road, or the other houses."

Bishop nodded and turned to Laurie. "Miss Laurie, do you have family, or friends, you could visit until we get this figured out?"

Charles added, "What about Dean and Gail?"

Laurie glanced at him then turned to Bishop. "Officer, this is my house. Folly Beach is my home." She pointed toward the north. "My husband is buried over there. I'm making good friends here, like Charles and Chris. I'm not going anywhere."

Bishop smiled. "It was simply a suggestion, Miss Laurie. I don't think there's anything else we can do here. I'll call Detective Callahan to see if he wants to send a forensics team. They could look around outside, dig the bullet out of the wall. Most likely, all they'll find will be the bullet. To be honest, I doubt they could find anything outside, other than a few beer cans, nothing useful. I'll talk to Chief LaMond, and we'll increase patrols in the area. Do you want me to help clean up the kitchen?"

Laurie's shaking was now limited to her hands. She made a brave effort to smile. "Thank you. My friends and I can get it cleaned up. I'll call the chief's husband at the hardware store."

"If you think of anything, regardless how inconsequential, please give us a call."

Laurie started to stand.

"Don't get up," Bishop said. "I'll find my way out."

I followed the officer to her car. Before she got in, she said, "Chris, how do you do it?"

I knew what she meant; I didn't respond beyond a shrug.

Bishop said, "I know, I know. It's a gift, a gift like a piñata full of pelican poop. You have any theories?"

"I did until a half hour ago."

Bishop said, "You thought she killed her husband then took the shot into the house the other day to throw us off?"

"Yes."

Bishop nodded toward Laurie's house. "I suppose this shoots the hell out of that theory. Pun intended."

"Yes."

By the time I returned to the house, Charles and Laurie were in the kitchen. Charles was sweeping up glass, while Laurie was wiping coffee off cabinet doors. I grabbed a roll of paper towels to help Charles with the glass.

"Laurie," Charles said, "I know you don't want to leave so how about calling Gail to see if she could come up to stay with you a few more days?"

"I don't know. She's been so irritating lately."

Charles said, "It'd be good for someone to be with you."

"Suppose I could put up with her a few more days." She stepped around the pile of glass Charles had swept to the center of the room. She grabbed the phone from her purse. Charles swept the pile of glass into a dustpan as Laurie sat at the table calling her friend.

Gail didn't answer, so Laurie left a message for her to return the call as soon as possible. She made another call, this time to Dean. From hearing one side of the conversation, I gathered that Gail was out of town for a couple of days and probably had left her phone in the hotel room. Dean said he would keep calling his wife to make sure she got Laurie's message.

Laurie may not have been the person shooting up her house, probably not the person who killed her husband, but she knew something that she wasn't telling the police. It was time to find out what.

Chapter Twenty-Seven

The kitchen was clean. Larry from Pewter Hardware agreed to stop by to fix the window. Laurie changed out of her coffee-stained blouse, and we'd returned to the living room. She sipped orange juice between bites of brownie, which, according to Charles, were both good for her health, and her nerves.

Laurie's hands had stopped shaking, so I thought it was an appropriate time to broach the subject. "Laurie, what aren't you telling the police?"

Her grip tightened on the juice glass. "What do you mean?"

"It's none of my business. You can tell me to butt out, if you want. You told us, and the police, that you and Anthony were at the Lighthouse Inlet Heritage Preserve searching for Civil War relics."

She mumbled, "Yes."

"I've heard from friends, who know way more about it than I do, that Civil War relics seldom hold great monetary worth other than sentimental value or value to a collector or museum."

Her eyes narrowed. "So?"

"Erik Swartz, a friend of mine, told me about a conversation he had with Anthony who told him all he planned to do in retirement was to fix up the house."

She continued to stare. "So?"

"Erik said he joked to Anthony that it sounded like a lot needed to be done. My friend referred to it as a money pit. Anthony told Erik he was right, but wasn't worried, because he'd dig up the money to do the work. I asked Erik if he thought Anthony meant it as a joke. He wasn't sure. Laurie, was it a joke?"

Charles had leaned back on the sofa as I prepared for an explosion.

Laurie reached for another brownie, changed her mind, and pulled her hand back. "When I visited Folly as a young girl, my granddad told me stories about buried Civil War relics."

She was speaking low, so Charles and I leaned closer to hear.

I said, "I remember you telling us that."

"I did, didn't I? What I didn't say was that Granddad also talked about how pirates stole tons of valuables from ships. That was long before the Civil War."

"A hundred years before," interrupted Charles.

Laurie nodded. "I learned some of it was buried out where we were." A tear formed in the corner of her eye. "We were looking for it when… when it happened."

"Wow," Charles said. "How'd you know it was there?"

Laurie wiped the tear from her face then looked at the floor. "It's cursed. Granddad told me stories. He told me about ghosts of pirates watching over buried treasure. He told me anyone who tried to find it will be struck dead. I thought he was telling stories to scare a little kid. I should've believed him. The curse killed Anthony."

I remembered William talking about pirates burying treasure along the coast, possibly in the Carolinas. He also talked about a curse on anyone who digs up the treasure. Laurie hadn't answered Charles's question, so it wouldn't be long before he repeated it.

"I've heard those stories," Charles said. "How'd you say you learned about the treasure being at the old Coast Guard station?"

"Charles, Anthony is dead. Someone's trying to kill me. It doesn't matter how I learned it." She pounded her glass on the table, effectively shutting down Charles's questions.

"Laurie, I understand," I said, even though I didn't. "Who else may've known where you and Anthony would be that day?"

She leaned back and took a deep breath. "I didn't tell anyone, honest to God I didn't. I can't speak for Anthony. From what you said, he told your friend, it's evident that Anthony told some of it to a stranger. He could've told others."

Charles said, "Anyone in particular?"

She hesitated, then said, "One day, we were in Bert's Market. Met some old guy. We were buying flashlight batteries when he made some crack about them being for our apple. I think it was a joke, you know, like an Apple iPhone. Out of the blue, Anthony started telling him about us relic hunting."

I'd already heard the story from the *old guy*, Stanley Kremitz. "Did you tell him when you were going to be out there?"

"Not then. I remember Anthony telling him more than I thought he should about what we were doing, especially since relic hunting was prohibited in the Preserve."

Charles said, "So you didn't tell him anything about specific times?"

"No. That doesn't mean Anthony didn't. Chris, I didn't know about his conversation with your friend."

"Have you met Abraham Gant, goes by Captain Gant?" I asked.

"Captain Gant. Didn't know his name was Abraham."

Charles said, "You know him?"

"No, Anthony told me about him. They about got in a fight."

I knew what the captain had said about meeting Anthony, how he thought Anthony was okay until he said something about relic hunting. "What happened?"

"Gant knew my granddad, said he liked him. Anthony and the captain were having a pleasant conversation, until the topic of relic hunting came up. The captain got mad. From what my husband said, Gant looked like he'd hit him."

Charles said, "Did Anthony tell the captain that you'd be out there that night?"

"He could've. He tended to open his mouth without thinking. That was cause for more than one argument. He didn't tell me he told Gant about it."

"You're certain you didn't tell anyone about where you were going to be that day?"

"Yes."

Laurie's phone rang. She said, "Hello," then moved to the bedroom.

Charles watched the bedroom door and said, "Aren't you glad I invited you to the party?"

"That's what friends are for. What do you think of her story?"

"Which story?"

"She didn't tell anyone they'd be out there that night."

"Even if she's telling the truth, hubby was a blabbermouth, he could've told anyone. And, what's with her not saying how they knew where to look for the buried treasure? The Preserve is a big plot of land to be roaming around hoping to dig up a fortune."

"She knows more than she's saying."

"Wow, Sherlock, you figure that out by yourself?"

I was working on an incredibly humorous, insightful retort when Laurie returned.

"That was Gail. She'll get back to Jacksonville tomorrow, will head over here the day after tomorrow."

Charles said, "That's great."

"Yes, you all can meet us for supper once she arrives."

What was it that I was saying about malaria?

Chapter Twenty-Eight

Charles was scheduled to make a delivery for Dude's surf shop, so I dropped him at his apartment then realized that I was hungry. After what I'd been through at Laurie's, I didn't want to eat at a restaurant, so I stopped at Woody's Pizza to get supper to go. Instead of ordering one of their pizzas, which I knew I'd eat too much of and later regret, I settled on a sub sandwich.

I'd opened my door when my phone rang. I considered not answering, and enjoying a peaceful meal at home, without any outside distractions. Seeing the name Cindy LaMond on the screen convinced me to answer. It's never wise to ignore a call from the chief.

"Hey, Chris, know where Theo is?"

"What makes you think I'd know that?"

"Figured you knew everything."

"That would be Charles."

"True. Charles hadn't spent time with Theo. Officer Bishop said she saw your car at Theo's this morning."

Nothing like small-town life. "I have no idea where he is."

"How about his daughter-in-law. Know where she is?"

"No, why?"

"I'm standing in Theo's drive, staring at a big ole' food truck. Its door was open, so being the good cop that I am, I peeked inside to make sure no one was dying, or dead. The good news is there were no bodies. Bad news is I'm no food-truck doctor yet, from my lay perspective, *Hot Diggity Dog!* has serious internal injuries. It may not be able to fix-up any more hot dogs."

"No one's at Theo's house?"

"Not even the one-man comedy show."

"When I was there this morning, neither Theo, nor Grace talked about going anywhere. Any idea what happened?"

I heard Cindy talking to someone then returned to talk to me. "I asked Officer Bishop to call Charleston to see if they could free up a crime scene tech. If there's nothing serious going on over there, they might send someone. It's unlikely they'll find anything. Whoever did this probably wore gloves. If not, there should be a thousand of their fingerprints. You wouldn't believe the mess."

"I'll be over," I said, hesitated while waiting for her to give me a lecture about it being a police matter, for me to stay away.

"What took you so long to decide?"

I PARKED on the street in front of Theo's house. Bishop was pulling away in her patrol car. Cindy's Ford F-150 was in the drive behind the food truck.

"Any word on Theo, or Grace?" I asked Cindy as she leaned against the truck.

"No. I called the number Grace gave me. It rolled over to voicemail. Do you know Theo's number, or if Sal has a phone?"

"I'll call Theo."

The homeowner answered and asked what was going on.

I asked if he knew where Grace was. He said that she was with him at the City Market in downtown Charleston. He was giving her a tour, and asked why I wanted to know. I told him where we were and why. He ended with saying they'd be back as soon as he could maneuver his way back to the car. Before I let him go, I asked if he knew where Sal was. Theo said that his brother had taken to walking around town sharing his unlimited supply of jokes with shop owners. He was probably irritating one of them.

I told the chief what he'd said, then asked what made the police stop at the truck.

"Officer Bishop was on patrol, saw the door open. She wanted to stop to check on Grace. Bishop knew Theo's daughter-in-law was shook after the first break in and wanted to see if she was okay. I was nearby and stopped to see what was going on."

"Good. Could I look inside?"

"Have at it." She chuckled. "Don't mess anything up."

A glance in the door told me why her comment was so funny. The inside of the truck looked as damaged as would a carton of eggs if someone took a sledgehammer to it. Not only was the equipment smashed, it was demolished. Everything breakable was broken; everything bendable bent. If the stainless-steel equipment, shelving, and cabinets had any value left, it was as scrap.

Cindy stood behind me. "Theo's cute little daughter-in-law has seriously pissed someone off."

I said, "That's an understatement."

It was hot in the truck, so I asked Cindy if she wanted to wait for Theo and Grace in my car.

She said that the air conditioning sounded good.

While we were waiting for the owner to arrive, I shared what Charles and I had learned from Laurie about what her grandfather had told her about gold being along the coast, that was what she and Anthony were looking for. I also shared what she'd said about stories that there was a curse on anyone who tried to find the treasure.

"I reckon Anthony Fitzsimmons is now a strong believer in the curse. You know those stories about buried treasure, pirates, ghosts that come in all shapes and sizes, and curses have been around for decades. So, the Fitzsimmons were out there looking for treasure instead of Civil War relics?"

I nodded.

"Which leads to a couple more questions. How in the ghost of Blackbeard did they think they could find something that hundreds, hell, probably thousands, of people who've turned over every rock, dug hole after hole, and gossiped about in local bars couldn't find?"

"I don't know why—"

Cindy waved her hand in my face. "Hold your blunderbuss, Pirate Chris, I'm not done. The more important question is if someone killed Anthony because of the gold instead of it being a random drug deal gone bad, how did the killer know the Fitzsimmonses would be there?"

"Hold my what?"

"Google it, or ask Charles. He knows everything."

I realized that I didn't care enough to do either. "Laurie hadn't told anyone here, or so she said. Anthony is another story." I shared what Erik Swartz had told me, what Laurie said about Anthony's annoying habit of talking too much, and about his confrontation with Captain Gant.

"I get it. It's no telling how many others Anthony told about hunting for relics, or buried treasure. That could increase the suspect pool to each living resident on our quaint island, not to mention ghosts residing here. It still doesn't answer how the couple thought they had the inside track on finding the treasure."

I agreed yet continued thinking that Laurie knew something she wasn't telling us; something I was determined to learn more about. My mind was wandering to how to find out, so must've missed part of what Cindy said.

"Cindy to Chris, stop daydreaming. It's possible, unlikely, I know, but possible, I said something important."

"Sorry, what?"

"I talked with Detective Callahan last night to see if he'd learned anything. He was more interested in telling me about the new murder investigation he'd caught yesterday morning. It's high profile, so the political bigwigs are pestering the sheriff for a quick close, which means that, like all, umm, excrement, it flows downhill. Callahan is supposed to put everything else aside to make the sheriff look good, good to those who vote for him. His sheriff can be persuasive like that."

"So Anthony's investigation is on the back burner?"

"Back burner, crap. I suspect it's no longer on the stove."

Theo's Mercedes pulled in behind Cindy's truck. Grace was looking in *Hot Diggity Dog!* before Theo made it out of the car.

Grace pounded on the side of the truck, screamed a profanity, jerked her head toward the rest of us, then yelled, "Why?"

No answer was forthcoming.

She climbed in the ransacked vehicle.

Theo asked Cindy what she knew.

She told him the same thing she'd told me, which was near nothing.

Grace came out of the truck, sat on the step, then cradled her head with her hands. Her shoulders sagged, tears streamed down her face. She looked like someone had run over her pet dog. I suppose that someone had.

Cindy reached out and put her hand on Grace's shoulder. "Grace, I'm so sorry. Do you have any idea who might've done this?"

She repeated what she'd said after the first break in.

Other than those standing around her now, she didn't know anyone on Folly.

Theo said it had to have happened after they left for Charleston and wondered if anyone had seen anything.

Cindy said that no one answered at the house next door. The people who lived across the street said they didn't hear or see anything. Theo said he saw Grace lock the truck before they'd left. He wondered how the person got in. Cindy told him it looked like the lock was loose from the first incident.

By now, Grace had regained her composure. She came over to Theo's car, where the rest of us were standing. "Chief LaMond, what's going to happen now?"

"One of my officers is contacting the crime scene techs in Charleston. If possible, they'll get prints. I doubt it'll do any good." She looked at the side of Theo's house and at the house next door. "Theo, you have cameras out here?"

"No."

She pointed at the neighbor's house. "Doesn't look like they do, either. That'd be too easy. Grace, unless you have anything to add, I'll be going."

Grace said that she didn't.

Cindy asked if she would be here all afternoon in case a tech arrives.

Grace said, "Maybe," and Theo said that he'd be here.

Cindy, once again, told Grace that she was sorry, adding that it was a pathetic introduction to her new home.

Chapter Twenty-Nine

As Cindy left, Grace paced the driveway, alternating between mumbling profanities and asking why. Theo and I had no answers. She looked at the truck, shook her head, and said, "I need to walk off some energy. Anyone want to go?"

Theo confessed that walking around the City Market had zapped him. Besides, he needed to stay home in case a crime scene tech showed up. I said that I'd go. We walked a block in silence before she turned back toward her father-in-law's house. "I'm glad the dear man didn't want to come. I've seen potted plants move faster." She covered her mouth with her hand. "Please don't tell him that."

I shared that I was an off-and-on member of a walking group Theo was in, and that he could always be counted on to be the last to arrive at our destination.

"He may be slow," she said, "but I don't know that I've met a nicer man." She laughed for the first time since she'd returned to his house. "Anyway, not a nicer man who's got a prejudice streak, who was on the outs with my husband, who lives with his brother, who's as funny as an ear of corn."

"I'm glad you're getting along. Like I told you, Theo is a wonderful person. From what I've seen, he would do anything for anyone."

"He told me I could stay as long as I wanted to." She shook her head. "After what's happened to my truck, it looks like that'll be a long time. I can't believe someone did that."

We were in front of Barb's Books, and I nodded toward the building, "Let's go in a minute. I'd like you to meet someone."

Barb met us at the door with, "I bet you're Grace, Theo's daughter-in-law."

"How'd you know?"

Barb chuckled. "When I moved here, it took me all of fifteen minutes to learn everybody knows everybody's business. Of course, newcomers are a challenge, so that was why it took fifteen minutes in my case. It's what makes Folly so great; it's what makes Folly so exasperating. Not only do I know who you are, I know your food truck was vandalized the other day."

Grace gave Barb an inquisitive look.

Barb smiled. "Heard it from Matty at the bike rental shop, and Paul at Mr. John's Beach Store."

Grace looked at her watch. "Let's see, it's been more than fifteen minutes. Heard anything about me today?"

Barb shook her head. "No, why?"

Grace grinned like she knew a secret that Barb didn't know.

I knew where Grace was going with her question. I wasn't ready to go there, so I formally introduced the ladies and told Grace that Barb and I had been dating. Three potential customers entered the bookstore cutting our conversation short. I told Barb that I'd call later. She put her arm around Grace's shoulder and said that she was glad to see another businesswoman on Folly.

We were crossing the street in front of the Folly Pier when Laurie came down the steps, heading our way. She gave a knowing nod when she saw me, and I introduced Grace to her. Laurie said it was nice meeting Grace before asking where Charles was. I told her that I didn't know.

Grace stepped closer to Laurie. "Oh, are you the lady who recently lost her husband?"

I thought lost was a poor choice of words, although I was impressed that Grace was catching on.

"Yes, he was murdered."

Grace touched Laurie's arm. "I'm terribly sorry,"

"Thank you. Have you lived here long?"

"Oh, yes. Nearly three days."

That brought a smile to Laurie's face, a welcomed sight.

"I'm a newcomer, too. Perhaps we can grab a meal sometime."

"I'd like that," Grace said.

They exchanged numbers, then Laurie said she needed to get home.

Grace and I continued our walk to the far end of the pier.

"Long pier," she said as we reached the two-level observation deck.

"If you stood it on end, it'd only be seventeen feet shorter than the Eiffel Tower."

Yes, Charles's penchant for trivia was rubbing off.

She looked down at the Atlantic. "That'd be a long way to fall."

I appreciated her sense of humor. "I don't think it's going anywhere."

Her smile faded as she looked back toward the beach. "Chris, I don't know what to think. Don't know what to do."

"About what happened to your truck?"

She nodded. "Why would someone do that? I don't think anything was taken. Why break in to destroy my stuff?"

"Two reasons I can think of. To steal something of value, or to try to stop you from opening."

Grace continued to look toward shore and said, "Nothing worth stealing was in there the first time, so why try again?"

"It's unlikely that that was the reason. If it was, there would've been no reason to do so much damage the second time. Grace, think back, have you met anyone since you've been here who acted strange toward you?"

She smiled. "Theo tells me there is no shortage of people who seem strange, so how would I tell the difference? Besides, I haven't been here long enough to talk to many people."

"How about anyone who's taken more than a cursory interest in the truck?"

She hesitated. "Not really. Matty, the bicycle man's been nice. A couple of the gals who waited on me at the restaurants said they'd seen the truck and were curious. There'd even been two people who stopped to ask if I was hiring." She smiled. "I didn't tell them that, if I didn't work free, I wouldn't be able to hire me."

After talking back and forth a few more minutes, it became clear that neither Grace nor I could shed light on why her truck had become a break-in magnet.

I said, "Let me change the subject. You were born in Kansas, grew up in the states, right?"

She nodded.

"I thought if the parent, or parents, were from another country, the children born here didn't share their parents' accent."

Grace gave a knowing grin. "You wonder why I have a Jamaican accent?"

"Yes."

"Chris, you're perceptive. The only accent I had growing up was Midwestern. When I started waiting on customers in the food industry, I started throwing in

Jamaican phrases and lilting some of my speech. It made customers happy. Happy customers bought more food, tipped better. The older I get, the more I sound like my dearly-departed father."

"Grace, you're a good actress, and pleasant to listen to."

"Thanks, mon."

I laughed.

She said that she should probably get back to see if the crime techs had arrived.

I offered to walk her back.

She thanked me, but said she'd be fine, before adding, if she could find Folly Beach from California, she could find Theo's mansion.

I remained on the pier, enjoying the warm ocean breeze and the melodic sound of the waves as they rolled to shore. The shrill ring of my phone shook me out of what some would call a nap, I refer to it as relaxing. Regardless, it was abruptly interrupted by Charles who said, "It's on. Tomorrow night, six, Snapper Jack's. See you there."

"What's on?"

"Supper. Gail, Laurie, you, me. See ya."

I'd hoped it was a dream, although I knew better.

Chapter Thirty

Snapper Jack's is a colorful, multi-level restaurant on the corner of Center Street and Ashley Avenue, the site of Folly's only traffic light. The restaurant's central location, reputed for good seafood and live music, often attracted diners in excess of its seating capacity. Tonight would be no exception. The temperature was in the low-eighties, so I was glad to see that Charles had adhered to his thirty-minute-early routine. He was waiting for me on the sidewalk in front of the restaurant. He wore tan shorts, a tan Tilley, and a light blue, long-sleeve T-shirt with UGF in large letters and Argos in smaller letters under it.

We'd beaten the supper rush and decided to head up the long flight of stairs to the rooftop bar where we could enjoy the panoramic view of downtown Folly, the nine-story Tides Hotel, plus a glimpse of the Atlantic Ocean thrown in to heighten the experience. Two tables were vacant along the railing overlooking the hotel. Charles gave one of his lovable smiles to the hostess as he pointed to the tables. He told her that there was going to be four of us, so she gave us our choice of tables.

A server, who told us that her name was Monique, but to call her Mo, arrived as soon as were seated.

Charles was quick to order a Budweiser, and told her that he'd probably need a lot more before the night was over.

I said water was fine, that I'd order something stronger once the others joined us.

Mo headed toward the covered outside bar, and Charles said that I'd sounded asleep when he called yesterday. He wondered if old age was catching up with me. I told him that I'd been enjoying the view from the pier which led into a discussion about why I'd been there. That led to telling him about Grace's unwelcomed visitor, which, of course, led to him asking me how *we* were going to find out who'd destroyed the interior of the food truck. Our drinks arrived while I was telling him that it was in good hands, that *we* didn't need to get involved. He took a gulp of beer then conceded I was probably right.

I was making progress until he added, "That'll give us more time to figure out who murdered Anthony, figure out who tried to kill Laurie."

"Charles, that's what the police—"

He waved his hand in my face. "Her life depends on it."

"Charles, that's why it's better left to the police."

He stopped me again. "Before you start blabbing on about why it's up to the police and none of our business, do you want to go down to wait for the ladies? They don't know we're up here."

"You go. Remember, I'm the one who wasn't invited."

Whether he saw the wisdom of my comment, or didn't want to argue, he headed for the steps. I stared at the ocean and admitted that he was right, followed by wondering how we could help the police, help before it was too late for Laurie.

It was quarter after six, so I was beginning to think that

our guests had stood us up, when I saw Charles and the two ladies heading my way.

Gail was looking at Charles's shirt, "What are Argos?"

Charles responded with words I'd seldom heard coming from his mouth. "I don't know."

I stood to greet the newcomers. Laurie didn't appear to care about Argos, and met me with a hug. She didn't seem upset that Charles had invited me. Gail was more fascinated with Charles's shirt than Laurie or I were.

"Hi, Chris," Gail said. "Charles was telling us that his shirt is from the University of Great Falls, that's in Montana."

"Interesting," I said, not meaning a syllable.

The server appeared and told the newcomers they could call her Mo.

With that out of the way, Laurie started to speak, but was interrupted by Gail. "She and I'll have white wine."

I was beginning to agree with Charles about the quantity of drinks we would need. I told Mo the same for me.

"Guys," Laurie said, "thanks for joining us. It's nice getting to know people here." She looked down. "Now that… now that Anthony's gone, it's lonely being in a strange place."

Gail leaned closer to Laurie. "Now, dear, I'm here with you. You know it would be best for you to come back to Jacksonville. You have many friends there."

Laurie said, "I appreciate you coming. This is my home."

I wondered how many times she'd have to tell that to Gail.

Charles said, "When did you get here?"

Gail glared at him like he'd interrupted her Jacksonville sales pitch.

"Gail arrived this morning."

It was refreshing seeing Laurie answer for Gail.

"I would've made it yesterday, but I'd been in a seminar in Saint Augustine, didn't get back until late yesterday."

"What kind of seminar?" asked Charles as Mo returned with our drinks.

Gail glanced at him. "Oh, I'm sure you'd not be interested."

"Sure, I am," he said.

Gail sighed. "It was about ways of searching for jobs, also assistance the state provides to employees whose companies are moving offshore. The company I worked for is moving operations to Mexico. I thought it'd help if I wanted to return to the workforce."

Charles nodded. "Learn anything?"

"Not really. It was boring, boring, boring."

"That's too bad," I said to get into the discussion.

"Not really. Dean's spending day and night at the store, I wouldn't have seen him much, anyway."

Laurie said, "Gail, I thought you wouldn't have to go back to work."

"Wishful thinking," Gail said. "Selling tires is getting fiercer and fiercer. Dean's store is having to compete with stores and national tire chains that buy tires by the ton."

Our drinks arrived, then Laurie tapped her friend's arm. "Let's talk about something more fun. It's so nice out tonight. Look at that view. This is my first time up here."

"It is a beautiful view," Gail said, as she turned to Charles. "Have the police learned anything about who killed Anthony, or who shot at Laurie?"

That's a fun topic, I thought.

Charles said, "I haven't heard."

Gail said, "Do they think the killer was after the treasure?"

"Gail," Laurie said, "they don't know why Anthony was killed. I doubt the person would've shot him over some Civil War relics. Chris and Charles think Anthony may've run across guys being where they shouldn't be, something about a boat delivering drugs. Isn't that right, Charles?"

"That's a theory."

Laurie pulled her chair up to the table, sat up straight, and said, "See, Gail, it doesn't have anything to do with the map, or anything we were doing out there." She abruptly turned to me. "Chris, it was nice meeting your friend Grace. I'll call her for lunch after Gail leaves." She turned away from Gail.

I didn't bother telling her that I'd known Grace for three days. I also didn't bother trying to steer the conversation back to the topic of Anthony's death, for she'd left no doubt the subject was now off limits.

The rest of the evening, we talked about everything but Anthony, the gunshots at Laurie's house, or anything else negative. Tension seemed to fall off Laurie's shoulders. Gail stopped interrupting everything Laurie tried to say. Charles attempted to be Charles a couple of times by asking questions that stepped over the none-of-your-business line, only to be deflected by Laurie. I couldn't tell if she was trying to hide something, or was determined to keep the topics light. Either way, it turned out to be a pleasant night spent with pleasant friends, new friends.

The feeling of a pleasant evening was hijacked while I was walking home. All I thought about was Laurie's brief mention of treasure, and the word that I hadn't heard her say before: map.

Chapter Thirty-One

I woke the next morning, remembering that, somewhere in the amorphous state between sleep and awake, I thought about something that Laurie had said during supper that was significant. The problem was that, now that I was awake, I couldn't put my finger on what it was. I convinced myself that a walk next door to Bert's to grab breakfast would jar the memory to the surface. Truth be told, I doubted that it would. I was searching for an excuse to buy a cinnamon roll.

The gooey delight was less appealing when I saw Stanley Kremitz in front of the case holding the high-calorie goodies. It became even less appealing when Stanley spotted me.

He looked my way, smiled, flapped his arms like they were wings, and said, "The early bird gets the worm."

"Hi, Stanley. Worms aren't my thing. The cinnamon rolls behind you are my weakness."

"It's an expression, Chris. An expression. I was about to grab one of those, myself. Told you we were as alike as two peas in a pod."

I wouldn't believe it, even if he told me until hell freezes over, I thought in Stanley speak.

He smiled, like he'd convinced me we were alike, then said, "Any word on who killed the relic hunter?"

"No. Have you heard anything?"

"Veronica and I were flapping our lips about it last night. She told me that she heard something at the beauty shop about Abraham Gant, you know, Captain Gant."

"Heard what?"

"Gant told someone that he knew where treasure was buried, that the money didn't mean anything to him."

"Why not?"

"Suppose because he's hung up on the past staying past."

"Did the person who told your wife say that was the reason?"

"Don't think so. I'm picturing the story about what Gant said being shared a few times from one person to another, to another. The story Veronica heard, most likely, ain't the version that started going around. A chain is only as strong as its weakest link."

The story may be convoluted although, if most of it's accurate, it's further evidence that Gant knew about the treasure map he told Charles and me about.

"Did Veronica specifically say that she'd heard the word treasure and not relics?"

"That's what she heard. It don't necessarily mean it's so."

"Who told her the story?"

"Maybelle Davis. Maybelle heard it from Francis something or other, who heard it from, umm, Francis didn't remember who she heard it from."

I lost track after Maybelle when I realized that following the chain to the initial source would be as successful as catching a seagull with a tablespoon.

"Stanley, let me know if you hear more about Gant."

"Sure will." He grabbed a roll out of the case. "Gotta head out. Promised Veronica I'd take her to Walmart." He shook his head. "She'll shop 'til she drops."

I watched him go, tried to erase several clichés from my mind, grabbed a cinnamon roll, then walked among the aisles long enough for Stanley to leave. Two things stuck with me about the conversation. First, it reinforced what Gant had told us about treasure and why Anthony and Laurie had been exploring the old Coast Guard property. Second, it appeared Stanley was determined to bring Abraham Gant into the discussion about Anthony's death. This wasn't the first time he'd pointed a finger at the captain. He'd asked again if I'd learned anything about the murder. Did the cliché king want to deflect suspicion from himself?

I microwaved the roll, paid, then headed home, only to find Chief LaMond's pickup truck in my drive. She stepped out of the vehicle when she saw me coming across the yard.

Cindy pointed to the house. "You're not in there."

I smiled. "Did you use all your chiefly skills to figure that out?"

"Nope. No answer after I pounded on the door gave it away."

"If I'd been home, what would I have done to receive a visit by the finest of Folly's finest?"

Instead of answering, Cindy sat on the step leading to my screened-in porch waving for me to join her.

"Well?" I said.

"Being that you're the second nosiest person I know, I wanted to share an update on the Anthony Fitzsimmons' murder."

Charles, of course, was the first, leading the pack by a longshot. "Share away."

Cindy watched a classic Volkswagen convertible pass and continued to stare at the road. "The update is there's no update. Or, I should have said the update is there's nothing new to update. No murder weapon, no forensic evidence, no eyewitnesses except Anthony, who unfortunately is in no condition to identify his killer."

"What happens now?"

"I talked to Detective Callahan this morning. He's up to his dimples in that high-profile case plus a couple of others. He said that he was still working it but sounded as optimistic as someone teaching a frog to pilot a helicopter."

"Does he think Laurie's telling the truth?"

She shook her head again. "Not really. Short of beating a confession out of her, his hands are tied."

"What about rumors that Anthony stumbled across a drug deal and paid for it with his life?"

"That's as good a story as any. Still, no evidence to indicate it's anything but a story."

"What about Abraham Gant?"

"Decent alibi, weak motive, no evidence."

I shared with the chief what Stanley Kremitz had said about Gant then what Laurie had said during supper about a map.

"Chris, I never bought her story about searching for Civil War relics. If she had a map from her grandfather, it would've been further proof she was lying. With that said, there's no map I've seen, no evidence, with only my gut reaction that she's involved. My gut don't mean squat when it comes to proof."

"So, you came to tell me that there's nothing."

"Frustrating as hell, isn't it?"

"Yes."

"Welcome to my world." She patted me on the knee before heading to her vehicle.

I watched her pull into the line of traffic, took a bite of cinnamon roll, and wondered what I could do to solve one more murder on my little slice of heaven. I may, or may not, succeed, although one thing was clear. The solution must start with Laurie.

I punched Charles's number in the phone. When he answered, said, "Ready to go?"

"Huh?"

I smiled at the reversal of what normally happens. "You home?"

"Yes."

"I'll pick you up in ten minutes." I hit *end call*.

I was beginning to see why he had so much fun doing the same thing to me. It was time to do what the police appeared to have a tough time doing.

Chapter Thirty-Two

I met Charles standing in front of his apartment, ignored his asking, several ways, where we were going, drove to Laurie's house, and pulled in behind her MINI.

"Did you forget something?" Laurie said as she opened the door. She jumped back when she saw us. "Oh, sorry. I thought you were Gail. She just left for the grocery." She looked at Charles. "Did I know you were coming?"

Charles pivoted to me.

I said, "We were nearby, so we thought we'd see if you were doing okay. I hope we're not interrupting anything."

"I think I'm okay. Umm, come in. Would you like coffee?"

Laurie wore tattered navy-blue shorts, a loose-fitting PINK T-shirt, and was barefoot. I felt a tinge of guilt for interrupting her morning. My guilt was short-lived. I said we'd love some.

We followed her to the kitchen, where she poured our drinks then pointed to the table. She surprised me when she chuckled. "Actually, I'm glad you stopped by. I sent Gail to the grocery to get her out of the house."

Charles said, "Why?"

"That woman's driving me crazy."

Charles looked toward the front door like he expected Gail to appear. "How?"

Laurie followed Charles's gaze. "After Anthony left us, this is the first time Gail and I've been together this long. Don't get me wrong, I love her."

She looked at Charles like she expected him to respond. He didn't disappoint.

"You're great friends."

She smiled at Charles. "We are." The smile disappeared. "Have you ever known someone who wouldn't stop talking, unless they're asleep or food's stuffed in their mouth?"

Charles wasn't that bad, although he came to mind. I responded, "Yes."

"I swear, guys, I can't complete a two-word sentence without her finishing it or she's veering off in another direction before I finish." She blinked twice then shook her head.

I said, "I'm sorry."

Laurie bit her lower lip, stared in her mug, and mumbled, "Sorry, hearing me bitch isn't why you're here."

Charles leaned forward. "That's okay. We don't mind."

She was right, that wasn't the reason we were here. I said, "Laurie, the other night at Snapper Jack's, you were talking about being with Anthony at the old Coast Guard station."

She nodded as she looked up from her drink.

"You said something about a map. I was wondering—"

She interrupted, "Map?"

"You and Gail were talking when you mentioned a map."

"Don't think so."

Okay, Charles, it's time that you stepped in to add you heard it.

No such luck, so I continued, "Gail said something about you all finding the treasure. You said map."

The look on Laurie's face screamed either confusion or that she was hiding something.

"Oh," Laurie said. "I must've been talking about that map beside the entrance to the Preserve. You know, the one where you donate a dollar to help protect the area."

I knew the map she was referring to. I also knew it wasn't the one she'd alluded to at supper.

Charles finally chipped in. "I hadn't thought of that one. That could've been it." He rubbed his hand through his three-day-old whiskers. "But, honest to Pete, I had the impression you were talking about a map you and Anthony had."

She hopped out of her chair, grabbed the coffee pot, and refilled our mugs. She then looked out the repaired window.

She paced the room as I reminded myself that I could be talking to Anthony's murderer. If she was guilty, I'll be walking in dangerous territory; if innocent, I wanted her to know that we cared. Either way, I wanted her to understand that I knew there was something about a map, not the one posted at the entrance to the Preserve. Besides, Stanley Kremitz had already told me about his experience with Harnell Levi, who'd talked about a map.

"Laurie, Charles, and I want to help. If there's something you aren't sharing, then it makes it hard for us to figure out what's going on. If you're afraid of going to the police, we could go with you."

She returned to her chair, took a sip, and in a faint voice said, "I've told you some about Granddad Levi, how I spent time here with him. He was a funny old bird. He could be cranky as a screech owl. Other times, he could spin tall tales with the best storytellers. Sadly, he could guzzle more alcohol than anyone I've ever known."

That was consistent with what Kremitz had said.

"I know people like that here," Charles added, hopefully not stopping Laurie's story.

She nodded at Charles. "During one of the calmer, sober moments, he took me in his den. He folded back a god-awful colored area rug and pried up a floorboard. I never would've seen it if he didn't show me. Under the floor was a tin container the size of a cigar box. Granddad got this big grin on his face, opened the box, took out a stack of cash. I'd never seen so much money in my life. Under the cash was a folded piece of paper." She smiled as she relived the memory. "He held the paper by the edges then unfolded it like it was the original Declaration of Independence. Know what he told me?"

Charles smiled. "Said it was a treasure map?"

Laurie shrugged. "Granddad put his arm around me. 'Laurie,' he said, 'this here's the most important piece of paper you'll ever see.' I remember it like it was yesterday because I thought the cash was as important as anything gets. He said the crinkly old map was to a treasure buried on Folly more than two hundred years ago, buried by pirates. He said he wanted me to have it. I was in my teens, no expert to say the least. To me, the map looked old, although not old enough to have been drawn by a pirate two hundred years earlier."

Charles asked, "What'd it look like?"

"I couldn't make hide nor hair of it. It had all these lines, squiggles, round things that I suppose were trees." Laurie hesitated.

Hesitated too long for Charles. "What'd he say?"

"I was right. He said it wasn't the original. Whoever got it first must've made a copy so that they could carry it around with them without ruining the original. Granddad said it didn't matter. He knew it was accurate."

I asked, "How'd he know?"

"He didn't say."

"Where'd he get it?" Charles asked.

"Funny thing. Granddad wouldn't tell me. All he said was he knew it was exactly like the original."

Charles said, "Had he looked for the treasure?"

Laurie nodded. "For years. The problem was according to the map, the treasure was buried on the Coast Guard property. For most of his years looking, it was under control of the military so he couldn't snoop around. Another problem was that over the years weather changed the face of the beach, maybe even most of the island.

"Landmarks from when the pirates buried the treasure had washed away by the tides, been blown away by hurricanes, trees grew, trees died, most everything changed. When the Coast Guard built the station, much of the landscape changed, buildings built, roads added. In other words, the map led him to the general area, but no closer."

"Why'd he give it to you?" I asked.

"It was one of the few times I saw him sober. He was in poor health. I think he knew he was too ill to keep looking." She shook her head. "He passed away two months after giving me the map."

Charles said, "What'd you do with it?"

"To tell the truth, I thought it was another of his tall tales. He was always talking about strange things happening on Folly. He told me, I think he believed it, that a spaceship landed behind what's now the Oceanfront Villas. He was also convinced, during World War II, a German submarine parked off the island sending three spies ashore in a small boat. I put his so-called treasure map in my keepsake box and went on with life, going to school, going to college, teaching, marrying Anthony."

"What changed?" I asked.

"We were moving to a new house about four years ago. I found my old keepsake box in the bottom of a carton of clothes. I remember laughing when I showed Anthony Granddad's map. I told him it was the key to our fortune. I was joking. Anthony wasn't. He didn't know Granddad, so he didn't know how quirky he was. Anthony said we needed to look for the treasure. That's what we did.

"Whenever we came here before retiring, we walked through the Preserve, looking for anything looking like what was marked on the map. A couple of times, we thought something could be like it was on the map, although we never felt we were close enough to dig. All we knew for certain was that the squiggles on the map represented the ocean. It was impossible to tell distances between the circles that looked like trees. Plus, the shoreline wasn't where it was when the map was drawn."

When we found her at the Preserve, she'd told us it was their first time exploring the property. "Laurie, didn't you tell us you'd never been at the Coast Guard property before the night Anthony was killed?"

She looked at the floor. "That was sort of a fib. You were strangers so I didn't want to tell you too much."

I let it go. "What about the night of Anthony's death?"

"The day before we'd been snooping around and found what we thought was one of the landmarks from the map. It wasn't exactly like the map, but close enough to try. There were a lot of people in the area. It was illegal to dig, so we decided to wait until the next day. Hoped for fewer people. That's when…"

She put her head down on the table. Tears streamed down her face. Charles and I sat in silence. What seemed like an eternity later, she wiped the tears away. "That's about it."

"Where's the map?" I asked.

She shook her head. "Don't know. Anthony had it. He had more pockets and didn't want to be walking around with it in his hands in case someone saw us. When the police said that I could pick up his personal effects, all they had was his wallet, watch, and clothes."

"The map was gone," said Charles, stating the obvious.

Laurie nodded.

We sipped our drinks in silence. Laurie started looking at the door every few seconds. I figured she was worried that

Gail would return and for some reason didn't want us to be here. I took the hint. I thanked her for sharing the story of the map then said we'd better be going. She didn't protest.

I was backing out of Laurie's drive when Charles said, "What do you think about her story?"

"I have trouble with a story about a treasure map. It sounds more like the myths that've been around for eons. Someone finds a map with an X on it, supposedly the location of buried treasure. Then, a bunch of people go on a wild goose chase. It makes an interesting television show. Great fiction."

"Your skeptic gene is showing."

"What do you think?"

"If she made it up, she inherited her granddad's story-telling skill."

"Okay, assume there was a map, that is, a copy of another map, let's say treasure was buried on the Preserve; what are the odds it'd be there after all these years? Most of the land had been occupied by the Coast Guard. They build numerous structures and had hundreds of coasties, guardians, or whatever you call Coast Guard members who were stationed there traipsing over every square foot of land. I find it hard to believe if there was treasure it wouldn't have been found."

"That may be true, although don't you think that if someone found a treasure chest filled with doubloons, it would've been big news?"

"If they told anyone."

"That's not the kind of secret people keep without bragging."

"I'll admit if she's lying, she's excellent at it. I still think she's the number one suspect. Treasure map or not, she has motive."

"Insurance?"

"Yes."

Charles looked out the windshield and tapped his hand on the armrest. "If she's guilty, how do you explain someone taking potshots at her?"

"She could've taken the first one herself. Remember, she told us a different version of where she was than she told the police. There were no witnesses."

"She couldn't have taken the second shot. We were there."

"That, I can't explain."

"See, it ain't her," Charles said, once again tapped his hand on the armrest. "What about other suspects? How about the story going around that Anthony stumbled on a drug transfer from a boat? That'd be an isolated spot for a transfer, especially since no one was supposed to be there after dark. It's easy to see how Anthony might've seen them and been awarded with a bullet."

"It's possible. It seems unlikely that the killer would wait days to take shots at Laurie. The odds she saw him at the Preserve would've been slim."

"Abraham Gant?"

"He'd talked to Anthony a few days before the murder. From what's been said, Anthony talked about a buried treasure more than was wise, so he could've told Gant. Everyone knows Gant goes bananas when there's talks about digging up things from the past, be it treasure, or Civil War uniform buttons."

"With him being a retired cop, he'd have a gun, and know how to use it," Charles said.

"Add to that, he knew about the murder before it was widespread knowledge. He didn't have qualms about saying he was glad Anthony was dead. Cindy questioned him. He didn't have a solid alibi for the time of the murder."

Charles turned to me as I pulled in his parking lot. "How are we going to prove he killed Anthony?"

"Charles, the police are aware of everything we know about Gant. I'm sure they're looking at him."

"Didn't Cindy tell you Detective Callahan is up to his coiffured hair with other cases? When's he going to have time to investigate Gant?"

"What do you propose?"

"Hey, you're the brains of our crime fighting duo. I'm the one who goes along then stumbles into catching bad guys."

I've worked hard over the years ignoring Charles's remarks about us being a *crime fighting duo*, or that he's a *private detective*. I was clueless about what to do to uncover Gant as the killer, so I ignored his comment.

Charles stared at me and must've figured a solution wasn't forthcoming. "Here's another thought. What about Gail?"

"What about her?"

"Think about it. She could've known about the treasure map since she was such good friends with Laurie. When someone first shot at Laurie, Gail was here. Allegedly, she'd gone to the grocery. It doesn't take a genius to figure she could've been the shooter."

That reminded me of the first time I talked with Gail when she'd said that she and Dean were supposed to be visiting Anthony and Laurie to search for relics. They knew about the search. Did they know about the treasure map?

"Charles, she was four hours away in Jacksonville when Anthony was shot."

"How do you know?"

"I don't. Do you think she and her never-speaking husband are in it together?"

"Probably not. Didn't you tell me Dean was somewhere other than Jacksonville? That was the reason they hadn't gone to visit Anthony and Laurie?"

"A tire retailers' meeting in Tallahassee."

Charles held out his arms and smiled, "Aha. Dean didn't know where Gail was. Her alibi about being in Jacksonville has more holes than a block of Swiss cheese."

Charles had a point, although I wasn't ready to move Gail to the top of the list. Time to throw out another possibility.

"What about Stanley Kremitz?"

Charles lowered his arms. "Stanley? You think he killed Anthony with a cliché?"

I grinned. "No. That would've been a slower, much more painful death. Think about it. Stanley knew Harnell Levi. According to Stanley, Levi told him about a map. Each time I've seen him since the murder, he's asked if I've heard anything about the killer then he pushes the theory it's Gant."

"I haven't given Stanley a speck of thought. I can't picture him shooting anyone."

"That doesn't mean he didn't."

"Does Cindy know your harebrained theory about the cliché king?"

"No."

"This is where if I told you what you told me you'd pat me on the back, then say it was none of our business, that I should take my ideas, regardless how stupid, to the police."

I hated it when Charles was right. "That's exactly what I'm going to do once I leave your parking lot."

I called Cindy on my way home. She was with Larry at a plumbing supply house in Charleston. I said that I could call her when she got back to Folly. She said my call was a gift from heaven. It would give her an excuse to not "ooh and ah" when Larry showed her the latest, greatest, high-tech toilets. I shared my ideas about possible suspects. When I finished, she said looking at toilets may not have been the worse idea after all.

Despite her faux lack of enthusiasm about my ideas, she'd take me seriously.

Theo called the next afternoon to share news about Grace's food truck. He'd talked to several local restaurant owners to explain what happened. Even though they competed for dining dollars, the owners were a tightknit group that helped each other in times of need. This was no exception. They pitched in to loan Grace the equipment needed to open *Hot Diggity Dog!*

Additionally, she had received her permit so, by the next day, she would be serving the best hot dogs found anywhere east of the Mississippi. Theo had done a taste test and couldn't swear hers were the best east of the Mississippi, but said it was the best he'd eaten. He ended by inviting me to a celebratory dinner with him and Grace the next evening at Magnolias, one of Charleston's finest restaurants. He was driving and buying. I asked what time.

Theo didn't have Charles's obsession about being early. He pulled in my drive at 6:00, the time he'd said he'd be there. I slid onto the soft leather backseat in his Mercedes. Grace rewarded me with a charming smile, while Theo thanked me for joining them. I told him I was honored to have been invited. Theo had on a navy sport coat and gray slacks, dressed more formally than I'd ever seen him. Grace wore a pale-yellow silk blouse and black linen slacks. I felt underdressed in a long-sleeve, blue striped shirt and tan chinos.

"Where's Sal?" I asked as we pulled off the island.

"I invited him. He declined, thank goodness. The night will be better without a joke machine with us. Said he'd met a couple of Folly old-timers who meet at the Crab Shack nearly every night to swap tall tales, share opinions on everything from the mayor to the president, while putting away a beverage or two. Sal said they love, he put air quotes around love, his jokes and stories from the comedy circuit.

They'd get over it, I thought, then lied saying I was sorry he couldn't make it.

I'd never been in Theo's car and was mesmerized by its smooth ride as we weaved through Charleston's streets lined with stately mansions and years of history on our way to the East Bay Street restaurant. I could get used to being chauffeured. A valet met us at the door, whisked the car off while another employee held the door of the restaurant known for its contemporary Lowcountry cuisine. I wasn't certain what that meant but, from everything I'd heard about the white-tablecloth restaurant, the food was outstanding. Besides, for once, someone else was paying.

We were seated by a window, overlooking the street, and greeted by a server who, with great flourish, handed Theo the wine list. I got a glimmer of Theo's life as a successful businessman before he retired in bohemian comfort on Folly when he ordered a bottle of expensive Champaign pronouncing its French name correctly, or so I assumed. Theo told the server we were celebrating the opening of another fine restaurant in the Lowcountry. Like the professional he was, the waiter said congratulations. He didn't enquire about what he could have perceived to be a new competitor.

"Grace," I said, "how was your first day of business?" I'd asked the same question on the ride over, but Theo said for us to wait until we were at the restaurant.

She gave me a high-wattage smile. "Exhilarating, and exhausting. I underestimated the quest for gourmet hot dogs on Folly."

Gourmet was not a word often bandied around on Folly, but I knew what she'd meant. "I'm thrilled for you."

The server returned with our bubbly, adroitly uncorked it, then poured a taste in Theo's flute. Theo waved it off saying he was certain it was acceptable. The server poured each glass to a third full then continued pouring until each flute was near full.

Theo raised his glass. "Here's to Folly's newest eating establishment and its lovely proprietress."

Grace looked around like she didn't know who Theo was referring to, then she said, "If, dear sir, you are referring to me, I'm honored."

I was pleased to see Theo and Grace on better terms than when they'd met.

Theo asked if we wanted an appetizer.

I said I'd get anything that the two of them wanted.

Grace took a sip of Champaign and tilted her flute to Theo. "Anything but hot dogs."

Theo laughed and said that he didn't think Magnolias was that fine a dining establishment. He waved the server over and ordered house-made potato chips and pimento cheese with Charleston flatbread.

"Did anything surprise you?" I asked the proprietress.

"California is known for its laid-back citizens. I wasn't certain what to expect on this side of the country. Mon, was I surprised. As dad would say, 'Gi laugh fi peas soup.' "

"Which means?" I said.

"The literal translation is, 'Give laughs for peas soup.' "

Theo tilted his head. "Which means?"

Grace laughed. "To joke around, to have a good time.

Everyone, okay, nearly everyone, who stepped up to the service window seemed happy. They joked. They laughed, smiled, were cheerful. It was, how shall I say it, umm energizing to feel so welcomed. Two men came back to buy more hot dogs. They said they would tell everyone how great they were."

Appetizers arrived and, while Grace and Theo grabbed a potato chip each, I said, "Are you going to hire someone to help?"

Grace put her hand in front of her mouth as she finished the chip. "That would be preferable although, with my expenses, plus the need to replace the damaged equipment, I'm afraid it will be a long time. That's what I told two young gentlemen who stopped by to see if I was hiring. It was the second time one of them stopped to ask. I told him to check back in a few weeks."

Theo nodded, "If business continues like today, that day might come sooner rather than later."

Grace raised her flute. "I'll drink to that."

Theo and I did as well.

A half hour later, Grace was eating blue crab stuffed rainbow trout, while Theo and I were savoring grilled fillets of beef. The festive conversation bounced around from the fantastic weather of the last week; Grace wondering how many hours the carriage horses worked in a day; Theo sharing stories from his world of work; and, I told how Charles and I managed to catch not one, but two murderers because of the walking group that Theo, Charles, and I were in. Grace's laughter was interspersed with yawns. I was amazed she'd managed to stay awake. I attributed it to my charm and winning personality. I suspected it was due to her being able to relax around her father-in-law.

Grace's phone interrupted a humorous story about one of her customers who wanted to pay with a fifty-euro banknote. She apologized for the interruption then answered.

Her face turned from a frown to a look of shock as she listened to whoever was on the other end. She put her hand over the phone and asked Theo, "How long will it take us to get to Folly?"

Theo said a half hour. Grace repeated that in the phone, then hit *end call*. She put her hand over her face and shook her head.

Theo put his arm around her shoulder. "What's wrong, dear?"

She threw her napkin on the table. "That was Chief LaMond. My truck's ablaze."

Chapter Thirty-Five

Theo may be one of the slowest walkers above ground. He may need police to stop traffic on Folly when he crosses streets with the walking group. Throw all that out the window when he's faced with a crisis. In fewer than five minutes, he'd paid the tab and summoned the valet to pull the Mercedes to the side of the building. Twenty minutes later, after running two yellow lights and, don't tell anyone, one red, we were crossing the bridge to Folly. Off to the left, I saw the flashing red lights from one of Folly's fire vehicles and blue lights from a police cruiser beside Theo's house.

Grace gasped.

Theo put his free hand on her arm as he turned on his street before skidding to a stop in his neighbors' gravel drive. Spotlights from the fire engine focused on the cab of the food truck backed into Theo's drive.

Two firefighters were rolling up hoses, one from a hydrant across the street, the other from the side of the fire apparatus. A wisp of smoke rose from the truck's blackened, cracked windshield.

Grace was already out of the car and being restrained by one of the firefighters after she tried to enter the truck. The logo wrap on the side had warped from the heat. A front tire was flat, melted rubber oozed from the door.

Theo and I approached the vehicle as the words *total loss* came to mind. I was heartbroken for Grace.

Chief LaMond came around the back of the vehicle and saw us standing with the distraught owner. She approached Grace. "I'm sorry."

Grace stared at the truck, her fists were balled, her shoulders sagged. I couldn't tell if she'd heard Cindy.

Theo moved to Grace's side then Cindy came over to where I was.

"We were fortunate," she said as she looked at the totaled vehicle.

Fortunate wouldn't have been a word I would've chosen to describe what I saw. The smell of burning rubber, mixed with a whiff of burnt meat, filled the air. "Fortunate?"

"The fire didn't reach the propane tank on the back of the truck avoiding an eruption, or explosion, which could've been catastrophic."

I shook my head.

"And," she continued, "when we got here the flames were pouring out the side of the truck, coming within a hair of Theo's house. If our guys hadn't gotten water on the house when they did, we'd be looking at a crispy McMansion."

Theo was still comforting Grace.

I said, "Cindy, any idea what caused it?"

"I'll let the arson investigator figure that out, but I'd guess it was set. It got too hot too quick. We were fortunate to contain the damage."

"*Hot Diggity Dog!* has been on Folly mere days and already broken in twice, now this," I said, more to myself than to Cindy.

She looked at the vehicle. "Don't guess we'll worry about more break ins."

"You may not want to comfort Grace with that insight."

Cindy rolled her eyes, then asked where Theo, Grace, and I had been when she called.

I explained where we were and why. Cindy muttered a profanity, then said, "Did Grace say anything about being afraid of anyone, or anything, strange happening to her?"

"Like someone telling her he was going to torch her truck?"

"That'd be a clue."

"The opposite," I said. "Her first day was a tremendous success. She was thrilled by the reception she'd received."

"I heard the same thing. I was planning on stopping by tomorrow for lunch. Suppose I'll have to change plans."

"Anyone see anybody around the truck?"

"None I know about. My guys canvassed the neighbors, who said that they hadn't seen anyone. Somebody driving by might have but, unless they do their civic duty and come forward, we'll never know."

The chief looked at her men loading the remaining fire-equipment on the truck. "I'll talk to Grace tomorrow after I have more information from the arson investigator, and she has time to get over the initial shock." She turned to head to her vehicle then stopped. "One more thing, Chris. I talked to Detective Callahan this afternoon. He said one of the other guys in his office was telling him there's been an uptick in drugs being offloaded from boats along the coast. One was caught last weekend near Edisto. He thinks there's a better than even chance the Fitzsimmonses were in the wrong place at the wrong time with Anthony stumbling on a drug deal."

"So Callahan's back on the case?"

"He's swamped. His drug guys are looking at it."

Anthony may've stumbled on a drug deal, but that didn't explain two attempts on Laurie's life. I asked Cindy to let me know if she learned anything. She said that she lived for the sole purpose of sharing everything law-enforcement related with me. I grinned as I thanked her. She mumbled another profanity then left to talk to Grace.

I looked in the truck where the smell of burnt rubber, incinerated hot dogs, and melted plastic was so strong that I had to step away from the vehicle. I couldn't fathom how *Hot Diggity Dog!* would serve another meal.

"Holy hot dog!" screamed Sal.

I turned to see him shuffle down the drive toward Theo and Grace.

He put his hand on his forehead psychic-style and said, "I see a fire sale in the future."

Theo waved his hand in Sal's face. "Sal, can it."

Sal stopped in front of Grace, leaned from side to side, possibly a result of hours sharing whatever he'd been sharing with his new buddies at the Crab Shack. He lowered his head. "Sorry, Grace. Sometimes, I'd like to smack myself for being so insensitive."

He'd have to get in line, I thought as I walked to the trio.

Grace, earning her name, put her hand on Sal's wobbly shoulder. "That's okay, Salvadore, you can't help yourself."

She was a quick learner. Theo wasn't as forgiving. He gave his brother a look that would stop a charging rhinoceros.

Sal ignored his brother's glare. "What happened?"

I joined the group to listen as Grace and Theo tag-teamed their explanation of what had occurred. Sal asked the same questions Cindy had asked and received the same answers until he asked a new question. "Was it insured?"

Grace lowered her head. "It was when we bought it. We had to have insurance in California. I didn't have enough money to keep it up. I didn't owe anything on the vehicle, so I dropped the comprehensive policy when I got here. I still have collision insurance."

Please, Sal, don't make a joke about the truck colliding with a match, or some other feeble attempt at humor.

He showed a glimmer of sensitivity when he said, "Grace, I'm so sorry."

She thanked him.

"Sal," said Theo after Sal's moment of concern. "Did you see anyone skulking around after we left for Charleston?"

"No. I headed to the Crab Shack before you got off the island. Been there ever since. I heard the fire trucks. Didn't know where they were going, or I would've followed."

Theo looked at the burned-out truck then turned to Grace. "Let's get in the house. I could use a spot of brandy."

Grace didn't say anything as she followed Theo.

Once again, Sal refrained from joking.

I walked by his side up the wide steps to Theo's house, the house spared by the quick-acting firefighters.

Theo went to get drinks, miracles continued when Sal offered to help.

Grace plopped down on the leather sofa in the great room. She twisted her hands together, looked at me, and said, "Why?"

I wish I had an answer.

Air conditioning, brandy, wine, and beer didn't reveal the answer to why someone set the fire, but calmed everyone's nerves.

Grace relaxed enough to joke that she knew today's sales were good, yet didn't realize they would be a record high.

Sal thought it was funny but didn't want to be topped so he added, "Did you hear about the new restaurant on the moon?"

Grace tilted her head. "Don't believe I did."

Theo sighed.

Sal said, "It has great food but no atmosphere."

I excused myself on that note.

Chapter Thirty-Six

I'd agreed to meet Charles for breakfast at the Dog. I arrived forty-five minutes before the designated time, in the hope of beating my buddy. I failed. He was sipping coffee at my favorite booth along the back wall. He saw me at the door then glanced at his bare wrist as I made my way to the table.

"You're early," he said. "I'm impressed."

Forty-five minutes early, I thought.

Charles wore a blue long-sleeved T-shirt with *Salve Regina University* in green on the front. I'd never heard of the school, yet still didn't mention it. I asked if he'd been here long.

"Not long. You walk?"

"Drove."

He shook his head and sighed at the same time, his way of saying poor, pitiful Chris.

He made a walking motion on the table with two fingers. "Thomas Jefferson said, 'Walking is the best possible exercise. Habituate yourself to walk very far.'"

"Chris Landrum said, 'Good morning, Charles.' "

Amber arrived at the table in time to hear my effort at bringing civility and less presidential history to the table. She pointed at Charles's T-shirt. "It's in Newport, Rhode Island."

Amber knew how much I tried to ignore Charles's T-shirts collection.

Charles beamed.

I wanted to go back to the car and instead of walking, drive, far away. I said, "Coffee, a lot of it."

Amber chuckled, bent down, and kissed the top of my balding head. I'd never admit it to them, but this kind of disjoined conversation was one of the reasons I loved living here. Amber went to fetch my drink.

Charles watched her go then turned serious. "Chris, I like Laurie. She's nice, but seems lost. I can't imagine how it would be to lose a spouse. She's got to be lonely. Look how many times she's asked us to be with her."

I wanted to point out that she asked him, not us, but I let it go.

He continued. "I'm worried about her."

"Why?"

"Is your old age killing off so many brain cells you've already forgotten two attempts on her life? If she'd been with Anthony when he was killed, she'd already be dead. Can't you see how much danger she's in?"

"I know that. I wondered if there was something else you were referring to. Have you talked to her since we were at her place?"

Amber returned with my drink and asked if I was ready to order. I told her French toast. She pretended to be shocked at the same thing I ordered ninety percent of the time.

After Amber headed to the kitchen, Charles said, "She called me around midnight. I was asleep. It must've taken me a long time to answer because she said she was afraid I wasn't going to."

"Was something wrong?"

"That was my thought. Calling me at midnight is like calling you geezers at ten. Snoresville."

I was only two years older than Charles, both of us senior citizens by any definition.

"Again, was anything wrong?"

"If there was, she didn't tell me. Said she was sitting in her dark house, needed someone to talk to. I asked if Gail was there. She said she'd gone back to Florida. Even if she was still on Folly, Laurie said she needed someone to talk to, not to listen to." He shook his head. I took a sip as I waited for him to continue. "Chris, she didn't give another reason for the call. She sounded scared."

"Did you learn anything?"

"Don't think so, but I may've dozed while she was talking. She rambled on about the night Anthony was killed. She'd said most of it to us before. She did talk more about the map, also wondered why it wasn't with the body. Seems to me the killer took it. For some reason, she doesn't want to believe that's what happened."

Amber returned with my breakfast, plus a drink refill for Charles, before moving to a group seated across from us.

Charles looked in his mug as he rubbed his chin. "Chris, I've been thinking."

"About?"

"We know there was a map."

"Not for sure."

"Whatever. Let's say there was. Anthony had it the night he was killed, but it wasn't on him when the cops came. The killer has it. So, what's the logical thing the killer will do?" Before I could respond, Charles said, "Try to find the treasure."

"Which, number one, may've been discovered years ago; two, the killer could've already found it; three, the map could've been a cruel joke drawn decades ago, leading to nothing."

"Yeah, yeah, yeah. Anyway, you said the police have pushed Anthony's death to the backburner, so it's up to us to solve it. We owe it to Laurie."

I was surprised, no, shocked, that I agreed. The most valuable lesson I'd learned, over my many years, was that friendships are more valuable than anything, and friends, devoted friends, would do anything for each other. Of course, it would be a stretch to count Laurie as a friend, a stretch for me. Charles didn't appear to have that reservation, but he was my friend.

"How do you propose we do that?"

"Stake out the Preserve. That's where the treasure is. That's where the killer will be looking."

"Charles, that's a huge piece of land. It's been days since the murder. The killer may have already found the treasure, that is, if it ever existed. What're we going to do if we discover someone looking? It's a long shot."

"A long shot's better than no shot. What's the downside?"

Wasting part of the life we have left. Getting countless mosquito bites. Being stuck in the woods with each other for hours. Oh, yeah, not to mention losing our lives to someone who's already killed once and tried twice other times.

After all that, I heard myself saying, "When do we start?"

Charles smiled; the smile he uses when he's won a major victory. We remained at the table another hour, getting ugly stares from customers waiting at the door for a table in the crowded restaurant. We hatched what could be considered a futile, harebrained plan to catch a killer. It was still peak vacation season, so most of the day the Lighthouse Inlet Heritage Preserve would be packed with vacationers, local fishermen, adventurous bicyclists. Like Anthony and Laurie, we'd limit our time at the Preserve to the late hours when attendance would be minimal.

At the end of our lengthy discussion, I was convinced that our chances of succeeding were miniscule. To paraphrase Charles and in terms our surfer friend, Dude, would be proud of, "Miniscule be better than no scule."

Chapter Thirty-Seven

It was four hours before Charles was to pick me up for our trip to the old Coast Guard property. The weather was perfect. Puffy high clouds meandered through the deep blue sky; the temperature was in the lower eighties; plus, a kind breeze provided nature's air conditioning. I hadn't seen Barb for a couple of days so decided a walk would do me good.

I was turning the corner in front of Snapper Jack's and nearly ran into Sal, standing in the middle of the sidewalk, looking at the traffic light. He saw me, smiled, and pointed at the light that'd turned yellow. "Why does someone believe you when you say there are four billion stars, yet has to check when you say paint is wet?"

"Ask Dude. He's the astronomer."

Sal sighed. "It was a joke, Chris."

"I know."

"You're supposed to laugh, not recommend an astronomer."

"I know."

He mumbled, "Tough audience."

"Yep. Where're you headed?"

"Nowhere, but making good time. Actually, I'm walking off my hearty lunch."

"At the Crab Shack?"

"How'd you know? Oh, wait, I forgot, everyone here knows everyone else's business."

"A lucky guess. Theo said you'd made friends with some regulars."

"One of the things I hated about spending years on the road, travelling from venue to venue, telling the same stale jokes night after night, was not making good friends."

"What about the comedians you travelled with?"

"We all knew each other, but we spent more time stabbing each other in the back than making friends. Getting to know some of the guys, and gals, at the Crab Shack is a welcomed treat. Most of them, anyway. One old gal must've fallen off her rocker before it landed on her head. One guy seems mad at everything, including everyone. Somebody told me he had a couple of businesses that went belly up. It may be true, but why take it out on me? I wasn't here when it happened." He shook his head. "Then, God didn't implant a sense of humor in a couple of them. They look at me like I'd barfed up a squirm of worms after I tell a hilarious joke."

I bit the inside of my cheek to keep from laughing, or from telling him that those were probably the people with the best sense of humor. Instead, I said, "It takes all kinds." Time to change the subject. "How's Grace?"

"Don't know. She was gone when I rolled out of bed at the crack of noon. I'm trying to get in the swing of getting up early like Theo, or you other early birds." He looked at his watch. "I'm getting better."

I'd heard enough about his quest to experience more daylight. Time to steer the conversation back to Grace. "Was she okay after I left last night?"

"I've seen worse. Often at my performances. She's

shook. She masks it with her Jamaican charm, but she's mad as hell." He glanced back at the light then at me. "Don't blame her."

"How's your brother adjusting to both of you staying with him?"

Sal tilted his head to the left then to the right. "Hard to answer. I don't know how the old boy was before I moved in, so I couldn't say which of his many quirks are because I'm there, or if he was always that way. You might've noticed I occasionally tend to tell a joke before my mind catches up reminding me it may not be appropriate."

"I've noticed."

"I'll admit, I'm an acquired taste, like opera, or bourbon. Theo's seems to be catching on. He'll occasionally laugh at something I say. To answer part of your question, I think he's beginning to adjust to having his smarter, better-looking, wiser brother shacking up with him."

I almost laughed then realized he may not have been joking. "What about Grace?"

"She thinks I'm hilarious."

Another joke?

"No, I meant how is Theo adjusting to her being there?"

"I knew what you meant. I was being funny."

So, it was a joke. Hard to tell.

"How's he doing?"

Sal rubbed the side of his head as he looked down at the sidewalk. "Theo took the death of his son mighty hard. They had an off again, off again relationship. My poor brother now knows that it'll never get better. That hurt more than he'll admit. I think when Grace arrived, it brought all of Theo's pent-up feelings about Teddy to a head. He didn't know what to think about her."

"His hurt, anger, frustration, and every other negative emotion he had stuck down in his gut erupted on the poor gal. I felt sorry for her at first. Here she was, losing her husband, moving from California, trying to start a new life, meeting her pap-in-law for the first time. Add to that, Theo treating her like she was Freddy Krueger knocking on his door."

This was the first time I'd seen Sal's sensitive, perceptive side. "Theo's gotten over most of the hard feelings, hasn't he?"

"Grace is a cutie, a charmer. Theo's happier now than since I got here."

"That's great."

"Yeah, I've made him a happy man."

"I thought it was Grace."

"Chris, it was a joke."

I smiled. "I'll let you get to your walk. Let me know if you hear anything, if any of your new friends have any ideas about who torched her truck."

He walked away without a parting joke. Was it my lucky day, or what?

Two customers were meandering through the book shelves when I entered Barb's Books. The store's namesake was helping a young lady search for something in the young adult section. Barb wore tan shorts, a red blouse and, around her neck, a silver chain with a starfish-shaped charm dangling from it. I smiled, remembering how happy she was when I gave her the necklace for her birthday.

She saw me in the doorway. "Don't run off. I've got something to tell you."

The young customer found what she was looking for. She took two books to the checkout counter. After the customer paid, Barb glanced at the other browser leafing through a book in the far corner of the room.

Barb pecked my cheek. "Good afternoon, Christopher. What brings you in this lovely day?"

"You, of course. How's business?"

She told me it had been steady, also that I'd missed William who'd left a few minutes earlier. She added that a woman brought in a box of recent best-sellers to trade. I didn't figure that those facts were what she wanted me to stay for. I reminded her that she wanted to tell me something.

She continued to look toward the customer. "Stanley Kremitz was in first thing this morning. After picking up a copy of *The Catcher in the Rye* and telling me that it was an oldie goldie, he started talking about Abraham Gant."

"What about him?"

"He hinted that Gant, Captain Gant, had been bragging that nobody was going to be digging up the past on his island. Gant said Anthony got what he deserved. The same fate would come to anybody else who's stupid enough to defile the past."

"Did Stanley think Gant was implying that he killed Anthony?"

"He didn't put it that way, yet I had the impression that's what Stanley meant."

"He say anything else?"

"This is where it got strange. After he told me about Gant, he said he'd heard you and I were dating, and you've been asking a bunch of questions around town about the murder. He said he'd bet his bottom dollar you'd be interested in what Gant said."

"Was he hinting for you to tell me?"

"No doubt."

I told Barb about how Stanley had hinted that Abraham Gant could be the killer.

"You think he's trying to deflect attention from himself?"

"Yes."

Her eyes narrowed. In a muffled voice, she said, "And you've told this to the police so they, not you, could follow up."

Not quite a subtle hint. "I shared it with Chief LaMond."

"Good." She'd made her point, knowing it wouldn't do

any good to reemphasize the part about the police following up.

The remaining customer approached the counter carrying several books, so I told Barb that I'd talk to her later.

Chapter Thirty-Eight

A dozen vehicles were parked along the street, and in the public parking area near the end of East Ashley Avenue, close to the entrance to the Lighthouse Inlet Heritage Preserve. Most likely, they belonged to a combination of residents at nearby rental houses, and vacationers who'd walked to the far end of the Preserve to view the Morris Island Lighthouse. Charles parked close to the houses so, if most of the vehicles left while we were there, his car would look like it belonged to one of the renters.

It was still more than an hour before sunset. I looked at Charles, who was wearing his black, long-sleeved NYPD T-shirt he reserves for times he's either meeting with cops, or pretending to be a detective. "Okay, Charles, this is your plan. What now?"

He tilted his Tilley back on his head. "Figured we'd sit a spell in air-conditioning while we watch for somebody walking toward the entrance, carrying a treasure map, and a shovel."

"No wonder you're the detective. In case that brilliant strategy doesn't work, what's Plan B?"

He twisted his head toward the Preserve. "We amble about, walk up and down the paths, spend time near where they found Anthony, and hope to see someone acting suspicious."

"Other than us?"

"You have a better idea?"

I shook my head, slid the seat back, and lowered the back. A family of five strolled toward the Preserve's entrance as an elderly couple walked arm-in-arm the other direction. The old Coast Guard property was one of Folly's most popular sites. During summer months, there were often traffic jams near the entrance. If nothing else, we would get a chance to people watch.

Charles was unusually quiet and had leaned back. I asked if he'd heard about the fire at *Hot Diggity Dog!*"

He sat up straight, jerking his head toward me. "Fire?"

I told him about going to supper with Theo and Grace then what'd happened while we were gone.

He growled, "Why didn't you tell me earlier?"

I explained it was late when it happened. Besides, I was telling him now.

"Are you certain it was arson?"

"Certain, no. Cindy thought so, but was waiting until she got a report from the arson investigator."

He pulled a phone from his pocket and punched in a number. A few seconds later, he said, "Please hold, chief. Chris Landrum has a question." He thrust the phone at me.

"What did I do to deserve to have my peaceful supper with Larry interrupted by a call from your secretary?"

I chuckled. "I'll tell my *secretary* you were upset."

Charles leaned back in the seat like I'd smacked him.

Cindy said, "Good."

"Have you heard from the arson investigator?"

"Yes."

The phone went dead.

I handed the phone to Charles as I relayed Cindy's one-word answer.

He tapped *redial*.

This time, Larry answered. "Chief LaMond's secretary speaking. Who may I ask is calling?"

I laughed, irritating Charles, but getting a chuckle from Larry. "You may tell her it's Nosy Charles with his young, handsome friend Chris."

Larry's chuckle turned to a laugh before he said, "The chief wanted me to tell you the fire was intentionally set. If you call one more time tonight, she'll issue warrants for both of you, the charge being first degree pissing off a police chief."

The phone went dead a second time.

I relayed the longer message to Charles, adding that, if he called a third time, not to hand me the phone.

He wisely chose not to call. Instead, he said, "Who'd want to torch a food truck? Who'd possibly have a problem with Grace? She's only been here a few days, open for business one day."

I told him those were the same questions Grace, Theo, and even Sal had asked, with no good answers forthcoming.

"Know any hot dog hating pyromaniacs?"

"I don't know any pyromaniacs who hate any of the food groups," I said. "Besides, the first two break ins happened before Grace sold a single hot dog here."

"Could someone with a grudge have followed her from California?"

"That's possible, although it's a long way to come to ruin her business. If there was anyone out there, he would've done something before she headed to South Carolina. I don't know of—"

His arm flailed. "Whoa. Hold that thought. Isn't that Stanley Cliché Kremitz?"

He pointed to a lone walker heading to the stanchion guarding the Preserve.

Stanley was heading toward the entrance to the Preserve. Instead of a treasure map, or a shovel, he carried a walking stick with binoculars strapped around his neck. "Doesn't look like he's ready to look for buried treasure."

Charles looked at me like I was a blue chipmunk. "Gee, Chris, don't you know a disguise when you see one?"

I thought the definition of a disguise was something you didn't recognize when you saw it. Instead of sharing that, I said, "If it is, it's a good one. Think he'll dig up the treasure with binoculars?"

"Don't know. Let's find out."

I had to admit it. I didn't have a better plan, so we began following Stanley. We grabbed our cameras so, if he saw us, we'd have a logical reason for being there. He was walking down the paved road that bisected the property so, if he looked back, he couldn't miss us.

Stanley stopped a third of the way shy of where the pavement ended, and a thick, sandy path continued to the beach. He looked at his phone then turned off the paved area where he moved down a narrow path toward the ocean.

We followed at a safe distance. When we reached the point where he left the road, I motioned for Charles to stop. The path that Stanley had taken was barely visible from the road as it weaved through a heavily wooded area. Windswept oaks and shrubs of all sizes were intertwined, blocking easy movement through the area unless you stayed on the sandy path. "If we follow him, there's a good chance he'll spot us."

Charles said, "What's our plan?"

I didn't point out that there was no "our" plan since it was his idea to be here.

"There's another path a hundred feet or so up the road. I think it meets this one near the beach. There's less chance of getting caught if we go that way."

"I knew you'd have a plan." Charles said, as he started walking.

We reached the second path as three men emerged. Their faces were covered with sweat, their white dress shirts soaked in perspiration, their black wingtips sand-covered.

I nodded.

One of them asked if it was always this hot.

A second man said, "Knew we should've gone to the afternoon's meeting."

The third one said, "It wasn't my idea to leave the pavement, to wander through brambles."

We wished them well, watched them reach the *pavement*, then laughed at their inappropriate dress before we continued in the direction that Stanley had taken.

The methodical sound of waves crashing against the shore told me that we were near the spot where the narrow path reached the foliage facing the beach. I thought that was where the path Stanley had taken merged with our trail. I motioned for Charles to stop so we could listen for anything that'd indicate Stanley's location.

We didn't have long to wait. Mixed with the sounds of the water slapping the shore, I heard laughter coming from more than one person; at least one male, possibly two females.

Charles leaned close and whispered, "Doesn't sound like a treasure-hunting party."

We moved a few yards closer to the sounds when I saw two men and two women. Stanley, the only one I recognized, put his forefinger to his mouth, a sign to silence the group, as he pointed toward the top of a nearby tree. The others stopped talking and raised binoculars to face the tree Stanley was motioning toward. I couldn't see what was so fascinating.

"Oh, great," Charles said. "We've caught a bevy of bird-watchers."

I smiled. "Maybe the pirates hid the gold in the top of that tree."

"Funny, Sal."

That hurt.

"Do you know any of them, other than Stanley?"

He shook his head. "No, just a group of bird-watchers."

"Birds of a feather flock together," I said with my best, albeit lousy, Stanley imitation.

Charles smacked my arm, pivoted, and started back toward the paved road. I didn't blame him.

Instead of heading to the car, we decided that, while we were here, we should walk the rest of the way to the beach overlooking the lighthouse. It was worth the walk. Sunset was approaching so that the low sun behind us illuminated the lighthouse. The tide was out. The remnants of Morris Island and sandbars closer to us were exposed, appearing golden brown in the fading sun.

We took several photos of the lighthouse, the subject of countless images over the years and, since sunset was close, I suggested that we return to the car. On the way, we passed the path that led to where the lifeless body of Anthony was discovered.

Charles said that it might be a good idea to start our next casing of the Preserve closer to that spot. He figured that, since Anthony was searching in the vicinity, the map must've shown him something to pick this spot. I agreed, since I didn't have a better suggestion. When we got to the car, there were three vehicles in the area as opposed to the dozen or so when we arrived. Lights were on in two of the eight houses closest to our car, so I assumed the vehicles belonged to the residents. If my assumption was accurate, all the visitors to the Preserve, including the bird-watchers, were gone.

"Same time, same place, tomorrow?" Charles said as he dropped me off at the house.

Same time, same place, same result, I thought.

Chapter Thirty-Nine

The phone jolted me awake. I blinked twice to focus my eyes then saw that it was after 11:00 p.m. I'd been asleep for an hour and nearly fell out of bed, reaching for the buzzing, exasperating piece of technology that woke me. It portended either a wrong number or a disaster. Everyone who knew me understood calling after ten o'clock was tantamount to a declaration of war.

I managed to hit the answer button. "Hello."

The cheery, wide-awake voice of someone I would've put last on the list of people I expected to call, said, "Chris, this is your good buddy, Sal. Didn't wake you, did I? Hey, did you know that a professor is someone who walks, umm, I mean talks in someone else's sleep?"

I held the phone away from my ear, shook my head awake. "Okay, yes, no."

"Huh?" Sal said, further proof that he not only ignores what others say, but he doesn't even listen to himself.

"Never mind. Other than waking me, what's up?"

"Cranky in your old age, aren't you?"

I heard voices and music in the background. "What is it, Sal?"

"I heard something I thought you might be interested in. Remember I told you about a guy at the Crab Shack who had a couple of businesses that flatlined?"

"What about him?"

"Ran into him tonight at, umm," he said. I heard him ask someone, "What's the name of this joint?" He returned. "The Washout, yeah, that's where I am. Umm, didn't wake you, did I?"

For the second time, I thought *Yes*, wondered how long Sal had been in the bar, and said, "The man with the businesses?"

"Oh, yeah. When I got here, two or it could've been three hours ago, he was spoused, umm, soused. The old boy was soused, plus plastered when he left, maybe fifteen minutes ago."

I had the strong suspicion that Sal was well on his way to soused plus plastered. "What about the man, Sal?"

"Marember, umm, remember, I told you he had two busted businesses?"

"Yes," I said through clenched teeth.

"Guess what he told me they were?"

I was close to hanging up, yet he called for a reason. During years of putting up with Charles's quirks, not to mention the idiosyncrasies of several other friends, I'd acquired a tolerance for thinking that was not only outside the box, but so far outside that you couldn't see the box.

"Sal, why don't you tell me?"

"You're no fun. Okay, here goes, one was a miniature golf course, can you believe that?"

That bit of trivia couldn't wait until the morning?

"Interesting," I said, with total insincerity.

"The other one was a food truck."

That got my attention. "Why was he telling you this?"

"Suppose because I'm a nice guy, someone folks can

easily talk to, a good listener." Sal laughed. "Kidding. Remember the soused part of my story? He was talking to me because I was sitting beside him at the bar. He could've been talking to the column that's holding up the roof on this here patio. Now that I think about it, that's what he was talking to when I sat down."

"Sal, what did he say that made you call?"

I heard him take a gulp of something, most likely beer, most likely his seventy-third of the night. "His golf course was in nowhere Ohio. His food truck was," Sal hesitated, and chuckled, "anywhere its wheels took it. It was a truck, get it?"

"Your point, Sal?"

"Has anyone told you you're no fun?"

"Many times."

"Okay, here's the skinny. He told me the reason his golf course went bust was because the only time anyone played miniature golf was in the slumber, umm, summer. Said even if the balls were orange, playing in the snow turned golfers off."

"Who would've guessed that?"

"The food truck hit the skids, figuratively speaking, I think, when the blankety, blank permit people harassed him so much, he couldn't stay open. A closed food truck don't sell much food."

He hesitated again, the music in the background got louder, and he continued, "My point is the guy told me ever since the blankety, blankety permit people shut him down, he's hated food trucks. They remind him of failing. Right before he fell off the bar stool, had to be led, or more like, carried out by two guys I didn't know, he slurred that if he had his way, all food trucks would be nuked."

"Sal, what's the man's name?"

"I'm not good with names. It's one of those Bible names. Like Matthew, or Mark, don't think it's puke, umm,

Luke. Wait, something's coming to me. Got it. I know it's not John."

"Did he say anything about Grace's truck?"

"Yes, sir, he did. Want to know what?"

Sal should be glad that I'm talking to him on the phone. If I was at The Washout, my hands would be around his neck.

"Yes, Sal."

"Thought so. He said, and this is a direct quote, '*Hot Diggity Dog!* Best damned fire I've ever seen.' Think that's a flew, umm, clue?"

"Sal, are you certain he said best fire he'd ever seen? Could it have been set instead of seen?"

I had to move the phone away from my ear when Sal shouted, "Barkeep, another brewski!" I heard a bottle hitting the bar and someone in the background talking about a baseball score before Sal returned to our conversation.

"What was the question again?"

I repeated it.

"Chris, I've had a couple of beers. My mind's not razor sharp, like it usually is. Give me a minute to ponder it."

From what I've observed, in the best of times, Sal's mind was as sharp as a tennis ball, so I wasn't optimistic about his recollections.

Apparently, the *barkeep* returned with Sal's drink. My near-soused "good buddy" mumbled, "Thanks." After what sounded like him taking a drink, he said, "Okay, think I've got the answer. You asked if he said set instead of seen, right?"

"Yes."

"Drum roll, please," he said. I heard his hand pounding on the bar. "The answer is maybe."

I closed my eyes, opened them, and stared at the phone. "Maybe?"

"Yes, sir, that's my best recollection. Maybe he did. Maybe he didn't. Think that's another clue?"

Maybe, I thought, then realized the odds of me getting anything useful out of Sal in his current condition was as likely as me measuring the circumference of the earth with a yardstick. I thanked him for calling. He said that he thought I'd called him.

The phone went dead.

I fell back on the bed, wondered, no hoped, that I'd dreamed the conversation with Sal, realized I was awake, and it really was my new, good "good buddy" on the phone. I decided that I'd sleep on what Sal had said then call Chief LaMond in the morning to share what he'd almost said.

BY 8:00, I grasped my wish to sleep on Sal's message had been elusive. I'd watched the clock pass each hour and pushed myself out of bed to head to the shower. Twenty minutes later, I felt as refreshed as I could after counting my sleep in minutes rather than hours. I punched Cindy's number into my phone.

She answered with a loud sigh before saying, "Unless you're dead, staring at a dead body, your house is on fire, or you want to give me a yacht, this is a recording. My office hours start at nine o'clock."

Not quite the mood I'd hoped to find her in, although it was encouraging that she hadn't already hung up.

"Good morning, chief. It's going to be a wonderful day."

I hadn't looked out the window, so I had no idea if it was true. Even if I had, my tired, watery eyes wouldn't have been able to see what kind of day it was.

"Yeah, yeah, Sugarmouth. What?"

I told her about my conversation with my "good buddy," Sal. Cindy either listened patiently without interrupting, or she had fallen asleep. I finished and said, "You still there?"

She chuckled. "Afraid so. Theo's not-funny brother was talking about Joseph Tannery."

"How do you get that from Matthew, or Mark? Oh, I get it, Joseph is a Biblical name."

"Chris, I'm many things. A Bible scholar ain't one of them. The miniature golf course gave it away."

"Huh?"

"Remember a couple of years after you moved here, somebody opened a miniature golf course on Center Street? It wasn't there long. Our guys had to arrest Joseph Tannery three times for disturbing the peace. The old boy would get drunk, stand near the entrance of the course, where he'd yell at customers not to waste money playing."

"Why'd he do that?"

"Chris, in addition to not being a Biblical scholar, I'm not a head shrink. I don't know what screws in his head came unthreaded. He told the cops he had a miniature golf course somewhere in the North. It went bust. He'd rant on that if he couldn't make it with kids hitting colorful golf balls through windmills and other stupid crap, the course on Folly shouldn't be able to."

"Who's Joseph Tannery?"

"Squatty-bodied guy, mid-fifties, jittery-like, harmless when sober. He was a big-time pain in our collective law-enforcement butts a few years back until some wise head doc suggested Mr. Tannery spend quality time in the nut house. He was gone a few years, returned a year ago, I haven't heard any negative reports on him since then."

"Did he ever mention anything about food trucks?"

Cindy was silent for a moment. Finally, she said, "I hadn't thought about it until now. When he got back from his mental respite, he caused a minor ruckus in front of Tokyo Crepes. I'll pull the report. I seem to recall him being upset because the food truck always had a line of customers. My guys didn't arrest him. Tannery apologized and went on his way. It appeared that his time having his noggin screwed back together did him good."

"That's it?"

"Pretty sure I would've remembered it if he said he was going to torch it. Tell you what, I'll review what happened at Tokyo Crepes, and see if I can find where he's staying. I'll have one of my guys ask if he wants to have a tour of our lovely police department so I can see what he knows about the weenie roast in Theo's drive."

I told her that sounded like a great idea. She told me that it was a police matter and to wring out of my brain the notion about getting involved. I told her I understood; understood, but not that I wouldn't get involved.

Chapter Forty

The phone rang two hours later, so I figured it was Cindy calling with a report on Joseph Tannery. Wrong. It was Charles inviting me to lunch at twelve-thirty at Rita's. He was buying. I should've known there was no such thing as a free lunch when he added that Laurie, Dean, and Gail would be joining us. Other than Charles, they wouldn't have been on my *A* list of people to eat with. I hesitated then he reminded me I had to eat somewhere.

It turned out to be the kind of wonderful day I'd only speculated about during my conversation with Cindy. I walked two blocks to the restaurant where I saw the others seated on the patio, enjoying the weather, two beers, and a glass of wine.

Charles waved me thought the patio's gate. He wore a smile, gray shorts, and a red and black, long-sleeved T-shirt with *FROSTBURG STATE UNIVERSITY BOBCATS* in block letters on the front. The other three at the table were dressed in traditional beach garb, not displaying allegiances to anything. Charles had pulled a fifth chair to the table and nodded for me to join them.

Laurie pointed at Charles's T-shirt, smiled, and said, "It's in Maryland."

"Oh," I said, hoping that ended the discussion about the shirt.

"Dean and I are glad you could make it. We got in this morning. Going to spend a few days with Laurie," Gail said, taking charge of the conversation. Surprise. Surprise.

Dean nodded agreement, a motion I suspected he was accustomed to making.

Kim, the server who'd waited on Barb and me during our recent visit, moved beside me to ask what I wanted to drink. I would have preferred a soft drink, but figured I'd need wine for lunch with Gail and Dean. I ordered Chardonnay.

We spent fifteen minutes sharing the niceties people who don't know each other well talk about: weather, traffic, food, and more weather. It was turning out to be a pleasant conversation, until Laurie said how glad she was Dean had taken time from his business to be here.

Gail jerked her head toward her husband and gripped the edge of the table so tightly her knuckles turned white. "Running from the feakin' bill collectors is more like it."

"Now, Gail," Laurie said as she touched her friend's arm. "Charles and Chris don't want to hear about it."

She was wrong about Charles. He wouldn't give up until he knew what "it" was.

Charles said, "That's okay, Laurie, you're among friends."

Dean blinked, then in a lower voice said, "It's no big deal. We've had a couple of financial setbacks. Nothing to worry about."

I thought Gail was going to spring over the table. "Nothing to worry about! Losing the business, losing our house is nothing to worry about?"

Laurie looked like she wanted to crawl under the table. She slowly shook her head and stared at her empty wine glass.

I caught a glimpse of Kim behind Laurie, so I motioned her to the table. With luck, an interruption might calm Gail.

Kim asked if we were ready to order.

Without checking with anyone else, Charles said that we were.

Gail started to speak, took a deep breath, then glanced at the menu. Tension subsided slightly as we went around the table making selections.

When it got to Dean, he told Kim that he wasn't hungry. He pushed away from the table and stormed out the gate.

Kim took it in stride, saying that she'd place our orders.

After an awkward silence, Gail said, "I apologize. I'm afraid the business is lost. Dean can't fight any longer. Folks, as goes the store, so goes our house. We've been living off credit cards for months. Sorry to dump this on you."

I was thinking how terrible it must be for them yet laying it on a friend who recently lost her husband seemed insensitive. I was thinking about Laurie's situation while Charles was telling Gail something about how sorry he was, when a comment by Gail joggled me back to reality.

She had thanked Charles for his sympathy and was talking to Laurie. "I'm leaving him."

Laurie stared at her friend. "What?"

"You heard me. I'm leaving Dean."

Laurie said, "Why?"

"He's having an affair."

I reminded myself that Charles was paying for this soap opera. I sat back to watch the show.

Laurie looked at the gate where Dean had exited. "How do you know?"

"Remember when we were supposed to be here with you relic hunting?"

"Sure."

Gail bobbed her head. "Dean said he couldn't come, that I should come by myself. He said he had to be at a tire meeting in Tallahassee."

Laurie said, "I remember."

"He wasn't."

"How do you know?"

"One of his tire buddies called the day Anthony was killed. He asked to talk to Dean, said Dean didn't answer his cell phone. I told him I thought my husband was with him in Tallahassee. He said he would've been if the meeting hadn't been cancelled. That wasn't the first time he'd lied about being out of town on business."

I wasn't nearly as interested in Dean and Gail's marital status as I was to learn that despite her earlier claims that she had been with her husband in Jacksonville when Anthony was killed, she wasn't. I also recalled that when I'd asked Laurie who knew she and Anthony would've been hunting for relics the night he was killed, she'd said she hadn't told anyone, which could've meant not told anyone on Folly.

I asked, "When did Dean get home?"

Gail turned to me and seemed stunned that I'd said anything. "Don't know. He was there when I got home, so I was more interested in where he'd been. He acted surprised I'd asked then gave me a song and dance about being in Tallahassee. I shut him up before he could weave his way through a pack of lies. I told him I knew he wasn't at a meeting."

Our food arrived. Laurie started on hers like she was starved. My guess was that she'd rather eat than join in the conversation. I was with her on that. Charles, on the other hand, was in his element. "Gail, how long—"

Gail pointed her fork at Charles. "Enough. I don't want to burden Laurie with my problems. Let's enjoy the weather, the food."

"That's okay," Laurie said, "I know it must—"

"I said enough," Gail said through a snarl.

The rest of our meal was eaten in peace, okay, silence, not peace.

After more than forty-five minutes of the most awkward meal I could remember, Charles paid the check.

Gail said she and Laurie needed to go to Harris Teeter to get cleaning supplies.

Laurie gave me a hug and a peck on the cheek then gave a longer hug to Charles and a super-sized peck on the cheek, more accurately, a kiss. She said that she'd call him later.

Charles and I moved to the bar to give the table to diners who'd been patiently waiting.

He told me he was still buying and added, "Wonder what took Dean so long to decide to leave Gail? That woman would drive me batty. Hope Dean's new squeeze knows he can talk."

Kim told the bartender what we'd been drinking, so he delivered beer to Charles, white wine to me, without our asking.

"Did you get what she'd said about Dean not being at the meeting in Tallahassee?"

Charles took a sip of beer. "Would've been hard to miss. I also remembered them saying they'd planned to be relic hunting with Anthony and Laurie but didn't make the trip because of Dean's meeting."

I added, "They knew Laurie and Anthony would be at the Preserve."

"Laurie said she didn't tell anyone here."

"She wasn't sure if Anthony told anyone."

Charles rubbed his chin. "Dean would've had a whopping motive to kill Anthony for the map."

"A failing store, losing his house, losing his wife."

"All good reasons. Remember, when the shot was taken at Laurie, Gail was here without Dean. He could've been with his new chick interest, or here shooting at Laurie."

"Before we accuse Dean, think about something else. Gail was already here and could've easily taken the shot. Remember what she said over there?" I pointed to the table where we'd been.

"Which part? She said a heap of hostile stuff."

"When I asked her when Dean got back from his alleged trip to Tallahassee, she said she wasn't there when he got home."

"So?"

"So," I said, "she could've been killing Anthony, stealing the map."

Charles dipped his head and tapped on the bar. "She could also have been at the grocery, getting a facial, dominating someone's conversation, or hanging with a friend making the friend's life miserable."

"True. What we do know is she was on Folly when the first shot was taken at Laurie; she wasn't with Dean when Anthony was killed."

Charles rubbed his temple. "Let's change the subject. All I get from thinking about this is a headache, a headache that started when dear, sweet Gail started unloading on Dean."

I nodded. "Do you know Joseph Tannery?"

"Whoa. I thought I'd cornered the market on abrupt turns in a conversation."

"I've learned from the best. Tannery?"

"Met him a couple of times. Don't know him well. Why?"

I shared what Sal had said about Tannery's discussion plus what Cindy had told me about the miniature golf course.

Charles stared at me. "You're taking crime-fighting advice from Sal?"

"Advice, no. Information, yes. What do you know about Tannery?"

"I remember the incident in front of the miniature golf course. I was there. I doubt Tannery remembers it. He was so drunk that if someone had walked by with a lit cigarette, his breath would've caught fire. I didn't see him for a few years after that. In fact, the next time I saw him was last week on the sidewalk. I nodded. He nodded. We didn't speak."

"Think he could've damaged and then burned Grace's food truck?"

"In the old days, he could've. I don't know about now. Do we need to find him so I can trick a confession out of him?"

"It's in the capable hands of the police."

"If you say so."

Chapter Forty-One

Hanging with Charles at the Preserve afternoon number two began a couple hours after we'd gone our separate ways from Rita's. I thought it was a futile effort. I didn't point that out when he picked me up at the house. If I'd mentioned it, he'd ask what I had better to do. I'd admit not a thing. I hopped in the car, put my Nikon on the back seat beside his.

He said, "Ready to catch a killer?"

I said sure.

There were more cars near the entrance than there were yesterday, most likely, belonging to vacationers.

Clouds had rolled in providing a welcomed relief from direct sunlight. The temperature was still in the upper eighties, yet tolerable. We followed a similar path to the one we'd taken the day before. There were no birdwatchers, and we returned to the pavement and walked most of the way to where the roadway ended, a spot where large elevated foundations left from the Coast Guard buildings had been recently removed.

During the half hour we sat on a couple of large rocks,

two dozen people walked past: two groups of four, a couple of men pulling fishing carts, three bicyclists, and several couples ranging in age from teenagers to seasoned citizens. None of them carried a shovel, or a metal detector.

Charles was unusually quiet most of the time.

I asked him twice what was wrong.

Both times, he said nothing.

I didn't believe him, but knew that he would tell me when he was ready. I suggested that we walk farther up the road to explore a path on the marsh side of the pavement.

He shrugged then moved beside me as I walked a hundred yards until I saw the narrow path leading to our left. Branches provided a low canopy over much of the way, so we walked single file through the tightest spots.

The path opened to a wide area overlooking the marsh. There were burnt logs in the clearing, evidence that someone had built a fire. What wasn't there was evidence of digging. We could hear voices coming from the beach fifty or so yards to our right, plus the sound of birds squawking about something.

Charles plopped down on a large, unburnt log, removed his Tilley and wiped his forehead with his arm. "Chris, I know you think this is a waste of time. It probably is. I'm worried about Laurie, don't know what else to do. We've seen too many of our friends hurt. I don't want her on that list."

"You like her, don't you?"

He looked at the sandy soil then kicked a piece of blackened wood. "I don't know. She's nice. For some reason, she latched onto me. She calls nearly every day. Look how many times she's wanted me to eat with her."

He rubbed a question mark in the sand with his foot. "I've seen videos of an animal, let's say a dog, rescuing another kind of critter, a baby duck, for example. The baby critter starts hanging around its rescuer, follows it wherever it goes, does stuff a duck would never do if it hadn't been rescued by the dog. I was the first person Laurie saw after that traumatic night. Could she be the baby duck, me the dog? Could that be why she's acting like that with me?"

"That'd make sense."

"I've had one serious romantic relationship in my million years on earth. That's not a lot of experience, so I don't know what to think, or do. I like her, think it's possible that, someday, it could turn to something more. If she's latched on me because of the dog/duck thing, I'd be barking up the wrong palmetto tree." He looked at me. "What do I do?"

I was stuck on the dog/duck thing and palmetto tree. I hesitated before saying, "Charles, time's the only thing that'll answer that question. You need to be yourself then see what happens."

"Gee, Chris, who but me can I be?"

"What I mean is don't try to be someone you're not. Don't try to change to be what you think she wants. You being you is wonderful."

"Thanks. That still doesn't help keep her safe. The only way that'll happen is for Anthony's killer to spend the rest of his life eating slop, while looking at concrete block walls and bars. How're we going to make that happen?"

I told him that I didn't know. I suggested that we weren't accomplishing anything out here. He grumbled, made a mild case for how it might help before kicking the ground one more time, then agreed with me.

We were getting in the car when Charles pointed to an older model, black Mercury Grand Marquis parked two cars over. "That's Captain Gant's car."

"You sure?"

"Yeah," Charles said as he opened the door and stepped out. "He told me he liked it because it reminded him of the Ford Crown Vics he drove when he was with the state cops. I also remember that AAA decal on the bumper. Let's find him." He started back toward the stanchions blocking the entrance to the Preserve before I made it out of the car. He didn't stay around long enough for me to suggest that Gant may be visiting one of the houses near his car instead of being at the Preserve.

I grabbed my camera then jogged to catch Charles. He had a renewed step in his gait while tapping his cane on the pavement like he was on a mission. I was less enthusiastic since we were charging off after a retired cop, a possible murderer. By the time I caught up with Charles, he was scanning each side of the road, reminding me of a coonhound sniffing the air in search of its prey. It was nearing sunset, so the number of walkers had thinned.

We passed the spot where we'd spent time earlier when Charles said, "This way. I think I saw someone."

He pushed the branches out of his face and bent down to miss higher hanging limbs as he made his way down a narrow path leading toward the beach. We had to walk single file, so I was a couple of feet behind him when someone barked, "Stop!"

I twisted around to see Captain Gant stepping out from behind a large tree. He wore a short-sleeved black shirt, baggy camouflage-patterned slacks, and a snarl that would terrify anyone under the age of sixteen. That wasn't what caught my eye. What grabbed my attention was the silver handgun pointed at my chest.

I turned to get a better look when he said, "Don't move. Slowly clasp your hands behind your head."

I was in no position to tell him we could do one or the other, not both. Charles moved beside me and mimicked the movement of my hands. Gant was too far away for me to grab the gun, yet close enough to not miss if he pulled the trigger.

He waved the handgun toward a log about five feet off the path. "Slowly walk over there and sit."

If Charles and I quickly split up, the odds were one of

us could get to the gun. The downside being one of us would most likely be shot.

Think quickly. What other options did we have?

Better to follow his command, for now.

We did. He looked at Charles then at me, before saying, "Where's the map?"

My voice crackled as I said, "We don't have it."

He pointed the gun at my shorts. "Empty your pockets."

I wasn't fast enough. He said, "Now! Back pockets, too."

We removed everything from our pockets, placing it on the log beside us. Gant looked at our wallets, car keys, a ballpoint pen I kept with me. "Where is it?"

I knew what he'd meant. I also knew how unhappy he'd be with my answer. "We don't have it. Why do you think we do?"

"Because you took it after killing that damned relic hunter."

That was the last answer I would've expected.

Charles took a deep breath. "We thought you killed him."

Gant looked at Charles like he'd seen the ghost of Blackbeard. "You what? That's preposterous. Crap, I'm a retired cop. You know, law and order. Why would I kill him?"

"Because you hated him, didn't want him digging up the past," Charles said.

"Holy smokes, Charles, I hate lots of people. If I went and killed all of them, this island would be near empty."

Charles said, "What are you doing out here? While you're thinking up an answer, could you lower that gun?"

"Not on your life. I'm here to catch whoever has the damned map and is trying to dig up the loot." He waved the gun at Charles. "What in the hell are you doing here?"

"We saw your car at the entrance, came looking for you. Chris thought you might be trying to find the treasure."

Thanks, Charles.

Gant continued staring at us. I suppose he didn't know

what to think. He wasn't alone. Beads of sweat rolled down his face.

"Captain," I said, "why don't you have a seat? Let's talk about it."

He must not have seen us as a threat. He sat on the log out of our reach, picked a sandspur off his camo pants, before turning to Charles. "I got intel someone was going to be out here digging, digging for Civil War relics or gold. What's buried must remain buried."

I was sick of hearing his tiring mantra. "What intel? Who told you?"

He turned my direction and scowled. He wasn't accustomed to being on the receiving side of an interrogation. "Bar talk. Don't know his name. He said word was going around someone got a treasure map off the dead guy. The guy said it was that nosy guy who was here when the cops found the body. That was you. If that's not why you're here, why are you?"

"It's a nice day, so Charles and I decided to walk out to where we could see the lighthouse to grab a photo, or two." I held my camera as part of my multi-media presentation.

It was a camera, not a shovel, so Gant appeared to buy my story. He rubbed his hands over his thighs, shook his head. "I'm too old for this crap. In my prime, I could stake out a spot for hours." Out of character, he chuckled. "That was back when I didn't have to pee every half hour. Damned prostate."

I nodded like I understood. Thankfully, I didn't.

He set the gun on the log, looked at me, then at Charles. "If one of you didn't shoot the guy, and I know I didn't, who did?"

Charles said, "That's what we're trying to find out."

"Did you tell Chief LaMond you thought I was the killer?"

Charles bowed. "We might've mentioned something about it."

Gant smiled. "Figures. That's why she came to my place to ask where I was when he was killed."

"Could be," Charles said, one of his rare understatements.

The Captain shook his head then repeated, "I'm getting too old for this."

So am I, I thought.

Charles didn't admit to aging. He said, "Any idea who might've shot him, other than us?"

"Probably the lovey-dovey wife. They're always the first in the line of suspects."

Charles sat up straighter. "She didn't do it."

"You sure?"

I wondered the same thing.

Charles said, "Yes."

Gant shrugged. "Suppose it's someone else, then." He nodded toward the handgun. "Fellas, sorry I pulled this on you. When I'm wrong, I admit it. Here's some advice. Instead of following strangers out here, leave it to the police. It's their job." He looked around. "I better head to the *casa* and let you get on your way."

We agreed and watched him walk away. I suggested that we wait on the log until he left the parking area before heading out. Charles said Gant was one more suspect to remove from the list. He didn't have a shovel with him today. In my mind, that still didn't eliminate him, although he was convincing when he accused us of being the killer. Add to that, he didn't appear to know the map's whereabouts. I shared my thoughts with Charles. He said, after our eventful lunch with Laurie and her "friends," his sharing his feelings about Laurie with me, the encounter with Gant and his gun, he was too tired to think straight. I wasn't far behind.

Chapter Forty-Two

The clouds that blanketed the area during the day turned ferocious overnight. Heavy rain pelted the tin roof, the accompanying wind whistled as it leaked through cracks around my ancient windows rattling the panes. I'm a heavy sleeper, so I would've missed most of the rain, and wind, had it not been for Anthony's murder bouncing around in my head. Gant was correct when he said we should leave it to the police. So why wasn't I willing to let it go?

I knew the answer, but simply didn't want to admit it. Charles and I were there when his body was found. Laurie latched onto us, no, latched onto Charles, who was my best friend. The more I got to know her, her friends, and others who were pulled into the situation, the closer I was to being involved.

The police should solve it, yet they'd already admitted the murder wasn't on top of their growing caseload. Besides, Charles and I'd already spent more time with Laurie and the potential suspects than had the police. Did I learn anything that would point to the killer? A clap of thunder rocked the house, and rocked me awake. It was a little past three and, regardless how much I wanted it to, sleep wouldn't return. I padded my way to the kitchen, started a pot of coffee, then stared at the darkness outside the rain-drenched window.

Despite Charles, and my encounter with Captain Gant and the story he'd shared, I wasn't convinced that he was innocent. His over-the-top reaction to anyone having the audacity to dig up the past made it easy for me to keep the door open to his guilt. Yet, if he was guilty, wouldn't he have the map? Then, what about the "intel" that someone told him in a bar that we had the missing document.

That brought me to Laurie. On the surface, she was the obvious suspect. Her story about getting separated from Anthony, finding the car, and falling asleep was nearly as farfetched as Gant's story that he heard about us in a bar. She was the only person we knew who'd been at the Preserve when her husband was shot. The insurance policy would've been a motive. She'd given us conflicting stories about getting separated from her husband, and more conflicting versions of where she was when the first shot was fired through her window. She may've killed her husband, but she couldn't have taken the shot when Charles and I were with her.

Was it possible that the shootings at her house had nothing to do with her husband's murder? Unlikely. Another possibility was that she had an accomplice. The second person could've taken the shot when we were there to deflect suspicion from Laurie. I tried to remember the sequence of events surrounding the shots fired into Laurie's house. Gail was there but had gone to the grocery the first time, so Laurie could've pulled the trigger. Nothing else from the first event had stuck out as being significant other than Laurie telling two versions of where she'd been.

The second shooting into the house left a larger impact since I was there. Laurie acted terrified. Real or faked? I took two large sips and remembered something that occurred after the shooting. Laurie called Gail to see if she could come stay with her for a few days. Gail hadn't answered, so Laurie called Dean who told her Gail was out of town and may've left her phone in the hotel room. He hadn't told Laurie where Gail was. Was it possible that she was standing outside Laurie's house?

Gail was pushy, always interrupting her friend, and someone I dreaded spending time with. I'd never considered her a murderer until the other day. She knew about the map. Her husband's business was in trouble, as was their marriage. She had said that she and Dean were supposed to be with Anthony and Laurie when Anthony was killed but didn't come because Dean was at a meeting out of town. That meant she could've been on Folly for all three incidents.

It was still raining, although the torrential downpour had eased. I must've drifted asleep in the chair. The sky had lightened, my clock indicated sunrise was minutes away. I stood. My back told me that not only had I fallen asleep, I'd fallen asleep in an awkward position. I got dressed and remembered the Captain's advice about leaving it to the police. I decided to tell the chief what'd happened with Gant in the Preserve and my suspicions about Gail. I also decided that I was hungry so the call to Cindy could wait until after breakfast. I drove to the Dog, which had just opened. The heavy rain had kept the crowds away, so I had my choice of tables and headed to my favorite. Kimberly, one of several friendly servers, was quick to the table with coffee and a cheerful greeting, both welcomed.

My need to call Chief LaMond ended when I saw her coming in the door. She took off her raincoat, wiped water off its shoulders, looked around the dining room, saw me, and came my way.

"Went by your house, and your car wasn't there." She slid in the booth opposite me. "Figured I'd find you here. What're you buying me for breakfast?"

"You went by the house to see if I wanted to take you to breakfast?"

"Nope." She nodded to the entrance. "That inspiration came when I got here, saw your car, and my stomach growled."

Kimberly was back at the table, so Cindy said, "Coffee, and the most expensive breakfast on the menu, whatever it is."

I told the server that I'd stick to French toast, even though there were more expensive options.

Kimberly headed to the kitchen, and I said, "Glad you're here. I've got something—"

Cindy put her hand in my face. "Cool your jets, me first." She didn't give me time to protest. "After you told me what Sal said about Joseph Tannery, I had my guys go to his apartment to invite him to the station for a chat. He wasn't home, so they went looking for him. They didn't have to look too hard. Dispatch got a call from a concerned citizen, who said he almost got run over while he was minding his business, whistling 'Dixie,' and walking in front of the post office."

She shrugged. "I added the 'Dixie' part. Anyway, it seems a car was weaving all over the place after it nearly squashed the concerned citizen. My guys took the citizen's statement then went looking for the weaver."

"I assume they found a car owned by Mr. Tannery."

"Yes, detective-wannabe. It was in the front yard of the house across the street from Theo's place. The driver was passed out under the influence of gallons of alcohol. My guys knew I was looking for Tannery, so they called me at home. Since I was sworn to serve and protect, I went to see Mr. Tannery in his then-current state of passed out."

"What happened?"

"Let's see. First Larry, my dear, sweet, hubby was pissed I was leaving. Now, don't worry, I made it up to him later. How is none of your business." She grinned. "Back to Tannery, he was coming to by the time I arrived. The boy smelled like a brewery. I asked him if he knew where he was. He said, 'I'm right here.' I asked him if he knew where 'here' was. I asked that since he was directly across from Theo's with the charcoal-broiled food truck in his drive. Know what he said?"

"What?"

"Interesting you ask. He looked out the window at the truck then mumbled something that sounded like, 'I had one of those.' So, I asked what he had. Here's the good part. He said, 'Tood fuc…' He giggled. 'I mean food truck.' Before I could stop him, he blurted out that the damned bank took it back then added, this is an exact quote, 'If I can't have one, neither can that wiener woman. Ha, ha. Burnt to a crisp. My finest hour.'"

Our food arrived. Cindy attacked it like she hadn't eaten in days. "What can I say? I'm a growing girl."

My safest response was no response. Instead, I said, "He confessed to torching Grace's truck?"

"Close enough, especially after he said something about trashing it twice before the fire. I read him his rights, although I doubt he understood anything I said. I suggested that, as soon as he sobers up, he should find a good lawyer and, because I was so nice I was going to provide him a bed for the night with a heart-unhealthy breakfast." She stared in her mug then slowly shook her head. "Chris, I don't think he even met Grace. Her truck represented something bad that'd been burning inside him for a long time. Sorry."

"And burned Grace's dream because of it."

"Yes. I'm glad you told me about what he was saying, or what you said Sal said he was saying. If you hadn't, Tannery would've been charged with DUI, never questioned about the fire. As much as it galls me to say it, thanks."

"Sal deserves most of the credit. Regardless, you're welcome."

She took another bite of her expensive meal, wiped her napkin across her lips, and said, 'What did you want to tell me?"

I realized that what I'd been thinking in the middle of the night seemed more significant then than now. I shared an abbreviated version of my thoughts on Laurie and Gail.

Cindy listened, although she kept shaking her head. I didn't blame her. When I started telling her about our encounter with the Captain at the Preserve, I thought she was going to hop on the table.

"You were where? You were doing what?"

I repeated that Charles and I were trying to catch someone digging for the fortune. She said she thought that's what I said, then spent what seemed like hours lambasting me for my stupid, idiotic, dangerous, plus a few other words I prefer not to repeat, actions. That was all before I got to the part where Gant pointed a gun at my stomach. That's when she fell back in her seat, bowed her head, rubbed her temples. Her hand covered her face so, when she made strange sounds, I couldn't tell if she was laughing or crying. I sipped water and waited.

Cindy finally moved her hand from her face, pulled her shoulders back, leaned closer to the table, and said, "Chris, are you and Charles okay?"

I told her that we were.

"Do you want me to arrest Gant?"

"For what?"

"I'm sure I can find some archaic law that prohibits sticking a gun in someone's bellybutton, even if the recipients are total idiots, while trying to rob said idiots of a treasure map."

"Let it go. He thought we'd killed Anthony. It wouldn't do any good having him arrested. I appreciate your concern."

"Okay, but you and your lamebrain friend are still idiots."

She got no argument from me.

Chapter Forty-Three

I called Theo to see if he and Grace were home. They were, and he said he'd be delighted for me to visit. They would be more delighted when I shared what I'd learned about the arsonist.

Instead of Theo, Grace greeted me at the door with a smile and a hug. "Wait until you hear the news," she said before she bounced up and down like a teenager telling her best friend that the coolest boy in school had invited her to the prom. "Pardon my manners, please, come in."

Grace turned to Theo, who'd moved beside her. "Can I tell him, or would you like the honor?"

Theo put his arm around her shoulder. "Grace, Chris asked to stop by. Why don't we let him tell us why?" He motioned for us to join him in the great room. "Then, you can share the news."

Grace was so excited that I wanted her to go first, until I imagined what I had to say was more important.

Theo offered coffee. I was already two cups past my limit, so I declined.

Grace sat opposite me and wrapped her arms around her legs. She was straining to hold back her glee.

"So," Theo said, "What brings you out this morning?"

"Is Sal here?"

Theo pointed to the ceiling then tilted his head and rested it on his hand. Asleep, I translated.

"Why?"

I began the story of Sal talking to me about the person he'd talked to in the bar and how that led to me talking to Cindy. By the time I got to the part about Joseph Tannery parked across the street, both Theo and Grace were sitting on the edge of their seats, staring at me. I seldom had this attentive an audience. I admit, I savored it longer than I should have before continuing the story ending with Tannery confessing; well, almost confessing, to trashing the truck then starting the fire that put Grace out of business.

Grace formed a confused look on her face. "I don't know who this Tannery person is. Did he know me? Did I somehow offend him?"

I shook my head. "Grace, it didn't have anything to do with you. It could've been any food truck. He's unstable. He took his anger out on your vehicle."

"Thank God," Theo added. "That's a good thing. Grace, you have nothing to worry about."

"I'm blessed," she said, before turning to Theo. "Can we tell him now?"

Theo smiled at her then nodded. Grace returned his smile and said, "Theo's setting me up in a restaurant. A real one. No wheels."

"Great. Where?"

Grace turned to Theo who said, "You know that little restaurant on West Huron just past what used to be the Wish Doctor?"

The restaurant had operated under several different names since I'd been on Folly; none lasted more than a year or two. I said that I knew the spot.

"I bought the building. It's a mess on the inside, but—"

Grace interrupted, "Not too big a mess for me. Teddy and I did a lot of renovating. No big deal for this tomboy."

Theo continued, "I'll be covering expenses until Grace gets on her feet. Heck, I may even wait tables."

With Theo's walking speed slightly faster than a live oak, I thought, *never in a million years*.

I mumbled, "That's an idea."

Grace clapped her hands. "Daddy would say, 'Enough fi stone dawg.' "

I said, "Which means?"

"Enough to stone a dog."

Theo said, "Which means?"

Grace chuckled. "An abundance of something. I'm blessed with an abundance of love, opportunity, family."

Theo asked before I did, "What's that have to do with stoning a dog?"

"Don't know. Think maybe it means that I have so much that I can do idle things, like stoning a dog."

It still didn't make sense. I also didn't think it was a good saying to throw around canine-friendly Folly.

"Grace, when do you think you'll be opening?"

"Theo doesn't own the building for another month, but the man who does says we can get in tomorrow to start working on it. I'm so excited."

"Grace, tell Chris what you're going to name it."

Her smile widened. "Teddy's Place."

Theo bobbed his head. "Isn't that wonderful?"

It was, and I told them so. My phone's ringtone interrupted their excitement. The screen read, *Charles*.

"Chris, this is Charles. Is this a good time to call?"

The voice was familiar, but the words didn't sound like any I'd ever heard from my friend.

"Umm, sure."

"I'm at Laurie's house. Could you come over?"

"Now?"

"Absolutely."

The conversation was getting stranger by the second. "Charles, is everything okay?"

He laughed like I'd said something funny. He said, "Nah."

"You can't talk?"

"That's right. How quick can you get here?"

"Five minutes; ten, tops."

"A half-hour, good." He hung up.

I excused myself to confused looks from my hosts and was in the car seconds later. The rain was pouring harder than it had been overnight. It was still hours before sunset, yet the sky was midnight dark. Water stood on the road, so I had to swerve to miss the deepest puddles.

I called Cindy as I turned on Laurie's street. I wanted her to know where I was going, and why. I got her voice mail, left a brief message, asking her to come to Laurie's house, that something might be wrong.

I was tempted to wait for her to call back, yet Charles's tone screamed he needed help now, not later.

Chapter Forty-Four

Laurie's MINI, Charles' vehicle, plus two cars with Florida plates were in the drive. I assumed that they belonged to Dean and Gail. I pulled off the road short of the house to wait for Cindy's call when I noticed the front door standing open. No doubt, something was wrong. I pulled in the drive, then stopped as close to the house as I could manage. There was a large puddle behind the closest car, so I had to park partially in the yard to avoid the tiny lake. Heavy rain continued, the wind howled. Whoever was inside may not have heard me.

I grabbed an umbrella from the back seat. The rain was blowing sideways and was so strong I had trouble opening the car door. A lightning bolt startled me enough that I was tempted to return to the car. The rapidly-expanding, large puddle was between me and the house, so I had to walk around it. I was afraid that the umbrella would blow inside out before I made it to the porch. My clothes were soaked by the time I got to the steps.

Through the open door, I saw it was darker inside than outside. Someone yelled, "Help!"

A pool of what looked like blood was in the doorway. I yelled, "Hello!" No one responded, or no one I heard.

The wind whipped around the side of the porch. Not only did I feel like I was in a wind tunnel, the sound of the blast of warm air made it impossible to hear anything in the house. I stepped around the pool of liquid as I moved to the living room. My eyes were getting accustomed to the darkened room. I wished they hadn't.

A woman was face down on the floor to the left of the door. I couldn't see her face, but her hair was the style of Gail's. There was a steady path of blood from the pool at the front door to the body. It looked like she'd tried to get to the door, was shot or stabbed, then made it back to where she was now before collapsing. She lay still, dead still.

I shook the sight out of my head as I looked around the room. Dean was on the floor to my right. He was in a seated position with his back against the wall. His left hand was covered with blood and was clutching his stomach. His eyes were closed. I started toward him when he opened his eyes and whispered, "I'll be okay. Check on Laurie." He nodded toward the door to the kitchen.

I turned to look in the direction that he had motioned. The light over the sink was bright enough for me to notice another body. The person was backlit, but I assumed it was Laurie. I stepped closer. The homeowner was lying face up with no visible wounds. She wasn't moving. I bent down to feel for a pulse when I heard a mumbled, agitated voice from the far corner of the kitchen.

Charles was on his side with his back to the cabinets. His hands were behind him wrapped together with the cord from a shattered lamp leaning against his side. A dishtowel was stuffed in his mouth.

Now what do I do? Was Laurie alive? Do I try to help her before untying Charles? Do I dial 9-1-1 instead of waiting for Cindy to return my call?

Charles was making louder noises and shaking his head. I stood, took a step toward my friend, when I heard the front door slam. Charles mumbled louder as I reached to untie his gag.

"I'd recommend not doing that," said someone behind me.

I jerked around to see Dean five feet away. He appeared well enough to be pointing a handgun at my face.

"What's going on?" My gaze went from the gun to his bloody shirt then to his hand dripping blood.

He looked at his hand. "Oh, the blood. It's Gail's. She didn't need it." He grinned. "Your friend there said it'd be a half hour before you showed so, when I heard you pull in the drive, I had to improvise. I wiped my hand in the blood beside my dear wife's silent, silent for once, body to look like I'd been shot. Had to buy time to figure out what to do. Worked, didn't it?" His grin turned to a smile.

I found nothing humorous in his comment. I was so shocked that I didn't hear my phone ring.

Dean did. He held out his bloodied hand and motioned for me to give him the phone.

I took it from my pocket, saw that the screen read *Cindy*, then handed it to him. Without lowering his gun, or taking his eyes off me, he dropped the phone then stomped on it. The screen shattered. My hope for a rescue shattered with it.

Dean motioned me to take a seat beside my gagged friend. I couldn't think of a better option, so I sat, my arm touching Charles's side. I knew that Dean wouldn't have known I'd been suspicious of Charles's out-of-character call enough to leave a message for Cindy to come to Laurie's. Our only hope was to stall long enough for her to get here.

"Dean, what happened?"

His smile disappeared. He glanced in the living room. "All I wanted was to save my store. I'm no killer." He shook his head. "Huh, don't suppose history will agree. Gail and I knew that Laurie had a map she got from her grandfather. I never knew him. Years ago, he convinced Laurie the map was authentic, that there was buried treasure.

"Laurie told us the story so many times I could recite it word for word. We knew they'd been looking out near the lighthouse for landmarks marked on the map. Anthony said that things had changed so much they didn't know if they'd ever find it."

Come on, Chief. Where are you? Time to stall longer.

"If they didn't know where to look, why'd you show up that night?"

"Anthony called, all excited. Said they'd found something he thought would help them find the treasure. He didn't say what. He said four sets of eyes would have a better chance of finding it than two. Said he'd wait for us before going out there. I knew that Gail wouldn't go along with stealing the map, or the treasure, from Anthony and Laurie, so I told her the story about going to a meeting in Tallahassee. I came here instead. I called Anthony to say that we wouldn't be coming. Told him to go without us."

"What happened?"

I was there before they arrived, parked in one of the drives near the entrance to the whatever you call that end of the island. The weather was like tonight, so I figured they wouldn't recognize my car. I was also afraid they wouldn't show. There was a break in the rain when they got there."

Still no sign the police were on their way. I was close enough to Charles to where I could move my left hand behind his back without Dean noticing. The electric cord was wrapped tight. It was possible, with enough time, that I could wiggle it enough to loosen its grip. *With enough time.*

"So you followed them on the old Coast Guard property?"

"It was getting darker by the minute. I didn't know who

was more stupid, them for coming out on such a horrible night, or me for following. Either way, we were there. My plan was to wait until they found something then step in to steal it. I wasn't going to kill anyone."

I wondered if he thought that Laurie and Anthony would let him steal the treasure without protest. How did he think he wasn't going to have to kill them?

"I understand," I said to stall.

"You've got to believe me," Dean said. He hesitated then shook his head. "Then it all went south. The rain started again, everything was black. I heard them debating what to do. Anthony finally said for Laurie to stay where she was. He'd find the way out, then come get her. He left. I don't know how, but he saw me while he was pushing through the underbrush. He grabbed a thick branch off the ground, pointed it at me, and asked what I was doing out there. I could barely see him, although, from what I could see, he knew I was up to no good."

Dean took a deep breath. "I started to explain how I needed money. Out of the blue, he lunged at me, raised the branch over his head, like he was going to clobber me." He looked down at his gun. "I ducked, pulled this out of my pocket. Pulled the trigger."

I took that brief opportunity to scoot closer to Charles, getting a better grip on the electric cord. From where I'd been, I managed to loosen it slightly, while Charles was twisting his hands for me to get a better grip on the jumble of wire.

Still no police.

"Why shoot at Laurie?"

"When I was there that terrible night watching the two of them arguing, Laurie stared directly at me. She didn't say anything. From what I've heard, she didn't mention it to anyone. Hell, maybe with it raining so hard she didn't see me. I couldn't take a chance that she'd remember later. I'd already killed her husband. Who'd believe I was defending myself. She had to go." He nodded toward Charles, then at me. "I didn't know you and your friend were with her the second time. I came to the wooded area beside her place from the road behind her house. I didn't see your car. Sorry if I scared you."

He's standing there after killing his wife, me not knowing what happened to Laurie, Charles being tied up and gagged, pointing a gun at my face, and he's apologizing for scaring us. I'm not looking at a rational man. Where were the police?

I said, "What happened tonight?" I was making slow, painstakingly slow progress on unknotting the cord.

Again, he tilted his head toward the living room, and snarled out, "She." He hesitated, took a deep breath, then continued, "She called to say that she knew what I'd done. I thought she was talking about killing Anthony. I drove up here to talk to her before she blabbed to everyone. Didn't know what I was going to do. Honest, I didn't." He took another deep breath. "I got here, found the three of them huddled in the living room, talking. Figured she'd told Laurie, and your buddy. Know what they were talking about? Know what she thought she knew?"

I shook my head as I continued making progress with the knot.

"Said I was having an affair. She was going to leave me. She didn't know a damned thing about me killing Anthony. Can you believe that?"

That didn't explain how the day turned violent. A huge sense of relief filled me when I heard Laurie moan, saw her hand move. Charles's hands were seconds from freedom. I had no idea what we would do then. I had to keep Dean talking.

"Then what happened?"

He shifted his gun's aim to Charles. "Gail said your

friend's nosy. I got here, and Gail pounced on me with both barrels. She started screaming about my affair. Laurie tried to welcome me. Gail wouldn't let her get in a word."

No surprise. He waved the gun back and forth between Charles and me.

"She said something about going to scream it to the world, then went to the front door, screaming the entire time. I snapped." He looked at the gun. "I yanked this out of my pocket. Pulled the trigger. Pulled it twice." He gave a sinister grin. "It felt good. She stood there, opened and closed her mouth with nothing coming out. A first. A first ever. She staggered to where she is now and collapsed. Laurie screamed and ran to Gail. Your friend started toward me. I pointed it at him. He stopped, put his hands in the air. Smart man."

I thought I heard police sirens in the distance. Or was it wishful thinking? I'd pulled the last bit of electric cord from Charles's wrists. I was afraid that Dean had seen Charles's arms moving. Fortunately, he was distracted by his story.

Laurie moaned. Dean glanced at her. "She screamed again and ran toward the kitchen to go out the back door. I took three steps toward her. Smacked her with the gun. She hit the floor like a sack of potatoes."

"Why am I here?" I asked.

"You and your friend have been nosing around. From what Laurie told me, you were good buds with the cops. Sooner or later, you were going to figure out what was going on. Charles was the only smart one in the room. That's why he's still alive and Gail isn't. Laurie will have the headache of the century. I told him to call you."

The sirens weren't my imagination. They were also not close to the house. Dean must've heard them as well. His eyes darted around the room. "Time's up."

Any hope Charles and I had was running out. I gave an abbreviated tilt of my head toward the back of the house.

Charles responded in kind. I figured that, if we separated quickly, then Dean wouldn't have time to shoot both of us. Either Charles, or I, could get to him. It was the same plan I'd rejected when Captain Gant had confronted us. This time, I didn't have options.

I rolled to my right.

Charles hurled the electric cord at Dean as he jumped up. The cord missed Dean but distracted him enough that he didn't fire the weapon. Charles reached for Dean's arm.

I dove for his legs. I expected a bullet to tear through my body.

Instead, Dean knocked Charles's hand away and twisted around enough to point the gun at my friend.

I slammed into Dean's left leg with my full weight. His leg buckled, throwing him off balance enough that he didn't get a shot off before falling awkwardly to the floor. I landed on Dean. The impact with the floor knocked the wind out of him.

Charles kicked the gun out of his hand.

Dean pushed up with his elbow, kicking my side before twisting toward Charles then punching him in the stomach. I reached to grab one of Dean's legs before he stood. I missed.

Charles was doubled over, gasping for breath. Dean would get away. There was little Charles, or I, could do to stop him.

Out of the corner of my eye, I saw movement beside Dean, saw a tea pitcher shatter over his head. Glass rained down on Charles, me, and Dean who staggered before collapsing.

Laurie towered over the three of us.

I could've hugged her, would have if Charles hadn't beaten me to it. His arms were around her before I caught my breath. He helped her to a kitchen chair.

She slowly touched her head where Dean's gun had smacked her.

I lowered myself back to the floor then felt my side. I'd bet ribs were broken.

The next thing I remembered was Officer Trula Bishop, along with an officer I didn't know, storm into the kitchen, weapons drawn. I was alive, so were Charles and Laurie. That was way more important than the pain in my side.

<h1 style="text-align:center">Epilogue</h1>

"**I**t seems like an eternity since Dean tried to bump us off," Charles said.

"Two months, three days," Laurie said, having caught on to Charles's penchant for accuracy.

It was the night before the grand opening of Teddy's Place. We were seated around two large, round tables in the newly painted and appointed dining room. Grace had put together the special event to celebrate not only her opening, but to honor her father-in-law for giving her the chance to carry her husband's legacy to the town where his father lives. She also wanted to celebrate Laurie's life being spared.

The gathering planned for six of us had expanded to nine, including Theo, the guest of honor, Charles, Laurie, Sal, Stanley Kremitz, Abraham Gant, Barb, and me and, of course, Grace who doubled as chef host.

I'd suffered two broken ribs. It had only been a week since I wasn't reminded daily about them. The doctor, who looked like he should have been in elementary school, said that, because of my "advanced age," recovery would be slower than for younger people. At least he didn't say because I was ancient.

Laurie had a concussion, suffered from headaches and occasional memory loss. Her doctor said that it would take months, possibly longer, before she fully recovered. Charles was keeping a close eye on her. He claimed it was what friends did. I knew it was more. Not only was Charles keeping an eye on her, Grace had moved in with her. Instead of paying rent, she was helping fix up the house. They'd become friends with one thing in common. They'd both suffered untimely losses. They had one significant difference. Laurie knew how she wanted to fix up her house, yet didn't have the skills. Grace was an experienced remodeler. Theo had been sad to see her leave his house but was pleased that she'd made a friend.

Wine, beer, and bourbon flowed freely. There was an ample supply of iced tea for Laurie since her doctor said she shouldn't drink alcohol until her concussion subsided. The appetizer was shrimp with cheese, and little pieces of something red stirred in the sauce. Grace tried to explain what it was but, considering my culinary skills, she would have been as successful explaining to me the Big Bang Theory in Hungarian.

I explained to Stanley, whom I hadn't seen since Dean's arrest, how Sal had been instrumental in catching the person who torched the food truck. Sal beamed when Stanley patted him on the back. Sal thanked him without cracking a joke. I don't know why it took me this long, but I realized that Sal had used jokes to feel needed, or wanted. Perhaps there was hope for him.

After we'd finished a fantastic steak and lobster entrée, Grace said that she wanted to say a few words. In her lovely, albeit fake, Jamaican accent, she praised Theo for accepting her and for the financial backing of the restaurant.

Theo choked back a tear and said, "That's what family is for. Teddy would be proud."

Grace wiped a tear from her cheek. "Yes, he would."

I could tell that she wanted to say more, but she shook her head and rushed to the kitchen. I suspected that she didn't want us to see her crying.

Stanley leaned across the table and said, "One thing confuses me. Did anyone find the treasure? What happened to the map?"

Laurie looked to see if anyone was going to answer. No one did, so she said, "We didn't find anything. Anthony thought he'd figured it out but, when we got to the spot where he thought the map indicated it should've been buried, the ocean had eroded most of it away. He thought he'd been reading the map wrong, but also thought he knew where we should go next. That's why we were out there, regardless of the weather."

Stanley said, "What happened to the map?"

Laurie shrugged. "Anthony had it when we went out there. The police didn't find it, so I figured whoever killed him took it."

Stanley said, "What did Dean do with it?"

Laurie said, "Don't know. Don't care. If there's treasure, it's cursed. I never want to hear about it again."

Captain Gant had been silent most of the evening, so I was surprised when he said, "Remember when someone broke into Dean's car?"

I doubted most of the people in the room remembered. After the police arrested Dean, his car was left in Laurie's drive. With everything going on, and Laurie suffering a concussion, no one seemed to pay attention to the vehicle.

Two days later, Chief LaMond went to Laurie's house to ask her more questions when she noticed the car's rear passenger's window had been smashed. Laurie didn't know anything about it. The chief had it towed.

Charles and I nodded. Laurie said that she remembered.

Gant sat up straight, took a sip of beer, and looked

around the room. "The past must remain in the past. There is no map."

Laurie said, "There was."

"No more," Gant said, grinned, then took a sip of his drink.

Faith

A FOLLY BEACH CHRISTMAS MYSTERY

Chapter One

The Folly Beach Christmas Parade is one of my favorite events of the year. Not only does it pay homage to the celebration that has a magical way of touching most of us on several levels, but it also gives my fellow residents an opportunity to show, no, to shout, their unique, quirky take on the holiday. Marching bagpipers sharing the same street with shiny waste-removal trucks, and golf carts overflowing with colorfully dressed elves. Add a UPS truck driver wearing a giant Santa's hat, city officials and other bigwigs chauffeured in vintage convertibles, riders dressed as reindeer riding yellow mopeds, and since Folly Beach, South Carolina, is not known as the snow capital of the country, a vehicle filling the air with artificial snow. Not a glimmer of beige interrupted the colorful feast for the eyes. Today was festive for children of all ages, for adults who want to relive their days of youth, and for those who simply love to see smiles. Count me among the latter group.

Today was perfect. It was approaching mid-December, yet the temperature was hovering in the tolerable sixties, the sky a crisp blue, with the unfiltered sun reflecting off every shiny surface. My friend Charles Fowler and I were watching the festivities from the ninth-floor walkway of the Tides Hotel, Folly's tallest building. We had a perfect, unobstructed view of the parade as it made its way four short blocks up Center Street, appropriately named since it roughly bisected the small, barrier island plus being its center of commerce. The crowd lining both sides of the street was treated to the festivities. Most of the children were waiting for the arrival of Santa, perched on one of Folly's fire engines instead of riding in a reindeer-propelled sleigh, while their parents reveled in laughing at or laughing with many of the parade participants. Charles and I were in the later stages of our sixties, so we didn't have young children to be sharing the sights and sounds with. We stood along the walkway's railing savoring the enjoyment of others.

The fire apparatus carrying the man most youngsters had come to see turned on Center Street when it stopped. Two firefighters jumped from the rig then moved to the rear of the vehicle while yelling something to Santa's helper. At the same time, the sound of laughter from paradegoers was interspersed with the high-pitched sirens of two police vehicles. A second fire engine pulled out of the combination City Hall and Department of Public Safety, a block from the parade's starting point. Police officers on foot stopped the parade to allow the emergency vehicles to cross the line of the parade. Onlookers scampered out of the way of the emergency vehicles as they crossed Center Street then sped up East Cooper Avenue, perpendicular to the parade route.

Santa was escorted off the fire engine as his handlers commandeered a golf cart holding two colorfully attired elves. The fire apparatus then backed up to turn east on Ashley Avenue, Folly's longest street.

Charles pointed to the police and fire vehicles moving away from the center of town. "Unless they're heading to another parade, something big is going on," he said, sharing one of his rare understatements.

A second parade was a nonstarter, but evicting Santa told me the emergency vehicles weren't responding to a cat stuck in a tree. A glance to the east reinforced my suspicion. Approximately four blocks east of Center Street billowing black smoke invaded the blue sky. From our elevated vantage point, I saw reddish-orange flames under the plume of smoke.

Before I pointed it out to Charles, he grabbed my shoulder, pushed me the direction of the elevator, and said, "Let's go."

I followed without needing convincing. What did take time was the wait for the elevator. It wasn't an eternity but seemed like it before the doors opened. Sure, we could've gone down the stairs, but don't forget our age. We weren't fit enough to traipse to ground level.

Center Street was lined with people enjoying the parade oblivious to what was happening a few blocks away. We weaved through the mass of people clogging the sidewalk along Center Street so we could follow the path Santa's former ride took. The fire was at least three blocks past my cottage on the other side of Bert's Market. Two engines from nearby James Island screamed past us. A few spectators from the parade had made their way the direction we were headed. Fires trump a parade almost every time.

I couldn't see what was burning but didn't doubt it was big. A couple of two-story apartment buildings were on East Ashley. From the number of emergency vehicles plus the amount of smoke filling the sky, I'd wager one of them was the subject of so much attention. The road was blocked two streets in front of us. Traffic was backed up from where it was being rerouted off Ashley. I was glad we were walking rather than stuck in the line of stopped vehicles.

We passed the first apartment building realizing the fire was in the other structure. Another fire truck pulled up behind us, siren blaring, with the added sounds of its horn attempting to get the stuck traffic to pull over so it could pass. It was having little success.

Charles tapped the handmade wooden cane he carries for no apparent reason on the pavement like it would give him extra speed. I slowed to catch my breath. The closer we got, the smell of burning wood, ashes floating in the air like leaves from a tree on a windy fall day, combined with shouts from firefighters, indicated little would be left from the burning structure still blocked from our view by two houses.

Allen Spencer, an officer with the Folly Beach Department of Public Safety I'd met when I first moved to Folly more than a decade ago, was in front of his patrol car which was diagonally parked blocking traffic. He was furiously waving his arms to get vehicles to turn off East Ashley. When I met Allen, he was new to the department, young, trim, and moved with the grace of a surfer, which he was. Since then, he'd gained thirty pounds. While still dedicated to work, he'd acquired the cynicism adopted by many law enforcement officials after years on the job. He considered me a friend, so he shared more than he would with most civilians.

We stopped beside Allen's patrol car where we got our first look at what was burning. The fire was, as I'd figured, in the two-story apartment building. The aging, wood-frame, six-unit structure was fully engulfed. Most of the roof had collapsed. Even though several hoses spewed water at the building, flames were still reaching out from the windows on two of the three first-floor apartments. The stairs to the second-floor walkway were barely attached to the building, appearing ready to collapse. It wouldn't have mattered since the walkway across the front of the building leading to the apartment doors had already fallen. Allen nodded in our direction but was too busy to tell us what he knew about the fire. We passed two Ford pickup trucks, a high-end SUV, and a Harley Davidson parked adjacent to the apartment's parking lot. Ashes rained from the sky like large, black, sinister snowflakes dotting the top of the vehicles.

Two ambulances from Charleston, seven miles from Folly, pulled up to Allen's car. He scurried to move it so the emergency vehicles could join the large gathering of first-responder vehicles. My first thought was that if anyone was in the building during the fire, ambulances would probably not be needed.

The building was a total loss, my prayer was that no residents were.

Chapter Two

Yellow police tape was strung fifty yards each direction from the burning structure. The group of bystanders, increasing by the minute, edged close to the barrier. Many of those gathered, Charles and I included, were startled when the remaining section of the roof collapsed. Smoke rolled toward us as fingers of flames darted from around the fallen roof. It may've startled us, but it didn't stop two couples from inching closer to the building, pushing the crime scene tape out of the way as they moved toward the fire.

Trula Bishop, another police officer I'd known since she moved to Folly four years ago, glared at the intruders. She yelled for them to move back as she rushed across the gravel lot to confront the trespassers. Fortunately, they obeyed. Trula saw Charles and me standing obediently behind the tape, then snarled at the offenders before coming over to us.

"Mr. Chris, Mr. Charles, should've known you'd be here. Something bad happens, you magically appear." She shook her head.

Trula was a double minority in the Folly Beach Department of Public Safety. She was one of the few women wearing a badge and even more in the minority being African American. Like most of Folly's first responders, Trula lived off-island. I knew little about her personal life but knew she was good at her job. Over the years, she'd helped me out of a couple of scrapes I'd gotten in while, along with a few of my friends, helping bring some serious criminals to justice.

That wouldn't have been unusual if my background had been in law enforcement. It was more than unusual since my entire working career was as a human resource professional with a large healthcare company in Kentucky. The closest I'd come to law enforcement or criminals before retiring to Folly was watching TV cop shows. Some cosmic switch was thrown when I crossed the Folly River the first time. My first week here, I stumbled on a murder victim as I was photographing the iconic Morris Island Lighthouse, visible from the east end of Folly. The murderer figured I may've seen him, which I hadn't by the way. His solution for silencing me was to do it permanently. I'm still around, so he clearly failed, but not by much. Oh well, that's a story for another time. In the years since that fateful encounter, I, along with some friends, had helped the police solve a few murders, murders that had either touched me or my close acquaintances. That's how Officer Bishop and I'd become acquainted.

I ignored her comment. "Trula, we were watching the Christmas parade from the Tides when—"

"When the jolly old man was dumped off the fire engine," Charles interrupted. "Chris said we'd better get nosy. So, here we are."

Not exactly how I remembered it, but it'd be a waste of words correcting him.

I said, "Trula, what happened?"

Charles interrupted, "Think someone was roasting chestnuts on an open fire and it got out of control?"

Trula stared at him.

"You know," Charles said, "Like in 'The Christmas Song'?"

The officer shook her head then glanced at the building, or what was left of it. Flames had died down, but black smoke still filled the air. "Chris, I don't know. It was fully engulfed when we arrived. I doubt there was anything we could've done to save it."

I followed her gaze, the one she gave after ignoring Charles's question. "Anyone in there when it started?"

"Our guys got a quick look in the three apartments on the first floor before the roof started falling. They didn't see anyone. The front walkway up there was already about to fall before we could get to the second floor. I hope no one was up there. If they were, well…."

"Any idea what started it?" Charles said.

Trula shook her head. "The building's old, wood, a fire waiting to happen. With that said, it went up fast, too fast."

I said, "Arson?"

"Mr. Chris, I'm no expert, but it wouldn't surprise me. If she hasn't already, The Chief will call in the Charleston Fire Department Fire Marshall Division. They're the experts. If it was arson, they'll figure it out. Fellas, I need to get back to playing cop."

"One more question," I said. "Do you know if any of the people standing around lived there?"

Trula looked at me with a slight smile. "Giving up your career as a private detective to become a fire investigator?"

I smiled. "Charles is the private detective. I'm the old, retired bureaucrat."

Years earlier, Charles self-proclaimed he was a private detective. He'd never studied to be a detective, nor had he ever worked under a licensed pro, a requirement in South Carolina. What he'd done, or claimed to have done, was read every novel in print featuring private detectives.

Charles beamed, apparently because I'd acknowledged

his self-imposed status. Note to self, make sarcastic remarks more apparent.

Charles said, "Don't worry, Officer Bishop, I'll remain a private detective, and my friend Chris will still be old."

Trula sighed. "Over with Chief LaMond. The woman with the boy."

Charles said, "Huh?"

"Mr. Charles, pay attention," Trula said. "Chris asked if anyone hanging around lived in the building."

"The woman with the kid lived there?"

"Mr. Charles, you are a detective after all."

Trula was better at sarcasm than I.

I said, "Who are they?"

Before she answered, the steps to the second floor pulled loose and crumbled to the ground stirring a cloud of dust. The smoke that bellowed moments earlier, was barely visible. A couple of firefighters were moving into the lower apartments, or what was left of them. I doubted they'd find anything usable. One of the ambulances was turning to start its trip back to Charleston. The good news was it would be returning without anyone needing medical attention.

"Yeah, who?" Charles added as if my asking wasn't enough.

Trula grinned. "Mr. Charles, I thought you knew everyone over here."

"Only everyone with pets," he said.

That wasn't much of an exaggeration.

"The woman is Rosalynn Wheeler, goes by Rose. Her son's Luke."

The woman Trula referred to appeared in her mid-forties, about five-foot-five, average weight, with curly brown hair. Luke was nine or ten, although I'm not good at guessing ages. He was chubby and looked at the ground and not at his mother as she talked to Chief Cindy LaMond.

I'd known Chief LaMond since she arrived on Folly a

year after I retired to the island. She moved up the ranks quickly, was named Chief three years ago.

"Does her name ring a bell?" Trula added.

"No," Charles said.

I shook my head.

"Wow, Mr. Charles. I know something such an outstanding private detective as yourself doesn't know."

"What would that be, Trula?"

"She's your Police Chief's sister."

Chapter Three

Cindy LaMond and I'd been friends going on a decade, but I knew little about her life before she arrived on Folly. She grew up near Knoxville, Tennessee, had worked for a Sheriff's Office before coming here, yet beyond that, not much. I didn't know she had a sibling.

I said, "Sister?"

"Don't feel bad, Cindy is my boss, I've worked closely with her, almost daily, for four years. I didn't know anything about a sister until she brought her by the station two weeks ago to introduce her."

"When did she get here?" I asked.

"Miss Rose arrived a few days before the Chief introduced us."

Charles said, "What else do you know about her?"

"Next to nothing. I'd guess she's recently divorced."

Charles glanced at Cindy, her sister, and Luke, then turned to Trula. "Did she say that?"

"No. Her ring finger has a white band of flesh where a wedding ring would go."

"She have pets?" Charles asked, as only he would.

Trula grinned. "Does a son count as a pet?"

"So, no pets?" Charles said.

Trula sighed. "None I'm aware of."

The fire appeared under control. Two James Island fire vehicles weaved their way out of the lot in front of the cremated building before pulling back on Ashley Avenue. Cindy, her sister, and Luke were moving out of the trucks' way when Cindy spotted us. She rolled her eyes, put her arm around her sister, then escorted her relatives our way.

"Chief," Trula said, "I caught these vagrants hanging around. Figured they were up to no good. Want me to arrest them?"

Cindy smiled. "Good police work, Officer Bishop. Tell you what, why don't you help Officer Spencer herd that line of traffic off Ashley. I'll take care of these troublemakers."

Cindy watched Trula leave, then turned toward Charles and me. "Guys, let me introduce you to Rosalynn Wheeler and her son Luke."

Rosalynn was two inches taller than Cindy. She shared Cindy's endearing smile, when she said, "Please call me Rose. It's nice to meet you. Cindy tells me you're a couple of her friends."

I said, "I'm honored to say that's true."

"We're a couple of her favorite citizens," Charles said, not to be left out.

Cindy tapped his arm. "That's compared to criminals, slimeballs, other assorted deviants I deal with."

Time to move along. "Rosalynn, umm, Rose, Officer Bishop told us you lived there." I nodded toward the smoldering pile of wood.

"Yes, we moved here three weeks ago and found an apartment there until we decide if we want to buy or rent."

Charles asked, "Where'd you move from?"

"Morristown, Tennessee. It's a small town northeast of Knoxville."

"What brings you to Folly?" Charles asked, never fearing to tread on personal ground.

Cindy stepped between Charles and Rose. "Guys, as you can see, no one will be returning to that building anytime soon, correction, anytime at all. They'll stay with Larry and me until they make other arrangements." She pointed to a row of vehicles in the parking lot. "That's Rose's Ford Explorer blocked by our fire apparatus, so it'll probably be a couple of hours before it can leave. Got a favor to ask. Could you walk Rose and Luke to my house so they can start settling in?"

"Cindy," Rose said, "I can find my way. I don't need an escort."

"Rose, I'd feel more comfortable if you'd let them go with you."

"It's no problem," I said. "I'd be glad to walk you and Luke. Cindy, does Larry know they're coming?"

Larry and Cindy had been married eight years and lived in a house on East Indian Avenue. While only six or so blocks from here, it's not a straight shot.

"Chris, you know hubby keeps himself handcuffed to the cash register this time of year. It's his big season. He's the only person I know who gets excited about someone buying a plunger to unclog a toilet. I'll be home long before he gets there and realizes we have boarders."

In addition to being married to Cindy, Larry owns Pewter Hardware, Folly's tiny hardware store.

I turned to Rose, "Ready to go?"

"Let me grab something out of my vehicle."

I nodded.

She walked to the Explorer with Luke matching her step for step.

Cindy watched them step over the firehoses snaked across the parking area, then said, "Chris, she's ten years younger than me, so I missed out on much of her life. I was already out of the house, moved out of our tiny hometown of Kodak, Tennessee, was working at various dead-end jobs in Knoxville during her junior-high and high-school years. The main thing I know is that she's by far the smarter chick of the two of us."

"Cindy, that's going some. You're as smart as most people I know."

"Yeah, maybe, but look who you're comparing me to." She pointed to Charles.

I laughed.

Charles said, "Chief, that makes you a genius."

That got a chuckle out of Cindy before she turned serious. "Don't know all the circumstances why she surprised me by showing up. I know she's fragile. Don't think it'd take much to break her from holding it together. I'd guess the only thing holding her together now is knowing she has to for Luke."

Charles kept an eye on Rose, yet said to Cindy, "You and Larry have a big house. How come they didn't move in with you until they found somewhere to live?"

"Excellent question, Charles. I asked the same thing. She said there was no way she was going to interrupt Larry and my way of life, whatever the hell that meant. Suppose that's going to change now."

Rose and Luke returned. She carried a small box. From the logo on it, I'd guess it held a new cell phone.

I didn't have to guess, when she said, "Got a new phone yesterday. My old one does everything well except make phone calls. The guy at the store said it'd cost more to fix than to replace. Fortunately, I hadn't gotten it out of the SUV. If I had, it'd be, well, you can see what it would've been." She nodded toward the apartment.

Cindy handed Rose a key to her house, then Charles said, "Chris, go on and escort Rose and Luke. I'll stay to talk to some of the folks gawking at the smoldering rubble."

Translating Charles speak, that meant he wanted to nose

into whatever happened; nose into things that were none of his business.

601

Chapter Four

We were a block from the apartment building before the air stopped smelling like burning wood, but we could still hear firefighters wrapping up.

Luke kept looking back at the frightening scene, before saying, "Mom, everything we have is gone. What're we going to do?"

Rose reached for his hand. He yanked it back. I didn't know if he was being a typical nine-year-old not wanting to show affection in front of a stranger, or something deeper.

She smiled. "Luke, you're right, our stuff is gone. Tell you what, let's look at it like an adventure. We'll get new things. Everything will be okay."

I was impressed with her attitude. I hoped she was sincere, not simply putting on a positive front for Luke.

"Mom, that's the same thing you said when we left home. Maybe we should go back to Tennessee where everything was okay." His voice broke, he hesitated, then said, "We had a house, we had stuff, we had friends. Mom, we had dad."

Rose's hand shook as she put it around Luke's shoulder. This time he didn't pull away. I didn't want to intrude on their personal moment, so I took a couple of strides ahead of them, then continued to Cindy's house.

The festivities on Center Street must've ended. Several groups of people passed us going the other direction, most laughing and enjoying the day with exceptional December weather. Then I saw a familiar face.

Dude Sloan was humming "Rudolph the Red-Nosed Reindeer," while skipping, yes, skipping, down the middle of the street followed by his Australian Terrier Pluto hooked to a rhinestone-studded leash. Dude would've been hard to miss in his white T-shirt with a large DayGlo red and green peace symbol on the front. Dude, real first name James, was a longtime resident of Folly, owner of the surf shop, looked like a five-foot-seven version of a cross between Willie Nelson and Arlo Guthrie, was in his mid-sixties, and comfortable living like an aging hippie stuck in the 1960s. Pluto looked like a shorter version of Dude. I was privileged to count Dude as a friend.

"Yo, Chrisster, Merry Christmas Parade. Got new family?"

Did I fail to mention Dude's vocabulary and speech pattern are challenging to say the least? That's appropriate since Dude's specialty is saying the least.

The first spark of life I'd seen in Luke was when he left his mom's side, then bent to rub Pluto's chin.

"What's his name?" asked the young man who appeared to have gotten over worrying about his future. He'd found a new friend.

"Pluto," Dude said. "Be named for dwarf planet. You be?"

Luke stood, shook Dude's hand, and said in a full, confident voice, "Luke Wheeler, pleased to meet you, Mr. Dude."

"No mister, just Dude."

"Dude," I said, "Luke is Chief LaMond's nephew. This is Rosalynn, Luke's mom."

"Woe, Dude not great at family branches. That make you Chieftress's sis?"

"Yes. Please call me Rose."

"Your sis be great gal. Nephew Luke be polite. Rare in youngins. Be visitin'?"

Rose smiled. "No, we've moved here from Tennessee."

"Cool. Rocky Top state," Dude said as Luke turned all his attention back to Pluto. "Where be livin'?"

Rose shook her head. "We were living in the apartment building that had the fire. Now we're heading to my sister's house until we find somewhere to relocate."

"Woe," Dude said for a second time. "You be in building that be giant weenie roast? You okay?"

"We're fine. Thanks for asking."

"Pluto plus me be at holiday parade, heard sirens like there be convention of fire folks. Someone said, Ashley Avenue apartment building gone. Glad you be okey dokey."

That was a long speech for Dude, so I told him we'd better be heading to Cindy's house.

"Cool. Be needin' anything. Clothes, surfboards, pup to hug, I be at surf shop. Don't be stranger."

Rose thanked him as he continued skipping to wherever.

"Interesting man," Rose said.

That was like calling an octopus an interesting looking creature.

"Mom, do we need a surfboard?"

"Think we need to get to Aunt Cindy's first, then get some clothes, food, then—"

"Got it," Luke said as he rolled his eyes.

"Rose," I said, "were you at the apartment when the fire started?"

"No, I was in Bert's Market yesterday when someone told me about the parade. Thought it'd be fun for Luke. We were standing by Snapper Jack's watching the festivities when I heard sirens. I didn't think much of it. I figured there'd be fire engines and police cars in the parade. They use their sirens when they're in the parades I've attended. Then more sirens, so I looked down Ashley toward our apartment. That's when I saw a fire truck heading toward the building. Luke pointed out the smoke. I didn't know what was burning but could tell it was near our place. We headed home to see for sure. You know the rest."

"That had to be terrifying."

"Not nearly as bad as it would've been if we were in the apartment."

"What floor were you on?"

"First, the unit nearest the street."

"Had you lived there long enough to meet other residents?"

"Not really. The middle unit, the one next to ours, was vacant, had been for five months, I'd heard. A man lived in the far unit, but I never met him. Upstairs there were two women, or that's what the landlord said, and a young man. He introduced himself to me the day I moved in. Think his name was Ty, didn't catch his last name. Sorry, that's all I know."

"Ty Striker?"

"Could be. Who's he?"

"Works at Bert's. He's the only Ty I know. Describe him?"

"Early twenties, tall, maybe six-foot-one, thin, face not yet out of the acne years. He was friendly, smiled a lot. Sorry, I don't know anything else."

"That's okay. I was curious."

"The landlord could give you the names."

"What's his name?"

"Russell O'Leary. I can give you his number. I don't think he lives on Folly."

Luke listened to our conversation, then interrupted.

"Mr. Landrum, does that Dude man surf? He looks old for a surfer."

I laughed. "He was a championship-level surfer a while back. He still goes out, mainly to help people wanting to learn."

"Think I'd like to learn. At home, guess that's our old home now, we've got this big, umm…What is it, mom?"

"Cherokee Reservoir."

"Yeah, the Reservoir. It's got a lot of water, but I don't think you can surf it. Maybe he can teach me. Mom, what do you think?"

"I think we need to get settled in your aunt's house, get new clothes, then we can think about surfing lessons. Deal?"

"If you say so." He lowered his head, not showing enthusiasm over her answer. He then raised his head. "Did you know mom is a professor?"

And I thought Charles could change subjects on the head of a pin. "I didn't know that, Luke. What does she teach?"

"English and books, umm…."

"Literature," Rose added. "Actually, I was only an associate professor at Walters State Community College in Morristown."

"How did you get there?" I asked.

"Got my master's in English from East Tennessee State University. After graduate school, I was fortunate to be offered the teaching job."

"That's where she met dad. He's a banker. They got married, had me, then didn't live happily ever after."

"Luke, I'm sure Chris doesn't want to hear all that."

The same couldn't have been said if Charles had been with us.

We'd made it to the front of Cindy's house. It was larger than the typical Folly house, was modern by island standards.

Rose patted my shoulder. "Thanks for walking us over.

We could've found it on our own, but my big sis still looks after me like I'm a little kid. Suppose she always will." She glanced at Luke who was paying more attention to a couple of women walking down the street than to us. "Cindy wanted us to move in with her. I didn't want her hovering over us, big sister like, so that's why we rented. We don't have a choice now."

"Rose, I didn't mind walking with you. Sorry about the rude welcome you received. Not every newcomer's house burns."

"Thank you anyway. Could I get your number in case I think of anything else about the others in my building?"

We exchanged numbers. She thanked me again for walking her to Cindy's.

"Mom," Luke said, "can we get a dog like Mr. Dude's?"

"Maybe someday."

I left on that vague promise.

Chapter Five

After depositing Rose and Luke at Cindy's, I called the Chief to let her know her relatives were safely at her house.

"How are they?"

"A little shook, as you can imagine, but overall I think they're fine. We ran into Dude along the way. Pluto distracted Luke, which was good."

Cindy laughed. "I'd also wager Dude distracted my sister, the English professor."

"She said she taught literature, so I imagine she's familiar with the strange versions of the English language throughout history."

"She didn't study anything resembling Dudespeak."

"True. Anyway, they're safe at your place. Know what started the fire?"

"Nothing official until the experts say. I'd put money on arson."

"Why?"

"It went up too fast. The fire spread faster than normal unless it was accelerant fed."

"Any idea who may've set it?"

"Chris, give me a break. I'm standing here looking at what used to be a building. If the arsonist left a written confession, it's part of the smoldering crap."

"Do you know who besides your sister lived there?"

She gave an audible sigh. "Tell me again why I answered the damn phone."

"Cindy, you never told me the first time. I assumed it was to enjoy a conversation with one of your favorite residents."

"Yeah, but then it was you."

"Other residents?"

"Five of the units were rented. Fortunately, we haven't found any bodies. Unfortunately, none of the residents, other than Rose have come to claim their ashes. They're either still milling around the events on Center Street, are on the beach, or off-island. I don't know who they are. We're running plates on the cars in the lot. With luck, that'll give us some names."

"Rose told me she'd only met one resident. The guy in the second-floor center unit is named Ty. She didn't know his last name. The only Ty I know is Ty Striker, a young man who works at Bert's."

"Thank you, detective Chris."

"Just sharing what your sister said. What about the landlord? Rose told me his name is Russell O'Leary. She doesn't think he lives on Folly."

"One of my guys tried to rent an apartment there a year ago. The units were full at the time, but he still had O'Leary's number. I tried it, but with my luck, it's disconnected."

"You can call your house to get the number Rose has. It'd be more recent."

"Thank you again, detective Chris."

I wasn't anxious to go home, so I passed my cottage on my way to Bert's, Folly's iconic grocery that prides itself on never closing. Hurricanes are the only thing that've messed with that tradition. I cook about as often as I skydive, which is never, so having a grocery next door was one of the appealing features when I bought my retirement home. Besides never closing, Bert's carries everything from bungee cords to beer, neither of which I have a need, but between the two, I could find snacks, breakfast items high on calories, an occasional sandwich, plus numerous items to meet my unhealthy penchant for sweets.

Today, I wasn't looking for food. Ty Striker was my focus. He was behind the register waiting on a lady tugging a sad-looking beagle behind her. Ty met the description of the man Rose said lived in her building. He was about six-foot-two-inches tall, thin, in his early twenties, with a narrow face with a long nose. He looked like he could play Ichabod Crane in a prequel to "The Legend of Sleepy Hollow." His long black hair was pulled in a ponytail with a multi-colored scrunchie. A few wayward hairs sprang out the side.

He gave his customer change while wishing her a pleasant day, then noticed me standing off to the side.

"Mr. Landrum, want a dog treat?" he said with a wide smile exposing crooked front teeth.

Bert's kept a supply of treats, normally reserved for canines. For some reason, Ty offers me one most every time he sees me in the store. For the record, I've never accepted one.

"Ty, thanks for the offer, but I'll decline."

"Your loss. What brings you in? Coffee, cinnamon roll, candy bar?"

He knew me well.

"Actually, came to see you."

"That's a first. What about?"

"The fire."

Ty turned to an employee stocking a shelf behind him. "Roger, could you take over a few minutes? I need to find something for Mr. Landrum."

He did and Ty motioned me to follow him to the back of the store near the restroom.

"Mr. Landrum, since you mentioned fire, then said you came to see me, I assume you know I live, lived, in the building that went up in smoke."

"I heard someone named Ty lived there. I hoped it wasn't you, but thought I'd ask. Guess my hoping didn't make it not true."

He nodded. "I've been working since eleven this morning. I wanted to see the Christmas parade, but that wasn't to be. A fire engine and two police cars zoomed past, so I went outside where I saw smoke." He looked toward the door to the office, before whispering, "I sneaked out for fifteen minutes; ran up the street to see what was going on." He shook his head. "My building was one big bonfire. Everything in it had to be burnt to a crisp." He stopped and stared at the floor.

"I'm so sorry. What'd you do then?"

"What else could I do? I hightailed it back here. Figured I'd need every penny I could make. Mr. Landrum, I ain't got clothes other than what you see. Didn't have much furniture, but what I had is gone, gone."

"I hate to hear it."

"Got lucky though."

"How?"

"Lost."

"Lost what?"

"Lost, that's my cat. He's safe."

That led to more questions than I could ask in the limited time Ty had before he needed to get back to work.

"Ty, was Lost outside when the fire started?"

"No, was in my car. On cool days like today, I bring him to work. I leave him in the car. When I get breaks, I go out to talk to him. He doesn't get mad at me, or yell because I'm not checking someone out fast enough."

"I'm glad, umm, Lost is safe. Any idea what started the fire?"

"Not really. I was afraid to ask, but I think the building was probably a fire trap. It was old, sort of run down. The wiring wasn't too good."

"Where are you going to live now that your apartment's gone?"

"For a while, I can live in my car. I've done it before. It's not much, a twenty-year-old Miata. Heck, it's only two years younger than me. It's mighty squinchy to sleep in, but I've managed." He looked toward the front of the store. "I'd better get to work. Can't afford to lose this job since I don't have anywhere to stay that ain't on wheels."

I repeated I was sorry about his apartment.

"Don't worry, me and Lost will be okay."

Chapter Six

The phone jarred me awake. The clock revealed it was seven-fifteen but felt earlier since I had a hard time getting to sleep, having managed to drift off around three. Thoughts about the fire and how lucky the residents had been by not being home dominated those awake hours. Charles's name popped up on the screen.

"Good morning, Charles. Isn't it a little early to—"

"Why aren't you here?" he interrupted.

I wiped the sleep out of my eyes. "Where is here? Why would I be there, wherever it is?"

"The Dog. Duh."

"Now I know where, how about why?"

"Figured you'd want to know what I learned after you sashayed off with Cindy's sis and her youngin'."

After more than a decade of conversations with Charles, talks bordering on Dudespeak, the safest, possibly only response was to say, "I'm on my way."

"Thought so," Charles said before hanging up.

The Lost Dog Cafe was Folly's go-to location for three things: great breakfasts, excellent lunches, and rumors. As

I've mentioned, my culinary skills coexist with nonexistent. If I want a meal that's not wrapped in aluminum foil or plastic wrap from Bert's, the Dog is my prime destination. I could almost walk to the colorful restaurant in my sleep. Today, I may be doing that since I was wiping sleep from my eyes as I headed to meet Charles. Fortunately, mild weather was hanging around. Sunday mornings were busy times for the restaurant located less than a block off Center Street. Two couples waited at the door for a table. Another couple leaned on the low railing decorated with a string of Christmas lights. I was glad Charles had commandeered a table. While it was unseasonably mild, it was too cool for dining on the two patios.

"About time you got here," said Amber Lewis, one of the restaurant's longest-term employees. She was one of the first people I met when I arrived on Folly. "Charles has been pestering me so much about when you would arrive, I thought I was going to have to go to your house to drag you out of bed."

The fifty-year-old server and I dated during my early years on Folly, then morphed into a close friendship. Along with her smile and talent for making customers feel at ease, Amber was one of the island's top sharers of rumors.

"Amber, I didn't know I was coming until Charles disturbed my sleep a half-hour ago."

"I know. He said he couldn't fathom why you weren't here when he showed up the second we opened."

Charles was at a table near the back of the restaurant watching my interaction with Amber. He glanced at his wrist where normal people wore a watch. Charles, anything but normal, didn't own one. The wrist glance was his way of saying I was late. He was wearing a navy-blue long-sleeve T-shirt with Wheaton in orange on the front.

"What took you so long?"

"Good morning, Charles. Nice day, isn't it?"

Amber delivered a steaming-hot mug of coffee before

Charles could continue chiding me for being late, which, of course, I wasn't. She asked if I wanted yogurt for breakfast, her effort to get me to eat healthier. I said French toast, my effort to resist her healthy suggestion. She smiled, feigned shock at the selection I chose for breakfast ninety percent or more of the time, then left to place my order.

Charles said, "Want to know about my shirt?"

My friend had a larger selection of T-shirts than all the T-shirt stores on Folly combined. I stopped asking about them years ago. That didn't stop him from sharing more than I wanted to know.

"No."

"Wheaton College, it's in Illinois. Know what it's got?"

Don't say you weren't warned.

"No."

"One of the oldest and largest Christmas festivals in the good old US of A."

"Is that why you wanted me to meet you?"

"Nope. That was a bonus, something to brighten your holiday spirit."

Charles took a bite of bacon, one of the few bites left on his plate, reinforcing he'd been here a while, then said, "Ready for the reason I called this meeting?"

I didn't even know it was a meeting. "Absolutely."

"While you were strolling through the streets of Folly with the police chief's lovely sister and her son, I was plying my well-honed detective skills at the site of the former, six-unit apartment building."

"I'm certain the Chief was thrilled with your help."

"Sarcasm doesn't suit you this early in the day."

Neither does trivia about Wheaton College, I thought.

I shrugged. "What'd you learn?"

"That's more like it. The main thing I learned was who lived there." He took another bite, then nodded like he'd discovered Colonel Sanders's fried chicken secret ingredients.

"Plan on sharing who?"

"Sure, once I finish enjoying knowing something you don't know."

Amber arrived with my breakfast allowing Charles to enjoy his knowledge a moment longer.

I poured syrup on my French toast while Charles finished gloating and started naming the residents.

"First, Janice Raque, the lady you accused of killing the bookie."

Charles and I met Janice months earlier when she became a prime suspect in the murder of a bookie whose body Charles and I unfortunately discovered. We also managed to catch the killer letting Janice off the hook. At the time, she was married, then her husband left her for a younger woman. After the divorce, she was forced to move out of her condo, but I didn't know where she'd landed.

"How'd you learn she lived there?"

"Outstanding detective work."

I stared at him.

"Okay, I was standing behind the police line when Janice tapped me on the arm, pointed to where the second floor used to be, and said, 'Oh my God, that was my apartment."

I grinned. "Wow, that's outstanding detective work."

"Sarcasm still doesn't suit you."

I smiled. "Who else?"

"Someone else you know. Would you believe Neil Wilson?"

I'd met Neil about the same time I'd become acquainted with Janice. In fact, he was another suspect in the bookie's murder. Neil's in his late forties, a former college football player, and built like someone I wouldn't want to argue with. He split his work career between being a bouncer in a bar in downtown Charleston, and part-time cook on Folly at Cal's Country Bar and Burgers.

"Neil and Janice in the same building. Weird."

"Neil lived there long before the bookie was killed, Janice moved in because it was the only place she could afford."

"I suppose you used your outstanding detective talents to learn he lived there."

"You're catching on. In fact, I used the age-old detective technique of developing an informant."

"Which means?"

"Listen closely, you can learn something from this. Ready?"

I nodded.

"I said, 'Janice, who else lived in the building?'"

I laughed, skipped the sarcasm, and jumped right to, "Who else?"

"That's where my skills deserted me."

I shared what I'd learned from Ty. I didn't attribute my knowledge to any detective skills.

Charles said, "Then, there was one other apartment, the one on the far side of the second floor. No one I talked to knew who rented it. Janice didn't know her name, but said it was a young, black woman. Janice is nearly sixty, so to her, young could be anyone between twenty and fifty. Janice didn't know much about the mystery woman. She saw her leaving the apartment a few times. Drives a black Dodge Ram pickup truck."

"Good job, Charles."

"You being sarcastic again?"

"Not this time. That's a lot more than Cindy knew when I called to tell her Rose and Luke were at her house."

"What'd she tell you?"

"Not much. She speculated the fire started in the vacant apartment in the middle of the first floor. She was fairly certain it was arson."

"A guy with the Charleston Fire Marshall Division was pulling in as I was leaving."

"Cindy called them."

"Speaking of Cindy, tell me about her sister."

I shared some of what I'd learned about Rose during the walk to Cindy's house. Charles, being Charles, asked me approximately seven thousand questions ranging from what Rose taught, not just what classes but how many students were in each class, why she got a divorce, what her ex-husband did for a living, ending with did she and Luke have pets when they were in Tennessee.

I was never happier to see anyone more than when Amber returned to refill our mugs. She poured coffee, then said, "Guys, where're the residents of the building going to live? Christmas is around the corner. Imagine how horrible it is for them."

I knew the answer for one of the tenants, but only one.

Chapter Seven

I left Charles at the Dog where he stopped to talk with a couple waiting for a table. They had a young border collie making it impossible for Charles to pass without talking to the canine, interrogating the couple about the enthusiastic pup's name, where the couple was from, and I don't know what else, since I told him I'd see him later then left him with the couple who I suspected were there for breakfast rather than an inquisition.

It was still warm for December, so I walked to the apartment building, more accurately, to what was left of the building. The smell of burnt debris assailed my nose a block before I got to the site. Part of the rear of the building and the right side were the only remnants of the structure standing. The roof, front wall, plus most of the left side of the building had collapsed and were barely recognizable in the rubble. Puddles of water from the firefighters' efforts had settled in low-lying sections of the ruins. Few items were identifiable. When the second floor burned through, refrigerators and stoves landed close to the ones in the first-floor units. Burned wood or steel frames were all that was left of the furniture. Glassware was shattered from the heat or from falling from the second floor. One item caught my attention. Inside what had been Rose and Luke's apartment, there was a blackened Christmas tree stand. The tree I pictured decked out with lights and ornaments, had been cremated.

It was hard to comprehend how five households were turned to worthless remnants in minutes. It may've been my imagination, but I thought I smelled gasoline, possibly the accelerant used to spread the fire making it impossible to save much. It was a sad sight to see anytime, but this close to Christmas, it was heartbreaking.

I was so focused on the devastation I didn't notice a black Dodge Ram pickup parked in the far corner of the deserted lot. The windows were tinted, but from the angle of the sun, I saw the outline of someone in the driver's seat. I remembered what Janice Raque told Charles about the building's still-unnamed resident, and what Cindy had said about a Dodge Ram being in the lot during the fire.

As I moved away from the rubble, the truck's door opened. An African-American female stepped out and smiled. She was in her late twenties or early thirties, thin, roughly five-foot-three, with a short afro, and wearing a dark-gray sweatshirt and black jeans. She hesitated before taking a couple of steps in my direction.

"Hi, I'm Chris Landrum." I pointed at the pile of burnt wood. "You lived there?"

Her smile turned to a look of surprise. "How'd you know?"

"I wasn't certain, but someone told me one of the residents drove a truck like yours."

"Oh." She stepped closer and held out her hand. "I'm Noelle Ward. Lived on the second floor."

"I'm terribly sorry about your apartment."

She shook her head. "Not nearly as sorry as I am. Do you live around here?"

"Near Bert's. Live here long?"

"Year next month."

"Did you lose everything?"

She nodded. "What you see is what I have left."

"Again, I'm sorry."

She turned to stare at what was left of the building, slowly shook her head, then barely above a whisper said, "Can't say I wasn't warned."

I wasn't sure I heard her correctly. "Sorry, what?"

"It's not important. Did you hear if everyone is safe?"

Not important wasn't my impression, but I didn't push.

"Yes, no one was in the building when it started. Where were you during the fire?"

"Researching something I'm writing. I was walking along the beach, almost made it to the west end of the island. I didn't know about the fire until late yesterday when I got back. Quite a shock, but glad no one was hurt."

"What are you writing?"

She smiled. "A novel."

No one's ever said that to me. "Your first?"

"Yes."

"What's it about?"

"Really want to know?"

"Sure."

"It's a murder mystery, set on a small imaginary island in Georgia. I picture it a place like Folly. That's why I moved here. I wanted to get my toes wet living and hanging around somewhere like where my novel takes place. You a reader?"

I smiled. "Afraid not. The newspaper is the extent of my reading material. I do have a friend who claims to have read every mystery novel written since Gutenberg."

She laughed. "A man after my own heart."

The more Noelle talked about her book, the more she relaxed, the more her voice, soft-spoken until now, became filled with confidence.

"If you've been around here a year, I'm surprised you haven't met him. His name's Charles Fowler."

She leaned on her truck's fender. "Don't recall the name, but I may have seen him. I'm terrible with names. He works on Folly?"

"He's retired. Occasionally, he helps some of the restaurants clean in the busy season. He also delivers local packages for the surf shop. Delivers them on his bike."

"Sounds like Mr. Fowler could be a character in my book."

"There's no doubt he's a character. If you're still around and he's with me, I'll introduce him. What are your plans now?"

"No idea. I spent last night in my truck."

"Sorry."

She smiled. "Don't be, the space in that big ole' Dodge is larger than the apartment I lived in while attending college. I still want to live over here. It's helping with my plot. You don't know of any little apartments for rent, do you? Don't want it to be too nice. My protagonist lives in a place I describe as a dump. That's the kind of apartment I'm looking for."

"Off the top of my head, I don't. If you don't mind giving me your number, I'll let you know if I hear of something."

"I'd appreciate it."

"Will you be okay until you find a new place?"

"Yes. Got a decent day job so I can buy clothes, food, other stuff. I'll be fine."

"Where do you work?"

I realized I was sounding like Charles with all the questions.

"Ad agency in downtown Charleston."

"Then I suppose writing comes easy."

She chuckled. "Yes and no. I have a degree in English, so I know how to string words together. Trouble is I'm good at writing copy for an ad or a television commercial where the word count can often be counted on my fingers plus toes. For my novel, I'll have to fill three hundred pages with words."

I couldn't imagine even writing enough to fill the television commercial.

"Sounds like a challenge, Noelle."

"You're telling me." She laughed. "Actually, my real name's Imani Marshall. Noelle's my pen name. With my background in advertising, I assure you, fewer people would buy a book written by Imani than Noelle."

Something was bothering me, so I figured that since she was more relaxed than when she got out of the truck, I could ask. "That makes sense. Got one more question. A little while ago when we were talking about when you learned of the fire, you said something like can't say I wasn't warned. What'd you mean?"

Her pleasant expression disappeared. "It's nothing important."

I didn't believe it but didn't know her enough to push for an explanation. "Okay. I'd better let you get on your way. I've enjoyed talking to you. Again, I'm sorry about your apartment."

Her smile returned, but not with the wattage from earlier.

"You too, Mr. Landrum."

She gave me her number. I promised to let her know if I heard about an apartment for rent.

She returned to her truck, slowly pulled out of the lot, then turned toward town. I watched her go, with one large unanswered question nagging me. What did she mean when she said she'd been warned?

Chapter Eight

After talking with two people who lost near everything and were spending nights in their vehicle, I began wondering about the others. Rose and Luke had somewhere to go, but what about Neil and Janice? I called Chief LaMond on the walk home.

"This better be good. This is my day off. Lo and behold, the wonderful, thoughtful, love of my life, brilliant hubby took me to brunch at Poogan's Porch. He—"

I interrupted, "He's listening, right?"

"Duh," Cindy said, answering my question. "He said it'd be a good way for me to get out of Dodge, or Folly, so I could enjoy a peaceful Sunday meal without being distracted by some idiot determined to ruin my day. Did I mention this is my day off—like in day to not work?"

"Sweetie," I heard Larry say in the background, "you may want to let him tell you why he called."

Cindy sighed. "Okay, Mr. Pest, what did I do to deserve a call on my day off?"

I didn't want to tell her after listening to her rant, I'd almost forgotten why I called.

"Chief, a couple of things. First, I was at the site of the fire where I ran into the lady who owned the Dodge pickup that was in the lot during the fire. Did you get a chance to talk to her?"

"Mr. Nosy Citizen, I also have a couple of things. First, why in hell were you at the site of the fire? In addition to nosing in police business and bumbling around catching killers, are you adding catching arsonists to your resume?"

"Chief, of course not. I can't add that to my resume until I catch one."

Cindy made a noise reminding me of a braying horse, then said, "Larry, order me another beer. I'm going to need it. Okay, Chris, the second thing is no, I haven't talked to the owner of the Dodge. What did you learn from her?"

Regardless of how hard a time Cindy gives me, she listens to what I say. I shared my conversation with Imani enlightening Cindy about Imani's pen name. I also gave her Noelle's number in case she wanted to contact her. I didn't share Noelle's comment about being warned since I didn't know what she'd meant. Cindy asked me to repeat Imani's pen name, saying her secretary, aka Larry, was better at running a hardware store than taking notes. I repeated it then added what Noelle said about writing a murder mystery.

"Chris, if you pester me again on my day off, Noelle will have a real murder to write about.'

I took the subtle hint, apologized for calling, then said I hoped she enjoyed the rest of her brunch.

"Whoa, Mr. Senior Citizen, you said there were a couple of reasons you called on, in case I haven't mentioned it, my day off. What's number two?"

Told you she listened.

"I know where Rose and Luke are staying, but I was worried about the others. Any idea what's happening to them?"

"I told all of them they could stay at your house. I

warned them not to expect a bed and breakfast. A bed, maybe. Breakfast, not a chance."

"Funny. Seriously, know anything about their plans?"

"I called the Red Cross yesterday; talked with a nice man in their disaster relief and recovery program. They'll provide money for food and will put the displaced residents up for two nights in one of three Charleston hotels. I've already told Neil Wilson, Janice Raque, and Ty Striker. Rose and Luke won't need help. Now that some busybody gave me the name of the other person on my day off, I'll contact her."

"Good. While I'm thinking about it, did you ever get in touch with the building's owner?"

"That's three things," she said before hanging up.

Must be her day off.

THE NEXT MORNING, I called Burl Costello, a friend who's pastor of First Light Church, Folly's newest house of worship; or more accurately, place of worship, since most of First Light's services are held on the beach. My call wasn't related to the church, but to Hope House, a halfway house Preacher Burl started two years ago. The large house was donated by a wealthy member of First Light under the condition Burl rents its rooms to people whom he felt needed the assist to get back to being productive members of the community. I asked Burl if he could spare a few minutes. He said he could but only if I shared a cup of coffee with him. He drove a hard bargain, but I relented.

Thirty minutes later, I was standing on the porch of the large, fifty-plus-year-old, wood-frame house on East Erie Avenue. White Christmas lights were strung around the door frame, giving it a holiday feel although the house had seen better days.

"Welcome, Brother Chris," Burl said as he waved me in. "Coffee's brewing."

Burl was in his mid-fifties, no more than five-foot-five, shaped like a football sitting on a kicking tee, topped by a face covered with a milk-chocolate colored mustache and balding head.

I followed him through the long center hallway to the large country-style kitchen.

"It's good to see you again," Burl said, as he poured my coffee and refilled his mug. "I've missed you at church."

At best, I was an irregular attendee at First Light.

"Sorry," I said with little enthusiasm.

"No need to apologize to me, Brother Chris. I'm not the one keeping score."

Time to move along.

"Burl, I'm sure you heard about the apartment building fire on East Ashley."

"It would've been hard to live on Folly without hearing of the conflagration. We had a prayer yesterday and a special offering to give to the survivors most in need. Brother Bernard is taking the love offering to the fire department this morning so they can distribute it to those displaced."

Bernard Prine was one of the Hope House residents I'd known for a couple of years. He's a military veteran suffering from PTSD, more recently called PTSI, post-traumatic stress injury, to lessen the stigma associated with the word disorder. Regardless of its name, Bernard had been kicked out of several homeless shelters for fighting before Burl worked his magic, making him feel like an important part of Hope House.

"Speaking of people in need, Preacher, do you have vacancies? I know two of the residents who're sleeping in their vehicles. There are two others I don't know about."

He took a sip, shook his head, and said, "Brother Chris, I'm saddened to say all six of my rooms are occupied. Two rooms that had been vacant were filled last week. Unless something unexpected occurs, I don't know any residents who've found other accommodations."

"Sorry to hear that, Preacher."

"Sorry to have to convey that news. But, Brother Chris, you know I'm an optimist. I have faith God, possibly working in strange and mysterious ways, will look over them to provide suitable accommodations."

"Preacher, I wish I had that much faith."

Burl smiled. "Ah, Brother Chris, we talk about things like faith on Sunday mornings. Perhaps a refresher would be helpful."

I mimicked his smile. "Subtle, Preacher Burl."

His smile turned to a laugh. "That's why I get paid the big bucks, Brother Chris." He turned serious. "I will keep the displaced residents in my prayers, but if that isn't enough by itself, I will enquire with others to see if there are alternatives we currently are unaware of."

"Thank you, Preacher. And, thanks for the coffee."

"Brother Chris, my coffee pot is always available to you."

Before I reached the car, the phone rang. Cindy's name appeared on the screen.

"Good morning, Chief."

"Did I tell you yesterday was my day off? Larry took me to Poogan's Porch where I had Chicken and Waffles."

I chuckled. "I believe you mentioned it."

"It was fantastic except for an exasperating call from one of Folly's nosiest residents. Can you believe he interrupted my scrumptious brunch to ask if I'd gotten ahold of the owner of the building that disappeared the other day?"

"A Chief's work is never done."

"You can say that again. In case you're interested, the answer is not yet."

"Where is he?"

"Could be swimming in the Mediterranean Sea,

skydiving over the Grand Canyon, hell, for all I know he could be floating around in the International Space Station. What I know is he's not answering the number he'd given Rose."

"So, what now?"

"I'll tell you the other bit of trivia I called for, then hang up so I can go to a budget meeting with the Mayor, a dream come true."

"The bit of trivia is?"

"The fire was arson. Don't ask, I don't know who set it."

Chapter Nine

One of Charles's numerous quirks was if I learned something he didn't know and didn't tell him in, oh, let's say, three flaps of a hummingbird's wing, a bucket of grief would follow. I'd exceeded that timeframe since meeting Noelle, so a call was overdue.

He was wheezing as he answered the phone.

"Where are you?" I asked.

"Jogging around the island."

I could count on fewer than one finger the number of times Charles had been jogging.

"Jogging?"

"Okay, maybe a brisk walk. Why?"

He took a brisk walk slightly more often than he jogged, but I let it go. "Where are you?"

"Getting ready to plop my rear on the picnic table at the Folly River Park."

Folly River Park is a small park bordered by the Folly River, Center Street, and East Indian Avenue. It's the site of art fairs throughout the year, but shines, figuratively and literally, during the holiday season as the location of Folly's official Christmas tree surrounded by large, colorfully lit seasonal displays.

"Plop down. I'll join you in about fifteen minutes."

Ten minutes later, I spotted him on the picnic table. He would've been hard to overlook wearing a cardinal red, long-sleeve sweatshirt with Arkansas Razorbacks and a fierce-looking hog on the front. He also wore a Tilley hat with nothing written on it, jeans, and tennis shoes that looked like they could've jogged hundreds of miles, although not on Charles's feet.

I nudged him to move over then scooted beside him on the table.

He stared at the Christmas tree, then said, "Why do bad things always happen at Christmas?"

"Bad things happen all the time. They seem worse this time of year."

"That sucks."

"Yes, but look at all the good things happening, especially during the Christmas season."

He glanced at the tree, then turned to me. "I thought I was the half-full kind of guy. You going to tell those folks who lived in the apartment building good things are happening?"

My friend had always been that half-full guy. In the last couple of years, he'd experienced some personal losses that jaded his outlook.

"Charles, I agree. Losing most everything was terrible. On the other hand, no one was injured. Cindy confirmed the fire was set which made it spread faster than would've been normal. They were lucky not to be home."

"When did the Chief tell you that?"

"Right before I called you."

I hoped that would get me off the hook, that is until I tell him about meeting the writer yesterday.

"If it was arson, why?"

I resisted the temptation to tell him to burn the building. Instead, I said, "What do you mean?"

"Whoever set it did it during the day when the odds were great its residents wouldn't be home or would've been awake enough to get out once they knew the building was ablaze. If the arsonist wanted to hurt or kill someone, wouldn't he or she have set it in the middle of the night when the intended victim was asleep?" He glanced at the tree again before turning back to me. "So, why set the fire?"

That reminded me of what Noelle shared about being warned.

"What if the arsonist wanted to scare one of the residents, not hurt him or her?"

"It would've scared the heebie-jeebies out of me if I'd seen everything I owned go up in smoke."

"Cindy also said she couldn't find the building's owner. What—"

"Whoa," he interrupted, "when did she say that?"

Don't say I didn't warn you about his quirk.

"Same time she confirmed it was arson. May I finish?"

He harrumphed then motioned me to continue.

I said, "What if the landlord torched his building?"

"Insurance?"

"Yes. It would've been a good time to do it when fewer tenants were at risk."

"How are we going to find out?"

"Charles, the police are looking at all possibilities. They'll figure it out."

"They can't even find the landlord. How do you think they'll prove he started the fire?"

"They'll find him. I didn't say it was the landlord, but it's my best guess."

"What about one of the tenants starting it?"

"Why?"

"Get out of paying rent. One of them may've been

behind, figuring he or she wouldn't have to pay if the apartment wasn't there."

"That's a possibility," I said but thought it unlikely since they'd be homeless as a result.

A man walking a boxer passed us on the paved path through the park. Charles, who could never let a dog pass without a brief conversation, hopped off the table then knelt to say a few words to the canine. He apparently ran out of canine-Charles conversation. The man and his dog continued around the park; Charles returned to the table.

"Where were the tenants when the fire started?" he asked as he watched the dog walk away.

"Ty was at Bert's. Rose and her son were watching the parade." I took a deep breath, preparing for an explosion, and said, "Noelle was walking on the beach. We don't—"

Charles's hand flew in front of my face. "Stop! Noelle?"

"I was walking by the site of the fire yesterday afternoon and saw the pickup truck that was there during the fire. The driver was looking at the ruins. Her name is Noelle Ward, actually, her name is Imani Marshall, but she goes by Noelle."

I paused anticipating Charles interrupting.

"Well, go on," he said, hinting he's not always predictable.

I gave him a brief bio on Noelle, including why she was using a pen name. Charles interrupted me twice to make sure she didn't already have published novels. Said if she did, he would've read them. I exhausted everything I knew about Noelle, repeated it twice before Charles felt he had enough information.

"Okay," he said, "what about Neil. Where was he?"

I told him I didn't know, then gave him the same answer when he asked if I knew where Janice was during the fire.

"Wonder how we're going to find out where they were?"

"Suppose we could use one of your well-honed detective skills. We could ask them."

Charles grabbed his phone and punched in a number.

"Yo, Cal, this is Charles, yeah, Charles Fowler. What other Charles do you know? Right. Is Neil there?"

Apparently, he was talking to our friend, Cal Ballew, at his bar where Neil was a part-time cook. Charles tapped his finger on the table while Cal said something. I could tell from the intensity of his tapping it wasn't to Charles's liking.

"Okay, thanks anyway."

He returned the phone to his pocket and shook his head. "Off today. Comes in at three tomorrow. You have Neil's number?"

"Why didn't you ask that before calling Cal's?"

"Well, do you?"

I scrolled through my contacts, tapped on Neil's number, then handed the phone to Charles. He didn't have as much luck as he had with Cal. He handed the phone back to me saying there was no answer.

Charles smiled and asked if I had Janice's number. I told him no before he proclaimed the day a total failure. His half-empty mood was back.

It went more downhill after he asked where the tenants would live.

"Rose and Luke will be fine," I said. "Cindy said the Red Cross was putting the others up for a couple of nights in a Charleston hotel."

"They think the landlord will wiggle his nose and a new building will rise from the ashes before two nights in a motel are used up?"

"That's all they can do."

"What about the others?" He snapped his fingers. "Got it. They could move to Hope House?"

I readied myself for another burst of irritation, then told him about my conversation with Burl.

"Crap. Christmas is around the corner and I doubt any of them could fit in a manger, even if we could find one for rent."

I interpreted that comment to be more out of frustration than my failure to tell him about meeting Burl. He got a far-away look in his eyes, a look I'd learned over the years not to interrupt.

He snapped his fingers a second time. "Got an idea."

I waited for him to share. When he didn't, I said, "What?"

"My apartment's too small for me to live in much less adding someone else."

Charles was right. In addition to being small, he'd added bookshelves to almost every wall, filled them with enough reading material to fill a small-town library. Other than his bed, every horizontal surface was covered with books, including much of the floor.

"I agree."

He smiled. "Your house is another story. Think about that extra bedroom that's only holding a computer with a printer. Acres of empty space. There'd be plenty of room for one of the poor, sad, displaced tenants to hang his hat until better accommodations come available." He nodded. "Great idea, if I say so myself."

I'd come to the same conclusion last night but didn't know if I was ready for a housemate. I'd lived alone for thirty years. Every time I'd considered other options, like adding a spouse, I broke out in cold sweats.

"Charles, there's no bed, besides, who's to say one of them would be interested?"

"You're right. Heck, I'm sure Ty is thrilled to be living like a pretzel in his Miata. Noelle must be feeling like a queen living in her pickup. We don't know anything about Neil or Janice. Think about it. I'll see if I can twist arms to help the others out. Surely I can guilt somebody by playing the Christmas card."

"I'll think about it."

"Good, you can tell me your decision tomorrow when we go to Cal's for a burger, a drink, a powwow with Neil."

Chapter Ten

The next morning began with me heading next door to grab a cinnamon Danish and cup of complimentary coffee. It was at least ten degrees colder than the last two days, so I pulled the collar of my lightweight jacket up around my neck. Over the years, I'd been tempted to buy a heavier coat, but refused telling myself Folly Beach was in the South so I wouldn't need anything warmer. Several times over the years, I'd regretted my stubbornness. This was one of those times.

Ty's Miata was parked in the lot between my house and Bert's. I was tempted to peek in to see if his cat was there. Instead, I rushed to the warmth of the store. Ty was behind the counter where three people waited to check out. He smiled when he saw me then went back to giving a woman change. My feet automatically took me to the case where oversized gooey delights would tempt me. I put a Danish in a paper bag then proceeded to the large coffee urn and filled a cup. By the time I made it to the register, Ty's customers were gone.

"Morning, Ty," I said as I put money on the counter for the Danish.

Ty's smile widened. "Mr. Landrum, it's a wonderful day."

His attitude was better than mine would be under similar circumstances.

"You seem happy this morning. Win the lottery?"

He continued to smile. "Afraid not, Mr. Landrum. I'm thankful Lost and I wasn't hurt in the fire. Things can always be worse, be worse."

"Is Lost in your car?"

"Not today, it's too cold for the little fellow. Left him in the hotel where the good folks from Red Cross are letting me bunk."

I knew the answer, but asked anyway, "How long will you be there?"

"Tonight will be it. It was nice of them to give me two nights."

"What'll happen then?"

"Suppose I'll move back in my car. Not quite luxury digs, but beggars can't be choosers, be choosers. I think that's how the saying goes."

A woman carrying a loaf of bread appeared behind me. I stepped aside so she could pay. Ty took her money, told her to have a wonderful day, then turned to me.

"Mr. Landrum, would you let me know if you hear of any cheap apartments for rent. Lost needs a better place to live than the car."

"What about you?"

He smiled. "Wouldn't mind it myself."

"I'll keep an eye out."

"Lost would appreciate it."

At the risk of sounding like Charles, curiosity got me to ask, "How'd you come up with the name Lost?"

He smiled. "Not the first time I've heard that question. Want the long or short version?"

I looked around and didn't see anyone vying for Ty's attention. "Whichever you have time for."

"I don't suppose you know anything about me other than what you see in here."

"True."

"I moved from Baltimore a little over a year ago. I came to Folly with a couple of friends I worked with at a roofing company. Tell you something, Mr. Landrum, slapping roofs on buildings when it's ninety degrees isn't high on the list of fun jobs, but see, I sort of barely got through high school. They said I was smart enough to go to college, but since I had a better time not being in school than when I was there, I figured I wouldn't be good for college. College wouldn't be good for me. That may not have been one of my better decisions. Anyway, my buds and me were coming here to vacation, surf, drink beer, then, drink more beer. Two days before we were to go back to roofing, we came in here to buy beer." He hesitated, then smiled. "I was standing right where you are when I saw a girl working behind the deli counter. Heard her tell someone her name was Aimee." His smile widened. "Mr. Landrum, she was the cutest girl I'd ever seen. I mean ever."

By now, I assumed, hoped, this was the long version of how Lost got his name. I took a sip of coffee and was tempted to pull some of the Danish out of the bag. I didn't but waited for Ty to continue.

"The next morning, I left my roommates sleeping. I came here, asked if the manager was around. The clerk pointed me his direction, so I asked if he was hiring. Figured it would be the best way to get to know Aimee, Aimee Mason I learned. Suppose you figured out he was hiring."

I nodded.

"Aimee and me got to talking when we were on overlapping shifts, and—"

"Ty!" someone yelled from the back of the store. "Let

Caroline take the register. I need your help unloading boxes."

Ty sighed. "The rest of the story will have to wait. Sorry, Mr. Landrum."

"Ty, before you go, do you have a number for your landlord?"

He pulled out his wallet, took out a folded piece of paper, and handed it to me. I unfolded the paper where I found the name Russell O'Leary plus a phone number. I put the number in my phone, returned the paper to Ty, then said we'd talk later.

Sitting at my seldom-used kitchen table, I ate the Danish while thinking about how unaffected Ty was about what was in my mind a horrible situation. I admired his outlook. I also wondered if the number he'd given me was the one the Chief had been using to reach the landlord. Today wasn't her day off, so I figured it'd be safe to call to give her the number.

"Good morning, one of my less-neurotic friends. You calling to apologize for interrupting one of my few days off?"

I smiled. "If it'll make you feel better, yes."

"Apology accepted. You going to say something now that'll need another apology?"

"Never, Chief. I was talking with Ty Striker a little while ago. He gave me a number for Russell O'Leary. I thought if it was different than the one you had; it may help you get in touch with the landlord."

She hesitated before speaking. "Just curious, why in holy hell were you asking Ty for the landlord's number? You want to rent an apartment or buy a bucket of soot?"

"Chief, you were having trouble reaching him. I wanted to help."

"Chris, don't treat me like you're talking to one of my dodo-brain officers. You're nosing in police business. Again."

Nothing would be gained by denying it. She wouldn't believe me. Neither would I. "Want the number?"

"Don't need it. I talked to O'Leary yesterday. Neil Wilson gave me a number I didn't have."

"What'd you learn from O'Leary?"

"Give me one reason I should answer that question?"

"Because—"

"Never mind. The only acceptable answer is because you'll pester me up to my eyeballs if I don't. I need that as much as I need the mayor threatening to fire me unless I start talking and acting like a police chief."

Mayor Newman had been on her case for as long as she'd been Chief. He knew she wasn't about to change, but that hadn't stopped him.

"What'd you learn from O'Leary?"

"Crap on a cucumber, Chris. Do you ever give up?"

See what the mayor meant?

I repeated, "O'Leary?"

"He swore he didn't know anything about the fire until the next day. Claims he was in Atlanta attending a seminar on buying real estate, getting filthy rich, without having to put any money down, or something like that."

"How'd he learn about the fire?"

"Claims he got back from Atlanta, drove by the building, where he perceptively noticed it was no longer there."

"Did you ask if he knew anyone who might've had reason to start the fire?"

"Gee, Chris, why didn't we professional investigators think to ask that."

Got it.

"What'd he say?"

"Claims he didn't know anyone."

"Cindy, why do I have the impression you don't believe his story?"

"What makes you say that?"

"You've used the word claims three times sharing his version."

"Damn, it's annoying you actually listen to me. Annoying and scary."

"Well?"

"I asked him the name of the seminar he allegedly attended. He couldn't remember. I asked when he got to Atlanta. He said a few days before the seminar. If I asked you that kind of question, wouldn't you name a specific day rather than 'a few days'? It's hard to judge someone's behavior over the phone, but my gut tells me he was lying about some of what he was saying."

"What next?"

"I'm going to call him later to schedule a face-to-face."

"Good luck."

"I'll need it if I want him to confess to torching his building."

Chapter Eleven

Cal Ballew took ownership of the bar eight years ago after Gregory Brile, the former owner, did what many people only dream of doing. He killed an attorney. Apparently, doing rather than dreaming has serious consequences. Gregory is in prison. The name of the bar switched from GB's to Cal's. The new owner, now in his mid-seventies, had spent most of his adult life traveling around the South, living out of his car, while playing his brand of traditional country music at any venue that would have him. He was performing at GB's when the owner moved from a comfortable house to a less-comfortable prison cell. Cal reluctantly took over even though he knew as much about owning a bar as a gecko knows about playing Chinese checkers.

Because of his decades on the road with nowhere to go on Christmas, when Cal took over, he was determined to hold an annual Christmas party so others who might share experiences similar to his would feel at home; a place where they could enjoy the spirit, fellowship, and calories of the holiday. His party has grown each year. It was now one of the highlights of the year, not only for those who had nowhere to go but for many of us who loved to share the joyous event with Cal. The singer who treated his patrons to a handful of sets during the week wasn't getting wealthy with the business but squirreled away money throughout the year so his Christmas party could provide free food and drinks to all comers.

I'd told Charles I'd meet him at Cal's but hadn't set a time. I was surprised he wasn't there when I arrived so he could tell me I was late. What was there brought a smile to my face. Four, seven-foot-tall artificial Christmas trees anchored the corners of the room. Multiple strands of colorful lights were attached to each non-moving vertical surface, more dangled from the ceiling. The bar spent most of the year looking tired, to put it kindly, but perked up come December. There were a dozen tables, plus a handful of barstools in front of the wooden bar on the side of the room. A twelve-by-twenty-foot laminate dance floor abutted a small stage in front of the room. The rest of the floor was covered with fraying indoor/outdoor carpet.

Seasonal sounds of Bing Crosby's "White Christmas" were coming from the antique Wurlitzer jukebox parked on a corner of the stage. Crosby's mellow voice competed with the country voice of Cal who was standing behind the bar drying a glass with a red, white, and blue bar towel. The owner was six-foot-three, toothpick thin with a spine that curved forward from bending down to a microphone plus living out of the back seat of his car for decades. Long, gray hair poked out from around the Stetson that'd traveled with him for more than forty years. In deference to the season, a strand of battery-operated, colorful lights was strung around the hat's crown. If Santa was anorexic, didn't have a beard, didn't wear a red suit, and didn't ride around the world transported by reindeer, Cal could be his double. I suspect Cal had a better singing voice, although I'd never heard Santa sing.

"Well if it isn't one of Santa's wise men," Cal said, mixing Christmas stories. He waved his hand around the room. "What do you think of this year's decorations?"

I thought they were overboard, but the same as last year. That wouldn't have been the correct answer, so I said, "Incredible, Cal, incredible."

"So you noticed the extra lights I've strung from the ceiling?"

Not really. I repeated, "Incredible."

Cal looked to see if anyone was nearby. No one was. "Truth be told, Neil did all the light stringing. This old broken-down body and ladders don't mix."

"Cal, it doesn't matter who decorated, it looks great. Would Neil happen to be here?"

He moved his head in the direction of the small kitchen. "In back, fixin' burgers for that table of guys by the wall, the ones looking like undertakers dressed in those suits. Must be a convention at the Tides."

Gene Autry began singing one of probably a thousand performers' versions of "Jingle Bells," as Cal handed me a glass of Cabernet, one I hadn't requested. He had my number.

"Chris, know what Charles told me about that song?"

Of course, I didn't, so I shook my head before taking a sip.

"Some cat wrote it back in eighteen-hundred-something as a Thanksgiving song. Can you believe that?"

If there was some archaic bit of trivia involved, I'd believe it. I limited my response to, "Who would've guessed?"

Neil walked out of the kitchen carrying a tray holding three hamburgers, two orders of fries, with an order of onion rings vying for space.

Neil said, "Hey, Chris."

Cal pointed to the table of men who ordered the burgers. Neil took the hint and headed their way.

Cal watched him move around two other tables. "You know about the fire at Neil's place, don't you?"

I nodded.

"Of course, you do, pard. You know everything bad that happens here."

I wouldn't have put it that way.

"How's Neil taking it?"

"Not as good as he wants everyone to think. He comes across as a big ole bruiser, living up to his part-time bouncer job downtown."

Neil could play that role well. He was six-three or four, in his late forties, looks like a former football player whose muscle turned to fat after his playing days ended. I remembered him coming across the way Cal described him earlier this year when he was a suspect in the bookie's murder. In fact, it was Cal who'd told me about a temper tantrum Neil had during a confrontation with the bookie.

I said, "That's the image he portrays."

"Dig deeper, pard, you'll find a big teddy bear. The boy's torn up about the fire, not just because it left him without a bed, but he feels horrible about the others who lost everything." Cal watched Neil as he left the food at the table and headed our way. "Don't tell him I said anything, okay, pard?"

"Deal."

Neil grabbed the colorful bar towel from Cal's shoulder, wiped his hands off, then shook my hand. "Good to see you, Chris."

"You too. I was sorry to hear about your apartment. I was there when firefighters were finishing up."

A new customer arrived and took a seat at the far end of the bar. Cal left to see what the newcomer wanted.

"Everything is gone but my old jalopy, plus some clothes I had in the trunk."

"Where were you when it happened?"

"Working. With the parade going on, it was a big day

here. I normally wouldn't have been here for lunch on Saturday, but Cal asked me to come in. I need all the hours I can get."

"I'm glad you weren't in your apartment. Any idea what started it?"

"I hear rumors it was arson. Got a couple of ideas, but nothing to back them up."

"What—"

Charles magically appeared behind me before I could get Neil to share his ideas.

"Hey, Neil, Chris, sorry I'm late."

"Late for what?" Neil said.

Excellent question, I thought.

"Meeting Chris. Figured I'd beat him like I always do."

"Neil," Cal said from behind the bar. "My buddy over there wants a cheeseburger. Let's don't keep him waiting."

"I'd better get cookin'," he said as he smiled at his boss.

"Did I miss anything?" Charles said as Neil headed to the kitchen.

Cal handed Charles a Budweiser, another correct assumption by the bartender. He and I headed to a vacant table. The only other customers were the man at the bar plus the three undertaker look-alikes.

Brenda Lee's version of "Rockin' Around the Christmas Tree" serenaded us as we sat and took a sip of our drinks.

"You didn't say anything to Neil about what we wanted to talk to him about, did you?"

"No," I said. "He was busy, then you interrupted us when he was getting ready to tell me about the fire."

"Good," Charles said as Brenda finished singing. He pivoted toward the bar. "Hey, Cal, old buddy. Chris here wants to talk to Neil when he gets a chance."

"No problem, pard. I'll mosey in the kitchen, tell him to drop everything he's doing. Stop fixing food. Rush out here to take a meeting with two old-timers. Will that work?"

"Good plan, Cal," Charles said, skipping over Cal's sarcasm.

Luckily, Cal laughed as he headed to the kitchen.

Cal delivered the hamburger to the customer at the bar as Neil came our way.

Neil turned a chair around, sat, then put his elbows on the back of the seat. "Cal said two old geezers want to talk to me."

Charles looked around the room, then said, "Don't see any. Since you're here, Chris said you were going to tell him something about the fire."

"I did?"

"Neil, you said you'd heard it was arson, that you had a couple of ideas about who may've started it."

Roger Miller's "King of the Road" proved Cal hadn't replaced all his classic country songs with Christmas music.

Neil looked at the jukebox then at me. "I'm being paranoid. Probably doesn't have anything to do with what I'm thinking. No need to get into it."

"Tell us anyway," Charles said. There was a zero chance he'd let Neil off that easy.

"Remember when Cal hired me?"

"Sure," I said.

"He'd heard I'd been fired from the private security job in Charleston."

Charles interrupted, "Yeah, your boss at that toy factory fired you because you were being questioned by the cops about the bookie's murder."

Neil nodded. "Doing my civic duty and that jackass kicked me out. Pissed me off."

Charles said, "So?"

Charles, let the man talk, I thought. "Neil, go on."

"I'd worked there for four years. You learn a lot about a place when you're a night watchman. Get to snoop when no one's around. Lots of hours with nothing to do. It'd be hard to find a thief who'd want to break in a kid's toy manufacturing company. Anyway, I started piecing together some papers of the owner, Paul Davidson's his name, by the way. Anyway, he was mighty careless about leaving tax papers and P&L statements on his desk. I'm no accountant, hell, I'm just a dumb country boy, but it didn't take a number cruncher to figure there was a bunch of revenue Paul wasn't reporting to the IRS."

"How'd you figure it out?" Charles asked.

Neil smiled. "Didn't have to. All I did after he fired me was make a couple of calls to the IRS office in Charleston. Guys, did you know they have a form you have to fill out to report fraud? They've got a form for everything." He shook his head. "Hell, I wasn't about to fill out a stupid form. I made the two calls, told them where and what, and if they wanted to catch a crook, they'd find him there. I wasn't going to do all the work for them."

"What happened?" Charles asked as if Neil wasn't going to tell us without being asked.

Cal hummed along with Charlie Rich's version of "Behind Closed Doors" as Neil took a sip of beer he'd brought with him to the table. No one else had entered the bar.

"One of the guys from the factory called a couple of weeks later, told me it was good I got out when I did." Neil laughed. "He didn't know I'd been fired. Said a group of suits swarmed all over the factory hauling out computers and everything from the file cabinets. My buddy wasn't sure what happened next, but Paul spent a lot of time talking to lawyers and storming around the factory looking like his head was going to explode. Best news I got in years."

"Neil," I said, "That's interesting. Sounds like he's getting what he deserves, but how's it related to the fire?"

"Suppose I left out an important part. Last week, my buddy at the factory called bitching about the extra work Paul was laying on him. He was always bitching about something. Anyway, he heard Paul telling one of his VPs he figured out who ratted him out to the Feds. Said he was going to get even with the SOB. Fellas, I'm that SOB."

I asked, "How would he have found out it was you?"

"Don't think he could. That's why I'm being paranoid. I didn't give the IRS my name. I never said anything at work hinting at me knowing about the business end of the company. Hell, I was just a dumb old night watchman."

Two customers arrived, sat at a table on the other side of the room, placed an order with Cal, who whistled for Neil, then pointed at the kitchen.

A subtle hint, it wasn't. Neil said he'd better do what Cal wanted. He didn't want to get fired from another job.

Ernest Tubb's version of "Blue Christmas" was playing, reminding everyone that Christmas was less than two weeks away.

Charles and I went separate ways after leaving Cal's. The temperature had become uncharacteristically warm for this time of year. Adding the bright sunshine made it feel warmer, so I walked a few short blocks to Pewter Hardware to ask Larry how his sister-in-law and nephew were adjusting to their new residence. This was the store's busiest time of year, so I wasn't surprised there were vehicles overflowing the small, crushed-shell parking lot.

The interior of the tiny store was more crowded than the lot. Three customers waited in line at the check-out counter, four were blocking the narrow aisle near the seasonal decorations, while two others were flipping through a battery display.

Larry manned the register. He wore a velvet Santa's hat, but at five-foot-one, weighing a hundred pounds after a Thanksgiving meal, he looked more like one of Santa's elves. He was self-conscious about his diminutive size, so the elf comparison was one he'd not hear from me.

I wasn't surprised by the crowd but was surprised seeing Luke beside Larry bagging purchases. Brandon, Larry's only full-time employee was helping a customer carry three sacks to the door.

The customers who'd been waiting to check out completed their purchases and headed for the exit. Larry saw me standing out of the flow of customers, smiled, then put his arms around Luke. The nine-year-old was only a half-foot shorter than Larry, another observation I'd keep to myself.

"Chris, check out my new employee."

I smiled. "Have the child-labor police been in yet?"

"Hi, Mr. Landrum," Luke said, ignoring my comment. "Uncle Larry says I'm a big help."

"You look like you're doing a great job. You need to ask your uncle for a raise."

Luke chuckled. "Uncle Larry says I'm earning my rent, but I can leave whenever I want."

I started to comment when someone tapped my shoulder. I turned to see Rose standing behind me wearing an orange Pewter Hardware sweatshirt.

"Don't tell me Larry's put both of you to work."

"He's not that cruel. As you know, I'm short on clothes so Larry contributed this to the cause. Cindy and I are going to the mall tomorrow to rectify the situation."

"Rose," Larry said, "why don't you get some fresh air. Luke and I can hold down the fort."

She nodded then turned to me. "Up for a walk?"

"I can cram one in my schedule."

"Mom, don't worry about me. Uncle Larry needs me here."

Another customer was ready to check out, so Rose and I left the store in the good hands of Larry, Luke, and, I suppose, Brandon.

"Which way?" Rose asked as we walked a block to Center Street.

"Have you been on the Folly Pier?"

"Luke and I started there once, but it was so cold we turned around. Today's nicer, I'm up for it if you are."

We walked six blocks to where Center Street dead-ends at the entrance to the Tides Hotel. Our walk was mostly silent, with Rose's only comments being about the illuminated sand dollar, dolphin, crab, and turtle decorations adorning light poles along the way. The Folly Beach Fishing Pier was adjacent to the Tides, so we turned at the hotel, before making our way up the long flight of steps to the pier's deck where a group of women were leaning against the railing watching the surf roll in. A middle-aged man was photographing two children sitting in a red chair big enough to hold someone the size of the Goodyear blimp.

"It's a lot warmer than the last time we were here. This is a great view of the beach."

I pointed to the far end of the thousand-foot-long structure. "It's even a better view from out there."

"What are we waiting for?" Rose said as she put her arm through mine and escorted me to the end of the pier.

When we reached the Atlantic end of the pier, we sat on a wooden picnic table and faced the shore. Rose was silent for a long time, before saying, "It's weird living in the house with Cindy."

"Were you close?"

I asked since Cindy had never mentioned a sister.

"Not really. With ten years between us, we had little in common. We have different fathers, you know."

"I didn't know. Cindy and I are good friends, but she seldom says anything about her life before moving to Folly."

Rose smiled. "That's no surprise. She's self-contained, irritatingly so at times."

I nodded.

"Her dad, Kenneth, was a coal miner near Evarts. That's in Harlan County, Eastern Kentucky. He'd dropped out of high school to work in the mines. Two years later, he married our mom, Ruth, then three years after that, Cindy came along."

"I thought she grew up in East Tennessee."

"Her dad didn't have much formal education, but was smart, or so mom said. She told me he realized if he kept working in the mines, his back would die before he did. He quit when Cindy was three. He'd heard about work in Tennessee from a friend who'd moved there a couple of years earlier. It was with the Sevier County Sheriff's Office. He packed up his family and moved to Kodak."

"Where you were born?"

She looked at the ocean for the longest time. I wasn't sure if she'd heard me. Finally, she said, "Three days shy of Kenneth's first anniversary with the Sheriff's Office, he pulled a man over for speeding. Nothing out of the ordinary. Nothing unusual until the man, later determined to be high on drugs, pulled a gun and shot Kenneth three times. He never had a chance. Cindy was four."

"That's horrible," I said, wondering if that's why Cindy seldom mentions her past.

"It got worse for Cindy. Five years later, Mom married a man named Boyd. He was a traveling shoe salesman, sold to small-town retail stores throughout the region. Mom was pregnant with me when they got married." She chuckled without a hint of humor then stared at the water. "Boyd told mom he could put up with one kid but not two. He left town, never to be heard from again." Cindy was Luke's age when I was born." She turned to me and smiled. "Cindy would kill me if she knew I was telling you."

"She won't hear it from me."

"Good. Not many years after that, Cindy graduated from high school. She had little interest in studying, but to keep mom happy, she moved in a dorm at the University of Tennessee, attended school off and on for three years before quitting. Instead of moving back to Kodak, she stayed in Knoxville. For eight years she bounced around dead-end jobs. She waited tables, tended bar, even sold encyclopedias door-to-door."

"She said she worked in law enforcement before moving here."

"She joined the same sheriff's office her dad was a member of. She never told me this, it's only amateur psycho-analyzing, but I think it was so her dad would've been proud of her following in his footsteps." She sighed. "Sure you won't tell her I told you?"

"You have my word."

She nodded. "Cindy said you were a pain in the ass but could be trusted. Otherwise, I wouldn't have said anything."

I laughed.

"While I'm spilling secrets, there's something else. I haven't told Cindy because I know her well enough to know if I did, she'd go all cop and blow it out of proportion."

"I can see that."

"The day before the apartment fire, my ex called. He was at the Crab Shack, wanted me to meet him."

"What'd you say?"

"Chris, I was shocked. I hadn't heard from him since I moved. He wanted to meet me without Luke. Probably shouldn't have, but I went. Told Luke I had to walk up the street for a few minutes and left him in the apartment. I felt bad about leaving him, but he was watching a monster movie and seemed okay." She turned to watch a large container ship lumber toward the entrance to the Charleston harbor.

I waited for her to continue.

"Lawrence, my ex, was sitting at a table acting smug. It's one of his more-practiced looks. He's a vice president at a Morristown bank, a job he got because his father is on the board. To put it mildly, I didn't greet him with open arms."

"What'd he want?"

"Us to come home—home to Morristown. Can you believe that? Mr. Hot Shot Bank Official got caught having an affair with a twenty-five-year-old teller at another bank. Now I'm supposed to come running back after the chickadee dumped him."

"What'd you tell him?"

She surprised me with a laugh. "With two college degrees in English, I'd learned several ways to tell him to go, umm, have intercourse with himself. I used all of them, then cracked open a peanut and threw the shell at him."

I struggled to hold back a laugh, then said, "How'd he respond?"

"It wasn't the reaction he'd expected. His face turned red, his hands gripped his drink so hard, I was afraid he'd break the glass. He dropped a twenty on the table, stared at me, and whispered, "You'll regret it.""

"Think he started the fire?"

She shook her head. "No. That's why I haven't told Cindy."

"What makes you think he didn't?"

"Oh, I wouldn't have put it past him if it were only me. There's no way he would've endangered Luke, even if there was a minuscule chance his son would've been in the apartment. No way."

It may've been my imagination, but the wind picked up and my skin felt like the temperature dropped twenty degrees. I wish I had her confidence.

Chapter Thirteen

After walking Rose to Larry's store, my growling stomach reminded me I'd skipped two meals, a rare event. Instead of heading home, I stopped at Snapper Jack's, a large, multi-level restaurant on the corner of Ashley Avenue and Center Street. The restaurant is easy to give directions to since it faces the island's only traffic light. A college-age hostess in an aqua Snapper Jack's T-shirt escorted me to a table by a large window overlooking Center Street. In-season it would've been nearly impossible to get a table so quickly.

A server greeted me with a smile, a menu, an introduction, her name is Marcia and an inquiry about my drink choice. She headed to the bar once I said a glass of Cabernet. Since the restaurant had few customers, Marcia had my drink on the table before I could study the menu. She asked if I was ready to order. I begged for additional time, to which she said she'd be near the bar, for me to wave when I was ready.

Instead of studying the menu, I replayed what Rose shared about Cindy's background plus her revelation about her ex-husband's visit. I understood why she was confident he didn't set the fire, but I wasn't as understanding. It struck me as more than a coincidence he was on Folly fewer than twenty-four hours before the fire. Did he return to Tennessee after their meeting or stay in the area?

How could I find out? On a couple of instances when I wanted to know where someone had been staying, Chief LaMond provided invaluable assistance. Her title and charm were more than enough to get hotel desk clerks to check guest registers to see if the people she asked about had stayed in their facility. I'd told Rose I wouldn't share what she'd said with her sister, so asking Cindy was off the table. I knew an employee at the Tides who might be able to remember Rose's ex staying there, but it'd be a long shot.

I nearly dropped my drink, when someone said, "Thought that was you."

I turned to see Janice Raque standing by the table. "Oh, hi, Janice."

Janice is in her late fifties, five-foot-four, with short brown hair with patches of gray sneaking in. She wore an oversized, navy-blue sweatshirt, and black slacks. She also had a bottle of Lagunitas IPA in her hand.

"You're, umm, now don't tell me, you're Chris, right?" She swung the bottle in rhythm with her words.

"Good memory."

"Remember talking to you a couple of times in Hal's, umm, Cal's."

Janice had been a regular in Cal's when she was married. According to Cal, she and her husband often got in arguments until one of them stormed out.

She looked at the bar-height stool on the other side of the table. I took the hint.

"I'm having an early supper. Want to join me?"

"Supper from a wineglass?" She chuckled. "This is my supper." She held up the beer bottle.

Instead of answering my question, she pulled out the stool.

I handed her the menu. "I was getting ready to order. Want something to eat?"

"This is my third, maybe fourth beer. Suppose I'd better eat something to sop the hops." She laughed.

I began wondering if she'd underestimated the number of beers she'd consumed for supper. I motioned for Marcia. I ordered fish and chips and asked Janice if she knew what she wanted. She ordered a Folly salad. I wasn't sure what it was since I eat salad as often as I eat chocolate-covered oyster shells. Marcia asked if we needed more drinks. I hadn't finished my wine, so I declined. Janice didn't decline. I doubted a Folly salad would sop up enough hops to prevent Janice from falling off the stool.

After Marcia left, I said, "Janice, didn't you live in the apartment building that burned?"

"Damn, Chris, has a secret ever escaped from this island without being caught by a gaggle of people?"

"Someone was talking about the people displaced by the fire. Your name was mentioned. I remembered you from Cal's."

I left out the part about remembering her because she'd been a murder suspect.

"Yes, I'm one of the unlucky people who're now homeless."

"Found somewhere to stay?"

"Why? Want me to shack up with you?"

She definitely underestimated the number of beers she'd consumed.

I smiled. "Afraid I don't have room."

"Well crapola."

I was saved when Marcia deposited Janice's beer, then said our food would be out shortly. Janice had the new bottle to her lips before Marcia reached the kitchen. Now to move past Janice's comment about moving in.

"I was asking because I heard the Red Cross provided housing for the fire victims."

She held up two fingers. "Two nights, period. Did they think the apartment building would be rebuilt in two days?"

"Sorry."

"Oh well, that's water under the dam, or over the bridge, or, crap, whatever the saying is. I'm at the Holliday Inn a couple of weeks until I figure something out."

The Holliday Inn, not to be confused with the national hotel chain spelled with one "l," is a fourteen room, locally-owned hotel that's been around since the late 1940s. It's a block from the ocean, has reasonably priced rooms, and is one of only two hotels on the island.

"It's good you have somewhere to go."

"I suppose. Some are living in their cars."

"Did you know many of the others?"

"Not really. I've been there a little over a year. Ever since, umm, never mind. Anyway, I know Neil pretty well. Nice guy. He's been there as long as I have. I only know him from Cal's. He cooks there, you know. Seldom saw him around the apartment." She took another sip. "The young guy, the one with the red sports car, don't know his name for certain. Something like Sly."

"Ty," I interrupted.

"Okay, Ty. Anyway, that's all I know about him. Oh wait, he's got a cat."

"Lost," I said.

"Lost what?"

"His cat's named Lost."

"Damned stupid name for a cat."

I didn't disagree. "What about the African-American lady?"

Janice shook her head. "All I know is she nearly ran me down with her big-ass truck."

"What happened?"

"I got food at Bert's and was carrying it home. I got to

our parking area when she whipped out of the lot, not looking where she was going. I was lucky or I wouldn't be here."

"Did she see you?"

"Said she didn't. She stopped, lowered her window, said she was sorry. It's no wonder she almost got me. It was dark, yet she had on these big sunglasses. Did she think she was a celebrity? Anyway, now you know all I know about her."

"What about the lady who moved in recently, the one with the young son?"

"She lived right under me. The kid kept the TV on loud. Thought about complaining. Knew it wouldn't do any good since the building was built cheap. Doubt there was a speck of insulation in it. Everyone could hear everything going on." Our meals arrived. Janice took a bite of salad, another sip of beer, then said, "That building was a fire waiting to happen. The damned landlord didn't fix anything. My bathroom sink leaked from the day I moved in. Suppose it don't leak no more." She laughed and took another drink. "Know what O'Leary, he's the landlord, was good at?"

"What?"

"Collecting rent. I could set my watch by the time he came knocking on the door the first of the month. I spilled the beans to everyone who asked me about renting there."

"Did many people ask?"

"A couple. The apartment on the first floor was vacant several months, so occasionally someone would see me outside and ask. Some guy, looked like a street person to me, asked. Told me he was Jeff, maybe Jerome. Anyway, he was looking for an apartment." She chuckled, took another sip of beer, then said, "Told him the apartment was fine unless the second floor fell on him. Chris, didn't know I was psychic, did you?"

I shook my head.

"Good ole Jeff or Jerome stopped asking me anything

after that. Then one time I was telling a woman named Kinsey or Kaycee exactly what I thought. She thanked me."

"Where'd you meet her?"

"Opening my door, in fact, she followed me upstairs. She told me she owned a couple of rental units and had someone looking for a place to rent, but hers were full. She was a fast talker; said a bunch of other stuff I can't remember now. I gave her the full load about how O'Leary doesn't take care of my place. She turned and left, not as fast as Jeff or Jerome, but close. She said something about— Whoops!" Janice slipped off the chair. I grabbed her before she hit the floor.

"You okay?" I said, knowing she wasn't.

She giggled, then finished her beer. "Sure I can't shack up with you?"

"Afraid not," I said and became fascinated with my fish and chips, rather than looking her in the eye.

Marcia returned to ask if the food was okay and if we wanted something else to drink. I said I was fine. Fortunately, Janice said the same—for now.

"Janice, have any idea who may've started the fire?"

She took another sip, played with her napkin, while she looked out the window, then back to me. "Absolutely."

Not the answer I expected.

"Who?"

"My ex."

"Horace?"

"Absolutely."

"Why think it was him?"

"Don't think, know it was."

"How do you know?"

"You know he left me for a floozie in Mt. Pleasant."

"I'd heard you got a divorce. Didn't know the details."

"Left me with nothing except his dirty underwear. I had to move out of our nice condo in Mariner's Cay. I couldn't afford a two-bit ambulance-chasing lawyer to go after

Horace for my share of what he had. Finally found one who'd do it on contingency." She chuckled. "He must've graduated last in his class. The poor fella was desperate to get a client. I told him Horace weren't no millionaire, but the shyster said he'd take the case anyway."

Interesting, I thought, but it didn't get me any closer to the reason Horace would've set the fire.

"Janice, why would Horace torch the building?"

"My attorney might not know how to get good-paying clients or have a fancy-schmancy office in downtown Charleston, but I'll tell you what he's good at. He's about driven Horace bananas harassing him for money, telling Horace's employer how much of a deadbeat his employee is."

I'll give it one more chance.

"Janice, why do you think Horace burned the building?"

"Chris, I don't know how many ways I can say it. It's as clear as day. Can't you see, he's pissed at me. Wants me to know it. Clear as day." She nodded like it was, well, clear as day, then took another drink.

It may be clear to her, although, in her current condition, I doubted anything was clear. I hadn't had four, maybe five, maybe no telling how many beers, but nothing she'd said led me to believe Horace had set the fire. Could he have? I suppose. Someone set it.

I made a couple more efforts to see if Janice could clarify how she "knew" her ex started the fire. I would've been more successful if I'd asked her to conjugate the verb imbibe in Hungarian. Then, I asked if she wanted me to walk her to her hotel. She declined and said she was moving to the bar and having one more for the road. Fortunately, her hotel was close, and she wouldn't be driving. As I walked away, she slurred one more effort to ask if she could shack up with me. I hoped she took my ignoring the question as no.

Chapter Fourteen

I had trouble sleeping; must've gone over today's conversations with the two fire victims a dozen times. Rose was certain her ex wouldn't have set the fire, but it still struck me as too great a coincidence that he was on Folly the day before the conflagration. He'd be near or at the top of my list of potential arsonists. On the other hand, Janice was certain her ex set it but provided nothing supporting her proclamation.

I attributed most of my sleeping problems to questions bouncing around in my head. It wasn't necessarily the questions that kept me awake, the lack of answers was my nemesis. Tonight, now this morning was the perfect example.

After three hours sleep, I decided a brisk walk in brisk weather to the Lost Dog Cafe would be good for my health. It would wake me up, provide me with a hearty breakfast, and allow my brain to find answers to the questions that'd kept me awake. Rationalizing was one of my strengths.

The restaurant was nearly full, so I was lucky to get one of the small tables against the front wall. I was even luckier when Amber appeared, set a mug of coffee in front of me, then asked what she could do to make my day better. I told her if she joined me at the table, it would make my day better. She laughed and said she'd have to improve my day by serving, not joining me. I said I'd take what I could get. She must've been in a good mood because she asked if I wanted French toast rather than trying to get me to eat healthier. I said yes, she said she wondered why she wasted time asking.

Before breakfast arrived, Cindy LaMond arrived, saw me, then headed my direction.

"Going to invite me to join you?" she said, as she pulled up a chair, not waiting on an answer.

I said, "You're always welcome to join me, Chief."

"Weren't you getting ready to ask if you could buy me breakfast?"

"Of course, I was," I said, not seeing a wise alternative.

Amber was quick to the table with coffee for Cindy, who smiled at the server, and said, "I'll have what he's having."

Amber returned the smile, and said, "How do you know—"

"French toast?"

Amber chuckled then headed to put in Cindy's order.

Cindy blew across the mug then cautiously took a sip, before saying, "I hear you sauntered to the end of the pier with my younger sister while she deserted her poor son stuck doing manual labor for a slave driver at a local hardware store."

"It's no wonder why you're Chief. You know everything that happens on your six-mile-long, half-mile-wide slice of earth."

"It helps that my confidential informant is a lad of nine who spent two hours last night gushing about how much fun he had at his uncle's store, while his mother gushed, not for two hours, but nevertheless gushed about how great it was talking to an adult without her son hearing every word. The only thing I disagreed with was her calling you an adult. I let her stay in her fantasy world and didn't tell her about the true you."

"Kind of you."

"She was too happy for me to ruin her mood. I wish she could be that happy all the time. Since the divorce, she's been having migraines, bouts of depression, and in general, miserable."

"She was in a good mood yesterday."

"She's coming out of it some. I'm afraid her moods are affecting Luke. Rose tries to shield him from everything bad, but he's perceptive."

"It's been rough on her, plus the fire didn't help. Time will take care of many of the bad moods."

"I hope you're right Psychiatrist Chris." Cindy took another sip as Amber arrived with our matching breakfasts.

We each focused for a moment on food, before I said, "Learn anything new about the fire?"

"Like who set it?"

"That'd be informative."

She rolled her eyes. "If only that easy. I did learn something interesting about the landlord, Russell O'Leary." She took another bite.

I waited for her to continue, hoping I wouldn't have to ask what. I was pleased she was more open to talking about it than she'd been when she accused me of butting into her business the first time I asked about O'Leary.

She finally continued, "Don't you want to know what?"

"Chief, what'd you learn?"

"That's better. For starters, Mr. O'Leary is three months behind on the building's mortgage."

"Was it well-insured?"

"Excellent question, motive-detector Chris. Mr. O'Leary is not only a landlord, he's psychic. Two months ago, he increased coverage on the building."

"Making him a candidate for arsonist of the year."

"If you weren't so old, so very very old, I'd put you on the force."

She could've left out the *very very* part, but I'll let it go. "What else?"

"What else what?"

"When you mentioned he was three months behind on his mortgage, you said, 'For starters,' so what else did you learn?"

"Chris, I wish you'd stop listening to everything I say."

I shrugged.

She took a bite of French toast, then a sip of coffee before continuing, "Remember I told you he said he was in Atlanta at some get-rich seminar the day of the fire?"

"I remember. Did you already forget I listen to every-thing you say?"

"Smartass."

I smiled.

"He said the seminar was at the Westin Peachtree Plaza in downtown Atlanta. Said he didn't stay there because it cost too much. He claimed to have stayed at a nearby cheaper hotel he—surprise, surprise—can't remember the name of. Before you ask, he said he paid cash so there wouldn't be a record of him staying there even if he could remember the name."

"He would've registered under his name; probably showed ID even if he paid cash."

"Probably, but know how many hotels there are in Atlanta? Besides, his entire story sounds off."

"Sounds fishy, doesn't it?"

"Ya think?"

"I do. Now what?"

"I finish my breakfast, cuss myself all the way back to the office for eating more calories than the total one-day consumption of everyone combined in a small, farming community in Tanzania, then close my office door so I can take a nap."

"I was thinking more about what you're going to do about Russell O'Leary."

"Hell if I know."

"Sounds like a plan."

Chapter Fifteen

While Cindy and I didn't solve who set the fire, or for that matter, didn't solve anything other than hunger, she said her plan was to learn more about Russell O'Leary's financial situation. I said my plan was to take a nap. She told me she was jealous.

Charles was parked on my front step when I got home. His 1961 Schwinn bicycle leaned against my screened-in porch. He wore a royal blue and white sweatshirt with Sierra Nevada College under the outline of an eagle on the front, his Tilley, and in a touch of irony, tan khaki work pants, an activity he hadn't participated in for decades.

"You're not home," he said as he pointed over his shoulder at the door.

"Am now. Did you run out of places to hang out?"

"Thought if we're going to catch whoever torched the building, we should talk."

"Who said we were going to catch the arsonist?"

"Me. Didn't you hear me?"

Arguing with Charles is like arguing with a clump of seaweed.

"Want to come in where we can talk in a warm room?"

"Why do you think I'm here?"

I started to open the door, when Charles grabbed my arm, tilted his head toward Bert's Market.

"Isn't that Ty?"

The young man was standing at the corner of the building talking to a man I knew to be homeless. "Yes."

Charles pulled me toward the store. "Look, he wants to talk to us."

I wasn't certain how Ty's talking to a homeless man meant he wanted to talk to us, but I was interested in asking if he'd heard anything new about the fire.

Ty saw us coming, told the man he had to go, then greeted Charles and me with a smile.

"Hey, Charles, you're big into animals. Want to meet Lost?"

"You bet."

Ty grinned like he was going to show Charles the Hope diamond. The Miata was tucked in the back of the small, sandy lot. The car was parked next to a dilapidated sailboat that looked like it hadn't been in the water since the flood that took Noah and his boat for a ride.

The feline's proud papa unlocked the passenger door. It opened to the scraping sound of metal against metal, followed by a meow loud enough to have come from a wildcat. The grey kitten he lifted out of the car didn't look like it could've made such a loud noise, but it was the vehicle's only occupant.

"Meet Lost," Ty said as he handed Charles the kitten.

"Wow," Charles said, "a polydactyl."

That sounded like some sort of a dinosaur.

I said, "A what?"

Charles shook his head like he was having to teach a robin how to catch worms.

"Chris, you never cease to amaze me." He pointed Lost at me then lifted the kitten's leg in my direction. "Polydactyl.

A furry little critter with six toes on one or more of its paws. See?"

The front right paw did have six toes. "Oh," I said, indicating I didn't have a future as a veterinarian.

"Ernest Hemingway became a big fan after someone gave him a white one. He named it Snow White. Today there are about fifty descendants of his cats at his former house in Key West."

"Half are polydactyl," Ty added, further reinforcing my ignorance.

Charles had run out of trivia, so he turned to Ty and asked how he got Lost, more importantly, how he'd come up with the name.

Ty proceeded to share the same story he'd told me about coming to Folly on vacation, seeing a girl named Aimee, staying here while his friends returned to Baltimore, getting the job at Bert's. That was as far as he got when he was telling me the first time he'd talked about her, so I began paying closer attention.

Charles suggested we move out of the shadows of the large trees on two sides of the lot and move to where the sun was peeking through so we could stay warm. Ty and I followed him to the side of the dumpster where Charles leaned on the large, industrial-sized waste container, petting Lost the entire time.

"After Aimee and I talked a few times, I wanted to give her something. You know, something to bond our love."

Charles said, "Love?"

Ty lowered his head. "Well, not love exactly. I liked her. A guy I met in the store told me he had three kittens he was trying to find homes. I went to see them. Lo and behold, this little one was the cutest. Just seeing it made me think of Aimee. How could I not take it? Gave it to Aimee a few days later." He stopped, shook his head, then continued, "Fellas, how could I know she was allergic to cats?"

"That's too bad," Charles said.

"That wasn't the baddest part," Ty said. "She was engaged. She didn't have a diamond ring on her finger, so how was I to know?"

Charles repeated, "That's too bad."

"You can say that again. I figured I could overcome the fiancée, but not the cat allergy. That's how I ended up with this little one. Also, how it got its name. I got the cat, lost the girl, so I named it Lost."

Charles said, "Sounds like the right name."

I thought it would've been a much shorter story if he'd named it Six Toes.

I realized we'd been standing outside for a fairly long time. So, I said, "Ty, are we keeping you from work?"

"No, I'm off. I worked most of the night. Going to head to the Walmart parking lot so I can curl up in the car to get some sleep."

Charles handed Lost back to Ty, then said, "Before you go, have any idea who burned your building?"

Unlike many people who talk to Charles, Ty didn't appear thrown by the change of directions

"Wish I knew. If I did, I'd make him sleep in my car a few nights. That's punishment for putting all of us out of our homes."

Charles nodded. "So, no idea?"

"Not for certain, but if I was a betting man, I'd put a few bucks on Nick Matthews."

"Who's he?" I asked.

"Aimee's fiancée."

Charles said, "Why him?"

Lost began meowing so Ty put him back in the car, said he'd be with him in a minute, then scraped his feet on the sandy parking lot surface. "Well, you know how I said I figured I could overcome the fiancée but not Aimee's allergy?"

Charles nodded.

"Well, I didn't give up easily. I think Aimee told Nick

how I was showing interest. I heard he had a temper, beat up another guy who'd been sniffing around his gal. Now, he never said anything to me at first, but I saw him in the store a few times after Aimee quit to take a waitressing job at Planet Follywood. He gave me the evil eye. The last time I saw him, he walked close to where I was stocking the bread shelf, and said something like, "You'll get yours."

Charles said, "You think he torched your building because of that comment?"

"Like I said, I'd put money on it, on it. Not a lot, though."

Ty yawned and Lost made a moaning sound from the car. I figured our conversation was over. I thanked him for telling us about Lost.

Chapter Sixteen

Charles had to deliver a wetsuit from the surf shop to a man from Seattle renting a house on West Ashley Avenue. We walked to my house where he straddled his bike, pedaled off, leaving me standing in the yard realizing I had nowhere to be, nor anything to do. After spending what seemed like a zillion years experiencing the daily grind working in a large healthcare company, it was a good feeling. Something else that made me feel good was spending time with Barbara Deanelli, owner of Barb's Books, a small, used bookstore on Center Street. We've dated for a couple of years. I hadn't seen her in more than a week, so it was time to rectify that situation. While Charles was delivering a wetsuit, I could get some much-needed exercise walking to her store. The bookstore was housed in the same space that had previously been Landrum Gallery, a photo gallery I'd owned until it became clear that losing thousands of dollars a year wasn't the wisest use of my limited retirement savings. Residents and vacationers could live without my photographic prints, so I swallowed my pride and closed the business.

Two customers were browsing rows of books as I entered. Barb had strung multi-colored Christmas lights across the top of the shelves facing the entry. On a small table at the front of one of the aisles, she'd arranged books with colorful dust jackets in a shape intended to resemble a Christmas tree. Three boxes the size that'd hold jewelry were wrapped and set beside the book tree. It looked more like a pyramid-shaped pile of books than a Christmas tree, but I'd keep that observation to myself. The store's decorations fell far short of Cal's display, but the overall impression should put visitors in the spirit of the season.

One of the customers moved to the counter and handed Barb a credit card. Barb was in her mid-sixties, looked younger, stood my height at five-foot-ten, but much thinner. She had short black hair, hazel eyes, and a captivating smile currently being used on her customer.

She didn't notice me standing in the entry until she'd finished bagging the purchase. She used another of her captivating smiles on me. The remaining customer was still flipping through books, so Barb came around to me, gave me a kiss on the cheek, pointed to the door leading to the small office in the back of the store, then asked if I wanted coffee. I nodded. She said for me to fix each of us one, that she'd join me once the customer leaves.

When I'd had a business in the space, the room she called her office served more as a hangout for my friends, where a few of us could goof off, sip on a beverage, and discuss the latest happenings on the island. In other words, share gossip and good company. Barb had transformed the space to look more like a law office rather than a backroom in a retail business. She'd been a successful attorney in Pennsylvania before moving to Folly, so the law office motif was understandable.

I brewed two mugs of coffee in the Keurig, then settled in a comfortable chrome and black leather chair to wait. I began thinking of what Ty shared about who he thought started the fire. I didn't know anything about Aimee's fiancée other than what Ty had said, so I had no way of knowing if he was capable of such a drastic move to, umm, to what? Was the fire intended to harm Ty? If so, wouldn't the boyfriend have been able to see if Ty was working when he started it? If he only wanted to scare Ty away from Aimee, was he evil or reckless enough to burn a building, possibly harming other residents? Did Nick even make the comment Ty thought he'd made, or was Ty's imagination or guilt over trying to steal Nick's fiancée working overtime?

"Chris, are you asleep, or is your head somewhere else?" Barb said.

She was reaching for the coffee.

"Sorry, guess I was daydreaming."

Seasonal sounds from the Trans-Siberian Orchestra flowed from a Bose sound system on the desk.

"Were visions of sugar plums dancing in your head?" she asked, as she rolled her desk chair closer to the door so she could see if anyone entered the store.

I didn't know what a sugar plum was but didn't share my ignorance. "Nothing that jolly. How's business?"

"Excellent. I'm surprised. There aren't many vacationers this time of year, but the locals have been fantastic. Seems there's an uptick in book sales, not only here, but in stores everywhere."

That wasn't something I ever said about photographs when I had the gallery.

"Fantastic. Thought I'd stop to see if you wanted to grab supper this evening."

She smiled. "Thought you'd never ask."

We set a time and location, then she said, "I suppose you heard about the fire out past your house."

"Charles and I walked out there while they were fighting it."

"You chose a fire over the Christmas Parade. I'm shocked." She laughed, then added, "Not."

"We figured it was big when we saw Santa kicked off the fire engine."

"Did you know any of the residents?"

"I knew three before the fire. Didn't know them well but had talked with each a few times."

Barb's eyes narrowed as she stared at me. "Three before the fire. Now how many do you know?"

I told her about meeting Rose Wheeler, her son Luke, and their relationship to Chief LaMond.

"One of my customers told me yesterday the Chief had a sister and her apartment was in the building. Did you know about the sister before meeting her?"

"No, Cindy doesn't share much about her past."

Barb agreed then said, "Do you know Noelle Ward?"

I was surprised she mentioned the name. "Met her in the apartment's parking lot after the fire. Why?"

"She's one of my better customers. Came in a few times when she moved here, but in the last few months, she's been in several times a week. If you've talked to her, you probably know she's writing a novel. She's bought several mysteries, says for research." Barb chuckled. "First time in, she was in the mystery section, then noticed me nearby. She looked at me, or I think she did, I couldn't tell for sure since she had on sunglasses. She looked in my direction and said, I remember it almost verbatim, 'One day my book will be right here, someone will've read it, sold it to you, to be read again.' She seemed both confident and naïve at the same time. I like that gal."

"She told me she was writing a novel but didn't say much about it other than it's set on an island like Folly. The main character is a female private detective."

"I'm surprised she said that much. She's not loquacious. I haven't seen her since the fire."

"She's living out of her truck, so I imagine she has a lot on her mind."

"That's too bad. Have the others found places to live?"

"Rose and her son have temporarily moved in with Cindy and Larry. Janice Raque is staying at the Holliday Inn. I don't think the others have found anything."

Barb took a sip of coffee, then said, "What about Hope House?"

"It's full. I talked to Burl the day after the fire. He's looking for other options."

"That's too bad. I hear it was arson. Does Cindy know who set it?"

"Not that I've heard."

"You mean you're not pestering her daily to find out what she knows?"

"Why would you say that?"

She looked in her coffee mug, then smiled. "Because that's what you do."

"She doesn't know," I said. "It started in a vacant apartment on the first floor, so there's no way of knowing intent."

"I suppose she's taking a hard look at the landlord. That's where I'd start."

"Cindy's checking. Do you know him?"

"What's his name?"

"Russell O'Leary."

"Doesn't ring a bell. What's his financial situation?"

"Three months behind on the mortgage. Spends near nothing on maintenance."

"In my other life, our firm represented a guy accused of torching his five-story office building."

"Did he do it?"

"Jury didn't think so."

"What did you think?"

"My gut said he did, but like a good defense attorney, I never asked. He had more debt than Portugal. Are you and Charles trying to find out?"

"We're more interested in helping the displaced residents find housing."

"Good. Arsonists are dangerous. They can look like

anyone, can be part of society like everyone else. In other words, they don't look or act like crooks, don't wave guns around announcing their intentions."

"I'll keep that in mind."

"Any luck finding living arrangements for the displaced residents?"

I shook my head.

Barb jumped up from the chair, said she was needed in front, but before she left, said, "Chris, I have faith you'll be able to help them."

I wish I shared her confidence.

Chapter Seventeen

It was four hours before I was to meet Barb. The unseasonably warm weather was still hanging around, so I decided to continue my off and on effort to walk wherever I needed to go around town. One of the New Year resolutions I'd been considering was to eat healthier combined with exercise, which in my dictionary meant walking, not other activities they torture people with in gyms. Why wait until January to begin?

I walked across the bridge heading off Folly then continued past where Center Street morphs into Folly Road. I turned on Mariner's Cay Drive and past the guardhouse with a gate that'd keep out unauthorized vehicles but did nothing to stop foot traffic. Over the years, I had known a few people who lived in Mariner's Cay, including Janice Raque. The large development consisted of a handful of residential buildings plus a marina. Several condos displayed colorful strands of Christmas lights around the perimeter of the screened-in patios, and on three balconies there were popular blow-up cartoon characters wearing Santa hats. I didn't walk through the development often, but it provided a different view than I was used to on my wanders around Folly.

I leaned against the rail on the walkway to the marina to watch several docked mid-size boats gently sway to the movement of the Folly River. I didn't know which building Janice had lived in or if they had a boat but being here gave me a chance to think more about her theory that Horace started the fire. I'd seen Horace a couple of times when they'd been in Cal's but had never spoken to him. From what I'd heard, he and Janice were in a rocky relationship. They'd often argue while at Cal's so I could only imagine how they'd gotten along in the privacy of their condo. Janice had a temper and according to an acquaintance who's a member of the Folly Beach City Council, she attended council meetings and wasn't shy about sharing opinions. What I didn't know was if Horace had built enough resentment to burn her building, nor did any significant revelations come to me as I watched the water flow by.

I crossed the bridge on my return to Folly then detoured on my walk home to stop by the Post Office to pick up what normally consisted of a "once in a lifetime" opportunity to get hearing aids at "unbelievable" low prices, a chance to consolidate all my credit cards into one so I could save thousands of dollars a year, or countless other "fantastic" offers for senior citizens.

I deposited the two "amazing" offers *du jour* in the trash receptacle the Post Office wisely placed near the exit. I thought about walking next door to Pewter Hardware to see Larry but rejected the idea after noticing his lot full and spaces along the road filled with vehicles. Cindy wasn't kidding when she said this was his busiest time of year.

Across the street, on a hill that led to the Folly River Park, Noelle Ward was seated in the shade. She was staring at her phone pointed toward the Post Office. At least, I assumed that's where her eyes were directed since I couldn't tell for sure. She wore her oversized sunglasses, a black sweatshirt, black jeans, and a dark gray jacket. I waved and she gave a tentative return wave as I walked over.

"Planning on robbing the Post Office?" I said, hoping to solicit a smile.

"They don't carry enough cash," she said, then laughed.

"Good point. I'm Chris, by the way. What brings you out here?"

She looked around, stood, and brushed off the back of her jeans. "I remember your name from the other day. I'm Noelle. It's getting cool in the shade. Want to move up there in the sun?"

"Lead on," I said.

She moved to the edge of the street, then fifty or so yards toward Center Street, before following the paved footpath into the park. The center of the small park was in full sun, so we sat at one of the picnic tables overlooking the city's Christmas tree.

She stretched her arms over her head, then turned to me. "Bet you're wondering what I was doing back there?"

"It crossed my mind."

"When we met, I told you I was writing a novel. Want to hear what it's about?"

That didn't answer why she was staring at the Post Office, but I was curious about her book. "Sure. You said it was a murder mystery. You were living here for research."

She smiled. "Good memory for someone who doesn't read."

I was surprised she remembered, especially since I told her while we were staring at her burned-out apartment building.

"You're the first author I've met, so I'm intrigued."

"My protagonist is a thirty-year-old, single, African-American female who's a fledgling private detective in a small, predominantly white town in Georgia."

"Sounds a lot like someone I know."

"Except for the private detective and Georgia part."

"Suppose that's why it's a novel and not non-fiction."

She smiled, which I was beginning to see as one of her most attractive and often-used traits.

"Shonda Black, the protagonist, opened a detective agency several months earlier and hasn't attracted any clients. She's depressed, on the verge of giving up, when a fifteen-year-old black teenager walks into her office. He came to her because she's the only black private eye in town." She hesitated, then said, "Let me back up a little. There'd been a bank robbery a week earlier in the next town over. Now to the kid walking in. He tells Shonda he saw the robbers in town when they were in a small grocery. It's a lot like Bert's Market. The boy, I call him Gabriel, tells Shonda he went to the police about seeing the bad guys. They laughed at him, told him he was seeing things, that the robbers had fled the state. That was why he was at her door. As you can probably guess, Gabriel doesn't have money to pay Shonda. She figured if she could catch the robbers the publicity would attract clients, the paying kind. I don't need to tell you more for you to guess Shonda catches the robbers. The end. My dream, only a dream at this point, is to make it the first book in a Shonda Black Mystery Series."

"That's great, Noelle."

"Thank you. Now all I need to do is finish writing it, write the second book in the series, and collect my Nobel Prize in Literature." She laughed and tapped my leg.

I laughed with her, then said, "Is a Post Office in your book?"

"Sorry, I drifted a little from telling you what I was doing."

"It was interesting."

"Interesting enough for you to read it when it comes out?"

"I'll not only read it, I'll write a letter to the Nobel Prize committee telling them they could stop looking. Your book is the winner."

She chuckled. "You make up stuff better than I do."

"The Post Office?"

"Research. Like I told you, the city where Shonda Black works is like Folly Beach. Small town, beach community, full of quirky characters. Most small towns are populated by people who are more similar than different, but I grew up in Missouri, no ocean nearby. Up until I decided to write the next Great American Novel, I wasn't good at observing people, how they dress, how they act, how they talk. I moved into the apartment that's now charcoal because it's like the place Shonda lives. Heck, I even bought the Dodge Ram 1500 pickup because it seemed like the kind Shonda would drive."

"You were researching people leaving the Post Office?"

"Yes. I've spent most every hour I'm not working watching people. Watching how they eat, how close they sit to each other, how some lean over when talking to someone else, how others speak loud not caring if their voice irritates others around them. I'm studying how they shop, how they move over so others can pass them in aisles, or on the sidewalks, all sorts of scenarios." She held up her phone. "I'm also taking videos so I can study people later."

"You're taking this seriously."

"I'm good at my day job, enjoy writing ad copy. If I want to be a good novelist, I have to study all phases of the process. One thing we do in the ad agency is to use focus groups to observe how people react to our various ads. For lack of better terms, Folly Beach is my large focus group."

"I'm not the person to ask about writing a novel, but it appears you know what you need to do."

"Time will tell, Chris."

"Changing the subject, have you found somewhere to live?"

"My Dodge condo."

"I was thinking somewhere without wheels."

"Not yet. I'm making the most of it. Think I'll add that

Shonda's apartment gets burned by the bank robbers, so she has to live in her truck."

"That's turning lemons into lemonade."

She laughed, "Hmm, turning lemons into lemonade. I need to put that in an ad someday." She turned serious. "Did I give you my number the other day?"

I patted my phone. "Right here."

"Living in a truck is good for research, not so good for my back. You'll let me know if you hear of any apartments?"

"Absolutely."

She started to rise.

"Noelle, one more thing. When we met and were talking about the fire, you said something about being warned. What'd you mean?"

"Oh, it was nothing."

She'd already used that line on me. Time to press. Charles would be proud of me.

"Noelle, it wasn't nothing or you wouldn't have said it. Please tell me what you meant?"

Her hand gripped the bottom of the picnic table's seat. I was afraid she wasn't going to respond until she said, "Two weeks before the fire, I found a note under the windshield wiper. It was printed on that kind of paper with all the little squares."

"Graph paper?"

"Yeah. It said, this is paraphrasing, if you know what's good for you, you'll pack up and get off Folly."

"Was that all?"

"Yes."

"You have an idea who it may've been from?"

"Wish I did."

"Had you angered anyone?"

"Not that I know of." She removed her sunglasses and squeezed the bridge of her nose. "Not anyone."

"Any ideas?"

"My first thought was someone put it there by mistake. It's not the only black Dodge Ram in town."

"Why did you change your mind?"

"Mine's the only truck like it at the apartment or at nearby houses. How could someone get it confused? I then thought it could've been from someone who saw me nosing around, watching people, shooting video. They could've been doing something wrong and thought I caught them. Something like that. Or it simply could've been someone who doesn't like black folk."

"Do you still have the note?"

She shook her head then shrugged. "It was in the apartment."

"Did you tell the police?"

"No. It'd be like Gabriel in my book going to the police. Nothing could be learned from a note on a piece of scrap paper. Unlike Gabriel, I'm trying to forget it."

"Do you think the person who left it started the fire?"

She stood a second time. "Chris, I don't know what to think," she hesitated, then added, "these are nice Christmas decorations."

That appeared to be her way of ending talk about the note. "They are nice."

"I'd better be going," she said, reached out and shook my hand. "Nice talking to you."

I agreed with her.

She left leaving me with more questions than when I arrived.

Chapter Eighteen

arb and I were to meet at Wiki Wiki Sandbar, one of
Folly's newest, and undoubtedly largest restaurants,
located a block from my cottage. I was standing
outside the multi-level, tiki-themed restaurant ten minutes
before our scheduled rendezvous. Barb, unlike Charles who
considered thirty-minutes early to be on time, arrived five
minutes later. She wore a lightweight tan jacket over a red
blouse, black slacks, and a smile that brightened the early-
evening darkness.

"Been waiting long?" she said then kissed my cheek.

"A couple of minutes. Hungry?"

She put her arm behind my back and nudged me
toward the entry. "Starved. This is my first time here. How
about you?"

"Once, but only to the bar. It's interesting."

She pointed to the other side of the L shaped structure.
"One of my customers told me the style is mid-century
modern, said there are five distinct rooms."

Before I could get a more-detailed architectural description of the building, a bubbly hostess escorted us to what she

called the Wave Room where we were seated under a sculpture featuring hundreds of glass balls anchored to the ceiling. We were handed menus and told Karen would be our server.

I looked around the modern-looking room, mid-century or otherwise, while Barb focused on the menu. As promised, Karen appeared at the table before I'd finished gazing around the room. She asked if we wanted something to drink. Barb, who'd already studied the drink choices, said she'd have an Aloha from the Edge, which a quick peek at the menu told me was vodka and passionfruit. I didn't want Barb to have to wait while I agonized over the menu trying to figure out what each drink was, so I said a glass of Cabernet. Karen headed to the bar while Barb continued studying the menu. I envied her metabolism. She could eat like a sumo wrestler yet never gain an ounce. She pointed at my menu and told me to stop looking around and decide what to order.

The server returned with our drinks as I made my decision, thank goodness. Barb ordered a Korean short rib, I went with the pork ribs, mainly because I was more familiar with the ribs than some of the other items.

With the pressure of ordering at a new restaurant out of the way, Barb asked what I'd been doing since I left the store earlier today. She added, what I was doing while she was hard at work.

I told her about my chance meeting with Noelle and what she'd said about the note on her truck.

"Think she was clueless about who put it there or why?"

I nodded. "Sounded convincing. I had to push to get her to tell me about it. I don't know if she was worried about it or thought it was so inconsequential it wasn't important enough to mention."

"Next time she's in, I'll see if I can get her to talk about it. Does she know we're dating?"

"Don't know. Why?"

"If she does, it'd give me a better entrée into the discussion about the note since you could've shared the information with me."

"True."

This was the first time Barb hadn't tried to discourage me from getting involved in something that clearly was none of my business, something best left to the police. I wanted to point out the historic moment but thought it wouldn't be wise, besides, Karen was at the table with our food. Little could keep my companion from grabbing a fork and digging in.

A few bites later, I said, "If you get a chance, check with some of your customers to see if they know of an apartment for Noelle. She's looking for what she calls a dump, something in line with where she was. She wants to stay in character with the protagonist in her novel."

Barb smiled. "So, you want me to ask customers if they know a dump for rent?"

"You could say it more lawyerly, something like a budget-priced rental unit."

Two bites later, she said, "Did Noelle think the fire was set because she didn't take the note's advice?"

"She didn't say. It seems more than a coincidence, although from what I've heard, she's not the only resident who'd upset someone enough to set the fire."

"Chris, remember I told you I defended an arsonist in my previous life?"

"Yes."

"To give him a proper defense, I researched arsonists. The consensus of experts profiled most as young males."

"That narrows it down to a few hundred folks over here."

"Chris, there's more, if you'll let me finish."

"Please do," I said before taking a sip of wine.

"In addition to being young guys, more than seventy-five percent were Caucasian."

I wanted to say that didn't eliminate many of Folly's young males. A dollop of wisdom made me nod instead of speaking.

"They also score relatively low on intelligence tests."

"Did that profile help with your client?"

"Sort of."

"Meaning?"

"He's Caucasian, a graduate of one of the nation's top business schools, plus, is in his late fifties. The profile of an arsonist typically refers to a serial arsonist, someone who's obsessed with starting fires. My client was accused of being a one-off arsonist. He allegedly set the fire for money, not kicks. There was no history of him starting others."

"So how did the profile sort of help in his defense?"

"Reasonable doubt. If I cluttered the defense with other possibilities, regardless of how remote, jurors' minds could be influenced."

"Were they?"

"I told you, he was found not guilty."

I smiled. "Not necessarily innocent."

She returned the smile.

"How does this relate to the apartment fire?"

"Are the police looking for a serial arsonist or someone who set the fire for a reason other than seeing a massive fire? Have there been other unexplained fires on Folly or in the area in recent days, weeks, months?"

"If there've been others, the apartment fire may've had nothing to do with Noelle or other residents. The motivation of the person starting it was to create a fire."

"You're catching on. Want dessert?"

A change of subject, a hint. Barb was motioning for the server before I could say yes.

Dessert was ordered, which led to more pleasant discussions, overall, a pleasant evening. On my way home after escorting Barb to her condo, I decided to call Chief LaMond in the morning to ask if she had any update on the fire. Additionally, I could ask if she was aware of other recent unsolved fires.

Chapter Nineteen

The Chief answered with, "Good morning, Chief LaMond speaking. How may I be of assistance?"

Her salutation couldn't have been clearer than if she'd said, "I can't talk. If you don't hang up, I'll have you arrested for pissing me off."

"Call when you get a chance."

"Of course."

I didn't expect to hear from her soon, so in quest of healthy exercise, I walked next door to Bert's for a heart-unhealthy cinnamon Danish plus coffee. I didn't realize until I was out the door that the weather had tanked overnight. The unseasonably warm December temperatures were gone, replaced by what must've been the mid-forties. To someone from the North, it would've felt mild, but to Lowcountry residents, it felt like the deep freeze. It was easier to keep heading to the store than return home for a jacket. In addition to getting breakfast, I also wanted to see how Ty was doing.

I succeeded in getting the Danish and coffee, but Ty was

nowhere to be seen. According to Caroline, another of Bert's helpful employees, Ty had the day off.

I was heading to the register, then home to eat my Danish in peace, when I heard a familiar voice coming from behind the nearby shelf.

"Morning, Mr. Photo Man. I see you're eating healthy as usual."

It's been a while since Charles greeted me with the Mr. Photo Man moniker. On a strange level, it was refreshing to hear. He wore a heavy gold sweatshirt with Wyoming Cowboys in brown letters on the front. No, I wasn't going to ask about the sweatshirt.

"Got to keep my energy level up," I said, "What're you doing on this side of town?"

Charles lived about seven blocks past Bert's but seldom frequented the store.

"Exercise. Teddy Roosevelt said, 'Let us rather run the risk of wearing out than rusting out.'"

Another of Charles's quirks is quoting United States Presidents. He says reading what they said keeps his mind active. I've attributed it to him wanting to be different, something he was without quoting anyone.

"There's little chance of you rusting." His hands were empty, so I added, "You getting something or working on wearing out."

"Out for a walk, but now that I see you, let me tell you about a brilliant idea I had in the middle of the night."

"Tell me, then I'll decide if it's brilliant."

"I'll go with you to your house where you can leave your breakfast, then we can saunter around town while you're listening to my brilliant idea."

I had nothing better to do, besides, I could get a jacket if we were going to saunter around. Charles said he'd get coffee while I paid. Five minutes later, I'd upgraded my wardrobe, took a bite of Danish, then headed toward the Folly Pier with my friend.

I was beginning to question the wisdom of walking on the pier. The stiff ocean breeze made it feel colder than the upper-forties. Why couldn't Charles tell me his brilliant idea in a restaurant or my cottage? We'd walked halfway to the end of the pier, when he said, "Got another idea."

"Is it as brilliant as the one you haven't shared yet?"

"Brilliant, no. Warmer, yes. Why don't we go to the hotel's lobby?"

I didn't know what his other idea was, but to my shivering body, his latest sounded brilliant.

Christmas decorations were scattered throughout the lobby of the oceanfront hotel. Jay, a friend who's worked at the hotel for years, greeted us with, "Merry Christmas, gentlemen. You two spreading tidings of comfort and joy?"

"Always," Charles said.

I wasn't as confident, so I shook Jay's hand and said it was nice seeing him before telling him we were getting out of the cold.

"You're always welcome here. Let me know if there's anything you need," Jay said and left us in the seating area off the lobby.

"Okay, Charles, let's hear your idea."

He warmed his hands by rubbing them together, gazed around the empty area, then said, "Brilliant idea. Ty has a cat, cute little thing." He stopped and nodded.

"Yes."

"Who else do you know with a cat?"

I wasn't ready for a quiz and took too long to answer.

"Well, who?"

"I've got it. Good old Mr. Sarnaw. He used to walk that big black cat with a leash down the sidewalk. First time I'd seen someone walking a cat."

Charles shook his head. "That would've been a good guess, except Mr. Sarnaw died in July. Don't worry, his neighbor took the cat to a friendly shelter where it was adopted. Don't know if the leash was part of the deal."

"Who are you talking about with a cat?"

"I'll give you one more guess. Here's another clue. Who do you know who has a pet snake?"

"Martha Wright," I said, feeling stupid not thinking of her first.

Charles and I met Martha a year ago when Dude Sloan's love of his life Pluto disappeared. After an island-wide search by numerous people, we discovered Martha had taken him in to join her menagerie which included some dozen animals. Martha gladly returned Pluto, apologized for inadvertently thinking he was a stray, and left a lasting impression on me, primarily because of her pet boa constrictor.

"Good guess."

"What about her?"

"She's got cats, Ty has a cat. Martha has a big house, Ty's living in a tiny-tiny four-wheel apartment. Now, the brilliant part. Martha takes in strays. Ty's a stray. Brilliant, right?"

"You think Martha will let Ty move in with her because she takes in strays?"

"How could she not?"

Truth be told, it wasn't a horrible idea. Far from brilliant, but not horrible.

"Why would she?"

"She's an eighty-year-old widow; her poor hubby bit the dust four years ago; she's living in that big house by herself. That lady needs a man around. Ty's almost a man, will do in a pinch. All you have to do is ask her."

"Me?"

"Don't worry, I'll go with you."

Before I could list thirty reasons it'd be a bad idea, the phone rang.

"Okay, troublemaker, what'd you want?" said the less-than-gleeful Cindy LaMond.

"I was talking with Barb at supper about the fire."

Cindy interrupted, "Cheery dinner talk. You sure know how to warm a woman's heart. Get it, fire, warm?"

"Yes, Cindy. Barb was talking about an arson suspect she'd defended. She said there were certain characteristics of most arsonists but was mainly talking about serial arsonists. Her client allegedly set fire to an office building he owned for the insurance."

She interrupted again, "Think you can get to the reason for pestering me before I retire?"

Charles waved for me to put the phone on speaker. Instead of having to repeat everything the Chief said, I hit the speaker icon.

"If the person who set the fire did it because he simply liked to start fires, it may not have anything to do with the residents or the building's owner."

Charles couldn't stand being left out of the conversation. "That makes sense, doesn't it, Chief?"

I heard an audible sigh on the other end of the line. "Chris, did you get a damned talking parrot, or was that your half-wit friend?"

"Cindy, you know the answer."

"That's what I was afraid of. Did I miss the point of your call somewhere in all that?"

"It's a simple question. Have there been other suspicious fires in the Charleston area?"

"I'm sure there were some in the 1800s. Suppose they were caused by the Yanks, or was it Rebels? Civil War history gets me confused. Charles, you were around then, which was it?"

I smiled and turned to Charles, who said, "Chief, I think Chris means something more recent."

She said, "No."

"No what?" Charles said.

She sighed again. "Did you forget the question? No suspicious fires in the last year or so."

I said, "You sure?"

"Yes, that's what the arson investigator told me when I asked the same question the day he told me it was arson. That means you can throw out the profile for the typical serial arsonist. You know, the profile you and that lovely lady discussed. The same lady who, for reasons beyond anything I can understand, enjoys spending time with you."

I was thinking of a humorous retort, although it would've been wasted. She'd hung up.

Chapter Twenty

Martha's house was four long blocks from the Tides, so I suggested we drive. Charles said it was a great idea, which, I suppose, wasn't as good as his "brilliant" idea that Martha would take Ty, the stray. Her house was a large, two-story, relatively new structure that backed up to the ocean. Martha met us with a look she probably would've given a Mormon missionary. She was no more than five-foot-two, slightly overweight, with dark black hair pulled in a bun. She opened the door a crack.

"Young men, I don't want any."

It was hard to understand what she'd said for the barking dogs nudging the door.

Charles, who didn't accept the concept of rejection, stepped forward, tipped his Tilley, then said, "Martha, I'm Charles Fowler. We met last year when we came looking for Pluto, Dude Sloan's dog. We've also talked in church a time or two."

I hadn't remembered, but Martha was a member of First Light where Charles was a regular.

Martha leaned on her cane, smiled, then said, "Oh, I

remember. Sorry, I thought you were some of those church kids going door-to-door, or worse, traveling salesmen. Give me a second to put my killer dogs in another room." She chuckled as she said it. It was at least two minutes before the door opened all the way. "Come in."

"Martha," Charles said as we followed her in the door. "You remember my friend, Chris Landrum, don't you?"

"Sure," she said, in a tone that failed to sound sincere. "Shall we retire to the sitting room?"

The room looked the same as it had a year ago, resembling an animal playhouse more than a sitting room. A three-foot-high, triple deck, carpeted cat tower occupied one corner. On a small table beside the cat tower, there was an oak cabinet like one I remembered from my childhood that contained a record player, or turntable, as they're called today. Assorted animal toys were scattered around. My eyes immediately went to the large aquarium beside one of the three wingback chairs. I was relieved to see the aquarium occupied, relieved because it held a boa constrictor that had to be a mile long. Okay, that's an exaggeration. On a previous visit, Martha shared she often let Squeezy—no, I'm not making that up—roam around the room. She'd said roam, I translated it to mean slither. I took the chair farthest from the aquarium.

Martha had already taken the second farthest chair from Squeezy, so Charles slowly lowered himself in the dog and cat hair infested remaining seat.

"Charles, want to hold Squeezy?"

"Perhaps another time, Martha. Speaking of pets, how many do you have now?"

Instead of answering, she popped up from the chair. "Fellas, want a hot toddy?"

One of the things I'd remembered about our visits last year, was her fondness for the drink, regardless of the time of day.

"No thank you, Martha," Charles said, and repeated, "Perhaps another time."

She lifted the top of the oak cabinet, fiddled with the record player, then said, "Then you can't say no to music of the season."

Neither Charles nor I had time to say, "Perhaps another time," before Alvin and the Chipmunks began their version of "Here Comes Santa Claus." I prayed the volume control wasn't broken since between the scratches on the record and the less-than-appealing voices of the three animated anthropomorphic chipmunks, a Boeing 757's engine would've been quieter.

Martha screamed, "My animals love the Chipmunks. I've got both of their Christmas albums."

Or, I thought that's what she said. The last part was drowned out by Alvin.

"Martha," I yelled, "don't you think it's a little loud?"

She tilted her head my direction, cupped her hand behind her ear, then reached in the cabinet. The volume lowered to bar-conversation levels.

"Sorry, want to repeat that, Chris? Couldn't hear you."

Now that my ears stopped ringing, I didn't feel the need to repeat what I'd said. Instead, I repeated Charles's question. "How many pets do you have?"

She returned to her chair, rubbed her chin, before saying, "Let's see. It's hard to keep up, you know." She looked toward the door where she'd herded her dogs when we arrived. "Four dogs: Pooch, Lady, Bowser, Ink Spot. No, it's five. I keep forgetting Little Dog. Still have three cats. I'm sure of that. There's Cat One, Cat Two, and Crazy." She shook her head. "Then, got to count Paul."

Charles said, "Your parrot?"

She nodded. "Still got to keep him upstairs, you know. His language would make a sailor blush. Danged hard to teach an old parrot new tricks, or words."

"Know what you mean," Charles said as he glanced my way.

I didn't know, didn't want to know if he wanted reinforcement, or was calling me old. "Martha," I said, "you still have Davy Crockett?"

She lowered her head, glanced around the room like someone was hiding behind one of the chairs, then said, "You know it's illegal to have a pet raccoon?"

I didn't know for certain, but she'd told us that before. I nodded.

"So, I can't count Davy," she said, winked, then whispered, "He's still around."

I nodded a second time.

Charles looked at the aquarium. "Don't forget Squeezy."

"Never, Charles, never." She smiled. "Sure you don't want to hold him?"

"Not this time, Martha."

Alvin and the Chipmunks were now butchering "Silver Bells." Time to move along.

"Martha, we stopped by to—"

She sat up straight in her chair. "I didn't do it."

"Do what?" I asked, figuring it was a reasonable question.

"Whatever you're here to accuse me of, young man."

"Martha, we're not here to accuse you of anything other than being a wonderful lady with some great pets," said Charles the suck-up.

"Oh. The last time you showed up at my door uninvited you accused me of dognapping, stealing that weird hippie's adorable Australian Terrier. Figured you had me on your suspect list if anything bad happens to critters."

"Now Martha," I said, "we know you were doing the right thing with Pluto. He didn't have a collar, he was hungry, you took him in."

"A good deed," Charles added. "Taking in strays is

admirable. I've told everyone I know how kind you were to little Pluto."

Told you he was a suck-up. Before Charles pulled out a violin, started singing more praise for Martha, in stark contrast to Alvin trying to sing "Jingle Bells," I'd better refocus the conversation.

"Martha, did you hear about the big, apartment building fire?"

"Lordy, Chris, how could I miss it? It was a block over. Smoke everywhere, sirens blaring. Made my dogs howl nearly as good as Alvin's singing."

"Do you know Ty Striker?"

"Can't say I do."

"He's in his early twenties, thin with long black hair, wears it a ponytail. Works at Bert's."

"Doesn't ring a bell. What about him? Isn't missing, is he?"

Charles piped up, "Not missing, but he's missing a place to live. He was one of the residents of the building that ain't there no more."

The record player groaned, then clanked, dropping another record on the turntable. Different record, same "performers." The Chipmunks started singing "Jingle Bell Rock."

A high-pitched howl came from the other room.

Martha smiled and nodded toward the room holding her dogs. "Bowser loves this song." She turned to Charles. "Where were we?"

"We were telling you about Ty. He has an adorable kitten, it's got six toes on one of its front paws."

Martha beamed. "A Polydactyl. Just like Hemingway's in Key West."

Charles nodded and I wondered if I was the only person in the country who didn't know about the six-pawed felines.

"Exactly," Charles said.

"What's its name?"

"Lost."

"Oh my, Ty's kitten's lost like that weird hippie's pup."

"No, Martha, Ty's cat is named Lost."

"Oh my, that's a ridiculous name for a cat."

That coming from someone who has cats named Cat One, Cat Two, and a dog named Little Dog.

"It's unusual," I said. "Charles, you want to tell Martha what you were thinking about Ty?"

"That's okay, Chris. You go ahead."

Thanks, coward.

"Martha, we were thinking." I generously didn't say Charles was thinking. "You love animals and have this wonderful large house. It had to be hard to lose your husband a few years back. I bet occasionally things need repairing or there are other things that could use a man's touch."

"You can say that again."

This was going better than expected, I thought.

"We were thinking you could let Ty move in one of your spare rooms until he finds somewhere permanently. He's sleeping in his tiny car."

Her hand flew to her mouth. It may've been my imagination, but her face seemed to turn white, snow-white in the vernacular of the season.

"Heavens to Betsy, no way, young man." Her hand left her face and gripped the arm of her chair. "What would Tommy and Dixie think? Me shacking up with a man. Lordy, no."

Tommy was her late husband, Dixie was her friend who lived across the street.

Alvin was singing "Have Yourself a Merry Little Christmas," but it was doing nothing to make my season bright, my heart feel light, or my troubles out of sight.

Charles appeared to wait for me to continue my sales pitch. I didn't.

"Martha," he said, "I'm certain Dixie would understand. She knows how you like to take in strays. You could consider Ty another stray."

"Young man, I've had a wonderful, long life. I'm not going out of it being accused of being a cougar."

From my limited understanding, Martha would be thirty years or so outside the range of cougars, women seeking younger men.

"Martha, I understand." I didn't. "Charles and I wanted to ask because we knew how kind and caring you were. We don't want to take more of your valuable time."

I stood to leave, when she said, "Now if that Ty fellow wants to bring Lost—I still can't believe he named a cat that —by to visit, that'd be fine. Cat One, Cat Two, and Crazy might like a visitor every now and then."

I said I'd share that information with Ty.

Alvin had stopped singing, Bowser had stopped barking harmony, and I felt anything but in the Christmas spirit as we left Martha leaning on her cane waving bye.

Chapter Twenty-One

"I need a hot toddy after that," Charles said as we got in the car.

"How about a beer at Cal's?"

"A close second."

It was early afternoon when we entered Cal's. The tables were vacant, but three men were seated at the bar drinking lunch. Loretta Lynn was singing "Silver Bells" from the jukebox that would've given Martha's record player a run for being the oldest music machine on the island. Cal was delivering a beer to one of the men. He saw us enter, nodded, then pointed around the room, his way of saying sit anywhere.

We chose a table close to the bar so Cal wouldn't have to go far to serve us. He seldom complained, but his knees were on their last legs, pun intended. Instead of asking what we wanted, he arrived at the table with a Budweiser for Charles, a glass of Cabernet for me.

"Hey, Cal," Charles said, "got anything by Alvin and the Chipmunks on the jukebox?"

Cal plopped down in a chair then squinted at Charles. "Pard, you lost your mind?"

"Don't think so, why?"

"Christmas is my favorite time of year. It's plum near here. This room's decorated, all cheery, festive, ready for that wonderful holiday. Then you come in and suck all the cheer out of me."

"Cal," I said, "what're you talking about?"

Cal looked at the bar to see if any customers needed anything, then back to us. "Back in the day when I was a fledgling country star, eighteen years old, with my first hit 'End of the Story,' I was traveling all over the South singing anywhere that'd have me." He looked at the ceiling. "Ah, those were the days. Anyway, was 1962, lord, I played a lot of bars. Not paying gigs, but tips weren't bad. They also let me sell my records. Most had jukeboxes like mine." He pointed to his ears. "Know what I had to subject these here listening devices to?"

It was beginning to make sense. "Alvin and the Chipmunks?"

"Those damned, fake, striped rodents, singing 'The Alvin Twist.' That horrible song, if you can call it a song, came out the same year my hit flew up the charts." He shook his head. "Can still hear '*If you wanna be smart, if you wanna be wise, take up your fun and exercise. Everybody, do the Alvin Twist.*' Know why I can still hear it?"

Charles, of course, had to know. "Why?"

"Because those damned rodents were singing it on every jukebox in every bar I went in. Over and over, over and over. It got worse after that. Those freakin' rodents came out with their first Christmas album the same year. Talk about kicking Christmas in the head. Why in holy vinyl are you asking about those damned rodents?"

Charles smiled. "So, you don't have any of their Christmas songs on the jukebox?"

Elvis, not Alvin, began singing "Blue Christmas," and I

was beginning to think we would have a blue one with Cal and his memories.

"It's not important, Cal," I said. "We wanted to stop to see if there's anything we can do to help you get ready for your party?"

Charles looked at me like, "We were?"

"I appreciate it, boys. Think everything's on schedule. My decorations are up. I got some volunteers coming to help with the food and drinks. Don't know how many folks have told me they're going to be here, but it's a bunch. Thanks for offering."

A customer whistled for Cal. The owner said he'd better earn his keep then headed to the bar.

Charles watched him go. "Think I ought to invite Martha to the Christmas party? She could bring her Chipmunks Christmas albums."

That didn't deserve an answer. I took a sip of wine before saying, "Think we need to talk about who might've set the fire."

"Whoa," Charles said, "you an alien that's done invaded Chris's body? I'm the guy who always wants to butt in police business. Chris always tells me it's none of my concern, that I need to leave it to the cops. What'd you do with my friend?"

"You're right. I know—"

"Of course, I'm right. Umm, remind me why?"

"Charles, I know each of the building's residents. Don't know them well, but it seems that I, we, might know more about them than the police know. It's worth discussing."

"Talk on," he said then took a long draw on his beer.

"Janice Raque is convinced her husband set the fire."

"Why would he? They're divorced, he's moved on with some floozy in Mt. Pleasant, Janice ain't around to fight with him every time they're in here, or wherever else they're butting heads."

"She thinks it's because her lawyer is on Horace's case to get her more support."

Charles said, "You buy that?"

"No, mainly because like you said, the fire was set during the day when there was little chance anyone would've been in the building, little chance anyone would've been hurt."

"Could've been to send a message. Leave me alone or I'll get you. A blazing building would be a powerful way to deliver a message."

"That's possible, but I'd put him low on my list."

"Okay, moving along, who would've wanted to burn Rose and Luke's apartment out from under them?"

I hadn't shared what Rose told me about her ex being on Folly the day before the fire. I took another sip knowing I'd need it once Charles started haranguing me for not telling him sooner. I took a deep breath then shared what Rose had told me.

Charles had started to take a drink, instead, he set the bottle on the table, more accurately, pounded the bottle on the table. "You didn't think that was important enough … never mind. Rose's hubby sounds too stupid to be a bank vice president if he thought she'd come crawling back to him if her apartment went up in smoke."

"I agree. I mentioned him because we know he was here the day before the fire. Don't you think that's a big coincidence?"

"Do we know if he was here the day of the fire?"

"No."

Charles pointed in the direction of the ocean. "I'll nose around the Tides. My innocent-looking face makes people tell me stuff they shouldn't."

His countless questions didn't hurt him getting information either. "Good idea, although there are many other places he could've stayed."

"Nick Matthews," Charles said.

"Aimee's fiancée?"

"He could've done it. Didn't Ty tell us he mumbled something like you'll get yours?"

"Yes."

"There you go. Suspect number one."

"How're we going to find out more about him?" I said out loud, although talking more to myself.

Charles picked my phone off the table, pointed it at me. "Call Cindy. Maybe Nick has a record or is known by the local cops for burning buildings."

"I'll call her later."

"Don't worry, I won't let you forget."

Cal returned to the table. "Get you boys anything else to drink?"

Charles looked at his bottle. "Not yet. What if we want something to eat?"

"I'll point you to some good restaurants," Cal said, then pushed his Stetson back on his head. "Neil ain't here, and I'm not in the mood for fixin' food."

"Speaking of Neil," Charles said, "know if he pissed off anyone enough to torch his building?"

"Don't know about him, but if it had a trio of damned chipmunks living there, I would've torched it myself."

Fifty years later, Alvin and his compatriots were still under Cal's skin.

"What about Neil?" I said to bring him back to the twenty-first century.

"I asked him. He said it could've been his old boss. Seems Neil turned the cheatin', thievin' crook's name over to the IRS. The feds came down on him like a pile of manure."

Neil had told Charles and me the same thing.

"That'd be a strong motive," Charles said.

I said, "He also mentioned something about a man he threw out of the bar."

"Don't remember that," Cal said.

"No," Charles said, "the bar in Charleston where he's a bouncer."

Cal said, "I'd stick with the IRS busted boss. Guys get thrown out of bars all the time. They bitch and groan, threaten everyone around, then sober up, before starting all over again. No biggie."

"You're probably right," I said. "Has Neil found a place to live?"

"Far as I know, he's still at the Holliday Inn. Says it costs him nearly everything he makes."

"It'd be nice, Christmaslike, if someone would take him in until he finds a cheaper place, wouldn't it?" Charles said, glancing at me out the corner of his eye.

One of the men at the bar called for another beer. Cal left to meet the need, and Hank Locklin broke the string of Christmas songs from the jukebox with "Please Help Me, I'm Falling."

"That brings us to Noelle," I said to move away from Neil's housing plight. "Let me tell you what she said yesterday."

"Is it like what you learned from Janice and didn't think it was important enough to tell me?"

"Charles, give me a chance, I'll tell you."

Charles held up his empty beer bottle. "Yo, Cal, I need another one of those. Chris is driving me to drink."

I told him about my encounter with Noelle after I saw her casing the Post Office. He was relatively calm until I got to the part about the note on her truck.

"You thought that clue wasn't important enough to lead this discussion with?"

Cal set a second Budweiser on the table then asked if I needed another glass of wine. I declined. Charles said he may need it before I drove him crazy.

Cal added, "Crazier," then headed to the bar.

"I don't know what we can do with that information," I said.

"You can add it to the list of things to talk to Cindy about."

"I'll do that. Let me tell you what Barb said about arsonists."

"Is it something else you should've told me before today?"

"No," I said, more defensively than I had intended. "Learned it last night."

I proceeded to tell him about Barb's research about arsonists, how it appeared whoever burned the apartment building probably wouldn't be considered a serial arsonist, but someone who burned it for a specific purpose. The most likely suspect would be the building's owner Russell O'Leary."

"Insurance?"

"Probably."

"He has money trouble?" Charles asked.

"Three months behind on the mortgage."

"Does Cindy know?"

"That's who told me. She's already looking into it. He also told her he was at a meeting in Atlanta, but the story was weak. He didn't remember where he stayed, paid cash, lots of wiggle room in his alibi."

Charles took a sip of the second beer, started peeling the label off the bottle, then said, "What do we do now?"

"Enjoy looking at Cal's Christmas decorations, his beautiful trees, then think how lucky we are to have a place to live."

Merle Haggard sang "If We Make It Through December."

Chapter Twenty-Two

I called Cindy after Charles and I had gone our separate ways.

"What now?" she said then sighed.

As strange as it seems, I was happier to hear that rude response than her trying to be friendly. Cindy was being Cindy.

"Have you talked to Noelle Ward about the fire?"

"You mean Imani Marshall?"

"Yes."

"She want to confess starting it?"

"Don't believe so, but if you say pretty please, she'll tell you about a note slipped under her windshield wiper a week before the fire."

"Did the person who wrote it say he or she was going to incinerate the building, then sign the note?"

"Noelle didn't mention it. It told her to get off the island or something like that."

"Was your new buddy Noelle ever going to share this with the police?"

"I asked. She said it wouldn't do any good." I didn't tell

Cindy that Noelle wasn't going to law enforcement because her novel's protagonist wouldn't.

"I'd like her to tell me that. Do you know where she's staying?"

"In her truck. I bet your crack police force could find one big Dodge Ram pickup without much trouble."

"You have more faith in them then I have. Would you happen to have Ms. Ward/Marshall's phone number?"

I not only told her I did but gave it to her.

"Cindy, now that you're on the phone, I have another question."

"Of course, you do, Charles in waiting."

"Do you know Nick Matthews?"

"No. Who's he?"

"How about Aimee Mason?"

"Chris, there are two thousand residents on Folly Beach. Are you planning on asking about each of them until I admit knowing someone?"

I chuckled. "No."

"So, who are Nick and Aimee?"

I shared what little I knew about them, omitting any mention of Lost, Ty's cat.

"Let me see if I have this straight. Ty was hitting on Aimee who happens to be Nick's fiancée. Nick didn't take kindly to it and maybe-kind-of-sort-of threatened Ty. How am I doing?"

"Perfect. No wonder you're Chief."

"Your theory is Nick thought Ty failed to grasp the importance of his maybe-kind-of-sort-of threat and burned an entire apartment building to communicate more strongly his objection to Ty's advances on his gal?"

"You've got it."

"That sounds like a stretch."

"Yes, but—"

Cindy interrupted, "Hold the but, the one with one T. Because you're such a friend, a pain in the butt with two Ts friend, I'll see if I can find Nick and have a pleasant talk. You don't happen to have his number, do you?"

"Sorry, no. By the way, how are Rose and Luke doing?"

"Luke's pestering Larry for a raise. Says he wants the extra money to buy his mom a nice Christmas present. Rose is trying to use some of her highfalutin education on me. Can you imagine her learnin' me proper grammar? I told her I'm dumber than a pretzel compared to her college students. I think she's figurin' that out."

Cindy is one of the smartest people I know. Her grammar may not always live up to textbook standards, but she's an effective communicator. She's also one of the most stubborn people I've run across. Rose will have her hands full. I wanted to ask if Rose told her about her ex's visit the day before the fire, but honored Rose's request that I not share it.

"Has she said much about the fire?"

"More about how rough it's been losing everything except the clothes on her back. She knows how lucky she and Luke were. The arson investigator figured the fire started in the apartment next to theirs, so they would've been close to the origination point if they'd been home."

"Does she think it had anything to do with them?"

"Why would it? She just moved here. They didn't know anybody, didn't even know others who lived in the building."

Which means Rose hadn't said anything about her ex's visit.

"Just curious."

Cindy laughed. "More than anything, Rose and Luke are putting their energy into decorating the house. Larry and I've never done anything more than put a wreath on the front door. No tree, no wrapped presents, no stockings hung by the chimney with care. Crap, we don't even have a chimney. By the time Christmas rolls around, Larry is shuffling around like an elf zombie. Tell him I said that, and you'll be hung by a rope by somebody's chimney."

I chuckled. "Your term of endearment is safe."

"Rose said our house shouldn't be decorated for Christmas the same way it is for Groundhog Day. She found an artificial tree in the attic, must've come with the place. They cleared a century of dust off it, plopped it down in the family room. Then Luke convinced Larry to give him strands of lights from the store so he and his mom could string them around the tree. Then Santa's little helpers went to Harris Teeter, bought wrapping paper, and candy canes. Now they're hanging on nearly everything you can hook a cane on."

"That's great, Cindy."

"I'll admit, it looks good. I put my foot down when she suggested I bake Christmas cookies. Luke said not to worry, he and his mom will bake them. I hope Larry will have enough energy left in his petite body to enjoy everything. Hell, I may even buy him a Christmas present. What man doesn't want a snow globe?"

"That's what we live for, Cindy."

"Perfect. I'll be sure to tell Larry you said that."

I hoped she was kidding. "Ho, Ho, Ho! Anything I can do to help?"

"Come to the house after Christmas to take down all the stuff Rose and Luke used to transform our humble abode into a Christmas village."

"Anything else?"

"Yeah, I'd love to spend more time talking about Christmas but I have to see if I can find Noelle, or whatever her name is, living in a pickup truck; Nick, the jealous fiancée; plus any other person who may've been on Folly in the last week who might've started the fire."

"That should keep you busy for a few minutes."

"I wish."

"One more thing before you go to solve the mystery. Don't forget Cal's annual Christmas bash."

"Gee, Chris, how could I forget, he only does it every

Christmas. I'm not old like you. I don't have to be reminded to get up every morning."

"I was thinking you and Larry might want to bring Rose and Luke by to meet some others on Folly."

"Good thought. I'll talk to them about it. Larry, of course, will sleep all day after he drags his tiny butt in from working ninety-four hours a day at the store."

"In addition to Rose teaching you proper grammar, you may see if she can refresh your knowledge of math."

I'm certain she was going to thank me for the suggestion, but the phone went dead before she had a chance.

Chapter Twenty-Three

The most likely person with a reason to burn the apartment building was its owner, Russell O'Leary. He was three months behind on his mortgage, one of the apartment units had been vacant for several months which would've made it more difficult to cover the mortgage. He claimed to have been in Atlanta at a meeting on the day of the fire but told Cindy he didn't stay at the hotel where the event was held. He said he'd rented a room at a nearby hotel whose name he couldn't remember. A feeble alibi at best. So, how do I prove it?

I didn't know Russell but knew someone who might. Bob Howard, a friend, and former Realtor who'd handled countless sales in the Charleston area.

"Good afternoon, Bob," I said after he answered on the third ring.

"Well if it isn't my worthless acquaintance who thinks he's too good to spend time with his good buddy."

Despite having had a successful career in real estate, Bob had the personality of a hippopotamus and nearly the same weight, yet, for reason's unknown, we'd become friends after he helped me find my cottage on Folly, the space I'd rented for Landrum Gallery, plus sharing information over the years allowing me to catch a couple of bad guys.

I ignored his comment, a wise decision when spending time around Bob. "Do you know Russell O'Leary?"

"Yes."

I waited for more. It was a waste of time.

"What do you know about him?"

"Chris, I figure the CIA, KGB, NCAA, or one of those other evil agencies has this phone bugged. Suppose you'll need to come over to hear it in person. Oh yeah, while you're here, you can buy a cheeseburger, double order of fries to share with me, plus some of that nasty red wine you sip in the winter."

"Will you be there in an hour?"

"Hell yes, damned slave-driver Al won't let me leave."

I hung up on him. It felt good.

When Bob retired from selling real estate, he bought Al's Bar near downtown Charleston. While it's too long a story to relay here, suffice to say Bob knew as much about running a bar as a jumbo shrimp knows about needlepoint. He bought it because his long-time friend Al Washington, the previous owner, was suffering serious health issues after running the bar for decades while raising nine adopted kids, much of that time as a single dad. Bob couldn't stand seeing Al suffer.

Forty-five minutes later, I was pulling in a rare empty parking space a half-block from Al's in an area of town near two hospital complexes. Other than the often-expanding health care facilities, much of the residential area would be considered pre-gentrification. If you'd called Al's Bar a hole in the wall, you'd be giving it too much credit. It was in a concrete-block building it shared with a Laundromat. The building hadn't been clothed in fresh paint since the Vietnam War. Regardless of its physical condition, I was certain Al's cheeseburgers were the best in the state. Bob claimed they were the best in the country. He could be right.

I stepped from late-afternoon daylight into cave-like darkness to be greeted by Al, who since Bob purchased the bar, served as the business's Walmart greeter.

"Praise the Lord, you're here," he said, gave me a warm, extended hug, then whispered, "Blubber Bob's been asking every two minutes if you were here yet."

The only illumination in the room came from a Budweiser and Budweiser Light neon signs behind the aging bar, but Bob was seated close enough to see each time the door opened. In other words, he had no reason to pester Al about my arrival.

Al was eighty-two-years-old, with short, gray hair, coffee-stained teeth, with skin the color somewhere between dark brown and light black. He looked as well-worn as the room's yard-sale tables and chairs.

"Old man," came a bellowing voice from the rear of the room, "stop hugging on the damned scrawny honkie so he can get over here and spend money. How in the hell am I going to pay your astronomical salary if you don't let customers blow their cash in here?"

That was Bob at his best. Al had the good sense not to remind Bob he was working free. Two men were seated at a table near the large plate-glass window, the lower-half painted black to provide privacy for the diners. They were sipping beer and playing cards. A pile of wooden matches was in front of each of them which I suspected had value other than for starting fires.

Other than the cardplayers, the bar was empty except for Al, Bob, and me. Al said he'd throw my cheeseburger on the grill if I promised to keep Bob quiet. I told him I'd do my best. During busy times, which were fewer and fewer, a part-time cook fixed the food. I hated that Al had to move around that much but knew that the chance of Bob manning the grill was about the same as him being named Pope.

"About time you got here," Bob said as I squeezed in my side of the booth, a space barely wide enough for me since Bob had taken up twice the normal space on the other side of the table. "Nosing in police business again?"

"Why do you say that?"

"Oh, could be because you called to ask if I knew Russell O'Leary who happens to own the building someone turned black and flat a couple of blocks from your house. Or, could be because you stick your pasty white nose in everything bad happening on Folly. How am I doing?"

Before I could answer, one of the cardplayers raised his hand and hollered to Al, "How about a couple more beers?"

Bob, being the customer-friendly, service-oriented bar owner, said, "Marvin, can't your Afro eyes see the man's busy fixing food for my young friend here?"

Bob was white; ninety-five percent of his customers African American. After Bob bought the bar, Al told me the main reason he wanted to stay on was to prevent a race riot in the place where he'd spent most of his work life. The more the regulars learned that Bob didn't like black people, they realized he didn't like brown, yellow, white, or any other color people. He was a textbook example of an equal-opportunity offender. He didn't like anyone, or so it appeared.

Marvin mumbled something under his breath, then went to the cooler and got the drinks. Bob mumbled something that sounded like, "Thanks, Marvin," but I had a hard time believing he could've said the word thanks.

Marvin returned to the card game, riot averted, for now. Bob turned back to me.

"Where was I," he said. "Oh yeah, you were going to tell me I was right about you nosing in police business."

I agreed but wasn't about to give him the satisfaction of hearing it.

"What do you know about O'Leary?"

"He's a heavy-truck mechanic at a shop over here. Decent income, but hard work, long hours. When his dad died a few years back, he inherited the building where you're snooping where you shouldn't."

Al made his way to the table, set a cheeseburger with a double order of fries in front of me. Before I'd arrived, Bob told him what I'd want, and what he'd want with the extra order of fries. Al also set a glass of wine beside my plate.

"Set your bony ass down while I tell my good-buddy Chris how brilliant I am."

Al lowered himself beside me. "Don't need to hear it. You say it every day."

"Old man, the truth will set you free."

Al rolled his eyes, as the sounds of the Four Tops' hit "Reach Out, I'll Be There," reverberated off the walls.

Bob yelled, "Marvin, you do that?"

Marvin smiled. "Yes, Master Bob. You needed some good music."

"Next time you punch those numbers in the jukebox I'm getting a restraining order to keep you from entering this fine dining, drinking establishment ever again."

Marvin's smile turned to a laugh. "Yes, Master Bob."

Bob turned back to Al and me. "Damned radicals."

"Bob, how do you know so much about O'Leary?"

"He walked into my office soon after inheriting the building. Said he knew everything there was to know about fixing a Peterbilt but nothing about owning an apartment building. Wanted to talk about selling. I worked up comps and met to talk to him about the details of selling a multi-unit structure. He pondered it for a couple of weeks before calling to say he and his wife talked it over. They have two teenagers, college-age by now, I guess. Much to my thinning wallet's dismay, they decided to hold on to the building. Said they wanted it to be a legacy they could leave to their kids, which meant no money for me to leave to my kids."

"Bob," Al said, "you ain't got no kids."

"Hell, Al, get with the program. I was being figurative-speaking-like, making the point that his gain was my loss."

"Sounded stupid-like to me," Al said.

I agreed with Al. "Bob, is that all you know about O'Leary?"

"That's more than you knew when you walked in."

"True. So, that's all?"

"Nope."

"Heavens, Bob. Tell the man what you know. Use plain English while you're doing it."

"Hush, old man. Let me tell the story the way I want."

Instead of smacking the fry out of Bob's mouth, Al smiled, then leaned back in the chair.

Despite tremendous differences ranging from skin color to socioeconomic background, to kindness to others, Bob and Al had been friends for decades; they'd do anything for each other.

"After you called to tell me you'd love to come over and buy a cheeseburger, I called a realtor I know over your way to see if he knew anything about Russell. He said rumors were flying that the mechanic turned landlord was in deep financial straits. Late paying bills, months behind on his mortgage, one kid in college, one in trouble with the law."

"Is that all?"

"What more do you want, his social security number and cholesterol level? I suppose you think he torched the building for the insurance."

"Maybe."

Bob stuffed another fry in his mouth, then said, "Hell, I know I would've."

Chapter Twenty-Four

Another below-average temperature the week before Christmas greeted me as I stepped outside for the walk next door for coffee, something to eat, and with luck, a chance to check on Ty. Three construction workers were standing around the large coffee urn—one pouring coffee, two adding sugar and milk to their caffeinated drink. I drew a cup after the workers headed to the exit, then moved to the cabinet holding three large Cinnamon rolls, where Preacher Burl Costello was holding two boxes of prepackaged donuts.

"Morning Burl, didn't your chef show up to fix breakfast?"

As he smiled, his milk-chocolate colored mustache wiggled like a caterpillar inching its way along his upper lip. "And a good morning to you as well, Brother Chris. One of my fantasy dreams is for a chef to take up residence at Hope House. Until then, the bakery in, umm," he looked at the bottom of the donut package. "Cleveland, Ohio, will have to prepare our morning meals. My skills are limited to burning toast and offering a prayer."

I pointed to the shelf where I was eying my breakfast. "Burning toast would be an upgrade in my culinary skills. Don't suppose you have vacancies since we talked the other day?"

Burl's smile transitioned to a frown plus a slow head shake. "Still full. Are some of the residents of the burned building still without somewhere to hang their hats?"

I glanced around looking for Ty, not seeing him, I said, "Unfortunately yes. Rose Wheeler and her son are the only ones who've found accommodations."

"Are they the relatives of our outstanding Chief?"

"She's Cindy's sister, Luke, Cindy's nephew. The others are living in their vehicles or staying at the Holliday Inn."

"Brother Chris, I have faith our community will come together to aid the displaced."

"I wish I had that much faith."

He smiled and patted my arm. "Tis the season of faith, Brother Chris. The season of faith."

As if on cue, Ty appeared at my side. He asked if he could help us find something. He had on what looked like the same shirt he'd been wearing the last time I'd seen him. His ponytail shined like it was covered with a layer of oil.

I introduced Ty to Preacher Burl.

"Preacher, Ty is one of the displaced residents I was talking about."

Burl set the donuts on the table, then put one arm around Ty. "Brother Ty, I'm terribly sorry about your loss of residence."

Ty took a step back from Burl. "No biggie, Preacher. I've lived in worse places than in my car. Besides, Lost is safe."

Burl looked at the young man like he'd look at three-legged deer. "Brother Ty, don't believe I understand."

I wouldn't have either if I hadn't known about Lost. "Preacher Burl, Ty is living in his Miata. Lost is the name of his adorable kitten that was in his car during the fire."

"Oh," Burl said, still looking confused. "It's nice meeting

you, Brother Ty. I have faith you'll find somewhere to live, perhaps with more living space than your car. Gentlemen, I hate to run but need to get back to the house with breakfast or I'll have several residents ready to move me to my vehicle."

"Preacher," I said, "will you be at Cal's Christmas party?"

"I wouldn't miss Brother Cal's event, although I'd be more inclined to be there if that old country singer didn't feel the need to drag me on stage to join him in a Christmas song."

The last two Christmas parties, Cal thought singing a duet with Burl was something the group would enjoy. The bar's owner said it combined the spirit of the holiday with the religious significance of the sacred event. Burl thought there must be better ways to communicate the message, but went along with Cal.

"Preacher, that's the highlight of the event."

"Not to me, Brother Chris. Not to me,"

Burl headed to the register.

Ty watched him go, then said, "He talks funny, doesn't he? Several customers told me they go to his church. I should give it a try. He has more faith than I have about me finding somewhere to live."

I shared more information about First Light, Hope House, then added, "Ty, another reason I came in was to see how you're doing."

"That's kind of you, Mr. Landrum. I'm doing peachy." He snapped his fingers. "There was one thing I wanted to mention when I saw you." He stared at me like he wanted me to say something.

"Now would be a good time."

He nodded. "Remember I told you about Aimee's fiancée?"

"Nick something."

"Nick Matthews. He came in yesterday. I didn't see him

at first. He was over by the beer cooler. I was stocking the book rack, know where I mean?"

"Yes."

"He got a six-pack, then walked close to me. He had this big look on his face. Looked like one of those Cheshire cat grins."

"Did he say anything?"

"Not a word, but figured the look was like him telling me he burnt the building, a smirk because he did it."

"Ty, you're certain he didn't say anything?"

"Certain."

I wasn't aware of laws against smirking but thought he should tell the police his suspicions.

"Ty, I doubt it'll do any good but I suggest you tell Chief Lamond the next time she's in."

"I will if you think it's a good idea but if I was the Chief and some kid told me he was reporting a smirk, I'd nod and forget it."

"Ty, she might do that but she's trying to figure out who set the fire. Anything related, regardless of how small or inconsequential, may help."

"If you say so," he said, sounding as convincing as I had suggesting it. "Better get back to work. Don't know what I'd do if I lost this job." He laughed. "I'd hate to have to give up my luxurious living quarters."

I was impressed by how well he was taking his uncomfortable situation. I couldn't handle it as well.

Chapter Twenty-Five

I called Neil after I got home. He'd told me a lot about the man he'd sicked the IRS on, but little about the person who'd threatened him after being bounced from the Charleston bar.

"Neil, are you at Cal's?"

"I go in at four. Why?"

"I was wondering about something you'd said. Thought I'd drop in if you were working."

"You can come tonight, or I could meet you somewhere now. The less time I spend in this room the better."

We agreed to meet at St. James Gate, a restaurant on the corner of Center Street and Ashley Avenue that prides itself on being a "proper Irish pub." From its distinct green and tan exterior to the dark wood and stone interior, the restaurant has the feel of how I pictured an Irish pub.

I would've preferred to sit on the back patio, but the temperature made that impractical, so I chose a table in front of the window facing Center Street. A half-dozen customers were at the bar. Four men sat at a table in the center of the room with two of them staring at laptop computers, most likely salespersons discussing whatever salespersons discuss. A server wearing a green and white T-shirt with a three-leaf clover over his heart was quick to the table. If I drank beer, I would've automatically ordered Guinness, the beer of choice in the pub. The server appeared disappointed when I stuck with water. He cheered slightly when I told him I was waiting on someone and might order more when my guest arrives.

I didn't wait long. Neil came in the door and headed my way. The server arrived with my water at the same time. Neil did what was expected in the Irish pub when he ordered Guinness and a menu. The server looked at me with an expression that said, "See, that's what you're supposed to do," then went to get Neil's drink.

"What's on your mind, Chris?"

Nothing like getting to the point, I thought. I told him I was wondering how he was doing, the same thing I'd said to Ty.

"Okay, I guess. Cal has been kind to give me extra hours, so I have enough money to replace some of the stuff lost in the fire. My car's a gas guzzler, so I cut back on my job in Charleston. Walking to Cal's helps save some."

"Still living in the Holliday Inn?"

"Yes, but I'd love to get out of there. They gave me a good rate, but I still can't afford it. Also, I can't stand being pent up in the small room. This time of year, it's even worse. It … never mind."

"Worse because of the holidays?"

"Sort of."

That's the kind of comment Charles would be all over. I liked to think I wasn't quite as pushy.

"Neil, when we were talking the other day, you said one of your customers in Charleston threatened you after you, umm, evicted him."

"Nothing unusual. It happens more than you might think. Alcohol does strange things to folks."

The gods of irony arrived the same time the server

arrived with Neil's alcoholic drink. The server asked if we were ready to order. Neil said the beer was all he needed for now, so I ordered a soft drink instead of food. I didn't know if Neil wasn't hungry or didn't have money for lunch.

"Neil, didn't you say the man you threw out threatened you?"

"Yeah." He chuckled. "They all do."

"Could he have started the fire for revenge?"

"I suppose so, but he didn't know where I lived."

"Could he have followed you home?"

Neil smiled. "Not that night. I don't think he was in any condition to find his nose, much less my apartment."

"Seen him since then?"

"Once or twice. He's a regular."

"He give you more trouble?"

"He made a couple of smart-ass comments, nothing more."

"No more threats?"

"Not really. I don't think he started the fire. If anyone did because of me, it was the guy who owns the plant where I worked."

"Do you have a reason to think that anything other than because he'd be angry?"

"He's got a temper. I remember several times where he yelled at an employee, or when he pounded his fist on a wall."

"Have you seen him since you turned him in?"

Neil took a sip of beer, looked out the window, then said, "No."

"He never directly threatened you?"

"No."

Other than two people who may have a beef with him, Neil didn't know anything to tie them to the fire, which brings me back to something he'd said, or more accurately, hadn't said about this time of year being worse than other times.

"Neil, what did you mean when you said this time of year was bad?"

He took another sip as he resumed staring out the window. I was afraid I'd irritated him.

He finally turned to me. "My dad died three days before Christmas. I was seventeen."

"Neil, I'm sorry. What happened?"

"Cancer. He'd been sick for months. We knew his time was short, but he told mom and me he wanted to be here one more Christmas. He didn't make it."

"That would be a good reason to be depressed this time of year. Again, I'm sorry."

He slowly shook his head. "There's more."

The server returned and asked if Neil wanted another beer. He nodded but didn't say anything. I told the server I was fine.

Neil watched him leave, then said, "I was married once."

"Oh," I said.

"She was the most wonderful person I ever knew. Married five years, five wonderful years."

Do I ask what happened? The server was back before I decided.

Neil took a long draw on the beer, then said, "Three years ago, Lisa, that was her name, went to visit her parents. They lived thirty miles from our house. Her car was T-boned by a drunk driver. Killed her instantly."

"Neil, I'm terribly sorry."

"Was Christmas Eve. Know what happened to the damned drunk?"

I shook my head.

"Airbag broke his little finger. Lisa dies and he gets his damned pinkie broke."

Not knowing what to say, I shook my head.

He took a sip, looked out the window, hopped out of the chair, and headed to the restroom. It was becoming clear why this time of the year was rough on Neil. It was also clear I was running out of ways to say sorry.

Neil returned, gave me a feeble smile, then said, "Know what I did the next Christmas?"

I was afraid to guess. "What?"

"Got arrested. Aggravated assault."

"What happened?"

"Sitting in a bar, feeling sorry for myself. Christmas Eve, a year to the day I lost Lisa." He held up his beer. "Drinking way too many of these. A guy sitting next to me started ragging on the gal bartender. Bitching about her being slow. I blew a gasket. Before I knew it, we were exchanging blows, then I was being hauled away by what must've been a dozen cops. Chris, ain't nothing good about spending Christmas in jail."

"Neil, no wonder this is a bad time of year."

"I'd be lying if I said it wasn't." He hesitated, then added, "You're the only person I've told all this to. I'd appreciate it if you didn't share it with anyone."

"It won't leave this table."

He smiled. "Thank you. Know what's picked me up more than anything?"

"What?"

"Cal. Watching that old crooner get so excited about Christmas. Helping him put up the trees, decorating the bar. Being part of something positive about the holiday has kept me from thinking too much about the bad ones. He's a lifesaver."

Before I left St. James Gate, Neil had put most of his negative thoughts behind him. I encouraged him to talk about working at Cal's. He shared a few humorous things he'd witnessed, how interesting it was to spend time with Cal reliving his experiences with many of the country legends from fifty years ago, and a few quirky regulars who frequented the bar. Neil said he wasn't a country music fan, but hanging around Cal, he had a new appreciation for the genre. He especially had a growing appreciation for Cal, his outlook on life, his tolerance of all people. I didn't know how long Neil's good mood would last since we were only a handful of days before Christmas, but when we went our separate ways, he was laughing.

I WAS CROSSING Center Street when I heard a horn, turned, and saw it was coming from a black Dodge Ram pickup. The truck, driven by Noelle, I assumed, pulled off the road in front of me. I moved to the driver's side and was greeted by a smiling Noelle Ward.

"Good to see you, Chris. Where you headed?"

"Nowhere in particular."

"Want to hop in? I could use some company."

I walked around to the passenger door, opened it, slid in, then looked at the back seat that held a sleeping bag, a small suitcase, and three Walmart bags.

"Still driving your apartment?"

Noelle, dressed in a black sweatshirt, black jeans, and red tennis shoes, laughed, then said, "Got some new duds at Walmart. All I have to do now is figure out how to get cable TV in here."

"Gets a little tight back there, doesn't it?"

She laughed. "One big advantage of being short and scrawny is I fit almost anywhere."

She waved at Ty standing in front of Bert's, drove past my house, then proceeded to her former residence.

She shook her head, then said, "Sad looking mess. It wasn't Shangri-La, but provided decent, almost decent housing."

The rubble looked exactly like it had the day after the fire.

"Sad, especially for those who were displaced."

"I have faith something will work out for all of us. After all, it's Christmas. Time for miracles, they say."

A blue Toyota Prius slowed, started to turn into the lot, then continued out Ashley Avenue.

Noelle watched the car slow and then leave. "That's the landlord."

"Have you talked to him since the fire?"

"No."

"Hear anything else about who started it?"

"Not really, or not really anything credible. I told you before that I'm spending time walking around observing people. Vacationers act different than locals, youngsters act way different than, umm, old-timers."

"Like me?"

She grinned. "No, not you, I mean old people."

"Ever thought about becoming a diplomat?"

"Too much work."

"For me, it'd be easier than writing a book."

"Anyway, in addition to observing folks, I've talked to several, mainly to see how they react to a stranger. A few want to talk about the fire." She chuckled. "It was hard getting some to stop talking about it. Besides the Christmas parade, the fire was the biggest thing that's happened around here in a while."

"It doesn't take much to get folks gossiping."

She stepped out of the truck and leaned against the hood. I joined her in front of the vehicle.

Noelle stared at the ruins then said, "One old man in the Crab Shack said he was certain the fire was started by a pyromaniac traveling from New York to Miami. The old guy said the man stopped here on his way to practice starting fires. He also said President Kennedy is living in a beach house on Kiawah."

"He lost credibility on that one, didn't he?"

"Did with me. Did you hear the fire started in the middle unit, first floor?"

"Yes, it was vacant, I believe."

"Vacant several months. Another guy at the Crab Shack told me he heard the fire was started by a kid sneaking in the empty apartment to smoke. The man couldn't explain how the kid spread gasoline around to make the fire accelerate."

"Noelle, that probably scratches the surface of rumors going around about the fire."

"Chris, there's one other thing. It could be my imagination." She smiled. "Novelists have big imaginations you know. Anyway, a couple of days before the fire, I noticed a guy standing back there." She pointed to the back of the lot. "Seems he was staring at my apartment. The reason he got my attention was that I'd swear I saw him three other times in recent weeks. I noticed because he was always looking around like he thought he was being followed."

"What'd he look like?"

"White dude, little older than me, long shaggy black hair."

"What about clothes?"

"Had them on every time I saw him," she said, then laughed.

"Cute."

"Sorry. He looked like every other dude. Jeans, sweatshirt, backward ball cap, think it was red."

"Anything else?"

"Not really. If I was putting him in my book, he'd be someone on the run, because of the way he kept looking around like he was worried about someone seeing him."

"Seen him since the fire?"

She looked toward the sky, then back at me, "Don't think so. Now you know everything I know about the guy."

"If you would, call me if you see him again. The police chief and I are friends. I can have her check him out."

"Deal. By the way, I was in the bookstore yesterday. The lady who owns it said you two are an item."

"We've been seeing each other a while."

"She's really nice."

I agreed.

Chapter Twenty-Six

I was to meet Barb for supper at Loggerhead's Beach Grill located across the street from her condo in the Charleston Oceanfront Villas. I was there fifteen minutes before the time we were to meet. The restaurant has one of the nicest outdoor decks on the island, but tonight was too cool to enjoy it. As I was walking across the parking lot, I noticed a man getting out of a blue Prius. He was middle-aged, six-foot-tall, average weight with a slight limp. I followed him up the steps and into the building where he took a stool at the bar. Most of the indoor tables were taken, so I was fortunate to get one along the wall. I wasn't certain, but the Prius was the color of the one Noelle said belonged to Russell O'Leary.

I didn't give the man another thought and ordered a Diet Coke while I waited for Barb. She was seldom late, but unlike Charles, she assumed on-time meant on-time, so I wasn't surprised she wasn't here yet. I was beginning to wonder when it was ten minutes after the time she was to arrive. I didn't wonder long. The phone rang with her name on the screen.

"On your way?"

"Not yet. Two groups came in as I was closing. It was as if they just realized Christmas was four days away. They're rummaging through the books trying to do all their Christmas shopping. It'll be a little while before I can get there. Want to postpone, or am I worth waiting for?"

I'm far from the smartest person in my orbit but knew there was only one acceptable answer. "Of course you're worth waiting for. Take your time."

"I appreciate it."

Three couples were at the door waiting for a table. Rather than hogging the real estate for no telling how long, I told the server I'd be at the bar. Besides, it'd give me a chance to introduce myself to the man I suspected to be the apartment building's owner. I took the bar-height seat next to him, then realized I had no logical way of identifying myself or asking about the fire. It didn't help that he was gripping his beer glass with both hands and staring at the liquid it contained like his mind was a thousand miles away.

I did my Charles imitation. "Hi, I'm Chris. You live around here?"

His hands never left the glass, but his head tilted slightly in my direction. "No."

Charles does Charles way better than I do.

"Then you probably didn't hear about the big fire on Folly a week ago."

This time he took one hand off the glass, then turned toward me. "Who'd you say you are again?"

"Chris Landrum."

He reached out in a motion I assumed meant to shake my hand. I shook his wet hand as he said, "I'm Russell O'Leary. You won't believe this, but it was my building that burned."

"You're kidding, that's terrible. I hear it's a total loss."

He sighed. "Unfortunately."

"What caused it?"

"They said arson."

"I'm sorry, Russell. Who would've done that?"

I thought that was better than asking if he'd torched it.

He shrugged.

"Own it long?"

"Been in the family twenty-three years. Dad had it until he passed a few years ago. I got the building. Inherited it and all its problems."

"Problems?"

He hesitated long enough for me to think my question had gone too far.

Finally, he said, "I'm a mechanic, big trucks. I didn't know anything about maintaining a building like that. Dad got the best years out of it, I got the leaky pipes, busted air-conditioners, wiring problems, outside constantly needing paint, that's not even counting deadbeat tenants who'd rather pay for cigarettes and cell phones than rent."

I remembered what Bob Howard had said about Russell considering selling the building.

"Ever think about selling?"

"Only every day, and twice in the middle of the night when I'd get a call about something wrong. What'd you say your name was again?"

His glass was empty. "Chris. Let me buy you another beer."

He glanced at his watch, then smiled, finally. "I never turn down a drink."

I waved for the bartender, ordered a beer for Russell, said I was okay with my drink.

"If it was such a headache, how come you didn't sell? From what I hear, the market's strong."

"Don't think I didn't come close a time or two. I've got two kids, guess they're not really kids anymore. They're eighteen and nineteen, almost grown men. Every time I said something about selling, they went bananas. Say they're going to take over, help do all the work, want it for their inheritance. My wife is on their side."

His second beer arrived, and he didn't waste time taking a long pull.

"How much help are the boys?"

"Chris, you got kids?"

I shook my head.

"Then I'll forgive you for that question. They're worthless. I was holding it to keep peace in the family."

"Going to rebuild?"

"Excellent question, my friend. Don't know."

"Were you at the fire?"

"I wasn't even in South Carolina, was at, umm, a meeting in Atlanta. I didn't know anything about it until the next day."

"That had to be a shock."

Another sip later, he said, "I probably shouldn't say it, but I'm glad it's gone. The insurance money will help clear some debts. With that said, I feel bad for my tenants."

"Have they found places to live?"

"The only one I've seen since the fire is a kid who works at Bert's. He said he's living in his car."

"That's rough."

"He's young, will be okay."

I remembered how Cindy said he'd been vague about the meeting he allegedly was attending and where he stayed in Atlanta.

"I haven't been to Atlanta in years. All I remember is construction downtown. Traffic was always disrupted. Is it still that way?"

"Don't know. I was a few miles from downtown."

Hadn't Cindy said the meeting was at a downtown hotel? I also couldn't figure a way to ask if he torched the building. Even if I had, I didn't get a chance. He looked at his watch for the third time since I sat down.

"Better get home. My wife will be calling out the police

if I don't show up soon. Thanks for the beer, Chris. Nice meeting you."

He slid off the chair and was out the door before I paid his tab. I not only bought his second beer, but the first was also on me.

Barb probably passed Russell on the way down the stairs. She arrived with a smile and proclaiming that she was starved, a common occurrence, or so it seems. The crowd had thinned so we had a choice of three tables. We ordered then Barb told me about her day, the closing-time rush, then a story about a customer who wanted Barb to gift wrap a dozen books he was giving to his three children. He eventually bought the books but was disappointed she didn't gift wrap.

I started to tell about meeting Russell O'Leary, but her body language told me she didn't want to talk about the fire. We found much more pleasant topics to enjoy with our meal. After supper, I walked her across the street to her condo, where our pleasant topics continued.

Chapter Twenty-Seven

B arb had kept my mind off the fire for several hours, but the next morning, I couldn't shake what Russell had said about being glad the building burned, and his comment about not being in downtown Atlanta. Had I misunderstood what Cindy shared about his meeting? A phone call would be a simple way to find out.

"Morning, Chief."

"Are you on your way to the Dog?"

"No, but I can be. Why?"

"Because if you're not here, how can you buy me breakfast."

"See you in a few minutes."

"Don't you love it when a plan comes together?" she said, then hung up.

The temperature was beginning to feel like Christmas, so I drove rather than walked. My half-hearted exercise plan would have to wait. There was a rare empty parking space in front of the restaurant, reducing my exercise by more steps.

Cindy was at a table in the center of the room. As I made my way over, she motioned for a server to bring a second cup of coffee.

"I thought you'd be home fixing bacon, eggs, hash browns, and toast for Rose, Luke, and Larry," I said, knowing that'd be the last thing she'd be doing.

"You've been hanging around Noelle Ward too long. She's the fiction writer."

I was surprised she knew Noelle. "Why did you mention Noelle?"

"She said she knew you."

"Where'd you meet her?"

"Did you forget there was a big-ass fire at her building?"

"No, but—"

"She stopped by the office yesterday. Said something about telling you about seeing someone nosing around the apartment. You said if she saw the guy again to call you, so you could tell me, or something like that."

My coffee arrived. Cindy interrupted her story to tell the server what she wanted for breakfast. I exhibited as much originality as I usually do when I ordered French toast.

"Your new writer friend said instead of dragging you in the middle of something that was none of your business, she told me directly about the guy who'd creeped her out."

I took a sip of coffee, then said, "Is that how Noelle said it?"

Cindy smiled. "I added none of your business."

"I figured. Did she give you anything that'd help find the guy?"

"Nothing that wouldn't describe a third of the population. I told her to call me—I repeat, call me—if she sees him again."

"Good plan."

"Chris, if memory serves me correct, you called me. Any particular reason other than to raise my blood pressure?"

"Didn't you tell me Russell O'Leary was in Atlanta the day of the fire?"

She took a small notebook out of her coat pocket, flipped through a few pages, then said, "The owner of a pile of charcoal said he was attending a get-rich-quick rip-off seminar in downtown Atlanta. He didn't say rip-off, that's my astute analysis of the hotel-meeting-room con-artist seminar."

"Are you sure he said downtown Atlanta?"

She flipped another page. "Said the seminar was at the Westin Peachtree Plaza, downtown Atlanta. Why did someone see him here?"

"I met him last night at Loggerhead's."

She shook her head. "Let me guess, you were minding your own business nibbling on a fry when low-and-behold Russell popped up out of nowhere and introduced himself."

"Close. I thought it was him, so I introduced myself."

"While minding your own business, I'm sure. Moving right along, why ask about Atlanta?"

Breakfast arrived. I poured syrup on the French toast, then said, "He told me he'd stayed a few miles outside downtown Atlanta."

"Pray tell, how did that come up in the conversation?" Cindy asked, then took a bite of toast.

"You'd told me he was in downtown Atlanta, so I said how bad construction had been the last time I was there. Asked if it was still bad."

Cindy rolled her eyes. "Chris, have you been to Atlanta since Sherman burned it?"

"Not quite that long ago."

"Charles must be learnin' you private detective techniques for tricking suspects. Did he say anything else about his trip?"

"Not about the trip, but said he was glad the building burned. Insurance would let him pay off debts."

"Suppose you would've already mentioned it if he told you he set the fire?"

"Chief, you would've been the first to know."

"Do you think he did?"

I shrugged. "Told me he wasn't good at maintaining the building; he hated getting called at all hours about problems; he threw out he wasn't fond of dealing with tenants. He didn't say it, but as you shared, he was behind on the mortgage."

"Does that mean you think he did it?"

"Cindy, I talked to the man for fifteen minutes. He seemed like a nice guy, but who knows. It bothers me he'd either lie to you or to me about where he was in Georgia, especially when it didn't matter one way or the other to me."

"And, he said he was glad the building burned."

I smiled. "That too."

"I suppose I'd better have another talk with the confused, former landlord."

"Sounds like the chiefly thing to do."

The server returned with refills on our drinks. Cindy took a sip of the refreshed coffee, then said, "Ho, Ho, Ho!"

"How are you and Larry adjusting to houseguests?"

"Larry hasn't been home enough to know they're there. When he gets home, he's so exhausted he flops in bed not acknowledging any of us. Sort of pleasant. Luke is still spending several hours a day at the store. He told me last night, Larry made him, how did he put it, umm, vice president of Christmas sales. It thrilled the heck out of the kid. I figure it was Larry's way of not giving Luke more money."

"How about Rose?"

"Fine most of the time."

"Most of the time?"

"Her a-hole ex keeps calling. It screws up her mood every time."

"What's he want?"

"What do you think? Wants her to come crawling back to Morristown."

"She thinking about it?"

"The first Thursday after hell freezes over."

"Good."

Cindy stuffed a bite of egg in her mouth, then mumbled, "Yep."

Chapter Twenty-Eight

An hour after breakfast with Cindy the phone rang. Her name appeared on the screen.

"Didn't get enough of me at breakfast?" I said.

"I'm beginning to see why you detest caller ID. How many favors have you asked me for since we've met?"

"The exact number?"

"Never mind. It's a zillion, give or take."

"Sounds right," I said, wondering where the conversation was headed.

"How many have I asked you for?"

"Way fewer than a zillion."

"How about fewer than three?"

"Close."

"I figure you owe me a few, quite a few."

"Cindy, you have a favor to ask?"

"Wow, you're smarter than the average bonehead I deal with."

"Flattery is not one of your strengths," I said, then chuckled. "What do you need?"

"Since Rose has been at the house, I've spent less time

with her than I've spent with the town drunk. Luke has been at the hardware store every day, but I know how tired of Larry someone can become. Plus, how many AA batteries can a nine-year-old put in bags before his battery runs down?"

"Your point?"

"Rose told me Luke has been wanting to eat at Planet Follywood, so today she's taking him there for lunch. Think you could miraculously happen in about the time they're arriving? I think conversation with someone other than the television would be good for Rose. Luke seems to like you. Heck if I know why."

"There you go with flattery again. When are they going?"

"I'm guessing noon, but Rose didn't say."

"I'll be there."

"Great. I would say I owe you one, but since you're a zillion favors behind, I'll leave it at thanks."

Planet Follywood was at the intersection of East Erie Avenue and Center Street and was one of Folly's most-established restaurants. It's also known for a large mural painted on the side of the building featuring larger-than-life paintings of Hollywood icons including John Wayne, Marilyn Monroe, Sammy Davis Jr, Elvis, plus a few others.

I arrived ten minutes before noon and stood across the street where I could see diners entering the restaurant. I wasn't there long; my intended targets arrived before noon. Luke pulled his mom past the entry where he pointed at the mural. Rose smiled then escorted her son to the door. I gave them a couple of minutes to settle before I "miraculously" entered.

The interior looked like what I imagine beach restaurants and bars looked like in days gone by. Luke and the food were probably the newest things in there. It was apparent why Planet Follywood was popular with residents and vacationers who wanted to relive their past. Neon beer signs were attached to most walls; another mural was painted on the concrete block wall to the left; wood paneling covered another wall and the ceiling. Overall, a warm, welcoming feel permeated the room. Luke and his mom were seated at a bar-height table in front of the mural and across from a Christmas tree. Luke wore a red sweatshirt that looked like it'd just come out of the package. It probably had. Rose had on a starched, white blouse and a tan lightweight jacket.

Luke spotted me standing in the entry. He waved then said something to his mom. She turned and waved me over.

"Hi, Chris, having lunch?"

I told her I was, then Luke said, "Want to sit with us?"

"I don't want to intrude," although, of course, I did.

"Nonsense," Rose said, "have a seat."

Luke watched me sit. "Been in here before?"

"Many times," I said. "How about you?"

"Our first," Rose answered for her son. "Luke's been talking about it since he saw the mural on the wall outside."

"Cool," he said. "Mom said all those people were in movies, like old movies."

"It was painted by a man from Charleston named James Christopher Hill."

"Think it was okay for him to paint all over that wall? I'd get in trouble if I did something like that."

"I'm sure he had permission."

A server arrived and took our drink orders.

The server left. Luke pointed at the Christmas tree. "Cool tree."

Guess we'd talked enough about the mural.

I said, "It is neat."

"Mom and me put up a tree in Aunt Cindy and Uncle Larry's living room."

Rose touched Luke's arm. "Mom and I."

Luke rolled his eyes, and said, "Mr. Landrum, never marry an English professor."

I smiled. "I'll keep that in mind."

The server returned with our drinks, saving Luke from more English lessons. She asked if we were ready to order. Rose said we needed a few more minutes. Luke took over the conversation from that point, telling me about working at the hardware store, about how cool his bedroom was, how he could see the Folly River and the marsh out his window, and several other things that were important to him but which I forgot as soon as he finished mentioning them. Rose sat back and watched her son share his day to day, almost moment to moment experiences.

The server tried again to see if we were ready to order. Rose asked Luke if he was. He turned to the server and asked if they had hot dogs. They did, so he ordered one, Rose stuck with a cheeseburger, and I ordered a chicken finger basket. Rose excused herself and headed to the restroom.

Luke watched her go, leaned close to me, then said, "Mr. Landrum, think you could do something for me?"

"Suppose it depends on what?"

"I want to get Mom something nice for Christmas. I heard you could find teeth from old, dead sharks on the beach. Can you believe that?"

I nodded.

Luke looked toward the restrooms, turned to me, and said, "Someone who came in the store said people make jewelry from the teeth. Do they sell them somewhere here?"

"In fact, they do. Barb's Books has several pieces of shark tooth jewelry made by Michelle, a local artist."

"Could you buy a necklace with a shark tooth on it for me to give Mom? If it's not too expensive. I have money Uncle Larry paid me for working, so I can pay you back."

"I'll be glad to."

He again glanced toward the restroom. "I'd also like to get one for Aunt Cindy. She's been nice to us."

"I'll do that, Luke."

"Make Aunt Cindy's a little cheaper than the one for Mom. I want Mom to know she's number one."

I smiled and said I would. "What about Uncle Larry?"

"All he wants for Christmas is to sleep for two days without being interrupted or hearing his cash register ding. I'm going to give him a quiet house. No TV, no playing loud."

"That's a great gift."

"What are you two men plotting out here?" Rose said as she returned to the table.

"Nothing, Mom. Guy talk."

"Luke, why don't you go wash your hands before our food arrives?"

He sighed, then slid off the chair.

"Rose, you have a great kid."

"Most of the time."

"Have you told Cindy about Kenneth's visit?"

"No."

"It's none of my business, but I think you should. I know you disagree, but he'd be a prime suspect in starting the fire. Cindy would have a good chance of learning if he was here the day of the fire. Don't you want to know?"

"Yes, but I don't want her going ballistic."

"Rose, I've known your sister a long time. She's at her best when faced with difficult situations. I'd trust her with my life. You can trust her with the truth."

Luke returned wiping his hands together. He smiled, then said, "What are you two grownups plotting out here?"

Touché.

Our conspiring ended when the food arrived. We spent the next hour enjoying the food, the eclectic restaurant, and each other. Cindy was right. Rose and Luke left the restaurant in better spirits and more relaxed than when they arrived. So did I.

Chapter Twenty-Nine

I headed to Barb's Books after leaving Rose and Luke full of food and smiles. A woman I didn't recognize was perusing the romance section while Barb was behind the counter thumbing through a book. She was wearing one of her signature red blouses and black slacks. She saw me at the door, closed the book, and smiled.

"What brings you in? I know it's not to buy a book."

"Right again," I said, then moved to a small table near the check-out counter that was covered with a white velour cloth. "I'm not looking for a book but a couple of these." On the velour, there were several silver necklaces, a couple of bracelets, plus five sets of earrings, all featuring black, shark teeth.

"Christopher, if I may be so bold, I suggest if you're looking to buy jewelry for a woman, you may not want to shop in a store owned by the lady you're dating."

I laughed. "I'll file that wise advice. Actually, I'm Christmas shopping for a gentleman I know." I then shared my assignment.

"In that case," Barb said, "I think these earrings would

be perfect for our Chief." Barb held one up to her ear. It had a half-inch long shark tooth dangling from the short chain. "First, they're pretty. Second, they could visually communicate to local miscreants not to mess with the Chief."

"Perfect. How about Rose?"

She modeled three necklaces before we agreed on one that not only had a shark tooth but a small, silver heart. She asked if I wanted her to gift-wrap the gifts.

"Didn't think you gift-wrapped."

She looked at the customer browsing in the romance section, then said, "I don't unless it's for someone special, someone like Luke."

"Or for me?"

"Nope. I'll also give your young friend the family discount."

I thanked her for the discount, to which she said she wasn't doing it for me, but for Luke. I told her about having lunch at Cindy's suggestion with Rose and Luke. She said she was glad Rose was getting out, hoping it'd keep her from thinking about the fire or losing most everything. I told her how I'd suggested, again, that she tell her sister about her ex-husband's visit to Folly the day before the fire.

"Speaking of fire victims," Barb said as she reached under the counter to pull out a roll of red and gold wrapping paper, "Noelle was in an hour ago. She's off work this week. Said without having an apartment to hang out in, she didn't know what to do with her time. She was heading to the library to work on her book."

"How's she doing?"

"She's young, adapts fairly well to adversity. Better than I would."

I shared what Noelle told me about thinking someone was watching her.

"She told me."

"Think she's right?"

Barb shrugged. "No way to know."

The browser carried a stack of books to the counter. Barb rang them up, then thanked the shopper, who left the store heavier than when she arrived.

Barb finished wrapping the gifts, waved off my attempt to pay, then said, "Let me bounce an idea off you. Noelle seems like a nice woman. She's funny, has a responsible job in Charleston, shows a huge amount of initiative with the book she's writing."

"I agree."

"I hate seeing her living out of her truck. I've got a spare bedroom going to waste. What do you think about me offering to let her stay in my condo until she finds the kind of apartment she's looking for?" Barb laughed. "The perfect dump she calls her dream apartment."

"Are you comfortable with it?"

"I'm leaning that way."

"I think it's a great idea, as long as you're comfortable."

THAT NIGHT BEGAN with me alternating between wondering if Rose would finally tell her sister about her ex-husband's visit, and my thoughts about Barb asking Noelle to move in with her.

My mind shifted to wondering who'd started the fire. Regardless of what Rose thought, I could see it being her ex. He could be eliminated if he was in Tennessee on the day of the fire. Ty could also have made Aimee's fiancée angry enough to start the fire. Most likely, he would've or could've known Ty was at work, so the fire was set to make a point rather than to harm Ty. That brought me to Horace, Janice's ex-husband. She was convinced he's the culprit, but it seems like a stretch. He'd moved on, although Janice's attorney was still after him for money. Was that reason enough to burn her building?

Neil's former boss had more than enough reason to want revenge for being turned in to the IRS. It'd been some time since Neil did that, so would he still be angry enough to set the fire? Then what about the customer Neil had unceremoniously thrown out of the bar? Granted, the man threatened Neil, but, as Cal said, that wasn't uncommon, and seldom led to anything. Could this be the exception?

Noelle was convinced someone was following her, or at least, keeping an eye on her, plus someone left her the note. Without knowing why there was no way to determine if she bothered someone enough to torch the building.

The most logical arsonist was Russell O'Leary. He was behind in his mortgage, appeared to have little means to catch up. His alibi for the time of the fire was suspect at best. Finally, he'd told me he didn't want the building in the first place.

From my limited time with Russell, he appeared to be a nice man, yet was in over his head maintaining the building. The fire was set when the building most likely would've been vacant. That seemed like something Russell would've taken into consideration.

Cindy knew everything I did about Russell, so I was confident she was following up. So, with all of that cleared up, I should be able to get a good night's sleep.

So, why didn't I?

Chapter Thirty

Despite little sleep, I was awake at six o'clock. I closed my eyes attempting to catch a few more minutes sleep. I failed. The next thing I knew, it was eight-thirty, far more than a few minutes later. While well-rested, I was hungry. The unseasonably warm weather from a few days ago had returned, so I walked next door. Ty was at the register adjusting a string of Christmas lights attached around the check-out stand.

"Hey, Mr. Landrum, want a treat?"

"No thanks, Ty. I wanted to stop by to see how you were doing."

"I'm doing better than these lights, Mr. Landrum."

"You're brighter than they are," I said. He could take it any way he wanted. "How's Lost?"

"Great. That little critter loves the warmer weather. She isn't a fan of staying in the car but handles it good when the temperature ain't too cold."

I nodded, thinking that'd apply to all of us.

Ty continued, "Anything I can help you with?"

"No. Grabbing coffee and something for breakfast."

"You know where it is. Merry Christmas."

"You going to Cal's Christmas party?"

"I don't know. I'll be working Bert's free community breakfast. It's over at ten, so I don't know if I'll be here longer than that. Besides, ain't most of the people at Cal's party old, umm, older than me?"

"All ages will be there," I said, although on average age he was right. "I'd love to see you."

"I'll ponder it," he said, then started waiting on a man who'd arrived at the counter.

I grabbed a cinnamon Danish, drew a cup of coffee, then returned to the register.

Ty took my money and said, "Done pondered it, Mr. Landrum. If I get out of here early enough, I'll be there."

"Fantastic."

I started home, smiled when I saw Ty's Miata in the back of the small parking lot, then jumped out of the way when an older-model white Chevrolet Malibu with a dent in the driver's door pulled in, nearly hitting me.

Janice Raque stepped out, gave me a dirty look like I had some nerve getting in the way of her car, hesitated, then smiled.

"Sorry, Chris. Didn't recognize you."

I wondered if that meant she wouldn't be sorry if she'd run down anyone else.

"Hi, Janice."

"Glad I ran into you." She smiled. "Didn't mean literally. Got something to tell you. Got a minute?"

I told her I did.

Her arms were wrapped around her torso like she was cold. "Let's get in the car? It's warmer."

I wasn't cold but agreed. Since she had something to say, I remained quiet and took a sip of coffee.

"Remember the other day when we were talking? I told you I was certain Horace was the one who set the fire."

That wasn't something I could easily forget. "Yes."

"Wasn't him."

"How do you know?"

"We had, guess still have, a mutual friend. Name's Sally. She called yesterday to see if I'd heard about Horace. I'd heard a bunch of things about the no-good, two-timing, goat herder. I wasn't sure what she was talking about, so I asked. You'll never guess what she told me."

She hesitated. I wondered if she wanted me to guess. Instead, I said, "What?"

"He had a stroke, happened two days before the fire. The two-timer was in the hospital in Mt. Pleasant. Nearly kicked the bucket."

"That's too bad."

She sighed. "Not bad enough. He didn't die. Got released yesterday. That's what Sally called to tell me. Like she thought I cared. No sir, I didn't."

"He couldn't have started the fire."

"I figured the stroke was caused by the old man pretending he was a youngster fiddlin' with that floozy he ran off with if you know what I mean." She offered a sly grin.

I did. Scratch one suspect. Which reminded me of something that'd bothered me since I had lunch with her in Snapper Jack's, something that contributed to me getting little sleep last night. It was something she said before nearly falling off the chair. Instead of following up at the time, I thought it better to catch her before she hit the floor.

"Janice, remember when we met the other day in Snapper Jack's?"

She smiled. "Not much. I was a bit under the weather if you know what I mean."

Drunk would have been the word I would've chosen.

"We were talking about the apartment building and you said people had asked you about living there. You mentioned two people, a man, I believe his name was Jeff, and a woman named something like Kaycee. Remember?"

"I remember them, but don't remember telling you. Sure it was me?"

Her not remembering didn't surprise me considering her condition at the time.

"What do you remember about them?"

"The guy, Jeff, or something like that, looked like a street person if you ask me. He stopped me in the parking lot one afternoon, said he was looking for somewhere to live and wanted to know what I thought about the apartment building. I told him I didn't think much of it, but that's about all."

"What about the woman? You started to tell me something, but, umm, we were interrupted." I didn't add, "by you falling off the chair."

"Let's see. I believe she said her name was Kaycee Ericson. She came knocking on my door, suppose a week or so before the fire." Janice closed her eyes, then tapped her fingers on the steering wheel. "Told me she owned some apartments. They were full and she had someone she was looking for a place to live. Think I told her about the vacant unit on the first floor. She then asked how long I lived there. If I liked living in the building. Then she asked how many people lived in my apartment. That got my dander up. I asked if she was a census taker or what. I wanted to find out if she was something official before I told her it was none of her damned business who lived in my apartment. Nearly slammed the door in her face." She could tell I was getting pissed." Janice looked out the side window, scratched the side of her face, then said, "She then told me she was looking at buying the place. That got my attention, so I let her in, offered her a beer, told her everything she wanted to know. Even told her about the leaky faucet, although I didn't have to since she could hear it drip, drip, drip all the way in the living room. Figured if she bought it, she couldn't be as bad a landlord as O'Leary. Our conversation then headed a direction I didn't like."

"How?"

"She started whispering like there were other people in the room nosing into what she was saying. Said she was trying to figure if she could fix the building up enough so she could increase rents enough to make the deal work." She looked at me and shrugged. "Didn't think it was too wise telling a tenant all that. I'm no math wizard, but it sounded like it would've had me digging deeper in my pocketbook to live there. Hell, Chris, if I could afford a higher rent, I wouldn't have been living in that dump."

"Janice, did she give you a card or her contact information?"

"Sure did."

"Do you have it?"

She frowned and looked at her hand on the steering wheel. "It was in the apartment." She clapped her hands together like she was wiping something off. "It's ashes."

"Janice, I appreciate you sharing. I don't want to keep you any longer."

"Chris, you ain't keeping me. All I have to do is go back to the damned hotel room."

"I'd better be going anyway. Are you going to be at Cal's Christmas party?"

She nodded. "Anything to get out of the hotel room."

Chapter Thirty-One

I finally made it home and to the cinnamon Danish I'd been carrying for a half hour. I microwaved the cold coffee then sat at the kitchen table. It was good eliminating Horace from the suspect list, although I never had him near the top.

Janice did say something that struck me as significant, more than anything about Horace. That was Kaycee Ericson's visit to Janice's apartment a week before the fire. She apparently was someone who wanted to buy the building. Was Russell O'Leary going to sell to her? I'd never heard of Kaycee Ericson until Janice shared her name. Was she local?

A call to Chief LaMond might provide answers.

"What do you want now?" she said.

I'd given up long ago trying to get my friends to answer with anything resembling a civil response.

"What do you know about Kaycee Ericson?"

"Chris, you've been around Charles way too much. What's Kaycee have to do with anything?"

I shared what Janice Raque had told me about the visit.

"Interesting. Are you trying to screw up my theory that O'Leary torched his building?"

"Cindy, you're Chief. I'm simply a lowly citizen sharing a story. I have no business sticking my nose in your investigation."

"Chris, I say this lovingly, you're as full of crap as Dumbo the elephant."

"Glad you said it lovingly."

"Want to pout or learn about Kaycee?"

"What do you think?"

"She lives in a condo across from Harris Teeter. Been here two years at the most. Someone said she moved from New Jersey, is connected to money. She's built a couple of new oceanfront McMansions, sold them for a tidy profit."

"How do you know all that?"

"I'm Chief. I know everything."

I waited, knowing once she got past the bluster, she'd elaborate.

"She's been all the talk around City Hall. With the two McMansions and now a condo building she wants to develop out West Ashley near the County Park, she's good at pushing the zoning regulation boundaries. So far, she hasn't crossed the line, but according to folks who know more about zoning than this lowly public servant, she's within millimeters of violating the regs."

"Cindy, is this enough for you to talk with Kaycee?"

"To be determined."

"Meaning?"

"Meaning, in fifteen minutes after I get a pesky citizen off the phone, Russell O'Leary will be in this big impressive office of Director of Public Safety. It's time for me to ram sharpened bamboo sticks under his fingernails to get the truth about his alleged visit to the metropolis of Atlanta. Truth like where he stayed, how long he was actually there, and if he's fortunate, proof he was there instead of here incinerating his building."

"Cindy, other than bamboo under his nails, that sounds like a good plan. Will you add questions about him selling the building?"

"Wasn't until three minutes ago. Bye."

Progress, she said bye before hanging up.

Thirty minutes later, the phone rang. At first, I thought it was Cindy, then realized she'd be talking to Russell. The screen read *Barb*.

"Good morning, my favorite bookstore owner."

"Only bookstore owner."

"You're my favorite, regardless how many bookstores there are. What did I do to deserve a call?"

"Nothing. I wanted to tell you something I did last night."

That got my attention. "What?"

"Invited Noelle to move in with me until she finds the kind of apartment she's looking for."

"That's wonderful. What did she say?"

"Short version, yes. Slightly longer version, she was thrilled. She said if she had to spend many more nights in her truck, she'd either have to find a chiropractor or a witch doctor to work on her back. Before she told me that, she kept saying she didn't want to inconvenience me. I told her she wouldn't. She kept offering to pay rent. I told her no. I couldn't tell for certain because of her sunglasses, but I think I saw tears."

"You're a kind person. She's lucky to have you as a friend."

"Don't know about that, but it made me feel good being able to help."

"The Christmas spirit in action."

"Tis the season. I met her at Loggerhead's. Before she left, know what she said?"

"I hope it was thank you."

Barb laughed. "She got serious, touched me on the arm, looked across the street at my condo building, and said something like, 'Don't take offense, Barb. Your condo is way too nice for what I'm looking for.' I told her I wasn't offended. She's moving in tonight."

I was touched by Barb's generosity. After her call, I got up from the table, carried my coffee cup to my office. Charles was right, all that was in the room was a small table holding my computer and printer, a chair, and a filing cabinet holding years of tax papers, plus other items I probably didn't need to save.

I sat, took a sip of coffee getting cold again, and punched in Neil Wilson's number. I didn't think he was going to answer, but he finally did. He sounded like the phone awakened him. It may have. I told him who was calling then asked if he was available for lunch. He said he was due at Cal's at three but could meet me at the Lost Dog Cafe in an hour.

Good to his word, he was standing in front of the restaurant when I arrived. He looked like he'd just climbed out of bed, although I knew he'd been awake an hour earlier. He wore a royal blue sweatshirt with The Griffon Pub in large block letters on the front, tan slacks with fraying cuffs. His hair was sticking out from a Charleston RiverDogs cap. He looked like he'd slept in his clothes.

We were escorted to a table in the center of the room. There were only four other tables occupied. Neil put his hat on the edge of the table, yawned, and ran his hand through his hair. It did little to get hairs going the same direction.

"Did you work last night?"

"Until two this morning. Can't you tell?"

I smiled. "Yes."

A server, who said her name was Anna, appeared with pen in hand.

"Coffee," Neil said. "That'll get my eyes open enough to read the menu."

I told her the same.

I filled the time until Anna returned by talking about the near-countless photos of dogs adorning the walls. Neil observed how different the decorations and colors were from those in Cal's. Anna returned with mugs of steaming hot coffee. She said she'd be back to take our order. Neil took three sips before speaking.

"I appreciate you calling," he said, then hesitated, "although it made me wonder why."

Good to her word, Anna returned asking if we were ready to order. While I'd told Neil the invitation was for lunch, he had breakfast on his mind. He started to order a bagel until I said I was buying. He switched to bacon and eggs; I went with French toast, surprise, surprise. Anna said, "Excellent choices," and headed to the kitchen. I wondered if she ever said, "Terrible choice."

"Chris, I appreciate you picking up the tab. Staying at the hotel is breaking me."

"That's what I wanted to talk to you about. I have an extra room at my place. If you want, you could move in until you find somewhere of your own."

He stared at me. "You're kidding."

"It's nothing luxurious. The room's small. Has a blowup mattress, no real bed."

Okay, it doesn't have a blowup mattress, but with luck, it will before he gets there.

"Not to be unappreciative," he said, "how much?"

"Nothing. It's yours until you find a place to stay."

He repeated, "You're kidding."

"I'm serious."

He stood, walked around the table, and shook my hand. "Thank you. I can't believe something good is happening to me at Christmas."

Anna arrived with our food, so Neil returned to his chair.

He took a bite of eggs, then said, "I won't be able to

move in until tomorrow. Besides, I've already paid the hotel for tonight. Wouldn't want that money to go to waste."

Good. That'll give me time to find a blowup mattress.

"That's fine, Neil."

Two more bites and he said, "Chris, you're really not kidding?"

Chapter Thirty-Two

Before leaving the Dog, Neil told me he needed to get to the hotel to take a shower before heading to work. He wanted to use as much of the hotel's water as he could to get his money's worth. I remained at the table to call Charles.

"Ready to go?" I said.

"Sure," he said, not asking where.

"I'll be there in ten minutes." I hung up on him, a move he'd perfected. It felt good being on this end of the line for a change.

Ten minutes later, I pulled in his crushed shell and gravel parking lot to see him standing in front of his apartment. He was wearing a maroon Texas A&M sweatshirt under a lightweight jacket, well-worn jeans, and his Tilley.

"We going to buy my Christmas present?" he said as he slid in the passenger seat.

"No," I said, then pulled out of the lot.

He snapped his fingers. "Done figured it out. We're going to catch a flight to Bora Bora for the holidays?"

"No," I repeated. This was nearly as much fun as hanging up on him.

We'd pulled off the island and past Harris Teeter.

"I see we're not grocery shopping. You can fill in our destination at any time."

Five minutes later, I pulled in Walmart's parking lot.

"Let me guess," he said, "we're going to Walmart."

"I see why you think you're a detective."

Before he could respond with one of his many smart-aleck remarks, the phone rang.

"Good afternoon, Cindy."

I parked and Charles motioned for me to put the phone on speaker. Rather than having to repeat everything she said, I tapped the speaker icon. Charles smiled.

"It's getting better by the minute," Cindy said. "Don't be surprised the next few days if you hear Russell O'Leary has been arrested for torching his apartment building."

"He confess?"

"It's not what he told me but what he didn't."

Charles leaned toward the phone. "What's that mean, Chief?"

"Chris, you done gone and got a talking disease. You sound like your worthless friend."

Charles said, "Chief, he doesn't sound anything like Bob Howard."

I heard her chuckle before saying, "His other worthless friend."

Enough! "Chief, what did Russell tell you?"

"He stuck to his story that sounds like a fairytale. Still claims he was in Atlanta, as in downtown Atlanta, attending a get-rich-quick seminar, sleeping in a nearby cheap hotel, paying cash, and not able to remember the name of where he stayed. His body language and failure to look me in the eyes made me not believe a word of it."

Charles said, "Who wouldn't want to look in such a lovely lady's eyes? He's definitely lying."

"Charles, your BS is appreciated, but it doesn't prove guilt."

"Cindy," I said, "if that's the case, why do you think he'll be arrested?"

"The only thing he appeared certain of in his far-fetched version of a trip to Atlanta, was where the seminar was held. After he left, I called the Westin Peachtree Plaza, the hotel he could remember. I had a pleasant talk with a nice lady with a cute southern accent. Seems she's in charge of meetings and seminars."

"Let me guess," I said, "there wasn't a get-rich-quick seminar the day of the apartment fire."

"Not that day, not the day before, not the day after, in fact, not the week before or after. The closest thing they hosted was a two-day meeting on financing options for large office buildings held two days after Russell returned to South Carolina."

Charles said, "So why isn't he sitting in a jail cell?"

"Charged with what, fibbing to the fuzz? We need more. I told him to bring proof, anything, gas receipts, restaurant receipts, hell, I'd even take a receipt written on toilet paper from a panhandler if Russell donated to the bum's liquor fund. Otherwise, my hands are tied until I have something more than a hunch to arrest him on."

"Cindy," I said, "you're convinced he did it?"

"Plum near a thousand percent."

"Have you talked to Kaycee Ericson?"

"I'm calling her as soon as I get off the phone with Folly's nosiest troublemakers."

It didn't take Charles's detective skills to know who she was talking about. I wished her luck.

"Did you drive me out here to sit in the parking lot?" Charles said after Cindy ended her call with the trou-blemakers.

Instead of telling him where we were going, I took the show him approach. It took several unsuccessful trips up aisles before I found the blowup mattresses in the sports and outdoors section. I savored the walk by not telling him what I was trying to find. Cruel, but sweet revenge for him doing similar things over the years.

I finally gave in and shared why I was looking at blowup mattresses.

"Wonderful. You took my advice about taking in Neil."

He'd suggested it, but I hated giving him the satisfaction of knowing he was right. Oh well, why not? After all, it's Christmas.

"Yes, it was your idea, a good one."

He beamed and curtsied. It was worth telling him the truth to see him happy. We studied our options when he came up with another good idea. I should buy an electric pump to inflate the mattress. It was a good idea, but he didn't have to add I'd need the pump because I was too old to blow it up with my fossilizing lungs.

On the way home, I called Bob Howard and hit the speaker button for Charles. While I had confidence Cindy was on the right trail with Russell, and that she'd contact Kaycee Ericson like she told me she would, I wasn't ready to convict the landlord. He seemed sincere with everything he'd told me. It also seemed counterproductive when he told me he was glad the building had been reduced to ashes. If anyone had dirt on or would know someone who would know anything bad about Kaycee, it'd be Bob.

Willie Nelson was singing "On the Road Again" in the background, when Bob answered with, "On your way to get a cheeseburger?"

"No."

"Then why are you wasting my valuable time?"

"Bob, I appreciate you taking time out of your busy day to talk to me," I said, exuding sarcasm.

"Damned right, I'm busy. You know how much energy it takes to sit, drink a beer, and watch the overpaid cook fixing burgers? What do you need?"

See why we're such good friends?

"What do you know about Kaycee Ericson?"

"You nosin' in something that's none of your business?"

"Yes."

"Figures. Don't know much. She's bought a few buildings over here, hear she's itching to be a big-time developer. Heard she either is or was married to Alan, who actually is a big-time developer. That's it, my well of information's dry."

"Thanks."

"Does this have something to do with the apartment building fire?"

"Yes."

"Think she set it?"

"Maybe."

"Let me make some calls to guys who'll know more about her than what I said."

"Bob, I'd appreciate it."

"Don't appreciate it enough to frequent this fine-dining establishment." He hung up.

I was impressed, first because Bob gave me some information without me having to buy food, and second, Charles hadn't interrupted.

Chapter Thirty-Three

After dropping Charles at his apartment, I went home to repurpose my office into a bedroom. I was glad Charles encouraged me to buy the pump, otherwise, it would've taken me five years and probably a heart attack to inflate the mattress with lung power. Using the pump, I had the bed inflated, covered with sheets that were too large, and added a pillow I'd forgotten I had. All Neil's bedroom lacked was a piece of chocolate on the pillow and a Gideon's Bible.

With my hotelier duties completed, I moved to the living room to review what, if anything, I'd learned during the extraordinarily busy day. Since I'd innocently walked to Bert's for breakfast and coffee, I'd talked with Ty, Janice, and Neil, residents of sixty percent of the five occupied apartments in the ill-fated building. Janice eliminated Horace as a suspect, while adding Kaycee. Two of the displaced residents, Noelle and Neil, had found somewhere to live. And, it appeared another suspect, Russell, was on the verge of being arrested.

While a lot had transpired, I wasn't closer to figuring out

who set the fire than I'd been on my walk to Bert's. My phone rang as I came to that realization.

Charles said, "I'll pick you up at nine in the morning."

"Going to buy my Christmas present, or taking a flight to Bora Bora?"

Silence was the response to what I thought was a humorous comment. He'd hung up.

Charles's definition of nine o'clock was eight-thirty, so I was waiting for him on my screened-in porch when he pulled in the drive.

"On time, good," he said as I slipped in the car.

He wore a navy-blue sweatshirt with Auburn University in orange on the front.

"Morning, Charles," I said, and resisted asking where we were going.

He drove two blocks then turned on East Arctic Avenue, before saying, "Know why I wore this sweatshirt?"

"To keep you warm?" I said, knowing it wasn't the answer he wanted.

"Guess again."

Then it struck me.

"Auburn has a well-known college of veterinarian medicine, so we're going to Martha Wright's zoo."

His head jerked my direction. "Wow! I may give you a promotion in my private detective agency."

"Charles, now that I know where we're going, how about why?"

"Martha called last night. Asked if I could stop by this morning."

"Why?"

"Suppose because of my charm, good looks, way with women."

I rolled my eyes. "Again, why?"

"Clueless. I'm bringing you in case she got a stray mountain lion."

I didn't waste time saying the mountain lion theory was

as remote as her wanting him to visit because of his good looks, charm, and way with women.

Martha greeted us at the door. I was surprised no barking dogs were surrounding her.

"Glad you could make it," she said. "I see you brought Chris."

She was smiling so I couldn't tell what she thought about Charles's plus one.

"Chris loves hearing about your animals, so I thought he'd enjoy visiting."

I did?

"Great," she said, with little enthusiasm. "Come in. We're gathered in the sitting room."

Other than Squeezy, I didn't know who "we" could include. Seconds later, that mystery was answered when I saw Martha's neighbor, Dixie Thompson, seated in one of the wingback chairs. I'd met Dixie before meeting Martha. She lived across the street from Martha and had been her friend for years. She was in her late-seventies, five-foot-eight, thin, with white hair that would put the whitest paint color to shame. Her hair looked even whiter compared to her tanned, leathery face.

Dixie stood, held up a tumbler holding an amber-colored liquid, and said, "Moscow."

Charles was the invited guest, so I let him respond, besides, I had no idea what to say.

"Huh?" he articulately said.

Dixie held the tumbler higher. "It's five o'clock somewhere."

Martha laughed. "In Moscow."

"Oh," Charles said.

Watching Dixie sway as she chuckled at Martha's remark, I wondered where it'd been five o'clock an hour or two earlier.

"Fellas," Martha said, "how about a hot toddy?"

"Or bourbon," Dixie added.

"No thanks," Charles said. "Wouldn't happen to have any coffee brewed?"

"Heaven's no," Martha said. "That stuff's not good for you. Let me grab a chair from the kitchen. Wouldn't want you to sit on the floor."

Charles said, "Martha, I'll get it."

She pointed her cane in the direction of the kitchen like Charles wouldn't know how to find it. Fortunately, Dixie was in the chair closest to Squeezy's occupied aquarium, so I sat on the only vacant seat. Charles returned and pulled the kitchen chair up beside Martha.

Martha waited for Charles to get comfortable, then said, "Gentlemen, I appreciate you coming over. I wanted to——"

Dixie interrupted, "Martha, God love her, wanted to be an unvarnished jackass. I told her so in no uncertain terms."

Martha pointed her cane at Dixie. "Dear, why don't you let me explain?"

Yes, Martha, please, I thought.

"It's your house," Dixie said, then took another sip.

"As you recall, when you visited the other day, you asked if I'd let the young man from Bert's stay here until he found satisfactory housing."

"Ty Striker," Charles said.

"Yes, anyway, I reacted strongly."

"Like a jackass," Dixie added, only to receive a dirty look from her friend.

"I was concerned about how my good friend Dixie and my dearly beloved deceased husband would react to a man moving in with me."

"Cut to the chase, Martha," Dixie said. "You thought we'd think it was for sex."

Martha's face turned red. "Dixie, I don't think that's appropriate talk——"

Again, Dixie interrupted, apparently one of her strengths, "Martha, you know that's what you thought. What did I tell you?"

"Dixie, I don't think—"

"I told you the man from Bert's was young enough to be your grandson, heavens, possibly great-grandson. The last time you had sex that peanut farmer from Georgia was President. I promise sex won't be popping in Ty's head when he sees you. I think it'd be great for you having someone who walks on two legs living in here not slithering around like Squeezy or walking on all fours like most of your family members."

"But, what about—"

"I know, I know. What would Tommy think? I told you he ain't doing a bit of thinking down in that hole in the ground. Not a bit."

Martha leaned forward in her chair, glared at her friend, then said, "Dixie, enough." She turned to Charles, then to me. "Guys, Dixie has some good points. Crudely put, but good. If you think the young man would be interested, I'd be honored for him to move in. As I think you said the last time you were here, this place is too large for me to keep up by myself."

Charles glanced at me. I said, "Martha, I think Ty would be thrilled."

"So would his kitten, Lost," Charles added.

"Martha," I said, "You'll make Ty's Christmas."

"Ladies," Charles said, "will you be at Cal's Christmas party?"

Dixie said, "Can't speak for Martha, but I'll be there. We always go to the potluck supper at Planet Follywood, but that's later."

"Don't know why you can't speak for me, you always do."

"Okay," Dixie said, "Martha will be there. She may even bring her new boy toy." She slapped her knee and laughed. "Then after we get home, he can come-a-courtin' over my way if Martha don't wear him out."

On that, it was time to leave. I told Martha I'd talk to Ty and get back with her.

In the car, I said, "At least we didn't have to put up with any of Martha's animals."

"You got enough dog hair on your butt from the chair to build a dog. I think I would've hugged Squeezy before listening more to Dixie."

"Good point," I said, "as long as it was you holding the boa."

Instead of turning in my drive, Charles drove a hundred feet farther and pulled in Bert's lot.

"Let's tell Ty," Charles said.

Ty was behind the register talking to Shawn, another friend of mine, holding his tiny dog Bruiser. He was paying for a loaf of bread while Ty was breaking a treat in half and giving it to Bruiser. Shawn left so Charles asked Ty if he had a few minutes. I was no expert, but it appeared Ty was working. I wondered how he'd have time for us. Charles added, "It's important."

A woman stepped behind us with a bag of chips. Ty looked around and asked a man working behind the deli counter if he could cover the register. The man nodded.

Ty said, "Let's go outside. I need to check on Lost."

On the way to his car, I asked if he knew Martha Wright.

"By reputation. Isn't she the woman who feeds strays, has a hundred pets?"

I smiled. "She does feed strays, but her pet count is closer to a dozen."

"Don't think I've talked to her, or if I have, I didn't know who she was. Why?"

I shared that we'd come from her house where she said she'd love for Ty to stay there until he found somewhere more suitable. I explained that Martha's house was on the ocean and had about two-thousand times more living space than his Miata.

"Why would a stranger want to take me in, me in?"

I resisted saying it was because she took in strays. "She knew about the fire, heard you were living in your car, and had Lost. She's an animal lover, so she thought her house would be perfect, that is, if you had any interest."

Yes, some of that was reimagining history, but I wanted it to sound like Martha's idea.

"I'd be thrilled for the opportunity," he said. "When can I meet her?"

I asked when he got off work. He told me six. I told him I'd let her know he'd accept her kind offer, and if okay with her, he could go to her house after work.

"How's that sound?"

"Wonderful."

I gave him Martha's address and Charles gave him her phone number in case he couldn't get there today.

"Oh, one more thing, Mr. Landrum. You were asking me if I knew of anyone who might know about the fire, anyone other than us who lived there."

I vaguely remembered saying something about it. "Yes."

"Did you see that lady behind you in line before we came out here?"

I noticed someone, but that was all. "Yes, why?"

"Today was the first time I've seen her since the fire. It reminded me she talked to me two, maybe three, weeks before the building burned. I was heading to my apartment and she was in the parking lot."

Charles said, "What'd she want?"

"Nothing important. Stuff like how I liked living there, how long I'd been there, if the landlord kept up the building good."

He was right, I didn't see how any of that was important. "Why'd you mention it?"

"I could be wrong, but I think I saw her near the building a time or two after that. Sort of thought it was a little strange, that's all."

"You saw her two or three times before the fire?" I said.

"Think so."

Charles said, "Did she give you her name?"

"Yeah. It was something like Kelsey."

I said, "Could it be Kaycee?"

Ty nodded. "Kaycee, umm. Could be."

I looked back toward the store. A blue SUV was pulling out of the lot, but the windows were tinted. I couldn't see the driver. "Ty, is that her in the blue SUV?"

He looked at the vehicle heading east on Ashley Avenue. "That's her car."

She was driving a Maserati SUV, a blue Maserati like the one parked adjacent to the apartment building's parking lot during the Christmas parade. Of course, there could be more than one blue Maserati SUV on Folly, but what were the odds?

"Ty," I said, "other than asking about the stuff you already mentioned, do you recall her saying anything else?"

He tapped on the Miata's window. Lost jumped from the seat to the headrest then gave Ty a *where's my food* look. Ty opened the door enough to get his hand in and wrapped it around Lost's stomach. The kitten purred as Ty lifted him out of the car, cradling him in the crook of his elbow. Charles being Charles stepped closer to Ty and rubbed Lost under his chin, then told the feline he was getting a new home, a home with animals to play with.

Ty handed Lost to Charles, then turned back to me. "Sorry, Mr. Landrum, what was the question?"

"Do you recall Kaycee saying anything else?"

"Not really. I think she must've been interested in renting an apartment."

Charles continued to rub the underside of his feline friend's chin, but said, "Why think that?"

"She wanted to know if there were vacant units."

He hadn't mentioned that earlier.

I said, "You sure?"

"Yeah. I told her the one on the first floor was empty. I offered to give her the landlord's name and number. Said she already had it."

Charles handed Lost back to Ty, and said, "Guess that's why she was asking how well he maintained the building."

"That's what I figured."

It could be as simple as that, I thought. Or not.

Charles said, "Did she say anything else?"

"Don't recall anything." He looked at his watch, then slipped Lost back in his car. "Guys, I'd better get back in there. I really need to keep this job."

I thanked him for talking with us and said I'd let Martha know he'd be stopping by after work.

He headed to the store. Charles headed to his car, until I said, "Charles, remember when we were on our way to the fire?"

"Duh, how could I forget? We were on—"

"Let me finish."

He shrugged. "So?"

"Do you remember seeing vehicles in the lot near the apartment building's parking area?"

"Chris, I remember black smoke, red flames, red fire trucks, and two ambulances that nearly ran us down. I don't remember what was parked nearby. Why?"

"One of the vehicles was a blue Maserati SUV."

Charles looked toward Bert's. "Like the one what's her name was driving?"

"Exactly."

"Coincidence?"

"What do you think?"

He continued looking at Bert's like the SUV would return. "Could she live in the building beside the apartment building?"

"No. Cindy told me she lives in a condo near Harris Teeter."

"Think you need to tell Cindy."

I said, "I will."

"I mean now."

I reached for my phone, when Charles added, "Don't forget to push that little speaker icon."

Instead of getting a live voice, Cindy's message informed me she was unable to take the call, for the caller to leave a message. I asked her to call when she got a chance. Charles harrumphed, then mumbled something about where were the police when you needed them.

I told him I'd let him know after I talked to the Chief. He asked if he needed to drive me home so I wouldn't have to walk thirty yards. I said I could manage the voyage. He left me standing in Bert's side parking area.

I was still in the lot when the phone rang. I figured Charles missed hearing Cindy by seconds, but I was wrong. Close, but wrong.

"Chris, this is Rose, Cindy's sister. Did I catch you at a bad time?"

I said no and resisted asking her if she could teach my friends phone etiquette.

"I'm calling as Luke's social secretary," she said then chuckled. "We're heading to Planet Follywood in a few minutes for lunch. Luke said how much you liked the restaurant. He wanted me to call to see if you'd join us."

I said I'd be honored. I also realized this was the first time in my adult life a pre-teen had his social secretary call to invite me to share a meal.

Chapter Thirty-Four

I approached Luke and Rose's table.

"Mr. Landrum," Luke said, "You said you loved eating here, so I asked mom to call you."

I thanked him for the invitation as a server arrived and put a glass of what appeared to be iced tea in front of Rose, a soft drink beside Luke. He asked if I wanted anything. I said water was fine.

"Luke," I said, "did Uncle Larry give you the day off?"

"No, he said with Christmas two days away, he needed all the help he could get. I told him even a little boy has to eat. He said I could bring mom here for lunch."

"You're a tough negotiator," I said.

He smiled like I'd called him king of the world.

"This is part of my Christmas gift," Rose said. "Luke is using his own money to buy lunch."

"Mr. Landrum, because you've been so nice to me, I want to buy yours too."

The phone rang before I told him that wasn't necessary. Bob Howard's name appeared on the screen.

"Hi, Bob."

"Aren't you going to insult me like you usually do?"

"It's Christmas, besides, you have that backward."

"Whatever. I have el scoopo on that woman you asked about."

"Hang on a second," I said, then told my lunch mates I needed to take the call then headed to the back of the restaurant.

"Okay," I said.

"If that was a second, you need a better watch. Ready for el scoopo?"

"Ready."

"Kaycee Ericson. Late-forties, good looking according to the old coots I talked to. She divorced Alan Ericson a while back. Alan is a big-time developer in Charleston, but he's done projects as far away as Asheville. Mostly large apartment complexes. Anyway, his ex took a bunch of money in the divorce. She built a small office building a half-block off Center Street in your town, and either two or three ocean-front McMansions. My source was vague on the number. As even you, as ignorant as you are about anything building wise, know, your zoning regulators are doing everything they can to limit new construction, especially super-sized buildings on property that originally held small beach houses. In other words, Kaycee has been running into brick walls instead of open arms from those in control."

I'd heard something similar from Cindy and shared that with Bob.

"Okay, know it all, did you hear she's trying to find properties, mostly multi-unit properties where the owners are, let's say, having financial difficulties?"

"That's new."

"Like all good storytellers, I saved the best for last."

I waited for him to continue, he didn't, so I assumed he wanted me to beg for the best. "What's that, Mr. Fount of Information?"

"That's better. One of my sources said several years ago,

one of Alan Ericson's apartment buildings had a horrible fire. Was it caused by lightning? No. Electrical problem? No. How about by Aunt Sally leaving something on the stove? Nope, again. Now that I've given you all the clues, think you can guess the cause?"

"Arson?"

"You're smarter than the average cucumber. There was a ton of speculation that Alan set the fire, but not an ounce of proof."

"You're saying that Kaycee is guilty by marriage?"

"Nope. I'm telling you what happened. You figure out the rest."

"Anything else?"

"Hell, do I have to get you a signed, notarized confession?"

"If you don't mind."

He must've minded. He hung up.

That didn't prove Kaycee started the fire but was information Cindy needed. Seeing Luke staring in my direction, it'd have to wait.

I returned to the table and Luke's broad smile.

"Mr. Landrum, I made an executive decision, although mom said I shouldn't."

"What was that, Luke?"

"I ordered your lunch. I got you the same thing you had when we were here the last time. I figured you liked it, or you wouldn't have got it then."

"Excellent decision, Luke."

His smile increased. "See Mom, told you so."

"Everything okay?" Rose said, then nodded her head in the direction where I'd been.

"Yes. Is your sister working today? I left her a message earlier but haven't heard from her."

"As far as I know. She said she had several meetings."

Luke interrupted, "Aunt Cindy said yucky meetings."

"Luke, you know not to interrupt," Rose said.

He bowed his head.

Rose turned to me. "You haven't heard from her today?"

"No, why?"

"Last night, she told me she had news about the fire. She was going to call you."

Lunch arrived. I wasn't the only one to order the same meal as last time. A hot dog was placed in front of Luke, a cheeseburger for Rose, and my chicken fingers. As much as I wanted to fight it, most of us are creatures of habit. We ate silently for a couple of minutes, but I kept going back to what Ty and Bob had said.

"Rose, this may be a strange question, but do you remember seeing a blue Maserati SUV parked near the apartment complex?"

"I don't pay much attention to cars, never have."

Luke said, "I do."

Rose said, "Luke's best friend's dad owns a Chevy dealership in Morristown."

"Len's dad is cool," Luke said. "He lets us roam around the lot. When the repair shop is closed, we can go in there. His dad says insurance wouldn't let us go in when mechanics are working."

That got my attention, about paying attention, not about his friend Len. "Do you mean you pay attention to cars, or do you remember seeing a blue SUV?"

Rose patted her son on the arm. "See, Luke, how you say things is important."

He sighed, "I know, mom. You tell me all the time."

I can't imagine how it would be growing up with an English teacher mom.

I said. "Luke, help me understand what you mean."

He glanced at Rose then turned to me. "It's sort of both, Mr. Landrum. I like looking at cars, especially new ones. And, I remember seeing a blue Maserati."

"Do you remember when you saw it?"

"Day after we moved in. I thought it was cool looking. I hadn't seen one."

"Was that the only time you saw it?"

"Umm, two more times, I think."

"When?"

"Suppose the next time was the day before the fire. It was close to our lot. Then I saw it the morning we were walking to watch the Christmas parade."

"Where was it?"

"Parked at the road. I figured the lady in it was going to move in our building."

"Why?"

"Mom and me were walking up our street when—"

"Mom and I, Luke," Rose said.

Luke made a noise that sounded like a braying horse. I bit the inside of my lip to keep from laughing.

"Yes, mom." He continued, "Mom and I were headed toward the street where the parade was going to be. I looked back and saw the lady carrying a large box, sort of like those boxes we packed stuff in to move here. I figured she was moving in."

"Luke, are you sure she came out of the blue SUV?"

Rose looked at Luke, then at me with narrowed eyes.

"Yes, sir. Know it was her. She didn't move in, did she? Someone said the next-door apartment was still empty when the fire started."

I ate the chicken fingers, but they could easily have been glued sawdust for all the attention I paid to them. I held my need to talk to Cindy in check and tried to make Luke's lunch for his mom and me as positive as possible.

I must not have shown as much anxiety as I felt. We finished and Luke said it'd been a wonderful Christmas lunch, that we ought to do it again.

All I wanted to do again was talk to Chief LaMond. She may be convinced that Russell O'Leary torched his building. I thought I had a persuasive argument she was wrong.

Chapter Thirty-Five

Instead of going home after lunch, I crossed Center Street and headed toward the combination City Hall and Department of Public Safety building. Cindy's pickup wasn't in the lot behind the building, so I changed direction to head home.

Patience may be a virtue, but with me, it's often in short supply. I was tempted to leave the Chief another message but knew she'd call when she got a chance. By five-thirty, my head was about to explode from waiting.

Fortunately, it didn't, so I was able to answer the phone. It was Cindy.

"Thank goodness you called," I said. "I've learned—"

"Hold that thought. Meet me at the Surf Bar in fifteen minutes. A day of meetings, boring meetings, and a trip downtown with the mayor, have me needing a cold beer more than anything you have to say."

The Surf Bar was across the street from the entrance to the Public Safety building, making it convenient for Cindy when she needed to escape her office. I got there in ten minutes to find her at a table near the door, gripping a beer in a Terrapin Beer Company glass. The turtle in the logo looked happier than the Chief.

"Rough day?" I said as I sat across from her at the small table.

"Spent most of it battling two councilmembers who think I'm spending too much money on overtime, one councilmember who thinks I need to increase police presence near his house, of course, then two hours in the car with our mayor listening to three million things he thinks the police need to do better. How do you think my day was?"

"You've had better."

"I've had better days at the dentist when she forgot to give me enough numbing juice before jackhammering on a molar. With griping out of the way, there is a bright side and a bad side."

"I suppose you're going to tell me both."

Cindy looked at the ceiling where dollar bills were attached to most non-moving surfaces. White Christmas lights were strung from the columns and roof trusses. I call them Christmas lights because that was their original purpose, but they're year-round fixtures in the Surf Bar.

"Chris, that's the least I can do since you're buying me this, and another, and another."

"It's my pleasure," I said with a tinge of sarcasm.

"Russell O'Leary," she said like that explained everything. "I had a nice long conversation with him this morning before every elected official in our fair city tried to take a chunk of my hide."

I've known the bartender for a few years, so he had a server bring me a glass of red wine without me having to say anything. That's one good thing about living in a small town. I took a sip, while Cindy stared at me.

I said, "What?"

"I'm waiting for your full attention. This is a fun-filled story."

"Proceed."

"Landlord Russell lied about where he was and why?"

"Is that the bright side?"

"Is for him. Seems he has a heart condition, some long Latin word I couldn't define, pronounce, or spell. Suffice to say, it's serious. His Charleston cardiologist referred him to some world-renowned specialist at the Emory University Hospital near Atlanta, the keyword being near, as opposed to being in downtown Atlanta. Russell didn't want his employer to know about the condition. He especially didn't want his wife and kids to know. Didn't want them to worry, he claimed." She took a sip of beer, shook her head, then continued. "He made up the whole story about being at a get-rich-quick seminar."

"Why'd he lie to you? Did he think you'd tell his employer or his wife?"

"Chris, in my entire life, I've never been a man. Most of the time, I don't know how you dudes think. Hell, I know how you act, but not think. Assuming you think. I don't know why he decided to stick me with the feeble story. He's still above ground, so I assume it worked with his wife."

"What did the Emery doctor say?"

"Said he has a heart. Whatever is wrong with it can be fixed with some expensive meds, or that's what Russell said. Since he's a proven liar, I don't know if I believe it. What I am certain is he was in Georgia when his building went up in smoke. He showed me a hotel bill, two gas receipts, and a food receipt from a Waffle House." She shook her head. "Who in the hell keeps Waffle House receipts?"

"You're a female, you wouldn't understand," I joked, or thought it was a joke.

Cindy didn't laugh, didn't smile, didn't say anything. Women often don't appreciate how witty men are.

"Chief, if that's the good side, what's the bad side?"

"I'm sitting here, feeling sorry for myself, without anyone to nominate for arsonist of the year."

I took a sip, smiled, then said, "Let me see if I can help. Did you get a chance to talk to Kaycee Ericson?"

"Not yet. Been wasting my time trying to prove Russell did something far worse than lie to his wife and me. Why? No, don't answer that. Did she start the fire? Do you have proof?"

"Proof, no, but let me tell you what I've learned."

She finished the beer and raised her glass for the server to bring a refill. "I'm all ears."

"I was talking with Ty who told me Kaycee approached him at the apartment building days before the fire. Started asking questions like how long he'd lived there, was the building well maintained, etc."

"What got Ty talking about that?"

"Charles and I went to Bert's to tell him that Martha Wright said he could stay at her place until he found somewhere else to live."

"Whoa, how'd that come about?"

I told her the story about approaching Martha a few days ago, her rejection of the idea, and why.

"Cindy almost choked on her beer, cleared her throat, then said, "Martha, the woman who's about two hundred years old, thought her neighbor would think she was a cougar? Crapola, I thought I'd heard it all."

I didn't add what Martha said her deceased husband would think. Instead, I told her about Martha's change of heart.

"That's great, but what does it have to do with Kaycee?"

"Nothing other than it's the reason Charles and I were talking to Ty."

"Charles was with you?"

I nodded.

"Figures. Okay, go ahead with something I'd be interested in."

"Kaycee asked Ty about vacant units. He thought she may want to rent one."

"More interesting. Like the vacant unit where the fire started?"

"That's the one. Ty also told us she was driving a blue Maserati SUV. He pointed it out in Bert's lot."

"That's important, how?"

"When Charles and I were walking up Ashley Avenue on our way to see what was burning, I saw a blue Maserati SUV in that small lot beside the apartment's parking area. Didn't you tell me Kaycee lives out by Harris Teeter?"

Cindy nodded.

"So, I wondered why her car, okay maybe not hers, but isn't it unlikely there're two blue Maserati SUVs over here?"

"I've never seen one. So, it's rare but not impossible. Go on."

I told her what Bob Howard's research uncovered, with emphasis on how Kaycee's ex-husband had been a suspect in an arson. I took a sip of wine, then added, "Do you know who I had lunch with today?"

"Dolly Parton?"

"Guess again."

"I'm guessed out. Who?"

"Your sister and nephew. Luke said he had so much fun eating with me last week, he had his mom invite me today."

"That boy needs to get out more and meet some fun people. How did Larry let him escape from the store?"

I laughed. "Luke said he told Larry that employees need to eat."

"Smart kid. I suppose there's a reason you're telling me this."

"Yes, a good one." I then bullet-pointed the highlights of our discussion.

"Are you telling me Luke saw Kaycee carrying a box to the apartment building less than an hour before the fire?"

"That's what I'm telling you."

"Let me wrap this around my undersized brain. I had

the most significant clue to who started the fire living under my roof."

I nodded.

"Crap, I should kick myself in the butt and turn in my badge."

I didn't ask how she planned to do the first part of that. Instead, I said, "Cindy, you couldn't have known. It only came up because I asked Luke about the blue SUV."

She lowered her head and stared in her beer. "Yet an old geezer with no law enforcement training figures it out."

I smiled. "Yeah, but Charles is teaching me all the tricks of being a detective."

She let out a string of profanities, none of which bear repeating.

I waited for her blood pressure to lower to non-stroke levels, then said, "It's a lot of circumstantial evidence, but what are the chances of getting a conviction on what you now know?"

"Slim, but it gives me a lot more to talk about tomorrow when I pay a Christmas Eve visit to Ms. Ericson."

"Excellent plan," I said, then told her I had to get home to wait for Neil Wilson, my new housemate, to arrive.

"You letting someone stay at your place. Will Christmas miracles never cease?"

Chapter Thirty-Six

Christmas Eve began with me sleeping late combined with rumbles of snores coming from my former office, current guest bedroom. It took a minute to remember why the snoring wasn't in my dreams but from my new houseguest. Neil had arrived last night, thanked me just under five hundred times for letting him stay, then adjusted to his new environment. He knew from working at Cal's I wasn't a beer drinker, so he brought a six-pack with him. Three cans were in the refrigerator this morning. He'd shared he often worked late, so I shouldn't expect to see him much in the mornings. I thought that was great since I'm a morning person who enjoys peace and quiet. I hadn't contemplated snoring.

I turned on the Mr. Coffee machine, then headed to Bert's for a box of donuts, and a chance to ask Ty about his move to Martha's. Ty wasn't at his usual hangout behind the register, so I asked if he was working. Denise, another of Bert's uber-helpful employees said he wasn't coming in until noon.

When I got home, Neil was at the kitchen table, wearing

orange and green flannel pajamas, and staring in one of my red I Love Folly Beach mugs. He continued staring in the mug, and said, "Did you know there's nothing to eat in your kitchen?"

I dropped the box of donuts on the table. "Bon Appetit."

I think he smiled, although it looked more like a frown.

"Sleep well?" I asked instead of telling him there was never food in the kitchen.

He opened the donuts, took a bite, then mumbled, "Think so."

Fifteen minutes later, with food in his stomach, caffeine in his veins, Neil reentered the world of the living with full sentences and stories about some of last night's more memorable customers. I suspected much of his conversation was from nervous energy rather than wanting me to know what each customer ordered, or what they were doing Christmas.

Ten o'clock rolled around quicker than it does with me here alone. I was wondering if Cindy had caught up with Kaycee Ericson. By eleven, I was tempted to call the Chief. Remember, patience isn't one of my virtues.

I didn't have to show the Chief my lack of patience. My phone rang at eleven fifteen revealing her name on the screen.

She began with, "Is this the Chris Landrum homeless shelter?"

"What'd you learn, Cindy?"

Okay, she was reminded of my lack of patience.

"Chill, it's Christmas Eve. Tis the season to be jolly."

I said, "Ho, Ho, Ho. What'd you learn?"

"You're no fun. Okay, at oh-nine-hundred this morning, I knocked on Kaycee's condo door. At nine-hundred one, nine-hundred two, nine-hundred three I knocked, all to no avail. Additionally, there wasn't a Maserati SUV in the lot. I used all my chiefly skills to deduce she wasn't home."

"What now?"

"Glad you asked. This is where it gets interesting. I returned to my majestic office and used my chiefly skills to access my secret, super-duper databases to check on Kaycee's said condo. Want to guess what I found?"

"It's too early for guessing."

"You wouldn't get it anyway. It seems the condo isn't owned by Kaycee but belongs to one Anthony Craft, a resident of Coral Gables, Florida. I called Mr. Craft, a call answered by his wife Madeline, who, once I assured her I wasn't Anthony's mistress, handed the phone to her hubby. I identified myself. then after explaining there wasn't anything wrong with his rental unit, he calmed down."

There was a long pause, so I said, "You still there?"

"Cool your jets. I'm looking for the rest of my notes. Got them. Okay, Anthony rented his condo to Kaycee two years ago. She occasionally was late on rent, but always paid, didn't complain about anything, and according to Anthony, was perfect for his condo, whatever that meant."

"I don't suppose he mentioned that she was an arsonist?"

"No, but know what he did share?"

"What?"

"His tenant called two days ago saying she was moving. Her lease expires the end of the month and she wouldn't be renewing. Anthony was saddened since she'd been such a good tenant, in other words, all he had to do was sit in beautiful Florida and cash rent checks."

"Did he say where she was going?"

"Nope. That would've been too easy. She said something about going back up north, which could be New England, Canada, the North Pole."

"What now?"

"I'm going to pick you up in ten minutes and we're going to make another visit to Anthony's condo."

"I thought you determined no one was there?"

"There isn't, but helpful Anthony gave me the keypad lock combination, plus the lawyerly super-important authorization to inspect the unit."

Cindy was out front blowing her horn five minutes later. Five minutes after that, we were standing in front of Kaycee's condo, with Cindy punching numbers on the keypad. She asked me to stand back as she entered. Not seeing anything amiss, or Kaycee pointing a gun at her, Cindy invited me in, reminding me not to touch anything.

The large, open floor plan unit was painted a cheery off-yellow with typical condo-package furniture. I didn't see anything indicating it'd been inhabited. There were no knickknacks or photos on the tables, no newspapers, magazines, or brochures setting around. Cindy took a quick scan around the room then went into the kitchen. I followed her and noticed a dirty plate, a butter knife, and three glasses in the sink. The Chief pulled out a tall trash container from under the counter. A used coffee filter, coffee grounds, and three pieces of paper torn in half were all the container held.

I followed Cindy down a narrow hall to the first bedroom. It looked like it'd never been used. A colorful bedspread was untouched, the pillow looked like it'd just come from the store. The closet was empty. The second bedroom didn't look any more used than the first.

The master bedroom was another story. The bedspread lay on the floor, the sheets mussed, the pillow dented where a head would've rested. Several hangers were strewn across the bed, two more on the floor, the closet door stood open, with more hangers on the rod. All were empty.

I was searching the corners of the closet, then looking under the bed, hoping to find anything indicating Kaycee was the arsonist. Cindy had begun pulling out dresser drawers.

She said, "Huh?"

"What?"

She pointed at two books she'd found in the bottom drawer. One was about buying real estate in both good and bad markets, the other on creative financing options. She was flipping through a copy-paper sized Office Depot wire-bound notebook.

"Where was that?"

"Under the books."

I moved closer to see what Cindy was seeing. Part of the first page had been ripped out. There were sketches on the next three pages. They looked like draft floor plans. What really got my attention was the paper, more accurately, graph paper.

"Cindy, remember I told you about the note under Noelle's windshield?"

"Politely telling her to get off Folly or no telling what?"

"That's the one."

"So what?"

"It was on graph paper."

"You didn't tell me that."

"Didn't think it was important."

"Bet you do now."

She didn't give me a chance to answer. She continued, "You said the note burned in the fire?"

I nodded.

She sighed. "More circumstantial evidence."

I took my phone out of my pocket and tapped in Noelle's number. She answered on the second ring.

"Noelle, this is Chris. Where are you?"

"Barb's Books, why?"

"If you're going to be there a few minutes, I'd like talk to you."

She said she'd wait. I hung up and turned to Cindy. "Let's visit Noelle."

"Why? The note's gone."

"I have an idea."

Cindy was kind not to push. "Okay."

"Take the notepad."

"Don't suppose you're going to tell me why?"

"Not yet."

Barb was behind the counter running a credit card through the machine then bagging three books.

She saw Cindy and me, pointed to the backroom, and said Noelle was waiting for us.

Noelle was pacing the small room. She wore a gray sweatshirt, jeans, and of course, sunglasses. She smiled when she saw me, the look turned inquisitive when she noticed the Chief behind me.

"Thanks for waiting. Have a seat."

She slowly lowered herself in the chair behind Barb's chrome and glass desk. "Is everything okay?"

"Yes," I said then pulled a chair up to the side of the desk. Cindy remained standing as I removed a sheet of copy paper from the printer.

"Noelle, didn't you tell me the note you found under your windshield was on paper that looked like it'd been torn from a larger sheet?"

She looked at Cindy, then her gaze turned to me. "Umm, yes. Why?"

"Noelle, this may seem silly, but bear with me." I handed her the piece of copy paper off Barb's printer. "Tear this about the size of the note you found."

"Chris, I don't remember exactly how big it was."

"I understand, give it your best shot."

She took the paper, began to rip it in half, stopped, then tore it about an inch lower than where she first started. She handed me the piece that was about one-third of the paper I'd handed her.

Cindy must've figured out what I was doing. She flipped open the pad she'd brought with her and set it on the desk. I took the piece Noelle had given me and laid it on the open pad. It wasn't a perfect match for what had been torn out of the pad, but close.

Noelle who hadn't said anything since she handed me the torn sheet, touched the pad, looked at Cindy, at me, then said, "Graph paper."

"Like the note you got," I added.

"Exactly."

Chapter Thirty-Seven

Christmas began with a call from Cindy wishing me Merry Christmas, then telling me there was an APB out on Kaycee Ericson's SUV. She hadn't been found, but she'd used her credit card to buy gas at an Interstate station in Lumberton, North Carolina, and later near Richmond, Virginia. She may not have been caught, but was heading away, far away, from Folly Beach, South Carolina. For that I was thankful.

I was then surprised when Neil stepped in the kitchen and handed me a bottle of Cabernet with a red ribbon tied around it.

My housemate said, "Merry Christmas."

I was touched. "Neil, you didn't have to do that. I didn't get you anything."

"Chris, hush. You gave me the best gift I could ever get. You gave me a place to stay and knowing someone cared enough to make it available."

I thanked him then asked what he was doing up so early.

"Cal's so excited about his party, he wants me to come

early to help get everything ready. I've never seen that old boy so amped."

"Christmas is his biggest day of the year." I told Neil about why having the party meant so much to the country crooner.

"I'll do whatever I can to make sure it's a success. Saying that, I'd better get dressed and over there. I'll grab something at Bert's community Christmas breakfast, so you won't have to fix anything fancy." He laughed at his joke, patted me on the back, then said he'd see me at the party.

Cal's Christmas gala was scheduled to begin at one o'clock, but the allure of free food and drink always brought attendees before the official opening. I wanted to be there early in case I could help.

I walked through the door surrounded by colorful lights at twelve-thirty. The room was already half full. Brenda Lee's "Rockin' Around the Christmas Tree" was playing, along with laughter coming from people at a table in the center of the room holding three bowls of salsa, avocado dip, and a basket of chips large enough to hold a beachball. Always early Charles was talking with Dude Sloan cradling Pluto in his arms. Dogs aren't allowed in Cal's, but it was Christmas. Besides, a good argument could be made Dude needed a service animal. I don't know what was said, but Charles was laughing louder than I'd heard in months.

All four trees were glowing brightly as were the countless strands of Christmas lights throughout the room. Cal was standing behind the bar pulling a beer out of the cooler. The LED lights on his Stetson blinked, his red polo shirt was so bright I suspected it'd glow in the dark. His smile was priceless. Neil was at the other end of the bar fiddling with a stack of red napkins.

Two men I didn't know arrived next. They waved at Cal who returned the wave then pointed toward the chips. They filled a paper plate with chips and headed to the bar where Cal shook their hands and offered each a drink. They didn't hesitate taking the drinks. Kristin, a part-time server who'd worked at Cal's for several years, and Joy, another server who'd joined Cal's a year ago, were moving a couple of tables around so there was more room for people to stand.

Burl arrived wearing a Santa hat and the sweater he wore to last year's party. It was easy to remember since it could win any ugly Christmas sweater contest.

"Merry Christmas, Brother Chris."

"The same to you, Preacher. Glad to see you. I know Cal will be happy you're here."

"Hope he's not happy enough to drag me on stage."

"Preacher, it's a Christmas tradition."

"Like grandpa getting drunk on eggnog," Burl said, then smiled.

Charles left Dude and Pluto talking with someone I didn't know and headed to the bar, where he said something to Neil, then grabbed a couple of drinks from the cooler. He handed the drinks to two men who were leaning against the bar. I smiled, knowing how much Charles loves helping others. He was in his element.

Gene Autry's version of "Here Comes Santa Claus" interrupted Burl's bemoaning the Christmas tradition. He said he'd better say hi to the host and left me standing near the front door enjoying the festive environment. I didn't see Martha Wright until she tapped me with her cane. She had a gleam in her eyes, either for being able to celebrate Christmas at Cal's or from Christmas morning hot toddies. Dixie was behind her. Each wore red Christmas sweaters; neither sweater could compete with Burl's for tackiness.

Dixie stepped in front of her neighbor. "Martha tells me this is one whale of a party."

Martha had attended for the first-time last year.

"She's right," I said. "Is Ty with you?"

"That boy's a gem," Martha said. "He was up at the crack of dawn. Fed my kids, fixed toast to go with my oatmeal, and," she chuckled. "Fixed me a hot toddy. Then he went to work for a few hours. Did I mention he was a gem?"

Yes, but didn't remind her. I didn't catch the answer to my question, so I repeated, "Is he here?"

"He's parking my car. I let him chauffeur us in the Lincoln. Told him he didn't even have to wear one of those chauffeur hats." She looked over my shoulder. "Heavens, here he is."

"Merry Christmas, Mr. Landrum," Ty said as we shook hands.

"Martha," Dixie said, "are we going to stand here and yak all day or we going to the bar?"

I had the impression she'd already found one. Martha put her arm around her neighbor and pulled her toward the drinks. Ty shrugged and followed the women. Three more people, two women and a man, I knew to be regulars entered and headed to the food.

Noelle, closely followed by Barb, stepped through the entry and looked around. Barb saw me and motioned for Noelle to join her as she gave me a hug and a kiss. I looked up to see if there was mistletoe. There wasn't. Noelle gave me a tentative hug. Both ladies wore red blouses and black slacks. I suspected Noelle's blouse came from Barb's closet.

We weaved our way through a group of people on our way to the salsa table, as Barb said, "Noelle told me about what you wanted with her in the store yesterday. Has Cindy found Kaycee?"

We got plates of food, Noelle went to thank Cal for hosting the party, and Barb and I moved to a corner of the room.

I told her Kaycee hadn't been caught, but she was several states away and traveling away from Folly.

"Good, Noelle was so worried, thinking she should have done something different when she got the note."

"I doubt it would've helped, besides what she told Cindy about the paper will be a big help."

"That's what I told her. Any idea why Kaycee set the fire?"

"The theory is so she could buy the lot from Russell O'Leary. He'd originally said he'd sell to her, then his kids and wife convinced him to keep it for their future. Kaycee probably figured he'd have no need for it if it was reduced to ashes."

"Putting on my lawyer's hat, they could probably get a conviction based on a decent amount of circumstantial evidence, especially the note. I'm still confused about why Kaycee wrote the note only to Noelle. If she was going to burn the building, and not harm anyone, why not warn everyone?"

"I suspect it had to do with Noelle spying on everyone around town while getting ideas for her novel. She could've seen Kaycee near the building. Kaycee could also have seen her and figured she was a loose end she needed to scare off before starting the fire."

"Makes sense."

"Know what makes more sense?"

"What?"

"Getting a drink, some food, and enjoying Cal's party."

We were on our way to the bar when I saw Rose, Luke, and Cindy at the door. Rose and Cindy were in red sweatshirts, Luke had on a white and red T-shirt. All wore huge smiles. With their entry, there was more red in here than at a University of Georgia football game.

Luke ran over, motioned me to lean down, and whispered, "Mom and Aunt Cindy love the shark jewelry. Thank you for helping me with it."

I told him it was my pleasure, took his hand, and walked him to the bar.

"Cal, you have a special drink back there for my young friend?"

"How about a root beer, partner?" Cal said and tipped his Stetson to Luke.

Luke laughed. "You're funny."

Cal fixed him his drink then he headed back to Rose.

Cindy had her phone to her ear, nodded, then headed out the door. I started to follow, but figured it was none of my business. She returned with a big smile on her face and motioned me over.

"Chris, guess who's spending Christmas day in the hoosegow in Hartford, Connecticut?"

"Our favorite arsonist?"

Her smile widened. "Yep."

"Sorry she's missing Cal's party, aren't you?"

"Nope."

"Me either."

"I'd better go tell my baby sister."

She headed toward Rose, and I moved closer to Noelle who was still standing beside Cal. She said, "Cal, this is my first time in here. I think I need to add a bar like this in my novel. Add a character like you."

Cal tipped his hat, this time at Noelle. "Darlin', I'm a whole novel all by myself."

Noelle laughed. No truer words had ever been spoken.

Cal excused himself, saying he had to say a word or two to the group that now was filling the room, with more arriving.

Fifteen minutes later, Cal tapped on the antique silver microphone in the center of the low stage, then said, "How about lending me an ear?" It took a second tap on the mic before Cal had everyone's attention. "Guys and gals, Merry Christmas. This here's our biggest Christmas shindig ever. Now let me tell from the get-go, I'm not going to be happy unless all of you are. We've all got a bunch to be thankful for, so let's celebrate it. After you eat and drink a bunch more, me and Preacher Burl will be entertaining you with a Christmas duet."

I saw Luke tug on his mom's shirt and whisper something to her, probably, "Cal should've said, Preacher and I, not me and Preacher." Rose smiled and fluffed his hair.

Janice Raque was standing in the doorway, looking around. I left the bar to meet her. Before I could make it through the crowd, Preacher Burl was talking with her. She looked toward the ceiling, then hugged Burl before I could reach the two.

Janice turned to me. "Chris, you'll never guess what Preacher Burl told me."

"What?"

"Someone moved out of Hope House yesterday afternoon. The preacher said I could have the room if I wanted it. You bet your as—umm, you bet I do."

Burl smiled. "Brother Chris, I told you I had faith it'd work out."

"That you did, Preacher."

Hank Williams Sr was finishing his classic version of "I Saw the Light" when Cal pulled the plug on the jukebox, stepped behind the silver mic, and said, "Y'all ready for it?" He cupped his hand behind his ear.

A few celebrators took the hint. "Yes."

"Preacher, get your holy body up here."

Burl was standing beside me and I was afraid he was going to bolt for the door. In the spirit of Christmas, he didn't. He sighed as he slowly made his way to the stage. Cal slung his guitar over his head, whispered something to Burl, then pushed the preacher close to the mic. Cal played two chords, nudged Burl's head closer to the mic, then sang:

"O Come, all ye faithful,

Joyful and triumphant,

O come ye, O come ye, to Bethlehem...."

About the Author

Bill Noel is the best-selling author of eighteen novels in the popular Folly Beach Mystery series. Besides being an award-winning novelist, Noel is a fine arts photographer and lives in Louisville, Kentucky, with his wife, Susan, and his off-kilter imagination. Learn more about the series, and the author by visiting www.billnoel.com.